FACE OF EVIL

FACE OF EVIL

RICHARD E. NICHOLSON JR.

PALMETTO
P U B L I S H I N G
Charleston, SC
www.PalmettoPublishing.com

Hardcover ISBN: 979-8-8229-5740-4
Paperback ISBN: 979-8-8229-5741-1
eBook ISBN: 979-8-8229-5742-8

SYNOPSIS

From the dense jungles of Vietnam to the mountain hollers of West Virginia.

Set in the early 1990s, *Face of Evil* tells the poignant story of a fierce war veteran and a young West Virginia war widow recovering from a brief, durable, but loveless marriage. Nuna Polinski grew up in an isolated deep mountain hollow and has flickering memories of growing up amid severe coal mining poverty. The story also centers on Captain Bryce Tucker, a handsome, vibrant military man who emerges as a fierce hero out of the dense jungles of Vietnam to become a legendary SEAL team captain, FBI special agent, and senior CIA special undercover operative.

It's a dramatic journey from the dense mangrove swamps and jungle waterways of Vietnam to the evil savagery of unseen corrupt forces at large in the rugged mountains of central West Virginia, culminating on a Bahamian island. It's a tale of raw heroism in battle, suspense, international and domestic corruption, shockingly heinous human trafficking, mystery, revenge, and romance that only gathers momentum with time.

Bryce distinguished himself in the ranks as a formidable and unmalleable operative, strategist, and adept killer. He is reasonably wealthy and well connected, though he is unknown to the public. His military records show that he honed his imaginative ability continuously to surprise the enemy and reverse their actions from offensive to defensive in a very short period of time. He has a stellar military reputation and was extensively trained and groomed on the infamous CIA base known as "The Farm" in Virginia. He excels in clandestine communications, airborne tactics, jungle combat and survival, and is a fourth-degree martial arts expert, as well as an expert in weapons and explosives. He also holds a master's degree in risk management and speaks several languages, including Vietnamese, Russian, Spanish, and Chinese.

ACKNOWLEDGMENTS

Researching and writing one's first novel is a monumental undertaking. I wish to express my gratitude to Alan Howell of Haddam, Connecticut who generously helped me edit and color the mosaic of this novel with the tiles of his knowledge, expertise, diligence and diplomatic criticism to make this novel better. In several instances where I felt it would enhance the narrative, I have taken literary license; but any factual errors are my responsibility and my responsibility alone.

For a really terrific family who always had my back and gave me unstinting support. You know who you are: My forever partner, Victoria Brady for her inspiration, technical support, acuity and patience while I wrote this novel. My brother, Jim Nicholson, who also served in Vietnam, my sisters Arlene and Mary. My two sons, Richard Nicholson III and Ryan Nicholson, my daughter-in-law Tracy Nicholson, and my two terrific grandchildren, Kendall Marie and Austin Ryan for their inspiration. Love you all!

I'm also very grateful for the professional support and diligence of Palmetto Publishing project manager, Anthony Ferrese and his team of editors and artist involved in this endeavor.

CHAPTER 1

It was zero dawn (0500 hours), November 14, 1967, and I—Lieutenant Bryce Tucker—was sitting on a wooden bench in pitch-black darkness. Back in Coronado, California, several days earlier, we had celebrated Cinco de Mayo on the white beach, raising hell before our departure.

The giant Pan American Boeing 707, with its four Rolls-Royce turbofan jet engines, eased itself into an early morning sky. The lights of Nome, Alaska, dwindled swiftly behind us. Our destination was the huge Da Nang Air Base. We had been in the air now for over 11 hours at 45,000 feet, averaging 475 knots since flying out of Nome, with a short 45-minute stop on Guam at the Anderson Military Base for refueling. No one was allowed off the plane, and the small widows didn't afford much of a view of the island. The pilot, Colonel Jeff Hunt, was a 37-year-old, 6-foot-3, 175-pound, pale-skinned, silver-haired native of Nashville, Tennessee, with a wife and three children.

Copilot former lieutenant George McCurry was a 35-year-old, 6-foot, 170-pound African American from New Orleans who had just recently married. Both pilots, having been former air force officers before opting for civilian life, had made this flight a dozen times now, and both would be relieved of the hazardous duty upon returning to Marks Air Force Base. As the colonel called it, this flight was a cakewalk to his retirement.

Sitting on hard wooden benches under military-mandated restrictive dim lighting with nothing but ocean under them was beginning to take its toll. The mood was becoming foul, and several of my inexperienced brethren were getting edgy with each other. During training, I had witnessed a fight between the two mountain boys back at the amphibious base. Scuttlebutt had it that Bubba and Zach, both West Virginian Irish mountain boys, both built like Greyhound buses, would fight like rabid dogs at the drop of a hat just for the sake of a bit of action, and they were the cockiest SOBs I had ever known. They also had an abominable vocabulary and would drink well beyond normal tolerance. But, all in all, our high spirits and sense of brotherhood had bonded us and made us a team of one.

Upon hearing the pilot's announcement directing our attention to the northern coast of the People's Republic of Vietnam off the right side of the aircraft, everyone went silent. "Thank you, gentlemen, for choosing Pan American Airlines. We hope you had a pleasant flight." The eight-thousand-mile trip had taken nearly twenty-two hours. He then announced that we were all to secure our belts and that we would be landing momentarily.

We were on the final approach and descending rapidly toward the ground. There were twenty-one of us lifting and picking up our back-packs, which had been used for seat cushions and pillows and were now being put back on and buckled. Helmet straps were being pulled tight. M16 rifles laden with cartridge belts filled with an assortment of M16 magazines, flares, machine-gun bandoliers, and hand grenades added to the weight each man was required to carry.

Standing, arms akimbo, I made one last check of the men. Strapped in next to their seabags, they had seventy pounds of gear on their backs and straining to look down at the approaching ground.

Da Nang was a sprawling American military base composed of an amalgamation of warehouses, tents, bunkers, landing docks, and air-fields covering hundreds of acres in the northern part of South Vietnam. Very little of it was visible outside the glass portals, save the blurred blue lights of the runway and the occasional outline of distant terrain as it cut against the shadowy skyline. However, as we descended lower and approached the landing strip with all lights out, I could see that a protective earth and sandbag revetment surrounded the runway along with a ten-foot-high cyclone fence topped with rolls upon rolls of barbed concertina razor wire.

With only a wall harness to hold us in place against the bulkhead, we all braced and held our breath as the plane slammed onto the runway with a sharp bump, wheels jostling and thumping along the tarmac, the four turbofans now reversing hard and screaming like the living dead as we taxied down the runway. As soon as we felt the plane come to a stop, we all joined in thunderous applause and hoopla as we unsnapped our harnesses. It was an exhilarating moment, echoing through the plane, and it would be fleeting. There was a collective sigh of relief as the exit door opened.

The pilots didn't shut down the engines as they were anxious to take off and get back in the air to Subic Bay in the Philippines, then California as soon as we exited. Every moment that plane sat in the open on this field made them a susceptible target for a guerrilla force known as the Vietcong (VC).

We had practiced this many times, and the movement of each sailor had a purpose as we prepared to disembark the rear of the plane. A deadly purpose. This time wasn't a drill. Their rifles were loaded with live ammo, and we were on Vietnamese soil per the orders of LBJ with the VC out there that wanted all of us dead. The men were ready and looking for action—no more drills or practice. Except for their training at the Coronado Amphibious Base, they were the rawest of new recruits, not one of them had ever crossed a time zone. They were scared shitless but wouldn't admit it. This was the moment when we did what we were trained to do. It was the moment when boys became men.

A Hollywood casting agency might have selected this gung-ho young brotherhood of cherries for a movie. While each one was unique in his own idiosyncrasy, they were all dressed in the same uniform, and they were all about the same age—eighteen—but each had their own distinctive aura. Looking back, they were the guileless cherry faces of youth that belonged in a high school album instead of the jungles of Vietnam. In addition, most of them were just starting to grow hair around their balls.

While everyone still clowned around and threw out jokes, they all presumably understood the danger they faced. The humor had a way of making the tension and suffocating pressure more tolerable. There were two big foul-mouthed Irish rednecks (Owen "Bubba" McKnight and Zachary Duff) from a coal-mining town of Bluefield, West Virginia, real roughhousing, obstreperous cannonballs who refused to pull their punches and shenanigans, with one always insulting, taunting, and bailing the other out. Fighting was the other activity in their repertoire. But if trouble came, you would want both to be covering your ass. Then there was an insolent Cajun traiteur from Vermilion Parish, Louisiana, always full of sarcasm and ready with a witty retort. There was, too, a slow-talking rabble-rouser hillbilly from Arkansas with an Ozark locution and a renegade Cherokee Indian with the moniker "Chief" named Eagle from South Carolina, always carping and looking for reparations.

Not to be left out, there was a hotshot muscular black pool player from a ghetto in New Jersey presumably with a checkered past who was nothing more than a supercilious jackass with an extra large set of gonads; a droll chicken farmer from Wisconsin with a round countenance, jovial face, and plentiful bluster, short reddish hair, always self-medicating with booze and whatever else he could find; a tough egotistical kid and self-proclaimed soprano from New York City with a facility with words who couldn't stop bloviating about his Sicilian heritage and wise guy connection to the movies; a Latino from San Juan with a reputation for being somewhat loquacious; a political wannabe from Culpepper, Virginia, who believed he was related to General Lee and was always making inflammatory comments related about the Civil War; two Mexican Americans from the barrio of East Harlem always craving tortillas and refried beans; and of course, a tall gangly Texan of Norwegian decent from Houston with a guitar longing for the boardwalk on Galveston Bay.

Rounding out the troop deployment were Mike Bogus EN1 and Mike Monroe SN1, two of the most sociable and simpatico men in the group. Both were from Connecticut, and both were cherries fresh out of boot camp at the Great Lakes Naval Base. As expected, both began to sweat and stress out even before the jumbo engines turned down. Nevertheless, all the men had been training together for the last four months at the Coronado Amphibious Base. They were now commiserating about their experiences on and off base. Bouts of spontaneous laughter erupted sporadically in the cabin as the discussions moved from family, muscle cars, and drinking to hot women.

Back in the briefing room at the naval airbase in Nome, we were again being made aware of the danger of enemy sniper attacks hitting us upon our landing in Da Nang, like so many other incoming and outbound flights before us.

This was my third and final Westpac tour, and the situation on the ground was still intense. However, we didn't have to wait long. Within moments of landing, I found myself edgy yet absorbed in my mission.

As we disembarked into the suffocating Indochina tropical heat, leaving behind the pale lights of the silver bird's cool cocoon, we immediately heard the sound of incoming fire from somewhere in the fog-shrouded early morning darkness beyond the fence. We bolted down the steps of the boarding ramp at the rear of the plane carrying rifles and seabags in a hell-for-leather manner.

Our reverie had been suddenly interrupted.

An AK-47 was my first thought as a second burst raked the rear fuselage and tail of the aircraft.

"Incoming" I yelled!

We all hit the ground and rolled away from the plane with our guns at the ready and the selector switches on full auto, searching for a target. "Shit!" In the next instant, before I could blink, I heard two distinct ghastly whistles in the night air above as I screamed, "Stay down!" They all dove back into the earth, getting as low to the ground as possible. Two 122 mm rockets simultaneously hit the airliner broadside with a massive, devastating explosion, blowing open its wing fuel tank and forward fuselage, sending a flaming fireball 90 feet into the air that then engulfed the aircraft. I heard a large piece of shrapnel whizzing perilously past my head and felt its burn. I was damn lucky: had the shard of metal been a couple of inches lower, I would have died a horrific death.

The rockets were accurate and profoundly lethal. Somewhere out there beyond the hurricane fencing topped with coils of razor wire was a camouflaged VC sniper and possibly a crack artillery unit positioned against the forested hills above the airfield who had us zeroed in their sights. Even in the darkness, with his face in the dirt, Eagle could see the shock waves radiating across the tarmac, like undulating ripples emanating from a stone thrown into the water. It was a sight unlike any other he had ever witnessed. Without question, our unit would soon encounter a landscape that was not a Shangri-la with an enemy that was not to be taken lightly.

Almost immediately, the security alarms began blasting their eerie "red alert" sirens, warning of incoming artillery. The base security defense teams responded with defensive countermeasures from several strategic locations, firing parachute-suspended pyrotechnic flares, lighting up the sky and illuminating the distant hillside. With salvos of interdiction fire raking the hillside with 57 mm recoilless cannons, .50 and .60 caliber machine guns, and 40 mm grenades fired in rapid succession from several launchers. Two air force Huey gunships had also joined the action. They were strafing the hillside from a higher elevation with a withering hail of retaliatory 20 mm cannon and 60 mm machine gunfire.

The incoming fire ceased almost immediately. Then there was a deadly silence; if any among the enemy had survived the deadly firefight, they had probably slithered and retreated into the dense undergrowth of the jungle. With bated breath, I quickly surveyed our team, ensuring that all twenty-five of us made it out of the plane. We froze, finding Mike face down no more than five feet off the ramp. He'd taken a bullet to the side of the head and had died instantly before he even hit the ground. I blanched and fell to my knees upon seeing the back of his head was missing. A sobering chill of horror went down my spine. Every muscle in my body revolted with raw, raging fury. Few knew Mike was to be my brother-in-law when we returned to the States.

Just as the shock of Mike's death took hold, another horrendous explosion ripped the PAN AM cargo area. Several pallets of black powder, which I estimated at 20,000 pounds, detonated with the thunderous concussion of a volcano, knocking us to our knees. With adrenaline still pumping and his ears ringing, Owen, cursing in his nasal mountain drawl, hefted Mike's lifeless body into a fireman's carry and, with a full tilt, frantically carried him away from the towering inferno. We all followed, running double time across the field for cover behind the bunker line ten yards out beyond the runway. The image of hell seared in my memory then: the cataclysm of fire, the intense heat, and the overall pandemonium generated by the surprise assault was inescapable.

The base fire crew and rescue personnel arrived quickly, but with the intense heat and ensuing munitions still detonating in the inferno, they were forced to let the fire burn itself out. The four-man aircrew didn't have time to escape the plane and had most likely perished in the first explosion—if not, definitely in the second one.

Several minutes later, two MPs drove up to us and asked if we were having a bad day, totally unaware that we had just suffered a casualty only moments before. It took six of the men to hold Owen back from attacking and beating the living hell out of them. Owen McKnight, one of the two West Virginians, was usually a good-natured guy to be with but was also a hard-drinking redneck who, at times, could quickly become hellacious and decimate someone abusing or insulting a friend of his. At six-foot-four, weighing in at 275 with the lightning speed of Cassius Clay, he was rumored to have never lost a fight. Apparently, this was not an uncommon event here.

Having apologized, they radioed for a medical response unit to take Mike's body to the base mortuary. The sergeant, with his eyes still cautiously focused on Owen, then instructed us to stay low and follow them to a marine cantonment next to the base infirmary, which would be our hooch for the coming days. Ordinarily, this would be music to our ears as it meant hot showers and a warm rack. Tonight would not be one of those nights. Without warning, a jagged spear of lightning lit up the darkened sky.

The naval Quonset hut, a half cylinder metal building, had been hit so many times that the hooch was covered in a drab-green tarp to keep out the daily monsoon rains. It still leaked like a sieve. With the mess hall already closed for the evening and no creature comforts available, we would be enjoying a C ration dinner by candlelight in our hut this night. Concertina wire glistened in the eerie moonlight. The men were already complaining about the torrid heat. The climate of the Vietnamese summer, coupled with the fine brown dust from the airfield, was indeed oppressive.

I stayed up and inspected every bunk, ensuring every man had a bunk and a blanket. We slept on military-issued cots surrounded by standing water with no linens or blankets. However, that didn't bother us unless you didn't mind taking a shower in your wet skivvies or sharing a crap with a million flies and other airborne insects. Rats scurrying around under our bunks proved a nuisance by dusk, and even more bothersome was not having mosquito netting.

We got little sleep, no thanks to frequent incoming and outgoing aircraft. But the worst of it was that it was steaming hot, muggy, and humid as hell. We spent most of the night either kicking away the rats or swatting the damned vectoring squadrons of blasted, bloodsucking mosquitoes, sand fleas, and other carnivorous insects. Some the size of my thumb were relentlessly boiling out of the stagnant pools of runoff like a biblical plague. Buzzing and droning into our mouths, our eyes, and around our ears, they were literally eating us alive.

By early morning, having fought a losing battle with the insects, we had produced so many welts from mosquitoes, red fire ants, and black cockroaches, we all fully expected to shiver to death with cerebral malaria. We all deserved mini Purple Hearts as we began to compare who had the most bites. There were no winners.

Overhead, the steady buzz of planes and helicopters taking off and landing within earshot of our hooch continued without interruption.

No one complained. Creature comforts were not on the menu. It was a scorching hot tropical morning, with the humidity forecasted to reach all-time highs for the next couple of days and thunderstorms, monsoon rain, and winds guaranteed. One could expect to lose a pound or so of water just walking to the water buffalo to fill up canteens on the other side of the base.

It sort of fit with what Mark Twain said: "Everyone complains about the weather, but no one ever does a fucking damn thing about it!"

"Welcome to Vietnam."

On our first night on the ground, every one of the sailors had lost their sense of humor and excitement. With their jaws tight and expressions tense with anger, they now wore a severe manifestation of hatred and revenge on their faces. In a matter of a couple of hours, they had morphed from boys on an exciting adventure to men with a sense of vengeance and a deadly mission. Emotionally drained and physically spent, none of them could or would put the day's events to rest for the rest of their lives. What they didn't know was that it was going to get worse. A lot worse!

Mike Monroe was seventeen years old, innocent and untouched by life, having just graduated high school, and of his own volition, he wanted to follow in his father's footsteps and fight in a war. He had also sworn an oath to himself to avenge the loss of two close friends who had graduated a year ahead of him and had both been killed in Nam nine months earlier. Being from Southington, Connecticut, we had all attended their military funerals. The community's display of grief and sadness was overwhelming. Mike's announcement that he was enlisting and volunteering to go to Vietnam had caused quite a hullabaloo that day. His parents, along with his sister and I, had all tried to talk him out of it, but despite all their efforts, there was no way they could mollify the anger in him with the loss of his friends. He was old enough to be cognizant of the danger before him but not wise enough to comprehend that the life he had known up to then could and would come to an end. They had had a big send-off dinner at his house the night before he left for boot camp.

Knowing that I was returning for another tour of duty, he had convinced his commander that he wanted to serve with me. His mission and his singular preoccupation with going to Vietnam were set.

I opined that it was a hell of a way to end a young life full of promise. With tears welling in my eyes, I had no idea how to deliver this heartbreaking news to his family, especially his sister Diane, other than providing it as naked, untarnished truth. This is one of those times in our lives when we cross a threshold and there is no chance of returning. The utter innocence of our youth that we once knew is irreconcilable with our new reality. She was going to be devastated.

Diane,

This is very difficult and by far the hardest letter I've ever written, but I deeply regret to confirm that Mike was killed in action on November 14, 1966, on the tarmac of Da Nang Air Base. He sustained a gunshot wound from hostile fire while exiting the plane. I and twenty other men were with him when he was hit. Having identified Mike, I will have a scar on my heart for as long as I live. The moment can never be more vivid. Please accept my sincere sympathy for the loss of your brother; my heart goes out to your entire family. I've been advised that your parents have already been notified. Mike's body is being processed and will be returned to Connecticut as soon as possible. Unfortunately, while I wanted to be with you in this desperate time, I've been advised that due to current enemy activity, I cannot accompany Mike's remains back to the states and must remain here. I love you, Diane!

I'm so, so sorry,

Bryce

The following morning, having dropped off the heartfelt letter at the FPO (fleet post office), I reported for duty to the Westpac commander of the Seventh Fleet Amphibious Force in charge of Assault Craft Unit

One, Division 4 Riverine Force, to which we were assigned. Seeing the sign in front of a Quonset hut identifying it as the home of the executive commanding officer, I knocked.

"Enter" came an unfriendly sounding voice from within.

Upon crossing the threshold, I said, "Sir, Lieutenant Tucker, reporting for duty."

"Take a seat, Lieutenant. I've been expecting you."

The meeting with our esteemed leader, Commander Roy Siddhartha, also known as the Douchebag Buddha (behind his back was a dour, stolid, taciturn, unpleasant officer who was always insinuating himself and his attributes onto others) was disappointingly quick and to the point. When he lifted his head from the maps on his desk, I immediately noticed that he was older than I had expected and the chest of his starched khaki uniform was full of medals. Moreover, looking at him now face-to-face, I saw he had a grizzled, heavily lined face that hadn't seen a razor in several days and was in a sour, belligerent mood for sure.

"What the hell took you so long to get here?" he screamed with an arched brow, catching me slightly off guard.

"We just landed last night from stateside, sir," I said, sounding apologetic. "We, unfortunately, lost a man to a sniper as we disembarked the plane on the tarmac."

"Lieutenant, I'm well aware of your casualty," he yelled in a basso that he'd most likely developed from years of smoking, drinking, and yelling. He looked at me with two dark, cold eyes.

"Get over it. There will be more," he said with strained belligerence.

From what I'd been told, he had a mean streak, and his method for motivating his officers was to scream, yell, and demean in front of others. He wasn't disappointing me. His bark was definitely greater than his bite. Word was that he was being sent back to the States next week, but for now, he was still the CO.

After venting his rage over losing a boat and crew a week earlier on the Chu Viet, he returned to business and gave me my orders. "Welcome aboard, Lieutenant, and now get the fuck out of here and let me do my work."

Our orders were to immediately leave the gargantuan air base and deploy across the Da Nang River, crossing the old French Bridge where we were to check in with the base officer at Bridge Ramp.

Upon leaving and responding with a sharp "Aye-aye, sir," I saluted, and he responded with a salute back. I did an about-face and departed his office in a precise military fashion. While he had a grouchy attitude, I couldn't help but see him as the hands on officer he would have been in the hell of battle. A week or two later, while sitting at the bar in the officers' lounge listening to a couple of captains, I learned that the crusty commander fully deserved my respect. He actually had a distinguished career, having spilled his blood at Pearl Harbor and Guadalcanal, and had been shot twice at the battle of Iwo Jima while transporting troops to the shore. I was proud to be his protégé on this tour.

Rounding out two and a half tours of combat duty, I was to split my team into three groups. Two of the crews would cross-train and familiarize themselves with the boat armaments on LCM 8s, and the other group would take command of the LCU 1601 to which I had been assigned.

An ex-smoker, I had the annoying habit of chewing on a toothpick, seemingly for emphasis when addressing others, including those superior to me in rank, such as Captain Siddhartha. In the leadup to this third tour in Nam, I had trained in amphibious warfare aboard the LCU 1501 at the amphibious base in Coronado. I had also completed six months of guerilla training at the SEAL One Division there too. Having graduated from university in Connecticut several years earlier, I had enlisted in the navy to see the world. I was fleet afoot and had always been a physically conditioned individual, weighing in at approximately 210 pounds, quite wiry at six-foot-four, with an imposing lean musculature, complemented by a full 'stache covering my upper lip. Always optimistic and simpatico, I gave my crew a generous share of my positive inner strength and demanded tremendous loyalty. I talked with a sense of confidence brought about by my extensive training. When I gave orders, they were carried out without question. I never had to raise my voice and didn't have much time for small talk. One of my famous sayings, delivered in a resonant baritone voice, was "God doesn't want us yet, and Satan is scared shitless that we might overrun hell." I was also great fun to be around because of my infectious laugh and hilarious and sometimes bawdy humor.

Accompanied by a platoon of marines, we loaded onto two 6-by-6 trucks in the morning and transported from the Da Nang Air Base to the Da Nang Naval Dock landing. Here we went through the tedium of processing again, standard briefings for new arrivals, paperwork, more shots, and standing in line for what seemed like forever. The men came away from the briefings with new knowledge of the various types of poisonous snakes and scorpions, as well as the numerous varieties of venereal disease. They would be shaking out their boots from now on and always carrying a condom. Up to this point, the men hadn't even seen a Vietnamese yet, man or woman. This was about to change.

CHAPTER 2

On January 27 we made ready at the first gesture of morning with a rising orange sun bringing sober life from gloomy darkness, the peace of dawn reluctantly making way for a frenetic new day. All three boats had been made ready for deployment, and we were to depart immediately for China Beach to load a bladder of JP4, two troops of marines from the 3rd Division, and munitions. For the past couple of monotonous months, we had been experiencing a lot of downtime in the oppressive heat. On some days, we would exchange harassing gunfire with the unseen VC shooting at us from the thick foliage on Elephant Mountain, but nothing more. There was great angst and uncertainty among the men.

Dressed in jungle fatigues like the rest of the men, I had pumped up and welded a disparate group of young men into a cohesive fighting force full of self-confidence and vigor. To our liking, no one was currently on R and R, and we would be going upriver soon with fully experienced naval crews and well-armed marines.

Excitement and a surge of jubilant motivation were in the air as most of the men believed through implicit noble convictions that they would be killing lots of gooks on this mission. In the ensuing days, there were a number shots being fired from Elephant Mountain. None found their mark. Now on my final tour of duty, I didn't share their enthusiasm, and they soon wouldn't either. While the enemy was less equipped than us, they were an experienced, formidable fighting force. Some of the men were nuts when they arrived in Nam, and others would go nuts while they were there. They were still too naïve to know the difference.

For the past twelve months, we had been ferrying jarheads and supplies from Da Nang up past the Imperial City of Hue to the Fork, otherwise known as the Thuan An Estuary, on the Perfume River. With the exception of a couple of LCMs running aground in the shallow river and a few sniper shots, all had been relatively uneventful up and down the wide river.

This mission would be different. Because of operational security, the destination for the Riverine Force operating under Task Force Clearwater would remain top secret until we were fully loaded and off the beach. Our destination was Dong Ha, otherwise known as Hell's Kitchen. Dong Ha was the northernmost marine combat base in South Vietnam and the main logistical base for the marine fire base of Kai San. Because of its location on the Chu Viet River, just ten kilometers below the DMZ, the support base could provide aviation fuel for the copters, ammunition, logistical supplies, and construction materials to both marine and army combat forces. Our short-term mission was to unload during the logistical transfer of supplies and provide protective firepower should the base come under mortar, rocket, artillery, and ground attack by the North Vietnamese Army (NVA). The trip would be dangerous as we would not only be subjected to possible attack by the NVA and/or VC but would also be subjected to high winds and harsh monsoon rains. The latest reconnaissance reported that the river was quiet, with no enemy sightings in the area. However, just outside the mouth of the Chu Viet, boats would be on constant alert for shifting sandbars that could ground them and subject them to rocket attacks from the shore.

I assigned twelve men to the LCU and put four men on each of the LCMs. In addition to our boat crews, each of the three boats would have two South Vietnamese soldiers working as interpreters on board. Usually, an LCU would have a contingent of thirteen men, but with the loss of Mike and no replacement available, we would be operating light.

The boats were each armed with two sets of twin .50 caliber machine guns on both starboard and port sides, along with a 40 mm automatic grenade launcher. The LCU also was outfitted with twin .50 and .60 caliber machine guns in armored turrets fore and aft, a 20 mm M55 weapon system, and a turret-mounted Zippo flamethrower system, located on the stern. We were armed to the teeth.

Looking at the team with unblinking eyes and knowing the agonies they'd been through the past several months, I said with a gravelly voice, "I'm hungry. So let's decompress and go eat and celebrate life in town!" Now, wasn't that an homage to political correctness?

The whole group chorused, "Yes."

The men hadn't had liberty off base in several months.

All had already exchanged their American greenbacks for funny money (military payment certificates), an all-paper currency that resembled Monopoly money to prevent profiteering on the black market.

The night was steaming hot, in the midnineties, and as humid as a mid-July night in New Orleans under a slender crescent moon. After getting enough funny money from the base exchange, we all forayed into the forbidden off-limits Old Quarter of Da Nang City to kick up some shit, as we all knew that the future was going to be a hell of a lot more ferocious.

This was my third and final tour of Nam. A tour in the navy was 329 days if you survived. The first and second tours had been literal horror stories. The casualties had been heavy, and six months into the first tour, the PBR I was on had sunk and Charlie had taken me prisoner. I had been wounded several times and tortured while in captivity. I recovered and returned to the unit each time as experienced men were in short supply. Men in Nam changed forever. A rule of thumb for a new recruit on the muddy rivers was that he had about five to six months before he was killed, wounded, or driven to the edge of insanity. We learned to be loyal but not to get too close to each other.

Fully armed with .45 caliber pistols strapped to our belts, we crossed the old French Bridge and made our way into Old Da Nang City. All were wearing flak jackets as a precaution should Victor Charlie show his face. A couple of the guys carried loaded M16s and gun belts for extra protection should it be needed. It seemed there was foot traffic everywhere despite the curfew. None of us wanted to see an MP walking in town any more than we'd want to see a priest giving mass in a brothel. We'd take care of ourselves.

We trudged into the fetid mud and filth of the gritty marketplace of open-air restaurants, flitting from one boisterous seedy bar to another. Truth to tell, we knew that this louche area of town was off-limits to military personnel, and we maintained our vigilance, keeping an alert eye for Victor Charlie and our MPs as we trolled from one dingy pub to another. I was fully aware that on some nights, this village hosted VC insurgents seeking comfort from the surrounding jungle.

Up the street, a bolt of lightning had speared downward, and there was an explosion where a slash of electricity had stabbed a building. A plume of flames shot upward, lighting the night sky. Locals and others still on the street just kept trudging forward, or in some cases staggering, as though explosions like this were to be expected.

Without the option of sidewalks, we negotiated and wended our way on abandoned wooded oak ammo skids up the muddied potholed gravel street still full of life, with locals selling their wares under traditional conical nón lá hats. The town was dirty, loud, and corrupt, full of prostitutes and street urchins begging for handouts. Then, we started our bar-hopping revelry at our leisure, with our first stop being a sleazy strip club the Bar De Colisee. The name spelled out in red neon letters hissed and crackled above the doorway. From there, we found the Kim-Son Bar on some little back street, which was nothing more than a raucous hole-in-the-wall turned meat factory streaming out tunes from the Beach Boys. Inside, the boisterous joint was smoky and reeking with the ripe odors of its rough clientele. "Gentlemen, let's give a hot welcome to the next group of intrepid ladies," the slovenly dressed DJ yelled. There was a stripper pole in the center of the room, a slim naked girl working it, her legs interlocked and circling around the shiny chrome.

Several other women in miniskirts and in various stages of naughty undress were sashaying about, working the tables and fulfilling American male erotic fantasies. This town did three things right—beer, slender women, and music—and we partook of all three, exploding in a frenzy of hell-raising throughout the night. The rowdy young sailors saw this as a luxury as they were barely eighteen. Da Nang proper was usually a safe place to be stationed and was considered to be a preferred duty with an abundance of local women to socialize and fraternize with. It also had a vibrant marketplace of colorful shops. Old Da Nang was the very opposite. Untamed and off-limits to hard-core, sex-starved, uncouth American soldiers. What the hell, we're sailors, we thought.

The Vietnamese girls were not great conversation partners with their mixed levels of English, but then they did look better and better with each beer. The men quickly blended right into the bar's general seediness, ambling along the row of barstools and the denizen riffraff. We walked across the well-worn wooden floor, which creaked with every step. A large wooden bar ran along the side wall from the front window almost to the wooden stairs leading upstairs to the guest rooms. Along the opposite wall were wooden tables with booths. The place was nearly half-full with a dozen haggard-looking battle-seasoned grunts fresh out of the bush exchanging scintillating braggadocio chatter and otherwise bloody war stories.

The air was a simmering stew and as dank as a Patriots locker room. As soon as I stepped through the doors, my nostrils were assailed by the smell of stale cigarette smoke, marijuana, and spilled booze. Both Bubba and Zach cackled and were wiggling their fingers at us from the bar. "Liquid gold," they yelled in their amped-up Southern drawl as they held ice-cold long-necked Buds in their right hands and groped two scantily clad barmaids with their lefts. The women had silky black hair down to their waist that could give a lonely soldier fresh out of the bush a nosebleed.

"Dumb and dumber," he blurted out with a thickened tongue.

A young Vietnamese woman standing in the doorway, dressed luridly in hot-yellow pants, stiletto heels, and a flesh-colored T-shirt, looked at us and smiled.

"It's OK, soldiers," she said in halting English. "We no bite you. You want come inside?"

Six or seven shapely girls in shorts and halter tops giggled and squealed behind the bouncer, who was dutifully flirting with them, and beckoned us to join the festivities inside. We stepped across the entrance, sailing into a cloud of cheap perfume, intoxicating pheromones, and rotating disco balls spraying the room with broken shards of light across the excited crowd of young chicks. Some of boom-boom girls in mini-dresses and short-shorts didn't look old enough to be out or wearing makeup at all, let alone drinking and on the prowl for American soldiers.

Oh well. Bubba, when inebriated, would bark and share his raffish foul-mouthed Irish proverbs with an elongated burr that would silence the entire bar. "As ye slide down the banister of life, may the splinters be goin' the wrong way," he said with a wry face to anyone who would listen.

Zach offered a crass verbal comeback as he downed a shot of JD with a beer chaser, canoodling and squeezing his barmaid's gyrating ass. "May your ups and downs always be under the sheets!"

It was going to be a testosterone night for sure. Swede belched with his unique vulpine smile. Nevertheless, the Texan was smiling with a peal of raw jocularity, laughter, and a dose of deft sarcasm. Zach looked at him with a lopsided grin from ear to ear, his eyes full of wicked, randy mischief.

A big, hard-looking grizzled bouncer in a black T-shirt came out from around the bar and blocked Zach's path to the stairs.

"You found something you like, bro?"

"I think I have. Now get the fuck out of my way."

"His language rather salty."

The crotchety bouncer responded, "Eighty-five now, and leave your gear on the bar. Anything extra, you talk and pay girl."

Zach nodded, pulled out his wallet along with his Smith & Wesson .45, and shoved it into the bouncer's mouth. A liquid puddle quickly formed at the base of the bouncer's feet.

Ten minutes later, with the grin of a feral Cheshire cat, he disappeared upstairs in the skivvy house with his boom-boom girl, who was wearing a fuck-me-please miniskirt that barely covered her crotch. I had to admire Zach's droll persona and his ability to laugh, crack out jokes when things got tense, and get the other guys laughing too. His devil-may-care flippancy was something we all seriously needed in this hell hole, particularly now. I knew that they were going to be confronting tougher times ahead and some would be spiraling up and passing through the pearly gates.

We soon found that we weren't alone in this no-man's-land as almost every bar we entered seemed to have a dozen or so sketchy-looking armed marines with dead eyes and unshaven faces quenching their thirst with cold beers and tranquilizing themselves with shots of tequila aplenty, all of them in need of an alcohol-laden detox. Some of the grunts were amped up and breezing through the night loud and rowdy, while the prattles of others was fading under a deluge of alcohol. An unmistakable scent of marijuana wafted in the air, but those partaking were very discreet, trying to impress us with bullshit stories of their recent firefights and village escapades with the local virgins, which got raunchier and less credible as the night wore on.

George and Lance, sitting at the bar, ordered a couple of Thit chó cheeseburgers to accompany their beers. The bartender, having delivered the burgers, smiled and moved back from the bacchanal. After taking his first bite, chewing on the bun-covered meat covered in a Vietnamese sauce, George suddenly stopped and swallowed. Lance also took a healthy bite and began chewing.

George asked the bartender, "What kind of beef is this?"

The bartender responded, "Thit chó."

"What's that in English?" he demanded.

A marine sitting beside him harrumphed, picking up his beer bottle. "Dog meat."

Lance turned green and promptly spat out what was left in his mouth on the bar.

The bartender came back, saying that dog meat was good for you—plenty of protein.

"You eat it, then," Lance said, pointing his pistol at the bartender's head. They watched as the nervous bartender chowed down the burgers with trembling hands. Both George and Lance proceeded to wash out their mouths with a bottle of vodka. Then, having no glasses, they began taking long swallows before putting the bottle back down on the bar.

It was around eleven thirty or maybe midnight as we were stumbling out of the dingy New York Bar, somewhat impaired, having imbibed the best alcohol available. We then headed for the Lisa Bar on the main drag, which we had passed on the way in. I spotted an American in faded Levi's slouching against a doorway with a cute-looking Vietnamese girl snuggled in his arms. He looked somewhat familiar as we got closer. It was my younger brother!

At first glance, it seemed he may have already had one too many, but when he cleared his throat, he yelled out my name with a dry rasp escaping his throat, telegraphing it across the wooden passage.

"Yo, James!" I yelled back. The enthusiastic shout took hold like a brush fire in the foothills of LA. He turned around, and we both just stood there, glaring at each other in the dim light. I was shocked, to say the least, and my pulse quickened. Then, without any further ado, we both flourished, moving forward, and gave each other bro hugs right there in the middle of the dusty road. Then I drew back, observing my younger brother. How the hell did you get over here? I thought. He was a noncommissioned army Huey mechanic; the last I knew, my brother had been stationed in Berlin, Germany. He obviously had somehow gotten a transfer to the Da Nang Army Air Base. My brother was a rakish Don Juan with an insatiable testosterone level and a tremendous gregarious appetite for women. Unrepentantly, he was a guy who could charm birds out of trees. From what he shared with me, he was now shacking up after hours and getting his rocks off shagging this hot hoochie-mama, who went by the moniker of "Peaches" off base. A definite no, no, no!

"Hey guys, meet my other half and all-around reprobate." By midnight, boundaries of behavior had begun to tilt under the influence of alcohol. Johnny Boy, barely coherent, swiveled on his stool, somewhat woozy and snickering, flourishing a well-used bottle of JD in a salute, and ogled aloud with derision. Then, in his deep Cajun accent and with a sappy grin, he said that he'd loved to taste Peaches tonight, before he realized what he had just intoned and felt his face go red with embarrassment. Suddenly, there was a portentous silence, like a lead curtain had been dropped over the room. Everyone in hearing distance was drawn to a possible bar brawl as moths to a flame. Jim's buoyant attitude instantly took a nosedive as he gnashed his teeth and flared his nostrils. Peaches swallowed visibly but said nothing.

My brother was no shrinking violet, and his anger torpedoed. "What the fuck did you just say, asshole," he yelled vociferously. "Excuse my fucking French, asshole!"

The vitriol of his words resonated deep into the barroom. I saw that the sour, astringent glare on my brother's face as he took a combative stance went beyond reproof: a capital sentence was to be handed down. It raised a few eyebrows, to say the least. Johnny Boy, now with a penitent snickered look on his unshaven puss, took a moment to process, then immediately apologized for the ribald joke, acknowledging that it was snarky and totally uncalled for. But, ahem, the image triggered more than a couple of visible chuckles and amoral gallows humor, notwithstanding a few derisive snorts from the other guys sitting at the bar hoping to witness *The Good, Bad, and the Ugly*. He slid off the barstool, and the floor silently seesawed and tilted, throwing him off balance and landing his ass on the hard floor. Sidling away unobtrusively, Jonny Boy, having now bridled his palooka tongue, then disappeared, his testosterone storm ghosting into the shadows.

Actually, we all took notice of her full breast and heart-shaped ass, barely covered by her white miniskirt. Anyway, a couple of hours and four or five beers followed by a few shots of Irish whiskey later, I traded a couple of high fives with my brother and wished him a safe return. "See you back home, bro. You're the best," I choked out as I watched him return to his wont, climbing the stairs, Peaches in tow behind him.

We all exited the Lisa Bar swaying a little, disheveled, and moving slowly and gracelessly like a dozen discombobulated rabid dogs. We somehow found our way back to base in the darkness, having secured a half dozen or more cyclos without a shot being fired and with no one left behind. I heard later that one cyclo missed a turn at the bridge and was last seen floating down the river. My brother seemingly had stayed as we left the bar and staggered back to base. I would not see Jim again alive. He was killed in a chopper crash several months later down in the Mekong Delta region.

To the best of my knowledge, we had all gotten sloshed, at least two drinks past inebriation. I finally got into my bunk before I fell down. But even with the collective level of bibulous debauchery, we'd all sobered up before reveille in the dank morning air that was saturated with dust and diesel fuel.

I have convinced myself that my brother never knew that during the final days of his romantic tryst, he had left Peaches in a family way.

CHAPTER 3

On the morning of April 7, 1997, at the crack of dawn in an eerie morning fog, we all had the standard insipid breakfast of coffee, congealed scrambled eggs, bacon, and toast before we began to prepare for what was thought to be a low-key voyage north hugging the white sands of the South China Sea coastline. All the men were dressed in olive T-shirts, field pants, and boots. LCM 325 was loaded with a highly volatile 10,000-gallon fuel bladder of Aviation JP4 fuel for helicopter refueling. LCM 326 was carrying 90 tons of munitions and 50 cases of beer, fresh water, C-rats, and other essential supplies for the troops. LCU 1601 was also carrying munitions and ferrying four platoons of seasoned combat-hardened grunts from the 1st Battalion, 3rd Marines, along with fifteen ARVN troops and an M48 tank in its well deck. The tank was to be deployed to the besieged Khe Sanh Combat Base as part of a reinforcement operation against the ongoing Tet Offensive. The marines used the waiting time to apply camouflage paint to each other's faces in case they encountered something unexpected and had to depart the boat in a hurry and enter the jungle. The boat crews watching the marines paint each other also got in the spirit and joined the makeup party.

Owen was watching Zach skeptically, getting his face done by a grunt. "If you weren't already so ugly, you wouldn't need that paint."

Zach's pulse rate accelerated, and he offered a well-articulated response: "Call me ugly one more time, and I'll put my Ruger up your fucking redneck ass!"

Owen sat down and got painted.

At 0500 hours the following morning, we got underway in the early morning darkness for the Cua Viet River north of Quang Tri Province, traveling approximately ninety-six clicks north, skirting up the coast to the base of the estuary. The thirty-minute wait as we double-checked everything before departure seemed like an eternity. A tang of salty sea breeze tickled my tongue. Just before we pulled out, the platoon commander and his three gunnery sergeants decided to redistribute the troops and firepower on the LCU, putting the first platoon of men on LCM 325 and the second platoon on LCM 326. The other two platoons would remain in the LCU. While not hearing any reports of VC activity and not expecting an attack, we were carrying a lot of valuable and much-needed aviation fuel, equipment, ammunition, and precious marine infantry replacements. We were now prepared for anything that might befall us. Two UH-1E Hueys would escort us out of the harbor and cover us for six klicks up the coast. We would be on our own for the rest of the mission, and we were well aware that convoys were ambushed regularly.

Due to aerial resupply from shoreline bases and offshore naval vessels being restricted based on distance, riverine units of Assault Craft Unit One utilizing LCUs and LCMs became the chief method of logistical replenishment for the forward units.

Our destination was the desolate northernmost marine combat logistical support base at Dong Ha, at the conflux of the Cua Viet and Bo Dieu tributaries, just a click and a half south of the DMZ. This firebase was essential to maintaining the continuous support of Khe Sanh Combat Base and several other marine firebases strategically strung out along the southern DMZ as they were all now under siege by the NVA and VC as part of the spring Tet Offensive. Of utmost importance was the continuous supply of ammunition, food, and aviation fuel for the choppers. Of less importance but still crucial to the moral of the troops was mail from home.

Because of the distance between the firebases, the choppers had to be refueled at Dong Ha Air Base. Our ETA was 1600 hours, cruising at 7 to 10 knots. As long as the weather cooperated and remained calm, we had a couple of hours to spare. Once we reached the estuary, we would rendezvous with two PBRs that would escort us up the river and provide additional fire support should we encounter trouble. We would all be on full alert as the fully laden U boats with life-essential supplies were susceptible targets for enemy snipers.

Unlike the Perfume River, which was wide with no jungle overhang, the Cua Viet River was a narrow serpentine channel with a triple-canopy jungle overhead all the way up to the firebase. We would all be at battle stations for the trip up these brown muddy waters, well known for enemy ambushes. The men had learned over the past several months to be aware of our surroundings on the river as the locals were not that forthcoming and might even be NVA and VC sympathizers. The murky estuary was brutally hot and smelled dank, and the humidity had to be 100 percent as the red rim of the sun climbed above the distant mountains. Unlike the thirty-meter-wide and deep Perfume River at the imperial citadel of Hue, which we skirted several hours earlier on our port side, the notorious silt-filled Cua Viet was dangerously shallow, narrow, a pest hole full of malaria, and barely navigable with shoals and strong currents.

The hot, oppressive sun radiated on the horizon across an ocean flecked with whitecaps. The sweltering, unfriendly environment was taking its toll, but the men were doing their jobs with alacrity and few complaints. We moved cautiously at 150 yards apart, slowly easing our way along the river through the triple-canopy jungle filled with pendulous vines always in our face. We stayed midstream as best we could from the bomb-cratered shoreline, constantly alert for an enemy sniper who would be invisible in the triple canopy above and might have us in his crosshairs, and then there were the venomous green vipers hanging from the vines. There were also the leeches clinging to the leaves zeroing in on our body heat and bloodsucking airborne mosquitoes the size of birds. Swede Westermarck, our navy sharpshooter, was on full alert, constantly looking off in the distance through his starlight scope mounted on his M21 sniper rifle toward where we are heading, scanning the trees for a sniper. Zachary Duff was also at full alert, manning his M2 machine gun mounted on the upper deck while the other guys went about their duties. The marines were watching the shoreline through field-issued binoculars from both sides of the boats with diligence, their M16s fully locked and loaded, at the ready.

The waterway resembled a mangrove more than a river, and danger lurked everywhere. Several areas along the riverbank were earthen dikes a couple of meters above the river's edge consisting of fertile rice paddies and some small dilapidated hamlets linked by hedgerows and an ever-changing concealment of paths and drainage ditches that provided the VC an ambush network. All were on high alert as we had received information that a small band of VC was in the area harassing the villagers. All five of the boats in convoy had their twin .50 caliber machine guns manned and pointed both port and starboard while underway upriver. We passed two PBRs conducting interdiction of traffic coming out of a mangrove canal and heading downriver. They reported no enemy activity.

We felt reasonably safe with four platoons of marines on board the boats, evening if they were cherries and only 50 percent of them were awake and on full alert at all times with their fingers on the triggers. However, they were under orders from battalion command that should we stumble upon the enemy, they were to pursue, engage, and destroy them in a short foray if at all possible without compromising the safety and security of the boats.

Having reached the mouth of the river with five to six hours of daylight still left, we rendezvoused with the two PBRs under the command of Chris Polinski, chief petty officer of PBR 718, and Doug Lasher, first class petty officer of PBR 724. Chris, showing off the maneuverability of his boat, took the controls away from his coxswain and did two 180-degree turns in his own wake.

Chris and I graduated from Teikyo Post University together, majoring in law enforcement, and had become friends. We had had some wild and often raucous times together back in the day. Back in San Diego, after an unusually tough day of training on Mare Island, Chris and I, along with a half dozen other officers, reconnected off base at a disreputable backwater tavern across the harbor. All of us were doing our best to deplete the pub's supply of beer, followed by shots of Hennessy and JD. One rowdy story led to another and another as we reminisced about our favorite antics back in the day. We were all making a lot of noise, laughing, and carrying on, creating new memories. All eleven of us got hammered that night and spent the night in a San Diego jail cell for disorderly conduct, cementing our brotherhood. I think that if I had to describe Chris, I would sketch him as a close amigo with a manic edge, a garrulous good-time Charlie, a connoisseur of fine cigars, anal-retentive, a rowdy political antagonist without a conscience, a butterfly for sure, a first class raconteur, and a frequent accomplice in humiliating antics unbecoming an officer. A true naval reprobate with no concept of self-control. He was genuinely incorrigible. Chris was a hellfire recalcitrant who always had a scheme and a plan to execute it. He always sought control. Scuttlebutt had it that he was receiving cases of smuggled booze from a corrupted navy quartermaster on base at below-bargain-basement pricing and reselling it to the troops at a premium.

Another story floating was that he was in cahoots with a couple of locals and had begun working as a middleman supplying weed, cocaine, heroin, and hash to the troops going out into the bush. There was no question that, unlike the rest of us, Chris always had plenty of money to buy rounds at the bar. From what he shared with us, he had recently married a very attractive young woman before enlisting. He had a gifted silver tongue and would talk on and on about females tirelessly and shamelessly, unabashedly adhering to a self-proclaimed double standard. He was obsessed with young Vietnamese women. While he drank a lot and obviously smoked a joint of two, he never seemed out of control, and to most of us, women seemed to be his preoccupation in life; they fell into his hands like fruit off trees. Doug Lasher, Chris's second-in-command, was another story. A pathetic one.

While he liked Chris and the courage he didn't have, Petty Officer Lasher had the courage needed but just wanted to survive and get home to a warm bed with clean sheets and his young wife of sixteen months. While Chris was absolutely fearless, oblivious to danger and physical pain, he was absolutely someone you wanted next to you if you found yourself in trouble. However, I kept my distance as I was too invested in my own career path to risk the taint of his growing reputation.

Upon entering the placid estuary of the Cua Viet, we allowed ourselves five hours max to cover the distance upriver to Dung Ha. My goal was to make it in four hours, fully alert for potential enemy activity. The scorching air was a steaming stew, and the jungle was humming with unrelenting mosquitoes and other flying irritants. We would proceed slowly, maintaining a distance of four boat lengths between boats upon veering port and starboard as the river was full of thick clumps of grasses and protruding stumps, some just below the surface of the murky water. We couldn't risk damaging our props and possibly disabling a boat. So the crew on relief and troops went to relaxed GQ and wolfed down their C-rats of cold ham and lima beans. Others, if they were lucky enough, had cold hot dogs and beans. All of it was dated 1945.

The convoy was arranged so that PBR 718, under the command of Chris Polinski, would be in the lead position one klick ahead, reconnoitering the passage, followed by George (Poncho) Viera on the LCM 326 in the second position 200 yards behind. The lumbering LCU 1601 piloted by Carlin Eagle would be in the middle, followed by George "Snake" Stone on the LCM 325. Finally, PBR 724, piloted by Doug Lasher, would be in the fourth position, maintaining a 200-yard distance and providing sweep protection for the rear. Swede always had the same bloodletting look behind the .50 caliber turret gun: eyes wide open and ready to kill any motherfucking gook lurking in the grass who dared to show his face. Swede, a navy gunner's mate, indeed followed the marine philosophy of "If in doubt, kill them all and let God sort it out later." He was a real piece of work, and I'm glad he was on our side. Maintaining radio silence, Chris gave the OK gesture with his left hand, and we began our journey up the muddy river in unison. Unfortunately, the pounding monsoon rains had come early on this day, making the trip upriver all the more miserable.

Several clicks upriver on our starboard side, we passed through a fecund vegetated marsh of rice paddies where a dilapidated old Buddhist shrine, a few small buildings, and thatched-roofed bamboo hooches dominated the bank of the river. This was a village of a hundred or more people, staunchly anti-communist, resting comfortably in the afternoon heat along the river's shoreline. Today, for some reason, only a dozen or so elderly mama Sans were visible on the banks. The young able-bodied men had most likely been taken by the VC and herded into the jungle, being taught the ridged doctrine of the VC.

Chris radioed back that all looked good but we should proceed with caution. A small contingent of indigenous peasant villagers with sunken cheekbones, wearing rice hats and holding their naked baby Sans, were swarming down to the river bank on our starboard side. In the pouring rain, they were doing antic pantomimes in their quest to communicate with us with waves of laughter. Some children are waving and yelling, "Hey, Joe" and "Give us chop-chop!" While the adults essentially just watched us in abandonment from the top of the tree-lined embankment, the children quickly learned enough English to yell for candy and food. While we couldn't give them money, we all threw them apples that were on board each boat for this very purpose. The VC would confiscate anything more valuable, such as chocolates or cans of C-rats, and the children would be either kidnapped or slaughtered for accepting the gifts. We all knew that the enemy didn't wear uniforms and was usually very near when the village locals and children stayed away from the river's edge. Small things can mean so much. We passed cautiously by without incident.

This village of small hovels was free of VC and NVA activity during the day. But after the sun went down, it was well-known that it was a haven for Charlie and that the villagers would be forced to feed them, care for their wounded before leaving, and take their rice with them. During the night they moved from village to village with complete impunity.

Operating under strict rules of engagement, a small platoon of marines was sent ashore to search for signs of Charlie within the village. Unless we came under heavy fire, we were restricted to holding our fire and not endangering the villagers. While Charlie was persistent, he learned and liked our rules.

Not finding any evidence of recent enemy activity, the convoy continued upriver, with our progress being noted indifferently by a corpulent water buffalo lazing close to the shore in the late day setting sun. It was a strangely peaceful sojourn upriver along peaceful riverbanks. While we were at relaxed GQ, we maintained constant vigilance for floating mines in the murky brown water and other dangers from the shoreline. The trip was uneventful, just the way everyone liked it. Still, no one dismissed that this steamy region of thick jungle, rainforest, and mangrove swamps, teeming with thriving wildlife and the bulbous heads of deadly snakes, was incredibly dangerous to your health.

This northern province bordering the DMZ and North Vietnam had largely been ceded to the NVA and was now the exclusive domain of the VC. Three weeks earlier, a riverine resupply convoy encountered hostile fire about 1,500 meters, or a click and a half, from where we were. They hit two river booby traps laid by the VC, with the last one destroying an LCM, wounding 15 marines and killing 3, including 4 sailors and 15 Vietnamese ARVN soldiers. Then, after a brief firefight with light machine gun fire from the south bank, the enemy fell back and disappeared into the jungle. Four marines and two ARVN interpreters were still listed as MIA.

We finally beached at the fortified Dong Ha boat ramp this day without incident in a grueling, suffocating heat. We landed just before dusk, lowered our bow ramps, and logged in at the base logistics master at 1900 hours. While Dung Ha was hardly the Garden of Eden, it did offer a little more security from the boonies and the dangers on the river. Concertina wire was strung everywhere, even hanging from the few trees that hadn't yet been cut down or blown up by the enemy.

The base was an abysmal, stifling, sweltering 150-degree sweatbox of Quonset huts, one with a canteen sign on top of it, water buffalo, shacks, and tents, resembling more of a ramshackle boomtown than a marine combat supply depot. The base was thrumming with activity. A busy assortment of military vehicles, not to mention the continuous landing and departures of Hueys and Chinooks carrying loads of carrion wrapped body bags being transported back to Da Nang, created dust clouds everywhere. Once a beautiful fine-grain sandy beach area in the middle of a lush rainforest, it was now a booming, clammy cantonment of dilapidated plywood huts, sandbag bunkers, unkempt latrines for officers, fifty-five-gallon shit drums for enlisted, miserable bunkers, and grimy mess halls. The base smelled of diesel fuel and burning shit. The forest tree line had been cut back two thousand yards around the site to facilitate helo traffic and deter any surprise enemy infiltration. Beyond that was a desolate no-man's-land. The perimeter was encased in thousands of yards of razor-sharp concertina wire and hundreds of Claymore mines and trip flares. Even with all the prevention in force, sappers still attempted to breach it and marines would pick them off. No one dared to venture from the security of the village. Once darkness fell, the landscape became a free-fire zone, and anyone out there was fair game. Local Vietnamese who were friendly by day often became the enemy by nightfall, leaving the firebase to give the VC coordinates of target positions in the camp to fire upon.

I radioed the logistics quartermaster upon our beaching, and marine logistical personnel began unloading the boats immediately with a half dozen military forklifts. The marine commander and gunnery sergeant began overseeing the unloading of the boats in between skimming through a well-used *Playboy* magazine. The logistic situation in Dung Ha was critical, and all replenishments were to be inventoried and secured with haste. In conjunction with ARVN forces at Dung Ha and Khe Sanh, American troops consumed twenty-six hundred tons of supplies daily, excluding bulk bladders of petroleum products, fuel for the tanks and other vehicles and the aviation fuel for the Huey gunships, Chinooks, and one thousand tons of munitions. In addition, fully armed soldiers were ambling all over the base landing zone seeking orders and command.

Not wanting to be idle during the unloading, the crews began checking for possible mechanical issues or possible improvements to be made to the boats. Owen "Bubba" McKnight, Lance Idler, and Shawn Russell disappeared into their engine compartments below deck, checking their engines and electrical components. The seamen—Ron Vargas, Zachary Duff, and Don Russell—were going over every inch of their boats from bow to stern, looking for deficiencies. None were found. The gunner's mates—Jake Cosciello from the LCU, along with Swede Westermarck and Dave Greeves from the LCMs—inspected, cleaned, and oiled all the ordnance, including deck guns, and double-checked munitions and grenade inventories. The three of them were more than capable of field-stripping all the artillery on board in the dark if necessary. Carlton Eagle, George Stone, and George Viera requisitioned a diesel tanker for refueling the boats.

Johnny Boy "Godfather" Soprano had completed his base commissary shopping and would be serving a well-deserved convivial spaghetti and meatball supper from the galley of the LCU. Chris magnanimously brought over two cases of ice-cold Schlitz along with a case of Hennessey that he must have somehow hijacked from the commissary storage shed. This brought cheers from the crew aboard the LCU 1501, including the crews of the PBRs. Apparently, only forty-five cases of beer were unloaded, and Chris looked furtively around for anyone stupid enough to question the apparent misappropriation.

The first class petty officer of PBR 724 was the stupid one. Only he had kept his eye on Johnny Boy and foolishly questioned the missing cases in front of the three boat crews. Chris stood over Doug and, staring him in the eye, asked, "You got a fucking problem, fella?" The galley went silent. "No one invited you over here for the party, asshole."

"No sir," he said pathetically. "I was saying how good the food and drink was, sir!"

"I'm not a 'sir,' asshole!"

The alcohol was kicking in, and there was devilment flickering in his eyes. Seemingly undaunted by the chief petty officer or his scowl, he laughed and finished his dish as Chris stormed past him, heading out of the galley belching every fucking obscenity he knew. We all ate, attacking the meatballs with voracity for the next hour or so.

Later we socialized, while some wrote letters back home and talked about what they did before enlisting, their wives and girlfriends, and what they planned to do when they got out. *If they got out.* Not one of the guys cared to talk about where we were headed. Any time we went on an operation upriver, there was a serious chance that some of us wouldn't be coming back. Lights went out at 2000 hours. An hour later, the sky opened up with a monsoon deluge.

Each U boat would set up an armed stern watch to stand guard for four-hour shifts throughout the moonless night, remaining vigilant for enemy swimmers. The LCU would have two additional armed sentries patrolling the forward beach perimeter line for the three U boats tethered together. Both the beachhead and harbor were classified as free-fire zones after dark, meaning they became areas where there was a strict curfew in effect, and any unidentified person who moved within that area could and would be considered a hostile enemy and dealt with summarily.

Chris and I took some time after he had cooled down, sat on a couple of ammo crates on the dock next to the boats, and reminisced about personal histories with a couple of mugs of coffee. The coffee was as thick as road tar, but it was tasty.

Later, over a couple of beers, we watched a swarm of fireflies dance on the surface of the blackish water as Chris blew perfect donuts of smoke from his Cuban cigar. While he had a wife back in San Diego, his true perdition was his lascivious zeal for Vietnamese Mama-Sans and their boom-boom girls back in Da Nang, which seemed to be his aphrodisiac. Chris was promiscuous as ever and didn't try to hide his philandering extramarital escapades and other indiscretions. For that reason and that reason alone, he was in a hurry to complete this supply run and get back to base. I didn't even bother to ask questions.

"Bryce, when was the last time you got laid?" A moment of protractive silence passed by. "OK, OK, none of my fucking business. Got it!"

Chris shrugged his shoulders and flashed a grin. Then he went on, "But you look about as much fun as a guy about to have a root canal. Tell you what, I'll set you up with a real Vietnamese Mama-San when you get back to base. A redhead, just your height with long legs; large, firm tits above her IQ; and an ass you'll be able to hold on to as you ride her. She'll speak English, will be none too bright, and will regard your cock as a magical wand."

That was his description of the perfect woman, which showed in his expressive grin. I found it nearly impossible not to laugh, but I gave it my best.

We continued to exchange small talk for an hour or so before calling it a night and nonchalantly said good night as we retreated to our bunks. Having listened to him talk about war atrocities and toot his raffish horn about the lurid prurient details of his promiscuous love life back at the base, I chose not to discuss my "Dear John" with him. Unfortunately, we all sometimes take departures from our better impetuous judgment, and it's usually due to the intensity to assuage our libidos. But unfortunately, Christ had a hair-trigger temper that had, on more than one occasion, ended with a frightening, mercurial mood shift that would set me on fire. Something in the finality of his tone sounded valedictory.

I took the opportunity of the brief hiatus to write what might very well be my final letter to Diane. We had corresponded several times since her brother's death. Still, I'd noticed that the length and level of fragrant affection within her spidery written letters began to diminish. The last one was her gut-wrenching "Dear John" letter.

Hi, Bryce,

I'm sorry. It's been several weeks since I've last written, but it's just so hard. Got your letters and pictures. It looks like you've lost weight! With you in Vietnam and everything going on here, it's difficult and confusing. All of my friends are protesting against the war. With the loss of my brother, I've recently joined them in denouncing your war and hopefully convincing the country that what you all are doing over there is immorally wrong and that my brother was murdered under your watch! The Vietnam War bloodshed horror is coming over loud and clear through the Walter Cronkite evening news every bloody night as the US body count grows higher and higher.

It's scaring the hell out of us back here at home. Two girls I know at the university have also recently lost their brothers there.

I don't know how to say this, so I'm just going to tell you straight out like it is: I've been dating an Ed Sterniac, and we've both fallen in love. He is the son of the captain of the Connecticut State Police, and he has been exempted from serving in the military. I swear I wasn't looking for anyone, but it just happened, and I now want to be his wife. We met at a country club dinner that my father sponsored with Ed's father, a friend of my father's. I'll send back the engagement ring to you, and I wish you a safe return and a happy life wherever you should end up.

Bryce, be careful and goodbye!

I was crushed and devastated! The bite of regret was sharp. Diane now saw me as having her brother's blood on my hands, and she was seemly involved in a tryst with my closest friend Ed Sterniac, whom I'd known and trusted since grammar school and was now intimately involved with Lorinda. I wanted to pour a tall glass of JD, maybe two, down my throat and smash something and everything in front of me with my fists. But as much as this had shattered me inside, I had to keep it private. Signs of depression, anxiety, and performance unbecoming an officer would soon attract attention and distract from our mission. Having read the letter several times now, I folded it again and stuffed it in my pocket. I would do my suffering in silence. After several weeks and a pang of silent hurt, I began to think less and less about her, eventually destroying the note.

I couldn't complain about my love life so far. I had sex a couple times back in the States but wasn't into cheap thrills or getting laid just to get a piece of ass. I respected women far too much to indulge in meaningless one-night flings. My relationships were few and far between, and I wasn't about to fuck my way through waves of women. I was OK. When the day came that I met the right woman, I'd be able to let her know I wasn't some man whore. Maybe I'd picked up some old-fashioned traits from my family, but I'd want her to know that she was special and that I was a special man as well. My parents and grandparents had brought me up to be respectful not only to others but also, just as importantly, to himself. If I couldn't respect myself, how could I expect respect from others? Over that, I really didn't much give a damn.

At 0200 hours on the following morning, we were awakened by an unrelenting driving rain outside being whipped into a frenzy by the monsoon's howling winds. The waves in the river surged and crashed against the sterns of our boats, which were tied and secured to the beach landing. A sliver of moon above was sheltered behind a thickening cloud cover. We all knew the tension of guard duty in Nam, the straining to see something in a pitch-black night. The monotonous ticking of time that seemed to tick seconds into hours. The terror of trying to decipher safety from harm. The rule was to shoot first to be sure.

Ka-pow, ka-pow, ka-pow…ka-pow! Boom!

We were suddenly all awakened to a volley of rapid gunfire from what sounded like a high-powered AK-47 rifle, seemingly coming from the stern of our LCU, positioned between the two LCMs. Having heard the distinctive report, we all bolted upright from our bunks, landing on our feet, grabbing our rifles, and almost certain we were under attack. We reached, fully armed and still in our skivvies, except for Bubba, who was buck naked, but no one noticed or cared as Zach met us there.

Then, as suddenly as it had begun, the firing stopped. A hush of silence hung in the air as some thirty half-naked men on three boats and on the shore searched the darkness with their rifles, trying to acquire their disoriented night vision on an almost moonless night so that they could identify target.

Zach quickly quelled the maelstrom in the darkness by assuring us that everything was OK, laughing hysterically as he said in a deep Irish brogue, "Ha are ya, ladies?"

Zach, who had the stern watch, had spotted what appeared to be an enemy swimmer in the darkened water and had fired four rounds from his captured and treasured AK-47 before lobbing a grenade at him for good measure, which also killed any fish that happened to be in close proximity to the sapper. Then, with the body floating on the surface face down some thirty yards out, Bubba, our self-proclaimed uncouth and underdeveloped redneck from Kentucky, dove into the dark, stagnant water commando. He back-stroked the bloody body back to shallow water by its hair before frog-walking it to shore. It hadn't been a banner day for that gook, Bryce thought.

Andrew, our sometimes hilarious combat medic, leaned over the body without touching it and positively identified it as a North Vietnamese swimmer now suitable for an explosive fish dinner. He was wearing Soviet scuba gear with a waterproof satchel of Chinese plastic explosives strapped to him that had failed to go off even after Zach riddled him with bullets. A marine explosive ordnance team was requested, and they carefully put the kamikaze back in the water, pulling the corpse out by boat into the middle of the harbor with a fifty-foot rope tethered around its neck. Releasing the rope, they detonated the motherfucking corpse from the shore with their own explosives. More dead fish soon began floating to the surface.

Time passed slowly, and the banter gradually diminished. The rest of the foul night was uneventful and quiet. There was no sense of exultation in the unrelenting humidity. We listened intently for sounds that would signal enemies in the area. We heard only the normal night sounds: frogs croaking, the river lapping at the shore as the tide changed, and night insects chirping.

The river was benign tonight, almost too quiet for my comfort. The men smoked cigarettes and scanned *Playboy* magazines; there was a light reckoning scent of cannabis in the air. Soon the banter ceased and the men tossed their cigarettes into the dark water.

The boat perimeter was reconnoitered, and as the night stretched into the morning, we got an early start on a new day as we had all gotten little sleep after the events of the night. The men rarely bathed now, and the smell was distinctive. Some during the afternoon would jump into the river fully clothed and sponge-wash themselves in the dark water, always on alert for venomous snakes. They wore the same sweat-soaked fatigues for weeks at a time, and some would never get the chance to change them.

CHAPTER 4

It had been two monotonous weeks since we left the base in Da Nang, and the lack of real intelligence and transparency from higher command was a major incipient concern for me. The heat only exacerbated my tension. Not having an official intelligence source, I had to rely on unofficial base dispatches and rabid scuttlebutt predicting a significant enemy buildup rapidly circulating from incoming recon patrols and Huey pilots. Two nights ago, during a torrent of monsoon rain, three VC were killed attempting to breach the fence, which gave me a compelling justification for my concern. Nobody disagreed that a major offensive was in the making. The VC, bolder than I had ever imagined possible, was gaining ground, which was unsettling. Each day that passed sitting idle here decreased the odds of us making it back.

Tick. Tick. Tick. It was eerily quiet that night. Glancing surreptitiously at my watch, I did a 360-degree look around me as I collapsed and crouched down against the starboard side of our boat, pondering our situation, hugging my fully loaded M16 and peering out into the jungle. While the two weeks that we had been docked in Dong Ha had been basically uneventful and the latest copy of the *Stars and Strips* repeated that General Westmorland was predicting that the end of the war was in view, I didn't see any evidence that the enemy was on the same frequency. I had a sinking prescience that trouble lay ahead, and it was eating at my gut like some insidious bacteria. Every nerve ending in my body was taut.

A beam of light came through the fronds and thick vines that hung above me. I squinted and sensed menacing danger. We'd been idle in Dong Ha for too long, waiting for orders to return. The days had become a frustrating, repetitive slog of finding things to do in the shade to eliminate boredom in the torrid, excruciating jungle heat. The command seemed to me to be suffering from almost total combat paralysis, leaving us stranded for no apparent purpose.

The men enjoyed the stand-down to relax, take baths in the river—some naked, some not so much—shave, brush teeth, and remove the stench of the jungle from their bodies. It was what was known in a combat zone as "relaxed grooming standards." Nevertheless, I had an uneasy suspicion that nagged at me, and I seriously wanted to get back to our Base facility in Da Nang. "Hurry up and wait," the normal military cliché, I said petulantly to himself. My gut feeling was that the VC was watching us, our uniquely psychedelic insanity amid the war on full display, and they would be waiting for our departure.

My forehead was corrugated with foreboding concern and uneasiness. My mouth felt as dry as the skin on my face, parched by the ever-present sun. As it stood, the Marine 3rd Division, consisting of 250 troops, had left during the night on five CH-47 Chinooks accompanied by a half dozen mortar units to reinforce beleaguered soldiers at besieged Khe Sanh Firebase. They left behind the 150 troops from the 3rd Battalion we had just brought up from Da Nang to protect the besieged Dong Ha Supply Dump from being attacked and overrun. Unease crawled through my gut, and nervous tension rippled down the tendons of my neck.

We ate our morning chow as we sat and waited for orders.

Observation, intelligence, and past experience all dictated to me that the VC was lurking nearby, a few hundred yards away at best, in the jungle perimeter just outside the razor wire.

The men that were able to got some shut-eye before stirring at 0600 hours the following morning. A serendipitous message was received. We were getting out of Dodge. At 0830 hours, having finally received confirming orders from naval support to return to Da Nang, I gave orders to make ready: "Lock and load, and let's get the hell out of here!"

Equipment and armaments were checked and double-checked. There was no luxury in Dong Ha, and it was time to haul ass before the local VC had time to set up a surprise party for this godforsaken base.

The conditions were miserable, and my sense of our vulnerability to an enemy assault would soon prove prescient.

I stepped off the LCU and quickly sprinted over to the PBRs tied up to the dock to give Chris and Doug the heads-up that we had received orders to return to Da Nang and would be leaving within the hour. What I found was that the jaded crew members were sprawled out on the deck drunk and soaked to the skin. It was obvious that they had been drinking heavily during the night. As I was surveying the chaos on deck, Chris stumbled out from the cabin below.

Having relayed the order, he responded, advising me that neither of the boats would be ready for a day or two as their propulsion water jets were jammed and inoperable. "Unfortunately, you're going to have to make do without us, big buddy," he said with a slumberous, intoxicated slur.

I could discern the distinct smell of weed wafting from below deck as he spoke, but with the overwhelming smell of diesel fuel and smoke in the air, it was a guess at best. Knowing his predilection for alcohol and marijuana, I was sure that Chris had been drinking and was too intoxicated to operate his boat. He gave me a wave before stumbling back down into the boat. Doug Lasher, the chief of the second boat, was nowhere to be found.

Breathing through clenched teeth, I was in no mood to be contrite and deal with this fubar moment. I had to make a decision and had to make it fast.

Seething inside at his betrayal, I squelched it. His inebriated callous condition was unbreachable. I would deal with their dereliction of duty when we got back to base. We had been in Dong Ha for two weeks, and no one had reported equipment failures or initiated any repairs.

We would make the precarious passage downriver without PBR protection. The one favorable change was that without the M48 tank and the fuel bladder, we would be going downriver a lot higher in the water than we had been coming up. Having completed our huddle, we all knew that danger might be lurking just outside the channel. We had formed a mutual admiration reflected in mild laughter, each of us knowing that this trip downriver could be the last any of us would experience. Ninety-eight worn-out marines, some wounded just returned from Khe Sanh recon patrols in the boonies with a hardened gunny would be accompanying us on the trip downriver.

At 0900 hours, after I made my last perusal of the channel opening, we broke the predawn silence. With the sky hanging low under a drab, gauzy gray cloud base, the three U" boats started their engines, raised their bow ramps, and as quietly as possible, backed out into the channel. Leaving the remote marine support base's unenviable protection behind, we all donned flak jackets and helmets as we began the three-hour journey back down the treacherous Chu Viet to the South China Sea, where we would turn north and follow the coastline back up to Da Nang. The oppressive air under the dense dispatches and rumors rapidly circulating from incoming recon patrols and Huey pilots predicted a significant enemy buildup. The VC, bolder than I ever imagined possible, was gaining ground, and that in itself was unsettling. Glancing surreptitiously at my watch, I did a 360-degree look around before crouching down against the starboard side of LCU, considering our situation and peering out into the hostile jungle. LCM 325 was 150 yards following our stern, and the LCM 326 was approximately 200 yards ahead of our bow in the lead.

A beam of light came through the fronds and thick vines that hung above the river's edge. I squinted and sensed menacing danger as we slowly penetrated the jungle. The oppressive air under the dense double canopy was stifling with the temperature climbing like the national debt. The air felt like the inside of truck that was baking in the sun with its windows all rolled up and filling with steam from the exhaust pipes. During the night, we were inundated with eight inches or more of torrential monsoon rain that hammered the deck. And while the rain had now abated, the swollen river was shrouded in a dense low-hanging fog that could provide cover for NVA and VC snipers. Talk about relative extrema; I had never seen a deluge like this.

We were leaving with 98 marines from Bravo Company, 3rd Battalion, 101st Airborne Division, carrying 70-pound rucksacks on their backs from the 1st Battalion who were being rotated and dispatched back to Da Nang for various medical injuries and other conditions. None of them were incapacitated. I was advised by Gunnery Sergeant Seth Miller, a fiery marine in charge of the grunts, that he was assigning a detail of 20 of his men to each LCM to boost its firepower in the event we ran into an ambush. The balance of his men were to go on the larger LCU due to capacity concerns with the LCMs. As it was still early morning, we were all on high alert at our battle stations but in relaxed GQ, savoring morning coffees. The relative calm of the moment was about to do a complete volte-face, however.

An hour later, at about eight klicks out of Dung Ha, just as we were passing the small fishing village of Chua Gia Do cautiously on our starboard side, George "Poncho" Viera, the coxswain in the lead LCM 326, radioed back, almost whispering to the lieutenant and Snake to be quiet and idle down. There was an eerie calm; something was wrong. I felt the menacing dull ache in my lower back that always accompanied ominous danger. There wasn't any sound of children on the sloping riverbanks, and even the monkeys had gone silent. We immediately went to full GQ. Every marine on board, with senses now sharpened, had their M16s unlocked as they nervously scanned the dense weeds and elephant grass on both riverbanks with owl-like eyes, swiveling their heads slowly back and forth like mechanical dolls.

A chill slithered up my spine as I stilled myself in a protracted silence, listening. I sensed something wasn't right. The men on all three boats were miming each other: "Shush." The riverbanks were eerily quiet, and there were no welding sounds of the jungle as there should have been: no sounds of birds, no screeching racket sounds of small monkeys as they swung from vine to vine in search of breakfast. And more concerning was that no children or locals were waving from the banks. Instead, they seemed to have melted and disappeared into the jungle. Beyond an occasional splash of a fish or a birdcall, the river was noiseless. Poncho from Texas took a knee on the deck and stilled as he sniffed the air of the mangrove swamp, his eyes riveted to the riverbanks. I surreptitiously took a deep breath and held it as I peered through the low-hanging fog.

"Something's wrong."

My pulse rate quickened, and I went on high alert, sensing a possible ambush. At that moment, a single bone-chilling shot rang out, and Poncho took a bullet through the windshield from a VC sniper and fell to the deck, mortally wounded.

"God all'mighty!" Someone screamed from the well deck.

Everybody hit the decks, looking for some cover. Some did not find it in time.

A terror-filled pandemonium followed, and all hell broke loose on the decks as we were hit with a seemingly endless lethal barrage of bullets, rifle-fired grenades, automatic weapons—the whole nine yards—from both sides of the river, the ammunition pinging off the steel walls like hailstones.

Ten marines facing the shoreline on the port side crumbled to the deck like prisoners at an execution. Two of the writhing soldiers screamed in horror, their last shriek, animalistic, harsh, and loud, was overwhelming as they dropped to their knees. They blindly began returning fire before they were cut down from the rear. Hundreds of faint muzzle flashes from the high shore grasses raked the decks, ricocheting everywhere. The beleaguered LCM 325 behind us then took three direct incoming rockets into its ammunition locker, blowing it out of the water in a flash of hellish light and exploding in a geyser of smoke and a ball of scarlet flames shooting upward over the jagged skyline of the jungle. The triple deafening concussions were like an earthquake on the water. Bullets and shrapnel ripped through flesh and muscle.

We felt the abysmal 105-degree heat and matching humidity on our skin. The explosion shocked every sense in my system, with the concussive waves turning me deaf and blinding me in a dense cloud of thick sulfur-laden smoke and going straight to my adrenal glands. Then, having inhaled the bitter taste of cordite, I coughed until my guts spasmed, and there another explosion a nanosecond later, knocking me back to the deck.

The gruesome ambush was devastating, with eighteen men slaughtered: four sailors, two Vietnamese interpreters, and twelve marines who didn't even have time to scream. Then, in one hideous instant, bodies were reduced to shredded meat and blood splatter. There were no bodies to recover, only mangled pieces of burning flesh, arms and legs of grotesque corpses floating away in the detritus. The twisted hulk, now engulfed in flames, lay smack in the middle of the muddy river, which had turned virtually blood red in a swirling death rotation.

The heavy stench of blood and smoke and the sulfurous smell of gunpowder filled the air as they watched helplessly only forty feet away. Some of the men were choking and coughing from the thick smoke. The war on the river had ratcheted up a couple of hundred notches on the desperation scale as we entered this macabre helter-skelter moment born in hell. Black smoke billowed up into the sky as lethal exploding ammunition threatened our presence, aborting any chance of a possible recovery.

When they awoke this morning in the fog of war, had any of them known that this would be the last day of their lives? I wondered.

LCU 1601 and LCM 326 were now quickly overwhelmed by the intense withering crossfire of enemy AK47s, taking a hellacious hailstorm of heavy machine gun fire, 61 mm mortar rounds, and recoilless rifle fire expelled from well-concealed undefined positions in the dense six-to-eight-foot elephant grass along both riverbanks. The marines in the well decks began dropping as bullets from enemy snipers in trees found their targets, resulting in the heartrending shrieks of the dying and wounded, bleeding from bullets and shrapnel wounds. Moans and desperate cries for help were coming from both boats. Then, a young marine radioman froze in the middle of the upper deck in shock and was cut to pieces by an enemy machine gun. Medics, some wounded themselves, were dressing wounds and giving shots of morphine to those with critical injuries. One of the marine medics crawled on the deck, working his way over to two severely wounded marines twitching, one holding his guts as they spilled out on the deck. One I had just had a conversation with before the attack; his legs were blown off at the knees. I ripped off his helmet and hugged him, murmuring empty words of comfort before life fled from him.

I felt emptied of life myself before a torrential rage of anger flowed into that void.

Covered in blood, not my own, I frantically radioed back to the Dong Ha quartermaster, somehow keeping my voice steady in the midst of the immediate contagion of panic, only to be advised that they also were under withering enemy fire and fierce, heavy artillery. A large enemy contingent of North Vietnam Regulars and VC guerrillas was besieging the base from three sides, and they would not be able to assist or help us. I could hear the sounds of incoming explosions in the background, punctuated by the staccato reports from heavy machine guns. The radio then went dead. I turned just as a barrage of enemy rounds began whizzing by me, ricocheting off the steel bulkhead of the pilothouse. One caught me in the left shoulder just above my flak jacket, slamming me with the force of a speeding locomotive, sending me backward, dazed, against the steel bulkhead. I screamed my own set of profanities as I felt the blood leaking down my chest inside the flak jacket from the bullet hole in my shoulder. Bullets and shrapnel were swirling in the air like confetti. The corpse of the coxswain lay on the steel deck, his body grotesquely contorted and bleeding out profusely from multiple bullet holes to the head, face, arms, and chest.

The marines, having taken protective refuge in the well deck, were fully engaged in the orgy and firing their M16s and M60s relentlessly from the well deck over the gunwales into the bush. Three of the grunts managed to set up a mortar unit in the well deck and began firing M19 projectiles with surprising accuracy into the bush at close quarters. Suddenly, they were cut down by an enemy machine gun in a tree. The ferocious sound of death, gunfire, and exploding shells was merciless. One of the grunts, having spotted the sniper, blew the fucking gook out of the tree with a .50 caliber machine gun, sending branches, leaves, and body parts everywhere. The gunny screamed that the mortar should be reset. Three grunts quickly righted it and loaded the mortar and began firing into the bush. Men were crying and screaming all around me as hundreds of white tracer rounds flew in every direction. Under cold fear and a moment of vertigo, I recovered my helmet and leveraged and pulled myself up off the deck as bullets whizzed through the air, hitting metal and ripping flesh.

The screams of dying and wounded men and the hellish stench of blood were everywhere, on the boats and the shores. A young marine next to me took an enemy sniper bullet in the face, with a second hitting him in his throat, splattering me with bone chips, blood, and brain tissue as he fell against me. He died instantly, and I lowered him to the deck. What was left of his boyish face was contorted in terror. I grappled the wheel for control as AK bullets clacked past my head, moving half-throttle ahead without knowing what terror might lay ahead of us. I sent Zach, the man from West Virginia, scurrying to the forward ramp via the inside gunwale to check for possible floating mines or other booby traps that the VC might have rigged up in the river. Steeling himself before ascending the ramp, Zachary reached the top and craned his head precariously over it with a horrified expression on his face, screaming back, "Six bogeys!"

There were four enemy sampans and two junks dead ahead now firing RPGs and machine guns at the ramp. Just then, we took a hit in the center of the ramp from an RPG, causing a jarring jolt and sending Zach rolling backward onto the well deck. Regaining his stance, Zach doggedly repositioned on the ramp with fear etched on his face and began firing his M16 into the sampans. No more than thirty seconds later, he let out a loud, protracted shriek, taking a bullet from a fucking VC sniper in the left leg, sending him screaming and staggering back into the well deck again, cringing and writhing in excruciating pain. Doc and a marine corpsman had their hands full with mass casualty triage on six critically wounded soldiers now pinned downed in the well deck from incoming rounds hitting and ricocheting off the gunwales. One must remember that these young, seventeen-, eighteen-, and nineteen-year-old, medics and corpsmen were not doctors. They had, on average, only four months of basic military medical training before being deployed, and they were expected to save lives by using tourniquets, applying battle dressings, and injecting morphine syrettes as needed. The doctors and medical surgeons were back at the base hospitals. The hail of savage mortal death from the triple canopy jungle was unrelenting, with confusion and wounded soldiers everywhere, but the medics never flinched. Zach winced and screamed in pain as the medic ripped open his bloodied trousers and patched the wound.

As Zach unleashed a tsunami of incoherent profanity, which was almost savage, the navy medic, ignoring the danger around him, rolled Zach over and jammed a morphine syrette into his thigh. That was the last injection the medic would ever give as he was riddled with bullets from a AK47 before standing up. At considerable risk to his own life, with a river of adrenaline coursing through his veins and coal-mountain courage heretofore unknown to us, Zach eeled his way forward in the well deck under withering fire and hauled himself back up the ramp with his M16, then began firing again at the sampans. "Take that, you motherfuckas."

Scanning frantically through the cacophony of hell, undeterred, with no way to maneuver around them, I slammed the throttle down. The boat crashed right through the ragtag enemy formation at full throttle, smashing all six enemy boats and toppling the VC guerillas into the rat-and-snake-infested water. Those who had survived the initial mass destruction were now frantically swimming in strong currents of boiling muddy water, desperate to avoid the hundreds of waterspouts and reach the riverbank. Not one of them made it. The gooks seemed to be everywhere, and we kept up the intense automatic fire from our M14s, M16s, our .30 and .50 caliber deck guns, slaughtering so many that they had to climb over their dead in the dense elephant grass to fire at us.

While Zach and two other marines were assessing the damage to the ramp, Godfather and Bubba were firing from both port and starboard .50 caliber machine gun turrets, killing gooks in the brown water like they were ducks trapped in a reedy pond oozing blood. Bubba and Johnny Boy of New Jersey later confirmed that not one of those savage bastards had made it to shore, stating, "Fucking kill them all; let God sort them out."

With no letup in action, all machine guns on both starboard and port gunwales, gun barrels overheating, were blazing and trading heavily, suppressing fire with the VC heavily camouflaged in dense nipa palms and elephant grass that lined the muddy riverbanks. Bits of trees, dirt, grass, and smoke flew into the air from the riverbanks, accompanied by screams of pain as our bullets found their mark.

Johnny Boy, gunner's mate GH5, reeling and sweat-soaked, his body raked with pain, hurried across the steel deck on his stomach over hundreds of sizzling hot spent cartridges to reach the Zippo on the stern. Just as he reached for the ignition switch, a frag grenade hit the deck alongside him. In that very nanosecond, Qui Nguyen, our South Vietnamese interpreter, holding what was left of his right arm, husbanding the last of his strength, instantly threw himself on it, absorbing the full impact of the explosion with his body. Johnny Boy, breathing erratically, quickly assimilated what had happened and, without a second of hesitation, stood upright. Then, finding his purchase and hitting the ignition switch, *whoosh*, he began sending a blazing hell of orange flame from the M9 flamethrower into the dense green elephant grass covering the muddy riverbank. He torched the VC out of their positions and forced them to bolt from the bush, thrashing their arms back and forth with horrifying screams coming from the scorched foliage and running into the river fully engulfed in flames only to be shot to hell by our blazing machine guns and rifles. The smell of diesel fuel, napalm, and burnt flesh filled our nostrils. Time became nonexistent.

A second later, an incoming RPG impacted the gyrocompass and took out the radio on the port side of the pilothouse. Jake Costello, gunner's mate GM4, from Kansas, was instantly decapitated, and eight other soldiers on the starboard side were seriously wounded, some gasping their last breath. What was left of Jake's corpse was pushed into the well deck along with his head. Carlin Eagle, sweating profusely, took a set of million dollar hits in both legs, sending him screaming "Goddamned motherfuckers" before crashing into the well deck below. Wincing and screaming in excruciating pain, he had severely fractured his right arm in the fall. Eagle, gravely wounded in both legs, was screaming that he couldn't move his legs. A corpsman went to his aid only to be shot dead as he knelt over Eagle, taking three bullets in the back from incoming AK47 machine gun fire. A split second later, six marines on the south well deck crumpled to their knees like prisoners at an execution, returning fire before pitching forward. Bullets ricocheted off the bullheads. A second rocket hit us in the hull, causing the boat to lurch violently to starboard, knocking out one of our two diesel engines. With forward engine speed now critically compromised at three knots, we were a floating duck ourselves in the reedy water.

I quickly signaled Ron Vargas on the LCM 326, already within ten yards of our stern, to come along our port side, tie up to us at the forward bow, and tow us out. Two marines immediately tossed bumper fenders over the side and took care of the bow and stern lines before one of them took a bullet in the back of the head and dropped back mortally wounded into the well deck, where he twitched spasmodically before going still. The back of his head had disintegrated, leaving only brain tissue to ooze out on the hot deck. A tall black marine with enormous hands, already blood-soaked, quickly pirouetted, took his place, and completed the cleating of the two boats before picking up the dead marine and carrying him over to the LCU on his shoulder. We began to pick up speed with the maximum throttle on our one starboard engine, reaching approximately four to five knots at best.

Most of the instrument panel in the pilothouse had been blown away with the first rocket. Bubba and one of the marine soul brothers had already jumped into the engine room to examine the damage and, hopefully, make repairs. While the marine was plugging up the hole in the hull with DC plugs, Bubba was jury-rigging the wiring on the bilge pump and then, with help from the marine, replacing the fuel line to the portside diesel that was severed by the blast. With two forward lookouts scanning the muddy water before them for floating mines, both boats were skimming the waters with their crews and marine counterparts raking the shoreline over the gunwales with 20 mm and .50 caliber machine guns cutting down anything in their path on both sides of the river. This wasn't any small ambush, as we were genuinely running the gauntlet through the steaming river channel of hell with nowhere to hide. We really needed some divine intervention at this point.

Swede Westermarck, gunner's mate GM5, on the LCM 326 still under fire from the port side, spotted and eyeballed another sniper with an RPG perched high in a bodhi tree approximately 50 yards out in front of us. Furious at having already been hit with two pieces of shrapnel in his right side, he still had enough anger and adrenaline to take the bastard out with a 30-second burst from his twin .50 caliber. He perforated and cut the motherfucker in half, dropping him out of the tree in two pieces. The sniper had tied himself high in the tree and now hung grotesquely like a rag doll as we passed by under him with his blood dripping from the body. That was one fucking gook that didn't receive the enlightenment that Siddhartha had.

"Requiescat in pace, you fucking bastard!" he screamed between gasps of gulping hot, humid air.

We were aware that a firmly entrenched PAVN force outnumbered us on both sides of the river. Our pathetically close quarters, abysmal situation was vulnerable, untenable, and rapidly deteriorating. The enemy was mauling us, and we no longer had enough able-bodied men, ammo, and hands to fight the enemy and do anything about the carnage that was happening on both sides of us.

"We can't stay here!" I yelled We had to haul ass and get the fucking hell out of there, and fast. Breakout was now or never. If we hesitated, we faced imminent death! The monsoon rain was now a torrential downpour coming from every direction, and we had to find an escape route on this treacherous steaming waterway. We made a run for it. Neither herbicides nor Agent Orange had yet been sprayed in this sector, and the triple canopy would give plenty of cover to snipers. To our right was a clearing of debris in the overflowing river to the jungle beyond. The locals would soon descend on the battle site and begin looting the bodies and weapons that littered the riverbanks.

My face was swollen with fear, my hair was matted with blood from a four-inch cut on the top of my throbbing head, and blood was trickling down my face. My bloody eyes were nearly shut, obscuring my vision as my mind darted back to the hellish scene of the smoldering wreckage of the LCM 325. It was seared into my brain, and I could still see the black smoke spiraling, shooting a smothering vortex of soot and ash upward before returning to the damaged boats still afloat and the wounded and damaged men still manning them. The jungle fragrance of the mangrove swamps, now morphed by the acrid smell of burning rubber and oil, created an eerie noxious odor.

Despite a devastating loss of life and a waning supply of ammunition, when the smoke cleared, we had successfully repelled and destroyed the communists on both flanks, decimated five enemy sampans, including their crews, and escaped the infernal ambush. Several of the marines were searching each of their dead and removing their bandoliers for precious ammo should it be needed. Charlie had taken heavy losses, paying a high price for the ambush, but so had we. Of the ninety-eight marines that we started with, only fifteen were still able to fight. We only had a small force of men left, aiming and firing M16 and M60 machine guns over the top of the gunwales covering our exit. The barrels were now red hot and untouchable. Unopposed, we cautiously left the smothering ambush.

With all the sonorous voice I had left, we continued our movement south. I kept screaming at the men, giving them courage with "We're not retreating." Blood had flowed on both sides, leaving behind a pall of death and carnage cascading over the muddy waters. The men were silent and said little, expecting another VC attack from the brush at any moment. Instead, Doc and another marine corpsman, displaying raw courage, were desperately doing triage on the grievously wounded, lying helplessly against the bulkheads in the well decks. Another marine medic was attending to Eagle, and the corpsman were working on the other eight critically wounded marines, patching wounds, closing holes and injecting morphine syrettes into each. Seven wounded marines, including Swede on the LCM, were moved to the LCU for medical attention.

Slowly the horrific, pounding din of war began to evanesce, and the pungent smell of nitroglycerin faded behind us, along with our composure, as we inched through the swollen, meandering, muddy channel of water through the gnarled jungle toward the sea. We had to adjust and adjust fast. Sweat was running like rivers from every pore in our bodies. Eyeballs peered out in every direction, absorbing sights and sounds from the jungle.

What remained of Charlie had been hurt badly. What remained of their numbers had scattered to the wind and evaporated into the jungle and maybe back north across the DMZ.

We were now at the mercy of the ferocity of the summer monsoons, which swamped the rivers of Southeast Asia every year during the July to September season without any predictable timeline. One by one, the medics and corpsmen on the LCM began transferring thirteen dead bodies over to the LCU. Three of the bodies came apart during the transfer, causing two hardened marines to buckle and vomit. The sight of the bodies and body parts was repulsive but under the dicey circumstances,

mandatory. Having separated and identified dog tags, the marine corpsman on the LCU had several men insert the corpses into a limited inventory of black plastic body bags, stacking them in the front well deck of
the LCU 326, covering the stack of corpses without bags.

Above, when we could see the sky, we watched AC-119 Stinger, and
AH-1 Cobra attack helicopters, along with AC-130E Spectre gunships
attacking enemy positions with rockets back upriver at the Dung Ha
firebase. Red smoke blossomed from the firebase. Under the triple canopy, they had no idea of the horror of our disposition.

George Stone, in the meantime, jammed a morphine syrette into
my arm, lifting me off the deck, grunting with effort, and supporting
me in the pilothouse against the controls while I reassessed our situation.
Then, standing on weakened and wobbly legs, with my body trembling,
I made a quick assessment. The LCU, with only one engine operating,
was listing at approximately twenty degrees with limited maneuvering
capacity, and Bubba EN5 was desperately working on both engines with
his skillful jury-rigging miracles. The listing LCM, with its bilge pump
alarm screaming from below deck, was still afloat, but it had so many
bullet holes that it looked more like metal Swiss cheese. Actually, both
boats had been grotesquely riddled with bullet and surface-to-air rocket
holes. The weather was taking a turn for the worse; treacherous wind and
rain began to pelt us as we continued our arduous journey downriver
away from the carnage.

The crew and troops had been bitching about everything for the past
week. Now they were seriously concentrating on survival, scavenging
limited munitions and weapons off dead marines and sailors to fight
back with. There was perceptible nervousness and fear among the men,
but this was largely offset when Bubba and the marine emerged out of
the engine room with Bubba yelling, "Start your fucking port engine!"

With both engines now online again, I ordered with labored breath
that the boats be untethered. We all moved and consoled each other with
exhilaration as we knew painfully well that we were damn lucky to be

still afloat and alive on this hellish river. All eyes were peeled on the river banks as we passed through a thick bamboo grove for any sign of a gook or other unforeseen complication in the water, such as a mine. Several sampans were seemingly abandoned on the shoreline. Sitting at the river's edge on its side was a downed marine medevac chopper that wasn't there when we last came up the river. A telling sign that the VC was or had been in the area. There was still a fragile hope that barring another ambush, we wouldn't get caught in another skirmish and maybe would have a haphazard chance for another day.

We pulled over to the still smoldering wreckage, and six marines went over the side of the boat to inspect the slick for any survivors. A door gunner from the downed slick hobbled out of the weeds, emerging from somewhere amid the thick elephant grass. He was wearing a flak jacket and his flight helmet and cradling a .50 caliber machine gun in his arms. The platoon sergeant immediately pushed him to the ground telling him, "Fuckin' lie low.?

"This place is hot with beaucoup VC!" the gunner screamed. "Man, you guys look wonderful."

They had been shot down by VC a day earlier by a surface-to-air rocket. He was the only survivor but had suffered serious burns to his arms and right leg. He told the gunny that they didn't have time before crashing to call in a mayday. He had watched from the bush as six VC appeared out of the jungle and stripped the three-man crew before machine-gunning them. Hopefully, they were already dead. The marines retrieved the bodies and carried back the three mutilated crew members, placing them in body bags found in the chopper. All their weapons were gone.

As long as we had engines moving us forward and didn't get broached on a sandbar in the fog bank as we navigated through the mangrove forest, we would most likely make it out of the Chu Viet channel by 1400 hours. We had to keep moving as fast as we could and treat fear and despair with absolute contempt. Unfortunately, without a working radio on either boat, leaving us entirely incommunicado, we couldn't request a medevac chopper to extract our wounded or even advise anyone of our position or status. With the NVA and VC attack taking place back at Dung Ha and no radio contact from us since early this morning, we were probably now listed as MIA.

CHAPTER 5

Exiting the channel at nightfall into a ferocious, turbulent, unforgiving fifty-to-sixty-mile-per-hour wind and a punishing biblical monsoon rain lashing across the well deck, we were now facing heaving mountains of waters in a crippled boat that was severely less than seaworthy. Unsympathetic, a large swell lifted the LCU, pushing it up and around like a rubber bath ducky toy. It seesawed violently. Dark clouds moved in over us promising us a dark night, scuttling low and wind-driven rain falling horizontally, reducing visibility to almost thirty feet off our bows.

Being trounced around in the open sea, I ordered all hatches to be buttoned down, life jackets to be put on, and the bow ramps to be checked and turnbuckles securely locked. This would be a white-knuckle adventure. We kept our rifles close.

Today could be a day without a tomorrow. I hurt all over. It hurt to breathe in the humid air. My shoulder hurt like sin itself, which was how I came to the realization that I was still alive. Clenching my left fist, I felt the burning pain go deep. Our throttles full out and our twin screws turning at full thrust, we were moving slowly against angry, white-capped, curling waves. The crew desperately fought against the incubating heat and the uncompromising incoming white-water surf crashing over our bow. The treacherous South China Sea, which had tried to force us back into the channel, was now trying to sink us. It was 1800 hours, and daylight was quickly fading to a hostile darkness.

My thoughts darkened as I gathered my waning energy, feeling a pall of dreaded trepidation settling over me. I was breathing slowly, desperately trying to stay awake, praying that my survival instinct would hold fast. The men were growing weaker, some on the verge of delirium, and a couple with sucking chest wounds were quietly begging and beseeching for morphine. Unfortunately, there wasn't any more to give them, and the deck was crimson with pools of blood. They wouldn't last the night as they lay mortally prostrate with others in a growing pool of blood from multiple shoulder and leg wounds. One marine, sitting against the well deck shaking uncontrollably, with a severed spine and missing half his face, was also crying and futilely asking for his mother. Another grunt, his face twisted and frozen in terror, was crying for his mother and pleading to God, as he was cupping his exposed intestines with his hands, screaming that he didn't want to die. While I never forswore my faith, I was never all that religious and didn't believe in the essence of epiphanies. Some might describe me as an agnostic. Neither would live through the night. Others, just hanging on to life, cried unashamedly, believing that the boat was their purgatory. One of the marines was slowly moving from one man to another, every step treacherously off balance, dispassionately passing out cigarettes and lighting them for whoever wanted one.

After what seemed like an eternity of being tossed in a boiling caldron, buffeted and diving down one trough and broaching the next in ten-to-fifteen-foot swells against an ugly driving rain, we began to lose the LCM. With each passing minute, the brutal, capricious wind was gaining in velocity and overwhelming the boats with tsunami-sized swells that threatened to flip them and drown the crew. Continuous jagged lightning bolts flashed all around us, followed by the threatening rumble of thunder in the sky.

Exhausted and seeing that the situation was dire, I yelled out and ordered that the boats again tether up and immediately transfer the men and bodies, and men only, over to the LCU: no personal equipment, artillery, or ammunition was to be salvaged from the boat. Before untethering from the LCM, the crew unlocked and opened the well deck ramp, jettisoning all unnecessary weight and gear overboard. When the last man came on board, we cut the lines and watched the boat quickly take on water and sink under the unmerciful waves. The LCM would become an artificial reef in the South China Sea.

There had been no time to save the artillery or the munitions as the waves began to hit us broadside. Finally, however, we got every one of the men off. Unfortunately, six were only expected to make it if they received medical attention soon. I was beginning to experience random thoughts, flitting like fireflies that came and went before I could grasp and assimilate them. However, I was still rational enough to recognize the onset of delirium. Sometime in the dark fog stealing across the bow, we had unfortunately passed the Perfume River entrance to the naval base at Hue.

For the next eight hours, most of it in thick soupy fog and pitched darkness under an eerie moonless sky, we fought the raw anger of Mother Nature. No amount of positive platitudes would be sufficient. The raging South China Sea, with ten-to-fifteen-foot swells, continued to threaten to swamp us, tossing us around like salad. If that wasn't enough, the pounding monsoon rain threatened to drown us throughout the night and into the morning hours. Hope as a narcotic soon wears off.

I found a small piece of beef jerky in one of my pockets. It tasted like filet mignon. We now knew that survival was a matter of taking it one day at a time, one hour at a time, one minute at a time until we were rescued and sent home. We also knew that this would not be the day, and I doubted it was going to be tomorrow either. lifted, leaving only tendrils that resembled wraiths moving across from one rolling wave to another. The bodies were beginning to bloat, and the stench was getting worse by the hour. We were battling a meteorological vortex with the monsoons drawing the summer energy of the day's scorching heat upon the land and seas, coupled with thick humidity and moist heated air blowing from the south. Even though we were a couple of feet apart, we had to yell and shout over the wind and pouring rain to communicate. Explosive thunderclaps and streaks of lighting seared across the dark sky above us. Time moved slowly in the darkness, and images of the battle drifted in and out of my consciousness. We had all agreed to take thirty-minute catnaps in rotation. When it was time for my watch, I wasn't sure if I had slept or not. It didn't matter much, as it was my time to be awake and fully alert.

Several times during the night, we had heard planes and choppers fly over and painfully craned our heads in the direction of the sound, but we couldn't see them, and they couldn't see us. Many of the men couldn't think of sleeping that night; all were ravaged by exhaustion and severe mental anguish. The image of the LCM being blown out of the water and bursting in flames with twenty-four men on board had imprinted itself on their memories with raw intensity. The nightmare would haunt us for the rest of our lives. Several of the badly wounded men in the well deck, still with bullets and shrapnel in them were lying in a stupor, too weak to scream anymore. The others found a spot on the steel deck, threw themselves down against the bulkheads, and laid their heads on their rucksacks as if they were down-filled pillows. The boat reeked of blood and urine. Time had ceased to exist for most of the men as they prayed for providence from the pain and prostration in the sweltering heat. Every four or five hours, two men would switch and take over the helm, keeping the boat heading south and fighting to keep it a klick or so from shore. Daylight brought us only more misery as the last can of C-rations was consumed.

Two days later
Still limping back maddeningly slowly down the coast to Da Nang with extensive damage to the LCU, we were in a less than somber mood as the boat tacked in an interminable zigzag pattern paralleling the coastline south. We were enshrouded in an early morning fog, barely making headway against the unrelenting tropical winds buffering the bow. Despite the direness of the circumstances, the seaworthiness of the boat was now a moment-by-moment proposition. We were oblivious to the relentless downpour swirling around us and now being driven by a maelstrom of strong tropical monsoon winds forcing us sideways, port, and then starboard. The boat began "porpoising" like a dolphin, swooping up and down in the pounding six-to-seven-foot waves. The men clung to anything bolted down under the seemingly gyrating sky above.

Any semblance of military professionalism had evaporated, depleted by hunger, thirst, and exposure.

You have to use your mind to leave your body behind. The pain in my shoulder receded more quickly than it had the day before. I craned my head to the side as far as I could and moved the collar of my shirt back over my shoulder; I immediately noticed that it didn't look good. Bright red and purple bruising was spreading, in every direction, beyond the white bandage that a medic had applied the day before. But none of the discoloration was migrating down my arm, which I took as a positive sign.

The men were tired, clothes wringing wet, and painfully miserable. We had no more C-rations, and we had to sip the rainwater sparingly from our pots. Bugs and flies were feasting on us round the clock. On the second night, I hunched forward, head hung down between my legs, my hair unruly, cursing myself under my breath, and then just as I lifted my head to stare up at the sky, *boom*, we were all startled awake by a gunshot in the well deck.

Swede, who had severe wounds to his chest and hips from shrapnel, had called upon a deity before putting his service revolver in his mouth and committing suicide, blowing his brains out in the far corner of the well deck. He had only two weeks left before he would have returned to Texas. We had lost eight more marines, all of whom had succumbed to their wounds during the night. One marine had gone mad believing that there was a rescue boat next to us, and he leaped overboard and drowned. None of us had had any water, food, sleep, or rest for the past seventy hours, and we were all saturated to the bone, weak, and utterly dehydrated, having only a ration of what little chlorinated water we had. Augmenting the arduous journey and dire conditions, we only had dated, almost inedible C-rations and MREs that tasted like coagulated grease to twenty-one half-naked, stressed-out men, all of them in torn and bloody T-shirts, shorts, and boots, half of whom were critically wounded, distraught, and nested in a bloodied well deck. The men had been tossed this way and that, wheezing, gagging, and unable to grasp the moment or comprehend the danger they were still in. The only medic still functioning was out of morphine syrettes.

The stifling air was a sultry simmering tropical stew, and I was physically and mentally suffocating in the sweltering, one-hundred-degree heat. The humidity, the smell of my sweat, and my drenched skin were beyond oppressive as I barely held myself up inside the pilothouse, bearing witness to my wounds and sinking spirits and a harrowing day from hell. I prayed for guidance and inspiration.

As dawn broke and the rain began to retreat, I could hear the guidance in the distance. We began to hear the faint *whup-whup-whup* of a helicopter getting closer. I felt nothing anywhere, inside my body as well as outside.

My vision was blurred, my eyes having been sunburned by the unforgiving blazing sun. When we were about six klicks from the mouth of the Da Nang Harbor, a base security chopper had been dispatched to check us out before allowing clearance into the high security harbor. As it vectored lower, hovering to get a closer look, the occupants were shocked to see forty-one bloodied, emaciated, wounded soldiers barely alive lying in the besmirched, blood-soaked welldeck on an LCU, so shot up from what looked like intense fire it was a miracle that it was still afloat. The scene below was akin to some netherworld between life and death, filled with the stench of blood, decaying body parts, and urine. Two Swift boats were immediately dispatched and soon came alongside with a half dozen or so medics and a boarding crew to take over control of the boat.

There was only a dead silence of horror where there should have been a feeling of tremendous exhilaration from the men. A dozen medics began handing out protein bars and canteens of water to those who could still lift their blistered arms and work their hands. Over a dozen ambulances with a platoon of medical corpsmen awaited us as the boat was beached and secured next to a pier.

We were filthy, unshaven, enfeebled, and no longer able to stand. Dozens of attendants carried us off the boat in stretchers, placing us in waiting ambulances. The fifteen or so bloated bodies were bagged and dispatched immediately to the base morgue. A lone journalist walked up with a photographer taking pictures and followed my stretcher as it was hurried toward an ambulance. He asked about our casualties. I gave him a stoic stare with a defeated expression as no words came out of my parched mouth to describe the hellish battle we had been through. Military MPs quickly dispatched him and confiscated his camera.

As word of our return and the number of casualties started to spider out through the base, a desire for revenge and a sense of anger began to take emotional hold at command headquarters.

We were all transported to the NSA combat casualty hospital in Da Nang and brought into emergency rooms, where even more paramedics, doctors, and nurses were scrubbed up and waiting with concerned faces. This was the second time I had become a resident of the hospital, having been mended and convalesced here for a month back in early 1966. Every man still lucky enough to be alive on the boat, shoulders hunched forward, heads sunk down between them, hair unruly, had either been shot or hit with shrapnel, some multiple times. All of us were in jungle fatigues and covered in blood from head to toe. Two would lose their legs to gangrene.

A military chaplain was standing next to the vehicles giving last rites as the bodies were carried on. They cut away what was left of my shirt and shorts and began washing the sweat and blood off me before inserting needles and injecting morphine into my emaciated torso. Still in a mental fog, having been sedated, I watched as they began cleaning my wounds with disinfectant. The doctor looked down at me and shook his head. I had two shards of shrapnel in my back, one in my leg, and a bullet in my shoulder. I was one of the lucky ones.

Except for Bubba, who was still down in the engine room below deck slaving away with his engines, all of us were beyond weak and had to be lifted and taken off in stretchers. I learned later that it took three MPs and a medic to enter the engine room and inject a sedative into him before they could remove him. Having been wounded by several pieces of shrapnel in the back, banged, bruised, and tossed around in the tight steaming compartment for the past harrowing eighteen hours, without food or water, he had the fortitude to still function and hurl imprecations at anyone in hearing distance. While he didn't realize it, he was suffocating in shock. But by some herculean miracle and a lot of good karma, he kept the bilge pumps and engines running! Bubba EN5 had gone beyond the call of duty, getting us out of the undeniable clusterfuck. Bubba didn't fear dying. His only fear was dying ignobly. We learned that he had slipped into a coma after the rescue and died from his wounds the following day with Zach at his side.

There was no other way to describe the hell and horror we miraculously managed to escape than that we were men who had played with death and cheated it. While we were all wounded and spilled our blood in one manner or another, we were still alive and would be having our first hot meal in three days.

None of us spoke of our wounds as we were fully aware of the negatives involved in our escape, and none wanted to deal with it immediately.

The following morning (or it may be had been the second morning), having heard the announcement of reveille at six o'clock, I slowly sat up in the bed with an IV in my arm and looked around the room. While now rehabilitating in the ward at the base hospital, I noticed that my men and troops occupied every bed. No one stood or even answered roll call, with most sleeping through it. Except for MPs at the entrance, only medical personnel were allowed in.

That is, with the exception of a general and a photographer with a Polaroid camera who was going from bed to bed handing out Purple Heart medals and professing in the name of the president of the United States and the United States Marine Corps that he was proud to present the medal and to send the pictures back to our families. I guessed that he didn't realize that some of us were navy.

Word came that Dung Ha was still under heavy siege from PAVN artillery attacking from two sides and that the Chu Viet River north of Chau

Gia Do was now entirely under enemy control. With heavy casualties, they had lost a lot of real estate, including four aircraft. The PAVN and Victor Charlie, on the first day, had hammered and decimated the supply depot, obliterating 150 tons of ammunition, damaging numerous buildings, killing 44 marines, including South Vietnamese soldiers, and wounding 25 others. The following day they again attacked at the break of day, killing 8 more South Vietnamese Marines and hitting the base's fuel farm with rockets, destroying 40,000 gallons of JP4, erupting the towering leviathans in a lethal flame that could be seen for miles. They had also blown up 2 disabled PBRs, killing both crews at their gun stations.

In quiet reflection, Chris, with an air of melancholy now surrounding him, said, "My friend?" He had been a friend of mine for several years and had just the night before shared with me that he was now a short-timer with only two weeks left on his third tour but had preconized that he probably wouldn't make it home.

Somewhat intoxicated and breathing erratically that night, he assuaged his guilt and lamented on his occasional infidelity off base as he thought of his quivering loins and not so much his brain. Chris had the hots for every female with a warm body to share. He looked straight into my eyes as he welled up and made me promise that if he didn't make it back, I would contact his wife and assure her he loved her. With a frisson of annoyance shooting up my spine yet not wanting to play the devil's advocate, I acquiesced. I wasn't sure I believed him, but his dire prediction carried the vomiting guilt to his grave.

Upon finishing my copy of *Stars and Stripes* at breakfast on the third day following our rescue, I was advised that I had visitors. A team of officials from the Department of Defense questioned me for the next several hours, conducting a standard debriefing on the circumstances surrounding our departure from Dung Ha and the ambush, including enemy casualties and our miraculous escape. I gave them a detailed account, starting at receiving orders to return to base immediately. I had yet to learn about the enemy's strength or casualty count. I also included my encounter with the chief of the two PBRs, who seemed intoxicated and declined to lead us out into the river due to mechanical issues. With what had happened on the river, I would never forgive that man, I said sagely under my breath.

The rescue brought jubilation to naval and marine headquarters as there had been no information on the ambush of five navel riverboats that had left the firebase that morning. While not confirmed, it had been assumed by the lack of radio communication for the past several days that all had been lost.

A medical captain stood over me and paused, giving me a once-over. "When's the last time you had a meal or looked in a mirror?"

I teared up. I, along with the other surviving men, was now all delirious from lack of food or water.

We were now combat tested and had returned as "the living dead."

We were completely unaware that the two PBRs that had stayed behind had been destroyed, with no survivors, in the attack on Dung Ha.

The next day, following my semiliquid lunch, I was advised that I had more visitors: a naval commander and a marine major, accompanied by twelve marines and seven sailors who had been wounded but had survived the attack, now surrounded my bed. The men seemed to be having difficulty expressing their feelings adequately to me about me leading them out of harm's way. I had always said that I wasn't the emotional type, but lying in bed in front of these men who had fought bravely with everything that they had, I relented. My eyes welled as each of them shared their stories.

The next night, the base came under attack again. NVA rockets landed and detonated close by, shaking the hospital. I tensed in bed, thinking that having survived the river attack, I might be terminated by a rocket hitting the hospital. However, the attack was soon repulsed and ebbed away.

A couple of days later, I was put on a plane for Clark Air Base in the Philippines to recoup from my injuries. Six weeks later, having survived military physical therapy and regained most of my strength, I began to feel a little bit stronger. My wounds were healing, and upon hearing that the NVA had initiated the Tet Offensive across the country, I requested to be returned to Da Nang and finish my third and final tour of duty. I had no immediate family left to speak of. As far as I was concerned, what was left of my family was still recovering in Da Nang.

CHAPTER 6

Four days later, in the wee hours of the morning, a combined river combat task force of six PBRs and five LCM-8s carrying troops and artillery left Da Nang for the Chu Viet River. Included in the task force were two LCUs, one carrying an M60 tank and munitions. The other carried an entire company of US Marines, a platoon of SEALs, and two platoons of South Vietnamese infantry. They were expected to reach and enter the estuary at 0700 hours as part of a counteroffensive assault and slowly preceded up the battle scarred Chu Viet to Dung Ha. The wind was still blowing, but the heavy rain had stopped, and it was forecasted to remain dry for the balance of the week. The marine support base at Dung Ha, having been under attack for several days, suffered heavy casualties. The NVA and VC also suffered significant losses before retreating back into the jungle. The troops were more than fully armed to fight their way up the Chu Viet and into Dung Ha, which was now a free-fire zone. South Vietnamese paratroopers were being deployed and dropped all around the enemy concentrations. The putrid smell of decomposing flesh and gunpowder was everywhere on the river due to the near massacre.

For the next two days, they poured heavy aerial rocket artillery fire into the enemy positions, inflicting numerous casualties as they kept up a furious combat tempo and advanced, tightening the noose around the remote military firebase. The demoralized enemy, who had made a determined effort to infiltrate the marine support base, was now desperately trying to escape the ever-closing trap they found themselves wedged into. Between the ground forces of the South Vietnamese Army, the US Marines and the naval assault units on the river were laying down a massive hail of suppressing fire along the riverbanks.

The brutal coordinated enemy assault that was the beginning of the Tet Offensive had failed, and they were now being annihilated by a beehive of Huey and Cobra gunships cutting them down as they attempted to disengage and retreat across the free-fire sectors of rice patties. The dense jungle was inflamed with napalm being dropped by F-100 Super Sabers. By the end of 48 hours of brutal combat, the 601st Battalion of PAVN, along with the 503rd Battalion of VC, had been mowed down and nearly annihilated, leaving 585 dead on the battlefield. An unknown number were floating down the river amid the carnage. The marines captured 25 VC alive and a vast assortment of weapons and munitions the escaping enemy left behind. LCM 251 and PBR 416, along with one PBR for security, had split from the riverine force where the ambush had taken place. Lowering their deck ramps, they began the grueling recovery of all the 25 men, now corpses, as well as grisly mangled body parts and bone fragments of the men lost on LCM 325 three days earlier. Since there were no identifying parts or bodies, the remnants were placed in unmarked body bags for return to Da Nang. All had been burned beyond recognition.

While the crews were hot, and physically and emotionally drained having finished the recovery effort, they stood on the lowered ramps in silence to pay tribute to the men who had perished there. They would be flown back to the States, where it would take weeks before they would be able to identify the remains through DNA testing and repatriate them. The locals were almost finished looting the bodies of the Charlies in the brush and on the riverbanks of the battle site. Either out of respect or fear of revenge, they had not touched the bloated bodies of the Americans snagged on the banks or those floating downriver in the muddy water. While the exact number of enemy casualties along the river was unknown, it was estimated to have been over two hundred.

Not one American, dead or alive, was left behind!

The LCU 1601 and LCM 326 had fought their way out and had left a hell of a lot of dead gooks in their wake, many of them piled like firewood on the riverbank. I was advised later that nothing stirred in that smoldering hellhole. Even the VC had abandoned it. Spent brass shell cartridges littered the shoreline and would be salvaged by the locals for scrap metal when we left. The enemy carcasses littered the gnarly banks on both sides of the river, and no one gave a fuckin' second look at the macabre carnage. Either they would become croc snacks, or the proliferating river rats, which were the size of cats, would feast on the decaying maggot-encrusted corpses for days to come. The attack on the firebase was major news, but the ambush of the riverboats remained classified and there was an apparent omission of the attack. There were no reports, bulletins, or footage on network television back home.

I lay in bed in the base infirmary in abject misery, somewhat jaded, recovering from my wounds and salted anger. As I raised my head off the pillow and rubbed the fatigue out of my eyes, a kaleidoscope of images of the ambush ran through my mind. No training could have prepared us for the trials and tribulations of river combat. I made an attempt to slide out of bed and stand, but a wave of vertigo hit me, sending me back onto the bed. I began to reflect on the carnage. I hadn't even realized that I had been hit with three pieces of shrapnel in the back after taking a bullet in the left shoulder that hurt like a bitch. It was hard to believe that we had been blasted from hell and back on our first day out. My lips quivered slightly, and the lower crescents of my eyelids filled. It was not difficult to understand how deeply my heart hurt for the men that had been lost. I would submit a detailed report on the brutal attack in the next day or so and the actions taken to mitigate it as soon as possible. I was reasonably sure that we had sunk three sampans and two enemy junks and destroyed most, if not all, of the attacking VC guerilla force. But in doing so, I had lost two LCMs, one with its entire crew of twenty-five men. I had also been informed that the two PBRs assigned to protect the convoy had been blown up at the dock and had been unfortunately hit with a napalm bomb during the attack on the harbor. They had been incinerated, and there were only pieces of bone and ash. We had also sustained considerable damage to the LCU 1601, with the loss of four men and the wounding of ten others, including myself. I was convinced that the battle had been intensely savage. In the face of grave personal destruction, every man on those three U boats showed extraordinary bravery, exemplary fighting spirit, and indomitable courage.

One by one, I'd send a short letter of condolence to each family, assuring that the deceased was now at peace and had gone to a better place. Some believed it, but I didn't. I simply cauterized the pain. Like our forefathers, we answered our country's call to arms. Our service in Nam didn't necessarily mean that we all agreed with the lexicon of US foreign policy. It did, however, express our patriotism as being part of the American military. Those who held the national angst against us, branded us baby killers, and defiled us would eventually be identified as cowards and dealt with appropriately.

Two days later, General Casey and Captain Smally made an appearance at the hospital with a small army of photojournalists. They delivered a warm laudatory address praising the troops for their performance and sacrifices. Every one of the men this day received a Purple Heart or two and a Silver Star for their combat performance; those that were KIA received these honors posthumously. I was awarded another Purple Heart, adding to my growing collection, but this time the navy commander awarded me the Navy Cross for extraordinary heroism in combat against the enemy. He also gave me a field promotion to the rank of captain.

The next four months were a nightmare on the rivers, with skirmishes and firefights seemingly taking place at every bend. The monsoons had been hell on the rivers, and the gooks used it to their advantage, attacking us with a rigorous vengeance. In the weeks that followed, the potential for being killed became palpable as we went into the hellish abyss. Death was all around us in every permutation one could possibly imagine as we held our shit together and navigated the boats up and down the muddy rivers.

We didn't know it yet, but this was just the beginning of the North Vietnamese Tet Offensive. The enemy had the wherewithal to ambush three heavily armed amphibious boats and do serious bodily harm to each of them as they attempted to make their way down the Chu Viet River to the South China Sea. Unfortunately, they miscalculated our perseverance and American resolve. We escaped annihilation at each turn by the narrowest of margins. At the same time, I had always been pragmatic and believed in luck. But this last tour had convinced me that our very survival had been either fate or the divine hand of God. I only prayed that the dead hadn't died for naught. Unlike the customs of home, in combat we had to endure gruesome deaths, amputations, and mental breakdowns without exhibiting or portraying weakness and move on. There were no wakes or funerals, and little time to grieve.

The casualty list included seven crew members, two South Vietnamese soldiers, and twenty-four marines. The crew members were:

Jake Cosciello, GN4 (gunner's mate); New Jersey; LCU 1601; KIA

George "Poncho" Viera, first class petty officer; Texas; LCM 325; KIA

Lance Idler, EN3 (engineman); West Virginia; LCM 325; KIA

Dave Greeves, GM5 (gunner's mate); Louisiana; LCM 325; KIA

Bubba, EN5 (engineman); LCU 1601; West Virginia; KIA

Don Russell, SN3; Massachusetts; LCM 325; KIA

Charlie "Swede" Westermarck; GM5 (gunner's mate); LCU 1500; Lubbock, Texas; KIA

The wounded list included five South Vietnamese soldiers and forty U.S. marines. The crew members were:

Captain Bryce Tucker, commander, Assault Craft Unit One; Connecticut; LCU 1601

Carlin Eagle, first class petty officer and coxswain; Arkansas; LCU 1601

Zachary Tuff, SN3; West Virginia; LCU 1601

George Stone, 1st class petty officer and coxswain; South Carolina; LCM 326

Ron Vargas, SN3; New York; LCM 326

Although only Zach knew I had received a "Dear John" letter from my heretofore future fiancée back in the States, I was hurting. The letter was devastating, especially given that I was in Nam, where my morale was not exactly improving. I learned from Zach that it had become common knowledge among the team that I had drunk myself into a stupor after dark on several occasions. I also smoked a joint and put my .38 caliber to my temple on a couple of occasions with the lame contemplation of blowing my brains out. Although I didn't know it at the time, I was under constant surveillance by my crew.

Having nearly finished my third and final tour of duty here in Nam, down to one hundred days and a wake up, I was ready to return to the States. I had been in Nam for three and a half years. Not that it mattered anymore, but two months ago, I had been promoted from captain to lieutenant commander with the expectation that I might reenlist. That wasn't going to happen. I had a higher calling. *Or so I thought.*

Upon being unceremoniously relieved of my command aboard LCU 1601, I began rechanneling and aligning my thoughts, focusing on my return to the States, which now almost seemed foreign to me. On that Friday evening, many of us officers headed to the officers' club for drinks and a meal. Despite the reality that we weren't quite home yet, it was an honor and a pleasure to be in the company of those who had served with me.

On Saturday morning, I headed straight for the administration headquarters, which was nothing more than a Quonset hut next to the officers club, to begin my processing back to the USA. Inside the Quonset hut the air was cool and refreshing compared to the wrenching 115-degree midday heat outside. I learned at the officers' club that a new marine recruit had died yesterday from heat stroke while standing guard duty at the bridge. Not something that his next of kin would want to hear. A young lieutenant advised me that the base commander wanted to see me before I left. The lieutenant directed me to the rear office of Commander Connelly.

I walked up to the desk, came to rigid attention, and saluted. The commander returned the salute. "Sit down, Bryce. I have a couple of cold beers in the fridge; care for one?" I accepted it, needing hydration. "Four Purple Hearts, one just recently, I see. Vietnam Campaign Medal and Ribbon, Combat Action Ribbon, Navy Cross, two Bronze Stars, Silver Star, Distinguished Navy Service Medal, Presidential Unit Citation—not bad. Cross of Gallantry with Palm. Hospitalized after being tortured by VC during captivity, hospitalized with malaria, gunshot, bayonet wounds, and shrapnel. Lieutenant Commander, I'm impressed."

The commander stood up, shook my hand, and wished me the best of luck. I saluted and did a 180-degree turn out the door.

As I had flown into Vietnam on a Pan Am, I would be flying out aboard a Lockheed Marine C130 Hercules from Da Nang. Quietly slouching against the open doorway of the Quonset hut and somewhat lost in morose reflection as I looked out into the darkness of the night, I raised a middle finger and swore under my breath. "Sayonara, Vietnam!" But as with all who had fought there, Vietnam would be etched in my mind forever.

The view from the air of the Vietnamese coastline was stunning. The brilliant white beaches contrasted with the deep-green farmlands and dense forest surrounding and hugging them. Elephant Mountain and other majestic peaks loomed far in the distance. The terrain below us, stretching out in all directions, was chopped up in random rice patty plots. The flight with thirty other soldiers returning to the States was peaceful and uneventful. Although personally thrilling, it was the first leg of my journey back to the world. I had to spruce up my "summer service" uniform, which was required for my return flight to the States. The last time I wore it was arriving in Vietnam on my first tour. It consisted of lightweight white trousers, a short-sleeved white shirt with an open collar, and the traditional navy web belt. Because of my new svelte appearance, I had to requisition a new uniform; I had lost fifty pounds since first arriving in Vietnam back in early 1966, going from 220 to

170. Not a negative thing as I was now all muscle, with just a few holes that had been patched up. I had also reduced my two-pack-a-day smoking habit to one every other day. Not that I didn't believe the medical advice, but the price had doubled, and the availability of filtered Marlboros was a challenge. My goal was to kick the habit altogether anyway.

My only personal consolation is that my almighty DEROS date and tour of duty had ended, and I had been pulled from the boat four weeks earlier, on January 3, to be discharged on my twenty-first birthday at the amphibious base in Coronado. The LCU 1601 had spent the last four months in dry dock being repaired and retrofitted for continued service on the rivers. I had written a reverent letter to the crew on my last night on board and, with tears welling in my eyes, had reminisced over our time together. The letter thanked them for their loyalty and added that the last year had been a great journey for me and their friendship and commitment had been very important. They were all now transferred from the LCU 1601, and heading back to the states.

We had fought the VC and NVA for almost three years, engaging them continuously for the last twelve months during Tet '68. Our unit had provided continuous riverine support to marine troops at Dung Ha and Khe Shan via the Chu Viet River. We had supported the troops at the Hue Citadel and the boat ramp via the Perfume River (Song Huong River) and given support with the cost of lives at the Battle of Quang Tri City just north of Hue on the eastern bank of the Thach Han River. During that year, we lost six LCM 8s, eight PBRs, and nearly the LCU 1601 exiting Dung Ha on the Chu Viet. Assault Craft Unit One, Division 4, had paid a heavy price. "The tip of the arrow." We sailors and Marines along with the ARVN of South Vietnam had all become a fighting unit, and it was an association that would stand the test of time.

We had fought through hell together, and none of us would ever forget the horrifying pilgrimage. There was no fanfare or welcoming placards from the populace to greet us as we returned from the war. Unlike in other wars, in which solders came home as units to welcoming celebration, here

I, like every other Vietnam veteran, came home alone with other strangers who may or may not have experienced combat. All were doused with the venom heaped on them by protesters and were treated as unstable outcasts and called baby killers.

Once the impertinent customs official had unceremoniously rifled through my sea bag at Hickam Air Force Base in Honolulu, we were transferred onto another C-130 for the flight to San Diego International. There was no welcoming committee to greet us there either. As we alighted the plane, we all bade farewell to each other inside the terminal. We formed a line and snaked out, going our separate ways straight into a gauntlet of anti-war protesters and the slangy sound of Hanoi Hannah and her new proverbial friend Hanoi Jane, Jane Fonda's voice delivering Hollywood's unrelenting propaganda, supporting their coming victory to Radio Hanoi at every exit. We came home to ridicule and hatred for fulfilling our duties and were unwelcome strangers in our own country, which was now almost foreign to us.

In a galling coup de grâce, on March 3, as I was enjoying a couple of much-needed drinks with a couple of officers at the base lounge, pickling our brains and preparing for discharge, I had picked up a copy of the *Stars and Stripes* and was shocked and appalled to learn that the LCU 1601 had been blown apart on February 27 while backloading munitions and black power at the bridge ramp in Da Nang. It had been hit with two rockets, instantly killing all thirteen men on board: the only survivor, a young lieutenant ashore receiving his command orders; he was my replacement. I had to sit down as I was buffeted with waves of catastrophic guilt for not being there with the men. Our drinking took on a much more somber tone.

Among the dead were Dale Fisher, BMC; Bob Burten, EN1; Charles Bush, EM1; Charles Swagler, SN; Richard Qebbie, CMG3; James Brurinda, FN; Mark Avery, CS2; Bert Demata, SN; Cecil Tavaras, FN; Dave Horton, BSM; David Fisher, BMC; Donald Hawryshko, BM2; and Reggie Yuhas, BM3.

I lamented the lost men. I had left the Coronado Amphibious Base with twenty-one men, and only three of us—Eagle, Duff, and I—had made it back alive. I had served three tours spanning twenty-eight months, during which time I had been shot four times and received three pieces shrapnel. I stared sightlessly at his hands. The price in blood had been high, but it was time to let the war fade, man up, and, most of all, keep going.

Stepping off the chopper at North Island, California, I was immediately assailed by a group of protesters pushing forward from a fence screaming "Child killer" and was pummeled by stones and other debris. The group of twenty or so tackled me to the ground and beat me until a MP group came to my rescue. The gang of juveniles had already disbanded across the field and my sea bag was nowhere to be found. That was a significant loss.

Having been honorably discharged as a lieutenant commander with a Silver Star, four Purple Hearts, and a Presidential Citation along with several other trinkets, I reset my goals, now in skivvies. I used my benefits to get a bachelor's degree in philosophy, but with no other civilian trade skills, I needed direction. Unfortunately, Vietnam veterans found themselves forgotten and unwanted by most, but we would move on and live a valuable and productive life. So instead of getting a job with the police or in a factory or going to work for the post office, as most expected me to do, I accepted an invitation from Captain Connelly to join an exclusive club. Two weeks later, I reenlisted in SEAL Team One, Special Operations, and continued my military service. The honor of being a lieutenant commander in SEAL Team One was like an inconceivable identify seared into the flesh. It would be with me the rest of my life. Now I knew who I was. I was no hero, but I liked being in the action. And even better, I was getting paid for it.

I was not the only one reenlisting and joining the infamous SEAL Team One on Coronado Island, so several of my fellow officers and I decided that we would enjoy one last night as civilians taking up residence at the terrace bar overlooking the white-sand beach across the street at the Hotel del Coronado, which stood in the sand alone in its Victorian splendor.

None of us made it back to base that night, but we only had to walk across the street and find our new home. While there wasn't time to forget the war, I did everything that I could to step away from it. By the end of the next several months of intense training at the SEAL Team One facilities, Indochina seemed a distant reality.

CHAPTER 7

The most tragic element of Chris Polinski's death was its timing and circumstances. His wife Nuna had already left their Gauley Bridge home in West Virginia on a euphoric high and traveled to San Diego via a Greyhound bus to be with Chris for his discharge on August 29. She had graduated from West Virginia University several years ago. She had a close friend in La

Jolla who practically begged her to come and stay with her for a couple of weeks until Chris arrived. With two weeks of unused vacation from her job, she graciously accepted the offer.

She returned to West Virginia, and what remained of Chris arrived in a closed casket the following week. Nuna was met by two naval mortuary personnel and taken to the Joint Forces Headquarters.

The remains were waiting in a small funeral chapel. Nuna stood nervously as two naval officers approached her carrying a folded blue military blanket. Only a half dozen bone fragments were on the blanket, including a piece of a human femur.

She and Chris had only been married for a year. And except for ten precious months, she had been alone. They had met in their senior year at a UCLA graduation dance in the summer of 1966. Chris had graduated from Post University in Connecticut the year before and was visiting a friend in Los Angeles. They met through several friends one night at the Eagles Nest Pub and learned that they had both been born and raised in West Virginia for the most part. Her father, having grown up in Elkins, West Virginia, was an air force sargaent and had relocated the family to Biloxi, Mississippi, when she was four years old and returned to Elkin's a year later having been medically discharged. He soon moved the family to Coaltown and took a job in a local mining operation. Thinking back on it, it seemed to her they fell in love that very night. It would always be a source of amazement to her that they had met at all.

Three months later, Chris came home gushing and rhapsodizing with the news that he had landed a job in Los Angeles as a financial adviser working for Bel Air Securities.

She hadn't planned on getting married so soon. She planned to get a master's degree in economics and pursue a career on Wall Street. She was already a self-trained computer programmer handling her church's external communication and organization.

* * *

Nuna

Marriage was not on my horizon at this time, and I was definitely not at the until-death-do-us-part stage of my life. But then Chris arrived on the scene and would not be dissuaded. I was smitten and fairly gaga all over. Our lives had entwined and then exploded in lust as he led me out of my salad days and down the primrose path. Both of us were glowing with love and romance."

Chris's parents were from Gauley Bridge, West Virginia, and they lived more lavishly than mine. His father was a sales agent for a real estate company. His mother was a vice president of a bank in Summersville, West Virginia. I had never met them, and other than that, I knew little of his past other than that he had been born with a congenital insensitivity to physical pain, a condition he bragged about from time to time as we dated.

Chris, relying on his skills at manipulation, was already salivating about his plans to earn his master's degree in business and then get a job as a Wall Street broker, which were tantalizingly close my plans. A dream plan, and we were going to share a life together and watch the money roll in. He didn't tell me the rest of his master plan until New Year's Eve aboard the *Queen Mary* almost four years ago.

Feeling orgiastic and quite beautiful, I was wearing a rented sapphire satin gown. My coiffed, flaxen hair was piled high on top of my head, compliments of Helena's Hair Salon. My mother had adorned me with faux diamond earrings, a faux diamond necklace, and a lacey low-cut gown with a risky décolletage to surpass Princess Diana's. With shoulder-length blond hair, Chris wore an exquisitely tailored black suit complemented by a black fedora redolent of an Italian godfather.

As we entered the catered event, I caught my toe and tripped up the second step, twisting my right foot. Chris moved like a bolt of lightning and caught me before hitting the steps. First, he gently sat my fanny down, removing my satin slipper. Then, seeing no apparent swelling in her ankle, he lifted me and supported me in the hall, sitting me at our assigned table in front of an enormous fieldstone fireplace. Inside, there was merriment and conviviality. The atmosphere was reminiscent of the classic nights aboard the *Titanic* at the turn of the century.

He asked me what I wanted to drink, and I told him a Captain Morgan and Coke would be great to start the evening with, and he made his way to the bar.

While he was standing at the bar ordering drinks, I noticed that a brunette was trying to make a pass at him and seemingly not taking no for an answer. Chris returned to the table with two drinks and a shit-eating grin on his face. Holding on to the edge of the table, I made an effort to stand up on one foot and give him my death stare, which seemed to wipe the grin off his face and dampen any interest he might have had while at the bar. He made a toast to us, proclaiming the drink an elixir guaranteed to induce love, and we clinked glasses. Then, performing an entertaining pirouette, he took my hand and led me through a pair of French doors and then up a spiral staircase to the observation deck overlooking the city's dazzling lights, across the harbor.

Finally, as the clock struck midnight, he went down, kneeling on one knee, and as a spectacular display of fireworks exploded over the Pacific Ocean, he asked me to marry him. If I didn't know better, I would have sworn that his move had been choreographed.

The words took me by surprise, and I was speechless.

He was still kneeling and dawdling with his hand resting on my knee. His beautiful blue eyes were asking "Well?"

"Chris, I need time to think about it," I said with a gentle sigh.

Of course, with the persuasion of Dom Pérignon laced with an adequate amount of liquid ecstasy and an impetuous wind of convivial passion, we spent the night in a luxurious stateroom on the upper deck. Upon entering the room, Chris closed the door and, without warning, put his arm around me and pulled my body fully against his. I literally went up in flames as I felt his enormous erection pressing against my abdomen. My drug-induced reaction was instantaneous and electrifying. I gasped and saw stars for a moment behind my sealed lids, and I instantly knew what he wanted. His kiss was uncompromisingly masculine, carnal, and hot. Very hot! It was the disarming kiss that I'd been craving for months. Mindlessly I obeyed his directions, moving my body in a tempestuous pagan ballet.

The penetration was swift and absolute. A branding hot pain shot through me as his steely manhood impaled the willing folds of my body. His hungry mouth took expert possession of my lips, and I moaned and seemingly lost focus on everything around me as his tongue grazed the inner linings of my teeth and lips. Then, as Chris drove his delicious swirling tongue past my lips, I instinctively opened and surrendered my lips for him with my eyes closed and gave him willingly all I had with moans of desire. As my mindless curiosity wandered into raging lust, Chris's possessive hands boldly roamed and groped uncharted territory. I offered no resistance as he removed my dress and slipped off my panties. I gently scratched my nails across his chin and heard him gasp as I lay naked and vulnerable under his warm weight.

The sound seemed far away, and I drifted into endless fervor. I whimpered and dizzily surrendered my last conscious thoughts, entrusting myself only to sensual instinct. I moaned as I felt my head sink against the silk pillow, and my moan could have been either a moan of protest or submission. I was lying on my back on the bed, my arms heavy and useless at my sides as though restrained by invisible bands. I had neither the energy nor the will to move or protest.

After that, I couldn't keep track of what was happening. Looking back, I sometimes wonder if he had put something in my drink that night. His tongue was in my mouth one moment and out the next, kissing me as if to suck the breath from me. He broke the kiss only to plant his hungry mouth at the base of my throat. He was nipping at my ears and working my neck in erotic sweeps, and I was reveling in shocking sensations never felt before.

Empowered, with a glint in his eyes, he grabbed a handful of my hair and yanked my head back, saying, "Your mine now!"

His chauvinistic declaration of possession rankled me, but I let it pass. My heart was melting like a snowball in the sun.

I wrapped her arms around his neck and drove my fingertips into his hair.

My responsive mouth meshed with his, and I worked my swirling tongue seductively around his, driving him crazy.

Driven by primal hunger, Chris walked me backward toward the bedroom, where he undid the zipper on the rear of my gown and let it drop to the floor.

He unsnapped my bra and tore the thong panties down my legs before focusing his eyes on the flaxen hair between my thighs.

His breathing was savage as he grappled with his belt buckle and the zipper of his slacks. Then, pushing me down on my back with my thighs apart, he thrust himself into me without foreplay.

He started driving and thrusting with escalating force into me, celebrating how good it felt to be inside me. I could tell he could feel the bite of my nails on his back. I was moaning and trashing as he pounded my womanhood. He didn't care if I was faking it or not. He liked it, making him feel like he had conquered me.

He climaxed intensely a minute later.

Regaining his breath, he levered himself up off me and tried to pull away.

"No," I cried, clutching at him as if I feared letting go. "No. Make love with me, Chris."

I mashed her pelvis against his in a gentle grind, wrapping my legs around him.

Forgetting about holding part of himself back and calling it a night, he instead drove his rock-hard cock again deep inside my moist vagina.

"You're my property," he whispered with a ragged breath.

With a soft cry, I arched my back off the bed, and my thighs squeezed his hips tightly. I know Chris felt my orgasm explode from the tip of his cock, now brutally buried deep inside me.

But no sooner had I realized the splendor of his possession that he began to push away from me.

The next morning, still woozy, still entranced, I drifted into a dream-less slumber. A single tear rolled from the corner of my eye. While my hair was a riot of flaxen silk atop the pillow, my lips were swollen and bruised. The smell of sex hung heavy in the room. A quiet agony flooded my eyes. Without any procrastination on his part, we were married two months later at the Rosewood Chapel in Charleston, West Virginia.

When I asked about meeting his parents, he became silent for a moment and then solemnly told me that they had been killed in an auto accident one night a year earlier when their car missed a turn on the midland trail and went over a cliff. With their demise, he—their only child—inherited their one-hundred-year-old ancestral home in Gauley Bridge on the western bank of the Kanawha River just south of the Hawks Nest, deep in the heart of Appalachia.

* * *

Gauley Bridge was a quaint mountain river town in Fayette County that didn't stand on too much ceremony. It had a population of 350 that had mostly stayed the same since the turn of the century. There was a post office, a sheriff's office, and town hall sharing the inside of an abandoned mill on Main Street. There was also small drugstore, a Baptist church, a farmer's market lot, and a turn-of-the-century diner. Several small streets off the main drag were residential, populated by small weathered clapboard houses with traditional front porches and beat-up vintage pickups and vans in the driveways spidering off the Midland Trail.

She envisioned that it would be here, in the blossoming tulip tree hallow of the hill-bounded Kanawha River, that they would begin their life together as a couple, rebuilding their antebellum roots. While the old-fashioned two-story clapboard stilted bungalow with its gingerbread trim only had two bedrooms and was on a small half-acre lot, it was a charming house that fit in nicely with the other well-tended homes of their neighbors. It was cozy, with a back porch facing an impenetrable forested mountainside, a front porch with two wicker rockers facing the Cathedral Falls, and a white picket fence in front. During the Civil War of 1861, the Union and Confederate Armies took possession of the house during their brief stay. Thankfully, they only burned the covered bridge at the confluence of the Gauley and the New rivers. Unfortunately, the ancient piers still projected out of the river, giving testimony to a violent past.

Decorating and furnishing the dated interior with eclectic furnishings had been a task that she had thoroughly enjoyed. Best of all, it was mortgage free. Nuna had a decorator's flair for enhancing the best features of a house. The dated yellow walls were now resplendent in forest greens and baby-blue trim. The hydrangea bushes in the front rock gardens added a perfect touch.

One of their biggest arguments was whether or not to have children. He had had a traumatic childhood, and bringing children into the world was not a question for him. While he never told her, she knew he had had a vasectomy before their marriage as he never used a condom later or requested that she take birth control pills.

Slowly, the things she'd found so romantic and charming about him began to fizzle and become silently oppressive. Things looked good on the surface, but there was a growing chasm of mercurial unrequited love opening between them, and there was a dark, simmering undercurrent of foreboding as she began to suspect that he had a roving eye. She had to seduce him into making love to her with desperate aggression. His kisses were becoming more platonic, with uncharacteristic insouciance. Nuna, with a heavy heart, felt the love that he had once had for her disappearing rapidly.

Then the quarrels began, primarily out of his resentment of her earning capacity and his lack of employment. She didn't yet pick up on the singles of marital disharmony. Something was eating at him. He was becoming an alcoholic, and he was becoming ever angrier, and something was frightening in his mannerisms.

It was almost like he was becoming unhinged, ranting about all the injustices in his life. She felt even more sorry for him. While she tried to rationalize with him that his unemployment was only a temporary setback, he only heard his rationalizations for his perceived failure. Chris was abject and still unemployed as the West Virginian economy was now in the toilet under President Johnson, with little hope for recovery. His obsession with his failure became a self-fulfilling prophecy, tearing him apart and weakening the underpinnings of their relationship.

Nuna didn't think their life could get any worse, and then it did. One afternoon he opened his mail and found that he was being drafted; he was to report for duty in two weeks at the Norfolk Naval Recruiting Station in Virginia.

Deep in thought and unbeknownst to her, he had come home sodden from a night out drinking with his male friends. Chris spent the better part of the evening nursing double shots of tequila on the back porch, backlit by moonlight, vacillating between the pros and cons of his options, his expression shifting constantly. At breakfast the following morning, he staggered into the kitchen and, pulsing with anger, told her that he had made up his mind and was enlisting in the navy.

She felt negative karma from him because he had made a deal with the devil. Instead of being a loyal, beaming wife hugging her husband, she was utterly shocked. All Nuna wanted was to be married to a man who loved her. This was her worst nightmare! Despite her pleading protests, he enlisted anyway, and her moral happiness plummeted. Chris's father and grandfather alike had been stern and taciturn military men and had both served proudly in the navy, and Chris wasn't about to refuse and break a family tradition of service. With passive acceptance, she listened to his family story.

The inevitable time of parting came, and he was shipped to the Great Lakes for training. When he came home on leave, he advised her that he was being sent to Coronado for training on PBRs at the Assault Craft Unit One Amphibious Base. Then, two months later, he wrote her that he was being transferred to Mare Island, California, for riverine training. Then, a month later, he wrote her that he was flying home for a few days before shipping out to Vietnam, where he would be assigned to a river patrol boat. Chris seemed to have only one goal now that he shared with her, and he was diving into it with a vengeance. That goal was to emulate the exalted military success of his father, who had been a chief petty officer aboard a tin can in World War II.

Chris packed his sea bag that morning without so much as a snivel, and after a quick breakfast, he gave her a quick hug and kiss and left in a taxi for the airport in Charleston. He said he didn't want her to drive him to the airport and have another emotional goodbye. She watched him exit the driveway with naked despair and what seemed to be unrequited love.

Her only connection to Chris now was watching Walter Cronkite every night giving the latest volatile summary of the Vietnam War. The stories bypassed the confusion, the taste and smell of blood, and the adrenaline rush as gunboats ran the daily gauntlet of hell, moving troops and logistics up and down the hostile rivers.

It was a clear, lazy April afternoon when the worst day of her life began. Her fears were realized the day a military car pulled up to her house in Coaltown with two Naval Officers at the front door delivering the shocking devastating news of his death. The lieutenant informed her without further ceremony that Chris had been killed in action. Handing her Chris's dog tags, he stated that what was left of his remains would be flown to Yeager Airport in Charleston. Did he suffer, she asked? The officer responded at once, "I'm sure he didn't." Nuna stood stoically in disbelief before closing the door, refusing to acknowledge or come to terms with the dolorous pain and emotional violence within her heart.

She would never see her Chris alive again. Only her eyes betrayed that she was feeling ineffable, wrenching pain. Prostrate with grief, she sat on the edge of her bed with her face buried in Chris's favorite shirt, holding it in her trembling hands, agonizing as the realization that she had lost her husband forever curled through her head. She cried in earnest. Her chagrin was agonizing and her grief intense as though her heart were being torn from her chest. She felt bereft of love and hope. It was heartbreaking and beyond bearing. The veil of indignant anger in her heart slowly peeled away, leaving her weakened, frail, and inconsolable. Ergo, what remained was a deep sadness for her loss. Every dream she had held for her life has evaporated.

Distraught and heartbroken, she was having trouble bearing the thought that Chris was actually gone from her world and she would never see him again.

"Did he suffer?" she asked.

The officer responded at once, "I'm sure he didn't."

She covered her eyes with both hands. "Thank God for that," she said despairingly and burst into tears again.

Chris Polinski's funeral service took place in the sanctuary of an obscure, outlying branch of the Christian Church. The structure itself was a one-story white clapboard building devoid of ornaments. When she reached the parking lot, there were already several cars parked.

Shockingly enough, when departing her house, she had encountered a few dozen protestors in the street, verbally celebrating his death, waving Vietnamese flags and calling him a "child murderer."

She wore a simple black dress with long sleeves, relieved of jewelry, to his funeral, which took place on a damp and overcast morning, adding to the solemnity of the lugubrious day. It was a lovely service with honor guards, sad and very touching. Her blond hair fell loose to her shoulders, as she had chosen to pass on wearing a hat and veil.

Rather than take a seat, she stood with her head up proud and with dignity, in perfect stillness, staring straight ahead at the flower-bedecked closed coffin before her. The pastor had composed a string of words before sailing into an all-encompassing prayer eulogizing a man he really didn't know. The funeral was a blur of agony, laying out the fleeting nature of their short existence together. Devastated and unable to speak or function, she stood stoic, angry with God. She was silent, allowing a unstemmable flow of thoughts and impressions to trickle randomly through her feeble and bereaved mind.

Since he had requested cremation in the advent of his death on his military documents, the few returned bones were cremated. Since there would be no actual body buried, the invocation and funeral were brief. An air of melancholy surrounded her. A small urn of ashes was presented to her. At the appointed time, in a fading afternoon light, a National Guard commander from Charleston gave a short, poignant eulogy stating that Chris had died honorably in combat along with his crewmates at the Battle of Dung Ha. A team of marine honor guards stood rigidly at attention, resplendent in their dress uniforms as taps was played. Upon firing the traditional twenty-one-gun salute, they presented her with the tricornered burial flag.

There wasn't a receiving line, but those in attendance made a point of coming up to her and giving her words of sympathy. Shaking hands and receiving kisses, she graciously greeted and thanked those who had converged upon her, her voice faltering with a slight tremor on the last few words. Unfortunately, no relatives or friends were in attendance to commiserate about her loss. Instead, his ashes would be scattered across the Kanawha River at Gauley Bridge with the Cathedral Falls cascading down off the mountain in the background, as he had requested in his living will. She pushed her welling tears away with a soggy Kleenex against her lips, suddenly looking bereft. She covered her eyes with her hands, and her body shook as her tenuous heart bled. Keening in grief, she wanted to scream his name but didn't. Instead, she had to deal with the inexorable corollary of depression and the self-doubt that followed.

While nothing was certain, everything was taking on a new meaning.

She lay in bed at night, thinking of their last conversations and reliving them in her head over and over again. Chris's departure from her life was wrenching, but the hard part of loving him was the hole it left in her heart. Now dripping with perturbation and lost in the tumult of her memories, she wondered, Did Chris really love her? Looking back, most of her memories of him were organic and, at best, three-dimensional, existing only in her mind, not her heart. Nevertheless, she still loved him and could not deny that indelible fact. The last time they truly had physical loving contact was the kiss they shared at the Rosewood Chapel on their wedding day. She wanted to be touched and appreciated as a woman again.

She needed more. Had she deluded herself into believing they were in love? Her love for Chris had waxed and cooled in the morose hollow of her heart, along with a terrible yawning emptiness. She reached up and brushed a lone tear from her eye. And it was that frightening, bittersweet unanswered question she now wished fervently she had considered before.

Returning to the house, she kissed and carefully packed the folded flag given to her as he was laid to rest into the sea chest on top of his other personal belongings and placed the chest in the attic. This was the last page of their brief life together. She felt utterly dehydrated. Her eyes were swollen and blurred as more tears welled up because of her ephemeral memory of the past year. It seemed that all she had done for the past week was cry.

She felt guilty for being mad at him when he enlisted and left. She felt hurt and angry that he had not sent her one letter or returned hers. She pulled the hatch closed and climbed back down the stairs with her eyes wide open, trying not to experience another emotional meltdown as she attempted to sanitize his memory. She forced herself to repress her bereaved grief as tears pooled in her eyes.

Ashes to ashes and dust to dust.

"Goodbye, Chris," she crooned, with a faraway look.

The wind outside whistled with a keening sound. This is the end of the Cinderella and Prince Charming story, she thought.

CHAPTER 8

Six years later

Tick. Tick. Tick. Nuna woke up one beckoning morning, inexplicably, at 4:00 a.m. with an excited longing for a new home. She had received notice of a position open with the Chase-Webster bank in Charleston and had accepted it after some back-and-forth negotiations on salary. She had sold the ramshackle cabin she had lived in all her life, a stone's throw outside the sleepy mining town Coalwood, with a population of three hundred souls still reminiscing about exaggerated stories of the Hatfield-McCoy feud. Having inherited it from her father several months back, she had been staying in a motel waiting for the rental lease to expire on the home she owned and had rented out a year ago in the eponymous bedroom town of Gauley Bridge, hidden in the folds of West Virginia's Monongahela Forest. It was one of the few things that Chris had bequeathed to her upon his death, having received it in a will from his deceased parents. She was tired of eating out at restaurants and diners and now wanted to put down roots and sleep in her own bed. Emotionally adrift, she had to rebuild her life without Chris and walk away from that sepulchral milestone. Still, the heartache, the throbbing desolation in her heart, and the sense of loss never went away.

At seven that morning, Nuna was on the road, heading through the pass that cut through the Appalachian Mountains. As the two-lane roadway crested, she was struck by the sweep of the undulating mountains before her. The rugged terrain was tinted a hazy blue-gray by the nature of the underlying rock. The road eased down in the valley, intersecting Highway 19 some fifteen miles beyond. Nuna shivered in amazement as her tires crunched the gravel beneath and she brought her Nissan Rogue to a stop. She stepped out of the car, savoring the crisp, languorous cool mountain air of the morning.

Tick. Tick. Tick. It was a little before nine o'clock, and she was losing time. The morning sun caused the aqua surface of the Kanawha River to glisten. A rooster strutted out of the next-door neighbor's yard. The bird cocked its head in her direction, rustled its feathers, and crowed loudly as she exited the jeep. Several chickens were running and pecking at the ground under a clothesline with a couple of sheets strung on it swaying lazily in the early morning breeze. Stepping onto the welcoming wraparound porch, she opened the whiny, groaning screen door, and having inserted her key into the lock, she pushed the door open.

"Voila! My new, beautiful home."

She sidestepped onto the creaky weathered wooden planks of the glassed-in front porch of her cozy 150-year-old postage-stamp-size English cottage. The house was surrounded by a weathered white picket fence on the bluff overlooking the Kanawha River. She glanced at the amazing ambiance of the mountainous landscape before her, cataloging and assessing. A large oak tree stood sentinel in her front yard, swaying as a gust of wind blew through it leafy branches. Several small songbirds flitted above the branches. It took her a dozen trips to the car to unload her clothes; cardboard boxes full of items including herbs and spices, kitchenware, and bedding; and three bags of groceries that she had purchased at the local village mart.

The house, with an asphalt roof that extended over a surrounding porch, was in need of some cosmetic attention, with a few cracked shutters, a loose rail board on the porch, et cetera. The siding needed a coat or two of paint, and the yard was slightly overgrown but only looked partially abandoned since her last visit two months earlier. In addition, the home had trapped the day's heat. She opened a few windows to let in the cool breeze that blew into the mountain holler. The house was recently rented to a young professional couple who had meticulously maintained it inside and out. Several weeks earlier, she had spent a week shopping for the home, buying window treatments, kitchen utensils, furnishings, her bed and bathroom linens, and a used coffee table and chairs.

Again, a clement fresh breeze came in through an open window. It had been sturdily constructed before the Civil War, withstanding the lashings and poundings of several dozen hurricanes, including the occupations of both Union and Confederate troops. White smoke was curling out of the ivy-covered stone chimney, compliments of her newly hired home maintenance man.

While the deceptively unpretentious two-story structure was dated, it had lots of charm. It had flourishing gingerbread trim that made it homey, even if it was indeed in need of some TLC. There was something about the retro feel of the house that gave her pleasure. An array of terra-cotta pots punctuated in thick moss along the flagstone walkway mingled with the intoxicating ambrosia perfumes of the riotous flowering fauna that blossomed in profusion, giving it that West Virginia charm. In the mountains on a quiet street, the home had a commanding view of the Kanawha River wending languidly below through the heart of Gauley Bridge like a coiled snake.

The town of Gauley Bridge, out yonder, wasn't much of a town: seven streets long and four deep, all bunched up against a mountain with an active train track running through backyard weeds and tall grasses. It had a population of 610 and was the kind of atavistic Mayberry-esque small town where everyone knew their neighbors. Its only notable feature was the cement pillars still standing like aging sentinels in the river, giving evidence of the historical wooden covered bridge burned by the Confederate Army back in 1862. The population was so modest the number wasn't even posted on a sigh anywhere.

The scene before her allowed her to relax fully, be whoever she was meant to be, and realize her essence as a woman. There was one drawback to the location. An active coal train track ran perpendicular across the very bottom of her driveway. It wasn't unusual to hear a fifty-car freight train in the morning chuffing its way up the mountain. A crocus of saffron, the West Virginia nectar, ran along the tracks.

With its lichen-covered stones and weathered white picket fence leading up to doors with porcelain knobs, it had that Norman Rockwell

presence, surrounded by patches of overgrown fescue set in the enchanted forest of a fairy tale.

A vintage Allis-Chalmers tractor with its derelict hand crank still
attached stood sentinel, rusting in a vacant lot next door in high grass
alongside a rusting swing set. On the far back of the lot, a forties-era out-
house with a disused appearance was leaning forward and succumbing
to nature, surrounded by moss, snarled papery-looking mountain laurel,
and dead leaves mingling with patches of fiddleheads.

The sunny, utilitarian knotty pine kitchen was small, with a jungle of
houseplants on the windowsill preceding a glimpse of the river across the
street. A corner étagère filled with miniature figurines, a walk-in pantry,
and a short Corian countertop abutting the stainless steel sink, stove, microwave, and refrigerator (free of magnets or mementos) were relatively
new. While the furniture was mostly hand-me-down and utilitarian, having been left by Chris's parents, the interior, with black-and-white photos
on the shelves dating back to the thirties, had a warm, secure feel, with
massive oak beams surrounded by a palette of soft blue, white, and pink.

The parquet oakwood floors were all recently sanded, varnished, and
covered with new area rugs, but they still creaked as she walked to the
parlor. The windows were adorned with lacy curtains trimmed with window boxes outside. The parlor and the dining alcove were encased in a
floral pastel chintz and furnished with turn-of-the-century Wedgewood
antiques that she had treasured and saved from her mother. A sliding
wall petition separated all the usual amenities. She particularly enjoyed
sitting on the sofa by the oversize fieldstone fireplace in the parlor with
its sloping ceiling, warming herself on a chilly night with both feet resting on the ottoman. Yes, the two-bedroom Cape was homey, cozy, and
as placid as one could ask for.

The bedroom had a queen-sized bed with nightstands on each side.
The other furnishings were a full dresser and a reading chair. Their large
closet, with its empty hangers on one side, looked forlorn. She shared the
home with a cat named Oscar, who spent much of his time chasing mice.

The one thing about having a cat is they're not judgmental as long as you feed them and scratch their backs from time to time.

The melodious sound of the Kanawha River perennially flowing along the front edge of her property calmed her, and the crisp mountain air was fresh and inviting as a warm wind ruffled her hair. A mockingbird was chirping out an alliteration of sonorous melodies on a strong Webster sycamore tree limb high above the front yard with an almost mystical dignity. Other birds drank at the lichen-covered century-old battle-scared stone pilings of a historical river bridge still standing sentinel in the middle of the river. Somewhere up the street, a couple of lawnmowers were chunking away, and the smell of burning charcoal hung in the air.

It was her oasis of serenity. She was still in the process of meeting her neighbors, who, for the most part, had lived there just off the CSX rail bed all their lives and exhibited the reality of a vibrant small-town life with a population of 605. It was a town where the local doctor still made house calls and the local farm overlooking Gauley Bridge still delivered fresh bottled milk in the morning. The small lot was remote on the hill overlooking the river with just a sprinkle of neighbors, but her desire for privacy was innate. She didn't have many friends, but it wasn't always that way. Since losing Chris, she had a lot of angst when it came to meeting new people. Most of the neighbors had lived in the sleepy mountain town of Gauley Bridge all of their lives and formed a close-knit, almost inbred, clannish community hailing from great-great-great grandparents. While they were mostly friendly and welcoming, they had been a little slow to accept her even though her late husband had grown up there and she was born and raised a couple of hundred miles north in Elkins.

After moving in, she decided that she should make every effort to become part of the enviable community. Without looking her in the eye, the women made euphemistic references to her loss and sorrow, but no one asked about her. Unfortunately, with her hectic work schedule, she always needed more time for coffee klatch friends.

The town of Gauley Bridge was rich in history, with that sleepy small-town Southern aura set in a shallow holler graced by fog-capped mountains. A sense of atavistic history and grace was laced in the moss hanging from the rocks and trees. The town was built along two streets that intersected the Midland 60, with ubiquitous rail lines all over town; one crossed the rear of her backyard. Scattered among the buildings were a half dozen small houses with sagging white picket fences and a couple of trailer homes. The other side of the road was sparser: a Handy Mart gas station, a Dollar General, a one-room dusty post office operated by an elderly clerk in her seventies, and a convenience store were all that was left. Empty storefronts and waist-high weeds on both sides shadowed Railroad Street. So that was the town of Gauley Bridge, population 614.

Since the trauma of her husband's death, it hadn't occurred to her that she didn't really have any close friends and hadn't really formed any lasting bonds with anyone. She now wanted the normalcy of small-town life, with its white church spires rising into the sky and antique-style streetlamps on every corner, and to be a part of the local fabric.

She had lived her whole life in West Virginia and had never become indifferent to its mountain beauty. Night had fallen without giving notice of its full buck moon enhancing the darkness. It had been an exhausting day for sure, and she now felt it appropriate to open a bottle of wine to celebrate her new home. Brushing some yellow pine needles off the rattan rocker on her front porch, she decided to sit a spell as the comforting sips of alcohol coursed her veins; she closed her eyes and raised her head to the starlit black velvet sky above. The sky was breathtakingly clear, and moonlight slanted through the trees. A breeze wafted against her face, brushing across her skin like a cool, fragrant kiss, and she smelled it again as her head lulled back: the scent of the mountains.

She hesitated to listen to the yipping of young fox cubs in the distance and the soft call of an owl in the forest, punctuating the night. A gathering of fireflies had taken up residence on her front lawn facing the river. Though a breeze had been blowing earlier, now the air was perfectly still. Not so much as a quiver of a leaf. Except for a high-pitched cicada chorus somewhere in the trees, there were no night sounds at all. She filled her nostrils with an inviting whiff of tantalizing fresh mountain air laced with honeysuckle and listened to the melodious cadence of the sounds of cicadas and crickets in the woodlands surrounding her. No cars passed on the road below. Somewhere across the street, a bullfrog croaked in the thick river weeds. It was what she had wanted for her own life. Her ardor became wistful. She enjoyed the cloistered tranquility of a simple life in the country, calling her in to watch a galaxy of glowworms on her lawn.

She had a beautiful wardrobe, even if it was a couple of years out of date. She had no credit card, wasn't in debt to anyone, and was financially stable. To her knowledge, she didn't have a single worry in the world.

* * *

The thickly wooded slope laced with wisteria vines was a place of renewal, peace, and tranquility and stretched upward against the background of a cerulean sky until it was lost in a froth of low-hanging, misty white cumulus clouds. Just then, she heard a clap of thunder in the distance and a gust of wind rattled the windows and abruptly interrupted her woolgathering. Another thunder boomer presaged a storm coming as dark clouds roiled above the tree line, prompting her to return to the kitchen just as a bolt of lightning slashed the darkening sky.

Long tendrils of kudzu vines hanging from the trees were turning ghostly and full of shadows. The air was stifling and thick with simmering midsummer humidity. Oppressive and horrendous but typical in the mountains of West Virginia this time of year.

Earlier that morning, lying atop summer-moist sheets, with the windows open to the relentless chorus of cicadas, she hung on to a faint hope of inhaling the fragrance of the wet earth and a hint of a mountain breeze. Later when, she had gone into town to do her marketing at the farmer's market and pick up her snail mail at the post office, a smattering of puffy clouds had dotted the sky over the predawn forest. Now they were steel gray and were filling it with an ominous warning. The celestial powers of nature were speaking loud and clear. A tempest was brewing in the distance, and the air felt charged and volatile. While waiting for the water to boil on the stove, she peered out the kitchen window above the sink as she cranked the window shut. Outside, the wind was now heralding the incoming storm from the other side of the mountain.

Nuna stuffed her hands in her jeans and smiled as she pushed her shoulder-length flaxen hair away from her eyes. I truly love it here, she thought. There's nothing like riding out a storm and looking out at the panoramic views of the Appalachian Mountains of West Virginia in the eastern skies. She was located just ten miles north of the tatterdemalion towns around the coal mines that were now mostly abandoned.

The small shed at the far end of the gravel driveway, with its creaking door rattling on its rusted hinges, was begging for attention. The rustic building across the way looked lonesome and enduring with its many shades of weathered siding. The house and yard needed serious TLC, and she could admit it. Yet, with conflicting emotions, she also felt an air of melancholy curling around her like an invisible shroud, with the devastating losses of both Chris in the war and now her father, who had just recently retired to his home in Hazzard Holler. I wish he were here right now, she thought. But that was not to be. Her father had been killed in a car accident six months ago, having missed a turn and plunged three hundred feet off a cliff. At least that's what the authorities said. That was a night she would never forget. The sheriff knocked on her front door at 11:00 p.m. and delivered the terrifying news.

The Tomblin Funeral Home in Elkins was like so many of them: everything pristine, sterile, and tasteful. The director was very gentle and thorough. The members of his church had arranged flowers. An easel was placed inside the entrance with a dozen black-and-white photographs of him and her mother at their wedding and in their happier days. They were happily married for forty-five years.

Being the only child with no known living relatives, she sat alone in the receiving line several feet from the open casket as they touched it and recited a short prayer. She worked hard to hold back the bubbling tears filling her eyes as she relived all the yonder years during which her daddy held her and supported her. Homesick memories of her childhood and the warm, loving father-daughter relationship growing up in deep Appalachia were unassailable. Approximately sixty-five members of his church came and offered their respects and blessings as they exited the visitation room.

Nuna spent the subsequent week closing and putting the dilapidated house on the market, and settling her father's estate. Still, deep in her mind, she didn't have closure over the cause of his death. While the official accident report stated excessive speed and intoxication, her seventy-five-year-old father rarely had more than a couple of weekly beers. He was a careful driver, never exceeding the speed limit. Something wasn't right, and she wasn't going to let go of it until she learned the truth. The only redeeming element of her dad's death was that he was now reunited with his loving wife, her mother, in heaven.

Despite her lingering sorrow, she had to stand strong, think of tomorrow, and move on with the next chapter of her life. She was not going to cling to a distant memory any longer. The Cape at Gauley Bridge was paid for, and she had a great job working for the Chase-Webster Bank in Charleston handling money transactions and catering to other requests for the Maduro Estate.

Nuna had changed into a pair of loose-fitting khaki pants and a short-sleeved shirt. She fixed herself a cup of tea and curled up on the Adirondack rocker on the porch barefoot in the gathering breeze and listened to the whisper of the trees and let her mind drift. The smell of citronella filled the air from a small flickering candle on a side table as she watched squirrels pursue their antics, chasing one another from one tree to another. The nocturnal night cadence deepened, and she heard the distant sound of booming thunder rolling across the sky in the waning light. Looking up as she sat curled up on her chair, looking at the cloud formations in the sky and the swaying treetops, she could see the anvil of a storm cloud slowly coming over the mountain, obscuring the silver image of a full buck moon on the river below. A strong wind was now beginning to blow out of the west with a nasty howl. No stars would be hovering over her home tonight. Somewhere up the mountain, she heard the distant primal ululation of a lone wolf. Lightning bugs winked at her from shadows in the grass under the leafy trees.

The barometric pressure was falling, and the heralds of a big storm in the stratosphere was brewing. She looked away, ran her fingers through her hair, and absently brushed a bug off her arm.

Having grown up in the mountains, Nuna could smell the distinctive heady fragrance and feel the impending storm in her bones. Then, several moments later, the wind picked up, blowing in the leading edge of the front-swaying treetops of the sycamores. The mist came in waves, almost a rain, but was so light it was more like a mysterious fog rolling in off the river and floating across the dewy grass.

A low rumble of thunder was echoing off the distant mountains, now shrouded in low clouds and thick fog. On cue, a brilliant bolt of lightning flashed across the darkening sky with a resounding clap of thunder. Within a few minutes, the temperature plummeted with the storm enveloping the area, and an unrelenting heavy rain lashed violently against the windows as the storm fully engaged. The explosive flashes of lightning spears were followed by the drumroll of thunder, forming an uneasy synchronicity that punctuated the intervals of deepening darkness across the river.

Rising to her feet and retreating back into the house, she padded back into the kitchen and made herself a cup of tea in the microwave, selecting a decaffeinated Earl Gray tea bag, and curled up on an overstuffed wicker armchair, taking off her slippers and tucking her legs beneath her as she enjoyed a contemplative moment. The clothes in the dryer were spinning and thumping. She sat on the enclosed porch in her father's oversized Giants nightshirt, watching the storm move across the mountains as it approached. The wind began to whip the rain into a frenzied maelstrom. Nocturnal fireflies flickered in the grass as she wilted into the cushions, cradling the hot cup in both hands before sipping another soothing mouthful of tea. Her only musical entertainment was the cicadas that buzzed in concert loudly but lazily in the thick cover of the mountainside forest behind her house, lulling her asleep on most nights.

Another crack of thunder, like Civil War cannon fire echoing through the narrow mountain hollows, obliterated all other sounds and caused the lights to flicker. They sputtered several more times and then fluttered out completely. It was going to be a candlelight night. She quickly pulled her flashlight out of the kitchen drawer and turned it on, then tested two battery-operated Coleman lanterns.

Losing power in the mountains was to be expected during a thunderstorm, and she was prepared. Until it happened, which it didn't, she had curled up on the couch with a new novel she had picked up and had been looking forward to reading. Reading novels was a passion of hers, and she hoped she one day to write one of her own.

It rained all night, one of those rare tropical storms that somehow find their way uninvited into the West Virginia mountains, transforming tranquil rivers into turgid, fast-moving white water. Thunder rumbled in the distance, and her windows flickered with blue flashes of lighting. The slanted rain escalated, and she would later wake at 5:00 a.m. to the sound of heavy raindrops drumming on her roof and bedroom windows.

She decided to call it a night, take a bath with a glass of wine in the claw-foot tub before curling up on the couch for an hours or so binging on another black-and-white episode of *Jeopardy*. While she tried to use her laptop to check out local news and Fox News and other websites, it was a gamble as coverage was only sometimes accommodating in the hollers of the mountains. Tonight was a washout. No internet, no moon, only the starlight glittering in the window. The night yawned before her, and she surrendered to the bedroom.

Good sleeping weather, she thought as she closed the venetian blinds and snuggled under the covers and gingerly lay down in bed. With her left hand, she turned the night light out, contently pushed the snooze button on the alarm clock, and closed her eyes. As she lay silent in the dark, resorting to her usual mantra, the baleful howl of a coyote cried in the distant forest, adding a soporific backdrop. No longer plagued by reoccurring insomnia, she fell into a deep slumber.

The storm had begun to abate when she woke at 6:00 a.m. Before long the rain had subsided to a light intermittent drizzle collecting in puddles, leaving behind a moisture-laden low-hanging fog obscuring the view of the river. The air was unmoving and had a texture almost as unyielding as the silence. Soon, crickets chirped from their hideouts. A lone croaking bullfrog was making his presence known somewhere on the riverbank as gauzy columns of fog rose off the surface.

Dawn had overcome the darkness only marginally as Nuna lifted her head from the plump pillows, having heard an unearthly screeching outside her bedroom window. She tossed the sheets and comforter aside into the footboard of her maple sleigh bed. Then, groping for the lamp on the end table and dragging herself from the languorous fog of sleep, she stretched, long and slow, like her still-sleeping cat, before peeling off the covers and stepping out of bed into her warm slippers.

The ozone gusting through the crack in the open window was cool and damp. The summer months of July and August are normally dry, and the flora tended to languish without moisture. She threw open the windows and breathed deeply of the mingled fragrances, allowing the mountain holler laced with honeysuckle to fill her nostrils. Having done a few perfunctory hamstring stretches, she was ready for a new day. She quickly used her inhaler. Breathing the summer air could promptly bring on an asthma attack.

The rains purified the humid air and were a welcome respite, with the forested summits wearing cowls of bottom-heavy opaque rain clouds and fog. Yet the humidity was oppressive, with the temperatures hovering in the mideighties. The summer winds roared through the mountains and screamed through the narrow hollows. Somewhere in the distant mountains, a coal train horn bleated. Nuna smiled and kicked off her shoes, going barefoot.

Stepping into the kitchen, she could hear the percolator sprucing out the rich aroma of mountain fresh coffee. Securing a mug from the cabinet, she poured herself the first of her customary three cups of dark-roasted coffee and ate a toasted bagel while turning on the TV to catch the day's news and weather. She had promised herself that she would reduce her caffeine intake, but like all good intentions, it would soon pass and go the way of most New Year's resolutions. She sipped the last dregs in her mug. That was OK: her vices were few and minor in nature.

With her stomach growling, she heated some leftover fried chicken from yesterday's fridge on the hibachi on the deck. She ate it with grits along with a couple of balls of falafel. She redeemed herself by throwing in a simple garden salad of tomatoes, cucumbers, snap peas, and beets, sprinkling a lemon vinaigrette and some bacon bits to top it off. Grabbing a bottle of water from the fridge and taking a long drink, she was assailed with the smell of real Southern fried chicken. She plunked down in the chair at the kitchen table and enjoyed her breakfast just the way she liked it. Simple and without complications.

It was now almost eight o'clock, and having placed her dishes in the sink, she hand-washed the dishes and utensils, laying each on a towel on the counter before drying her hands with another dish towel. She then putzed around the kitchen, cleaned and rinsed the coffee maker, and took out the trash. She was frugal and didn't have a dishwasher or a clothes dryer, even though she could afford both. She had a clothes washer, but like her mom and grandmother before her, she still hung on to atavistic tradition and practiced the old-fashioned way of cranking clothes through a wooded wringer and latching them to a clothesline in the backyard to dry. For the most part, to her knowledge, everyone else in town did the same.

The silence of the morning was shattered as she opened the light-blocking shades. She leaned against the windowsill and listened to the morning sounds of warbling songbirds in the trees. Fluffy gossamer curtains fluttered in the soft West Virginia morning breeze under white cumulus clouds dappling the sky. On the lawn before her was a rooster strutting purposefully toward several hens, crowing his lungs out. Now, she remembered seeing a sign on her neighbor's lawn advertising "Fresh Eggs." The cloud cover in the thickly forested mountains overlooking the holler was heavy and low with morning shadows.

She inhaled the scent of fresh lavender in the shower and rinsed herself clean.

Stepping out of the shower with water droplets trickling into her eyes, she grabbed a towel and dried herself off, standing before the bathroom mirror. Then, taking a smaller towel, she wrapped it around her hair, much like a turban. She brushed her teeth and did a couple more stretches.

Completing her morning ministrations, Nuna threw on a top, tied her hair back in a ponytail, got into her knee-length black spandex shorts, and put on her sneakers. After a half hour workout in her makeshift gym, she went for a four-mile jog east, crossing the bridge where the confluence of the Gauley River and the New River formed the Kanawha River, taking her over to the Cathedral Falls, which cascaded sixty feet down off Gauley Mountain into a narrow canyon just off the Midland Trail. A half dozen hardy motorcyclists on Harley-Davidsons with out-of-state plates were already parked at the base of the waterfall taking pictures. The morning was chilly and foggy, the ground still saturated from the rain during the night.

Taking a five-minute break, she sat on a rock, deeply inhaled the fresh July air, and listened to the sounds of the musical chirping birds and the water crashing over the rocks, forming a symphony of sound, a façade of forested mountain harmony. An unseen scurry of tree squirrels chittered in unison in the trees above. It was her way of reconnecting with nature and escaping the worries of business life for a while. From there, she reversed her direction and jogged over to the Kanawha Falls on the river's east bank and back. A cool veil of mist floated above the water, merging with the road pavement. She stopped momentarily and watched an inconspicuous blue heron just off the riverbank ferociously skewer and swallow a small frog. This was her piece of heaven. She spent the rest of the day mowing the front and rear lawns and getting acquainted with her new home.

The horizon was turning a salmon pink as the sun crept over the mountains and into view. Nuna loved the mountains, the forest, and the people who lived in the simplicity of this rural setting.

She removed her baseball cap and ran a hand through her damp dewy hair. Walking into the kitchen, she made herself a bowl of hot oatmeal with fresh strawberries and maple syrup. It was her go-to breakfast. She was a morning person and loved everything about the first meal of her day, including two mugs of freshly brewed coffee. She loved life. She now owned a home of her own. Her life was quiet and beautiful, but having been isolated and cloistered away in the isolated mountains most of her life, she now found herself without any close friends or family. There was a yawning abyss of loneliness in her soul that silently cried for desperate understanding and a true, loving romance.

The phone rang, and she lunged at it. The call was from customer relations at the Chase-Webster bank in Charleston. Maria Manduro had called and was requesting that Nuna meet with her at the Manduro compound ASAP.

CHAPTER 9

On a lazy Saturday afternoon in late June, Captain Bryce Tucker was angled back in faded denim and his trademark well-worn Lucchese cowboy boots, relaxed on a rattan glider with a longneck Corona on the rear wraparound deck of his new sprawling rustic ranch house. Relaxed, he felt very much at ease, for jeans and Western boots were the norm in this part of West Virginia. His home was on the spine of a remote ridge line overlooking the New River George. Ash, maple, oak, pine, and other evergreens rose and flourished on all corners of the land.

He was rocking back and forth, drumming his fingers on the armrest and basking in his historical handmade glider. He looked down at the white water rapids roaring and churning over glacial boulders as the river cascaded through the deep one-thousand-foot canyon below. Before him, on the other side of the gorge, a flock of blackbirds was hassling a hawk, diving on the larger bird like F-15 jet-fighters on a B-27 bomber. On the mountain, there were no traffic noises, only the sound of a breeze blowing through the tops of towering trees. It was the house that he built with a large family in mind, but it would be his, with no one waiting in the wings. He hadn't allowed anyone that close.

During the winter, the weather could get bitterly cold, but the summers were generally warm and relaxing. Several white cumulus puffy clouds benevolently floated across the sky, blocking the scorching sun.

"It's peaceful here," he whispered as he ran his fingers through his disheveled hair and wiped a bead of sweat from his forehead before it leached into his eyes. He sat back and stared up into the sky, lost in thought. He truly enjoyed his easygoing laissez-faire bachelorhood. The town of Fayetteville, with just over two thousand populations, enjoyed a well-deserved reputation for having an almost imperceptible crime rate.

It was one of the felicitous reasons he had chosen Fayetteville as home. The second was the allure of the mountains. The New River wound through the southern Allegheny Mountains of West Virginia, and it was renowned for class IV white water rafting and kayaking through the wild rapids of Fayetteville. With the advent of summer, the calmer waters were beautiful, attracting thousands of tourists during the warmer months.

* * *

Bryce

I called my pistol-packing, eccentric, incorrigible biological redneck cousin Ray Palmer, whom I hadn't seen in all of the last fifteen years or so, and set a date to meet him at my new house. I had thought his older cousin would now be fragile and vulnerable having lived in the mountains for so long. Instead he looked hale and healthy, in his prime. Ray had grown up traipsing here in the West Virginia Appalachian Mountains and knew his neck of the woods like the back of his weathered hands. It didn't take me long to reunderstand that we stood in stark cultural contrast to one another. As he always stated, the trees were here before he was born and would still stand tall when he left. A gleam of ebullience suffused his restless, unflappable blue eyes whenever he spoke of the mountains. Ray was an unimposing bohemian living embodiment of Appalachia. It was one of his little idiosyncrasies. I would supply the beer and Ray a fresh jug of moonshine, and we would sit and shoot the shit for hours while he whittled on a branch of sugar maple regaling the past.

Not having seen Ray in all these years, I had expected his wizened face to have whittled down and paled, but that was not the Ray I was now looking at, with his halting beatific smile, as he fiddled with the jaunty red kerchief knotted around his neck and the brim of his well-worn straw hat. Ray had a hardened, crusty face as weathered as a barn and a lion's mane of unruly white hair; a competing beard that hadn't seen a barber or a razor in nigh a year or more was constantly blowing in the wind. He was dressed in a back-woods style in shoulder-strapped britches, and one could describe Ray as an enamored stodgy, crusty throwback, with a good-ol'-boy mentality, to the bygone 1940s backwoods generation. His skin was tan and lined with deep wrinkles. It matched his untrimmed beard, which was all of ten inches. His eyes were dark blue and probing, his beatific jowls heavy. Ray always had a curved Civil War pipe in his mouth when he wasn't packing it with his favorite Highland whiskey and black cherry concoction. Sending a pungent cloud of smoke above his head, he swore his daddy's grandpa stole it from an intoxicated Confederate when they occupied Gauley Bridge. Yeah, another story.

He had sidestepped and scorned most of modernity, and his stock-in-trade was the New River Outfitters Sporting Goods store at the base of Gauley Mountain on the New River, which he owned. The plan for today was to grab a couple of six-packs of beer and spend some quality time canoeing from Cathedral Falls on the New River to the Gorge located in Fayetteville under the New River Bridge. Ray was also a Vietnam veteran and, while he was now pushing fifty-five years old, give or take a couple, was still hale and hearty. He was a good-natured, gregarious character for sure, always radiating zesty bonhomie with his anachronistic mountain appearance, which always included his legendary denim overalls. Born with a natural proclivity for storytelling, he could fill the tedium of a hot summer day. Ray would sit a spell on a rock or stump next to a crick, whittling with gnarled fingers and a knife on a branch of ash, regaling me and others around him with his extensive repertoire of rustic yarns and myths about bygone days in the mountains, the good-ol'-boy ways of the past. Some were true, others apocryphal. He was an expert kayaker and loved the river, but arthritis in his shoulders stifled that activity.

Ray was a master raconteur with endless anecdotes, and for the most part, they were accompanied by his plucking at the strings of his fiddle, sounding out cherished lyrics of mountain fiddle melodies, though he knew none of them by name.

Ray shared with me that he never knew his father or his mother, whom he learned later on in life was a seventeen-year-old druggie.

She abandoned him at birth, left town abruptly, and never came back. His hillbilly grandparents quickly adopted him upon learning of their daughter's disgraceful decision. Ray became their only son, and he still referred to his grandfather as Papaw. Papaw was a lumberjack and volunteer firefighter and had passed away years before he should have, and his overwhelmed ninety-year-old grandmother, known as Mamaw, followed him a short year later, from a broken heart. By his own admission, he couldn't remember a single event of his childhood growing up. It was for these reasons Ray never married.

Ray was a redneck Appalachian rebel with a beer belly and a deep twang who loved everything but rules, which explained the three monster marijuana plants growing behind his store. Sensing my concern, he quickly responded, "Medical, medicinal needs," with a mischievous smile, assuaging my skepticism. He lived as was expected of one who had grown up in the Appalachian hills and just barely graduated from a one-room K–12 schoolhouse at the tender age of seventeen. Shortly after getting his diploma, he enlisted. He was now an aging hillbilly with the mouth and war medals of a backwoods soldier. With the exception of his sporting goods shack on the river, he didn't really own much. He'd never voted in his life, and from what I had come to believe, he'd never paid a dime of income tax.

One gruesome but romantic tale was about a young white Confederate major from a wealthy Virginia family being smitten by a black runaway slave, resulting in a zealous love affair between the two. It has been said that the officer was stripped of his uniform, and the two of them were bound and set adrift on a rickety raft on Gauley Bridge at the confluence of the Kanawha River and the New River. Confederate troops, watching them from a high cliff overlooking the deep gorge of the New River, reported them drifting down and breaking apart against the large boulders and drowning in the powerful currents and violent white rapids.

Years later, after the war, the town of Fayetteville became known for its healthy population of hardworking mulattos. It was believed that they were all descendants of the despised mixed-race couple set adrift on the doomed raft two decades earlier.

"Unabashed. It's a myth. Probable untrue, then maybe not." He would say any story worth telling was worth exaggerating. While Ray currently lived in the small coal mining town of Mabscott, he grew up in Kanawha Falls and, with fifty some years under his belt and a West Virginia lilt, knew the area like the back of his hand. He was definitely a good ol' mountain boy, living a rhapsodized singularly solitary existence with bittersweet memories forming a collage of joy and despair. His bohemian mantra was simple and uncomplicated, coupled with a healthy skepticism of the local, state, and federal government. He boasted the look of a sclerotic Appalachian mountaineer caricature straight off the cover of the *Saturday Evening Post*.

"One doesn't git to eat the bread unless you plant the grain," he would say. Since retiring as fire chief of Mabscott, his small outpost store in Gauley Bridge was his life. It was filled with bittersweet memories, forming a remembered collage of joy and despair. It earned him little, and he needed even less. He spent much of his time sitting on the weathered wooden deck of his shop carving and whittling a piece of ash and would most likely do so right into his dotage.

As this was a small burg of a town, most of his proclivities on the river were common knowledge. No rafter had ever drowned on his rides in the punishing rapids of the New River at Fayetteville. Having little trust in banks or the bureaucracy of doing business with them, Ray kept his money stashed in mason jars, still holding onto a Depression mentality. With plenty of free time on his hands, he periodically took care of Thor during my away-from-home assignments, which was a real plus in my line of work. But Ray, who loved to howl with laughter, also had a reticent side to him, and he could be cantankerous at times; I chose to overlook and not to breach his standoffish periods.

Ray was a stand-up guy and understandably profoundly lonely but refused to discuss his experiences in Vietnam or before. Having served two tours in the Mekong Delta region as part of the Special Forces, he had been wounded twice and received several medals before opting out of the mayhem. He had seen a bunch of nasty-ass shit that no human should ever have to witness. Few combat veterans were willing to share their combat vicissitudes. I knew, better than most, that men who actually killed or endured a firefight were wary of divulging details of their own culpability for violent actions that might offend the untarnished sensitivities of civilians and families. Unfortunately, in Ray's defense, he was seriously beaten up and robbed by a gang of university students upon his return from the war shortly after he deplaned in Los Angeles. To this day, that incident haunted him and gave him the feeling that America had abandoned him.

Alongside me in the fading light of the afternoon lay Thor, my incredibly loyal three-year-old German shepherd. I had personally trained him during his recent year of covert SEAL training at the Coronado Naval Amphibious Base. Thor cozied up next to my foot but had his ears peaked for the slightest command from his master.

While I looked out over the ridge from my deck, which cantilevered out over the mountainside, a nuthatch landed on the rail in front of me. Startled by my presence, it didn't stay long and took flight. My hand would reach down and randomly scratch the top of Thor's head and behind his ears as I snoozed in the afternoon sun. Then, one afternoon, I had been sleeping on the porch in rapt silence when Thor growled and leaped across the wooden deck at the lighting speed of a cheetah and severed the head of a timber rattlesnake with his razor-sharp teeth. The snake had made it within three feet of my bare foot.

The house I designed was for a family that I hoped to have one day. Though I had no immediate plans, it was my home. I had no women in mind and no one waiting in the wings. I didn't even have one to consider, having not allowed anyone to get close. I wanted nothing more than to come home to a loving wife and children after being away on a mission. But for now, the house and property with its electronic iron gate and state-of-the-art security system stood as a symbol of my hopes for the future.

I had reenlisted several times and now have twenty years in the navy. Upon completing pilot training in helicopters, I was selected to become a Secret Service operative and was awaiting orders from the Pentagon in Washington, DC. Wistfully, having lost the love of my life several years earlier and with no chance of resurrection of the relationship, I sold my home in Connecticut and moved to Fayetteville, West Virginia, for a quieter life and a new start, leaving behind a stash of fond memories. While I sometimes fantasized about having a committed relationship with a woman, that had ended with Lorinda. Marriage was working for my friends, but it seemed outside my future. I enjoyed being free to do what I was trained to do and kept my life simple to do just that. My life assumed a predictable cadence: adventure and no personal complications.

Look at me now, thirty-eight years old, with no family left other than Ray and precious few friends other than Ray and Thor to go home to. Living the dream, I thought wryly. I might have made a mistake somewhere in the adventure but would work my way through it. I spent my adolescent years growing up in Connecticut at my grandparents' house, which was a fine place to be a kid, with my younger brother, but only rarely did we visit with our parents, who were local legends in the medical community at their home on Martha's Vineyard. Being part of Doctors without Borders, they were rarely there themselves. Our upbringing was more nontraditional than most. While I believe that our parents truly loved us, they tried in their own way to equate money with love and affection. Not even my closest friends knew that we actually lived full-time with my grandparents.

The air was clear, the sky was forever, and high school was closed all summer, though summers were not always carefree for a teenager growing up in the 1960s. Apple orchards and chicken farms dominated the town culture, and if one wanted to have enough money to engage in social circles, he was forced to find summer employment. All of the gifts of life, such as sports, cars, dates, and sex with girlfriends like Kathy Spencer and Patty Parson, required money, which I was never really lacking. For the most part, sex with girlfriends was practiced in the back seat of cars borrowed from sleeping neighbors. While my parents were generous enough, they could be frugal with our allowances.

That's when they weren't traveling to some third-world country. So for most of our teenage years, we were under the strict care of our grandparents. For the most part, I had an adventurous zing and a rebellious itch growing up. One might say that I was not a malleable child. I was fired from several early summer jobs for horsing around during work. I was fired from Raskins Chicken Farm for using chickens for football kicking practice when I was supposed to collect eggs. Another time, I was fired from a Cheshire Apple Orchard for practicing pitching using apples that were supposed to be carefully placed in a basket. Another time, I was working as a dishwasher at the Highway Restaurant in the center of town. While carrying a stack of a dozen freshly washed dishes to the shelf, I spotted my girlfriend in a booth with another guy. I stopped in my tracks and dropped the stack of dishes to the floor, breaking every one of the plates. The management didn't understand or tolerate my deviant behavior. While my brother was a shadow behind me, he knew to keep a distance.

In the summer of my sixteenth year, a friend named Thomas Cramer borrowed his father's new Lincoln Continental one night from the Meriden Air Port while he was away on a business trip in Chicago. The state of Connecticut at the time was building a new Route 84 through town with a straight, freshly paved two-mile-long run through the corn fields into Cheshire, an adjacent village to Southington. We, along with a dozen other teens, one late night used it for drag racing. We won one of the races at over 110 miles per hour.

Yup, growing up had its treasured moments and challenges. Not always, of course, but for the most part, life was good. I had become the

Blue Knights High School's favorite varsity quarterback and won three all-expense scholarships. Fortunately, for my sake, my generous parents and grandparents never gave up on me, and I became a mensch. According to my grandmother, I eventually grew up, maturing and becoming an overachiever, immersing myself in my studies and graduating from Post College in Connecticut second in my class.

I asked my grandmother, "Why have I changed?" Her response was to keep going and follow the path. But then my grandfather, having retired from the army, stepped in, laying out his two cents of advice: "Don't forget your country. Carry a big stick, and know when to use it."

At first, my grandmother scoffed. Four years in the military would help me become a man, I told myself, and become the man I wanted to be. My brother followed me a year later into the military, enlisting in the army. My last correspondence from him was from Berlin, Germany.

The year was early 1966, and two of my best friends from town that had enlisted earlier that year had been killed in combat in Vietnam. Putting my own personal celebration on hold, I took that as a calling of revenge and enlisted in the navy, requesting combat duty in Vietnam. I reminded myself that my country needed me and that I'd regret not participating in America's newest war. Twelve weeks later, I was assigned and attached to the Naval Assault Unit, Division Eleven, on Coronado Island. Having trained for five months with SEAL Team One on the sands of Coronado and three months later at the marine combat base at Camp Pendleton, I was ready.

I was wrong. The screaming drill instructors, the constant physical routines of exercise that pushed my out-of-shape body to its limits, the separation from my friends and grandparents scared and shook the hell out of me. That, too, would change my rapidly changing character forever.

On January 1967, I was assigned to a PBR with a crew of four to an unnamed tributary in the Mekong Delta region of Vietnam.

* * *

The Appalachian Mountains and the rich history of the Mountain State inspired me with their backwoods tranquilly. Many of the homes, storefronts, and saloons in town dated back to the turn of the twentieth century, when the town was a bustling coal mining hub on the New River. Having done my due diligence, I purchased a four-thousand square foot, four-bedroom Blue Ridge log cabin on a hundred-acre ranch situated on an ancient bluff overlooking the verdant New River Gorge in Fayetteville. The plot was surrounded by tall fir trees and seventy-foot ancient hardwoods fusing harmoniously with the scent of blooming wild mountain rhododendrons, the perfume of the mountain. I watched the restless surge of the treetops, swaying indiscriminately in the breeze. While the cabin was larger than I needed, the location was a godsend as I prized the quiet splendor and serene solitude above the river. Having hired an architect to update and redesign the structure totally, I went ahead and moved in. While I needed action, conversation, and challenges leading to the capture of bad guys, this was a special place to take a step back and escape into peaceful and serene obscurity. This was my new home and sanctuary away from the evils of the world.

The cabin was twenty minutes from town via the old Fayetteville service road, which was a paved serpentine road of mountain curves and switchbacks with steep inclines tracing the outer edges of cliffs. The road definitely didn't encourage the average tourist or even local traffic but added to the exclusiveness of my new home. The thickness of the trees and flora of this location to the mountains, a thousand miles in the making, was as incredible offering of privacy. Yet the charming village of Fayetteville, with its famous New River Bridge, was within reasonable proximity for convenience should I decide to socialize. It was a small village where everyone knew each other, drug issues were almost nonexistent, and the streets were mainly safe at night.

Standing on the porch, I felt the beauty of the surrounding forest and the sanctuary of my new home descend upon me like a soothing balm. A song sparrow let loose with its three piping cheerful notes, followed by a rapid slur of a smaller trill. Inside, the solid wide-planked floors were polished cedar, the walls and lofts were all cut from West Virginia poplar hardwood, and huge bay windows on all sides offered spectacular views of the landscape. The million-dollar view from my bed, overlooking the north rim of the gorge, was awesome. While the cabin was only five years old, I had the entire structure refinished inside and out and equipped with the latest high-tech appliances and equipment, including security alarms and surveillance cameras.

My parents had both been medical professionals associated with Doctors without Borders and had been kidnapped and murdered by rebels four years ago in Somalia. Nevertheless, they had done well in the tech stock and medical markets, leaving behind a substantial trust fund of over four-million dollars upon the disbursal of their Cape Cod estate. My only living relative was Ray Palmer.

The following day, I awoke to the sound of birds chirping out back. It was still early, with the sun rising above the mountains and the sighs of a summer breeze. Finally, after trying to wrestle my way through his jumbled emotions, I surrendered, set the security alarms, and closed my eyes for a period of quiet reflection. My sleep had been fitfully deep and dreamless, which was not always the case. When the alarm went off, waking me from a deep sleep at the crack of dawn, I threw off the covers and levered himself off the bed, pandiculating to work the cramps out of my muscles. Waking up fast and in complete control of my senses, with my neurons firing on all cylinders, was an ingrained habit and necessary ability I'd acquired as part of my training over the years. The sharp ringing of the church bells echoing from the steeple of the New River Baptist Church in the center of Fayetteville beckoned from the top of the mountain down into the holler below as sunlight flooded the room.

I thought of going for a jog in the cool of the morning but decided against it. I would consider it later. Instead, I would have a hasty breakfast and work out downstairs in the gym. Working my way through the regular one-hour routine with four rotations of thirty to forty push-ups on rotating stands, and two-hundred ab crunches, lower back exercised, lateral rows, sit-ups, more push-ups, pull-ups, leg extensions, leg curls, chest and shoulder presses, and various other exercises for the biceps and triceps.

I was pumped up and euphoric, and perspiration was pouring out of my body, collecting in strands of dark, curly chest hair and trickling down to my midriff and navel. Raising my arm to clear the sweat dripping from my brow, I went into the bathroom, turned on the new deluxe rainforest shower, and stepped in under the steaming hot water, letting the pelting water course over my face and run in rivulets down my back. The shower had become a cloud of moisture. I stepped out of the shower, toweling myself vigorously, dried my face, reached out, swiped the fog off the mirror with my towel, and began the morning maintenance routine with a cup of steaming black joe liberally doused with a packet of Sweet'N Low.

The morning broke bright and sunny with cotton candy clouds, and it looked like the day was promising to be a pretty nice one. Mechanically, I dressed, stepping into jeans and a T-shirt. I opened the windows wide to let in the purifying halcyon mountain air as the whiff of freshly roasted coffee beans brewing in the kitchen wafted through the house. A couple of deer appeared at the edge of the woods, searching for fescue and flora.

I pulled a carton of eggs from the refrigerator and poured a glass of V-8 and another cup of coffee. I started the grill on the rear deck and, in several cast-iron skillets, cooked a man-size breakfast of thick Canadian bacon, three eggs sunny-side up, sizzling home fries, and whole-wheat toast, waiting to spit out of the toaster. Looking at Thor in the corner of the kitchen, I slathered the muffins with apple and peanut butter and took a bite. Thor was close by, wolfing down his morning breakfast and slurping water to wash it down. After resetting the rumpled pillows and tangled sheets, all traces of breakfast cleared away, I washed and seasoned the iron skillets and hung them on the wall. I now had a yen to go for a seven-mile jog with Thor on the old Fayette Station Road loop through the forest down into the chasm before the sun made its full assault.

A little more than a month past the summer solstice, the warm June breeze was redolent of rich floral mountain scents and a trifecta of pungent herbs growing along the well-worn pathway to the edge of the ridge. Fragrant hues of mountain laurel pervaded the trail down the mountain. The large backyard lawn and the gardens along the path had been laid out long ago by a previous owner affording an unobstructed view of the mountain gorge in either direction. had now assumed the position of gardener as it was a passion of his and a welcomed hand for me. A couple of innocuous squirrels were scurrying about hither and yon. Some of the hollies, greenbriers, and rose bushes were over a century old. I got out the hose and watered the holly bushes to scrub off some of the rude "prayer offerings" dropped by the birds. I received a scolding from a territorial blue jay from above. After that, Thor shadowed his every move.

Having closed the lid of the Weber over three hearty marinated rib eyes, I leaned out over the deck railing with a beer in one hand and a kitchen spatula in the other. I couldn't help but note the sizzling behind me under the cover and the grease-laden smoke exiting the side ports. The aroma of the garlic, onion, oregano, and other seasonings, which boasted a huge cookout melt-in-your-mouth aroma, now wafted through the air and made my mouth water. Throwing open the lid and flipping the thick rib eyes over with the kitchen spatula brought an angry flame through the grates, singeing my knuckles. I needed to purchase a grilling spatula soon.

I, as a rule, did not cook for one. There was always my four-legged friend, Thor, who was now drooling at my feet. "You do know that you have a drinking problem, don't you?" I asked. It would be two rib eyes for me and one for Thor. As he looked at me from the corner of the deck, his tail was wagging, he gave a single bark. "Enjoy, my friend," I said.

I had always loved to cook; when I was young, my grandparents taught him well. This thought now brought me back to my childhood and happy days.

After lunch, having plated my dinner, I returned to the deck, Thor following.

With the sun reaching high in the sky and a wilting, unseasonably oppressive temperature now in the midnineties, I decided to take a morning jog down into the steep gorge along an old coal mining path through the blanket of thick forest down to the verge of the river, a thousand feet below.

Several times a week, I jogged at a rapid clip, making my way down to the river and back up to the ledge with just enough fortitude to complete the route, cutting himself no slack. The dog tagged along at my side, loping and keeping pace, sometimes flitting in and out of the underbrush. Thor would chase a curious squirrel or maybe a rabbit but never more than several feet from my presence. The hush was profound, except for a whispering breeze in the treetops. There wasn't another human around for miles, and I treasured taking a reflective sojourn in the woods.

Finally reaching the river's sandy shore and not breathing hard, I shed my sneakers, jeans, and T-shirt. Now totally nude in an isolated cove, I dove into the refreshing New River with Thor loyally following his master into the cool water escaping the cloying heat. A fish leaped and splashed into the water behind me. The only people who frequented this swimming hole were young locals who seemed to enjoy swimming naked and basking on boulders under the ancient trestle bridge a hundred yards upriver. It was deserted today, a welcome reprieve. A painted turtle appeared on a log and stared at us as it basked languorously, absorbing the rays of the warm summer sun. The swimming hole, just five hundred yards north of the lower gorge with its class 4 white-water rapids, would have made Huckleberry Finn feel right at home. Two bald eagles nested above. Swimming head-to-head with his master as he had been trained, Thor lapped at my face knowingly in a stand-down mode.

Casually whistling, with Thor beside me, I followed the trail back up the mountain, breathing measured and calm. The sun was beginning to drop behind the mountains, bathing the horizon with its vermilion afterglow. The afternoon had culminated in another glorious West Virginia sunset. The atmosphere of the landscape was warm, still, and silent. A mournful darkness would soon swallow up the mountains. On the summit of a mountain, there was no ambient light to interfere with the sky's darkness and the infinite, spectacular display of stars. Insects chirped their indifference as a light breeze blew through the trees.

Later that night, after I lit the logs in the fireplace, the dog sprawled out and snoozed in front of the flickering glow of the stone-walled fireplace. We were both exhausted from the seven-mile jog and then the one-mile trek down to the river and back up the mountain in a deepening twilight. While it could climb to the nineties in the afternoon, it got chilly up in the mountains at night.

The stars began to come out of the darkening sky, showering the mountaintop. Somewhere in the forest, bullfrogs bellowed out their baritone mating calls from their muddy lairs along the river, and a lone coyote was baying mournfully at the quarter moon in the yawning darkness. Whippoorwills were calling each other in the woods with their melancholy whistling songs of the evening. The soothing silence that followed was broken only by the crackling and snapping of the burning logs. I flopped down and was ensconced in the deep buttery texture of the leather couch with my feet resting on the leather hassock as I gazed at the cozy flickering fire. Every once in a while, I got up to stoke the flames while munching on a cornichon, half listening to the play-by-play of the Yankees and Red Sox game on TV; they were tied at the bottom of the ninth. There was a mouthwatering aroma of buttery popcorn lingering in the air coming the microwave in the kitchen.

Suddenly my reverie was broken by the ringing of the secured landline phone on the end table beside me. Being a Secret Service agent, I was used to getting calls on the secured line at odd hours. I grabbed the receiver and curtly answered on the second ring.

"Tucker," I said politely. My shoulders went tight instantly, and my expression turned seriously somber as only one person called that number. I had been on a two-month hiatus from another successful covert operation in Montenegro. Nevertheless, my curiosity was piqued, and I sat straight up, swinging my feet to the floor.

"Yes, sir, I'll be there at nine a.m. sharp tomorrow."

The call went silent, followed by a dial tone, and I returned the receiver to its cradle. Admiral Connelly wasn't known for superfluous chitchat; without preamble, he summoned me to meet forthwith with him tomorrow at Langley. I stared down at Thor, who hadn't budged but was all ears. As a Special Forces CIA operative, I was on call to duty 24-7 and could be sent anywhere in the world with little notice.

Since it was almost 10:00 pm, I pushed off my size-eleven boots using alternate feet to free my foothold. Unsnapping my jeans and dropping the fly, I stepped out of the jeans, peeled off my shirt, and balled it up, tossing it into the hamper, followed by my socks. Reaching the bed with nothing on other than my skivvies, I flung back the covers and attempted to called it a night. Unfortunately, tonight sleep would be elusive.

A CIA helicopter would be at Raleigh Memorial Airport at 8:00 a.m. to shuttle me to headquarters. It was a Sunday morning, and having Admiral Connelly call me and summon me meant that there was an urgent mission to be assigned and anything on my schedule was now moot. I had been a special counterintelligence operative for over eight years, and so I was expected to be available for sensitive missions, and everything else in my personal life fell to second place. I had called Ray and advised him of my appointment; he would be at the house by no later than 5:00 a.m.

With the windows open, I shut off the TV and checked the motion detectors and camera monitors before calling it a night again. The white sound of the river in the gorge below soon had me profoundly asleep.

CHAPTER 10

I awoke the following morning, a Monday, to a predawn gray. My gaze flitted to the clock on the wall. It was 0500 hours, and I could smell fresh coffee percolating and waft through the morning air. I preferred to use a military time clock rather than a standard one. Breakfast was a toasted English muffin with peanut butter, scrambled eggs with home fries, and Canadian bacon. Ray had arrived early before the maid came and couldn't wait to put his culinary talents to use and cook in the new kitchen.

Having completed my morning ministrations, leaving the crumpled pillows and wrinkled sheets covering the bed behind, I dressed in full military uniform and made my way down to the kitchen. Sitting at the kitchen table in deep thought, neither of us said much as we finished the last dregs of Green Mountain brews. Having known each other for years, Ray and I didn't need to converse in useless banter. I thanked Ray with a firm handshake and hugged Thor, who was having morning breakfast, then I pulled my Jeep Cherokee out of the garage and drove to Raleigh Memorial Airport in Beckley. I boarded the Bell helicopter that the admiral's office had prearranged for my trip.

The weather was startlingly clear. I strapped in, and thirty minutes later, the landing port at CIA headquarters in Langley, Virginia, was in sight. In the distance an American flag flapped in the breeze atop a forty-foot stainless flagpole. "Cleared for a visual approach to Langley Air Force Base," the controller said. The pilot descended and turned right downwind for the south #14 heliport, having been cleared to land.

After we touched down smoothly at the cloistered heliport at 8:30 a.m., I unstrapped and exited the chopper. I walked to the NHB gate of the moated fortress, where I entered my seven-digit code and proffered my security badge to the marine security guard at the entrance of the secured landing area. It had only been a six weeks since I had been summoned by the admiral to use my commando training to take down three armed Houthi gunmen from Yemen threatening to blow up a commercial airline on the tarmac at the O'Hare Airport in Chicago. With the assistance of other two agents, all three were terminated without civilian casualties.

Old Glory was blowing full from the flagpole in a stiff wind under a blue sky and rising morning sun.

"State your purpose here today, sir."

"I have an appointment with Admiral Connelly."

The guard scanned a conventional-looking telephone panel before passing me through.

Upon walking into the building vestibule, I again entered my seven-digit code into the keypad, proffered my security badge, and went through a security metal detector monitored by video 24-7. The alarm went off instantly. Standing behind the bulletproof glass, the young marine guard, with a dour expression on his face, touched the grip of his pistol and excitedly demanded that I surrender my weapon and cell phone.

"I can't do that, Sergeant."

"Sir, you're not allowed to be armed or carry a cell phone in this building."

"You've seen my credentials, Sergeant! I'm authorized to be armed 24-7, anywhere in the world."

"Sorry, sir, I have my orders and have to insist." He drew his weapon.

"Sergeant, the only way you're going to get my gun and phone is to take it from my fucking dead body! Now get on that goddamned phone, call Admiral Connelly's office, and get clearance."

Having reholstered his weapon, he made the call. After hanging up the telephone receiver three minutes later, the unsmiling sergeant looked at me. Then, having lost his enthusiasm, visually shaken, he stiffened his back with indignation; he pushed the button and opened the locked steel door, waving me through, apologizing with angry resignation as he led me down a long corridor filled with exhibits outlining the history of the CIA before stopping at a brass elevator.

"Marine, the next time you draw your weapon, shoot it without hesitation. You don't realize how close you came to being shot and killed. Do you understand me?"

"Yes, sir." He saluted.

Stepping into the mahogany-paneled elevator, I was silently whisked to the prominent seventh floor with its high coffered ceiling. A faint ping announced the arrival of the elevator. When the stainless-steel double doors whooshed open, I was met by another security agent, and I again offered my security badge and stood before a facial recognition screen before being allowed to enter the esteemed Special Operations Executive Office area. The hallowed halls of this floor were bristling and humming with official military activity.

I checked in with Admiral Connelly's secretary as she was talking into the telephone cradled between her shoulder and chin, and she quickly checked out my security credentials before deferentially announcing my arrival to the admiral. She protected his office chamber as if it were a lair.

The admiral's door opened, and he stood in the doorway. His name and title were etched on a brass plaque to the right of the entrance. Then, without preamble, he ushered me into his hallowed, commodious chamber before closing the heavy oak door behind him.

The admiral extended his well-manicured hand, warmly proffered with respectful cordiality.

"How are you, Commander Tucker?"

"I'm fine, thank you, sir."

"Do you know why you're here?"

"No, sir."

"Please sit down, Commander," he said succinctly.

Sitting down behind his desk, he told me brusquely to take a seat as he called his receptionist on the two-way intercom.

"Jill, I don't want to be disturbed until further notice."

"Yes, Admiral."

"Good morning, Bryce," he said with candor, flashing a benign smile and making a tent of his fingers on the desk. "Please relax."

A pulsating breeze from the ceiling fan's twirling paddles cooled the air.

The admiral was my mentor, boss, friend, and SEAL team instructor twelve years ago. To me, it was an immense honor to serve under the admiral, whom I found to be have a delicious, unassailable wit that was paradoxically both merciless and forgiving.

"In as much as the FBI director had to fly to New York to deal with a serious personal tragedy and won't be joining us, we might as well get to it and cut to the chase," the admiral said succinctly.

Admiral Connelly was a United States Naval Academy graduate who admired and epitomized the military career of the esteemed Admiral Chester W. Nimitz, who in a storied career served as the commander in chief of the Pacific Fleet during World War II in the Pacific Theater. With the exception of the electronic wall map of the world, where several areas were flashing in red, denoting active spots, the rest of the polished mahogany walls were pedantically adorned with pictures of Admiral Nimitz. These included several pictures with Admiral Connelly shaking hands and receiving the Navy Cross from the legendary admiral aboard the USS *Enterprise* in 1942.

Wearing an impeccable black Armani suit with a gray tie, the admiral was an imposing, heavyset man, just shy of 65, 6-foot-4, 225 pounds, and as steady as a Swiss watch, with razor-sharp instincts. He was the most brilliant man I'd ever met and carried an air of gravitas that commanded respect and proclaimed absolute authority and obedience. His voice had a commanding lilt and throatiness gained only with seasoning. He had a formidable, erudite intellect and a mind that could quickly absorb and process reams of unrelenting arcane minutiae. He separated macros from micros and devised a sage strategy based on unfathomable logic, putting forth a mode of action and a sound solution to a problem in minutes. While balding with a ruddy complexion, he had eyes that spoke of a venerable lifetime of geopolitical intrigue and a profile that belonged on a Roman coin. While radiating esteemed dignity, he had an air of absolute, unerring self-confidence, and one could mistake his fastidious formality and sageness for arrogance unless one knew him well.

I sat ramrod straight in the chair directly in front of the admiral's massive mahogany naval desk. I remained stolid, deferential, and shrewdly silent. My right leg was straight, while my left was crossed over the other at the shin, casual and relaxed. I had a nagging, unfazed presage that whatever was coming would not be routine and as always, my life would be on the line. The admiral's fossilized patrician expression exuded an innate brutish strength that belied the uneasiness of his unblinking incisive eyes as he jotted notes on the leather-bound desk blotter in front of him.

"Bryce," he said emphatically without preamble, "we have a nascent problem in Charleston, West Virginia, with salient tentacles extending out globally."

"What is it?"

"According to several trenchant CIA preliminary reports, a terrorist organization headed by a charismatic and ruthless Colombian known as Hugo Maduro is supplying military-grade weapons to various terrorist and rebel groups in South America and other third-world countries in the Middle East. The scope and sophistication of his operation is daunting, and he is becoming a growing power here in the United States and offshore locations. The unconfirmed report also states that the Maduro organization is well connected to the Mexican Sinaloa Cartel and the Cartel of the Suns in Venezuela, trading drugs and prospering from international money laundering, graft, and sex trafficking of young kidnapped children across the borders. It's also being suggested that the Maduro organization may be eyeing a strong-arm, unprecedented takeover of Mara Salvatrucha, the brutal Hispanic gang otherwise known as MS-13, and expanding their operations south of the border. From all reports, the man is well connected, methodical, and shockingly lacking in empathy.

"Bryce, twenty-four hours ago, the director of national intelligence, along with the president, signed a directive stating that the Maduro organization was a clear and present terrorist threat and a danger to the security of the United States. With that, he is suspending the Posse Comitatus Act. He has ordered that the CIA and NSA immediately initiate covert operations in conjunction with the Navy SEALs and take down and exterminate the organization domestically and internationally."

I was listening in rapt absorption to the vehemence of the admiral, interrupting only for occasional clarification if needed.

"It's still a mystery where Maduro is purchasing his weapons. It is generally thought to be from Iran, Libya, and countries in South America, places that have excessive weapons inventories but need more cash reserves. His narrative is to create unrest in the Middle East and profit from the proliferation of arms sales to all sides. We need to infiltrate the nest and follow the wasp.

"A revelation of disturbing but salient information received just last week from an anonymous source adds another wrinkle to the operation. The nexus of the actual violence now extends past arms trafficking, money laundering, and incessant kidnappings. The organization has begun to compromise law enforcement in West Virginia and Kentucky with intimidation and payoffs to cover the commission of their criminal activities. There is evidence that there has been rampant bribery and corruption within the local political and law enforcement agencies of both states.

"It's also disturbing that a couple of senators who happen to be sitting on the Congressional Intelligence Committee may be culpably linked to the Maduro crime organization and protecting the operation with classified insider information. The agency has had both senators on our radar for over a year, but to date we haven't had enough to arrest them. Their travel patterns have been suspicious to say the least, with several visits to Cuba and Venezuela. The region's counties have plunged into economic malaise, tax revenues have plummeted to record lows, and law enforcement has suffered as a consequence. We don't have any hard evidence, and I sincerely hope this proves wrong, but the information being gathered gives sound indications that it is a strong possibility.

"With that in mind, and being careful not to inject conjecture without a solid basis, this mission must be handled anomalously."

I was getting the picture. No wonder the admiral was briefing me alone and discreetly rather than with the Congressional Intelligence Committee. With the possibility of one or more senators being involved, the admiral's rationale was projected clearly. While the information was credible, it was still circumstantial. The team of the informed on this assignment would be goddamned tight, and the admiral would need solid tangential evidence of any conclusion moving forward.

Admiral Connelly had Jill bring us a couple cups of coffee. "It's because of our expertise in deep undercover surveillance that we've been assigned this mission."

The admiral as I knew him was a man of few words but packed lots of action. He was issuing a presidential warrant to bring this organization down.

"Two months ago, the FBI infiltrated the Maduro organization with two deep undercover operatives providing information to the department almost daily through a secure line. Then, four days ago, the sporadic communications went dead. Dominic Formosa and Ken Carrabba are both highly experienced covert operatives. There's a gut feeling by their handler that they may have been compromised."

I arched my eyebrows. While I didn't know them well, I had briefly worked with them several years ago in Nicaragua. Reflecting, I remembered that they were both highly intelligent and physical. They also spoke Russian and Spanish fluently, making them a perfect fit for the assignment.

"Bryce, we have a serious situation on our hands. Three days ago, orders from the House Intelligence Committee came down to abort the operation immediately."

From the admiral's indignant frown and the raising of his gravelly voice, I could tell he emphatically opposed the decision. *Vehemently.*

"Bryce, we need you to find the operatives, dead or alive, and advise."

"Yes, sir. What else?" I said obligingly.

"Tucker, this is where there may be a problem. I do not want Hugo dead." Spacing his words, he enunciated, "I want Hugo Manduro alive." Sounding deceptively calm, he leaned forward. "I need you to bring him alive, along with his support lieutenants and political cohorts. Without the money, his operation will no longer be able to foment the terrorism that he's instigating and no longer be able to pervasively pit one country against another to create demand for his operation and threaten the civilized world. We want him alive so that we can track down his bank accounts and identify his support sources. We want to put together a dossier on every politician and/or corporation involved with his operation. We will also want to locate and seize the Colombian's money before the bastard or one of his lieutenants can start another coup elsewhere.

"After we have the information and control of the assets, accidents can happen…well, off the books. Your job is to bring him in alive along with the others. Others within the agency will break them."

This last order was a verbal codicil; the admiral always tacked on to mission assignments.

I resisted the urge to squirm as I didn't relish the idea of taking down US senators. But *duty* and *honor* weren't just words used by the special operatives of the CIA; they were the bedrock of our moral character and the uncompromising code of integrity to abide by. So, like it or not, I would not think twice about bringing down or taking out a couple of corrupt individuals who dared to breach the trust and taint the exalted reputation of the US Congress, and compromise the mission.

While I didn't say anything, I was somewhat pessimistic about the prospects of bringing Maduro in alive.

The admiral shrugged and leaned forward. "So let's get down to the details. Only a small select troika is involved in this mission, Bryce, and you will be operating off the grid without congressional or administrative oversight. Powerful interests are arrayed all over this operation, and I assure you they need to be aligned with our interests. While we don't yet have verifiable proof of senatorial corruption, the two senators seem to have been bought and paid for by the Maduro operation. You will have to gather solid conclusive evidence to prove their involvement in the insidious alliance. With that said, you will have to move with delicate secrecy. Your team will be free of toxic politics and other regulatory constraints, but resources will be limited. The flip side is we don't have any bureaucracy to hinder the operation and your purview of operational authority will be without restrictive constraints. I want you to precipitate the demise of his organization and take it down by whatever means necessary, period.

I responded by reciting the French metaphor "You can't make an omelet without breaking some eggs."

"You and I understand the objective. We sent two highly trained, curated operatives to Charleston three months ago to begin our undercover investigation. Special Agent Glenn Nunez has since joined the Maduro organization through an employment agency under the guise of an unemployed ex-linebacker. He's employed as an armed 'gate guard' at the entrance to the estate. He's a young, dedicated, pragmatic operative of Venezuelan descent who has proven his mettle and wherewithal several times in undercover operations. Agent Nunez is not only an excellent covert operative, he is also muscular, with a lot of honed sinews. He is a dead shot under fire with a forty-five caliber pistol at one hundred yards.

"He's been communicating with Agent Bomen a couple of times a week."

I met Agent Nunez about a year ago while working undercover in Spain. The four-man team there respected him for his sheer doggedness in handling a difficult situation. His command of the Spanish language and lilt was excellent.

"Special Agent Austin Bomen is an astute intelligence collection analyst and paramilitary operative specializing in gathering and monitoring electronic communications," the admiral continued. "And that's a gross understatement. He's also a philologist with an affinity for languages and is fluent in English, Russian, Mexican, Spanish, and Arabic. As a mission analyst, his service has been exemplary, and his probity and assiduous intelligence are almost an anomaly among NSA nerds. Agent Bomen has proved his mettle time and time again and has a sterling record of achievements. He has been monitoring the Maduro estates in West Virginia and Norman's Cay, Bahamas. He will work directly with you as support and update you and me on the latest information being gathered. Agent Bomen will initiate contact with you tomorrow at 1400 hours at the Residence Inn in Charleston.

"Literally speaking, Bryce, no one in special ops has more extensive training or better odds of handling the operation and surviving than you. Lieutenant Commander, you have distinguished yourself in the ranks as a formidable and unmalleable operative and strategist, and autonomously adept killer. You have honed your imaginative ability continuously to surprise the enemy and reverse their actions from offensive to defensive before they know what is happening. As a pragmatic special Secret Service operative and former SEAL commander with a stellar military reputation, you have been extensively trained and groomed on the 'Farm.' You've excelled in clandestine communications, airborne tactics, jungle combat and survival, fourth-degree martial arts including Krav Maga and jujitsu, weapons, and explosives. You have a master's degree in risk management, and you fluently speak five languages besides English: Russian, Chinese, Spanish, French, and German. Your grit, innate toughness, and dogged determination have made you a legend in your own time.

"Bryce, because of the unmitigated gravity of the mission, I want you to lead this operation."

"I appreciate your confidence," I said sheepishly.

The admiral nodded and took a sip of his coffee, holding the cup by its handle.

His pupils narrowed to pinpoints, and his jaded expression exuded an inner pain as if what he was about to say soured his mouth. "Are your life insurance and beneficiaries up to date, your power of attorney current, your last will and testament executed and duly notarized?"

"Yes, sir!"

"Excellent." Penning his signature on the document before him, the admiral closed the file folder and slid it across the desk to me. "Bryce Tucker, you're to report only to me and on the secure line." The admiral's expression was opaque. "This team is being activated to address an unconventional threat without interference from the bureaucracy of either the intelligence or congressional establishments."

"Yes, sir."

"Any questions?"

A myriad of them floated in my head. But none I would venture to ask. My first priority would be to insulate the president and the admiral from scandal should something go wrong. The information I needed would be in the bulging Redweld file containing the dossiers the admiral just slid across the desk; each was stamped *CONFIDENTIAL—PROPERTY OF THE CIA*. I would read, digest, commit to memory, and then secure them in my safe. "No, sir."

In looking at the size of the accordion folder, I could tell his secretary had done a lot of Xeroxing.

The admiral let out a dry sigh. "There's one more thing that you need to know and will have to address. Bizarrely, there is a woman involved with the Maduro organization that you have an indirect connection to, dating back to the Vietnam War. The woman works for the Chase-Webster Bank in Charleston, where the Maduro's have over a half billion dollars on deposit. From what we've been able to ascertain, her whole function is to cater to the financial instructions of the Colombian. In short, whether she's aware of it or not, her job is to facilitate the laundering of illegal sums of money around the globe.

"Her name is Nuna Polinski, and her late husband, Chris Polinski, I understand, was an acquaintance of yours in Vietnam.

My rapt curiosity was piqued.

"Our information shows that you two went to college together and reconnected on a mission up the Dung Ha River back in early 1968. Unfortunately, Chris Polinski was killed in combat during that mission at Dung Ha. The record also shows that you had him and his crew written up in your final report to the base commanding officer upon your return for drug addiction, drunkenness, and dereliction of duty at Dung Ha. This information is still classified in his record and was never published. Therefore, we'd like you to insinuate yourself and enlist his widow's cooperation in taking the Maduro organization down. Be advised that some of our intel suggests that her life may also be in danger.

"Eight months ago, a bank employee of the Chase-Webster Bank in Charleston was found by a local fisherman floating face down in the Gauley River. The autopsy revealed that he had been heavily drugged with meth and most likely had overdosed. Our sources determined that he was a strict conservative Jew and had never touched drugs or alcohol in his life. It was also learned that he was potamophobic. Because of Chase-Webster public relations and local political pressure, the murder was classified as an unfortunate accident and received zero fanfare. Nuna was hired six weeks later to replace him.

"That's it, I'm in," I said, meeting the admiral's stare with serious aplomb.

The admiral let that sink in and disseminate for a moment and then dismissed him by saying, "That will be all, Commander. Thank you for your service, and good luck."

I extended my hand, and the admiral nodded and shook it.

"I'll report as soon as I have some information."

I stood up, saluted and pivoted, walking with stiff shoulders to the door, opened it, and left without a backward glance or another word being said. I was looking for a fight, but my prime objective was to rescue the girls.

Against this backdrop, visions of Nuna flickered through my mind as Chris had once shown me a picture of her he carried in his wallet.

He called her his feisty trophy wife. An icy shiver raced up my spine as I began to understand that I had a dilemma to overcome. While Chris had asked me to contact his wife in the event of his death, I was nettled by the request. I wistfully chose not to get involved in the possible crumbling foundation of their relationship, knowing the dark, philandering side of Chris's capricious infidelity. Addicted to adrenaline and fast women as night followed day, Chris had been both a friend and a walking disaster. That ambivalence nagged at me now, but I felt no remorse as my rational side was my strongest one and it said "Let her go." I would never reveal the nocturnal indiscretions of Chris to Nuna. Now I had no options and would have to address questions undaunted that had bedeviled me for nearly ten years.

CHAPTER 11

An hour later, I landed in Beckley in a glowing twilight. After alighting the chopper with my gear, I proceeded to the visitor parking area. Checking my rear mirror in the jeep, I lowered my window and took a slow, meandering drive home on mediocre back roads that were stultifying, driving with the windows down under a canopy of trees, puttering along at thirty-five miles an hour, enjoying the white noise, and digesting the particulars of the assignment before arriving home just before 9:00 p.m. The undulating rural mountain roads were, for the most part, empty. Outside the window, grassy fields of farmland and sprawling pastures scrolled by, and the sun hovered over the horizon, illuminating the clouds to the west in a spectacular fiery glow. My headlights cut through the growing darkness before washing over my front lawn as I drove into the driveway and entered the open automatic garage doors.

The air was still, and I stood a moment, listening to the imperturbable quiet. As I looked up into the dark sky, my eyes began tracing one constellation after another before finally spotting the Big Dipper. I activated the key code to open the gate and waited for it to swing open. The tight security was a reality of my life. Pulling into the garage and stepping out of the jeep with the garage door closing behind me, I could smell the lingering scent of fried Cajun-seasoned catfish that Ray had cooked earlier; it was so appetizing that my quaking stomach began to growl in anticipation.

Having laid my attaché case on the counter, I found Ray sacked out on the rear deck in a semistupor, catnapping and slowly rocking in the Adirondack slider with Thor at his feet, listening to the saccharine sounds of the crickets chirping in the woods under the soft purple of the evening mountain sky. Thor's tail went ballistic and wagged in joy with merriment at the my presence, and he sniffed every inch of my jeans. I patted my thigh, and Thor was immediately at my side.

Planting a foot down on the deck and stopping the swing, Ray awoke, putting a fist over his mouth and chocking off a yawn as he exited the slider.

"Care for a brew?" he asked.

"I do," I replied with a negligent wave of my hand.

Ray got up, retreated into the kitchen, and reappeared with two longneck Coronas, a basket of home-fried chicken breasts, and a bag of potato chips. Ray wasn't known for being nutritionally correct.

"Thanks," I said, parking my boots on the railing.

Ray sat back in the rocker, chewing on a toothpick, a habit he picked up several years ago when he decided to quit smoking.

Life was good. The sky was black, with a full moon as luminous as a pearl hanging high above a carpet of glittering stars celebrating a somnolent summer evening.

The conversation drifted from woods to my choice of weapons for the upcoming operation.

Ray never directly asked for details.

He and I casually reminisced about the good old times before discussing my agenda and strategy over the next couple of hours, then adjourning to the kitchen and calling it a night. "Take care of yourself," Ray exhorted as he retired to his room.

The temperature in the mountain air was dropping almost palpably, and a fog bank seemed to be moving in, overtaking the cobalt blue of the night sky. Since it was now too late to drive home, he decided to stay over and retired to the guest room for the night. The wind was picking up, and a storm was making its way up the East Coast, moving up through the mountains. From Ray's perspective, as long as the storm didn't interrupt the cable signal, it could be raining cats and dogs all night.

This assignment was unlike any that I had been assigned before. As a highly skilled special ops agent, I was usually thousands of miles away in a foreign country, working under deep cover in some godforsaken location with orders to eliminate a leader and destroy a targeted rebel movement. Simply put, I was to capture the target using any means at my disposal and make the operation disappear from the face of the earth.

With this assignment, I would be basically working in my backyard in West Virginia and taking down an international terrorist organization located in Charleston without killing its leader. Having recently moved to West Virginia from New England, I was little known. Perhaps if he escaped again, my next assignment would be to kill him, and there would be no remorse or mercy.

Later that night, I sat back at my desk, marshaling my thoughts, opened the thick file, and began reading and mulling over the data, memorizing each of the five dossiers along with my orders, which I would shed later. I analyzed and reanalyzed the information, trying to read between the lines for more profound insight. Nothing was leaping out at me as unwonted.

After reconnoitering the situations in Charleston and Norman's Cay, I judiciously laid out an operations plan. I would first work my way into the Maduro operation and observe, search for his weaknesses, strengths, and defenses, and lay out a plan to confront and destroy the organization without killing him.

I settled on the couch and closed my lids, ruminating and trying to force my mind blank, but I was too amped up, and sleep tonight would be evasive, leaving little room for dalliance. So I got up and paced the floor before returning to my desk with my third cup of decaffeinated coffee that night, turned on the computer, and began methodically reading and studying the contents of each of the dossiers.

Hugo Maduro: Elusive, secretive, and ferocious, Hugo Maduro is a psychopath and head of the notorious Maduro Crime Cartel. He was born in Guyana City as Luis Cabrera. Now age sixty, he is a swarthy bastardized Venezuelan-born Russian of mixed decent born to upper-middle class parents. Two hundred and forty pounds; six-foot-three, muscular, he has a coiled cobra tattooed on the left side of his neck. He is not exactly handsome: his face is sallow and severely pockmarked from the acne he'd suffered as a teenager. But he is extremely bright.

On his sixteenth birthday, he and his sister were accused by his step-mother of stealing her jewelry and turned in to the police. He spent the next several years in jail before being released. His sister was spared partly due to her beauty and newly acquired political connections. None of which was offered to his defense. His mother died from cancer, and his father was murdered while he was incarcerated. Coming out and now homeless, he took to the streets and began dealing drugs and engaging in small-time theft. It wasn't long before he acquired a gun, and by the age of twenty, he had become a hitman for a local drug dealer.

Somewhere along the way, he graduated to political terrorism, working with a local cartel, and became a cold-blooded son of a bitch, killing his sister for her political stance against the cartel. It was an extremely gory death as she was tortured from head to foot. He had changed his identity six times over the years, but since arriving in the United States and securing a US passport, he had kept his current identity for almost four years.

He rose from poverty as a slum lord in a ghetto north of Caracas to build an extensive business empire. He received an atypical honor-ary rank of general in the Venezuelan Army in 1973. Within one year, he had cobbled together a band of disgruntled military officers, gaining substantial political weight, and began plotting and financing a political coup to take control of the Venezuelan government. Somehow, he had gained entry into the Central Bank of Venezuela and began channeling laundered funds to Manuel Velez, the leader of FARC, to finance a coup attempt. On the night of November 4, 1974, they initiated a failed coup against the Venezuelan government of Carlos Pérez and were cashiered and sentenced to death by hanging. Manuel, along with ninety-two oth-ers, managed to escape into the mountains. Just hours before the attack, more than $1.75 billion in the bank vanished. Months of investigation by the Venezuelan authorities failed to locate the missing funds, but all the avenues pointed to the renegade Hugo Maduro.

Incarcerated and facing the gallows for the abortive coup and the missing assets, he escaped the Ramo Verde Prison, a maximum-security military prison facility in Venezuela, into the mountains of Colombia and went into exile. While he was in prison, Venezuelan prison guards tortured Hugo by slicing his face to get him to divulge the location of the money he stole.

Maria Maduro had been accused, convicted, and sentenced in absentia to life in prison for orchestrating her erstwhile husband's escape from prison. Two years later, he resurfaced in Havana. He returned and aligned himself with the FARC rebels, quickly becoming a persona grata, rising in rank and providing an array of weapons. Maduro quickly put all his energy into the business end, successfully buying arms from the collapse of the Soviet Union and selling to and/or bartering with dozens of African revolutionaries or any other terrorist group with the funds or products to purchase and trade.

He leads a flamboyant lifestyle, living in strategically located villas in Cuba, Italy, Tunica, Germany, France, Brazil, Costa Rica, and the Bahamas, where he owns Norman's Cay. And most recently, according to town records, he purchased a five-hundred-acre spread, formerly a US military training base during World War II, and built a heavily protected mansion on the Slaty Fork Mountain summit just inside the Monongahela National Forest at a cost of $15 million. The property has several secret military bunkers, one of them quite elaborate, with a conference room, bathrooms, a shooting range, cells for housing prisoners of war should it had been necessary, and last but not least, a water purification facility.

None of this has been recorded, and tax records have disappeared.

Working closely with the "command-and-control structure" of the Sinaloa cartel, he is conspiring to distribute large quantities of drugs in the United States. It been learned that his army of sicarios, or hit men, is under orders to kidnap, torture, and kill anyone who gets in the way.

The island of Norman's Cay consists of a marina, a yacht club, approximately 100 abandoned bungalows, and a 35,000-fot paved private airstrip for Maduro's Learjet. The island is six miles long and about 250 feet or more in width. He employs approximately 50 armed Mexican and Bohemian guards and a half dozen attack dogs that patrol the airstrip and the shores 24-7. In the mid-1970s, Maduro began buying up property and threatening the island's residents to leave. One of the residents refused to sell. Not long after that, a fishing boat belonging to the single resisting resident was found drifting off the coast with the corpses of its owners aboard. The rest of his family was nowhere to be found. Soon after, Maduro purchased the entire island for less than $15 million from the Bohemian governor.

The Caribbean cay is suspected of being a tropical hideaway and playground for Hugo and his associates. The island is also suspected of being a major hub for his illicit drug and arms enterprises, including human trafficking. He deals in the wholesale distribution of cannabis, coke, meth, hash, and smack. The island is protected by radar, bodyguards, and attack Doberman pinschers. He has a Learjet at the Charleston Airport, two helicopters, a sixty-five-foot yacht, and armed speedboats that patrol Norman's Cay.

"What was a former FARC guerrilla doing in the US with a US passport?"

"You would have to ask him. Money, guns, and women are my guess."

"Supposedly, he's not personally into arms trafficking anymore. Instead, he now owns a number of offshore shell companies along and has a veritable army of old associates shielding him from the obvious illegal stuff."

The new façade of Hugo Maduro is still that of a remorseless, cold-blooded killer, but now he has sprouted new sophisticated wings. He currently lives the high life of a West Virginia socialite as a respected and respectable international commodities broker of oil, diamonds, timber, whatever one corrupt country or group wants to sell and another wants to buy. Nothing with money in it is off the table. He has the patience of a jaguar and the instinct of a covert operative. But unfortunately, he also has a reputation for having a vicious temper.

Maduro has a pilot's license to fly his helicopter to and from his private heliport in West Virginia. In addition, he has a sixty-five-foot luxury yacht, the *Lady Maria*, docked in Virginia that he uses to sail to the Bahamas. Hugo is litigious and often embroiled in lawsuits requiring him to sell several businesses to settle for missing funds estimated in the hundreds of millions of pounds and dollars. In 1970 his stepson's body and that of his first wife were found floating in the Atlantic Ocean several miles from shore off San Juan, and their deaths were officially classified at the inquest as unfortunate accidental drownings after falling overboard out at sea. His son was presumed to have fallen overboard from the yacht while taking a leak in the nude over the side, as he was well known to do. His mother most likely jumped over the side in an effort to try and rescue him. The judge ruled out murder and suicide, and Maduro received $10 million from the life insurance policies.

He speaks four different languages and is an expert at deception, using numerous aliases to escape identification and capture. The CIA has been tracking him for over a half dozen years, and he has disappeared every time we feel we have a solid link.

The Colombian is the leader of the Cartel of the Suns, a corrupt arm of the Venezuelan Armed Forces of unquestioned loyalty to him. He made about half a billion dollars selling covert arms to North Vietnam, Laos, Iran, Ethiopia, and both sides of the Egyptian and Syria war, including the Black September Terrorist group responsible for the Munich massacre. He is also a significant player in the drug trafficking trade dealing heavily in opium through the Golden Triangle of Southeast Asia.

In his latest venture out of his West Virginia estate, he lobbied and corralled a compromised senator, several lobbyists, and ruthless lawyers for a more significant piece of the pork. He has also purchased tons of small arms, RPGs, and artillery from Russia, China, Iran, and other trading partners. He has purchased a fleet of cargo planes along with pilots from the Venezuelan Air Force so he can transport them and resell them to militias all over the African continent at a considerable profit. The latest Intelligence shows that he's made half a billion dollars ramping up the violence between the African nations and tribes. In addition, it is now speculated that he is a major player in the international sex trafficking trade.

In July 1974 Maduro and his wife were arrested in Mexico and charged with five federal crimes, including money laundering, drug, and sex trafficking, transportation of a minor to engage in criminal sexual activity, and conspiracy to entice minors to travel to engage in an illegal sex act. All this allegedly arose out of his operation of a sex-trafficking ring with the Mexican wing of the Cartel of the Suns. Both escaped conviction and were released as not one timorous witness could be found alive to testify against them. However, the charge files of both were expurgated.

Yeah, he's one bright son of bitch. One way or another, it's always going to be about money, I thought to myself.

My fingers were twirling a pencil I had been doodling with; now, it snapped in two. I threw both pieces into the wastebasket with bridled anger.

Maria Maduro: Maria is 60–20 years younger than her husband. They have been together for over fifteen years. Of almond complexion, brunette, with capped teeth, 145 pounds, she was a gold-digging, persnickety Brazilian trollop and exotic dancer before becoming a "Brazilian supermodel." She has given Hugo three children and is deeply involved in promoting the Maduro business operations. She grew up in a Brazilian ghetto, dropped out of school in the eighth grade, and was discovered by a fashion scout who personally taught her how to look sexy and entertain.

She speaks English and Spanish" her mother was an American prostitute and her father was a farmer. She and her husband have been indicted several times by US prosecutors for drug smuggling, narco-terrorism, and sex trafficking, which has landed two of her convicted nephews in a Florida penitentiary. The Brazilian information minister, Jorge Rodriquez, bolstering his puissant position and wealth, has rejected all subpoenas and has called the US indictment of the Maduros vile, slanderous, and offensive. He declined to elaborate further.

Pablo Escobar: Age 49, he is a beholden hitman and confederate of Hugo Maduro with a propensity for violence. Mixed German-Honduran descent. A rogue contract ice-cold pathological assassin and drug addict. An illegal immigrant and nasty amigo with a thick, greasy mop of unruly shoulder-length black hair. He speaks English with a heavy Mexican accent. Information on his adolescent years is as blank as a flyleaf. Heavyset, 5-foot-3, approximately 180 pounds, coffee-colored skin, with a flat hangdog face and a prominent fat nose twice as broad as it is long. Born in an obscure ramshackle barrio in the mountains of Armenia, Mexico. Education: "School of Hard Knocks"—illiterate with a sixth-grade education max.

He spent a five-year stint in a Mexican prison for manufacturing and smuggling both meth and cocaine. He is a former Colombian drug protector and hitman for the Medellin Cartel. He's known to have a hatred of Gringos. His expertise is execution, murder, smuggling, kidnapping, and drug and human trafficking between the United States, Mexico, and Colombia. Along with several other "coyotes," he manages several drop houses between Charleston and Nogales, Arizona.

Although this is not yet confirmed, he may also be an enforcer and assassin for the Los Zetas based just south of Brownsville, Texas. He specializes in the use of a garrote and a knife. Pablo Escobar is extremely dangerous. He likes to rape and beat women into submission. Two years ago, he was arrested and formally charged with rape, aggravated battery, and murder of her husband. While he was incarcerated and awaiting trial, there was an undisclosed settlement with money exchanging hands with the Mexican federales on the take. Maduro is suspected of putting up the cash. The next day, the woman could not remember her assailant, and all charges were dropped against Pablo. He walked away with charges wholly neutered. The woman also disappeared several days later without a trace. He's one bad hombre with a litany of crimes to his name, and killing doesn't bother him.

Senator Sahra Assad: Assad, age 40, 100 pounds, 5-foot-4, brown hair, hazel eyes, is a bastard of Somali decent born following her mother's monthlong dalliance with her Palestinian cousin Ahmad Bashiir, whom she never saw or heard from again. Never compelled to work, the senator has devoted her time to social causes and charities that may be cover for more clandestine activities. She studied in Beirut, Lebanon, and obtained a bachelor's degree in political science from Cairo University before receiving her master's from Yale University.

She sits on the Senate Intelligence Committee representing the Democratic Party. It has been noted in a recent unpublished CIA report that she has a warped perspective on her responsibilities following her push to dismantle the US economy and political system. She is also being investigated for her blocking vote of several recent covert operations in Somalia that had to be aborted and for secretly leaking classified information of renewed interest regarding NSA surveillance anonymously to the media.

Following the end of her incestuous marriage to her cousin, she had within weeks married a Mexican politician with indirect ties to both the Sinaloa Cartel and the Cartel of the Suns in Venezuela. According to reliable sources, she was arrested at age twenty-four in Beirut for the attempted murder of a cousin she had been schmoozing with, but the record was expunged, and the United States never got wind of it. The *Washington Post* reported that last year, the senator and her husband received over $300,000 from Hugo Maduro for consulting and research services along with a $200,000 donation to the senator's reelection campaign. All of it was processed through an offshore bank in Saint Martins. Several complaints against her for ethics violations and other nefarious activities by the National Legal and Policy Center are still being litigated. She has attended several galas at the Maduro estate in West Virginia over the past two years. Records indicate that she has initiated a number of investigations using unethical means and disenfranchised several opponents of Maduro's political expansion in West Virginia.

There was no mention in the file of her ongoing affair with Senator Schiff, which might have been an oversight, or it was erased.

Senator Alan Schiff: Senator Schiff, age 60, is a sleazy lawyer of Venezuelan descent, 240 pounds, 6-foot, brown eyes, balding. He received a BA and MA in political science from the Virginia Commonwealth University of Georgia, finishing toward the bottom of his class. He also carved out time from his classes to participate in turbocharged radical protests against the Vietnam War, burn his draft card, and march against civil rights demonstrations, including attending sit-ins and getting arrested. He's survived three failed marriages, which were costly settlements—and is currently married to an investment banker at Chase-Webster who is fifteen years his junior. He has a history of making poor choices in wives, business partners, and real estate investments.

He sits on the Senate Intelligence Committee and has been central to several boondoggle controversies during his latest term. He represents West Virginia and has served the district for over eighteen years representing the Democratic Party. It was learned through several unconfirmed channels that he had engaged in a less-than-appropriate relationship with Senator Assad during two of her trips to the Maduro estate. He is also being investigated for possible conspiracy and money laundering, having received over half a million dollars in cash from a Mexican politician named Néstor Lamas, who is well connected to the international drug and sex trade in Mexico and Venezuela. During a congressional hearing in March, the senator denied all the accusations.

Having been with the CIA now for over five years, this was my first exposure to humanity's dark side, which included human trafficking, brutal rape, and general depravity.

Nuna Polinski: Age 27, of Danish-American descent, voluptuous, blond, blue eyes, 125 pounds, 5-foot-7, widowed, no children or immediate family. She was born and raised between Elkins and Coalwood, West Virginia, as the only child of Liza and Bart Penksa with genes apparently from a Confederate general. Her only affiliation is with the United Daughters of the Confederacy. She is currently residing in a single-family home in the small town of Gauley Bridge, West Virginia. She has a BS Degree in economics with a major in international finance. Her father retired on a medical discharge from the Marine Corps as a master sergeant and was a coal miner who met his untimely death in an auto accident under mysterious circumstances when his car lost control and careened over a three-hundred-foot cliff just south of Hawks Nest on Route 60, dropping over three hundred feet into the river below. According to the owner of the garage who hauled up and removed the crumpled vehicle from the riverbed, the brake lines had been cut, but the incurious police never investigated or reported it. His accident was similar to a number of other untimely deaths of drug gang people murdered during that period. She is currently working as a finance consultant and investment banker for the Chase-Webster Bank in Charleston, following in her father's footsteps, a paragon of competence and virtue. She doesn't seem to be obsessed with feminine affectations and vanity.

An examination of her credit card purchases for the past couple of years shows that she lives a low-key existence indulging on a couple of bottles of Oster Bay Sauvignon Blanc each month, along with lots vegetarian cuisine.

Lieutenant Glenn Nunez: "Bloody brilliant," age 39, 6-foot-3, 200 pounds with a Doberman build, fluent in English and Spanish, West Point graduate and ex-linebacker. Since he is an Army ranger and special forces operative on assignment with the CIA, he has already sated my curiosity with an impeccable record in covert computer sciences.

He is a Vietnam veteran of three tours; during the third he was behind enemy lines for over seven months, facilitating the escape of twenty-three

POWs from deep jungle prisons. He has been wounded several times and was awarded the Congressional Medal of Honor in 1973 by President Nixon for his valor beyond the call of duty in combat. He has three Purple Hearts and has been awarded both the Bronze and Silver Stars.

Lieutenant Austin Bomen: Age 41, 6-foot, 190 pounds, dark hair, speaks four languages, MIT graduate, capable, Vietnam veteran with two tours with SEAL Team One. He has three Purple Hearts and was awarded the Silver Star for continuously flying wounded marines out of Kai San even when he had been seriously wounded by enemy fire during the 1968 Tet Offensive. The man is unflappable, and in looking at his file photo, I saw he is a Charles Bronson look-alike. Lieutenant Bomen has access to technology and federal databases, excels in computers and electronics, and has an unsurpassed talent for performing algorithm research. He is already in place and has set up a surveillance camp atop a mountain approximately two miles from the Maduro compound. He is conducting round-the-clock surveillance of activities in the compound via satellite.

He has set up a Gulfstream V as a disguise, and it's now his de facto war room, full of computers and other surveillance equipment. Both of these men have garnered impressive reviews from the admiral.

* * *

Not the type to dawdle, Bryce surveyed the kitchen and, having tucked his laptop into its case, prepared his gear, went to his bedroom, undressed, climbed into bed, and turned off his bed lamp. Stacking his hands beneath his head, he called it a night. The lazy circling blades of the fan cast swirling shadows on the ceiling. The droning hum of its motor was mesmerizing. As he drifted off to sleep, his mission followed him into la-la land.

Waking in the morning, he grabbed his jacket and headed out. The breaking dawn came early, and having had his reservations confirmed, he drove straight to Charleston: after the clear and cloudless morning, the fog was coming in and now obscured most of the street in front of him.

CHAPTER 12

At a little before ten, Nuna arrived a half hour early at Hugo and Maria Maduro's ostentatious main entrance gate. The stout eight-foot-tall well-secured iron gate was the type that slid to the side; therefore no hinges were required. It could only be accessed through the gatehouse on the other side and was without weak spots.

The sprawling pillared Greek revival antebellum-style palace on the mountaintop eminence of the unassuming village of Slaty Forks was frozen in time, tucked into the edge of the Monongahela National Forest just north of Marlinton. Completed four years ago, the twenty—thousand-square-foot grand chateau, named Sapphire del Monongahela, had a terra-cotta roof and sat on nine hundred acres of expensive, picturesque countryside with a commanding view of the hollows and mountain environs below. Undulating acres of grassy fields crisscrossed with miles of four-board white fences holding in half a dozen grazing thoroughbred horses. The double doors were made from hardwood trees felled to clear the construction site for the mansion. The interior included Brazilian mahogany cornices and carved balustrades complemented by gleaming Bahia granite and polished Italian marble embellished, adorned with the opulence of priceless eighteenth- and nineteenth-century paintings and other eclectic European artwork.

According to bank records, the wealthy Manduro family estate was worth gazillions and the couple had paid more than twenty-five million for the opulent mega estate, which consisted of an eighteen-hole golf course, several guest cottages, lavish staff quarters, a magnificent stable, a private theater, an Olympic-size heated saltwater infinity pool complete with a grotto and waterfall, complemented by a terraced Jacuzzi with a stunningly ineffable panoramic view of the surrounding tranquil

mountain vistas, recreational facilities surrounded by an enchanted terraced garden, and state-of-art security system, including several fortified rooms, roaming armed guards with canines, and a guarded electric
gate at the bottom of the mountain. They even had a heliport atop the
theater with a gleaming French EC120 Colibri Hummingbird and a
pilot on call 24-7 for executive orders. The flamboyant Hugo Maduro,
having served in the Venezuelan Air Force for two years, was also a certified pilot, and he was known to fly the Hummingbird without advance
notice to his luxury yacht docked at the Pier 41 Marina in Bermuda.
When not in Bermuda, he and his wife could be found riding their
thoroughbred collection, including an Arabian, a quarter horse, and an
Andalusian.

Not everyone serving the Manduro family was formally employed
by them. With more than $1 billion on deposit with Chase-Webster,
they were entitled to a highly unusual level of professional service. Nuna
Polinski was a customer service manager at Chase-Webster and was assigned to be their personal financial girl Friday who paid their bills and
moved money among their many domestic and offshore accounts, including covering overdrafts and shortfalls. She also made house calls to
Sapphire del Monongahela to pick up deposits and drop off receipts as
needed. As instructed, she openly pooh-poohed the trappings of international financial power, no questions asked. It was an abysmal assignment,
definitely not her dream job, but it paid the bills.

It was just another spectacular summer day in the pristine mountains of West Virginia under a cerulean blue sky dotted by a handful of
white clouds that looked like fluffy sheep floating in the air. The heat
was palpable, wrapping around her like a moist blanket as she waited
for the security guard to come out of his bunker and buzz her through
the gate. She gazed at the flowering rosebushes and begonias blossoming
prodigiously in front of the massive twelve-foot-high stone walls on each
side of the entrance. Gardeners were pruning and trimming, speaking
languages other than English.

The stalwart uniformed security guard with an intimidating, Doberman-like, lean and muscular body was on the phone with, she assumed, Mrs. Manduro but was taking every opportunity he could with frank curiosity to look into her window and check out her legs. He was handsome but in an aggressive way that never actually appealed to her. His unembellished khaki uniform was starched and crisply pressed, the slacks looking like they'd been professionally tailored to fit. He had long arms and big hands decorated by a fraternity ring of some sort. He was in his midthirties, just over six feet tall, clean-shaven, and had a full head of glossy black hair. He wore aviator glasses with wire frames, and his square hatchet jaw looked like it could compete with the Old Man of the Mountain in New Hampshire.

Finally stepping out of the bunker with a big effusive enigmatic grin on his face, he said, "Mrs. Manduro says you can go up. But be advised," he added benevolently, somewhat snarkily, "that she is somewhat querulous this morning. Hugo is back. From the night log, I reckon he got in late last night with his bodyguards chauffeuring him in the Bentley. But from what I learned this morning during the shift change, he's attending a sale of thoroughbreds out by the track on Talbut Mountain."

He leaned into the window and whispered in her ear, "Actually, I think something here is askew. I've actually never seen him this agitated in daylight, either."

Nuna rolled her eyes and took a calming breath, making a tsking sound. "Sir, he's a worldly, globe-trotting, brilliant business magnate. You should be more understanding and less censorious.

Glenn nodded absently. "All right, and what business might that include?" he asked in a palsy-walsy way. "Drugs, prostitution, human trafficking?" He guffawed.

Nuna gave him an incredulous look and then laughed and shook her head as his incessant questioning was beyond the pale. Trying not to come across as sententious, she simply said that Mr. Manduro lived a frenetic lifestyle trading in international oil and other natural resources. "Now open the gate before you cause me to be late."

Reluctantly and unabashedly, Glenn, with a deadpan expression, stepped back from her jeep and engaged the gate mechanism as he pointed to the 5 miles per hour sign. The gate began to open, sliding to the right. While Glenn was handsome, he struck her as a feckless muscle-bound buffoon and naive lackey of the establishment without a smidgen of common sense. Looking at him askance, she waved goodbye and rolled through the twenty-foot heavy-duty cast iron gates, amused and roiling at his security guard's persistent avid interest in their employer. She could handle the smiling come-ons, along with his prattle, but the Maduros put a high value on their physical and fiscal privacy. Wealthy families were targets for everyone, from civic and political fundraisers to thieves and kidnappers. The wealthy kept the world at bay with strong iron gates, security cameras, and a thick layer of guards, servants, lawyers, and bankers.

If in Maduros shoes, she would have done the same. Especially as they had three teenage children to protect from the world's predators.

Slowly, she drove up the one-mile Belgium block driveway with its winding twenty-degree incline, through the spacious grounds, noting the cathedrals of red maple trees and the glory of the well-tended lush beds of manicured summer flowers and chrysanthemums and other succulents bedecking the hilly front yard of the huge, ostentatious mansion.

She parked her car in the circular drive alongside Maria's Bentley and walked up the Italian marble walkway, along a manicured lawn lined with topiaries to the portico entrance with a massive double front doors, pressing the doorbell.

The air was morning crisp and smelled of fresh-cut grass.

The front doorbell triggered an impressive set of deep chimes worthy of a Vatican chapel on Easter Sunday. She listened to the chimes peal and fade into the unseen vastness of the interior. Even though she had been here several times, she stood all atwitter. The massive oak door opened inward with barely a whoosh. An elusive scent of potpourri wafted out into the summer air. A thirtysomething, stiffly arrogant doorman with a sober expression on his face and an extremely muscular frame answered and greeted her. He was apparently a new employee, Latino, either ex-military or a bodybuilder, wearing an impeccable conservative black-and-white butler uniform similar to those worn by British butlers in the early twentieth century. Doorkeepers were supposed to be friendly, but this butler was anything but. Stone-faced and dour, he stared scrutinizing me before asking, "Can I help you?"

When she gave him her name, he gave her a stolid look; his eyes remained riveted on her in a dignified manner but never met her eyes.

"Mrs. Maduro is expecting you. This way, please," he said, ushering her in. He shepherded her through the palatial marble vestibule, which was a magnificent montage of pink granite, and down a wide opulent corridor with high ceilings and gilded skylights lined with floral arrangements of red poinsettias and white amaryllis that led to a large garden patio. Nuna's footsteps were silent on the plush hallway carpet; the sounds of water were everywhere as it cascaded down from terrace to terrace in small waterfalls.

The residence was a treasure. The sound of soft classical Brazilian music mingled with the sound of chirping birds. Spring was here: it was only two weeks before Memorial Day.

"You're late." Her lips pursed, Maria said peevishly with a waxed, eloquent Brazilian Portuguese intonation as she sat ramrod straight with crossed legs sipping her morning brew at the far side of the terrace under a cascade of superfluous flora above her. She looked as prosperous and well-kept as her surroundings. She lowered and folded her newspaper on the table, her curiosity satiated. The doorman seemed to have evaporated unnoticed as the two women faced each other in sumptuous opulence.

Maria's unctuous tone was graciously frosty as usual but sounded miffed and not exactly filled with warmth. The Asscher cut diamond on her finely manicured finger gleaming in the morning sun was no less than thirty carats. "But I'll have Luis make you a demitasse." It was a perfunctory offer, but Nuna, unperturbed, accepted it with a placating tone even though she didn't really want a coffee. A stack of ivory inlaid bangles glistened on Maria's wrist as she gestured for her servant's attention.

"Please," she said, graciously sweeping her open bejeweled hand and gesturing Nuna toward a chair opposite hers.

"Mrs. Maduro, I left my house as soon as Mr. Siniscalo called me telling me that you wished to see me this morning."

"Nuna, sit down, please," she said conversationally in a throaty voice.

Nuna pulled up a wicker chair and sat gingerly beneath the cabana casually cross-legged, placing her leather briefcase at her feet as she preened her cotton shift.

"What do you need of me this morning, Mrs. Maduro?" she asked with a self-deprecating smile complemented by a professional crispness in her voice as she pulled out of her purse a small digital recorder for audio notes.

Everything was copacetic.

Maria took a slow, deliberate sip of her coffee, not hedging on Nuna's question but aligning her thoughts into words first with prim hauteur. The uniformed waiter wheeled over a serving cart and graciously poured her coffee, placing the cup and saucer on the table in front of her. As the waiter turned, Maria murmured to him, and he nodded and left.

"Yes," Nuna said after apologizing profusely, "but you can blame that on your new Machiavellian security guard, who keeps stalling me at the gate and trying to seduce me into a date every time I come by," she cooed in a brittle voice.

Maria eloquently gave her the awe-inspiring mesmeric porcelain smile of an international South American beauty queen who had graced the cover of *Vogue* not once but twice. "Of course he would. You're an attractive, intoxicating young woman with a Pilates body who's doing well in life, and he's a hapless former football linebacker who has lost his moment of fame and no longer has the incentive to do anything constructive with his life other than protect me."

The elite social fey charm of the Illuminati and the extroverted sybaritic enthusiasm in the process were without question all Maria. While she was seriously bipolar, and the flippancy of her droll mood swings was at times astonishing, she had a polished, vibrant, pompous, pretentious, high-maintenance pulchritude laced with a mysterious, elegant demeanor. Maria was in a spatial center with her long, dark obsidian-like hair and her popular hourglass figure, reputedly rumored to have turned the heads of the entire Brazilian Naval Academy in Rio de Janeiro. She had the luminous looks of Sophia Loren, was shrewd, extroverted, socially ambitious, and arrogant in an inexorable manner that only a beautiful Brazilian woman with flamboyance and half a billion dollars in banks spread around the world could be. Not only was Maria Maduro a ravishing coquette with legs like a gazelle and eyes like a cunning fox, she was also amazingly intelligent for someone with only a high school education. With Hugo's blessings, she fully invested her time and expertise in managing the Maduro financial network according to her personal caprices and whims.

While Nuna was impressed with Maria's beauty and accomplishments, she wasn't dazzled. Her beauty might be the result of either face peels or Botox injections or both, she thought. In the back of her mind, Nuna admitted that she despised Maria for her hectoring, condescending arrogance, mirthless smiles, beguiling laughter, and capricious inclinations and didn't trust her. Yet she saw through the transparent veneer of her beauty to the cunning and guile beneath. There was something vicariously sinister about her that spelled evil.

Maria had been at a charity dinner with her agent and had been introduced to Hugo Maduro by an up-and-coming cartel lord. That night, she had abandoned her date and engaged in ultra sex with Hugo on the elevator all the way up to his suite. Within three months of that memorable evening, she was Mrs. Hugo Maduro. Maria had walked away from her budding modeling career to become Hugo's adoring trophy wife, his strongest advocate, ardent lover, and devoted mother of their children.

Hugo loved and trusted her beyond measure, and she made damn sure that was never compromised. Then there was the fact that Maria was a loving mother to three energetic, utterly confident children who were now adults in their early to late twenties.

Born and raised just outside the abysmal Brazilian slums, Maria had been steeled with that unsparing awareness of the difference between poverty and wealth. Yet no matter what Nuna might have thought Maria as a person, she respected her client's dedication to her children. Austin, who was the oldest and married to a Georgian princess, was now a financial analyst for Goldman Sachs; Casandra, like her mother, was a striking fair-skinned brunette and had just recently married a marketing executive of Hanover Investments; and Victor, the youngest of the three, unfortunately was obstreperous and a rebellious druggy. All three of the children had been highly educated at home by the ministration of their mother. Maria was convinced that the private parochial schools in America weren't equipped to handle wealthy kidnap targets.

Maria offered a weak apology for the digression.

"Have you done everything I requested of you for the polo gala?"

Nuna, having listened raptly, didn't need to review her notes. The Maduros were her most esteemed clients. Actually, they were her only clients. "The funds are all in the entertainment account as requested," Nuna said.

"Along with the decorators' requests, I've also decided to festoon the entire gala with bouquets of flowers, and I'm sure we depleted the wholesale inventories of all the florists for miles."

She was well aware that Maria demanded optimum performance from everyone and had a reputation for being vindictive. Mistakes and failures weren't tolerated. Insolence or slipshod service was grounds for immediate dismissal or termination. In that event, scurrilous allegations would be introduced, "termination" being a euphemism for killed.

"Excelente." Maria Maduro made no secret of the fact that she wanted her face and her surgically refreshed cleavage discreetly present in the elite society pages at least once a month.

She had even contacted the *Charleston Gazette* and suggested they do a feature article with a full-color photo of her in the Sunday paper.

Having taken off her sunglasses, Maria removed an envelope from under her dish and slid it over to Nuna. "Please have this deposited into my entertainment account before closing today."

Nuna opened the envelope and removed a handwritten check. It had been drawn on a foreign bank that she'd never heard of. Her eyes bulged in stupefaction, and the levity of her expression left her face as she gave Maria an incredulous look.

"Twenty-two million dollars," she said. "There must be some mistake." She stared at the check, flabbergasted. "Maria, even with your punctiliousness, you couldn't spend that much on a party."

The silence was immediate and profound. The morning joviality died at the table.

Her anger went from zero to sixty in a nanosecond, with no warning signs and no time for anyone to get out of the way.

Seething with unmitigated waspish anger, Maria snapped her head with a flash of her raging, tempestuous temper, pursed her lips, and rabidly glared straight at Nuna with glowing gimlet eyes. Then, surging to her feet and splattering the garden with shouted obscenities and wild gesticulations, she said, "How dare you question me!"

Nuna's ebullience fizzled, and she felt the earth drop under her.

Cheeks flaming, eyes flashing, Maria added, "Who do you think you are? Your job isn't to fucking judge my expenditures."

Maria's voice was now at a hysterical fulminating pitch and as cold and infuriated as her glacial, icy stare, her lashes thick with mascara. Her faint Latin accent deepened, and she barely contained her bitter hostility as she lambasted Nuna. "Your sole function is to deposit and withdraw money at my desire," she said imperiously. Her expression grew hideous, all the ugliness in her suddenly evident as her façade fell away in her tirade and she unleashed a torrent of expletives.

Nuna was completely confounded; her expression calcified with stupefaction. She cringed and stared at Maria wordlessly until the eruption, which was on the scale of Vesuvius, had subsided. The shocked silence of the tête-à-tête at the table would surely lead to a heated argument. She took a deep breath to conjure up her strength. Nuna's stomach knotted as she looked away, visually shaken based on her long, puissant stare, and sighed heavily.

"Maria, apropos the check, I'll be happy to process it in any account you specify," Nuna said in a quavering voice. "But not being familiar with the account numbers and the offshore bank the check is being drawn on, I'm required by law and regulatory procedures to ask some pertinent questions." Compliant and complicit accountants were no longer legally immune from the implications of their professional activities. Nuna was well aware of the ramifications of international money laundering. Comprehension unknotted her brows. "Please understand," she said, genuinely contrite, "I'm not an advocate of the current rules, but I can't change the laws. If I don't comply with the laws, Chase-Webster will fire me on the spot for sure."

"It's too late to worry about your fucking job," Hugo Maduro said lividly, coming up behind Nuna in an icy rage and interrupting ruthlessly with a wild, vexed, snarling look in his turbulent eyes.

The rasping acidity in his belligerent voice was so intense that she could see the blood-red pulsing veins in his face and neck, shattering her composure into a million lacerated shards. "Worry about your fucking freedom instead."

Shocked, she blanched with the unexpected volume of his voice. But Nuna was nonplussed and let the petrified silence expand as she looked up at Maduro, now standing almost on top of her. His obnoxious and menacing smile addled her brain, and her knees turned to jelly as he ratcheted up the horrifying rhetoric. In silent contemplation, she couldn't help but flinch, cursing under her breath. Her future was imploding and looking dimmer and dimmer, and she now understood that she was standing on a foundation of sand, that it could shift at the click of his finger and her career would crash.

She was emphatically a West Virginia coal miner's daughter, born and raised in the Appalachian Mountains. She rode, shot, and killed snakes with her folding knife. But she had a cold feeling that the brazened Hugo Manduro was way beyond her varmint-killing skills.

"It's too late to worry about your fucking job, bitch! Worry about your fucking life instead!" And with glaring asperity in his eyes and an unrepentant dastardly shrug, Hugo's nostrils flared as he reached across the table and grabbed her recorder, tossing it to the marbled floor and smashing it under the heel of his boot. Nuna remained silent. She didn't want to provoke him further. She had never seen eyes as ice-cold and terrifying as his. If Maria's arrogant smile was meant to soothe Nuna's equanimity, it didn't.

Nuna pursed her lips and clenched her hands in her lap as she stared at the frightening Maduros across the table from her and silently maintained her equanimity. She sensed that the less she said, the less she'd sink into the quagmire that suddenly had become an abomination. Waves of poleaxed nausea trashed her stomach, forcing her to consider retching.

Hugo slid down next to Nuna and put his right arm around her, pulling her close. With his left, he reached across the table and placed the plain white envelope back in front of her. Nuna pushed away in circumspection as a response to the mortal danger that he posed to her now in spades. She wasn't about to deceive herself into believing otherwise. He had donned an air of huffiness that she found repugnant. His aura of power and aggressive persona were now menacing, starting with his chilling icy-cold flinty eyes and the pronounced angular structure of his face.

"You will do as you're told," Hugo said with a hectoring attitude, "or you may lose your fucking life. The choice is yours."

Nuna swallowed hard with trepidation and prayed that her stammering voice sounded less afraid than she was. "What choice?"

"It's quite simple, chica." He rested his hand upon hers. "You now belong to me," he said callously with a wicked grin as his flinty eyes bored into hers.

"What?" She snorted as she pulled her hand back quickly, girding herself for battle. She was aghast at the statement. The words slammed into her then with all the force of a speeding train.

CHAPTER 13

The next morning, a Friday, Nuna, now under extraordinary pressure and after considerable internal debate, felt her indignant anger begin to overtake her fear and trepidation. Her tension was high, and a knot of hatred seemed to coalesce in her chest as she made a valiant attempt to keep the anger at bay. Nuna's weary heart was pounding furiously and felt like it was being put through a meat grinder. She had lost her laid-back country girl demeanor, and her voice was crisp. To buy herself time to think about the hapless purgatory that the despicable narcissist had put her in, she had been going through the bank escrow documents again, painfully, very slowly, page by page.

She wasn't about to commit the ultimate folly of becoming a felon for the Maduros. Going to jail for something as unethical as money laundering, which she had no control over, was an unnerving lingering possibility causing her to rethink my career choice. She thought she could hear somewhere in the back of her mind the harsh clanging of cell-block iron closing behind her.

She drove past the gated entry several times to steel her resolve before entering. Still, truth be told, her heart was relentlessly pounding like a drum, the voice in her head whimpering and then screaming for courage, her breath desperately shallow and wheezing, her skin prickling with fear at the thought of becoming a felon and possibly going to prison. To shake off the combination of abiding anger and doubt, she kept reminding herself that none of this was even remotely her fault. Her stomach was rolling, and her palms were slick with perspiration as she was led by the butler to the outside patio.

Thank God I'm wearing these dark bug-eyed sunglasses, she thought as her lashes glistened and her eyes welled with insufferable tears.

She scowled at Hugo defiantly; he was her blackmailer and the tormentor in charge of her life. The tension was running like a hot electrical synapse firing through her nerves. She was the gazelle frozen with fear, her nostrils flared, her ears twitching, and the lion threatening to pounce on her.

"When in doubt, brazen it out and soldier through the fear." She recalled the saying by rote.

"Mr. Maduro…" she said, taking a deep breath and steeling herself, barely able to swallow. Then with a shaky breath and a seething look on her face, she said loathingly, "Let's get this straight." With her Polish temper ignited and a charged look of steely inner resolve, she bolstered herself again, took a deep breath, and looked boldly into his eyes. "I'm not your property and never will be, Hugo!"

Her ice-formed façade of composure was now on the verge of melting as a chill ran down her spine and her insides quivered. She gave him a cold stare that was at once forthright and defiant. After a pregnant pause, Maduro looked surprised, then blatantly disregarded her protest, glaring at her with an angry stone face oozing menace over her. The blood vessels in his temples were pounding and expanding to a level of excruciating pain, but he held back.

Nuna steeled herself, glared back at him unblinking with a cold, narrow-eyed combative look, and gave him a hardened, astringent smile, refusing to kowtow to his inexorable belligerence.

Her chest was pulsing rapidly, as though the intensity of the vituperation she had been subjected to, now locked within her, was creating violent emotional turbulence.

"Mr. Maduro," she asked without preamble but at a lower timbre, "I don't suppose there's any way I can opt out of this charming business venture?" Nuna was controlling her anger, hoping for détente, but the effort was bleeding into the tone of her voice.

Silently Maduro registered mild surprise over her snappishness but managed to keep his restrained countenance as he considered her defiant deportment.

Then he turned to Maria, who had a furious expression of granite. Nuna was scared shitless.

Maria handed him the envelope and flavored Nuna with a sour inimical look that oozed hatred as Nuna locked eyes with her in the ensuing silence, rife with smoldering hatred and hostility. "If she doesn't, there's going to be hell to pay."

Maduro's baleful eyes narrowed and burned into Nuna's. His irises were so dark that they were almost indistinguishable from his pupils. He bore down on her like a hawk on a chipmunk until she had to bow her head back to look up at him. Nuna felt the weight of his clenched jaw muscles and his blazing eyes on her. His breathing was now heavy and volatile, ragged with raw rage. He came close and leered at her expansively with a haughty, outlandish smirking grin. His rough hand stroked her cheek. The coldness of his touch almost made her retch.

"Maria already fucking told you what she wants!" Maduro yelled. He threw the envelope at her. "Deposit this fucking check immediately! There will be more coming. Be prepared to transfer this deposit from her entertainment account to an overseas account as soon as the bank opens on Monday morning. Maria will give you the account and routing information on Monday morning." He smiled with a glint in his dark, evil eyes. "After that, I don't believe any more special banking services will be required of you."

Nuna quailed before him but kept her expression defiant.

"Another banking arrangement will be made. And we'll forget that we ever had this little talk. I assume you expect me to ignore the regulations that require me to be sure the money was legitimately obtained and not filthy lucre."

"Yes, and from this minute on, you'll do anything I tell you to do. Do we have an understanding?"

His tone was dismissive, making it sound like a fait accompli. His grin reeked of arrogant self-confidence at her growing discomfiture, and his tone made it an implicit threat. He stood up and rounded the table, looking at her through dark, narrowed eyes. His voice, gravelly from years of smoking cigars, vibrated with anger.

Nuna felt her pulse quicken, and her blood turned to ice at Hugo's words. She refused to quail before him. The thought of him controlling her was untenable. She inhaled, counting to five before exhaling.

With no immediate options, she gritted her teeth and steeled her spine.

"One minute," Maduro said with an austere expression revealing no emotion and eyes as stone cold as a frozen fjord, his strident, amplified voice commanding attention. He picked up the Aruban Bank draft and, with scolding reproof, held it out to her, forcing her to take it.

"Now deposit this fucking immediately. And I mean immediately." Raw savagery radiated from his tone.

With trembling fingers and angst about the possibility of losing her job, Nuna took the check. There wasn't a hell of a lot that she could do at this point. She was trapped and helpless, having blindly and stupidly gotten involved with a ruthless, implacable monster. She felt the earth shift beneath her feet, and sweat began damping her palms. He was a callous, unfeeling bastard and had unscrupulously manipulated and exploited her to his advantage. This, without question, marked the end of her innocence.

Chagrin washed through her, and she waited for the heat to burn her face. Rather than yell and remonstrate with him, Nuna, resigned to the vagary of her fate, turned and in silent acquiesce flipped them the bird and gave him a "screw you" smile, icily. She decided that while she walked away in a huff, without a hint of totter, she would persevere and steel her resolve, one-foot landing in front of the other.

Her palms were damp. She dried them on her skirt. Sliding her legs out from beneath the table, she surged to her feet and stumbled back, her weight faltering and coming down on her insole. Gnawing on her full bottom lip, she hitched her purse over her shoulder and pushed Hugo aside, swallowing the explosive anger that threatened to choke her. Nuna

Polinski would never quail from his heartless words. She refrained from saying another word. Her fragile features seemed to welter. Far from being vanquished, however, she stood up. With chin up, shoulders squared, she straightened her carriage and sidestepped Maria as she stormed out in high dudgeon on the walkway, cutting diagonally across the parking area. She could feel the white heat of her anger on the back of her neck as all the blood drained from her head. Conquering unseen tears and emotions that conspired to unbalance her, she gave off an air of calm composure as she walked determinedly to her car. She was ticked off.

Her petiteness was incongruous with her combative stride across the parking lot before doing a fast fade. Her heart was pounding, and she could feel the dampness of perspiration in the small of her back. Her eyes prickled with tears. The Maduros watched her make fleet and surefooted progress down the steps and walk away, huffing with rage.

Without looking back over her shoulder, she regarded Hugo with repugnance. She balled her fists until her fingernails made deep half-moons in the palms of her hands. There was nothing to say as she made her way to her car. A journey of perhaps fifty feet, but it felt impossibly far.

She wiped the welling tears back and swallowed hard to ease the lump in her throat.

If she crumpled, if she gave way to his threat, then they would win. She would be damned before she would give him that satisfaction. She slid into the driver's seat, started the car, tighten the seat belt, and left in a cloud of dust.

"I chastise myself for misjudging her," he murmured. I" did give her too long of a leash. Her moral righteousness is not what I expected," he added quietly, maintaining his composure. "I will say she has gumption and fortitude worthy of admiration."

Now in a stormy disposition, Maria pursed her lips and threw Nuna a quick, harried glance as she departed the parking lot, laying rubber off both rear tires. Her face showed more than its usual tic of agitation. "I no longer trust her, and I'm not comfortable having her out there running around free," Maria said, her silky voice carrying sinister undertones as she shrugged her shoulders. "Pablo has been instructed to shadow her every move. Her house, car, and phone are tapped, and if she's asinine enough to go to the authorities, Pablo will stop her."

Laughing, Maduro sighed. "After the final deposits are made, I'll give her to Pablo for his exclusive entertainment for a week or so before adding her to the stable. Her virtuous spirit will have been broken by then. In the meantime, he has to keep her alive until the final funds transfer is made."

Hugo shuffled some ecstasy aside and then a large bag of coke.

He ran his hand through her hair and rested it on her shoulder. "Maria, you are tense and overwrought. I can feel it."

She was being placated, and it angered her. He was a little reckless. His eyes were glittery, partially attributable to a couple of lines of coke or a slug of heroin, both of which he was known to enjoy as a recreational pastime.

"Be that as it may," Maria, with lips pursed caustically, chimed in, radiating hostility like rays from a searing sun. Then, intensely exasperated, with her nostrils flaring, she gave him a sharp scornful rebuke with a searing skeptical look. "I've lost all faith in her. There's a lot at stake here, and that still leaves too much fucking time and opportunity for her to expose us before you eliminate her." Maria's eyes took on a furtive cast. "She's a dangerous loose end that needs to be terminated soon."

With mockery on his face as he reached out and again tangled his fingers in her well-maintained streaked blond hair, he said, "My lioness, money always is, and no one is going to stop me from having everything that I want. That's why we have so much and others have so little. We take risks. Don't worry," he said dismissively. "Her tenure with us is going to be short. As soon as Nuna transfers all the funds, her services will no longer be needed, and Pablo will take her out of circulation." Hugo comforted himself with that solipsism. "She will be collateral damage. The rebels will have the arms to topple the Venezuelan regime, and the oil concessions will be mine. Everything will be copacetic. Let's enjoy our wealth and celebrate our life. Subject dropped!" Hugo disliked being second-guessed and gave Maria a scathing look that muted her. Indeed, he resented even a hint of criticism, especially coming from a woman.

The agitation on Maria's face didn't reveal even a fraction of the turbulent fury raging within her.

"Nuna will be collateral damage?" Maria was patently suspicious and seethed silently. Nuna was fraying her nerves. "That's what you think," she silently whispered to herself.

Hugo raised his hand, and a man in a starched white jacket appeared with a tray holding a bottle of Saint Feliciano Cabernet Sauvignon and two glasses.

Hugo patted her hand sedately, having grown attached to her but asking himself if he really loved Maria. He couldn't answer. *Love* was just a word denoting little feeling or emotion to him. His own calm more than matched hers amid their current marital détente.

"I think you're underestimating her resolve," she said snidely. "In her eyes, we are wealthy and therefore evil."

Hugo evoked a quick, aborted smile. He loved to argue to argue. He also always won.

His military training had taught him to live by the code "Only trust large stones and the dead, and beware of stones as they sometimes may roll."

CHAPTER 14

One thirty in the afternoon. A day had come and gone. Nuna's mind was racing. Her chest was tight with anxiety fluttering through her jangled nerves, and she struggled to hold back a river of tears welling in her stormy eyes as hot as her bitter anger. During some of the drive, she wished that my eyes had windshield wipers. Disgruntled, she had hastily left the Maduro compound in her black Nissan, which she had recently purchased before moving to Gauley Bridge, and driven back home, a two-and-a-half-hour lonely drive on sparsely populated Route 39, a circuitous 120-mile hot macadam country back road banked on both sides by dense forest. One had to be especially careful at this time of day as fully loaded eighteen-wheel logging trucks would be barreling down the mountain, making their final delivery run for the day. One such truck was pulled off on the shoulder with the driver outside inspecting a lopsided load. She was tempted to stop and grab a bite to eat, but she could hear a peanut butter and pickle sandwich calling her from home.

It was still daylight up on the mountain ridgeline. Waning sunlight was casting long shadows on the serpentine passageway as she descended a hairpin turn into the holler below. The sunlight quickly vanished in the rearview mirror and disappeared behind the mountain's shadow. With trembling hands, she stewed over Hugo's threatening diatribe, still drumming in her head, with hysteria rampaging through her mind all the way to Gauley Bridge. She was in a serious quandary and bit her lip in vexation.

Fear, indignation, and general malaise filled her head as she cried and gave vent to the tears that had been welling up since the scene at the Maduros. She was now exhausted, distraught, angry, vulnerable, and finding it difficult to maintain her equanimity. Despair had semi-immobilized her.

Up until this point, her life had been uneventful. However, a single event today had turned her world on its axis, and she now needed some time to decompress and align her scattered thoughts. Nuna wasn't prone to dawdling. She wondered if she could have done things differently and avoided this earthquake. Suppose I had been wiser and possibly more cautious? There are better times for introspection, she thought.

It was almost dusk when Nuna reached the sanctuary of her home, fatigued and miserable, her blood pulsing through her veins and pounding in her temples as she parked the car under the carport alongside her house and killed the engine. Fourth of July decorations adorned her front lawn for the upcoming parade down the main street. As she stepped out of the car, the intense heat of the day actually felt good after the air-conditioning. She clumsily fumbled with her keys to open the door to her kitchen. She stepped into the kitchen, closed and locked and bolted the door, tossed her keys into her purse, and placed the purse on the kitchen counter before standing before the mirror in the hallway, nonplussed. Her dejected spirit was as flat as three-day-old champagne. She was mentally and emotionally drained and fighting off hysteria. Still reeling and shaken to the core by Hugo's vituperative words, she verged precariously on tears.

The nocturnal sounds of cicadas penetrated the darkness, and the implacable scent of the mountain dampness filled her nostrils with earthiness. Gathering her strength, she went into the living room and closed the sliding door behind her, securing her respite, undressing, looking in the mirror as she washed her face, removing her makeup, before taking a Valium and putting on her almond lotion. Staring into the mirror, she whispered to her reflection with a quavering voice, "How could this happen?"

On wobbly knees, she was feeling bilious and had an incipient killer headache that, no doubt, was caused by the crisis-filled past several tumultuous hours.

Nuna, in stony silence, wilted and sank to the floor of the parlor and cradled her face in her raised knees as she sorted through her emotions. Dust motes danced in the shard of light as crazily as her pulse. Hauling herself to her feet with trembling hands, she secured her handbag from the kitchen and feebly trudged up the narrow staircase, leaning heavily upon the balustrade to her bedroom, in need of a shower or a long, soothing hot bath. Instead, she was surrounded by cold raw loneliness. She was no stranger to the stabbing pain as she had lived with it for years. Ablutions would need to wait. Nuna placed her purse on the top of the bureau, kicked off her shoes, undressed, folding her clothes, positioned her slippers, turned off the bedside lamp, and climbed into bed naked. She began to feel the heat and tension ebbing out of her body. Then, with her eyes closed, her thoughts involuntarily returned to her hasty exit from the Maduros. Lethargically she beat the pillows into submission before collapsing onto the soft cotton linens and pulling the covers over her. Within seconds of closing her eyes and willing her exhaustive and depleted body and mind to shut down, her indefinite soliloquy melted into the rapt silence of imagination and, brushing off insomnia, she went asleep.

In the horror of the moment and the muddled aggrieved state of her mind, she was playing mind games with herself, thinking of various options and possible scenarios (hopefully) at her disposal. The thought of going to jail snaked into her consciousness surreptitiously like a low-hanging morning fog. A clandestine escape into the mountains. A tall leap off the New River Bridge. Each fleeting thought was overridden by the next, and she found it impossible to focus, concentrate, or think rationally. Drained, she fell backward into her bed and sprawled like a rag doll with her arms extended. Not a good time for introspection, staring pensively into space. The skull-cracking headache that had been smoldering for the past hour or so finally passed, and she stretched out on the bed, closed her eyes, and massaged her temples. She slowly opened her eyes, continued staring at the ceiling for over an hour, and cursed the man who had kept a tortured sleep at bay all night.

Breathing slowly, she soon felt the tension of the day ebbing from her mind. She pulled back the covers, turned off the lights, and soon was fast asleep. The cicadas trilled on.

Contrary to her best intentions, Nuna awoke in the dark before daybreak, having lost all track of time to the insistent full volume of the alarm clock. She reached out bleary-eyed, groping for the digital clock before slapping it twice and silencing it, savoring the moment of peace. She was in a surly mood and lay propped up against the pillows motionless, desperately wanting to sleep forever. She sighed before opening her eyes. Her body was languid with total lassitude. Her inactivity was delicious for sure. Her chemise was clinging to her back with damp and nervous sweat.

She had had a bad, restless night of fitful sleep interspersed with unbidden dreams, but who wouldn't have under the circumstances that lay ahead of her? Sometime during the bleak hours of the night, the voice came as a dark, menacing echo of a whisper murmuring in her head, "You now belong to me, and you'll do anything I tell you to do." In her state of despondency, his voice was almost palpable. Her head was pounding, and her heart was shuddering from thoughts she didn't want to entertain.

Soon enough, the agonizing nightmare of being blackmailed reemerged, and she had the urgent need to get outside and breathe fresh air. She was whizzing and suffocating under the sheet and now tottering and gasping for air. She needed to breathe as she sorted through the muddle of truth making up her feelings. The galling shock of yesterday was fading, but the reality of being coaxed to commit a felony was arching its ugly head before her all over again. His egregious parting words now seemed ominous, almost prophetic, as she began to understand the undertones: while she was now an asset that he needed, she would soon be a liability to the Maduros. Nuna was well aware of the consequences.

Finally, she garnered enough energy to rise to a new day. Yawning, she stretched. She shoved the sheet aside and eased from the bed, bleary-eyed, dancing around her addled brain and ignoring the queasiness that attacked her stomach as she sat up and swung her bare feet to the floor, running her fingers through her tangled hair. She had tossed and turned all night and arisen at 6:00 a.m. She quickly cinched the sash of her robe, padded barefoot to the bathroom, and washed down two Tylenol and two Pepto-Bismol tablets before tiptoeing to the kitchen to brew morning coffee. She desperately needed a caffeine jolt to lift her morning fog. Taking a dark red terrycloth robe from the closet, she put it on and tied the sash.

As she opened the front door with a mug of steaming fresh drip coffee in one hand to a slowly rising sun filtering into her screened-in porch, a light wind whispered through the tree branches, carrying the fermented scent of early morning mountain dew. Dust particles were dancing in the bright morning rays. The distant whistle of a train echoed off the mountain as she made her way to the doorway. The air was cool, and the lawn was still damp as she stood quietly, lost in thought. The glaring sun was beginning to rise over the mountains, painting the sky red and pink. As her eyes acclimatized to the brightness, she focused on her surroundings, took a deep cleansing breath, and exhaled as if she'd been suffocating. There was an early morning chill, but the air from the now-dissipating dreary cloud cover was muggy.

She pulled out her inhaler and took a couple of restorative puffs. The morning humidity wasn't good for her asthma. The final dregs of fresh-brewed Folgers fell into the mug, and she topped it off with some cream and sugar. She blew on her mug. The first couple of sips were hot and instantly got her attention. The grass and weeds in the yard had grown rampantly this year, and rather than face the ire of her neighbors, she would have to take some time to do some yard grooming soon. She enjoyed the smell of freshly cut grass, but she knew today would be an unfavorable day for mowing the lawn.

Bewildered, Nuna went back into the bedroom full of unbridled consternation, leaned against the wall, folded her arms around her chest, and addressed her reflection in the mirror. Hugo Maduro was the topic on her mind this day. She shook her head quietly, saying, "No" to her reflection in the mirrored closet door. Nuna had no idea what she wanted to become or if she would become anything other than a forlorn, homespun, unemployed single woman living a solitary and ponderous life in Appalachia. Still, she had no misgivings about selling her unblemished soul to hold this job, and its enticements had not been in her plans. Steadfast, rebellious, resilient determination had been inculcated into her by some voiceless omnipotent power, and she had been imbued with a will to survive. In her heart of hearts, she was sure she was doing the right thing. Slowly, she would map out a plan for her future and free herself from the unwarranted trepidation.

Since Chris's death, she had lived by her own pragmatic devices, learning life as she went from her own mistakes. She was not wealthy by any means but not destitute either. She had kept herself isolated from any external intervention or improprieties, especially from men. When she entrusted her life to the hands of a man she truly loved, it ended in a disastrous, heartfelt moment of suffering. She had pledged irrevocably never again to allow herself to fall in love and become attached to and dependent on a man.

I'm a good and honest woman with unwavering virtues, and I will not slide from grace, she said to herself. But, as a woman of the mountains, I might choose to resign to living the rest of my life in total obscurity.

She had lost her mother early in life to an untimely death and had been reared by her father to mature quickly, think for herself, and trust her instincts. She knew she was pretty, college educated, and was well aware that she had an IQ of 180.

She was now lonely and had no one to talk to, but she knew she wanted her freedom back and to escape this predicament. She leaned against the doorframe and buried her face in her hands but refused to weep. Hugo Manduro was weighing heavy on her mind.

She wasn't about to let tears break through the floodgates. They might never stop. That in itself, along with a sudden spritz of electricity coursing through her veins, was enough to keep her forging doggedly ahead and abandoning any thoughts of self-flagellation. Every strand of self-defense in her DNA was screaming *Don't give in.*

Fate, for whatever reason, had steamed, rolled her, and dealt her a wrongful hand of spades. If she had no choice but to obey and play, she would resolutely damn well play to win. She would have to outthink him and square her shoulders in preparation. The thought strengthened her. It cleared her head and fired her determination. I can do this, she thought. She had her career and personal life to worry about; wallowing in angst would only worsen the situation. Nuna would never acquiesce to his tempest of demands. The very thought made her nauseous. The Maduros had underestimated her tenacity and Appalachian spirit.

* * *

The morning unfurled with rays of brilliant summer sun radiating through open windows. While she had had a restless sleep, her churning thoughts plaguing her for the better part of the night, she felt the sudden acceleration of her pulse and the tingling feeling of purifying halcyon mountain air prickle throughout her body. "To hell with the Maduros," she said emphatically. Waking in tangled sheets, she swung her legs over the side of her bed and padded to the bathroom naked. Her throat clenched tight as she prayed for deliverance and shed haunted dreams.

She stepped into the shower, having adjusted the temperature settings, letting the tepid water sluice over her. Steam filled the room, leaving the mirror above the sink coated with a fine layer of misty fog. After stepping out of the shower and towel-drying off the residue of a labyrinth of bad dreams, she brushed her teeth and then laved herself with an afterbath splash. She brushed her long hair vigorously and thought of leaving it to hang freely before deciding against it and tying it into a haphazard ponytail with a pink ribbon. Padding back into the bedroom with a bathrobe wrapped around her, she stood in front of her closet mirror.

Finishing her second steaming cup of coffee and feeling slightly better due to her verbalized self-assurance, she turned on her heels. She retraced her steps back to the bathroom to attend to her morning toilette ministrations, determined to look nice even if she was a tired calamity inside.

Stepping up to the mirror and toweling the steam off it, she studied her naked visage for a moment before blowing her hair dry. Muttering a curse or two at her reflection, she began running a brush through her hair as she studied her pale complexion in the mirror. She wrung her hands, agonized about what to do, and finally decided she couldn't dither any longer. Nuna donned a pair of jeans slim enough to fit her tight ass and legs long enough to get attention should she want it. Then she slipped into a knit cotton sweater.

She again pulled her hair back into a low haphazard ponytail, exited the bathroom, and returned to the kitchen. It wasn't easy being a single female with above-average looks, not in a magazine sense but by the standards of the mountains of West Virginia. Prominent cheekbones, deep blue eyes, and thin lips gave her a patrician air, except for her gently rounded nose. She took good care of herself, not out of vanity and not for someone else, but just for herself and her moral self-being. After looking into the refrigerator, searching for some forgotten treasures, she closed it in utter disappointment.

Since it was Saturday, she decided to drive into town, do her weekly marketing, and take care of a couple of errands. Lack of activity had never suited her. Not known for procrastinating, she had made her bed and would take up the house cleaning later. She emptied the remaining dregs of lukewarm coffee into a travel mug, tugged on her boots, and headed out the door. The sun was beginning to ignite the blue sky to the east with just a touch of a delicious chill in the air. Pulling out onto Route 60, she began the steep climb up Miner's Mountain with a ground fog curling across the pavement like soft puffs of smoke, stopping briefly to view Cathedral Falls, glittering like cascading diamonds in the reflecting rays of the early morning sun. From the top of the Midland Trail, she could look out across the valley shrouded with mist all the way to Sander's Mountain.

Passing the Chimney Corner Luncheonette, the local mom-and-pop hub of the burg of Amsted, an adorable little town just up the road a

bit from Gauley Bridge, she turned around and parked in the pine-nee-
dle-covered parking space on the side of the building. From what she had
heard, the luncheonette had been a staple in town for over fifty years,
offering the nostalgia of a bygone era. Several elderly men were smoking
cigarettes in the shade under an oak tree at the edge of the parking lot. She
hadn't eaten since breakfast the day before and now, already feeling slight
pangs of hunger, she became suddenly famished. The place was bustling
as usual, with a cacophony of good-natured voices and clinking silverware
and the clatter of stoneware. The aroma of coffee permeated the air.

The eatery was packed with the local diehard breakfast crowd, mostly guys wearing overalls and John Deere caps sitting at the counter eating
morning grits with Canadian fried bacon, reading and discussing the
local morning newspapers scattered over the countertop. She stepped
in, and none of them paid her any heed as she passed, a sign of a very
rural country neighborhood. She paused to read the breakfast specials on
the whiteboard set up on an easel just inside the front doorway before
threading her way down the narrow aisle, finding a duct-taped maroon
vinyl-covered swivel seat at the far end of the Formica lunch counter.

She hung her purse on the hook under the counter and sidled up to
the counter and began slowly perusing the interior, regaling in nostalgia
and the laidback ambiance while she waited for the waitress. The pungent smell of sizzling grease on the griddle and fresh percolating coffee
burbling from a coffeemaker wafted in the air. It was the kind of eatery where you knew the food would be good. A no-nonsense, matronly, middle-aged, blowsy waitress behind the counter with large limbs, a
harried expression, and pendulous breasts was plunging her hands into
the soapy water and washing and rinsing coffee mugs. Drying her hands
with a towel, she strutted her way over to Nuna across the rubber mesh
grating on the floor, brushing crumbs off her white apron as she navigated around the short-order cook at the grill and without any exchange of
pleasantries or so much as even looking Nuna in the eye, placed a steaming mug of coffee in front of her along with a setup and a glass of water.

"So whaddaya have, honey?" she chortled with a gravelly voice and a pencil poised over her pad. She had bleached blond hair piled high in a bun, was as plump as a partridge, with deep dark eyes accentuated with blue liner and heavy mascara and lips outrageously glossed in iridescent red lipstick. She then took Nuna's request for a cheese-and-mushroom omelet, home fries, rye toast with marmalade on the side, and orange juice. She watched the short-order cook crack a couple of eggs on the grill and lay down four strips of bacon beside a couple of sizzling sausages as she idly stirred cream and stared into her coffee cup as if seeing visions there and took a tentative sip of the steaming brew. Eyeing a newspaper lying on the counter, she picked it up and began surfing the front page.

The luncheonette was a narrow space with a checkered tile floor leading to a battered red door at the end of the counter marked *RESTROOM*.

The waitress returned within a couple of minutes, setting the plate down in front of her as she moved back, giving the waitress room to serve her dish and freshen her coffee. She began eating slowly as she garnished the plate with salt and pepper, put a dollop of butter on the toast, and then sliced it into the omelet with her knife and fork; the melted cheese within oozed out. She nonchalantly placed the fork down and, using the last slice of the rye toast, proceeded to clean her plate.

The headache was fading fast, and she began plotting the rest of her day as she scanned the newspaper. The laughter and town gossip roared around her. The "breaking news" on the front page concerned three young girls who had disappeared in West Virginia during the past couple of months without a trace. According to the article, the general speculation was that they might have all been runaways.

A comely fortysomething redheaded woman with green eyes and peaches-and-cream skin, generously built, wearing a red cotton long-sleeve dress and canvas tennis shoes showing swollen red ankles entered the diner. She was carrying herself well from what Nuna could see out of her peripheral vision. She came up from behind and tapped Nuna on the left shoulder.

"Morning, stranger, how ya doin?" she chimed lamely as she graciously took the stool beside her, nudging her knee as she slid her legs beneath the counter.

"Mind if I join you?" she asked feebly.

Instinctually Nuna swiveled around on her stool, craning her neck and glancing to her left. She instantly recognized her.

Nuna had just put the last slice of her toast from her breakfast plate into her mouth and didn't respond until she finished chewing.

"Not at all," she murmured solemnly with a manufactured smile.

It was her meddlesome neighbor from up the street whom she barely knew and rarely saw since moving to Gauley Bridge several years ago. Now, three years later, Nuna still didn't know her name, nor did she care to share her heartiness. The woman wasn't the sharpest pencil in the neighborhood and had a nasty foible of being the local one-woman gossip queen and rumor mill of Gauley Bridge. She began fretting and chatting on in a breezy manner.

"Isn't it a glorious day outside? It's marvelous, and the air seems so invigorating."

It was obvious that she kept up with the weatherman. Nuna responded, "I'm afraid that I don't share your enthusiasm. My experience is that the weather forecasts are not that reliable. I believe nature will decide on what the weather will be, and I will just live with it."

Nuna, in somewhat of a snarky mood, had no interest in talking weather or exchanging recipes or listening to the copious episodes of small-town sappy intermarrying gossip being bantered. At the age of seventy-two, the other woman was a retired waitress, involved now in catering tea parties for elderly ladies in town.

"Haven't seen you in here in a while. Welcome back," she said unevenly with an ingratiating smile.

"Thank you. How have you been?"

"Same as ever, aging graciously," she whispered, paying attention to the volume of her voice. "Betsy Bourdieu. Remember me?"

Nuna pushed her empty plate aside and nodded her head like a parrot. "Yep!"

"You sure aren't doing a lot of smiling these days," she teased as she jabbed cheekily into Nuna's side with her elbow. "How have you been doing since losing Chris?"

Nuna chose to not respond.

The waitress cleared Nuna's empty dish, wiped the counter with a rag, and refilled her mug along with Betsy's with fresh coffee poured from a steaming glass carafe.

"Careful, hon, it's freshly percolated and hot," she said to Betsy as she placed a hot Danish in front of her before going back and watching the news channel on the overhead black-and-white TV.

Betsy said without commiseration, "You're young, Nuna, and you seem to be holding up well. Everybody in town says so, you know."

Nuna stewed, wanting to lash out at her, but constrained her hostility. Ever mindful of eavesdroppers, she smiled and let the statement vaporize. News and information in this small town traveled by gossip, sly innuendo, and/or osmosis at warp speed.

After exchanging a few pleasantries, Betsy began to prattle nonstop with the latest local drivel, nattering away from one juicy subject to another with a random assortment of almost comical anecdotes. She then asked a few vague questions about Nuna's life before offering meaningless blather about staying in contact.

Underwhelmed and now grated, Nuna didn't need to listen to her drivel as she stared into her steaming coffee mug, running her fingers idly around and around the rim, waiting for it to cool. She wasn't known for being loquacious and now had enough problems of her own without engaging with a hyperbolic schmoozer frothing at the mouth with vacuous chatter and yearning with a lust to know all the titillating details of her life. Bristling and in a turbulent mood, she felt the muscles in her back tighten. Nuna finally upended the insipid coffee mug, set it down, pushing it away, and cleared her throat, savoring the last sip of dregs.

She deflected the daft questions nicely and, glancing at her watch, gave her voluble neighbor a nod and the magnanimous impression that she had an important appointment to make.

The crusty, rotund waitress with chubby cheeks and a mottled freckled complexion, obviously stressed out, slipped her bill under her cup and gave her a diminishing apathetic smile. Cognizant of a line of people at the entrance patiently waiting to secure a seat, Nuna tossed a couple of dollars on the counter and then demurely rose to leave, pay the deadpan-looking waitress at the register, and exit the eatery.

She swiveled out on her stool, stood up, and closed the conversation with a perfunctory handshake. "Yes'm, I'm running late," she said with vituperation. "Places to be, things to do. The story of my life."

Betsy just looked at Nuna nonplussed and huffed a reproachful sigh. As this was a small mountain river town, she knew that the locals were probably all kissing cousins and had a propensity for nosiness. Like a hair beauty shop or a nail salon, this eatery was a cesspool of tawdry gossip and other malicious innuendos. Betsy would have derived savage ecstasy if she knew Nuna's predicament. But, that being what it is, Nuna didn't want to listen to a lengthy annoying discourse on the latest events in town or, worse, be added to the local scandalous fodder to be bandied about. If the old harridan knew a fraction of what she was involved in, the gossip about her would reach epic proportions.

Nuna breathed a heartfelt sigh of relief that the situation had been mollified without further explanation.

Maduro had Pablo and another hired gun following Nuna and keeping her under 24-7 surveillance. Her phone had been wiretapped and compromised, with Pablo listening to all her telephone conversations. In addition, a magnetic transmitter had been placed in the trunk of her car, emitting a constant GPS signal and the location of every place she went.

Nuna was feeling isolated and lonelier by the day and had an uncanny foreboding feeling that she was being watched. Still, she had seen nothing to suggest that she was under surveillance and had to keep going. She had a low residual level of anxiety humming inside her as she drove home. She was still shaken by what Hugo had said the other day and had a strange feeling of being watched. She was praying that it was just my paranoia.

She made a quick stop at the Piggy Wiggly for some groceries: a Cornish hen, cold cuts from the deli, and a bottle of wine. She was heading back home now under the ashy light of the early afternoon before the ice cream turned to soup. Any more than basics, and she would have to drive south for another hour to Beckley. They even had a Walmart store there. Having unlocked the side door, she walked into the kitchen with an armful of groceries, which she quickly heaved onto the kitchen counter.

Having put away the milk, butter, and eggs in the vintage refrigerator, she opened the kitchen windows. Without her knowledge, she was being closely watched. Pablo had monitored her movements as she stopped at the Go-Mart gas station to fill her tank, its windows covered in posters for Keno and Mega Millions tickets.

The Fayetteville village was soon fading behind her as she unbound her hair and let the cool breeze play with it, taking in gulps of fresh mountain air. She drove her way across one holler after another, navigating the serpentine switchbacks of the Midland Route 60 back to the sleepy hollow of Gauley Bridge. She parked under the carport, carried the pokes of groceries to the side door with her keys in hand, opened the door, and stepped into the kitchen, placing her grocery bags on the counter.

She spent the latter part of her afternoon doing housework, dusting, doing laundry, doing her nails, paying bills, and mowing the lawn. Dusk arrived early that night without fanfare in the central mountains of West Virginia as daylight faded to indigo. The winding empty back roads became narrower and alive with haunting shadows as she passed through green farmlands, with a copse of trees separating open fields. The sounds of the crickets in the endless forest were nearly eclipsed by the roaring treats of Hugo, still pounding and reverberating in her ears.

As a nightly precaution, she checked and double-checked the windows and the locks on the side, rear, and front doors an hour before calling it a night. The moon rose over the gables of the house next door as a flock of Canadian geese descended to the river's edge.

Her home was cozy, and she was more than content to be back home. After plunking a couple of pokes of groceries down on the counter, she put them all away before she made herself a cup of tea and opened the living room shade, letting in a cascade of the late afternoon sun. Her hands were curled around her mug as she inhaled the steaming aroma stepping out onto the front porch. She could hear the swarms of mosquitoes humming on the outside as clouds began to obscure the fading afternoon sun.

A lone coyote howled and yipped an eerie socializing melody somewhere up on the mountain behind her house. It was a dark night with only a partial crescent moon, now obscured by clouds. Nuna smothering a yawn, stood motionless for several minutes, watching the clouds float across the night sky. The wind blew through the holler, sharp and chilled. The screening on the porch was the best thing she had done this year. Somewhere in the woods behind her house, she heard the occasional hoot of an owl piercing the deafening, forbidden silence of the night. It was a melancholy, solitary sound in the yawning silence of the forest, otherwise broken only by the leaves dancing in the breeze.

Stepping back into the kitchen, she stole a celery stick out of the refrigerator. Feeling some pangs of hunger creeping up on her, she heated up a square of the lasagna she had made a day or two ago and arranged a fresh Italian vegetable salad for herself. Then, finishing dinner without procrastinating, she did the dishes and put in another load of laundry before retrieving a much-deserved bottle of Oyster Bay Sauvignon Blanc from the refrigerator and finishing it off as she continued going through the mail

It was now just after 10:00 p.m., and she spooned a measure of her special black tea into an old Georgian pot, poured boiling water over the leaves, moseyed up to the bathroom, and took a long, soothing hot bath. Then, putting on yoga pants and a loose light cotton sweater, she escaped to the living room. A pile of unsorted laundry, which she would attack later, sat on the washer. Ensconced on the couch in the living room, her tea nicely steeped in her favorite mug, she turned on the TV, studying the large rococo ceramic lamp on the end table next to her. It was one of the few touches of exuberance among her otherwise minimalist furnishings. She dimmed the lamp and tried to contemplate all that had happened in the past twenty-four hours.

She wanted to go to sleep, but it was a fruitless endeavor to stop the chatter of her thoughts. A chilly mountain breeze sliced through the starless, somber night air. The past few days had been an emotional roller coaster in her mind, generating a weariness now masquerading as depression.

The bedroom was as dark as black ink. Her skin crawled at the uncanny feeling that someone was watching her every move as she walked from one room to another. There was a faint tingle up her spine and a prickling of the hairs on her neck.

"Overimaginative" she could almost hear her father saying.

But still, the feeling of someone watching her was horridly intense. Finally climbing into bed and burrowing into the covers, she started reading a sappy novel. Time passed quickly. Just as soon as her head touched the pillow, she somehow, miraculously drifted into la-la land.

As she walked from the living room to the bedroom, she switched off all the lights and checked that all the doors and windows were locked and curtains pulled tightly closed before retiring to the bedroom and closing the door. She removed the decorative throw pillows from the bed and folded back the handmade comforter before going to the bathroom to brush her teeth and wash her face.

Instead, she spent the next several hours wired and twisting with fear, her heart running the gauntlet of the myriad things that had gone wrong in the past days. Sighing with resignation, she lay awake an hour or two, staring into darkness and allowing the night to flow over her torpor. She finally dozed off around midnight on the couch, hoping for a happy ending. Something about this night was unsettling her. For a brief moment, she had a strange, disquieting sense of being watched by someone. But she was too tired and emotionally wrung out to put her finger on it. Likewise, her body was utterly depleted and desperate for a much needed hibernation. So embracing her false bravado, she went to bed and got some well-deserved sleep.

She woke several hours later, gaze unfocused but with a clearer head. Restless and needing to busy herself, she threw off the covers, disentangled her arms and legs, stretched, and landed her feet on the floor. She went into her kitchen, filled the tea strainer with some of the herbal tisanes she had purchased online, and grabbed a bag of forbidden potato chips to nibble on. She shouldn't be munching on them, but throwing them out would be wasting food, which was a sin. At least that was her bland justification. Of course, she could stop buying them, but every time she went marketing, she ended up with a jumbled bag of Cape Cod kettle chips in her carriage.

She was in her nightgown and robe. She put the chips away and turned down the lights. The water in the kettle began to boil. She removed the pot, poured the steaming hot water into a mug, and waited for the scalding water to cool. The gentle, soothing aroma of the herbs in the strainer wafted across the room. She moved the strainer from the mug and set it on the counter beside the kettle. Then, carrying the mug in her right hand, she went into the parlor to catch up on her reading and possibly do some channel surfing. Her slippers made no sound on the bare hardwood floor.

Pain overpowered and hammered her head like a sledgehammer. The ensuing silence of the night was almost palpable. A nasty musky odor filled her nostrils, and then she heard his raspy and uneven breathing in the darkness. Don't move, she told herself through bleary eyes, hoping that he might go away. With adrenaline pumping through her bloodstream, her heart was pounding so hard she thought her chest would explode. Instead, his fetid scent grew stronger as she felt him move closer. She wanted to scream but couldn't. She lay coiled under her covers. Her lips were numb, her arms and legs were dead weight, and her whole body felt paralyzed. Panic was threatening to overwhelm her.

He climbed on top of her and covered her mouth with one hand while his other ripped the blanket off her. His body was crushing and pinning her under his weight. She wanted to strike out and hit him and tear his eyes out with her nails, but her body wouldn't obey her commands, and the incubus persona was overwhelming. Terrified, she began screaming. Silent screams of horror tore through her body. Suddenly, jolted awake, the subliminal alarm in her head sounded, and she bolted straight upright, flailing and shuddering helplessly, screaming, and all the horror of the imaginary terror vanished. As the last vestiges of the nightmare faded and she returned to her senses, she opened her eyes and found no one in her room.

Nuna sat there in bed, breathing hard as she found her way back to the present. A small end lamp and the glowing digital clock were still on in the dawning light as her disoriented body, stunned by the vividness of the nightmare, began to come back to life. She placed her hands on both sides of her head and tried to concentrate on what she last remembered. He had no face. Why was my skin all crawly, like someone evil out yonder is watching me? she wondered. She went into the bathroom, turned on the faucet, and splashed cold water on her face.

The landscaping of her world was changing fast. Yet most of the time, she managed her life well. She was professional at work, polite, and friendly to her associates, and she had a new home. Still, not yet fully secure with the underpinnings of her life, she preferred to remain remote.

CHAPTER 15

Bryce
5:00 a.m.

I flicked open my eyes and lay prone for a few seconds, clearing the mental cobwebs of the night. Then, finally, I slid out of bed without needing my alarm. There were artificial beams of light coming from the parking area through several cracks between the drape and the wall. I shuffled to the bathroom, showered, and changed into a fresh set of clothes. The sky was still dark and covered with clouds, but little by little, slivers of dawn were starting to build. I looked outside, and the air was still filled with thick West Virginia mountain morning moisture.

As I came out of the mountains just before dusk, there were occasional wildlife sightings and little traffic, and I now could see the glittering Charleston jigsaw skyline come into view in the distance. Charleston swam in neon color, and spotlights crowned new glass and polished stone towers nestled among the Appalachian Mountains, on the banks of the Kanawha River flowing out of Ohio on the west into the confluence of the Kanawha and New rivers at Gauley Bridge to the east. But, true to form, for several miles on narrow roads winding through the countryside east of Charleston, I had encountered a bridge out. I was forced to take a detour following the foul wake of a dated pickup truck rumbling ahead and spewing blue-black exhaust out of its pipes. If I hadn't shut my windows, I probably would have succumbed to black lung disease. It was still early, but the cacophony of morning traffic was building, with horns blowing, and having encountered a couple of clogged highways, it took me another twenty minutes to reach the hotel.

Pulling into the porte cochere of the Residence Inn, I was still coughing up my lungs as I stepped out. Recovering, I walked into the hotel, rang the bell at the reception desk, and checked in.

The concierge behind the desk pulled her blond hair back; the name tag on her dark blue suit jacket read Gloria. She asked if I'd be having brunch, which was now being served in the dining room. Having had a hearty breakfast before leaving the house, I politely declined the offer and gave her a withering look as she handed me a key card. I had chosen a one-bedroom suite on the second floor and was provided with a city map. Locating a parking slot close to my room, I tucked the Jeep Wrangler into the parking space. Then, I reentered the hotel from the back parking lot and took the elevator to the second floor.

Upon stepping out of the elevator, I was immediately hit with a noxious smell of fresh paint and a faint hint of chlorine coming from the inside pool down the hall. I could hear laughing and splashing from the swimmers in the pool. Without breaking stride, I quickly found my suite, inserted the key card into the lock, opened the door, slid the sliders to the balcony open, and unpacked my duffel bag. I had packed light so as to be unencumbered. The inn was a four-star boutique hotel just minutes walking from downtown and a little over an hour and a half drive to the Maduro estate. Historic Charleston proper, at the confluence of the Elk and Kanawha rivers, was a beautiful metropolis of city lights, trendy restaurants, and boutiques, nestled between the two magnificent rivers and surrounded by the majestic forested foothills of the Allegheny Mountains.

The imposing, glittering concrete jungle of strip malls and shopping centers was in stark contrast to the forty-mile desolate stretch of darkened, ruddy rural back roads that I had just traversed, passing through one hardscrabble mountain holler after another. I had moved through disconsolate stretch of squalid, washboarded, impoverished lined roads with rusted lantern posts dotting the main drag, where roots and frost heaves cracked the pavement on both sides with knee-high ragweed and

a mix of sunflowers penetrating rusted skeletons of derelict automo-
biles rotting away and sagging wire fences. Canted ramshackle houses
in scraggly yards littered the roadside with sagging front porches stained
by acid rain and rusted tin roofs sporting rabbit ears covered in coal
dust, laundry hanging on outdoor clotheslines to dry, fecund gardens
sprouting assorted produce. Abandoned coal mines, boarded-up stores,
factories and indigent warehouses littered the decaying Depression-era
countryside of West Virginia. Undernourished stray dogs lolled and suffered under abandoned cars choked by weeds and bleeding rust, while
neglected barefoot kids in worn hand-me-down mealy colored clothing
bleached by the sun sat in a puddle of stagnant water on the steaming
pavement playing with worms. An old tire swing hung by a rope from
an ancient oak tree limb that grew in the front yard. A succession of
business owners had failed to make a go of whatever businesses they
had started there. The prosperity and mountaineering pride that one
flourished in the backwoods mountain hollers had now been tainted and
replaced by desolation, poverty, despair, and pestilent destitution. A gust
of welcoming breeze blew through, flapping laundry and a few missing
pages of the morning newspapers. Thin undernourished men who once
stood tall and risked their lives in the mines were now rocking idly on
rickety porches in dire need of repair and were strumming old hand-me-
down fiddles as they endured a hardscrabble, impoverished lives. An epi-
demic of drug addiction had taken root. They were no more than a mere
couple of miles apart in mountain distance but encompassed an entirely
different world of prosperity and contradictions in every other respect.

The second-floor corner one-bedroom suite was comfortable and
neat, with a spaciously furnished bedroom with a queen-sized bed, a
large dresser, closet, credenza, and a sliding glass window overlooking
the parking lot. The tiled bathroom just off the bedroom had a walk-
in shower stall, a recessed sink, a wall-mounted shelf, and a toilet. The
living room was comfortable and had the usual amenities: a desk, sofa,
TV, and telephone. A large sliding window with curtains overlooked the

suburban area of Charleston in the distance. Adjacent to the living room was a fully equipped kitchenette for extended stays.

Having methodically perused the intel jackets and reread the briefing papers, each stamped *Classified*, doing background reading for the umpteenth time gleaning small nuggets of data on each and making notations, I sat back in his chair and lowered the top of my laptop, putting it into sleep mode while I immersed and ruminated. The howl of a fire engine passed somewhere in the distance.

It had been a short one-hour drive from Fayetteville to Charleston. I decided to go to the Charleston town hall and check out the property records and any archived transaction records that might be connected to the Maduros before taking a brief tour of the city. After negotiating the gauntlet of homeless persons camped on the main street, I arrived at the library. It was much like any library in any city. The space was airy and open, the noise level subdued. The vinyl floor was a mottled beige, polished to a dull gleam. The air smelled pleasantly like fresh lavender furniture polish. I found an empty table in the reference department and began my due diligence digging into Maduro's business operation in West Virginia. The library tables were sparsely occupied, and the reference desk was being handled by one elderly lady who looked to be sixty if a day.

It didn't take long for me to find what I was looking for in the ranks of books. A vast panoply of information came up on Hugo Maduro and the Maduro organization. Reviewing his property deeds and tax records, I found no outstanding tax liabilities. As I dug further, it appeared that Senator Alan Schiff had approved a state tax official to give the Maduro organization a 100 percent property tax exemption for being a foreign religious organization doing confidential consulting for West Virginia. I attempted to check his income tax returns, but again, there weren't any. Apparently, Hugo was registered as a foreign national with dual citizenship, and all his income was offshore. Yet he was plundering the West Virginia treasury through tax evasions and tax avoidances. The utter banality of the face of evil.

More interesting was what I found on the large map attached to the wall.

There were now several women in the room who were staring at me as I traced my finger across the Maduro estate. Locating the correct reference number, I went to the smaller maps and was surprised by what I found. The Maduro estate encompassed over nine-hundred acres of prime West Virginia real estate that had seemingly been either donated or bequeathed to Hugo Maduro. I copied the deed register along with the page numbers and replaced the register on the rack. Next, I walked to the Register of Deeds Department and spoke to the elderly woman across the counter. "Can you help me?"

For a moment, she looked at me blankly, before saying, "Yes, sir. What can I help you with?"

After I handed her the slip of paper, she had me follow her to the other end of the counter, where she obligingly pulled a large book off the shelf and laid it on the counter. Thumbing through the pages until she found the correct one, she spun the book around to face me.

"This what you're looking for?" she asked.

I skimmed the somewhat straightforward language; the pages reflected the deeds of transfer covering over a dozen transfers dating back six years. The clerk looked surprised, and she glanced at the pages.

"That's interesting," she whispered sagely.

I rested my chin on my steeped fingers. "What?" I asked dryly.

She took her frail finger, pointed at several deeds, and then, flipping the pages, gasped. "No tax stamps," she said.

I nodded absently, also pitching my voice to a near whisper. "Explain, please."

Then, she juxtaposed several property transfers during the same period with the Maduros'.

Leaning down and reading the fine print on the deeds, she responded, somewhat surprised, "It means that most of these deed transfers were bequeathed to the Maduro organization tax-free." Looking up, she pointed to a colored tax stamp affixed to the right-hand corner of a deed covering one hundred acres in Slaty Forks. She said this was the only real estate Hugo Maduro had actually purchased in West Virginia. The rest of the eight-hundred-acres had been either donated or bequeathed to him through wills, all signed and officiated by the local law office of Schiff & Sons.

I noted that Maduro had had a minor battle with the local building inspector while constructing the mansion over the location of the heli-port on his property. The inspector refused to issue the permit and was subsequently terminated by the mayor several days later due to a budget cut seemingly brought on at the instruction of Maduro. Unfortunately, the inspector filed a civil complaint over the firing, but he and his wife died in a fire at their home a week later, and nothing more came of it. The fire marshal called the fire suspicious. Of particular interest was the fact that the mayor of Slaty Forks was Senator Schiff's brother.

I then stopped at the public library and went through a month's worth of Sunday *Charleston Times* collected in the periodicals room. I carefully read the main story and related articles, absorbing all the relevant de-tails. Finally, I returned to the hotel, having spent the afternoon walking the sidewalks around the city, navigating through the mire of swarming crowds of lively pedestrians, listening to car horns blaring, wailing sirens, and watching through Persol aviators citified dog walkers, business peo-ple, and pullulating weekend tourist moving in all directions.

Kicking off my boots, I lingered a moment to calm my thoughts be-fore I started up my laptop again, bringing it back to life and did another gleaning skim over the dossiers, which clicked by my fingertips until my eyes burned and my vision blurred. Then, having burned the midnight oil, with streetlights slicing through the blinds, I called it a night just after 0100 hours and let my consciousness ebb away.

I woke up shortly after five thirty in the morning, having had a rest-less night punctuated by a seemingly incessant thrumming cacophony of traffic and sirens waxing and waning, fading off in the distance. Yet, even with all-night revelers' periodic shouts and laughter down the hall, I was still invigorated and anxious for the new day to start. Morning broke bright and sunny, and the day promised to be nice. Having completed my matutinal ministration ritual proficiently, I clicked around a few TV channels. I watched the local weather station and *Breaking News Overnight*. I got dressed, selecting a pair of jeans, a fresh white shirt, and a tan micro-suede sport jacket. Checking my reflection in the mirror one last time, I stepped into my boots, left the room, and walked down the stairway to the first floor before sauntering down the dimly lit corridor to the hotel's austere dining room, where I had a hearty breakfast satisfying a wolfish hunger. Now, at almost seven o'clock, the restaurant was teeming with a motley group of convivial tourists and white water enthusiasts ravenously wolfing down their complimentary continental breakfast, eager to test their skills in the rapids of the New and Gauley rivers. The breakfast crowd ebbed and flowed.

Picking up a copy of the morning newspaper and thumbing through it, I sat there finishing the last dregs of my coffee before returning to my room to wait for Agent Bomen and Agent Nunez to arrive for their prearranged midmorning meeting. Bright, radiant sunlight streamed through the open vertical balcony blinds, causing me to squint. As I was scanning the newspaper, I couldn't help but take notice of the extensive coverage of the Maduro Polo Gala being hosted tomorrow by Mrs. Maria Maduro. Yet as I read the full front page and the social event story, including each sidebar connected to the article, Hugo Maduro's name had yet to be mentioned. "Interesting," I said to myself.

Having arrived on time, Agent Bomen and Agent Nunez called from the lobby, and I directed them to my suite. After I opened the door, we exchanged perfunctory greetings, and I beckoned for both to enter. I hung a *Do Not Disturb* tag outside the door. Then, I gave both a once-over with scrutinizing eyes. From prior experience, I would first try to divine the innermost thoughts and motives of the two agents from their exteriors as they both sat ramrod straight in their chairs.

"Men, the admiral thinks very highly of you both."

The agents responded simultaneously, "Well, it's reciprocated, sir."

Agent Bomen, at six-foot-four and thirty-six years of age, was an affable guy of heavier than average build with a toothy smile that could have easily landed him in a dental commercial. But unfortunately, it didn't enhance the pleasure of meeting him, nor did his appearance predispose my favor. For lack of a better description, Agent Bomen resembled a Tom Cruise on steroids with a square jaw and a slender nose between thick dark eyebrows.

A lithe, fit agent in his midthirties, Agent Nunez, a pit bull in disguise with a serious rakish mien, could have been the younger brother of New England Patriots quarterback Aaron Hernandez with his close-cropped black hair, dark complexion, and slate gray deep, threatening eyes. He stood at 6-foot-2, was 215 pounds, had broad shoulders, and moved with an easy self-possessed athleticism. With his Ray-Bans tucked into the breast pocket of his jacket, there was a coiled energy about him that belied the calmness of his gravelly voice.

I gave both a penetrating look as they entered. Both had a professional look, calm, with relaxed alertness that I was accustomed to. But, on the other hand, they both had the serious eyes of law enforcement. Observant, suspicious, and expectant. Both were carrying glock-19s under their jackets as we sat down at the oversize living room table, which was about to become the primitive nerve center of the operation.

After coffee and a few minutes of innocuous agency intercourse, they both began to fill me in on the miscellaneous information they had gathered on the Maduro operation, reminding me that it was still sketchy. Austin's laptop logged in an email, and Glenn laid out a topographic map of the Maduro complex, which included an eight-foot-high electric chain-link fence surrounding the perimeter. Motion detection cameras were mounted on twelve-foot polls every one-hundred yards. There were only two entrances, one in front and a service entrance on the west side from an access road for employees and domestic deliveries. Both gates were guarded.

During the conversation, the admiral's name came up, and Austin assured me that he would deny everything the admiral might have said about him, and I returned the grin. Austin was shorter than me, but he was built like a resolute Marine Corp pit bull and sported the legendary crew cut and a fierce face to match. I wasn't fond of exchanging pleasantries or personal information with other agents, but be that as it may, both of us had proffered their hands, and I shook it as my eyes blandly sized the agents up. Both had firm countenance in their handshakes, and a quick release was appreciated. They were both hands-on federal agents, neither showboaters nor politically inclined. They were both rock solid. If there was warmth in the gesture, I couldn't detect it as their eyes bored into me. Having experienced the hell of a battle in Vietnam, I was of the mind that the less you know about your associates, the better off you are should they be compromised.

"Cut to the chase." Fisting my hands and tenting them on the table, I gestured for the two agents to continue with their recent omniscient findings as I leaned back in my chair and interlaced my hands around the back of my neck. Austin had tapped into Interpol's Criminal Information System and found a montage of hundreds of documents related to Hugo Maduro's inglorious military history, arrests, tax rolls, imprisonments, and laundry list of other idiosyncrasies. While nothing had directly tied him to a criminal organization, he was listed as a person of interest. He had been seen affiliating with known criminals in shady locations, but to date, he had no arrests or indictment history in West Virginia. The rest of his intelligence data came from satellite surveillance of phone calls, electronic text messaging deciphered, and other high-tech equipment. The reports from Interpol across Europe and the Middle East all pointed to the fact that the acts of terror taking place in the Middle East were the work of a network of one man: Hugo Maduro.

I was all ears as I shrewdly listened to his narrated erudite summary and warily watched Agent Nunez's PowerPoint presentation outlining and confirming the copious adamantine data he had accumulated over the past couple of months, monitoring and logging the comings and go-ings of individuals from the front guardhouse. I was focused and enjoyed a few moments of listening and analyzing this new information.

"Coming from an impoverished bumfucked ghetto in Caracas, Hugo became a juvenile gang leader hardened like a railroad tie. Hav-ing found a gun in a trash can, he began to commit armed robberies and jack cars. Soon after, he began taking orders from a local cartel for high-valued sports cars and other selections, transporting them to Mex-ico. Having established himself in Mexico with a well-organized gang, he was savvy enough to know when to diversify, offering protection to restaurants he soon owned.

"With temerity, at fifteen years old, he quickly began laundering money through the restaurants for the cartels. Still young with a shark-like, restless ego, he enlisted in the army and rose to a commander in the special forces. Sources describe him as intelligent, extremely dangerous, competitive, and a natural-born leader. Two decades later, he had be-come a multimillionaire.

"The Maduros have a very profitable import/export enterprise, which is, as I see it, a shell company using money gained from his criminal operations. There is no corporate address and there are no brick-and-motor assets other than his two homes. His financials are of interest in that the Manduro Enterprise takes in large amounts of cash from foreign banks, which is in turn deposited through a labyrinth of banks, one being the Chase-Webster Bank in Charleston. Raising a red flag is the fact that the Maduros instruct the bank to maneuver and redeposit the exact same amount to his accounts in the Caribbean or Cuba, Ven-ezuela, and Colombia. My guess is Maduro is unequivocally laundering a lot of dirty cash through the Chase-Webster quietly as part of his oper-ations. Of concern is that they never personally make the deposits. They currently are using a bank employee assigned by the bank manager by the name of Nuna Polinski to personally make the deposits—and only to the bank manager.

"He has become a wealthy oil broker and a ruthless renegade, playing middleman between South American regimes on one side and oil-soaked Middle Eastern regimes on the other. His jet is kept at Yeager Airport; on any given day, he might be in Moscow, Paris, or Madrid. One might say he is high up in the terrorist chain of command and global geopolitical power is his raison d'être. Maduro is now rich beyond the dreams of avarice and a dominating juggernaut not to be reckoned with.

"Bryce, Maduro has an unscrupulous credo: if you don't go forward and conquer your competitor, you go backward and lose. He is the epitome of money and power and, with his colossal ego, can bully and cajole whoever to get whatever he wants with impunity.

"After the collapse of the Berlin Wall, he formed a powerful coalition of shell companies with several Eastern European and Persian Gulf states and a slew of banana republics with anemic economies willing and able to supply him surplus weaponry and drugs of all flavors. In the aftermath of the fall of the Soviet Union, several Russian oligarchs operating out of Amsterdam and Prague began to supply him with shiploads of stolen Russian tanks, surface-to-air missiles, and other heavy artillery. He has a transnational rolodex of this ilk: former IRA clients, terrorists, guerrillas, and corrupt politicians looking to move money out of their countries, willing to do his bidding and enforce his savage and brutal decisions, which includes procured assassinations.

"Having overheard a conversation between two of his soldiers, Hugo rigged an auction for several ships in Madrid and walked away owning two of them for nothing. Three competitors formally complained to the police, and two quickly disappeared without a trace in the harbor. Having heard of the news regarding the other two, the third one packed up and made a vain attempt to reach his private jet. Just as it was preparing to depart on the runway, it blew up and burned with no survivors. The investigation found no evidence of explosives, and the case was closed within a week as an unfortunate accident caused by pilot error. This is Hugo's unique way of doing business. As of this time, there is no accurate data on his actual worth due to his numerous offshore global accounts.

"As for his West Virginia aspirations, he has big plans with unfettered tentacles reaching into the pockets of political and governing powers behind an elaborate facade. Hugo revels in his political connections gained through local social organizations and personal magnetism. He has been brought in and questioned twice for complaints but has never been arrested. But he has a number of business associates who do have criminal ties to cartels. He now has a cabal of some serious political clout, and his insidious evil intent is flourishing.

"He recently purchased several shopping centers, truck stops, and strip malls with legitimate businesses such as restaurants, nightclubs, and home improvement centers and a fifty percent interest in the Mardi Casino in Charleston. From what I've gathered, both the truck stops and nightclubs are spurious fronts for illegal sports betting. According to records in both Morgantown and Charleston, all these acquisitions have been approved and pushed through with the omnipotent blessings of a Senator Schiff out of Charleston and a Senator Assad from upstate West Virginia. Both have recently come into wealth, presumably through investments, buying expensive cars, gambling trips to Las Vegas, and extended vacations to South America.

"Several of the strip malls are located in the Charleston area and have cash-only coffee shops, Chinese fast-food restaurants, smoke shops, and pawn shops, bought cheap for profit in gentrifying neighborhoods. We're investigating and looking at the contracts and ownership of each with the thought that they may be fronts for his money laundering activities.

"Another project he's involved with is two large state construction projects. Two years ago, he purchased the La Rossa Construction Company in Charleston and added it to his business empire. Rumors, yet to be substantiated, have it that he is undermining the local labor union and substituting materials of lesser quality on two bridge replacement projects in Mercer and McDowell counties. Senator Alan Schiff and Senator Sahra Assad have been found to have played instrumental roles in enabling the La Rossa Construction Company to win both bids; this may involve crimes of venality.

"For the most part, the Maduro underground conglomerate is run solely by Hugo with the supporting alliance of a shadowy consigliere operating out of Cuba and an auspicious rogue acolyte by the name of General Garcia in the Venezuelan army. The operation's nexus is mainly run from the benighted private island of Norman's Cay in the Bahamas, the de facto headquarters of his crime syndicate. Norman's Cay is owned by Hugo Maduro and allows him to leave West Virginia at will and live in safety and relative luxury, escaping the laws of the United States.

"Focusing on the best intel we currently have, the island is the locus from which all transactions and directives originate and are brokered."

"Do we have any proof yet?" I asked brusquely.

"Not yet, but we're close, having recently intercepted a scripted communication from the island brokering a high-level supply agreement with an Afghan to deliver heroin on a monthly basis. The transaction was to the tune of a hundred million bucks a month, with the proceeds being split between Hugo and the warlords of Afghanistan.

"A lot of ink and time has been devoted to conjecture and speculation, some of it credible, some of it not so much. I have a host of unanswered questions that needed answers.

"With a seemingly endless supply of funds, Maduro purchased the island from the Bahamian government and then bribed and bullied virtually every political official on the island into acquiescence. The sun-drenched island is no paradise as far as the penurious locals are concerned. Mexican and Venezuelan gangsters patrol every inch of the island, and the locals chafe under a dictatorial code of silence. From that location, he has constructed a small private runway on the island's eastern side for his Gulfstream, which has a transcontinental range. He rarely flies commercial, leaving no trace of his movements or activities.

"They're directing the shipping of arms and explosives to terrorist organizations operating in Africa, the Persian Gulf, South America, and anywhere else where armed conflict can be assured. Hugo has left a steady trail of bodies from Moscow to Geneva to Beirut, Mexico and beyond. The weapons and components are being purchased in shiploads out of Libya, Morocco, Yemen, and a number of other Levantine states for vast sums of money and other offerings, including drugs and human slavery. One of my informants described the sale of young females as his latest venture. Wealthy pedophiles who want their fantasies fulfilled are willing to spend six figures for the purchase. My sources have also traced several large shipments of cocaine, crystal methamphetamine, fentanyl, and heroin weighing over eighteen thousand pounds out of Uruguay, Colombia, and Venezuela with the targeted destinations of Europe, Africa, and the United States.

"Operating on the same wavelength as the Mexican cartels, Maduro has an extensive list of attorneys and politicians willing to grease the palms of local law enforcement and state officials to protect his operations. According to my contacts, the movements of the Maduro operations are rarely detected or followed by law enforcement. When, on a rare occasion, it does happen, as it did a year ago with a drug shipment being intercepted by an alert customs agent, the unfortunate incident is quietly dispensed with and swept away before ever going to court. The source also informed me that the rookie customs agent who made the bust disappeared without a trace. Maduro mules never go to trial, and if by some unforeseen circumstance they are incarcerated, they are freed by police within hours, escaping and leaving by the back door.

"Hugo Maduro has also pursued and developed his own personal breeding program on Norman's Cay for the past fifteen years. Per one resilient girl who managed to escape from the island by hiding in an empty flour drum on a logistics shuttle. Hugo personally impregnates ten to fifteen percent of the most attractive females he procures before he resells them to clients. She describes Hugo as having a streak of sadism in him. Apparently only the healthiest and prettiest female infants are kept and trained from birth for their security forces and future entertainment. The male babies and others deemed not worthy are sold or taken out and tossed into the sea as shark bate.

"On many occasions over the course of the year she was held as a kitchen waitress, she witnessed Hugo, along with two of his close friends, known to her only as Jeffery and Chris, abuse a number of young girls and make little or no attempt to conceal the debauchery. It was like watching a party of serial killers dancing on the patio in broad daylight. It wasn't unusual, according to her statement, for her and the girls to be paraded on the beach nude for his and his guest's entertainment. Rumor had it that Fidel Castro was a frequent guest at the compound but was never seen by staff. His handpicked employees and security staff of well-trained women on the island are sworn to secrecy and subjected to intimidation and elimination as needed. They are also rewarded with large semiannual bonuses as an monitory incentive to overlook and ignore his activities. Overall, Maduro reigns as the supreme dictator on the island, and they know that their future is in his hands. His security force knows that Hugo supports and supposedly generously greases the hands of the political establishment on the Bahamian chain so none of the island authorities will initiate an investigation or even consider intervening in his activities.

"Per my latest communication with Glenn, his wife Maria knows of his sexual indulgences and accepts them as long as he keeps his extracurricular activities restricted to the island. She is rewarded with his wealth. This allows for her prodigal expenditures, their home, their social influence, and her personal comforts, which includes occasional infidelity on her part.

"Hugo and Maria are a huge success story to the world at large and are seen as pillars of the community, running a respectable international business organization. They both serve on all the local charity boards and belonged to the best clubs in Charleston and the surrounding areas. She traded up a few economic levels when she married Hugo, whom she knew was innately evil. Hugo was a stickler for accuracy, and he traveled a lot. Maria had her own busy schedule with the fashion industry so they were apart more than together. They were married on a Saturday in Caracas and flew back to West Virginia the following day. No mess, no fuss, no records in the US: a perfect modern marriage. They were the personification of the American dream, and Hugo wasn't about to lose it.

"Glenn also informed me that Maduro's security team at the Slaty Forks operation is doubled at night, almost as if he might be expecting a raid. In the morning, the security team is reduced to five guards, all armed."

I fought back another rousing wave of angst and growing repugnance as a growing heat coursed through my veins. I paused as I parsed the statement.

"Utter bullshit," I snapped. "The bastard is a ruthless sociopath deluding not only the public but his own wife. He kills women and children as easily as brushing his teeth. He has no emotions and kills without remorse." Just listening to Glenn's report had my blood boiling.

Glenn rejoined, "That's a succinct way to summarize it."

Austin grimaced in acknowledgment.

Maduro was narcissistic and notorious for his criminal ambitions, now moving around in West Virginia with impunity. The obstinate son of a bitch was an abomination, manipulative, and moved his pieces cunningly and tactically. He didn't mind sacrificing a pawn or even a queen as long as it didn't compromise his hold on his power and wealth. With deadly indifference to human carnage, Maduro viewed lives as though they were debits and credits to be manipulated at will. He thought nothing of replacing a thriving democracy with a bloodthirsty dictatorship. And it was now well-known that when things went wrong in his conquests, he would be unrelenting and swindle his way out of it. Nevertheless, he held on to his evil enterprise by insulating himself with calculating manipulations and, through a web of blackmailed and corrupt political associations, seized opportunities with surprising swiftness.

* * *

Bryce's emotions veered between anxiety, anticipation, and rage. He sighed with irritation and leaned back in his chair, marshaling his thoughts.

"Agent Bomen, Agent Nunez," he said in a remonstrative tone, "Hugo Maduro must be taken down."

Bryce adamantly shook his head, giving an angry sigh. Having spent the better part of the last two days ruminating and meticulously reading between the lines and following the bittersweet threads of Nuna Polinski's life in the Appalachian Mountains of West Virginia, he was now perusing notes in Nuna Polinski's dossier and making notes of his own, forming a sense of her Viking character: this woman seemed to have a hell of a lot of substance. Unfortunately, death seemed to be part of Nuna's life. Her mother died when she was a young teen her father was killed recently in an auto accident, and her husband, whom he had personally known, had been killed in Vietnam shortly after they had married. She had grown up in abject poverty, her parents scratching out a hand-to-mouth existence in a run-down cabin next to a coal mine. Beneath her veneer of self-reliance, she had become skilled in cauterizing deep emotional pain.

Bryce had secured her school records and high school diary, and the information gleaned from the records led him to understand that Nuna had to staunchly endure the indignity of being a prosaic coal miner's daughter through most of her adolescence years. Having a single hand mirror from her mother, she looked upon herself as a depressing simple mountain girl. In her mind, she was nothing special and no boy would want to date a dourly mountain girl like her, with a couple patches of acne on her face. Her wardrobe amounted to two worn-out summer dresses handmade by her mother and a faded pair of patched blue jeans. Her home-cut flaxen hair was always hopelessly tangled and impossible to manage.

During her time in high school, Nuna donned an armor of indifference shielding her from attacks from other students. After school, instead of getting involved with sports, she would go to the school library and bring home books of every genre to read at night before class the next morning. It was a two-mile walk on a dusty dirt road to school, and she would wake up every morning early and never missed a class. While she had a family horse, she chose not take it to school and leave it unattended, preferring to leave it in their barn, where it would be protected.

She seemed to have escaped the deep anger and resentment harbored by her social peers who spurned and ridiculed her cruelly for being poor. Nuna was a precocious twelve-year-old child homeschooled until her heavyset, doting mother passed away from cancer.

She was no ditz, Bryce thought as he pondered her accomplishments. Born and bred in the remote Appalachian mountain holler of Coalwood, West Virginia, she was the only daughter of a genteel, poverty-stricken, but deeply religious coal-mining hillbilly family. Her Appalachian mountain heritage was ingrained into her ebullient spirit as she had been forced to grow up quickly from the age of a ten. In reading between the lines, Bryce concluded Nuna Polinski could have been a poster child for West Virginia poverty.

It seemed that she had a wary, arm's length relationship with her teachers, who misinterpreted her lonely standoffishness as conceitedness. At the age of fifteen, she took notice that her body was beginning to show the beginnings of being a ripening woman complete with periods, and she made note of that in her diary. Her adolescent body was beginning to take shape, her breasts were enlarging, and her facial acne was fading. She desperately wanted to be pretty and educated, and at times it would engulf her in a huge wave of unbearable pain.

Undeterred by deep woods, venomous snakes, steep inclines, deep rivers, and mosquitoes, she was a gangly backwoods country girl and a hellion tomboy at heart who enjoyed casing turtles rather than boys. She was an Appalachian mountain girl to her core. Trained by her austere father, she was a marksman with a .30 caliber Remington rifle, 12-gauge Mossberg, and a .38 caliber Smith & Wesson before age ten.

Her mother worked long hours at a local diner waiting on tables. As a result, there were many nights when their supper was leftovers from the dinner the night before.

Her mother died from a virulent strain of metastatic breast cancer when Nuna was just ten years old. It was Nuna's first confrontation with death. Their financial problems became acute without her mother's weekly income. Her upbringing after that fell on her virtuous father, who was known to be strict with no gray areas where honesty and integrity were concerned. Somewhere down the road after her mother died, her father seemingly became disconsolate and retreated into himself and never remarried. Reading her diary, Bryce learned Nuna and her father both fell into a poignant sadness. For unknown reasons known to her father only, he began a fierce one-person grassroots local religious crusade against strip clubs, drugs, and prostitution in West Virginia. He was beginning to draw serious media attention to his message.

Through deep emotional drive, knowing there was no money for college, she studied hard in high school, reaching the top of her class and graduating as the valedictorian. She received a four-year full scholarship, including room and board, to the University of West Virginia. A week after moving to Morgantown to attend classes, she secured a part-time job at night waitressing. While prudent with her money, she purchased new clothing from a small Goodwill thrift store.

At some point during her sophomore year at the university, she realized that all the girls were talking of nothing but their sexual exploits. It was then that she first realized that she was possibly the only nineteen-year-old virgin on the campus and logged it. Having immersed herself in her studies, she again graduated at top of her class, earning a bachelor's degree in finance. The university awarded Nuna a full scholarship to pursue her master's degree at the University of Kentucky. She took double classes and graduated summa cum laude.

She had been married for just a little over a year when she was notified that her husband was killed in Vietnam, leaving her with a painful emptiness. One month later, her life was further shattered when she learned that her father had been tragically killed in a car accident when his car caromed off an oak tree and went over a cliff in the middle of the night just two miles from home. The rudimentary police report stated that there were no witnesses and that he was heavily intoxicated and had most likely been out celebrating and lost control. Responding paramedics who pulled the body out of the mangled vehicle reported that the driver had been killed on impact by a large boulder at the bottom of the chasm before going over the cliff at high speed. He had won a hearing to take place the following week before the West Virginia State Supreme Court involving several popular strip clubs. A broken bottle of local white lightening was found on the front seat, and his shirt and front seat were wreaked of illegal alcohol.

Yet, according to the coroner that examined him the next day, there was no mention of alcohol in his system. Several sources that knew him well, including the local folks, all confirmed that he was hale and hearty and lived an ascetic lifestyle. While not a Bible-thumping man, he was a deeply religious man with the highest of morals and never had more than one or two beers a week. Nuna worshiped him. She vehemently believed that the cursory DUI ruling on her father's death was dubious from the night it happened.

Unfortunately, the incurious accident investigation had been brief, and there was never any evidence that the crash had been anything more than an unfortunate alcohol-related accident. What Bryce found most disturbing was the fact that the official autopsy report showed no evidence and made no reference of alcohol in his blood. For some unknown reason, the inscrutable proof that her father had found and considered the smoking gun for the argument he was basing everything on to stop the political corruption was reclassified upon his death as confidential and then subsequently misplaced or lost. The Maduros obtained a permit to build three more strip clubs a month later. All of these were approved by the town council and given the blessing by Senator Schiff and Senator Assad, who claimed they would bring life back to the area by employing laid-off miners.

Nuna didn't gamble, rarely drank more than a glass of wine, had no drug additions that could be found, and seemingly had a simple flair for a life of simplicity. Morally anchored, she was definitely not a bimbo trailer-trash hillbilly and had a lot of her father's moral spirit in her. She hadn't had a relationship with a man since her husband's death, seemingly unwilling to give her body and soul to a man again. She was self-confident, assiduous, and had a strong sense of self-worth, living frugally, relying on no one, and never forgetting her hillbilly roots and humble upbringing.

Overall, she was a pragmatic overachiever and a committed, focused, hardworking young middle-class widow, capable but underpaid and woefully underappreciated. She seemingly had a reverence for individuality. Until recently, her associates described her as a bundle of energy and infectious enthusiasm, a stalwart employee, scrupulously honest, ambitious but cautious, savvy to a fault, effervescent, gregarious, optimistic, full of charisma, with a sunny Pollyanna disposition. For the past four years, she'd organized and run a successful Red Cross fundraiser in Charleston, and when they were short drivers, she delivered food for Meals on Wheels.

She was a headstrong woman with a lot of moxie and liked to be busy. She had a caged, daunting energy about her that made her seem bred for survival. She was being described now as dour, depressed, moodier, distant, far from her effervescent self and preoccupied with something that she would not discuss with her associates or peers.

Somehow Bryce was surmising that Maduro was browbeating her and attempting to twist her otherwise exemplary moral compass. But, unfortunately, at this point in the investigation, there was no way to corroborate that.

He didn't yet see that she would become a phenomenon in his life.

"God damn it, Austin," Bryce belched. "It's how the son of a bitch gets what he wants," he went on, pointing his finger with emphatic fervor at Agent Bomen.

Bryce's smile had vanished. He was amped. He raked a hand through his hair and leveled his trenchant gaze.

"So…" He hedged a bit. "From the data, you and the bureau have managed to compile, are you postulating that this woman is a willing agent of Manduro?" he asked tartly, belligerently, and almost antagonistically.

An uneasy, long moment of protracted silence echoed within the four walls of the suite as he watched Agents Bomen and Nunez very steadily.

There was not a sound, only a kind of tightness.

Austin and Glenn glanced sharply at Bryce and his abrupt segue.

For no reason that he could articulate, he didn't need to hear the answer as he glared at Agent Bomen with a gathering frown.

"Exactly," he said as Agent Bomen nodded sagely. "For Chrissake."

It was all there in the CIA dossier and Agent Bomen's computer files. He went back to looking at various pictures of Nuna Polinski. Every report added nuance, color, and data to what he was already aware of. She was an outlier.

Good or bad, all the profile pictures depicted an indubitably attractive woman in a conservative business suit, with a pale complexion and long blond hair, blue eyes, high Slavic cheekbones, and a sharp, imperial nose suggesting Polish or Norwegian descent. Her guileless smile exuded warmth and nervous energy. Not a typical mug shot of a criminal by any means.

Quietly, Bryce raised his head and leaned close, murmuring in Agent Bomen's ear without harboring any lingering doubts that this was all bullshit.

"She may have a minor foible or two, but she's not a crook, and there's not a scintilla of evidence to the contrary," he said with certitude, even though he knew deep in his mind that it was still a matter of avid conjecture. But he had to fall back on his axiom "Everything is important until proven not to be."

That's for damn sure, he thought. She's being used as a pawn and doesn't even know she's on the board.

His visceral instincts were sizzling like burning logs in a fire. A picture was beginning to come into focus. His loathsomeness for Maduro was proliferating: the very name of the son of a bitch was constitutionally nasty and roiling uneasily in his gut.

Bryce stared at Agent Nunez intently and, with a gimlet eye, asked, "How did you come to be indoctrinated into the CIA?" Bryce had a slight niggling of discomfort in the back of his head.

"They promised me a life of intriguing adventure," he responded.

Bryce grunted with mock comprehension. Everything about Agent Nunez pointed to an abstemious discipline. He was unmarried and a workaholic in his early forties.

Glenn shrugged modestly. He said, "There's really not much to tell," taking a moment to organize his thoughts. "Do you want the long or short version?"

"Just the basics."

"I was born on a small farm in Caracas, Venezuela, and raised there in poverty along with three older sisters. When the government collapsed, the militias fought each other for control. They began terrorizing the benighted local farmers into surrendering their land and forcing them to manufacture cocaine and crystal meth. My parents refused and were murdered one night, and my sisters were taken by twelve men carrying machetes. I never saw them again. I still hear the screams of terror, smell the gunpowder odor and death. I remember one of them was a very big man with a Cobra tattoo on the left side of his neck. He roughed me up, gave me seventy-six lashes on my back and legs, and then stuck me in a shed. I managed to escape by digging a hole under the shed wall and fled. I found the naked bodies of my father and mother in a shallow grave in our vegetable garden as I fled into the hills. That in itself marked me indelibly.

"I spent many months traveling at night on foot, heading north, taking refuge in dwellings so ramshackle they couldn't even be called houses. Windows were papered over to keep out the rain, old cars riddled by bullets rusting on front lawns protecting rats and snakes. It was like that all the way to Mexico City. I finally got to the embassy in Mexico City, where I applied for asylum in the US. A strange and remarkable country you Americans have. In Caracas, one either joins a gang, goes to prison, or dies young. I got lucky and deracinated from hell and lived.

"Having reached America, I began a sojourn up and down the California coast, working odd farm jobs and reading voraciously, eventually learning to speak English fluently. A year later, I started taking night courses at a local community college and received my associate's degree in English.

"Anyway, a Latino woman that I had met in San Diego and began dating was an active-duty navy nurse who got me to enlist in the navy, where I earned a scholarship and received a BS degree in political science and a master's in criminal justice. Eventually, I became a member of SEAL Team One, serving two tours in Iraq before being recruited into the CIA as a covert agent in Afghanistan. I speak Spanish, Arabic, Farsi, French, and English."

Bryce said, "Agent Bomen, give me a brief summary of your enlistment, beyond your résumé, which I've already perused."

"Doggedly, twenty years later, with a master's degree in electronic intelligence, I retired and was, within a couple of months, recruited into the CIA. The rest of my profile can be found in my file," he said with intense earnestness. Bryce nodded his head with paternal benevolence.

Bryce took out a file from his briefcase and went over its contents. Then, taking a cleansing breath, he said, "We need factual information on his operation" and slid a list of directives to both agents.

Concluding the meeting, they nodded sagely to each other as their goals had been laid out and would be methodically accomplished. They had discussed protocol, and Bryce gave both implicit directives to have little or minimum contact with local authorities as, from what he had so far gathered, most of the local law enforcement spent most of their time hoisting back a few beers and shooting off ammo in the woods. No one was to be trusted, and he damn well didn't want to lose one of his team. Nevertheless, he was satisfied that both Austin and Glenn would be laser-focused and had the talents to accomplish the tasks before them.

As they stood to leave, Bryce gave them instructions that until the operation was complete, they were to address each other on a first-name

code basis and bag the military courtesies. Eyeing the two, Bryce reflected on their über disparity. Glenn was of muscle, whereas Austin was
a computer nerd with a keen analytical mind and a highly perceptive
digital investigator. But they were by any fair measure physically fit, and
both had the traits and capabilities that would be needed: patience, dedication, and tenacity. The ingression phase of this operation had been
accomplished. Bryce demanded perfection of himself and expected the
same from his team. Both Austin and Glenn had the focus and zeal to
perform their respective functions.

CHAPTER 16

After lying in the predawn darkness for half an hour, Nuna opened her groggy eyes. The matutinal sun, arriving from the east at the twilight of the morning and rising over the mountains, was shooting rays of sunlight across the sky.

From her fetal position, she dispiritedly pushed back the fresh sheets and rose from the sanctuary of the bed, swinging her feet to the floor and nesting in her slippers. Standing in front of the bedroom window, she began her morning pandiculation routine, stretching out one side of her body and then the other. Slowly, she made my way down to the kitchen. With the timer set, she could hear the percolator perking and smell the heady aroma of fresh coffee brewing and wafting out of the kitchen.

Nuna stood under the shower, letting the hot water sluice over her slender body, simmering and knowing that today would be inauspicious, to say the least. After stepping out of the shower, she vigorously toweled myself, brushed her teeth, blow-dried her hair, tied it into a bun, applied her makeup and lip gloss, slipped into her pantyhose, and dressed in a light gray business suit. Having given the task a great deal of thought, she would take the check to Chase-Webster Bank and deliver it to the account executive. Her heart was pounding; somehow, she had to squelch her anger and mounting anxiety. Her anger warred with anxiety and doubt about what she was about to do. The imposing image of Hugo Maduro briefly flitted across her mind.

She had been incessantly torturing herself about it for three days, and she finally decided to go to the bank and address it in person.

The Maduro's saw her as a meek, mildly obedient, and malleable young woman with her head in the clouds. "Stupid and dumb Nuna" is what they thought of her. She was brooding at home, bedraggled and wallowing in her forsaken, self-inflicted torment.

How mistaken they were. Brooding, venting, propulsive—feeling threatened now, with nothing to lose, and feeling somewhat pathetic, she chose to fortify herself with a deep breath and brazen it out. She called her congressman and requested an appointment to discuss a pressing banking issue. Not to her surprise, she got the answering service and left a brief message.

Hugo had physically threatened her with an icy ultimatum of violence that terrified her. The Maduros had revealed an aspect of themselves that appalled, repelled, and scared her. She would not work another day with a client who hinted at violence so effectively that she believed him capable of it. Nuna again opened the envelope tremulously and looked at the check. Not known for procrastinating, less than an hour later, she drove to the bank.

At the customer service desk, Nuna took a deep breath.

An affable middle-aged woman with the punctilious look of a librarian did a double-take at the check and looked up at her with suspicious eyes.

Nuna nodded and gave her a look back. Her tears came unbidden and as hot as her bitter anger.

She gave her the check and walked away, knowing that she might have to take up waitressing at Denny's. But somehow, she knew she wouldn't let the Maduros continue to get away with this. She knew she wasn't a superhero, but she had to stand up for what was right. I'm not going to be the disposable hillbilly to the Maduros, she thought. She wasn't going to back down and sit quietly in the corner.

She would never kowtow to the Maduro operation and slide down the slippery slope to becoming a felon. In the end, all she was certain of was her moral ambivalence.

Nuna loved her job as a customer service agent working for the bank. It was a complete surprise to her friends and associates when she resigned from her position.

Mr. Siniscalo, president of the Charleston bank, was immediately disconcerted and anxious over her sudden resignation and asked her for a reason. Her answer was blunt and truthful: she would never work with or for the Maduro organization again.

David Siniscalo was a meticulous person and demanded top performance from his employees. But outside the office, he was affable; some would consider him likable. She had had lunch with him several times over the past year, discussing the banking business. Somewhere along the way, the lunches had become more intimate and frequent.

Nuna at first thought his increasing interest in her was related to her business relationship with the Maduro organization. But it soon became apparent that he was looking for more and his hungry eyes were becoming serious. Upon sensing the motive, she began to decline his invitations and veiled passes. David was married but separated from a very attractive wife with two young children living in the suburbs of Charleston.

Lying on her bed, she recalled her last encounter with him. It was Monday evening as she was packing up and calling it a day. It had been an exhausting day as she was planning her exit from the Maduros. The bank was now closed, and most of the employees had left. David walked into her office and, framing the doorway, closed the door behind him.

He gave her a coy smile, walked to the front of her desk, leaned over, placed his hands on the desk, and looked her straight in the eyes.

"How about we have dinner together tonight?" His voice was seductive, and his motive precise.

Nuna looked at him and smiled. "Not tonight. I'm tired and going home to relax and call it a night."

"You've been working all day and haven't had lunch. You have to be hungry."

"I have some leftovers in the refrigerator."

"Doesn't sound very appetizing to me." He grimaced.

"It will satisfy my hunger," she said.

She stood up, picked up her purse from under her desk, and stepped away.

Before she got two feet from her desk, he reached for her hand and turned her around so she was facing him. He tried to ease her purse from her hand, but she firmly held on to it.

"Nuna," he said with a heavy sigh, looking into her beautiful glacier-blue eyes, "what is the real reason you won't have dinner with me?" David's fingers brushed her cheek, but she stood stoic and unaffected.

Nuna replied, "First, you're married, and second, I'm not interested in having a relationship." She couldn't believe that he had the unmitigated gall to attempt a dalliance with her. Nuna would not deign to engage in a relationship with a married man, especially her boss.

He took a step closer, grabbed her ass with his left hand, and pulled her into his crushing embrace as he lowered his head and attempted to kiss her on the mouth. She fought his raw attempt to force her lips to open, tightened her lips, and turned her head in revulsion. Desperately, she frantically tried to push away from him, using both hands against his chest, but couldn't escape his masculine grip.

"Mr. Siniscalo, pleasssse. This is wrong!" she screamed.

She gathered her strength and, using the right palm of her hand, slapped him hard in the face as hard as she could. Then, when he still didn't release her, she slapped him again and again, then kneed him with her right knee in the groin, using all her strength.

He screamed, reeling in pain as he released her, and dropped to his knees, calling her every expletive he could muster.

"You bastard!" she screamed. "Don't you ever touch me again!"

The unbending lines of her resolute expression and the ice of her eyes froze him. He knew that he had gone too far.

"Touch me again, and I'll file a sexual harassment claim against you. I may even do it now!" she screamed.

"You'll pay for this, bitch. You're fired!" he screamed. "No one is going to come to your defense against me. I'm the president, your boss, and everyone has seen us together many times, and I actively acted in a manly way." He made a scoffing sound as he got up, holding his groin, and straightened his shirt and jacket. "Nuna, you'll learn to be obedient one way or another. It was only at the insistence of Hugo that you were hired in the first place."

She stared at him desperately, hoping she hadn't heard him correctly. His eyes were pained, and she knew that he wasn't lying. The man she hated the most had given her the job at the bank representing him.

"Yes, he wields a lot of power."

She stared at him in stunned shock. Her face paled with consternation.

"That's not possible," she said. Her tone was acerbic. "I applied and sent a résumé for the opening as advertised. How could Hugo Manduro have known I was looking for a job? And you turned me down based on my application. Then, a week later, you called me and told me that after careful consideration by management, I was being considered for the position."

"That's true," he said. "Hugo Maduro paid the branch manager a visit and threatened to remove his money and place it elsewhere if the bank didn't hire you for the position. Shortly after he left the branch manager's office, I was summoned. Nuna, you have yet to learn of the clout the Maduros wield. You were to be hired immediately, with no ifs or buts."

Almost screaming, she said, "He couldn't have known anything of my background!"

David shrugged. "The Maduros make it their business to know everything they can about their investments. And Ms. Polinski, for the record, you were part of that transaction," he said heatedly.

Mr. Siniscalo glaring at her allowed her a couple of moments of introspection.

With a cautionary finger in the air, he went on, "Can I tell Mr. Maduro that you've reconsidered and would love to have dinner with both of us tonight?"

Her entire body vibrated with indignation as she stared at him. Without another word being said, she pivoted and pushed past him in a fit of pique and left without pause, slamming the door behind her. She knew her time with the bank was over, and she was proffering her resignation and leaving proudly. Staying on beyond this juncture would be imbecilic. He was right. She wouldn't file sexual harassment charges against him. He was the president of Chase-Webster Bank, a pillar in the community, and she was a nobody in the West Virginia scheme of things. She knew that no one would risk losing their job to come forward and stand with her, even if it might be in their better interest later on.

David Siniscalo was the catalyst she needed to make the decision she knew she had to make. She wasn't going to go out quietly, she said archly to herself, absently reaching up to smooth her hair. She was morose and silent all the way home.

David Siniscalo's self-assured expression was suddenly emblazoned with that of Hugo Maduro in her mind, which only enflamed her more. The gall of this man and his insouciance infuriated her to no end, and the thought nagged at her like a hangnail on a dry cuticle. She would stand tall and maintain control. Her father had ingrained into her that control was one way to combat fear.

He called her a week later, presumably to apologize, but she fobbed him off in as firm a voice as she could muster. She was a small petite package of a woman, but when riled, she was as hot as a stick of dyna-mite. Unperturbed by his warning and intimidating message, she hung up the phone before he could say another word. He was in no hurry to tell Hugo, he fired her for his own personal sexual flaw. She was feeling her blood pressure rise as she sought to banish the angry edginess that bothered her all day. She would not submit to this coercion. The fol-lowing day, with steeled courage, she resigned and left the company of her own volition, triumphantly. The severance from the bank and the Maduro organization would be swift and irrevocable. She was young, educated, and would find other remunerative opportunities.

Determinedly, she channeled her mind toward fulfilling her last two weeks of her contract working for the Maduro's.

But she spent much time the following day trying to sort out what Mr. Siniscalo had divulged and why the Maduros had gone to such lengths to manipulate her life.

"Well," Nuna said inaudibly, apropos of nothing. A couple minutes later, she did something she rarely did: she burst into tears.

Any thoughts of continuing and reconciling her employment with the bank were stultified, and the perfidy of Mr. Siniscalo was banished. She was adamantly against notifying the authorities and initiating a vituperative attack. She didn't want to get drawn into the quagmire of financial corruption and face the further wrath of the Manduro Organization and possible death.

Her death.

Nuna couldn't shake the feeling she was being followed. She had had the same feeling before, but the feeling was stronger now. She stopped moving, looked around but saw and heard nothing but a frog belching in the fog. Later that night, having agonized most of the day over the information she'd been given, she called it an early night. She double-checked the locks on the doors and dropped the shades. Satisfied that she was safe and secure, she slid into bed and gingerly pulled her down comforter higher, snuggled her head deep into the pillows, and shut her eyes. It was only seconds before they popped open. She ended up staring at the ceiling, counting sheep as a last resort.

CHAPTER 17

Operations had contacted the newspaper and made all the arrangements to get Bryce and Austin on their payroll immediately. While Bryce would still be using his real name, the bureau had issued him a new social security number, driver's license, vehicle registration, marker plates, credit card, and a Charleston address complete with a freelance reporter work history. Austin and Glenn already had their identity's changed. As quid pro quo, they would have exclusive rights to the story upon the mission's conclusion. Bryce would be employed as a bona fide entertainment reporter, and Austin would be the videographer for the *Charleston Gazette-Mail* covering Charleston's social events, including the equine extravaganza and the upcoming wedding of Maduro's daughter.

While it was not expected that anyone would be checking out their background history, it would be untraceable if someone did. Leaving Fayetteville behind, Bryce drove to Charleston and leased a suite overlooking the Kanawha River.

When the chiming alarm went off on his phone at 0500, Bryce woke up as he always did at the crack of dawn: panting, drenched in sweat, trying to remember something in the hues of the nightmares that he couldn't. Waking fast and in the full perception of his surroundings was an acquired trait that he'd developed in his line of work. The merest noise in the night would be enough to wake him. Before his feet hit the floor, he was pandiculating and yawning like a lion. Kicking off the crumbled sheets and covers, he crawled out from the bed and followed the morning scent of fresh coffee brewing in the kitchen.

Returning to the living room, he pulled the curtains open, peered outside, and turned on the TV to catch the morning weather channel and any breaking news he might want to be aware of. The day itself was uplifting, a sunny, crisp morning. Retrieving a second cup of coffee, he headed to the bathroom and began the morning maintenance protocol with the shower. Before dressing, he wired a micro recorder to his chest with his belt buckle serving as the remote. Austin designed it, and he would be wearing one, also. They would also wear highly sophisticated watches that doubled as state-of-the-art cameras and audio recorders.

Bryce methodically pulled on a pair of crisp black jeans and a pressed white shirt with the cuffs rolled back precisely once. Then, stepping into his saddle-brown Western Lucchese boots, he stood ramrod straight at six foot, four inches, with a solid muscular definition from head to toe.

He slipped his wallet into the back pocket of his jeans, put his PR identification necklace around his neck, and inserted his loaded .40 caliber glock into his shoulder holster, which nested comfortably under his left armpit. Two magazine clips were holstered inside his boots. Concealing the armament, he threw on a Nautica suede tan sport coat. What made him attractive to women was the way he carried himself, displaying an air of absolute self-confidence in his distinctive strut, along with the cynical intelligence reflected in his vivid cobalt blue eyes.

Having locked his room and collected his cell phone, a notepad, and the Canon XF705 camera supplied by the *Charleston Gazette*, he walked down the stairs and over to the manager's office, where he requested to use their shredder.

Having shredded the dossiers, he walked to the parking lot, where he noticed the morning hotel maintenance crew huddled, getting their instructions. Judging at a distance, he estimated there were about eight women and two men verbally grousing, mostly a mix of black and Hispanic as well as several Anglos, all in gray hotel uniforms. Having completed his morning analysis, he left in his nondescript rental car, maintaining anonymity. He drove to the *Charleston Gazette* corporate office parking lot on Virginia Street downtown in Charleston proper, where he was met by Austin, working under the guise of his cameraman. He was casually dressed in chinos and a plaid button-down and would also serve as his driver. Having discretely parked his car, they left in a commandeered Chevy Tahoe with *Charleston Gazette* plastered on both sides for maximum public exposure. It had rained during the early morning hours, and the pavement was still steaming as they left.

Austin put the Tahoe in gear and pulled out of the garage with Bryce riding shotgun. He was cursing and venting at the feel of the steering and the lack of power that the eight-cylinder vehicle had compared to that of his new Ford Mustang. He drove north on Lee Street through the heart of the Haddad Riverfront Park ghetto, which was the notorious crime-infested cesspool of the city flanking the Kanawha River, before taking a weak unannounced right from the left lane onto the bridge crossing the reiver; there he got a burst of horns and waves consisting of single digits.

Bryce checked his watch. It was 0800 hours.

Suddenly ravenous, realizing that he hadn't eaten since the morning's single slice of cold pizza, he asked, Have you had breakfast yet?"

"No, not yet."

"Hungry?"

"Yes, having skipped breakfast at the hotel this morning, I'm damn starved!"

"Good, I'm hungry as a wolf staring down a chicken."

Spotting the blinking neon sign spelling out *Sunny Day Diner* in one convoluted loop, Bryce said, "Pull in, and let's get some breakfast."

Austin hit his turn signal and pulled into the parking stall in front of the diner. They could smell the bacon grease. Neither Austin nor Bryce had ever been to this unpretentious diner. However, upon entering the bustling eatery, they were amused and aroused by the old-fashioned diner ambiance, circa 1956, and the tantalizing aroma of freshly brewed coffee wafting through the air. It was busy, but they secured a booth across from the counter bar and grill. A couple of truckers were ranting with the cook over their scrambled eggs. Sliding across the nostalgically red vinyl Naugahyde bench seats and finding a coin-fed table jukebox was definitely a trip back down memory row. They noted the best seat in the house, with no duct tape holding it together. The walls were full of fifties memorabilia tacked haphazardly end to end.

"Morning, y'all" A friendly, rail-thin, angelic-looking waitress with tawny skin in a pale pink uniform with lupine cow eyes and a heart-melting southern West Virginia accent stood standing at attention. Bryce asked her to bring us coffee and a glass of water, mine black with a packet of Sweet'N Low. She quickly brought over two heavy gray mugs of steaming black coffee and glasses of water bearing the diner logo. Having introduced herself as Tina-Louise, she asked diffidently in her most genteel schmoozing West Virginia drawl, "Will y'all be needing breakfast menus?"

Reorienting one shoulder toward her, "I reckon we do," Austin responded brazenly with his unauthentic mountain accent as his eyes rapaciously slid over the overendowed cleavage swelling above her undersized top with practiced mien. Looking fresh out of high school and barely of legal drinking age, with colorful tattooed Disney fairies on both of her wrists, she had clearly come from a gritty past. Her double-Ds and electrifying innocent country-girl façade were meant to collect appreciation and healthy tips from men, and she was clearly a firm believer in "If you got it, flaunt it."

Not waiting to let the simpering waitress read off the specials, Austin ordered a "Lumberjack," which included three eggs sunny-side up, two sausage links, four strips of Canadian bacon, hash browns, and wheat toast. He also requested two packs of Splenda for his coffee. The fresh smells permeated the kitchen air, and the aroma of steaming fresh Colombian coffee wafting out of the kitchen titillated Bryce's olfactory nerves as he perused the menu.

Austin was exchanging a pleasantry with the cute twenty-something Latino waitress with a figure of a model with a tight ass and flat belly trapped inside a prick-tease blouse with breasts threatening to burst her buttons.

"And you, sir?"

"I'll have the morning breakfast special." It was a Chesapeake Bay benedict omelet made with succulent lumps of blue crab, home-grown onions, bell peppers, celery, mushrooms, and cheese. Also included with the dish were home fries, sage sausage, and two biscuits still warm from the oven and light as a feather. "I would also like a double cappuccino with two packs of Sweet'N Low and half-and-half, and I will also need a copious amount of water to wash it all down."

"Coming right up," she said with an infectious country smile. "Holla if you be needing anything else, y'all hear."

She coltishly walked away with a sass in her stride, stealing a covert look back at Austin.

The waitress sauntered back several minutes later and graciously delivered their meals. While they enjoyed and devoured the meals, Austin made Bryce aware that nearly 15 percent of the Charleston police force had recently left through early retirement and resignation due to a lack of political support and half-assed direction from the state administration. With that, thugs were now roaming the deserted streets at night unchecked. As a result, crime had exploded across the city, with people being robbed, raped, and stabbed across the metropolis. In addition, the kidnappings of young girls and boys were up over 25 percent in the past year with zero recoveries.

"Not a good situation," he said, forking up the last of his eggs.

They finished our meals, not leaving a single morsel behind. Then, with Bryce's stomach thoroughly sated, he licked the grease and excess butter off his fingers and leaned back in the booth.

Austin inadvertently picked up the check and gestured the flirtatious waitress over to the table.

"I've got the tab," he said, filching the check from my hand.

Having satisfied the check, Austin gave her a big fawning smile and said in a fake West Virginia drawl, "It's time to skedaddle, but y'all can be sure we'll be back."

"I'll hold you to that," she chimed in frivolously in her Southern mellifluous voice.

With a discerning eye, Bryce just nodded, shook his head in resignation, and smiled.

As Austin returned to the table beaming, he handed him a napkin.

"What's this for?" he said, swallowing his coffee.

"Traditionally, for wiping food from one's mouth. You, however, might want to wipe your chin. You're drooling all over."

Having tried to remain stone-faced and stifle a smile, he failed and busted out laughing, coughing up a little of his coffee.

"Really that visible, huh?"

"Uh-huh." Bryce let out a short, aborted chuckle; he was entertained by the inanity of the remark.

He again just shook his head and chortled as he wiped the crumbs from the table into his hand. Austin was high on octane and low on subtlety, but his dark bodacious Latin looks and his gift of witty repartee attracted women like moths to a flame. For all his bravado, Austin now suddenly seemed more like a teenager.

Grabbing two capped Styrofoam cups of coffee to go, Bryce said, "Let's get the hell out of here." He was amped and ready for action.

Having belted up, they left the eatery fully sated. The leafy country roads that led to Slaty Forks were narrow, winding back roads that crossed a series of bridges that arched over meandering creaks and lined the mortarless fieldstone walls that had been constructed by Irish immigrants back in the 1700s. Several deer and moose crossing warning signs appeared along the side of the road, and having noticed Austin's foot somewhat heavy on the gas, Bryce told him to slow down a bit on the curves. "You don't want to hit a moose this morning."

"You're right, a moose probably weighs as much as this Tahoe, maybe more, and they are known to have nasty dispositions."

"How is it that you know so much about moose?"

Austin responded, "I'm a big fan of Animal Planet."

They drove for another couple of hours or so. No moose, no deer, and just a few squirrels, some lucky, some not so much.

CHAPTER 18

Bryce

Three hours and 126 miles later, having recollected ourselves, we were snaking the circuitous Route 219 heading through the Monongahela National Forest to the isolated burg of Slaty Forks Mountain. The drive was uneventful with one exception, a covey of quail taking their sweet time crossing the road. Having blasted them with our horn, we continued through a number of sleepy mountain towns with nothing more than rusting mobile homes lining the two-lane passageway. The villages all looked the same, each having a combination gas station, a grocery store, and maybe a post office with the American flag flying proudly from a flagpole.

"The locals are unquestionably patriotic," I said drily.

Local speculation, as we learned from the last gas station attendant before entering Slaty Forks, had it that the mountain town of Slaty Forks might possibly be renamed Maduro after the next referendum.

The final curve was marked by an elaborate, well taken care of sculpture garden. Having shown our credentials and been cleared through the ostentatious main gate of the massive mountaintop estate, Austin parked the SUV in the designated tree-shaded spot. We couldn't help but notice a Black Tahoe bearing diplomatic government license plates in the slot next to us. I poured the dregs of my cup on the macadam pavement, and we both scanned the parking lot and photographed the vehicles and license plates. There was a phalanx of cars resembling a collector's car show: Rolls-Royces, Bentleys, Porsches, Saabs, Mercedes. Our Tahoe was just another classic one, albeit not the nicest one. After gathering our gear, we alighted the SUV. The revelry had already begun.

Austin and I put on their aviators and slowly ghosted our way toward a buzz of activity on foot ascending the hill in different directions as part of our covert observations, basically getting a lay of the land at this point. Austin was to work his way around the perimeter videoing the grounds and the thoroughbred racehorses being kept in the air-conditioned barns, including the saddling up and the polo event. If possible, he would map out the gravel service road on the back side, which seemed to meander in a serpentine fashion through the middle of an undeveloped section of abandoned farmland for a couple of miles to the south. The security gate was locked 24-7 and monitored by closed-circuit cameras at a second guard station with a high heavy-duty iron sliding gate. He would tap into the system and look for and document all that ingress and egress, along with any anomalous behavior associated with the event. I would cover the event's festivities, interviewing and taking photos as I went. Feeling relaxed, I rolled up my shirtsleeves and jacket cuff halfway over my wrist, grabbed my camera from the back seat, and exited the car.

As I sauntered up the marble walkway to the main gathering, I couldn't help but notice Maduro's chopper. The glistening blue Bell 206B sat on a concrete pad surrounded by well-manicured grass next to a couple of tennis courts. Several golf carts were parked nearby. The courts could also be used as a helipad if needed. Standing beside the tethered chopper were two burly guys in uniform conversing. One was most likely the pilot, and the other a guard shouldering a menacing-looking Uzi.

I slowly wended my way unostentatiously through the gaggle of soulless, carelessly dressed paparazzi barracudas already gathered on the meticulously manicured lawn hoping for a titillating story about Maria Maduro to sell to the *National Enquirer* and other sensational supermarket tabloids. With a plastic bottle of Evian cradled in my left hand, a small dish of fresh hors d'oeuvres in my right, and a bulky Nikon digital camera slung around my shoulder, I continued to meander about the rich, famous, or influential. Or a combination of all. There were surveillance cameras everywhere. Locating Nunez already aligned with the crowd, I gave him an inconspicuous nudge as we moved away from the periphery of the media cluster and went in different directions to reconnoiter. A reggae band played by the rose garden.

Nunez, having applied his charismatic indefatigable persuasion with just a stroke of rakish serendipity, had insidiously inveigled his way into the trust of Maria and had been fortuitously reassigned by her to be a roving undercover security guard for the polo gala. His penetration of the Maduro operation was on schedule, and he could survey the compound for points of interest and vulnerability without drawing attention. With a well-trained, keen eye, I quickly noticed that he was wearing a congruous shoulder holster under his denim shirt, which was unbuttoned over a tank top and cargo shorts. I was carrying as well, but my pistol was tucked into the back waistband of my jeans under a field jacket.

I was killing time, scoping out the mingling crowds of indistinguishable guests and other swirls of microsocializing gatherings with trained and practiced eyes disciplined by battle, always moving. I wore the leather jacket to carry a lot of stuff. Pockets were necessary as a freelance photographer. Today my pockets were stuffed with extra batteries, film lenses, and all sorts of tools of the trade including maps of the property, various forms of identification, and concealed cash. Wandering the campus, clicking away, I was staggered by the estate's opulence and ambitions. As I walked the grounds, my eyes roamed, probed, pierced, and incised the glistening gaiety. Always on the point, I was able to make quick discriminations and judgments as I went.

Glenn had already alerted us that security cameras were in ten sections of the compound. Nevertheless, I kept my emotions in check, and my facial expressions didn't change.

Austin was out back interviewing and photographing the participants in the lavish polo event. One smile like the one he was bestowing would draw people to him, especially women. His charisma and sex appeal would be doled out as necessary to accomplish his task. Men and women were attracted to him, wanting to be his friend.

It was a balmy first day of July. All the women were eagerly cavorting and flaunting their sartorial prosperity under flowery parasols. They were all enshrined in glittering pearls, diamonds, and other jewels normally sequestered in a safe or bank vault. The pageantry of glitter-polished nails before me bespoke affluence. All were flamboyantly embellished in bright flowery summer dresses and jumpsuits, wearing an astounding array of wide-brimmed floral feathery bonnets set at various jaunty angles, each striking and specially designed for formal display at the event. Their posture was so rigid that they walked like they all had sticks up their haute couture asses. But it was an eclectic crowd.

As I moved casually through it, a couple of women turned and ogled me. Paying them no observable attention, I moved on doggedly, wending my way slowly through the crowd. Most of the men were presumably sports figures, entertainers, bankers, and prominent people with aristocratic political clout indulging in casual folderol. I suspected that there might even be one or two cartel ambassadors roaming the grounds. All aspired to a dapper look, fedoras included, displaying the latest vogue in clothing. Most were wearing crested linen blazers with matching slacks and loafers. Several wore more serious faces and were lurking in the shadows watching for unfestive activities. They were obviously part of Maduro's security detail.

All were walking around trading old tales and proffering new ones. The babble of conviviality and laughter was everywhere. The others were being ambushed and jostled by one rapacious reporter after another, pointing cameras and recorders at them in a desperate attempt to get a media exclusive.

For a moment, I thought I might be at the Kentucky Derby, and while my shirt and jeans were clean, I felt dressed for the stables. Nuna, slowly moving across the well-manicured turf at the leisurely gait of summer under azure-blue skies speckled with lazy drifting clouds, came to an abrupt halt as she spotted an unusual man standing with an expensive camera several yards before her. By virtue of his sheer physicality and apparent masculine strength, he was drawing her attention away from the activities at hand as he couldn't or maybe shouldn't be ignored. However, she couldn't help noticing the bulge of his shoulders as his shirt pulled tight against them and decided to move closer and take his measure.

Having threaded my way through the undulating gatherings, I stepped back to make a minor adjustment to the camera's strobe. The fragrant pheromone scent of Obsession wafted buoyantly in the sultry air around my head. The subtlety of the scent alone held me in thrall, identifying that it was a woman standing behind me, and very close. If she hadn't moved away quickly, I'd likely have backed up right into her. I inhaled deeply and meted the air out ever so slowly.

As I turned around, our gazes locked. Seconds ticked off ponderously while we continued to stare at each other as if mesmerized. I was staring into her cerulean topaz eyes set in high Slavic cheekbones, noting her imperial nose surrounded by a thick, lustrous crown of long flaxen sun-kissed hair cascading below her shoulders. Despite an absence of adornment, she was drop-dead gorgeous and of my age, tall, svelte, on high tensile alertness, her well-endowed, firm bosom heaving fetchingly in the sunlight, with a smoldering air of innocence. The other women there would pay handsomely to have what this Grecian goddess had. But she wasn't flaunting affectations in any way, shape, or form.

I felt my pulse jump as I immediately recognized her from her file and, for some unexplained reason, was smitten by her presence. But, of course, having seen her up close, I realized the file photo didn't do her justice. She was much prettier than she appeared in her photo and captivated my attention as it had never been captivated before. Nuna actually could be a twin voluptuous sister of Goldie Hawn, without a trace of lasciviousness. Just below her deep mischievous blue eyes was a magical dusting of light freckles, and I found myself longing to place a kiss on each one. Our eyes beseechingly locked in one of those shining, scrupulous moments of epiphany.

I stilled and waited rapaciously in consternation for her to say something, giving her a long connoisseur's appreciation. She didn't, instead she smiled with a voluptuous mouth flickering upward and putting on a demure and reticent look. I raised my eyes to hers and returned the smile covertly as I slowly set my camera down.

There was a moment of prolonged silence as I gave her a disarming grin. I'm ordinarily comfortable conversing with women, but I was momentarily mute for a protracted moment. A very brief moment.

"Hello, ma'am," I said breezily and without preamble, unable to think of anything at that second more intelligent, my radar beeping like an incessant alarm. "I don't believe we've met," I added with an intriguing covert smile and a measured look, extending my arm and greeting her with a cursory handshake. "But you certainly attracted my attention. I might add, you smell amazing."

My attraction to her was distinctly masculine, and I responded the way any heterosexual man would to that feminine stimuli. While desire slammed into my groin like nothing had ever before, I willed my erection down.

Not going there. Not yet, I thought. I wasn't proud of my desire, but I wasn't ashamed of it either.

Barely managing a delicate smile, she could barely form a coherent thought, much less engage in converse with this man exuding a self-assurance that reflected an intelligence that bordered on shrewdness.

My first thought was that the surveillance photos that had been taken hadn't done her physical endowments justice. Not one of the photos of her had prepared me for my first glimpse of her in the flesh. She was slim and lithe and had to be spending some serious time in a gym.

Nuna wasn't just pretty; she was beautiful.

While one could easily see the melancholy air of loneliness and depression in her arresting blue topaz eyes, I could also see that she exuded a beauty that was deeper than her extraordinarily flawless complexion, bereft of makeup. She also radiated an intense, fearsome intellectual sparkle in her eyes that arrested my attention. She had the aura of a delicate, bewitching young woman but was strong as a willow. It would be easy to spew some uplifting platitudes, but they would only insult her intelligence, and we both knew it. Even without makeup, her slanting almond shaped blue eyes eyes were arresting. With her sunlit hair, she looked summery and golden.

Unlike the other women strolling the jubilant festivities and circulating among the party guests in the unseasonable heat, she was poised, sculpted, graceful, and not ostentatious. Nuna wasn't a slavish follower of the glamour party dress code for some inexplicable reason. She was demure, quiet, and wasn't toting a parasol, wasn't wearing a bonnet or a flowing dress. Instead, she dressed casually in an elegantly simple trendy gray pencil knee-length skirt that perfectly fit her lithe size-six body. She was wearing low, sensible heels and a silky white sleeveless cotton blouse cut to reveal just a suggestion of provocative cleavage. Her mane of blond hair cascaded down the nape of her neck on both sides, framing her exotic face. Her chiseled features, naturally tan and unblemished, stood out prominently, and above them, her beguiling eyes were sultry. Her rosebud lips were painted in glistening eggplant gloss, her nails and eyebrows were manicured, and she had a vivacious self-possessed demure bearing about her that was stunning and bespoke the professional class. I was having a hard time believing that this coveted svelte goddess was so close to me. Her separatism intrigued me.

* * *

Bryce, standing still and looking around through aviator sunglasses in a deceptively casual pose, radiated tangible aloofness, masculine strength, a brooding intelligence, and a calming influence of self-confidence. Apparently, he worked out at a gymnasium daily, she thought, noticing the corded tendons in his forearms.

Nuna looked at him coyly with a quick, comprehensive glance and was again mesmerized by his daunting, dangerous size and rugged,

windblown, sunbaked attractiveness that almost personified the gravitas of a Greek God who had somehow come to life. Enthralled, she
drew in a quick, sudden breath and smiled demurely. This man topped
most men by several inches, even those considered tall by normal standards. Somehow she expected reporters to be myopic, rangy, and garru-
lously annoying, with a light meter dangling from a cord around their
necks. This absurdly deeply tanned, square-jawed formidable hunk of a
man with the honed herculean body wasn't any of those things. This was
a man that wasn't to be messed with. He screamed badass from head to
toe. Six-foot-five, 220 pounds, suave, swarthiness to his skin, provocative shape to his mouth, teeth white and straight, devilishly and devastatingly handsome, weathered angular face, a corded neck nearly a head
taller than her, clean-shaven and stern, a craggy face, lithe, long-legged,
muscular arms with broad shoulders, a tight butt, and a shoulder-length
thick mane of unruly dark blond hair and compelling dark storm-cloud
cobalt blue eyes that could etch steel. He exuded a pugnacious brooding
in his snug jeans, with sleeves rolled up and an arresting virility that
confounded her but a sort of benevolence, too, even in repose. That
unidentified sonorous quality in his voice was dangerously erotic, virile,
totally alluring, and potentially a fatal attraction, leaving her with a
sense of profound helplessness.

He wore ironed jeans, a white shirt covered by a corduroy sport coat
with patches at the elbows, and Western boots. She was unaware of the
fully loaded glock holstered in his belt under the jacket. The burning
sizzle and invisible shivery little tendrils of desire that suddenly coursed
through her body, stirring the hair on the nape of her neck, were making
her body throb and go all gooey inside. She fantasized about running her
hands over all that sculptured hard-bodied splendor and kissing every
nuance of that chiseled mouth.

Nuna was experiencing a feeling she had never felt before as she
looked into his unwavering blue eyes, which spoke of considerable masculine experience and danger. But what should have been sinister was

actually scintillating. He gazed back at her like a steady emerald flame. Self-conscious at having been caught staring, she turned and looked away. Her usually well-restrained emotions were now in upheaval, and she had just met him. He was female catnip.

She had unbidden thoughts floating through her mind of butterflies taking flight and a pang in her heart fantasizing about him coaxing her into his bed and having mind-blowing sex with her. But it wasn't going to happen, not yet anyway, she told herself, taking a step back and rocking her head from side to side as if she were debating whether or not to give him her name.

She would rely on her professional demeanor and an accent so thick that Bryce could swear that she had never left the hollers of the mountains. Two days ago, she couldn't have imagined a man like him. Nor could she have imagined that she'd be feeling the way she was feeling at the moment. Her life didn't allow for such weakness.

"My name is Ms. Nuna Polinski," she drawled coquettishly in a soft pronounced Southern West Virginia–tinged voice that wandered up and down the scale like the mountain switchbacks without a hint of inflection.

"And yours might be?" she asked coyly, pushing back a tendril of her blond hair.

He processed a plethora of possible clandestine undercover aliases before deciding on covert affectation. "Bryce Tucker, ma'am," he said with a low, controlled cello-mellow voice, a smirk in his grin, and a hint of an Irish lilt. He was treading a delicate line here.

Bryce was surprisingly amused by his own discomfiture.

Proffering his hand out to her gingerly, he continued, "I'm a photojournalist currently filling in as a social event reporter with the *Charleston Gazette*."

She reciprocated with a warm, ceremonious handshake, and electricity flared between them as their eyes met. The hand that she shook heartily was nothing close to what she had expected. His hand was solid, calloused with hardened knuckles and nails clipped and clean. Not the hands of a writer or one that only attacked keyboards. Her dubious gaze was both skeptical and searching as she slanted her head, scrutinizing the press pass hanging around his neck.

Meeting the intriguing Nuna Polinski at the Maduro event was fortuitous, he thought silently to himself as he scanned the grounds, getting the lay of the land. From what he understood, over two hundred people were attending the gala. Thoughts began to percolate through his head.

"Are you not partaking in the festivities?" he asked conversationally as they moved at a casual pace with him swiping a stray hair off his brow.

"I don't want to be looked upon as a brooding person. I only wish that this equine lollapalooza had a higher, benevolent purpose, like feeding the hungry or helping homeless veterans," she whispered, maintaining her professional persona. Her composed façade and gracious smile belied the tumult and quivering agony within.

Bryce almost choked but managed a tight nod. It was as if his mind had become opaque, and she, with uncanny accuracy, was on to him, having penetrated his inner thoughts about the gala.

'I'm somewhat confused as to what you mean," he cajoled, not wanting to embarrass her.

She gazed up at him and obliquely smiled a tad defensively.

"My female intuition says that I think you do," she said wryly. "But don't worry. My lips are sealed." She gave him a skeptical look. "I'm sure Mrs. Maduro will be most interested in you interviewing her. Your article will aggrandize her and subsequently place her on the top of the Charleston social pedestal and reward her with the social grace and prominence from the coterie of politicians she seeks."

Bryce quietly looked at her in perplexity. So what's a woman like Nuna doing working for the likes of the Maduros? He thought "From what I've read, the mistress of the manor is unfailingly all careless sophistication and ageless beauty and grace."

She indulged him with a conservative laugh.

"Y'all studied her well, and yes, she's not a cerebral slouch by any stretch of the imagination."

With the lingering scent of Obsession in his lungs, he continued to stare at her fine features and assess her attributes.

"You say that like it's a bad thing," he said dubiously with a hint of mirth as he shortened his long stride to accommodate her slow Southern gait.

"No. I'm sorry, but I'm not quite myself today, that's all. I'm just somewhat envious," she said unequivocally, feigning a sweet smile. The words came out before she had time to consider them.

Bryce gave in to temptation and glanced briefly at Nuna. She was half turned away from him. He was astounded that if you didn't look in her eyes, she seemed younger than he knew she was. Her body, athletically fit and so tightly strung, rightly or wrongly implied confidence and imperturbability. She all but vibrated with verve and ardor. Lightly tan skin, a gray pencil skirt, and a silky white cotton blouse that just revealed a small rose tattoo on her collarbone. He wanted to lick it.

She had an enigmatic expression on her face, a blend of elfin innocence, sensuality, and quiet lament without a hint of affectation. She had an air of precise delicacy about her.

CHAPTER 19

This is one hell of a bad time to get a boner, he thought to himself as he chortled fervently.

But here she was, being dwarfed by him in his shadow. Her dossier had intrigued him; his attraction to her effervescent personality felt visceral, and her candor was beyond description. Something was challenging and flinty about her eloquence, but at the same time, she was vulnerable, with a susceptible heart, and he wanted to take her into his arms and care for her for eternity. I would also like to lick the red lipstick off her lips, he thought. The warmth she radiated, the intellectual honesty of her voice, and the mesmeric sensitivity in her eyes were filled with an unintentional seductive appeal.

Looking around restlessly but inconspicuously with a keen discerning eye, he mentally cataloged those that attended the gala as they slowly meandered, chatted inconsequentially, and tread around at a languid pace engaging in desultory conversation.

He said, "Given the high-profile nature of this event, I was under the impression that everybody here would be of high society caliber and be either of old money or new money, a celebrity, a well-heeled luminary, a powerful politician, or a filthy rich, influential landowner."

Bryce was looking at her quizzically, waiting for an answer.

Being careful to ameliorate her tone, she replied haltingly in a sibilant whisper as she absently hooked strands of her long hair behind her ears. "Not everyone," she said somewhat piously, giving him a single comprehensive glance. "The Maduros only invite those who can enhance their political power and financial enterprise."

"As for the staff," she averred, "the Maduros employ a phalanx of benighted servants, gofers, guards, secretaries, butlers, maids, chefs, chauffeurs, gardeners, some permanent, some temporary. And some of us are expendable factotum outside contractors providing professional services as needed. We all get to enjoy the festivities, but first, we have to be vetted and prove our devout obedience and shameless sycophancy to the king and queen. After that, the staff will shine shoes, make beds, wash floors, cook, clean toilets, wash dishes, and do whatever else the Maduros tell them to do. And since many are either downtrodden undocumented immigrants or unemployed locals, they've all been subjugated to their rule and are seemingly grateful for the chance to work on the estate regardless of their exploitation."

Nuna hoped Bryce didn't catch the harsh bitterness in her choice of words.

Her words were a surprise and instantly had his attention.

With a perceptible pause, he looked at her and smiled, giving her a truncated nod of understanding.

"Nothing surprises me anymore," he grumbled with chagrin.

"Yeah, I've heard that the Maduros are a couple of self-righteous fanatical bastards," Bryce said sotto voce.

"They're both narcissistic," she whispered conspiratorially in a shaky voice. "They're like two active volcanos, and you never know which one is going to explode. Whatever they ask for is expected to be complied with without a quibble. Noncompliance with their wishes is met with a veiled threat of severe consequences for which there is no appeal."

"I don't believe that I've seen him. Is he here today?" he said coaxingly.

He gave her a long, searching look as he continued to listen to her pejorative description of the Maduros.

"While I can't personally attest to it, rumor has it that they live separate lives despite being a married couple. As a result, they have separate suites and separate libraries on the second floor."

"Have you ever been inside their mansion?"

"Yes. Mrs. Maduro has had me join her in her library a couple of times. Mr. Maduro also owns an island in the Bahamas; as rumor has it,

Maria has yet to go. But, as with this gala, they do occasionally entertain together," she said through pursed lips. She knew her pensive response was too loathing and curt, but she couldn't help herself. Maduro flat-out terrified her.

Nuna suddenly became catatonic, in the process, Bryce divined, of concealing her fear.

"Forgive my indelicacy, Mr. Tucker." Nuna looked uncomfortably at him with keen perception. "I may be out of line saying this, but it's been festering in my mind. In hindsight, I am trying to remember your name on the invitation list I put together."

She gave him a quelling look. Bryce squelched a grimace, turned away from her gaze, and repeated that he was researching the possibility of doing a feature article on Mrs. Maria Maduro. The original entertainment reporter that was assigned had a medical emergency and had to leave unexpectedly on a flight to Alberta. He pushed his fingers through his mane of hair, then ran his hand around the back of his neck. "I'm taking his place during his absence."

Her wide blue eyes were now slits of suspicion. When he looked at her again, she was still dubiously looking at him with a furrowed brow and a hint of skepticism. While she hesitated, he sensed her reluctance and unwilling curiosity.

Bryce found himself in a precarious position. He couldn't reveal his identity to her without exposing his mission. She was still suspected until proven to be an innocent pawn of the Maduros. He was hamstrung but had to continue to act out his role with aplomb stealthily. Should Maduro learn of his intent, he would immediately be persona non grata on these grounds.

"Mr. Tucker, you look better suited to cover an NFL game as a former quarterback."

Bryce shrugged noncommittally, answering evasively. "I'm a freelanced reporter, and while I love to watch football, I go where the editor sends me," he said, smirking.

Casting a quick, furtive glance over her shoulder, Nuna tracked him like one of those mysterious paintings that appear to follow your every move. She gave him a bewildered, quizzical look of latent incredulity, a bit wary, a bit skeptical, but she didn't probe further.

He'd seen many beautiful women in his life, but none had the ability to be hypnotic and blow his concentration to hell as she did. She was goddamn stunning.

Nuna, with a feeling of awe, stared at him with a saccharine smile. She was suddenly conscious of a warm glow pulsing deep inside her as she was finding him to be not only charismatic but a very masculine specimen of a man of intense beauty. She'd successfully blocked feelings of intimacy, but now they were glaringly obvious, and his presence was making her feel more alive than she had been in years. It was a new chapter in her life that she would have to deal with.

Mere days ago, she thought that her world was collapsing. Now it was beginning to come alive with a new, exciting glow.

A woman's sudden burst of beguiling laughter rose above the sound of the soft Latin music as she threw her head back in histrionic abandon. Statuesque was Bryce's initial impression of Maria Maduro as she posed for various shots dressed to the nines and larger than life, in her element. Maria waxed poetic at the microphone and was skilled at turning on bedazzled charm at will to disarm an adversary or critic and promote herself. She made a single superfluous gesture, then turned, or bowed, barely touching the hands that reached out to her. Bryce stepped forward and fired a half dozen shots before snapping one last shot of the mansion in the background. She had a reputation for arrogance and pomposity, and she made it her business to be photographed with an array of politicians, important state dignitaries, and other officials as often as possible. She was wearing a set of colorful feathered bonnets atop her carefully coiffed hair with unmistakable gravitas and panache, standing tall in shimmering four-inch stiletto heels and wearing what looked like a two-thousand-dollar summer dress with equine patterns and an enormous string of pearlescent pearls around her neck. Maria Maduro was truly svelte and sophisticated, with a figure that most women in their twenties would have coveted, he thought sophomorically. Her hair flaring out graciously from her bonnet was perfectly coiffed, her nails flawlessly embellished, and her waist was pathologically trim. She was gesticulating, making her rudimentary introductions, acknowledging the enthusiastic plaudits and claques from the crowd, and now responding uproariously to some obviously ecstatic witticism that a Spanish-looking young man had said to her. Then, with just a trace of her patented sunny smile, she suddenly hesitated, apparently considering the correct posture to affect.

"The glacial queen?" Bryce asked, craning his neck and squinting with one eye to get a better view. "See a lot of her in the society pages. Haven't seen any evidence of the glacial king, though."

She waited for a beat of prolonged silence, then responded with an even voice, "He's a very private man, and his desire for privacy is legendary among his legions of associates. This is the first event he's ever made an appearance at that I'm aware of. Maria is public face and gloating spokesperson for this equine exposition and the debutante ball that follows. Maria is a snob to most, but her skill of urbane prodigal elocution elevates her as a regaled sweetheart to those in power—who could be used to advance her status further."

"I take it that this is an extraordinary circus," Bryce said.

"I reckon it is," she whispered. "I'm betting that Mrs. Maduro expects this desultory shindig to cement her position on the board of directors of the Charleston Art Museum."

"That's important to her?" Bryce asked as he removed a large coin from his jeans pocket and deftly rolled it back and forth across the backs of his fingers.

"She has no compunction about using her beaucoup money and guile to get on the board of directors," Nuna said absently, staring at Bryce incredulously. "She has become involved in a number of local social charities and ramrodded herself into becoming West Virginia's foremost advocate for a half dozen other local causes, all of which are self-serving charades for the Brazilian virago. Unfortunately, none help the homeless or provide food or medical treatment to the poor."

Maria stepped to the podium at a sedate pace with her feigned panache and Mona Lisa smile, enthused by the turnout, and began an elaborate, cultured, amplified welcoming speech over the din of the up-market glitterati in attendance, thanking all for coming to the Maduro polo gala and paying homage to them. As the dignified host of the lavish reception with incalculable wealth, Maria had spared no expense for the affair and deported herself as one of West Virginia's preeminent hostesses. Important, influential people vied for an invitation to her social events. The ruby-and-diamond necklace around her slender throat was exquisite and outshone the jewelry of the other women in attendance.

She then made a gracious gesture with a gold-rimmed stemmed goblet of champagne held aloft, and an army of starched-white-jacketed livery began rolling out a bounty of sumptuous delights on carts. She seemed to be launching into a long monologue but then suddenly aborted. Her apercu elicited an uproarious merriment of champagne-fueled cheers from the crowd.

There was champagne, a dizzying assortment of French and Argentinean sparkling wines. On long tables covered in white linens, there was a cornucopia of wild-caught salmon, fresh trout from the Mountaineer Trout Farm, mounds of freshly caught shrimp sill pink and ready to be peeled and dunked into spicy sauces shrimp, oysters, and a surfeit of locally sourced loaves of bread, ham, fruits, along with a wide selection of hot and cold Spanish hors d'oeuvres, Southern fried chicken, corn on the cob, seasoned rice, baked yams, and Southern homemade cornbread. As if that wasn't enough, peach cobbler complemented with apple pie was on the table to satisfy the sweet tooth. Vast charcoal pits contained large quantities of sizzling barbecued ribs, and the smell of beef filled the air. There was a loud applause of assent.

A white-uniformed waitress with dazzlingly beautiful blond hair and stunning green eyes offered each of them a flute of Cristal champagne. She smiled impishly yet decorously at Bryce as she disappeared into the chattering crowd.

Bryce politely accepted the champagne and thanked her, questioning why he had even accepted it. She backed away, smiling bashfully. Bryce took Nuna's arm, trying not to be too obvious about it, as they continued their meandering walk.

As the wine flowed, several of the guests chatting within earshot of Bryce made some snide contemptuous comments about the host, but nothing Maria would have been able to hear. No one wanted to throttle the enthusiasm of the event.

"Mrs. Maduro has invested millions of dollars in the name of the Phoenix Museum in Charleston, so it is essential to her. Not to mention how she twisted arms and called in favors so that most of the critical socialites and half the politicians of West Virginia are here."

Bryce could hear fundamental ambivalence in Nuna's tone and saw a twinge of pain rippling in her eyes. He thought that her pain was almost touchable.

Then Nuna heard her unbidden words echo in her head and cringed at her gaffe and indiscretion. "Your concern is understandable," she said with sincerity emanating through a thin-lipped smile. "I'm sorry, I've never told anyone that before. I can't discuss a client. It isn't ethical. Professional private accountants shouldn't gossip about their clients. It's a fast way to get terminated." She whispered in a barely audible voice, "Terminated is a euphemism for murder."

She pantomimed shooting herself in the temple as they ambled on.

"Forget I said that," she said quickly, covering her dissing misstep. "But, unfortunately, I wasn't paying enough attention to my incautious words.

"Forget you said what? Forgive me, I didn't hear you, ma'am," he said, suppressing a smile with an almost imperceptible chuckle.

Nuna smiled sheepishly and deftly dodged the issue "And stop calling me ma'am! I'm not your great aunt."

He heard her long breath of relief as he backed off, and she almost smiled. He didn't blame her for being nervous. Hugo Maduro might not be called the Colombian anymore, but beneath the designer suits and political firewalls, he was still a vicious, conscienceless predator and a very nasty egotistical son of a bitch. Anyone sullying the truculent heathen could count on having a short future.

Nuna was frightened and vulnerable.

Under the pretext of looking beyond her, Bryce turned sideways, keeping a discerning eye on her, coming closer to her, and inhaling Obsession. Her blond hair was streaked by the rays of the sun. Her ice-blue eyes, minimal makeup, and that damned tempting butterfly tattoo on her rear shoulder made her one hell of a sassy woman.

I hope you're as innocent as I believe you are, Bryce thought grimly, desperately keeping his inchoate thoughts and perspective. All that he was sure of was that this covert operation was responsible for the congruence of their lives and that he hoped they could find a future with each other. But innocent or not, his focus was mission-centric. We're stuck with each other at the moment, he thought.

CHAPTER 20

As noon elongated into midafternoon under a warm sun, they continued to traverse the grounds, wandering and maneuvering through the diverse crowd. His gaze roamed the gala, always alert for a familiar face of interest. His plan for taking down Maduro and possibly a senator or two was still vague, a necessary improvisation of gathering information cultivated by his own honed covert instincts. The information he'd been given on the senators' involvement in vast money laundering schemes and political corruption was still highly inscrutable and circumstantial. Still, if taken together, the evidence of a nefarious affiliation would create a significant disruption to the criminal activities taking place in West Virginia. What Bryce needed was solid, incontrovertible proof of an alliance.

"Excuse me, dear." They both turned, and suddenly, a lithe Muslim woman smartly dressed, in her early forties, unceremoniously appeared behind them and congenially extended her unsolicited hand to Nuna, introducing herself as Senator Sahra Assad. She was wearing a trendy knee-length dress with a black hijab scarf and wore glasses with tortoise-shell rims; when she removed them, her eyes were revealed to be a luminous hazel. She was mild and polite with a saccharine tone, so subtle in her affect that it was hard to believe that she had congressional power.

After Bryce and Nuna introduced themselves and went through the obligatory social pleasantries, she asked in florid prose where the nearest loo might be found. Nuna, with an ingratiating smile, quickly directed her to the pool area behind the main house. "Go through the sliding glass doors, and it's on your immediate left."

She thanked us and tottered away. Bryce had never heard the word *loo* in his thirty-five years, but Nuna clearly recognized it. They both knew that she may have had one too many cocktails already. While he recognized the senator from the dossier, he gave her a swift, inquisitive once-over. Nuna didn't take notice, and they continued moving through the merriment.

"Your hands look too rough and callused for someone who writes articles for a living," Nuna said without thinking.

"They come in handy from time to time," he said, laconically skirting the issue.

An awkward moment passed. She nonchalantly groaned at the pun. He grinned, feeling emboldened. Curious, she studied his effortless swagger rather than looking around at the other guests. She studied his black jeans, loose-fitting shirt, and black leather boots. She turned and looked up at him, her sparkling blue eyes lit by curiosity and a touch of humor.

"Bryce, you aren't from around these parts, are you?" she asked politely in a melodious Southern drawl, then quickly apologized for the inane question, covering her mouth in embarrassment. "I'm so sorry. You seem to have corrupted my senses."

Bryce smiled at her, giving her a sideways glance that piqued her heartbeat. "Sounds promising," he said facetiously.

She gave him a look of alacrity that spoke volumes. The polite, stilted conversation began to evaporate.

As they continued their walk, they drifted into asking trivial but anomalous questions, bantering, and jesting. By her nature, she was somewhat reticent to discuss her personal life with a stranger. Still, little by little, in examining life's vicissitudes, they were getting to know a bit more about each other, which she liked.

Bryce, unable to deflect the intuit question, shared that he had just recently purchased a home in Fayetteville. He said before that he had spent most of his time in Connecticut and Upstate New York, in the Adirondacks.

"Currently, I'm staying at the Resident Inn in Charleston, close to the newspaper headquarters." He then asked Nuna, "How long have you lived here in the Mountain State?"

While being extremely reticent to reveal her personal history, she responded, "All my life. I was borne in Elkins and bred in Coalwood, an only child, making me a denizen of the mountains."

"Do your parents still live in Coalwood?"

"No, my mama passed away a while back from cancer, and my daddy was recently killed in an auto accident, so the authorities say. I still don't believe it. So now it's just me," she said ruefully. "All that is left of my family are memories and fading pictures set on my shelves or hung on the walls of my house. And yours?"

Not being comfortable with small talk, Bryce preferred to listen to others, but at this moment, he decided to relent. He looked up at the sky with an expression of mock concentration, as though striving to separate the momentous from the consequential. He felt the familiar ache in his chest that made it difficult to speak.

"No, my parents are both deceased also and my brother was killed in Vietnam. My parents were both doctors with Doctors without Borders. Both were murdered in Angola."

"I'm so sorry, Bryce That must have been terrible for you," she ventured.

"It's was, but it's OK now," Bryce answered simply. "I'm over it, and they died doing exactly what they lived for."

"What were they like?"

Smiling reminiscently, he said, "Professional, energetic, humorous, affectionate. I loved them immensely." There was a short moment of stoic silence before he asked, "Do you have children?"

"No." She laughed, shaking her head. "My late husband didn't want children. I did, and it had been a source of contention between us. In retrospect, it was just as well. I wouldn't have wanted a child to grow up in the impermanence of our brief marriage."

"Are you married now?" Bryce asked.

"No, I'm a widow," she said solemnly, wiping away a tear and a memory.

"Have you ever considered getting married again?"

"In the years going forth, I've never found Mr. Right. That would include my late husband."

"I'm sure you've had a number of suitors."

"I have, yes," she said cryptically. "However, what they were pursuing me for was not necessarily what I saw as marriage."

"OK, sorry I asked," he said with a commiserating smile.

Bryce heard something sad beneath the words.

"For the love of God, I have no idea why I'm sharing this information with you," she said.

"Maybe because we're sort of becoming friends," Bryce said. That seemed to give her pause. "Are you working now?"

She responded, "Sort of."

Acutely aware of the sadness now showing in her eyes, he directed the conversation in another direction.

"How'd you come to be employed by the Maduros?"

Bryce's tone was so serious that she felt a slight prickle of alarm

"I'm not, at least not in the conventional sense. I'm their personal customer service agent. I actually work for the Chase-Webster Bank in Charleston, and most of my employment up to this point has been quite interesting. At least for now," she added, then wished she hadn't. This morning's confrontation with the Maduros had terrified her more than she'd realized. Whenever she reflected on her naiveté, it depressed her.

"So you're not married. But are you seeing anyone right now?"

"No, I'm not. Back at you," she wheezed.

Bryce shook his head. "No, I've never been married, and I have no illegitimate children either," he responded in an unguarded manner.

"You're not currently involved with anyone?" She persisted in a voice tinged with curiosity.

"No, not since my last tour in Vietnam, when I received a 'Dear John' from my fiancé."

"Surely you must have someone you care about in your life," she said solicitously.

Amused at her stammering, he laughed. It was something Bryce had asked himself a number of times. "Unfortunately, not yet," he solemnly responded with a reticence that he hoped would discourage further prying. "One might say I'm an unreformed bachelor with periods of semi-monogamy punctuated by moments of random curiosity."

It wasn't often she found a man with the body of a linebacker and the relaxed disposition of a mellow librarian.

"Bryce, you look like you came back from the war all right," she said. "What do you do for fun?" She added, "Stupid question."

"Not at all," he said. "I guess my work leaves little time for fun. And you?"

"Like you, my work leaves practically no time for fun. With what happed here yesterday I expect to change that," she said.

"Sounds like you're jonesing for another job," Bryce said. He stared at her, perplexed.

Nuna gave him a whimsical look. "You never know. Everybody needs a new challenge in life from time to time," she said. "So I've bided my time. I've been pondering a career change."

"You don't like finance?" Bryce looked at her quizzically.

Her voice cracked as she spoke, and her face softened fractionally. For the first time, Nuna realized that she wasn't completely enthralled with banking. At least not anymore. "It's always about money." She had recently learned that money doesn't always bring out the best in people.

"Reporters don't know much about money," he said. "But it's enough to keep a roof over your head and food on the table." Serenely, he added, "If I wasn't doing what I'm doing right now, I'd be sunning myself in the hammock on my back deck sucking an ice-cold Corona."

In the back recesses of his mind, he was processing the thought of eventually retiring, after seven more years. One could retire after twenty years of military service, and he could definitely find ways to occupy his time. If he got bored or needed some additional funds, he could always hire out as a covert mercenary.

"And it always comes down to the question of what one will do to keep from starving to death, right?" she asked.

Her expression showed the sadness that she was experiencing.

"In all honesty, I don't know."

With a slow nod, she said, "Life is quite strange, you know."

"How so?" Bryce asked.

"You have a vision after graduation, a predetermined idea of how your life will be. And then it all collapses." Bitterness tainted her verbiage as she abruptly changed the subject, not wanting to reveal more of her situation than was judicious. Right there, he found her to be brooding and highly intelligent.

Time flew by while they meandered, revealing inconsequential, sketchy aspects of their lives, past and present.

"Pretty much," he said. "Speaking of food, what are you doing after this? I know this is extremely presumptuous on my part, having just met you. Still, you look like an outgoing, adventuresome young woman sojourning through life, and I was considering whether or not you might throw caution to the wind and have dinner with me tonight." Staring at her levelly, he asked, "What's the matter? Hasn't a man ever asked you out for dinner?"

Nuna turned and retorted crisply, giving him a stormy look. "Not thirty minutes after I first met him and not an hour after somebody else asked me to meet him in the garden at six p.m. I may have an instinctive aversion to someone carrying a camera and following people around, possibly hoping for a compromising situation."

To her surprise, he laughed.

"I'm too late?" he asked lightly in a plaintive, lilting tone, nettling her as he glanced at his watch covertly.

Bryce had learned early in his career to keep his professional life and his personal life separate. Until Nuna came along, he had done an excellent job of it. But there was something about her that had lit a fire inside him. Looking at her made him restless, and her infectious laugh and passion for life were incredible. The urge to take her into his arms and kiss her was so intense that he had to use all his willpower to hold himself in check.

"Unfortunately, I sort of have another commitment," she murmured.

Her solemn, downcast expression told him she didn't really want to fulfill this commitment.

"Can you break it?" he asked solicitously.

"It's not that easy." She temporized. "But I'm considering the consequences of doing just that," she added obliquely, deliberately being noncommittal.

"So," he said with a look of perplexity on his face, "I'm not entirely out of the running, am I?" Bryce gave her a searching look.

There was a perceptible pause before she turned and responded with the stubborn jut of her chin, "Why is it that, for some inexplicable reason, I feel hunted?"

Bryce continued to walk closely at her side before turning with an impish smile. "My strategy may need some tweaking, but I aim to swoop you up on my horse and gallop away to dinner."

Nuna smiled in stunned silence at his bluntness but was thinking to herself that she would be a fool if she didn't at least give this budding attraction between them a chance. She was feeling awkwardly stiff and a little off-kilter with the invitation. While a part of her was trying to concentrate on Bryce, the other half was dealing with the Maduros and their demands.

Nuna cleared her throat and asked, taking umbrage, shaking her shoulder-length hair away from her face. "For pity's sake, can I have a rain check?"

"Absolutely," he responded.

"That's very chivalrous of you, Bryce, to give me such an easy out."

As the hot and muggy afternoon dragged on forever, they slowly walked about the grounds together.

CHAPTER 21

In the periphery of Bryce's vision, he detected four men walking toward them. HE squinted in the afternoon sun. Providentially, he recognized three of the odious Manduro characters but kept it to himself at this point.

His prodigious memory kicked in. Dossiers were attaching themselves to vaguely familiar faces from surveillance photographs.

Nuna turned, craning her neck, and looked over her shoulder. Her smile faded at once, with her manner turning cold and disdainful as she spotted Maduro and the other three protégés striding toward her. The first two seemed engaged in lively discussion as they walked. Bryce studied their body language from a distance. All three had an ominous presence. They reeked of menace.

Assuming a pose of casual conversation, Bryce scanned the grounds. Nuna averted her head, and for a couple of ponderous moments, neither said a word.

"The big beefy guy on the right with the beetled brow;, crow-black pomaded, Brylcreemed, gelled hair; and thick gold chain around his muscular twenty-inch bull neck, thick with wattles and a cobra tattoo on the left side is Mr. Maduro," she said quietly. "Be advised that he is not only physically imposing, with an approximately twenty-one-inch bicep, but also has a brutal temperament."

He was a formidable lean fifty-something guy for sure, with a buzz cut, neatly dressed in pressed khakis slacks, impeccably polished Fifth Avenue wingtip shoes, wearing a short-sleeved lavender silk Ralph Lauren golf shirt open wide from his neck to his chest with an HM monogram, sporting what looked like a gold Rolex on his left wrist and Ray-Bans covering his eyes. Bryce's gaze was glued on the man. Maduro looked like he had owned a tattoo parlor as his deeply tanned arms and neck were covered in faded designs. Hugo continued to stroke his beard, which covered two deep, nasty scars running from his lower chin to his forehead. Reportedly from a drug deal gone wrong while he was imprisoned in Venezuela. From what Bryce could see from this distance, he looked like the meanest son of a bitch one would ever expect to encounter this side of hell. His face had a fierce stamp of brutality. He had the hulking chest of a mastiff, the contented, self-important look of scary, no-nonsense, hard-faced looking bastard starting to put on extra weight. He had the bearing of a man in charge.

Bryce immediately sensed an edge of controlled contempt in her tone.

"The unscrupulous Senator Adam Schiff is the hefty guy on the left with the wholly unprepossessing pallid complexion and the jaunty swagger, in his perfectly pressed dapper gray suit."

His aquiline face made him look like a man of privilege, and there was an arrogant glaze to his mien. Bryce couldn't help but notice that he was wearing a tailored suit; he was also wearing a pair of well-worn loafers without socks indicating an implied devil-may-care attitude of wealth. He kind of looked like a strutting peacock. Bryce loathed him immediately.

"The slender bespectacled, cigar-smoking one walking parallel to the senator with the swagger is relatively new to most of us, and I know little of him. According to rumor, he's an Estonian adviser from Eastern Europe and goes by the moniker of Doc."

He was a wiry, reed-thin individual with an unprepossessing, gaunt, hatched face, protuberant eyes, lupine teeth, an aquiline nose, ropy arms covered with black hair, and a disturbingly dark tan, but his skin was not leathery. He spoke English with a fractured accent and broken grammar. He actually looked like a belligerent pit bull, with a large set of suspicious canted eyes and a flashy gold chain around his neck, who could be dangerous and destroy a person deliberately and with malice aforethought. A large dark mustache covered his upper lip and matched his eyebrows, which covered ferret eyes. Bryce studied his impassive profile. His guess was that he was in his forties but looked older. He was five-foot-eight, had a swarthy complexion and a supercilious expression on his face. He lifted an expensive white straw fedora off his head and dabbed at his forehead with a handkerchief as he kept pace with Maduro.

"The diminutive, barrel-chested rogue Mexican with the large scar on his face, a drinker's nose, and a thicket of disheveled dark brown shaggy hair hanging down to his shoulders walking in tow behind Hugo is Pablo."

Pablo was his obsequious, hostile bodyguard and right-hand man and was always alert and on guard. It was rumored that Hugo had saved the disreputable reprobate from a Mexican court-mandated life sentence behind bars and made him agree to an offer he couldn't refuse. Sizing him up, Bryce noted he wasn't that big in stature but he had the wiry musculature physique of a tree stump that suggested strength for his size. There was something manic about him, a hint of rabid truculent tension in his movements. His eyes were restless, and his neck looked like the neck of an ox. His head and arms were covered in what looked like amateur jailhouse tribal tattoos of skulls and screaming ghoulish faces, apparently applied in a vain effort to cover severe acne that left his face permanently scarred. He cracked his knuckles as he walked and had a dour Spanish weathered visage that only a mother gargoyle could love. Coupled with the sunbaked darkness of his skin, his front teeth were nicotine-stained and broken. His tawdry, uncouth appearance reminded Bryce of Scarface in bell-bottoms. Long tufts of underarm hair were visible. Bryce couldn't help but notice the sheathed fifteen-inch jungle knife attached to his belt under his ratty Adidas sweatshirt and the glock 40 Roscoe at the back of his worn jeans. The unsavory parasite was a well-armed thug.

"Ah, Mr. Maduro," he said distractively, "the mysterious puissant host with the beaucoup bucks." He hoped his portentous tone of voice didn't reflect the adrenaline hammering through his body, bringing him to fight-or-flight alert. "Should I know the dapper one with a paunch in the dark suit with him?" he asked. "Senator Davis is an important man, huh?"

She looked at him warily. "A very well-connected, influential maven," she intoned, conspiratorially whispering in a low pitch, almost inaudible. "He's a ranking member of the House Ways and Means Committee. They control the money, so yeah, one might consider him important."

Bryce asked, "Do you know him?"

"I know of him. I don't personally know him, and I kind of dislike him heartily," she said dryly and without a hint of inflection. "He's somewhat standoffish."

Maduro and Senator Davis stopped next to a large copse of gnarled oak trees and, after a short monologue and what looked like an animated conversation, closed with a conspiratorial smile and shook hands, indicating they were finished talking. From Bryce's location, they both looked to be of the same vintage, radiating evil vibes. The senator turned and looked furtively around before sideling away, heading back to the festivities, and circulating, mainly with females.

Bryce could only guess what the egomaniacal SOB was discussing. Just as soon as the unassuming senator left, Maduro turned 180 degrees and stretched his head to one side and then the other with a wolfish grin spread across his face. He was extremely proud of his physique. He headed our way with a surly look on his face like he was pissed at something the senator had said.

Spotting Nuna standing on the hill, he smiled like a Cheshire cat about to lunge on a mouse as he toyed with the sizable sparkling diamond in his right ear and started walking toward her. As he approached, Bryce turned around and walked away, giving them some distance.

Maduro, an inscrutable phony smile on his face, approached Nuna with the bearing of a military general about to address a corporal and gave her an arrogant and invasive leer before stepping into her personal space. Removing his Ray-Bans, he whispered into her ear, "Don't forget, my *bonito uno*, eight tonight at the pool." His dark eyes leered and brazenly surveyed her breasts beneath her white blouse as he stood before her. A grin spread across his face, and he ran his hand through his hair. He arched his back slightly and flexed his chest.

"A bathing suit won't be necessary," he intoned while leering lecherously at her, giving her a slow predatory once-over as he moved closer, then closer still, until she could smell the odor of alcohol in his breath. "I'm sure that I'll find your naked body delectable." His belligerent eyes reflected the crass arrogance of knowing he was indisputably in charge of the county and could rule as he pleased.

His smile was insolent.

She could feel his lecherous, incisive eyes examining her body with sexual merriment.

Bryce took notice of his eyebrows now that he had removed his glasses. Bushy and thick, they seemed to grow together as one single untamed strip across the bridge of his nose.

"What?" she yelled with an incredulous gasp.

Hugo angled his head back, allowing him to look down at her with a cocky grin and an attitude of arrogant dominance, his eyes exuberant with unscrupulous malice.

"You heard me correctly. I'm going to enjoy your treasures tonight." He grinned unrepentantly with unmitigated contempt as he continued to accost her.

She had an insane compulsion to run and scream. His mordant words crept under her skin.

Seething inside with extreme antagonism, she rolled her eyes in exasperation, stepped back, staving him off, swallowed a growl, ignoring his lascivious smirk, and gave him a bitter and astringent, poisonous stare. He looked her straight in the eyes, impervious to her pain. The man was insufferable, and she hated the insolent tone of his voice.

Her mouth went dry in response to Maduro's bold testiness. His crudeness didn't scare her as it was obviously intended to. To the contrary, it only fueled her resolve.

"Hugo, I can't make it tonight as I have another commitment," she replied deadpan, looping a hank of hair behind her ear.

"Nuna, Nuna, Nuna," he said blatantly as he ogled her breasts and legs, enunciating his words in a gravelly gruff voice, "eight p.m. or else, *comprendo, mi bonito uno…*" he said with a faint taunting glacial smile, slicing the air with his hand as he jovially tapped her on her ass. Nuna balled her hands into a fist.

She instantly spun on her heels and swung her fist at him, but he caught her hand and pulled her in proprietarily close to his chest, forcing an indulgent sloppy kiss on her lips. The shock had momentarily rendered her immobile. She pushed the bile in her stomach back from leaching up into her throat. Her nostrils flared in revulsion as heated anger sluiced from the top of her head to her toes. .

"Nuna," he said, slanting his mouth into a wicked condescending grin, "you're my property, and I'm going to fuck you, and don't forget it."

Driven by raw and raging panic, she hastily backed away from him with aplomb but cold civility, trying not to cause a scene. She swallowed visibly but said nothing. He tilted his head back and laughed again, a victorious chortle.

Turning away, he gave Bryce a thousand-yard reproachful stare and a baleful nod with a glancing stolid look that turned into a derisive sneer as he swaggered overconfidently back to the house, temporarily mollified as he vaporized into invisibility. He was oblivious to the interplay in progress. Having looked at his picture in the file, Bryce thought his mesmerizing eyes had an evil way of hooking one into them, even on paper. Looking at him in person, he saw they were even colder as he addressed Nuna condescendingly. The pompous bastard had an ego the size of West Virginia.

Bryce, quelling his antipathy and the murderous rage billowing through him like a storm, maintained his forbearance, remained calm even though his hands were fisted tight. Keeping a solicitous eye on the arrogant, egotistical, chauvinist prick, he ran a litany of foul expletives under his breath. Nothing was going to stymie the taking down of Hugo, and when it happened, the misogynistic brute would get no mercy.

Appearances had to be preserved, but Bryce had little doubt of the ruthlessness of Maduro. He, to start, had a venomous ego that was somewhere in the outer limits of the stratosphere. If furtive stares were bullets, Bryce thought both he and Hugo would be dead.

His jaw ridged as he gnashed his teeth; the muscles along with it were flexing incipient anger, all without uttering a word. Bryce wanted the thought to sink in. He was seething on the inside. "I'm coming for you, Hugo," he said with vehemence, inaudibly. Bryce stood rigid as a statue, whispering to himself, "You're dead meat, you pompous SOB, and I will be your worst nightmare." He wasn't using hyperbole for effect. He watched Maduro in suspense, then quickly averted his head.

Nuna, with pursed lips, did not so much as deign a glance as he walked away, but she trembled with a cold foreboding. Her temerity was visibly disparate with her size.

Silently Bryce whistled, noting the change in her disposition. "The lady is pissed and scared shitless," he whispered to himself, barely concealing his pall of ire. He grudgingly grinned as he eyed her quizzically. She had turned out to be far stubborner than he'd understood her to be.

Vexed and refusing to cower to his insolence, Nuna was muttering to herself as her face went pale, her hatred oozing out of her pores like rancid sweat. She was full of defiant nervous energy and gave Hugo a venomous look.

Bryce hovered, staying his distance for a palpable beat. Having reined in his anger, he then moved closer to her, all the while keeping his eyes trained on Maduro, now well out of hearing distance.

To her credit, Nuna didn't even flinch, but her hackles were up for sure.

She stood her ground unflinching and had looked Hugo straight in the eye with repugnance, ignoring his threat.

Bryce said, guilelessly, "Based on the transgressions I think I heard, you can haul his predatory ass up on sexual harassment charges."

"Hugo, unfortunately, is as unfathomably brilliant as he is ruthless," she said cryptically. "He is a cad and a chauvinistic reprobate of the highest level. He employs several foreign secretarial assistants, all trained on

Norman's Cay. I can assure you from my occasional contact with them that each one of them is filled with intense angst and trepidation of him. Possibly illegal immigrants, they wouldn't even consider going to the authorities and filing sexual harassment charges. Instead, they submit to his daily fifteen-minute irreverent trysts on the couch and hope for a better future." She still kept her personal plight to herself. "In spades."

Bryce gave her a wary look. "You aren't one of them?" he replied deadpan.

She shrugged one shoulder contemptuously. She was piqued. Her head tilted quizzically as the combativeness in her eyes receded. "So does that make me finicky or stupid?" she asked rhetorically. She groused, her arms akimbo, giving him a blistering tetchily look, with eyes filled with turbulence and seething contempt.

"You're a long way from being stupid, " he said hesitantly. "May I call you Nuna?"

The guarded look in her eyes receded, taking the edge off her tone, and her voice rose an octave.

"Anything but *mi bonito*, or I'll deck you." She snorted, laughing dismissively, eyes averted as she raised her arms in a gesture of helplessness.

In a feigned riposte, Bryce gave her a slicing, sideways look with an impish smile. "OK, gorgeous," he said quietly. "But only if you call me Bryce."

She punched him in the shoulder playfully and reflectively said, "*Aren't you a comic?*" She scowled. He feigned a flinch.

She surprised both of them by laughing like a teenager at his unblushing use of flattery to get her attention. "Thanks, handsome."

He was feeling smudged, and he responded with an unrepentant gesture. He was again amazed by her air of complete confidence. She oozed it.

"Nuna, I have a premonition that Hugo's ardor is going to cool under a deserved comeuppance in the very near future."

She took several swift swallows of wine to take the bitter taste out of her mouth. It was her second glass. As she took another several quick swallows, draining her glass, she looked at him and then at her wine stem. She held it out toward Bryce, who refilled it. She was honest enough to admit that she was attracted to him and disgusted enough to wish she weren't. He was a charmer and a user.

Her eyes were brimming with excitement. Did he know just how discombobulated she was?

Bryce ignored the brittle edge in the tone of her voice and choice of words. He smiled and then drained his water bottle as he checked his watch.

"Where would you like to go for dinner?"

She squinted and gave him a pensive look. "I've lost my appetite," she replied tetchily. "I'll take a rain check." She winked at him saucily. "Believe me, I hate to be rude and run, but I'm going to have to run after I visit the lady's room."

Bryce shook his head, miming wonder. An hour earlier, she had been ravenously hungry, but now her digestive system was simmering on the verge of a nervous meltdown. He couldn't help but notice that she was jittery and feeling threatened.

Bryce, appearing unfazed, stood up to help with her chair, but as Nuna stood and backed up, her heel caught in one of the many electrical cables feeding the camera lights. With the speed and agility of a cougar, he caught her with his right hand and held her upright.

My God, he's fast, she thought, startled. And so strong.

"I haven't," he groused.

"What?" she said curtly.

"Lost my appetite."

The thought of going out to dinner was repugnant. Bryce eyed her askance with a tomcat grin. With feral eyes, she looked into his gray-green eyes and, for a moment, forgot to breathe.

"Dinner is optional," he said jokingly, gently releasing her from his arms.

Her smile was noncommittal. "Bryce, I declare that you are the politest man I've met in quite a while. You have a friendly smile when you let it out," she said. "Has anyone ever told you that?"

"Not until just now," he said beseechingly with a warming smile, holding up both hands in mock surrender. "Nuna, as you get to know me better, you may discover that *politeness* isn't exactly my strong suit."

Nuna wondered if she was the only one who noticed the difference in Bryce's eyes when he looked at his hostess. He enjoyed Maria's beauty, but he didn't want her.

Is he picky or stupid? Because he sure isn't blind. And he sure isn't stupid, she thought.

Nuna told herself not to be flattered. She was anyway.

"Aren't you afraid that Maria will discover her new lapdog is jonesing for another lap?" Nuna asked, irritated and curious at once.

"Even lapdogs have teeth." Bryce showed her a double row of his. "So I know when to bite, shut up, and wag."

"Wagging draws the better paycheck. But there are more important things than money."

"Easier for you to say." Bryce grunted as he spoke through clenched teeth. "You have no idea what's at stake," he said with deep sense of foreboding.

He thought, And I'm a fool for caring what she thinks of me. This isn't about a bonehead with a boner.

Nuna was too attractive and much too vulnerable.

"Please," she said, "can I think about it tonight? I'm consumed by my work, as you may have noticed. It has been a long time since I've seen or been with anyone. And I'm not looking for a relationship at this time." Several hours had elapsed since their initial meeting. "Good night, Bryce," she whispered with rheumy eyes, placing her hand on his arm affectionately.

She smiled encouragingly. Just then Bryce took hold of her shoulders, bringing her toward him, and gave her a gentle but warm kiss on her mouth. Nuna, having been caught by total surprise, had not realized just how hungry she was for him until she felt him slide his tongue between her lips. It had been years since she had felt sexual pleasure, and she closed her eyes and returned his kiss with abandonment. Bryce, and maybe the wine, was having a strange effect on her. All the unpleasant calamities that had fallen upon her that morning seemed to fade away. She was aware of the expectations twisting inside her, but she was also aware of her pounding pulse, which was now skittering with pure exhilaration. She was a woman, and atavistic or not, she had a deep longing for the touch and protectiveness of a real man. That real man would be Bryce Tucker.

"Nuna, I have a distinct prophetic vision that my future includes the inevitability of dinner plans with you," he said with a wink and another kiss. The statement silenced her. She was not accustomed to kindness from a man.

At the last minute, he again forestalled her. "Wait, I need your phone number."

Wordlessly, she sashayed away with a blazing smile, thinking that that kiss wasn't a mere kiss. Instead, it was a prelude to things to come. She was starting to like him and was undoubtedly becoming attracted to him. What girl wouldn't be? Their eyes had connected in a way that had warm overtones of an inevitability that had been postponed over some time.

The kiss had been worth the wait.

Bryce thought to himself, I couldn't help but watch her leave.

Connecting with her this morning was strangely providential.

The cell phone on his belt vibrated, but he ignored. He had to refocus on his assignment as it was his one true talent. In his life, every success or accomplishment had come down to the singleness of purpose, his tenacious ability to focus, plan, and leave out everything not attached to the matter.

Without question, she was beautiful woman and had a hidden wealth of sass. But he saw bewilderment in her beautiful blue eyes, and he saw a hurting loneliness and a suffering anger like a pall deep inside her. So he had to somehow overcome her emotional reticence and get her to lighten up.

But be that as it may, she was a mere means to an end. He was acutely mindful that Nuna was the woman he'd been given to use with this assignment, and he would dispassionately execute it and firewall his feelings. He didn't expect her to be a willing agent of Maduro, but he had learned the hard way not to let a person get in the way of the objective. He was a linear creature, which meant that he wouldn't allow any ancillary issues to muddy the waters of his conscience. So, little by little, with detached stoicism, he was doing his due diligence and picking up little nuggets of information on the Maduro operation. Even so, Bryce felt his pulse skitter.

He walked her out to her car, a late model Honda.

"It was very nice meeting you, Mr. Bryce Tucker," Nuna said with West Virginia mock formality.

"It was my pleasure spending the afternoon with you, Ms. Nuna Polinski."

She gave him a dazzling smile and said, looking at her watch, that she would love to continue their talk later but she had an appointment with a plumber scheduled to be at her house in a couple of hours to fix a drain issue.

With that, she gave him her phone number, and he surreptitiously mimed a kiss, and she returned an elfin smile.

"See ya," she said, walking away without further explanation and feeling a prickle travel up her spine. She had to escape the captivating eyes, his compelling voice, his seductive presence, and her now treacherous susceptibility to all three. She wasn't looking forward to a date, but it was nice to be pursued.

He watched as her taillights retreated down the driveway. The guests had dwindled. The fading light of day had mellowed, leaving the mountains awash in a soft pinkish glow of the approaching sunset. He stood there for a moment, inhaling the cool mountain air, thinking he hadn't felt that good in a long time. Then, much to his chagrin, he caught himself remembering how it felt to be close to her, inhaling her fragrance. I may be on the path to something special, he thought. She was definitely a fascinating female and, by far, the damnedest woman he'd ever met. Nuna Polinski could be hilarious, confident in a way that stood out, and utterly genuine.

* * *

Upon arriving home, Nuna went upstairs and showered, slid naked between the cool sheets, closed her burning eyes, and willed her mind to shut down and allow her body to fall asleep.

But neither her mind nor her body cooperated. Thoughts of Bryce Tucker persisted. Images of them in sexual scenarios flitted through her mind, making her body restless, actually feverish in places impossible to ignore, places where she wanted to feel his eyes and hands and mouth.

CHAPTER 22

In being sure that he was not deluding himself, he would now stay close to her like the tail of a fox, but at the moment, his train of thought derailed. Returning to the car stealthy, he found Austin waiting and going over his notes and scanning the photos he had taken. He had opened the windows in the vehicle to dissipate the oppressively hot air from the afternoon heat. As Bryce got into the overheated passenger seat, Austin showed him the most interesting shots he had taken. He had taken a number of staged photos of Maria posing on her horse, trotting and prancing along the race track and coursing the estate's perimeter. The second set of shots was much more interesting. It showed Senator Schiff and Senator Assad furtively entering a guest cottage together, which would have been shortly after he had left Maduro on the upper lawn. Austin had called Glenn and got assurance that the hidden surveillance cameras of the guest cottage area had been turned off for the polo gala to give privacy to guests staying the night. That didn't mean that the hidden internal cameras had been turned off. The other set, taken an hour or so later with a zoom lens, caught both of them leaving, looking a little disheveled, like they had enjoyed an afternoon tryst in bed.

Walking out the door, Senator Assad was still aligning her hijab as she glanced around surreptitiously, obviously concerned that someone might notice her leaving the guesthouse. Several other political subjects were being recorded this afternoon in the bedrooms. Austin, burning with anxiety, couldn't wait to show Bryce another set he had taken through a crack in the venetian blinds with his watch pressed against the cottage window. The two senators were stark naked, and she was being fucked repeatedly on the queen-sized bed.

The mic taped to his chest was iterating but a necessity. The camera in his watch indeed captured the image.

The new information now merited a call reporting back to the admiral and giving him a summary of what Bryce had learned so far, but not until he'd had a chance to sift through the binder and maybe, just maybe, discover what information would lead him to the two missing agents.

* * *

Bryce

At this point, Bryce Tucker, CIA Special Agent, was a distant memory, like someone I knew long ago. I was now trying to fit in and melt into the social fabric.

Working undercover and pretending to be someone you're not while trying to keep all the lies straight is taxing, to say the least. On the bright side, it was time well spent. Though I didn't learn anything earth-shattering, I met the one person that I wanted to meet. And Austin now had confirmation of the extramarital tryst taking place between Senator Schiff and Senator Assad.

Austin and I drove out of the parking lot and into the late afternoon sun heading down the mountain. Arriving back at the hotel and unlocking the door, I kicked off my boots and headed to the frig. I wanted a hot shower and a few hours of downtime before calling the admiral and updating him on the information we'd garnered to date, including the sexual rendezvous that Austin had recorded of the senators in Maduro's backyard.

I pulled out my cell phone.

"I've been expecting your call, Bryce," the admiral began without a preamble.

"Admiral, I just emailed you a file with some background summarizing what's been happening here. Unfortunately, the data is still sketchy and still being compiled and disseminated by Austin and Glenn. Sorry about that. But on another note, Glenn, having found his way into Hugo's library, uncovered a map in Hugo's desk that identified the location of Maduro's ships, warehouses on Norman's Cay, and arms warehouse in Cuba. A shadowy American expatriate by the name of Chris Vallarta, which may be an alias, manages and controls the Puerto Rico operation out of the deep-water port of Mariel Bay. As of yet, little is known of him, but we have an undercover contact working on the island. We expect to have more information on him shortly.

"Like a spider crack in a windshield, another interesting piece of information we've uncovered is that Congressman Swift and Congresswoman Assad have large mortgages and bank accounts with the Chase-Webster Bank in Charleston. In looking deeper into the ownership of this bank, we found it is partly owned by a Wall Street consortium of investment bankers with an elaborately concealed obfuscation of Venezuelan and Mexican controlling interest to the Grand Cayman Bank.

"Austin also found a funds-transfer pattern between the Grand Cayman Bank and the Chase-Webster Bank that you might find quite interesting. We believe that someone at the bank is blackmailing the congressman and leaking both proprietary transfers and personal information as needed.

"Glenn, having swiftly pierced the sanctum of Hugo's wife's wood-paneled library during the weeks following the gala, disabled the security cameras that were tucked into the crown molding at every corner of her office and deftly placed a bug under the front drawer of her massive burnished mahogany desk, and in doing so, he accidentally found and gleaned their encrypted algorithm taped under the keyboard. He also discovered a secret wall safe in her bedroom during his random inspection of the rooms. Glenn cracked the code and, in opening the closet safe, found approximately a million dollars in thousand-dollar wraps and a leather jewelry case filled with a flask of diamonds and emeralds of excellent cut and color. He estimated it was worth a couple of million dollars.

"In addition, he placed miniature microphones with transmitting devices the size of a tiny ladybug in every room throughout the mansion, including Hugo's private library and limo. Glenn was a pro. Hugo Manduro takes his personal security very seriously. In his limo he has an armed driver behind darkened windows and two armed security men with Uzi submachine guns with him at all times. The car has been retrofitted with a skin of Kevlar between its frame and the metal exterior.

"Austin, with the support of the NSA and a specialized department known as the CAF, is now able to tap into their phones and communication equipment via satellite, and we're now deciphering their codes and following their calls, faxes, email transmissions, and the movement of several large cash transactions offshore. Moreover, with the password and wiretaps in place, we can now listen to and decrypt the telephonic signals to and from the island in real time.

"Nasty stuff, though.

"With the help from Glenn, Austin is in the process of zeroing in on the browser history and looking at the files that seem to have been manually erased. The file attached is a record of wire transfer payments to no less than a couple of dozen accounts out of the Grand Caymans, Colombia, Mexico, Venezuela, Cuba, Somalia, Libya, West Virginia, and the list goes on. The record shows that Maduro is moving immense amounts of money and power, and now, with the addition of his Liberian-flagged ships, he stands to increase that tenfold! The transfers range from one hundred thousand dollars to hundreds of thousands; several were triple those numbers. All of it is foreign, laundered, and untraceable.

"The names on the accounts are shocking, and yes, both senators have been recipients of several large cash deposits from an offshore account. Additionally, the Maduro organization has been using bribery, blackmail, and extortion to elicit political influence across the globe, including right here in West Virginia.

"Somehow, the once reputable Chase-Webster Bank got involved in the money-laundering business, including channeling funds for political bribes. You'll understand after reading it that for security reasons, Austin had the file re-encrypted."

I nodded ruminatively, my thoughts now far away. The clock was ticking for Hugo.

After ending my conversation with the admiral, Austin and I looked at each other for a brief moment and, without a word, shared a high-five salute and then sat quietly for a moment with our eyes closed. Maduro, Senator Schiff, and Senator Assad, a most interesting triumvirate when you think about it. Let's take them down, I thought.

I considered the fact that the day was slipping away, sliding from afternoon to evening, as I got into Austin's car. We were both psyched and determined, and we were still wired. Darkness swallowed the taillights.

* * *

Nuna arrived home and made a beeline for the refrigerator. She was now famished. No, make that starved. Inside, the last sunlight cast an array of dim shadows. She hadn't known many men and had certainly never had a relationship with anyone since Chris's death. She had learned to be independent and guarded her independence fiercely. But the man she had met today could very well change that.

The July Fourth holiday came and went. The omnipresent mountains gave way to holler and flat lands as Austin and I returned to the hotel. After grabbing an early dinner at the restaurant by the lobby, we called it a night. It was currently a sultry eighty-one degrees with 100 percent humidity. We were indeed in the dog days of the summer.

A couple of hectic weeks went by as Austin and Bryce continued our investigation of the prosaic details of the Maduro organization.

The following Sunday morning, he decided to call her.

When the phone rang, Nuna had just returned from morning mass and was cleaning the breakfast dishes. Her hand hovered above the vintage Princess wall phone for a second or so before she lifted it from its cradle. It was rare for her phone to ring at nine o'clock on a Sunday morning.

"Ms. Polinski," she said immediately after saying hello.

"Bryce Tucker."

"Good morning, Mr. Tucker. How are you doing on this fine summer morning?"

"Absolutely fine, and you?"

"I hope I didn't catch you at a bad time."

"No. I just got back from morning mass and was washing the morning dishes."

She thought, Is he serious? I could have only dreamed of a call from this man. Actually, it was one of my prayers in church this morning. Hope began to flare in her heart like a hot ember, not quite dead in the ashes. A short pause yawned between them, and it seemed to span infinity. It was a silence rife with allusive innuendo as Bryce was already aware of her Sunday morning routine.

"Oh, I hope I'm not interrupting anything."

The insinuation was so blatantly covert and bold that she had to take a deep breath to respond.

"No, Mr. Tucker, you're not," she said earnestly as she walked around the breakfast bar and sat down at the kitchen table.

"Nuna, could we meet to discuss the connection between the Manduro operation and the Chase-Webster Bank?"

"And here I was hoping that you'd called just because you wanted to ask me to walk with you on this fine sunny afternoon." Nuna was cautiously flirting with him.

"Nuna," Bryce said, "we could do both. Can I pick you up in an hour?"

"Mr. Tucker, that would be fine." She had the sudden insane urge to kiss him on the phone.

She had an ingratiating smile on her face as they finished the conversation and she disconnected, putting the phone down in its cradle and spent the next five minutes thinking of a life with him. He somehow made her feel less alone. Because that's what she was feeling. Alone and bereft. No matter how much she steeled herself and tried to pretend otherwise.

"Damn," she swore under her breath as she struggled with the zipper on her jeans.

By the end of the day and a long three-mile walk, Nuna had answered all his questions and given him a summation of her ordeals with
the Maduros from start to finish. She was unaware of the horrors that
lay ahead.

CHAPTER 23

Bryce

I lost the coin flip, so I drove. An unyielding heavy cloud cover with a misting drizzle overhung the mountains, blacking out the moon and stars. With three miles still to go, we could see the glow of Charleston looming in the distance before us.

It was just after ten o'clock when we arrived back at the hotel. Austin and I had stopped at Graziani's Pizza on the way back for a bite of NY-style pizza before calling it a night. Graziani's had a basic Italian menu, and the food was served promptly; they were very hospitable. An hour later, having reviewed and summarized the events of the day and now somewhat tired, we decided to split the remaining pizza and take it back to our rooms.

Having undressed and now in my robe, I took the pizza and a glass of wine into the living room and sat with my feet propped up on the coffee table, watching a late show and thinking of Nuna.

I rubbed my knuckles over my eyes, trying to wipe out the fatigue. I was tired and a little bleary-eyed. I'd barely gotten four hours of sleep the night before, and it wasn't long before my eyes began to grow heavy. I dozed off into a fitful sleep right there on the couch. But sleep didn't come quickly. Stirring restlessly, I tossed and turned all night, unable to shake his conviction that Hugo Maduro was a murderer. I was hot with the covers on and cold without them.

This would prove another shallow night filled with nightmares jolting me awake. Locked-away images of the horrors of Vietnam, images of floating body parts in the river. Horrific visions of a SEAL Team tortured, decapitated, and left for vultures in the Iraq desert. I awoke at 5:00 a.m., shaved, showered, and went straight to my desk. It was cluttered with every photo and piece of information we had collected during the Maduro gala. In addition, every sliver of evidence we had so far on the connections between Hugo Maduro and the West Virginia and Kentucky Democratic Senators was beginning to show a criminal alliance with the Maduro organization. My goal was to get enough evidence to send the bastards to prison for life at a level six.

It jelled and hit me like a ton of bricks. Two of our agents had been killed and dumped in the river.

Both had been shot in the head. When I shot Pablo's driver and he dropped his gun on the payment, we retrieved it. Austin had advised me that ballistics was looking into whether there was a match to the bullets that had killed the agents. Pablo had returned fire and may have hit the car. Those also needed to be checked immediately. If there was a match, that would tie the murders to the Maduro organization.

The morning dawned to rain. The drops tapped at my window, not hard but continuously. Sometimes a mist, other times ramping up to a drizzle with water dripping from the broad leaves of the magnolias.

As I brushed my teeth, the phone rang; it was Austin. I'd been up for almost an hour, having consumed a couple of cups of coffee and reviewed notes and other data at the kitchen table.

Austin said, "Sometime between noon and three o'clock yesterday, two thirteen-year-old white twin sisters were presumed to have been kidnapped while riding their bikes home from school a half mile from their farm. Their names are Salina and Crystal Gorder. Seven hours later, the Marlinton Police located their bikes on a rural two-lane at an abandoned logging camp four miles from town."

Austin's hesitation and nuanced tone caused me to grit my teeth. He went on, "Five days later, a volunteer search team found Crystal's nude, headless body in a clearing off a dirt path a mile down the road in the brush. No sign of her sister.

"She had been bound, sexually assaulted, and brutalized before having her throat cut. Her severed head was found in the woods several yards from her body. Possibly dragged by some animal." My stomach lurched, and I had to turn away and compose myself for a moment. "She had been dead for several days, and the body was already putrefying in the heat. Unfortunately, it had rained heavily last night, and according to initial reports, the scene yielded nothing in the form of forensics other than her tattered clothing and sneakers."

I pursed my lips before regaining my cold professionalism. Cicadas and mosquitoes bussed from thickets somewhere ahead.

"Of particular interest to the ME was that her tongue was cut out and missing. Again, there's no trace of her sister. Following normal protocol, they are interviewing all the registered sex offenders, friends, neighbors, teachers, and anyone with even the remotest connection to the girls. So far, they've got no witnesses or leads."

An hour later after I received the call, Austin and I entered the Monongahela Forest region. We were at the scene. It was now eight thirty in the morning. We had driven for an hour and a half, rounding curve after curve and wasting no time for breakfast. Yet, surprisingly, with only five hours of sleep, I felt reasonably OK.

Temporary barricades of yellow tape had been set up upon sawhorses along the road and surrounding area to prevent contamination by media and others bent on seeing a body bag and getting a slant on another local tragedy. Having shown our badges to a uniformed officer, we were escorted across wet leaves and damp earth to the victim, now covered in plastic, with a couple of detectives and the coroner standing next to it, snapping pictures. The young girl was on her back, shoulder-length blond hair now caked in blood, partially covering what had been an angelic face. There didn't seem to be any effort to conceal or bury the body.

From the evidence, it looked like he raped her and then had her run naked in the woods for her life before tackling her to the ground and killing her where she lay. I felt my body cringe with revolting repugnance.

The road was ablaze with flashing police and first responder strobe lights. Beyond the yellow tape were the usual responders, a coroner's van, a crime scene unit, and two unmarked Crown Victorias. A blue sky illuminated a colossal rock cliff that was bereft of trees.

About a half mile down the road, a gravel passage on our left caught our interest, and we took it to the mountain's summit. A sign at the top said that we were now at 4,360 feet above sea level. The sky was an endless blue dome with a temperature in the midseventies. Of particular interest was the fact that using binoculars, we could see not only the flashing lights of the crime site below but also the Gorder farm just up the street and the Maduro estate a mile or so north. I noted the similarities to several other girls that had been murdered in West Virginia during the past two-year period and had had their tongues cut out.

"Are you thinking that the Maduro organization had something to do with this?" I asked.

"It's a possibility. Hugo brought Pablo to West Virginia from Mexico two years ago. While the bastard has never been arrested in the US, he is a suspect in the disappearance and deaths of several young adolescent girls in Tijuana, Mexico. It may be time to have some dialog with the Mexican authorities.

"The MO is the same. All the victims were young teenage girls between thirteen and sixteen years old; all of them were petite blondes of the same average height, abducted from rural roads in both West Virginia and eastern Kentucky, and sexually assaulted. All were found face up with their hands bound behind their backs, throats slashed, their tongues cut out. Five other girls believed to have been abducted have disappeared without a trace."

CHAPTER 24

Four weeks passed before I finally convinced Nuna to spend a day with me. I stole away for a quick early breakfast in the morning with her. For the past several weeks, we had been conversing on the phone daily about this and that as I continued to collect and compile data in the investigation of the Maduro organization. We had agreed not to discuss her connection to the Maduros, but it was lurking in the background. She adroitly dodged talking about the couple and was still pondering resigning from the bank. She agreed to meet me in Fayetteville as she had an early morning appointment for a cleaning with her dentist.

The morning special at the Wood Iron Eatery was blueberry pancakes and/or waffles with locally harvested West Virginia fruits and maple syrup. Fruit stands heaped with early summer produce lined both sides of the roadway. In Fayetteville, the dining options were limited, but this one was known as a local gem with its outside umbrella-covered patio. It had been remodeled several times and now had that rugged mountain look. Since it was now after the morning rush hour, the waitress came up and escorted Nuna to the counter where I sat. I looked up to one beautiful woman standing before me. "I's here," she whispered in her West Virginia drawl. I immediately stood and politely took her hand.

Several booths next to the front windows were occupied, so we took a booth at the back. A half dozen locals were sitting and chatting at the thick wooden counter, nursing coffee and playing chess with their home fries. Several of the guys looked up as we entered but quickly returned to their plates and chatter. Two short-order cooks were busy behind the counter flipping pancakes and eggs, never looking back.

The friendly redheaded waitress was young, athletically fit, tattooed on both arms, carrying a pot of coffee in one hand and two mugs in the other.

"Coffee?" she asked.

"Yes, please," Nuna said tersely.

"Cream?"

Nuna looked up, giving me an inquiring look.

"No," I said, "black with one pack of Sweet'N Low, please."

Nuna and I perused the menu, but in the end, she chose the pancakes, hash, and blueberry grits, while I ordered two eggs sunny-side up, bacon, sausage, toast, and home fries. The waitress, with pencil and pad in hand, graciously took our orders and skittered back to the kitchen.

When the orders came, her pancakes were four layers high. She placed a pancake and a healthy spoonful of grits on my dish, and I responded in kind with a wolfish smile by placing a sausage link and a strip of bacon on hers. For the next hour or so, we talked about this and that, both of us getting to know the other a little better.

Having wiped out the last of my catsup-covered home fries, I signaled the waitress and insisted on paying for the breakfast, and then we went our separate ways with no hugs or kisses, promising to contact each other soon.

For two days, we lived our separate lives, taking care of business but wondering what the other was doing and longing for each other. Then, finally, that morning, I made the first move and, having done my routine surveillance, parked in a nearby lot one hundred yards north of her driveway.

The sun was burning down with unseasonable ferocity for July.

I had heard nothing from Austin for three days as he had flown to Cuba under their radar, hitchhiking on a Navy minisub, and gone underground ashore to connect with his informants.

"Nuna, have you ever gone kayaking?" I asked.

She looked surprised. "Yes, I have done it several times when not rock climbing up Seneca Rocks. Why?"

The bodacious timbre of my voice drew her eyes to me.

"I have a cousin who owns New River Outfitters and rents kayaks and canoes on the New River. It's going to be hot tomorrow, and I was wondering if you might care to join me."

Nuna, finishing her coffee and thinking that she didn't want to give up this opportunity, surrendered and said, "Yes. Actually, that sounds exciting."

"OK, I'll meet you at noon," I said, tacking on a mischievous grin. "You said you rock climb?"

"Yes, I've always enjoyed the challenge of scaling a cliff."

"I used to do rock climbing as part of my hobby and exercise routine. You know, using climbing ropes, D-Links, and other equipment as necessary."

The following day, I met her at the Fayetteville Visitor Center wearing my long bathing trunks and took her upriver in my jeep on the rutted mountain road leading down into the hollow to Ray's store. Walking across the unpainted slats of his porch, we passed his lazy hound lying in the shade, giving us no attention as we passed. Opening the screen door, we found Ray inside on his knees, cleaning his bate tank, which would have been considered an aquarium in a more refined setting. He spun around so suddenly that he almost toppled off his knee scooter.

"You son of a bitch, you almost scared the Jesus out of me!"

I interrupted dryly, "There is a lady with me. Nuna, meet my wayward cousin, and pay no mind to his highfalutin attitude."

Upon my introducing Nuna, Ray, without further introduction, gave her a whopping bear hug and welcomed her to his mountain holler. Nuna graciously accepted the hug. The structure resurrected atavistic memories of the cabin she had grown up in. Next, Ray led us to a desk, which needed to be more organized than the rest of his store. Finally, he pulled up an extra crate for Nuna and nodded toward another for me. Having conversed with Ray for a half hour, we secured our gear in the kayaks and dragged them over to the dock at the river's edge.

"I don't think I've ever seen water this clear," she said as we dragged the kayaks in and began paddling with the deceptively fast current.

The forest was spectacular. The ancient evergreen trees were tall, straight, and symmetrically reflective in the water. The unseasonable heat blazing down from the clear blue sky was a plus.

She had changed into a yellow bikini top under her life jacket and a pair of white cotton hip-hugger shorts. With her hair pulled back in a ponytail, wearing a West Virginia Mountaineers football cap turned backward, she was a beautiful sight, a true backwoods country girl.

I said, watching her dipping the paddle in and out of the water as we moved with the current synchronized, "You're really good at this."

We paddled, negotiating the currents around rocks to navigate the sharp curves of the river.

Nuna yelled across with exuberant energy, "When I was at West Virginia University in my younger days, I was with the Division IV rowing team slicing the waters of the Monongahela River. I love the water."

"OK, so you're a natural," I'd said sardonically.

The military tattoo on his bulging right bicep caught her eye, as well as the lack of a wedding ring, and like the rest of his masculine physique, embarrassingly piqued the excitement in her.

The azure sky was placid without the whisper of a cloud.

Before reaching the white water rapids beyond the trestle bridge and under the New River bridge, we pulled into the shallow and disembarked the kayaks onto the shore. Ray would retrieve the boats later in the afternoon.

Eons ago, this river had gouged a deep canyon through the Adirondack Mountains, creating steep cliffs towering over the swift-running waters. Just a couple hundred yards downriver were class 4 white water rapids, a tourist favorite.

"Care to swim?" I asked as I beached his kayak on the sandy shore.

"Sure," she responded, following me to the shore.

Nuna slid out of her life jacket and shorts and tossed her tennis shoes as I removed my life jacket but not my T-shirt. I could tell she thought this strange for someone of my stature but decided to not say a word.

I was amazed at her physical attributes. She was lean and defined, without an ounce of fat anywhere on her body. Without a doubt, she had all the right curves in all the right places.

With the sun's fierce heat beating down on her back, penetrating her naked skin, before I had even removed my sneakers, she dove into the river and coquettishly went under in an explosion of water before surfacing and treading water in the swift current. I could see that there wasn't a timorous bone in her body as she was laughing, throwing back her wet hair, and wading out farther into the eddies of the swirling water.

"You are coming in, right?" she yelled out with contagious laughter, enslaving my senses.

She was free-spirited, blithe and laughing, carefree, totally without constraint as she frolicked in the river.

Looking around, I saw no other kayakers were in evidence at this bend in the river.

With my T-shirt still on, I quickly dove in, slicing the refreshing cold water with my hands, and came up very close to her, now treading water. My heart pounded with male excitement as I get close to her. Rivulets of water were running down her face.

"The cool water feels refreshing, doesn't it?" she said.

He wore a hint of a smile as she took in my muscled body with penetrating eyes.

"She's checking me out!" I said quietly under my breath.

A compelling desire surged through me. I will claim her one day, I thought.

Across the river, a lone osprey decided that there was too much distraction and took flight. We waded and frolicked in the river for at least an hour or so before retreating with brisk, determined strides across the pebbly bottom back to the sandy shore.

She wrung out her hair, grabbed a towel from the kayak, and toweled off before we lay on a flat rock at the water's edge with our toes in the water, letting the sun dry our skin. She was grinning like a forest imp; her mood was effervescent.

"Bryce, this place is beautiful," she said reverently. She sighed deeply and shut her eyes for a languorous moment, reveling in the idyll of relative peace. Then, opening her eyes, she watched the sunlight's reflection on the river's clear pristine water pass by. For the moment, she escaped from the Maduro threat and renewed herself amid the mountain environs.

She froze and watched several large butterflies flitting around a flowering patch of wild mountain lilacs bursting with purple flowers. Two were yellow swallowtails, and the other was a magnificent orange monarch with almost psychedelic wings.

"Do you come here often?" she asked

"I do. Actually, I live on the top of this mountain behind us."

"Really!"

"Really," I said wryly.

She looked at me with both interest and puzzlement.

"Interested in some lunch?" I asked. "I'm starving," she said.

Nuna slipped back into her T-shirt and shorts, put on her sneakers, and tied her hair back with a black scrunchie.

I couldn't believe how voluptuous she was. She bewitched me for sure.

I reached for her hand as she sat beside me, bringing her fractionally closer, then slowly kissing her on the lips.

"I like being with you, Bryce," she said as she looked into my eyes and brushed back a lock of hair from my creased forehead. I kissed her again, my tongue outlining her mouth, memorizing her unique taste, infusing her lips with my nectar.

We retrieved the Styrofoam box lunches from the small cooler that Ray had provided and ate deli sandwiches of crispy fried Southern chicken, boiled taters, and collard greens picnic style on the rock as we waited for Ray to arrive with his boat.

Nuna, famished, demolished her lunch, including the surprise Hershey chocolate bar. A gray squirrel darted across the rocks, suddenly stopping and rising up on its haunches, an acorn clutched in its front paws, and then scampering up the side of a large oak tree.

Nuna lay prone face down on her towel with her head nested on her crossed arms, letting the sun bathe her body with its warm rays. Unfortunately, her bikini provided little protection from the heated rays.

"Bryce, can you do me a favor and rub my tanning lotion on my back?"

"Sure," I said, kneeling beside her.

This wasn't a favor but an endearing privilege.

My hands smoothed the thick emulsion on her firm back with a gifted sculptor's strong evocative massaging strokes. Then, working my way down from her shoulders with languid motions and a generous amount of lotion, I went beyond kneading the small of her back, applying the lotion to the back of her long, firm legs. Nuna drifted into a relaxed, heavy languor that anchored her to the towel.

* * *

When Bryce finished, withdrawing his hand, and recapped the tube, she experienced an intense longing that begged to be assuaged. Instead, to her mortification, her breast began to riot against the soft material of her top. Coupled with the sounds of the river and the deep sound of his voice, she was beckoned into a deeper lassitude. She couldn't remember when she felt more secure in a man's hands than she was feeling now.

Bryce didn't have an issue with sunburn. His body was a dark bronze all over, she assumed. For some strange reason unknown to her, he wore a dark T-shirt all day, even when swimming in the river. Having noticed a couple of nasty scars on his legs earlier, she chose not to ask any questions.

Looking out over the water with the sun still high in the sky, they could hear the cadence of insects chirping and the slow, meandering trickle of the river as it worked its way past them. Otherwise, the forested landscape was silent.

Ray arrived about a half hour later as Nuna donned her windbreaker. Bryce helped her gather her belongings before loading the kayaks onto the recovery boat.

Later that night, Nuna sat on her porch, tilting her head back, gazing at the night sky. It was almost impossible to remove his poignant image from her mind. She surmised that the day seemed truncated and that he felt the same.

She didn't want to feel this way. She was a mature woman, and she now found herself wanting to be his woman. Bryce had the sophistication, the classiness, and an indefinable distinction that set him apart from every man she had ever known.

Nuna was sure that he had a story, and he didn't seem to want to talk about himself. Why should he? They'd only known each other for a couple of days. Seemed like much longer somehow.

The following day, while Austin was out talking to and interviewing local townspeople and merchants in Slaty Forks proper, Bryce called Nuna and asked if she would have breakfast with him.

He turned his hands palms up in capitulation. "I'll pick you up at eight."

Bryce and Nuna decided on a day trip south to visit the Beckley Exhibition Coal Mine and then go to the Tamarack in Beckley for lunch. The drive entailed a topography of winding rides over several mountains and a series of stomach-churning switchbacks and hairpin turns.

A couple of veteran miners dressed in coal-miner gear, including hard hats with battery-operated lights, took them into the darkness of the vintage underground passage, giving them a hands-on tour of the turn-of-the-century coal mine. While Nuna had lived in West Virginia all her life, she had never actually stepped foot into a darkened coal mine.

"My father and grandfather were miners at one time," she said. "So there were times in my younger years when they came home at night. I thought that they were black men until they washed their faces."

Later, having driven her home, he opened the passenger door for her. As she alighted, he stepped forward, bending his head down and slanting his mouth over hers.

His lips touched hers, silencing any protest. The kiss was long, delicious, and held her in breathless suspension.

"We had a great day, no?" He put his hand to her cheek, and surprisingly, his fingers were gentle despite being rough and calloused. As he leaned into her, she breathed his manly scent of sweat.

Before she realized what had happened, he pulled away, turned, and walked to his jeep, raising a hand and giving her a farewell wave. Then, with a smile and a wink, he was gone.

She silently watched him fade away as the celestial flaming orb went low in the western sky.

As Scarlett O'Hara so famously put it in Gone with the Wind, tomorrow was another day.

Grinning with a change of thought, she filled the tub and took a hot bath. Then, after exiting and toweling, she could see her true reflection in the mirror, where she critically examined herself. Five-foot-six, she weighed one hundred and ten pounds, which was ten pounds less than she weighed four years ago. She lay down on top of summer-moist sheets with the windows open to the relentless comforting chorus of cicadas punctuating the night and a faint hope that a tiny breeze would slither through the sultry night air. The darkness of the night left her feeling alone and adrift on a dark sea of nothingness. Somewhere on the mountain, yipping fox cubs and a lonely hoot of an owl in the distance gave the sounds of a haunting phantom lost in the darkness. The gentle waves of nothingness finally lulled her to sleep.

Nuna woke from the fog of sleep and yawned into the pillow and stretched her pointed painted toes out as far as she could beneath the covers, slowly raking her disarrayed hair out of her eyes, still trying to focus on a new day. She heard the tumbling of the freight train, on schedule, like clockwork, as it passed on the nearby tracks.

The mundane, routine days fell into a pattern, but this day was different. Her thoughts of sexuality had lain dormant until a couple of hours ago. Now she was secretly preoccupied with thoughts of Bryce Tucker.

CHAPTER 25

Sunday morning arrived with the sound of church bells clanging in the distance. Slowly opening her eyes and staggering over to the window, Nuna opened the shades to a brilliant globe floating in a deep cerulean sky without a trace of a cloud. The eastern sky is ablaze with color when she descend the stairs. Bryce called her and asked if she might be interested in a motorcycle ride. Having never been on a motorcycle, she politely declined.

"When's was the last time you did something spontaneous?"

"With an infinitesimal pause, she said, "I can't remember.""

"Nuna, I've been riding a Harley for the past ten years, and I assure you that you'll love it."

Nuna gnawed the inside of her mouth in indecision. While she didn't exactly accept the invitation with alacrity, she did finally agree as a delicious weakness was spilling through her.

"Oh, all right." Nuna surrendered to the wild temptation, pursing her lips. The idea of the impetuous adventure was exciting. She whispered under her breath, "I hope it won't be a train wreck."

It was a glorious morning: the sun was shining bright, the air was mountain crisp, and the scent of her roses was in the air. Having washed and towel-dried her dishes and put them away, she went back upstairs to change. She pulled on tight jeans and put on a navy pullover before stepping into her black Reeboks and checking her appearance in the mirror. She did a quick review of the contents of her small leather pouch and headed downstairs.

Bryce picked her up at her house. He rode past it twice before pulling into the driveway. The house and yard were tidy: green lawn, bright flowers, no weeds. Nuna was indeed a thorough and meticulous woman in all her wild mountain elegance. She came out, locking the door behind her, as he dismounted the Harley. The dazzling sunlight glinted off his mirrored glasses as he walked toward her. He gave her his now familiar charismatic smile and waggled an eyebrow at her, giving her reassurance. She acquiesced while watching him with intense eyes. After giving her some basic instructions and showing her how to mount the pillow, he mounted the Heritage and had her wrap her hands tightly around his midsection.

"Hold on tight and don't be scared," he said.

"I won't be scared." She lied. A small thrill of fear and anxiety zipped up her spine.

She closed her eyes and held him tightly as he started and revved the engine, bringing the beast (as he called it) alive. Bryce pushed off the ground and put the Harley into motion. Her head was spinning, and her skin prickled with excitement. The endorphins coursing through her blood provided a thrilling uplifting high.

They rode out of Gulley Bridge on Route 60 before merging onto US 19 north to Durban for lunch before moving into the lumbering town of Cass in Pocahontas Country. There, Bryce plucked her off the bike and put her on her feet. Having had a pub lunch at a café, we took a four-hour locomotive steam train ride eleven miles up through fertile green meadows up the bucolic splendor of wooded hills to the breathtaking forty-eight-hundred-foot summit of Bald Knob. She had to admit to him that she had never ridden on a motorcycle before, any more than she had ever ridden a coal-fired locomotive for as long as she had lived in West Virginia. Nuna was enjoying this day for sure.

"How do you like it?" he shouted back over his shoulder at her as they roared out of Cass over the mountain macadam on two wheels.

"I love it!" she said, laughing breathlessly against his neck. "It's so rejuvenating," she averred, shouting into the cool lash of wind roaring past her. Nuna's body was pressed against his, and she felt his muscles ebbing like waves against her pelvis.

Bryce laughed as he felt her fingers digging into his torso. As soon as they hit the open road of Route 60, he gunned them, forward having swerved around a smashed possum. Her arms convulsed around his abdomen, and she held on for dear life. She was burning with excitement.

The sun beat at them mercilessly as they rode through the sweltering mountain hollers on a winding ribbon of pavement through the Monongahela National Forest. Her thighs cradled his hips as she held on to him, feeling how the air smelled, so sharp and fresh. She felt recklessly and beautifully alive in a way she never had before.

They rode back to her house, where Bryce brought the bike to an idle before shutting it down. He let Nuna alight first while he removed his helmet and stepped off the bike. Her knees nearly buckled beneath her as she stepped off the Harley. The excitement of the adventure had surely robbed her of her equilibrium.

She bowed her head and wiped her eyes. "I can't allow myself to become a criminal. I just can't."

Bryce stepped up to her. "You're not a criminal, and you're not going to jail."

Nuna lifted her head and looked up at him with damp, dewy, imploring eyes. "I'm scared," she said.

She dropped her head forward and left it resting against his chest. He lifted a strand of her hair that had been lying against her cheek and rubbed it between his thumb and fingers. He placed his hands on her waist and gathered her sweater. He moved slowly, allowing her to object or slap him. She didn't.

He leaned in to whisk his lips across hers as he continued to raise her sweater until it cleared her chest. Her arms went up. He pulled it over her head and let it fall to the floor.

She lowered her arms but otherwise didn't move.

Bryce took advantage of her passiveness to drink in the sight. The slender column of her neck, the shallow triangle at its base, a bosom mad for pillowing. Her bra was the color of the sky.

* * *

Now Nuna missed his weight on her, the tickle of hair against places where her body was smooth, the scent of his skin, the overall feel of him on her and inside her. The tumult was over, but she wasn't done savoring the aftermath.

They said our goodbyes, which included a long hug. Nuna took the opportunity to give him a quick kiss on the cheek. Her eyes were wide and full of hilarity.

"You taste like chocolate," he said after a warm kiss.

"I'm sorry."

"I'm not complaining," Bryce said. "I love chocolate. You're delicious."

Her eyes widened in a pantomime of bewilderment. "Delicious?"

"It was a compliment," Bryce assured with a smile.

"See ya, Bryce," she said with an alluring certainty as she waltzed away. She was a grown-up woman, not a girl, and she was mature enough to recognize desire in a man's eyes when she saw it. And Bryce Tucker definitely desired her. From the first moment they met at Maduro's polo gala, there'd been an undeniable chemistry between them simmering just below the surface.

She was going to act on it and do her best to entice and reel him in. Her heart thundered anew.

* * *

That was a month ago, and in the intervening weeks, their relationship had developed markedly. Over the next four weeks, they busied themselves: several plays and a concert in Charleston, a couple of cinemas, and lunches at the local diners. While Bryce remained focused on his mission, Nuna was eyeing him as the man that would truly make her happy and would stand the test of time.

Now back home before dusk, Bryce walked her to her front door, said good night to her, giving her a perfunctory kiss before he went back to the motorcycle and left. She drew herself a hot bath, a hot bubbly bath, as she reviewed messages left on her phone. Ninety percent of them work-related, from the bank. The gnawing feeling beginning in her stomach had nothing to do with physical hunger; it was primal.

Austin, having acquired some more information on Pablo's sleazy past, shared it with Bryce later that night. The next day would take them into Pablo's inner world.

CHAPTER 26

Bryce

Glenn fed us scraps of information on the location where Pablo supposedly lived. Hence, it was time for Austin and I to pay an unheralded visit
to Pablo's turf; we knew that he and a couple of his soldiers were down
in the border town of Ciudad Juarez on business for Maduro. His home
was a room that he called home above the ramshackle, marginally safe
Red Dog Saloon in a sketchy part of Durham, a Podunk flyspeck town
of rough and rowdy bikers, small-time drug dealers, and honky-tonk
unemployed loggers and coal miners. A very different socioeconomic
class from that of the Maduros.

The neighborhood had probably been charming once, but gangs had
gradually overtaken it, and now there was no more than a hapless mix
of tasteless lowlifes living in ramshackle houses next to vacant lots overgrown with high weeds and boxed in by rusted hurricane fencing. A few
television sets could be heard through open windows. Several sunbaked,
rusting cars with open hoods sat on blocks across the street with tall
weeds growing through them. Several local derelicts were sleeping alongside the roadway across from a sordid vacant lot littered with broken
glass and trash and other detritus. One was doing his business behind a
broken wood fence. Citizens minded their own business in this section
of town, either out of fear or indifference.

Durham, located in the badlands of Pocahontas County, was a neglected town of struggling dysfunctional denizen families with gang-
banger teens about an hour outside Slaty Forks. The sinister-looking
clapboard building just off Main Street looked like it hadn't seen paint
since the turn of the century. No activity in the area. A rusting Jeep
Cherokee, minus its engine, squatted in the yard in front of the sagging

porch. A dozen or so bikes gleamed on chrome and black leather saddlebags angled with military precision. A marauding pack of feral cats roamed the porch looking for scraps.

Having acquired a couple of Harleys and donned our "don't fuckwith-me" biker disguises, we pulled into the open space in front of the ramshackle honky-tonk, killed the ignitions, put the kickstands down, locked the ignitions, dismounted, and walked around a couple of wizened old men with no teeth sitting on the front porch chewing tobacco before stepping up and through the dented metal door and threshold of the unsavory one-room biker bar. Having stepped in, Austin and I immediately began processing the scenery. The room was hot and stuffy, and the floor was covered in a thin layer of sawdust. Several sombreros, along with a number of bras and panties, were hanging from the knotty pine paneled walls.

A couple of bikers to our right were sitting and chatting at the window. Neither lifted their head as we went by them. We were immediately assaulted with the darkness and the comingled disreputableness. A miasma of stale beer, sweat, mold, perfume, and vile cigar smoke hung in the air. Crossing the room, we were assailed by the stench of urine, and the pungent citrus disinfectant being used to cover and fumigate the odious stench of the urinals escaping from the broken door hanging on one hinge to the men's room did little. An occasional faint whiff of sickly sweet cannabis wafted from the men's room. There wasn't a ladies' room; then again, no ladies were expected. A silent baseball game was playing on a large TV screen on one wall, but none of the customers paid it any attention. The place vibrated with raucous laughter and throbbing brass mariachi music coming out of a vintage jukebox on a far wall. A scruffy badass gang consisting of a half dozen local unsavory miscreants were sitting at the beer-soaked particleboard bar with names, dates, and vulgarities carved into it, drinking and smoking up a storm. A couple of the raunchy, hardened faces of the denizens looked like they belonged on a post office bulletin board.

None of them really looked hard-core types. More like poseurs or wannabes. There were everal pitchers of beer, a couple of mugs, and a dozen empty shot glasses on the bar. As we watched out of our peripheral vision, they clinked glasses, said something we couldn't hear, and swallowed without another word. They were seemingly cavorting with several somewhat coquettishly dishabille biker chicks wearing lurid crotch-hugging red leather hot pants, cheap stiletto heels, and tank tops that barely contained their breasts. Their crass body language suggested that they were involved in some raucous diss jokes. One of the beer-swilling roughnecks sitting alongside a diminutive brunette lolling against his shoulder had his hand exploring inside the woman's top as his tongue played with her ear. Several platters of nachos had been reduced to crumbles. They were either feisty promiscuous hookers or jaded wives of unemployed, inattentive miners working a second profession for tips. Either way, they certainly weren't virtuous, and chivalrous men would not be found here. Bottom line was, no respectable woman would come to this place.

A haggard-looking geriatric hard-core alkie with a foot-long goatee, looking like hammered shit, hunched over the bar at the far end, snoring with one arm dangling lifelessly at his side. He was wearing a faded wifebeater that probably hadn't been washed in a couple of years and now was the color of urine, and it smelled it. A couple of other unsavory cretins, one a diminutive Mexican, the other a belligerent black Hispanic with long dreads and a gold nose stud, smoked unfiltered Marlboro cigarettes dangling from their mouths; they both seemed to be waiting for the light of a Zippo. Wearing the colors of Mongols, they were arguing about the Giants and the 49ers, one coughing spasmodically. Both were sitting in rickety booths that harkened back to the 1950s, watching vacuously out the front window over the bikes and probably keeping watch for the local police or health authorities. Maybe both. The one with the dreads kept picking at them like a monkey inspecting itself for fleas.

The foul-smelling rabble was a mix of rowdy unsavory blue-collared yahoos, Mexicans, Cajuns, and German and Italian gringos. These were Pablo's malicious lackeys. The jaunty thumping sound of Kenny Roger's "Gambler" was playing out of a jukebox on the back wall: "You gotta know when to hold 'em, know when to fold 'em"

After that ended, the music played was mainly the gut-wrenching pulsing lyrics of Hispanic hip-hop.

With the exception of the front window, all the walls and ceiling were decorated with illuminated posters of Marilyn Monroe, Farrah Fawcett, and countless other seminude celebrities punctuated by gaudy kitsch Mexican beer signs.

Hundreds of lurid bras, pairs of panties, hosieries, and thongs of every imaginable color and flavor had either been voluntarily or involuntarily given up and hung on display from the ceilings without any concession for aesthetics.

We made our way around the burgundy felt pool table, currently sitting vacant in the center of the room with a cherubic-looking Latina perched on a corner obviously on the prowl putting out her hand waving us over to her with a sultry smile. "Hey, hiya, wanna party?" She wore a hip-hugging fuck-me red leather miniskirt and a see-through white baby-doll tank top allowing a liberal view of her tattoo peeking from the open collar of her oversize breasts. The cloying essence of her cheap perfume mixed with a stench emanating from a nearby restroom. With her dangling shapely legs capped with red spike-heeled shoes, she also had three earrings hanging off her left ear. She tossed her shaggy mane of punk blond hair in a tacky way she thought was sexy. Both Austin and I politely declined the invitation before moving on.

Having scoped the pub clientele, we had to assume that her clothing was a required condition of her employment.

Austin and I edged our way to the bar, and I secured a couple of wobbly leg stools at the end of the bar, claiming temporary ownership. We ordered a couple of beers and a small platter of buffalo wings from a

weathered, hard-faced, downtrodden, bleached blond waif of a bartender. She came up behind the bar with watery, desolation eyes that could
barely see us.

The querulous bartender had just finished dragging a case of Bud
longnecks up from the cellar and restocked the ice chest under the bar.
Tall and wasp-thin, she acknowledged us with a bland smile and stepped
forward, tossing her hair back and waving wisps of smoke in the air from
her face. Soaking wet she wouldn't have topped one hundred pounds on
a scale. A synthetic diamond chip pierced her left nostril. She had dark,
coppery skin and a giant lotus blossom tattoo on her right arm and wore
a thin, skimpy T-shirt with a faded Harley-Davidson logo cut low across
her ample breasts and a miniskirt with dark nylons that left very little to
the imagination. Her clothes looked crumbled, like she'd slept in them
for a week. She spoke halting English with a slurred Spanish accent, and
her glare bored into Austin at eye level. We immediately saw from her
countenance that she was hurting inside.

Fatigue? Weariness? Sorrow?

"Whatch y'all drinkin'?"

"Two Coronas," I said.

"Sí, amigo," she responded dully.

As she set two longnecks on the bar in front of us hard enough to
bring foam out of the neck, we instinctively stepped back. She reeked of
stale beer. I took a long swig of the cold beer before wiping my mouth
with the back of my hand and nodded appreciatively. Then, with just a
hint of a smile, she wiped down the bar in front of us.

Austin and I chatted on about nothing of immediate personal importance as we cast an idle glance around the room. I pulled out my
wallet and slapped two bills onto the bar. Money in hand, the bartender
moved down the bar, leaving us alone. Austin and I were both fluent in
Spanish and listened to the mismatched conversations of the patrons.
From what we had seen so far, we were the only sober customers in the
joint, and it was only two o'clock in the afternoon.

The bartender noticed that we were both staring at the grizzled, be-draggled elderly fellow several stools down slouching with his head on the bar sleeping it off and snoring loudly with a pack of Marlboros crushed in his fist. He had a sodden face, was obese and obviously seriously inebriated. We could smell the bourbon fumes emanating from him from our seats, and it could have been considered an accelerant. We both looked him over as we leaned back on the stools, which creaked ominously. He had a cadaverous football-shaped head, long grayish-white hair, a diminutive chin, and glossy, dime-sized eyes with pronounced bags under them when he opened them. Every couple of minutes, the doddering old hippie would come awake and show his withered face, displaying a set of worn yellow teeth, before canting his jowly head toward the floor and belching a loud, gurgling burp, then laying his head back down on the bar with folded arms slower than a centipede in molasses. Evidently, he had imbibed more than his share of alcohol and was now oblivious and alone at life's outpost, just waiting for his moment of darkness.

"Been that way for an hour or so," the chain-smoking bartender volunteered. "He's a maudlin, ornery, curmudgeonly eighty-eight-year-old coot," she added, shaking her head and grimacing. "The gringo lost his wife to cancer four years ago and now comes in every day and quaffs pint after pint of bourbon until he's sloshed and collapses incoherently in a stupor on the bar."

We drank slowly and ordered a couple of chili dogs to give us time to assess the place and survey its customers. The microwaved hot dogs encased in cold, stale bunds struggled toward mediocrity. The vacuous bartender was thirtyish-something and, with her downcast eyes, looked every day of it. She was once a pretty girl but now had bleach blond hair with the roots already showing and a nasty scar across her face that make-up wouldn't cover. She continued telling us that she had lived through some harsh times. It wasn't long before we started a conversation with her, learning that she was Mexican and that her name was Consuela. Here I hoped to elicit information on Pablo.

Consuela was quite loquacious but most likely had the IQ of a tree stump. We learned from her that Pablo owned the place and that she was the bastard's personal property. She seemed drawn to Austin and began to babble about a lot of mundane stuff, including her work schedule and when her shift ended. We listened. Just then, a burst of uproariously harsh testosterone-driven phlegmy laughter erupted with quarrelsome undertones from the bikers at the other end of the bar, apparently from a tedious bawdy joke. One of the bikers yelled for a "fucking beer," and she flipped him a finger, almost habitually, as another biker slid behind the bar and groped her ass. Her response was devoid of authority, and she brought them their beers. There was another hoot of ribald laughter.

Pablo had been the one that, with blinding speed, took out his wrath on her and decorated her face for getting too friendly with one of the local bikers. She was lucky. He stabbed the biker to death, slashing him from chin to hairline right in front of a half dozen regulars no more than three feet from where we were sitting. Everyone in the bar that night watched the atrocity, but not one of the raunchy homeboys stepped forward to stop it.

Consuela conveyed that while the crowd was all full of machismo bluster, they were pathetic wimps when Pablo was in their midst. "Moments later, he opened the bar and ungraciously ordered two of them to bring me out from behind it. He pulled his knife, and before everyone in the bar, he slashed and ruined my face before sending me upstairs screaming in pain to fend for myself."

Consuela was about five-foot-six and rail thin, with a narrow, skeletal face and an untidy tangle of black hair halfway down her back. Her vapid eyes, sad, glum with resignation, were deep and dark, and she had long fake eyelashes. Surprisingly, she spoke of Pablo without rancor or resentment. She and the giddy barmaid waif with tattoos on her neck and a ring in her nose were braless under their Red Dog Saloon T-shirts, and their miniskirts barely covered their womanhood. Neither would be intellectually stimulating, but their sultry voices, ribald wit, and infectious laughs did add some entertainment.

Consuela, we later determined, was an illegal immigrant that Pablo had acquired in a pool game a year ago. Even with her discernible scar, she was warm to everyone and exchanged endless ribald jokes with the local vermin; all of them she knew by name, along with their preferred drinks. For some unknown reason, probably the drugs she was taking in the back room, she had a natural reticence, and she prattled on and became unwittingly generous with uncensored gauche information. We learned that nothing was sacred to Pablo, not God, country, or even human life. He and Consuela had respect for nothing, neither persons, pets, nor property, including his own. An obnoxious guy with an anger management problem for sure yelled for another beer, followed by a couple of lewd innuendos. "Fuck you, amigo" she yelled back. And then there was another round of laughter.

Unfazed, she asked, "Y'all want me get you another beer?" while nursing one of her own. She slammed her beer down, wiping her wet lips with the back of one hand and now slurring her words with a cigarette dangling from her mouth. We declined. She shrugged, giving us a mischievous smile, her eyes at half-mast as she ground her second cigarette butt in an overflowing ashtray before skittering down the bar a little unsteadily to refill empty glasses.

Slipping off the barstool, I left a ten dollar bill on the bar to settle the tab as we left unobtrusively. Assured by Glenn that the rabid Pablo would not be returning tonight, we mounted the bikes and road off quietly, parking the bikes a block away in a dimly lit parking lot. It was now pushing eight, and the light was fading fast. An old homeless peon with a shopping cart was picking through a trash container. He never noticed our presence and seemingly went about his business. We walked back, did a 360-degree check, and slipped noiselessly upstairs through the back alleyway stairway. As Austin and I studied the backside of the saloon, *decrepit* was the word that came to mind.

Consuela, now too pickled and drug-addled to have noticed our exit, would only be leaving the bar downstairs for a couple of hours, maybe longer. A dog began barking from across the street as we slowly ascended the rickety stairs, its owner barked louder, and all went quiet, with no one paying them any heed. Austin narrowed his eyes, searching for any telltale signs of an alarm before methodically scrub-picking the door lock under a low glimmer of ambient light in less than thirty seconds. The agency hadn't taught him that. He had learned that trick of the trade on his own with his own dime. Having put on latex gloves and thanked ourselves for keeping up our tetanus boosters, we slowly opened the door an inch at a time; it squealed on hinges that had most likely never had seen lubricant. Closing the door, a moment later, with our Maglites on, we covertly entered and slowly began prowling through the darkened, unoccupied flophouse. For what we didn't quite know. There were only two windows, and both were covered with tattered sheets. The floorboards creaked under our footfalls, and there was a constant whining sound of a window fan. Other annoying sounds formed a chorus of complaints. The decrepitude was so intense you could smell it: the redolent stench of sour milk, rancid meat, rotten bananas, and who knew what else.

The interior of the squalid flophouse was a depressing collage of cheap paneled walls. Other than Nuna, Pablo was our only direct connection to the Maduro operation. But as the saying goes, "Old sins cast long shadows." We were looking for secrets or anything relevant to the Maduro operation down the road. The sordid room had a bare, low-wattage yellow light bulb of no more than forty watts hanging from the ceiling plugged into an electrical socket on the wall. There was a small round kitchen table with two mismatched wooden chairs. The effluvium smell in the room was obnoxiously foul and stunk terribly to high heaven with a mélange of mawkish odors. The place looked like a hoarder's paradise, with piles of detritus crap everywhere. No amount of lemon Pledge would erase the toxic footprint of decrepitude. It was hard to believe that even Pablo could live in such abhorrent, abysmal conditions. Again, both of us were thankful for keeping up to date on our tetanus booster shots.

We moved stealthily through the squalor, listening and alert to the tiniest nuance and looking for anything out of the ordinary. As we stepped over discarded pieces of clothing strewn about, the filthy wooden floor squeaked beneath our heavy boots. The apartment, although sparse, was a filthy mess.

Moving into the adjacent kitchenette, we quickly noted that the appliances were several decades old and set amid dilapidated yellow Formica countertops with peeling veneer on the particleboard cabinets. The electric stove was graced with a skillet containing two fossilized breakfast sausages links. Austin opened the fridge, and the disgusting stink from rotting food instantly assailed his nostrils. The skink faucet had a steady drip every couple of seconds. Dirty dishes, pots, flatware in a stained porcelain sink, empty whiskey and beer bottles and glasses covered the filthy countertop, which was also littered with ashtrays and leftover marijuana roaches, two open boxes of Wheat Thins, and partially eaten fast-food left rotting. Rummaging through the kitchen drawers and cabinets, we found the first held wrinkled towels, the second a mixed collection of cooking utensils and drug paraphernalia including a crack pipe, empty crack vials, a set of broken earphones and several generic-brand bottles of ibuprofen possibly used by Pablo to do his drug alchemy. The place reeked of stale cigar smoke and garbage that smelled like it hadn't been taken out in a week or more. Bad housecleaning, for sure.

What we found in the living room was mismatched odds and ends of furniture, a dilapidated couch, a fake plant, a hodgepodge of pornography, sleazy true-crime magazines everywhere, rolled up and flattened tubes of toothpaste, and other used or empty toiletries. Despite the label, a couple of OxyContin bottles weren't prescription quality. A relic of a thirteen-inch TV rested on an apple crate. There were over-the-counter medications and several toothbrushes with bristles splayed left and right, looking like they were universally used for brushing teeth and cleaning the wax off his motorcycle. Moving into the minuscule bedroom, we found a hideous twin-size bed that looked like it hadn't been made in months and stank of an effluvium of body sweat and just a hint of pungent marijuana. Open condom packages littered the floor. The drawers of a single dresser were open, spilling out underwear and small empty plastic containers that smelled of ammonia, leading us to conclude that they were using methamphetamine. Piles of junk mail, discarded catalogs, and discarded bills were everywhere.

A summer storm had been forecasted earlier, and that was now proving to be accurate. A heavy rain was pouring down outside, pelting the roof above us.

A bolt of lightning illuminated the room, followed immediately by a loud crack of thunder in the mountains.

The bathroom looked more like a public latrine. The floor was littered with empty tubes of toothpaste, shampoo bottles, and disintegrating clumps of wet tissues. The glass shower door had been cracked and mended with masking tape. The toilet was beyond description and looked like it was ready to overflow with the next flush. The refrigerator in the kitchen, with a constant humming, underscored the silence in the small, dark room. It was stocked full of longnecks and recycled leftovers from downstairs. Just as we were getting ready to exit, my eyes gravitated to a slight depression in the floor. Upon lifting the worn-out rug, we found the jackpot. In the closet, one of his boots tipped over, spilling out a .38 caliber Smith & Wesson and a handful of loose ammo. It also revealed a small three-foot-square locked compartment built into the floor and covered with a tattered burlap rug.

Austin did his magic and opened it, finding another .38 caliber Smith & Wesson, along with what appeared to be a kilo bag of cocaine and possibly heroin, broken down into smaller 32-ounce bags, and a half dozen bundles of cash wrapped in paper bands. Assuming that they were all used one-hundred dollar bills, there was over $50,000 of drug money in the cache that hadn't found its way back to Hugo. I decided to let that settle as they backtracked.

Pablo was either secretly ripping off his boss or freelancing on the side. In checking the other boot, we found a 9 mm glock loaded with loose ammo. But this boot also contained a disturbing photo. The picture was of Nuna. Given the presence of the picture, I decided to confiscate the guns, ammo, and cash. Having taken several pictures of the contents, including the three weapons and the serial numbers on the guns, we meticulously put it all back as found, less the guns and stash. We had now gleaned more information about the character of Pablo and knew there was nothing more of interest to be found, so we left unobtrusively, backtracking and retracing our steps out the way we had entered, emerging in the rear of the building. This Mexican was treacherous and high-octane dangerous.

Returning to the bikes, which now soaking wet under dark skies, we left the area as quietly as two Harleys could in a heavy rain.

Little happened over the next thirty-six hours. Austin sent the guns, ammo, and cash to Langley for analysis. With the hope of lighting a fire in the Maduro camp, we anonymously sent a couple of pictures of our find to Hugo for his perusal.

CHAPTER 27

At 8:00 p.m. the following day, Hugo visualized his latest product delivery being shipped to the island later in the week. He was achieving new heights as a master human trafficker. Walking up the spiral staircase to his bedroom, he found Maria sitting in the upper living room looking out into the distant mountains, indulging herself by sipping her nightly bedtime scotch.

The view of the mountains from this room was dazzling, but tonight it had been obscured by rain and fog. So he poured himself a three-finger glass of bourbon to induce sleep or, even better, let his genius mind free-float about his forthcoming transaction. For the moment, all was copacetic.

He'd finished the drink and gone through his nightly bedtime routine. Now feeling lethargic, he turned off the lights and retired to the bed, pulling his silk sheets and cashmere blanket over him. But, unfortunately, sleep eluded him and the alcohol only dulled his thoughts.

The morning had come much too early.

His maid knocked and opened the door to Hugo's bedroom. "Coffee, Hugo?"

Only half-attentive to her presence, he snapped a reproachful "No, get out of here." He then instantly ameliorated his tone, offering no apologies as he quickly looked at his watch, flashing her a scornful look. The housekeepers weren't expected to report for another couple of hours. Maria and his daughter had already left for their hair appointment in Charleston.

They had planned to spend the better part of the day having lunch and shopping at the Tamarack Marketplace in Beckley before returning home. Architecturally the Tamarack resembled an Appalachian village, and it consisted of diverse eateries, boutiques, and craft shops offering everything from Waterford crystal to fresh donuts to unique handcrafted wooden statues. Hugo was sure they wouldn't return until late in the evening.

With the maid having retreated downstairs, he pushed the fresh sheets back and slid out of bed. Stiffness and arthritic aches growled and barked through his body as he began his morning pandiculation routine, stretching out one knotted muscle and then another as he made his way to the bathroom. Then, with a pulsating hangover, he went through the motions of brushing his teeth before stepping into the shower.

He made his way downstairs, stopping at the gym to stretch and loosen some muscles before taking his seat in the breakfast lounge. He looked rough and rugged, with his open-neck shirt showing a muscular hairy chest beneath it. His eyes were dark, his hair mussed, and he had a day's stubble on his face.

He watched the young twenty-three-year-old buxom brunette maid enter the room, setting down the coffee before him.

"What might you desire for your breakfast, *signor*?" she asked.

He watched her as intensively as she did him.

"Come here," he demanded with asperity, patting his lap with the palm of his hand. With her head downcast, she cowered to his demand and obeyed, sitting down ever so gently on his lap. "That's a good girl," he said mockingly, his face impassive.

Slowly running his questing hand under her skirt and up her inner thighs, he felt her stiffen a bit as he slowly messaged her womanhood with his deft fingers.

"Relax, Francisca; all is well."

"Mr. Hugo, please…I don't wish you to do this," she cried.

"Francisca, yes, you do," he chortled. "Would you and your husband be happier as sharecroppers in Venezuela?"

"No, no…please, Mr. Hugo. We must not go back there."

"Is not your husband happy working the grounds? Are you both not paid well for your services?"

"*Sí*…Mr. Hugo, we are very happy," she whimpered.

Pulling her lips to his and forcing his tongue between hers before working back to her ear, he whispered, "You will continue to honor our little secret, Francisca. Do you agree, *señorita*?"

With a slight whimper and downcast eyes, she responded, surrendering to her servitude, ""Sí… Senor Hugo."

"Now, feed me, *senorita*." He pushed her off him and slapped her on her malleable ass as she quickly clacked across the marble floor and retreated to the kitchen. She soon returned, refreshing his coffee, and served him a Canadian ham and pepper omelet with a warm bagel and cheese. Hugo was reading the morning newspaper and barely looked up as he quickly waved her off.

He was in deep thought, thinking of the jaded confrontation he and Maria had had with Nuna a couple of days ago. He knew that he had made a mistake in judgment when he accepted Nuna as his banking representative. Anyway, she would soon be taken care of and would never breathe a word again.

Retreating to his private library at the rear of the mansion, he found his private secretary and receptionist in the reception area behind her desk, already on the phone taking care of daily operations and solicitous contractors. Walking past her, he cordially said, "Bueno días, Joanna." He continued, "I have a full plate of issues to take care of today, and I don't want to be bothered or interrupted for the balance of the day."

He unlocked his heavy oak door and disappeared into his office without saying another word.

He was interrupted by a light tap on the door. He looked up at the sound of Joanna opening it just a crack but enough to peek in and let him know that she was shutting down her computer and closing up for the day.

Joanna Paloma was a forty-five-year-old voluptuous redheaded beauty of Mexican-Venezuelan decent, deeply tanned, with a figure that still turned heads. One of the benefits of working for Hugo was that she could freely use the spa, pool, and massage parlor, complete with a tanning booth. So naturally, Mrs. Paloma, having lots of time on her hands after work, took full use of the opportunities available to her.

She met his eyes with the look of an intimate confidante. "Signor Hugo, I'm available if you interested before I go home," she said in a dulcet voice.

Having finished most of his business, and given that it was getting late in the day, he decided to dally a bit and take her up on her offer. Joanna was older than Maria, a matronly woman with her brownish-red hair made up in a retro beehive. While not quite as pretty as Maria, she was still very attractive and much more enthusiastic in bed or on the leather office couch. Joanna actually reminded him a lot of the Hollywood actress Susan Sarandon with her wild hairstyles and impressive breasts. Wearing rectangular glasses and a form-fitting white diaphanous blouse with a black pencil skirt, she looked like she was trying out for a hot librarian part in a porn movie. It was indeed an ideal arrangement. Mrs. Joanna Paloma's husband was a senior produce buyer for a grocery chain up in Morgantown and was constantly on the road and out of state for weeks on end.

According to Joanna, he was a good provider, a loyal husband, and a decent father to their attractive fifteen-year-old daughter. Unfortunately, she complained, he was always tired when at home. Worst, he was a complete bore in bed, with the frequency of sex dropping precipitously. While Joanna wasn't exactly the sharpest pencil on the block, she was attractive, with singular femininity and charisma, efficient on the phone, and most impressive, she had a great set of well pronounced tits and excelled in the skill of sex, which was unfulfilled at home.

"Is everything all right?" she asked, stepping beyond the doorway and into the soundproof library. Hugo gave her a perfunctory nod. Joanna fanned her face with a file in her hand as if she was suddenly hot, then unfastened the top three buttons of her blouse so that the lacy camisole she was wearing peeked out. Then, sotto voce, she added, "Whew, it's warm in here."

Hugo paid her well, twice what she had been making as a cashier at the Kroger's grocery market where she previously worked. He had already removed his sport jacket and rolled up his sleeves earlier in the day because of the afternoon heat. Her Chanel No. 5 perfume, which he occasionally provided her with, had the essence of spring flowers after a light rain.

"No, there just happens to be a lot of shit going on at the moment."

"Maybe I can offer you a distraction that will take your mind off the shit, Señor Hugo, no?

She stepped in and slowly wiggled into the office, crooning. Stepping behind him as he sat relaxed behind his desk, she began to slowly massage his shoulders with her experienced, splayed hands, whispering soft, lewd encouragements in his ear. He put his head back against her ample cleavage, and he let out a low moan, fully enjoying the massage.

Having locked the door, Joanna removed her glasses and placed them on the desk before slowly sauntering around to the side of his chair and, with a dazzling smile and visceral instincts, giving him a mischievous smile, kissing him on the lips, stifling any instinct he might have to object. She knew better than to push him: Hugo could explode from silent brooding to explosive rage in a second.

On the contrary, Hugo's pulse jumped into overdrive and turned fierce with hunger. Giving her a dangerously knowing smile, he took hold of her, pulling her down to him, angled her head so that it faced his, and parted her lips and savagely claimed her mouth like he was starving for a taste of the woman. He knew that she was vulnerable and planned to use her sexual energy to control and manipulate her to his advantage. She enjoyed being used and manhandled by Hugo. His rolled-back sleeves lying across the top of his desk showed muscular forearms covered with black curly hair. His white shirt opened at the neck and stretched across his sculpted chest, masking the raw masculinity within.

Joanna's heart was pulsating so hard that it almost frightened her. Her emotions were confused as she was sexually overly excited about touching him.

"Señor Hugo, would you like some music?" she asked.

"Si, señorita," he said.

She turned on a narcocorrido recording that she knew Hugo especially liked.

"Would you like me to stimulate you with my mouth?" she quietly mewed in his ear.

Her voice was low, intimate, and sexually stirring.

Hugo, exhibiting a wicked smile, reached up, took her hand, and brought her around. She obediently twirled and knelt on the floor before him obediently giving him absolute possession. Without another word being said, she let her hair down, unbuttoned her blouse, and slowly removed it along with her bra exposing her 38D tits, which were firm and high. She couldn't resist the overwhelming macho power of Hugo Maduro. He unfastened his holstered gun and placed it on the desk. Slowly, deliberately, she unbuckled his belt, unzipped his slacks, and slid them down to his ankles. She knew exactly how to arouse him. He reached down and began pinching her nipples and kneading her ample breasts. Joanna moaned and mumbled something under her breath as she expertly massaged his cock up and down between her warm breasts. She could feel his pulse pumping against her palm and fingers. His cock swelled against her warm hand, which she held fast. With Hugo now rock solid, she went after him with renewed enthusiasm, taking him deeper and deeper down her throat. Finally, he took hold of her head and began deep fucking her mouth until he couldn't hold back anymore and exploded, filling her mouth with his semen. She writhed uncontrollable and heard Hugo's muttered curse.

Pulling out of her mouth, he ordered her to lick it clean. Mrs. Paloma, without looking up, obediently licked every drop off his penis before gently licking and gently kissing both of his balls. Hugo picked her up and laid her gently across his desktop on her back. With her naked legs spread wide hanging off the desk, her ass on the edge, he went down on her, licking and caressing her furry cunt with his tongue as she cried for mercy. "Going to taste that sweet pussy of yours," he breathed out. Her entire body spasmed and shuddered as raw pleasure rolled through it. His hands slid over her breasts and stomach, caressing her hips and touching her sensitive parts. There was a reverence in his hold of her that mystified her.

He fucked her hard in perfect synchronization with her hips until her orgasm exploded in erotic lust. She began to scream as she felt both his hands tighten on her ass, his cock diving through her pussy savagely with ownership.

Hugo stood up, looked her naked body up and down, and then pulled the limp and motionless Mrs. Paloma up with him. "You're not afraid of me, are you, *senora*?"

She hesitated and then said, "No, not at all, Signor Hugo." Pulling her naked breasts into his chest, he pulled her head back by her hair before running his fingers through her wild mane, kissing her on the forehead, and sending her on her way. She gave him a pouting glance as she grabbed her blouse and skirt and fished her bra and panties off the floor, then slowly put them back on as she stood before Hugo's predatory eyes. She headed out the door flattening and smoothing her pencil skirt and changed her high heels for tennis shoes, placing them in a box and storing them in a file cabinet under her desk.

Despite her mediocre clerical and computer skills, Joanna felt secure at her job. She would be back at her desk tomorrow morning just like she had for the past three years since her sister's unfortunate car accident. Her sister, Colleen, who had been Hugo's private secretary for just shy of a year, had shared with Joanna how much she loved her job. She had lied. Unfortunately, she had been killed by a hit-and-run driver as she crossed a two-lane road on a dark, unlit night in front of her apartment. The driver was never found. Hugo had not lost any sleep over the accident, as he had grown tired of her moral character anyway. She had recently threatened him with sexual harassment if he continued to touch her. He made a secret wish that the bitch would soon be no longer.

Wishes do sometimes come true, he thought to himself at the time.

Upon meeting her sister Joanna at the wake that he had decided to attend for appearances, and again at the funeral, he found her sexually interesting. He arranged to have several lunches with her later that month. She was pretty open about herself, and he listened intently as she discussed how bored she was at her job and her domestic failings at home.

Having learned that Joanna didn't share the moral standings of her sister, he offered her the job.

She didn't hesitate and graciously accepted it without further ado. Within the first several weeks, she quickly learned the requirements of her position well. But, unbeknownst to her, she was recorded by several strategically placed hidden video cameras every time she entered his office.

He thought, Joanna Paloma is about to be my personal paramour and my personal property. She may be married to her husband, but she is my property to use as I want.

He owned her and hadn't let her petite fifteen-year-old daughter go unnoticed either. With eyes of pure evil, he drained his glass of scotch. This was an end-of-day ritual to him.

The following day

Two men arrived in a SUV at night driving to the back gate before reaching the office of Hugo Maduro. When the gates opened, the interior lights were dimmed. Both rough-looking men were dressed in business clothing and each had a bulge under their left arm. The driver was at least six-feet and broad-shouldered. The other man was shorter, also broad-shouldered, with dark eyes searching left and right, moving in both apposition and in concordance, with little compassion for anyone or anything that might threaten them. One of Hugo's security guards opened the door and gestured for them to enter.

Hugo knew both of them. Indeed, they both worked for him. He walked assertively across the carpeted floor as if he were crossing a conference room to greet his colleagues.

"I believe that I have a couple more problems within my organization that needs immediate attention," he said. As the capo of the Maduro cartel, Hugo held his darkest thoughts in check. He was smart and
ruthless.

A week later, Joanna's husband, who hadn't attended her sister's funeral or even called, disappeared, leaving a note that he was relocating
to Mexico and leaving her for another woman. No one ever saw Senor
Paloma again, not alive anyway. Fortunately, Joanna wasn't at all overly
distraught with the untimely news and filed for divorce soon after. Unable to cover the expense of her apartment anymore with one paycheck,
she eagerly accepted Hugo's proposal that both she and her daughter
live rent-free on his estate for as long as she worked for him. Of course
there would be conditions attached. One, her salary would be reduced
accordingly. Two, she was to be available to him 24-7. Joanna, having
no other options, accepted immediately, signing his contract. What she
didn't realize was that she was expendable and that her daughter was now
his property occupying his dark thoughts, just as Nuna Polinski did.
Timing was everything.

CHAPTER 28

In his line of work, Bryce had to deal with those who turned his stomach. He had to compartmentalize and separate his feelings, swim with uncontrollable squids and ignore the savagery of the sharks. Maduro was a large, avaricious squid with many camouflaged tentacles and his major bête noire. He was into illegal arms trading, drugs, money laundering, and the human trafficking business. From Norman's Cay, he was procuring kidnapped girls who had been eking out a living on the streets from all of South America, Mexico, Asia, Europe, and even the United States, selling and shipping them like fresh fruit off a tree to the brothels of the Middle East, Africa, Russia, and anywhere else there was a demand.

He was ruthless, vile, and despicable. He ran a professional, well-planned, well-executed smuggling operation with total impunity, an unlimited budget, and plenty of manpower to do his bidding.

Unknown to Bryce and his associates until just recently, Maduro had formed a potent nefarious alliance with a rogue incognito American arms broker based in Cuba locally known for, as they say in Spanish, his *la vida loca*. The latest intel from their operative on the island had it that the imperious American was being remunerated exceptionally well by Maduro for strategically overseeing his warehouse logistics on the island and acting as an essential conduit for his international black-market operations. Hugo had met with the American through another renegade rebel contact while exiled in Cuba in the midseventies. According to the growing bloody dossier, the American was approximately 6 feet in height, 200 pounds, about 30 to 35 years old, unmarried, and of unknown origin but had been described as having dark, brooding, menacing eyes where nothing lived and a faint but recognizable lilt indicating a Southern American accent.

Of immediate concern was that it was recently learned that Senator Schiff has visited and stayed at Vallarta's huge twenty-two-room villa numerous times over the past year, with his most recent visit being only two weeks ago on his return from Venezuela. The villa stood on a half acre, a spacious lot by local standards. It had commanding views of the ocean and the surrounding villages. It was surrounded by high stone walls, and entry was afforded by a wrought-iron gate and an armed security guard. Built in 1938, the villa had six bedrooms, each with a full bath. A master suite was on the top floor, and there was a spacious kitchen, sunken living room, covered veranda, five fireplaces, and a windowless maid's quarters next to a guard's barracks on the ground floor. Vallarta didn't employ any maids. He had trained female servants who had been mentally broken and now subversively fit the bill. When he purchased the villa, he made a number of alterations to accommodate his lifestyle. Local day workers and contractors had done all the work quietly without government permits. The rooms had been soundproofed, with several secretly ensconced rooms behind solid oak walls holding his helpless young urchin captives.

Two weeks later, an international warrant was issued out of Venezuela. He was being sought as a person of interest for questioning in the assassination of a Venezuelan oil minister and his family while they were on vacation in Costa Rica. Mr. Vallarta suddenly disappeared quietly off international radar without a trace.

From what was understood, Vallarta was a shady, elusive, inscrutable, freewheeling American businessman notorious in Asia for being deeply involved in a number of shadowy international business deals, including human trafficking. He had a reputation for acting as a middleman and a logistics czar for a number of crime syndicates, including the Asian and Russian mafia operating out of Asia and several outlaw states in the Persian Gulf, Africa, and South America. In addition, it was alleged that he had secured substantial holdings now in Bacardi and Domino's Cuban sugar cane operations.

Both the FBI and CIA had recently found hundreds of millions of dollars in offshore bank accounts now identified as belonging to a Cuban international real estate developer by the name of Chris Vallarta. He was also known to be volatile, a coldhearted assassin and a procurer of assassinations for a price. It was rumored and later reported by the police that he blew up a grammar school for girls in Nan Hai, Cambodia, to facilitate his escape on his yacht. One hundred twenty-five children perished without witnesses or informants willing to talk. Even the local police, notorious for being corrupt and inept, stood back, refusing to investigate further, fearing his zealous bestial depravity. Unable to quell the grieving parents' anger and keening and hindered by a ransom demand, they went silent and pressured the local populace to do the same, fearing reprisal from the Vallarta cartel and fraying any hope for justice.

Vallarta was seemingly a fast-talking elusive figure with several aliases and had never been arrested. His current alias was known to only a select few in the business, such as Hugo Maduro, Fidel Castro, and Jeffrey Epstein. There was always the foreboding risk of being unmasked, being hailed by one name when he had identified himself by another. The risk came with the turf and was an occupational hazard for a demon.

It was also learned based on extraneous information that his coterie of elites included Castro, who had become a close personal friend of Vallarta's and frequently was an overnight VIP guest at his compound. While Maduro had arranged a number of lavish meetings with him at his luxury compound at Mariel Bay, just twenty-eight miles west of Havana, they hadn't been seen together in over four years. But in his line of business, that wasn't all that unusual.

From what little they'd learned about Chris Vallarta, it seemed he was extremely selective in terms of whom he met with and would not set foot on American soil for fear of federal arrest and prosecution. While he occasionally traveled internationally out of Cuba via his private jet or yacht, the country could not have an extradition treaty with the United States or Canada.

Intelligence had it that he rarely left his villa without armed security guards and, to the best of their knowledge, he had never visited any mob-run Cuban casinos.

He was insulated under the protective umbrella provided by Castro and Maduro. When he did venture out in his armored Humvee, he had a driver and an armed guard and never maintained the same profile during the sojourn. He changed hats, shirts, jackets, scarves, and shoes several times daily.

Like Maduro, Vallarta was paranoid about his personal security and didn't allow any pictures to be taken of him, and he always wore gloves, leaving no fingerprints. With what little there was to see of his hairline, it seemed his hair was silver-gray, with the variegated tones of a blond man who had gone prematurely gray. His glacial eyes had been described as dark gray and turbulent, like a killer's. In addition, it was rumored that his hands and face were seriously scarred. Described as a reclusive megalomaniac figure, he always covered his head with a black wide-brim straw fedora. In addition, he wore dark aviator glasses and a balaclava when out in public, feigning a paranoia about germs. No one alive could describe his face, not even the female companions he periodically purchased and sometimes received as gifts from Maduro. However, his prodigious and malevolent appetite for women, especially young virgins, was well established.

Austin made several calls and arranged for a high-tech surveillance camera to be set up on the roof of a high-rise two blocks away from the compound. While there was an array of tall buildings in the area, the one that held his interest lacked a maintenance staff and gave him an unobstructed view. Having affixed a long lens and sighted in the electronic camera on the compound, it was just a matter of waiting it out.

Several days later, Austin got a call from his disembodied contact in Mariel Bay. Austin had solicited and assured the contact that he would be paid well for the intelligence should it be well documented. It was.

He explained, "From what the contact has been able to extract through a hacked government database, Chris Vallarta, as he is known, doesn't exist. He is unmanly jaded and doesn't process an iota of compassion for anyone but himself. From the surveillance cameras that were set up above his meticulously built villa, we know he comes out in the salmon-colored courtyard around noon each day with different teenage girls in various stages of undress. He relaxes in his chaise lounge by the pool like a sated feral pig with a large, elegant Cuban Cohiba in one hand, already trimmed, nursing a cocktail in the other. In contrast, one of the young mamacitas lathers him in sunscreen and pleasures him by kneading his genitals, while the other entertains him from the crystal-clear waters of the pool. The agent keeps clicking away and electronically photographing the bizarre activity. The lens coverage is perfect; it's like we're sitting next to him.

"While he is blasé, wearing a bathing suit soaking up the rays, he is self-effacing when it comes to his diabolical face, which is fully covered by a balaclava, and his gloved hands. Though we don't have a good close-up, it almost looks like his upper chest might have been scarred from burns received in a fire.

"Also, the perimeter of his eight-foot concrete walled villa, including the entrance, is heavily guarded by an armed security detail of large men further inflated by the Kevlar vests they are wearing under their jackets. The villa is located in the older section of town and is surrounded by a dilapidated labyrinth of steep and untended narrow streets.

"It's exigent that we get some eyes on the ground inside his little fiefdom."

Just then, Bryce had an epiphany: Senator Schiff.

In detail, he and Austin reviewed the video and stills pensively on the table before them. They portrayed the enigma of a masked man, over a period of ten years, who looked slightly different in every picture.

The man, maybe in his late thirties, was slim, wearing a white blousy shirt and Western jeans inside a Vietnamese hostess bar. If this was Chris Polinski, he didn't look anything like the Chris that Bryce had known. The following clip had him exiting a dark Mercedes outside a massage parlor with two young girls on the Khao San Road in Havana, flanked by two Cuban guards armed with 9 mm submachine guns. There were a number of shots like these, all vague, taken from a distance by Austin's contact, all show him conversing and shaking hands with dangerous-looking individuals in empty parking lots, abandoned warehouses, and red-light alleyways.

Bryce got a haunting feeling and had a dark, rancid taste on his tongue that rankled him. While this sleazy son of a bitch wasn't a dead ringer for the Chris that he had known, there was something poignant about the spectral image he projected: his age, his build, his posture, and the way he held his head. As he was about to put the photo back down, he noticed Vallarta's left-handed pointed ring gesture in the image. Looking closely, Bryce was paying particular attention to the nuance of the oblique angle of his arm, positioned to the right, holding the cigar in the air, and the belligerent tilt of his chin as he exhaled a perfect smoke ring into the air. He felt a horrifying cold finger run down his spine, hearkening his back to that last night on the dock in Dung Ha. The thoughts were chilling as he took in another shot of him idly belching out another vaporous O into the air. Did Chris actually commit a heinous parricide, killing his parents to inherit their money and home?

That day, Chris's driver took him to Havana, where he boarded a private jet owned by the Maduro organization, which left just before noon. In checking the flight plan, also through a hacked database, they found Chris was flying on a Gulfstream to Norman's Cay in the Bahamas, which was no more than a thirty-minute flight. Having landed a half hour later, he took a jeep and drove to the main house, where he would be staying for a couple of days of business and pleasure. A shipment of girls would be delivered, and he would be a part of the inspection team salivating to taste the fruit.

Having unpacked in his guest room, he went out on the patio and was met by an attractive waitress and offered a gift of appreciation from Hugo, which included a drink, the waitress if desired, and a pretrimmed

Cuban cigar. Chris made a show of licking it just to his liking, fired it up, and exhaled a cloud of aromatic smoke.

One week later
Rumor had it that this delightfully unscrupulous American scamp with the moniker "Scarface" turned up one-day terra incognita in Phnom Penh, Cambodia, after roving the Vietnamese highlands with nothing but a rogue amoral talent for cavorting, pimping, subjugating, and selling downtrodden children and young girls and other orphaned street urchins into prostitution for cash. Being skillful and highly elusive, with an unprecedented pattern of corruption, he soon began to up the ante to a new height, smuggling out small amounts of antiquities via the gray market by bribing customs officials with young girls recruited off the streets. Shortly after, he began to blackmail corrupt South Vietnamese generals and politicians, smuggling out excess American weaponry, even guns and explosives, from captured and overrun military sites in South Vietnam. After the war, he audaciously relocated to the Ha Long Bay area, which connected to the Gulf of Tonkin in North Vietnam.

Though the authorities were unaware, he now resided on a sixty-five-foot yacht of unknown provenance and using his natural charisma and subterfuge, had begun a budding business of debauchery, carousing and buying and selling scores of prepubescent Amerasian girls left behind in a decadent society for the taking on the streets of Saigon by American soldiers exiting the country. He had become a psychopathic killer and looked upon them as cute, pointless lemmings to be collected, corralled, and bred for profits. *His profits.* Bodies of prostitutes, children, call girls, escorts, and women he picked up in bars and impregnated began showing up in dumpsters, alleyways, and abandoned cars, with Mr. Vallarta disavowing any knowledge of the macabre carnage.

All of them were brutally murdered and expunged, except one who escaped the brutal carnage only because her seat belt released as they sat at a traffic light late one night. She threw open the van door and ran for her life into and through the narrow alleyways as his bullets rained around her.

Repulsed in every possible way, she found it almost impossible to describe the horror she had been subjected to. She claimed that he was a belligerent monster with gluttony for alcohol and cocaine and an insatiable sexual compulsion for ultrarough sadistic sex, including asphyxiation games. His preferred passion was torturing and strangling young adolescent girls to death as he raped them. Then, like the predator Tyrannosaurus rex scavenging for a meal, he preyed on young homeless early teen girls on the street who had no family, place to stay, money, education, or means or opportunity to support themselves. To him, they were "cotton candy" for the taking, easy prey.

She had seen him with her own eyes rape and squeeze the life out of a sixteen-year-old-girl who refused to be waxed between her thighs for religious reasons. He broke each of her finger bones, her arms, and then legs with his bare hands and listening to her beg from the floor, sobbing and screaming for his mercy as he smiled and slowly squeezed her slender neck until her despairing eyes bulged and her heart stopped. While she had no evidence, she had heard rumors that the bodies are put aboard his yacht and disposed of out at sea as shark bait.

He was a sadistic psychopath who believed in the vexation of the spirit without any taboos or moral boundaries. He had become an avatar of evil, tolling out torture and bloodshed, makin the Marquis de Sade seem like an amateur in comparison.

The local police had reported a notable trend of young Eurasian girls disappearing from nightclubs and raves, never to be heard from again; if they were found, they were in pieces. Young women in their early teens walking the streets, Vietnamese, Blacks, Filipinas, Latinas, and Malaysians, were being kidnapped, brutally murdered, and left like trash.

The murders only stopped after he left the territory and disappeared. Another grisly report described the growing trafficking of women and young teen girls out of Cambodia and their subsequent torture and sexual slavery into prostitution. The evidence against him was staggering and repulsive. But, unfortunately, the whole sinister enterprise was nearly impossible to prevent or prosecute because of the corrupt police and the collusion with organized crime, and the unwillingness of the women who had been rescued to identify their captors.

He later added illegal arms and explosives to his growing business, supplying Asian insurgencies and providing military grade weapons, ammunition, and other equipment to the communist regime of North Vietnam. He currently had multiple warrants from Cambodia and Vietnam for murder, extortion, theft of a yacht, and human trafficking. Yet the authorities simply turned their eyes, allowing him to disappeared again. Two years later, he resurfaced in Cuba, apparently now affluent. It wasn't long before Chris Vallarta brokered a partnership with Hugo Maduro and the Castro regime on the island.

* * *

Bryce

I just sat there in total stupefaction, reviewing the psychological profile. Chris had become a venomous psychopath with an insatiable penchant for sadomasochism, dominating and sexually abusing young virgin girls. A killer. He had somehow become the antithesis of everything that Nuna remembered about him.

Suddenly, fears that had fractured in the back of my head began gelling. I had an unbidden epiphany, with images and sequences hearkening from the past, harassing me in the periphery of my consciousness as they rushed forward to the present. It was a memory of my last encounter with Chris that still made my blood boil. I asked Austin to again look into the circumstances surrounding the death of Chris's parents in detail. I also requested that the same be done with the death of Nuna's father. I needed to know. This blighted psychopath was not only a murderer; he was also a criminal directly responsible for the hedonistic enslavement and death of countless women and young girls.

"I promise this ephebophile will be condemned to eternal damnation for what he did," I said.

Senil touched a mouse, and the image of Chris Vallarta came on the screen.

"What is it that you want me to do with it?"

"I want to change the image, Senil. See if it matches someone I know."

He clicked the mouse again. A grid appeared over the image. "OK?"

"First, I want to lose the mask."

Senil typed in a few coordinates, and they immediately narrowed into just a square of the suspect's face. Then, using a cursor, he outlined the area of the mask. Gently, he moved his cursor back and forth, as if he were airbrushing, while guiding the cursor like a surgeon. "Did this guy change his face on you?"

"Not sure, just working on a hunch."

"This process is called grafting and displacement. Essentially, we eliminate a field: skin tone, a scar, in this case, a mask." Instantly, the facial area was blank, and Senil retrieved a section of skin from another part of the image and filled in the space. "Then we graft onto it." Next, he smoothed out the facial lines. "Cut and paste."

"That's great," I said, leaning over his shoulder. "Now, what do you say we try and alter the hair? Make it short and close to the skull. Now set the hairline back a bit around the sides."

Senil started playing around with the cursor again. "Yes, like that?" It took about a minute more of grafting and displacement before my suspicion was validated.

The image on the screen almost knocked me to the floor.

"Anything else, Bryce? If you're not satisfied, give me a word."

"No, Senil." I patted his shoulder. "I think we're done."

The person in the screen, whom I had known during the Vietnam War, was incongruent with the monster now called Chris Vallarta.

But I was looking with apprehension at Chris Polinski a.k.a. Chris Vallarta.

Chris now stood at the guest room window in Maduro's mansion on Norman's Cay, looking out at the magnificent ocean and then looking down at the paltry stream of humanity working the gardens below. His thoughts drifted back to Asia, where war-weary girls would gather around him, the masked American. He would bribe the very best with promises of blissful escape from their benighted homeland to America. Then, feeding and protecting them from the harsh street life and bone-numbing rain and dampness of the night they were coming from, he could bed any of them.

In letting them wallow in the numbing bliss of marijuana and cocaine, he could lead them back to his compound just outside the city and do whatever he wanted them to do. They willingly put their dismal future in his hands.

He was the epitome of a face of evil.

Due to the injuries that he lived with, it was plausible that he eschewed all contact with any groups. He was totally confident and depended only on himself, answering only to himself. Living off the grid, eluding apprehension, he had somehow become arrogant, his narcissism escalating to all-out grandiosity. The perfect assassin: swift, silent, and deadly.

Vallarta's warped moral soul didn't possess a tinge of repentance or remorse for all the girls and women he had murdered. Instead, he believed in the vexation of spirit and that he had a right to all that mattered to him in this life. So he liked to hurt the girls and demean them to his mindless satisfaction. He also believed that virgins awaited him in paradise. He was tired of Asian whores, but the cash flow was enormous and continuous.

Unbeknownst to anyone alive, Chris also lived with a deep, hardwired hatred of his parents.

They had always been ultrareligious and military disciplined, and he, in his mind, suffered a strict unnatural upbringing of damnation. He had stood at the edge of the road looking over the cliff at the crumbled remains of his parent's car, which had caromed off the guardrail, flipping over a one-hundred-foot cliff. He had cut the brake lines. Then, without remorse and needing to be sure that neither had survived the crash, he had climbed down and tossed a match into the leaking gas. Chris justified it as poetic justice. He now would receive their house, a sizable financial inheritance, not to mention a life insurance policy.

I saw the blackness at his center, the virulent purple flashes of his narcissism and his pride in himself.

"We don't have a driver's license, birth date, a social security number for Chris Vallarta, and he doesn't use a credit card. He is almost a ghost. A man that doesn't exist and to date hasn't been taken down for his crimes. Pinning a crime on him would be like harpooning a whale with a toothpick."

I nodded. "We need a larger toothpick. He could be found guilty of pseudocide, or faking or falsifying one's own death. Vallarta is an evil man that cannot take criticism and is now totally beyond the pale of human decency."

Chris was two different men occupying one body. We closely watched Vallarta's movements and communications with a high-tech surveillance team at three locations monitoring every telecommunication and physical movement within the predator's compound. We needed to know all the dimensions of his sexual debauchery. While I knew that he was reckless, it never occurred to me that Chris Polinski had a dubious morality and unfathomable appetite for torture and murder.

There was a time when he and I were friends, and even though we were opposites in most respects, I genuinely liked Chris. That was ancient history now. If this lecherous, cold-blooded bastard was indeed the Chris I had known and I had failed to see his barbaric appetites, there would be no absolution in his future.

There would be no mercy.

CHAPTER 29

In the summer, lunchtime at the Foxfire Grill on Snowshoe Mountain was a bustle of tourists, backpackers, and hikers looking for a relaxing meal in the unique rustic ambiance of the trendy, overpriced mountain oasis with incredible scenery. It also provided a chance to decompress and brainstorm while listening to the aspen highland music floating in from the village speakers. No less than twenty-five turbines arranged in rows like whirligigs graced the summits of the wind farms before us. Austin, Glenn, and I rendezvoused in the Snow Shoe parking lot at noon before walking in the front door and just barely heard the jingles of the bell announcing our entrance over the din of the small but energized crowd of diners.

A rush of warm air tinged with competing scents of garlic, oregano, warm homemade bread, and grilled steaks wafted upward in the air and made my stomach growl. Several large HD TVs were locked on a baseball game between the Red Socks and the Yankees. The crowd was intense, and emotions were high.

Taking three stools at the bar next to the window overlooking the slope, the three of us sat observing the crowd with mixed expressions. The Red Socks hit a home run with two on base, and the crowd, with all eyes on the screens, broke out yelling and roaring.

Bryce quickly scanned the restaurant, ensuring no one was seated nearby or in the vicinity to overhear their conversation. The restaurant was crowded, and the background din around them was welcoming. Having ordered a round of beers from the bar, the three glanced around, doubly ensuring that we recognized no one and that no one was paying us any unnecessary attention. We were subtly disguised to mask our identities in public.

We had all taken notice of the security cameras over the bar area that Austin had disconnected moments earlier.

The waitress came to the bar and advised us that the table we had requested was now available. Taking us to the table and filling our glasses with water, she handed us menus and, having graciously identified herself as Heidi, said she would be our server. Her soft voice held that lyrical touch of Appalachia. She then graciously read us the specials before walking back to the bar.

Upon her return to the table, Glenn and I ordered the Wednesday special: roast beef dinner, mashed potatoes, and green beans. Austin's voracious appetite, on the other hand, succumbed to a full rack of ribs, baked beans, and a large helping of mash potatoes.

Glenn then took the lead and began updating us of his findings inside the Maduro mansion. Having deciphered the locks on Hugo's office and library, he had methodically searched each room several times. Glenn unsnapped his briefcase and spun it around, facing Austin and me. Inside was the Slaty Forks mansion's floor plan, with the floor plan and site plan of Norman's Cay next to it. Also in the briefcase were three one-inch-thick file folders of documents that Glenn had meticulously copied from files and off the Maduro computers. Glenn gave Austin Maduro's computer password, username, and pseudonym for further investigation into his nefarious activities.

The first file contained the Maduros' financial records going back twelve years to the present. The second one contained records of their financial transactions, which included disbursements, receipts, and offshore accounts owned by Maduro Enterprises. The third and final one contained a wealth of emails, transactions, and pictures of young females nude and dressed as received, along with the names, origination, names, and titles of all contacts involved in the human transaction. A number of them featured Maduro, Chris Vallarta, and the Doc abusing adolescent girls at Norman's Cay.

"Glenn, great job," I said.

"Thanks, but there's still more that I need to get to."

The tension at the table had hit a fever pitch. Austin was cracking his knuckles, anxious to make a move. I kept it all in check.

"Austin and I will review the data tonight and forward it to the admiral for his perusal in the morning," I said.

Our meals arrived: roast beef piled high on a slice of rye, a humongous spear of a pickle, and a generous portion of garlic mashed potatoes. Unfortunately, Austin was less than impressed as he noshed his three inches of ribs, which looked like they might have been shared with another meal. He did have an ample portion of baked beans and sweet potato fries, though.

Having finished our meals, our stomachs sated, Austin, Glenn, and I enumerated the details of the upcoming transaction with Pablo. I went to one of the rest rooms and air-dried my hands for lack of paper towels. Returning to the table, I picked up the tab, dropping several bills on the table, and we wended our way out just as the social activity in the restaurant began to pick up considerably. We drove away from the village resort parking lot in separate cars and descended the mountain.

The next few days were grueling. Nuna seemed solemnly preoccupied, her face taut with anxiety. Austin and I were busy reviewing Glenn's shared data on the Maduros and focusing on Senator Davis and Senator Assad.

The pace of the operation was such that Nuna and I were too busy to pursue a personal relationship further at this point in time.

Austin was a master hacker. He had assembled a workstation in his room on the hotel's upper level. He had six advanced supercomputers, each with double monitors, all connected to an ominous black box. The floor was covered with power cords and cables connecting the computers, audio enhancers, monitors, and printers. He, Glenn, and another operative from the NSA had masterfully attached and installed wireless USB transmitters and micro video cameras in various locations at the Maduro residence, helicopter, and island residence, as well as the homes and living accommodations of both senators. This included bugging their vehicles' GPS and tapping their cell phones and landlines. Austin had hacked into Maduro's Blackberry and, with the help of the bureau and NSA, compromised his clandestine secret code system.

On the room's wall was a large electronic screen outlining the details of the island and displaying satellite imagery of the complex. We diligently monitored Maduro's operations by listening to phone chatter and viewing his email communications. It was soon learned that Hugo always traveled unannounced with a half dozen well-armed burly Mexican and Venezuelan bodyguards. So there could have been more we didn't know about in the trenches surrounding the island.

Through Maduro's coded communications, it was learned that Pablo and one of his ruthless henchmen by the name of Heriberto Lazaro, who had a reputation for being dumber than a turkey, would be meeting a member of the Los Zetas Cartel by the name of Del Loco Estrada in the parking lot at the summit of Spruce Knob the next day at 10:00 a.m.

Austin and I left early in the morning with a small contingent of FBI and DEA agents. As Estrada's private jet landed at the Charleston airport at 5:00 a.m., Austin and I followed him to the Hertz rental desk, where he rented a Jeep Cherokee. As he walked away from the rental desk into the terminal, he made a brief stop at the men's room, and we immediately took him into custody without incident. At the same time, FBI and DEA law enforcement agents were on the tarmac, arresting the pilot and taking possession of the aircraft before moving it to a secured hangar along with the Jeep. In searching the plane, they found a large stash of nineteen kilograms, or forty-one pounds, of uncut cocaine hydrochloride hidden in a backpack stashed in the technical space section of the plane. The estimated value was $1.4 million. Because of the size of the load, we had to assume that something was in the works that we weren't yet aware of.

* * *

Bryce, sitting in the back seat of the rented Jeep, having undergone a makeup session compliments of the FBI, now looked like Del Loco as Austin, who also now looked like a Hispanic Mexican goon, slowly drove up the gravel service road leading to the summit of Spruce Knob at 4,862 feet. The top of Spruce Knob was an ideal location for a drug transaction: remote and offering a clear view for miles of anyone coming up or flying in.

Having undergone several hours of intense interrogation, which included a brief but very effective waterboarding session, Estrada had given them all the information they wanted and more.

There was bad blood between Pablo and Estrada, and they learned by happenstance he was planning on killing Pablo during the exchange.

Austin crested the mountain and spotted their car, which was the only one in the weedy parking lot. With his window rolled down, he stuck his arm out, gesturing toward another vehicle that was parked several perpendicular spaces away on the verge of the lot, giving the occupants an unimpeded view of the pending exchange. Pablo was sitting in the passenger seat with the door open smoking a cigarette. The driver, wearing a hoodie, had his head slightly bent down, trying not to show his face.

Austin parked and killed the engine while watching the other vehicle with a suspicious countenance.

With a considerable sense of foreboding, Bryce stepped out of the car, his eyes ranging the parking lot, and slowly walked thirty yards toward Pablo's vehicle, stopping midway. The Mexican alighted the vehicle, arched his back, rolled his shoulders, cracked his knuckles, looked stupidly fierce, and began walking toward Bryce, meeting his unrelenting gaze as they faced off on the asphalt without shifting his myopic eyes one iota.

If he was nervous, he wasn't showing it.

Bryce's size and demeanor were possibly intimidating.

For a brief moment, there was an immeasurable ocean of silence between them.

"Hola, amigo," Pablo said with the phlegmy voice of a smoker.

They spoke in Spanish, with Bryce not even hinting at an American accent.

"Buenos tardes," said Bryce.

"Si, senor."

"Did you bring the goods for me?" Bryce asked.

"Si, senor."

"Gracias."

"Do you have the money?" Pablo asked.

"Si, senor. One hundred thousand in US currency, as agreed."

"Bueno," Pablo called out, giving a feigned thumbs-up.

Pablo tipped his hat, put his hand to his face, and faked a cough into it as if giving a moronic signal of some sort. The spider veins on his crooked nose and cheeks were telltale signs of his alcohol and drug addiction.

Bryce, unblinking, with a granite expression and a prickle of unease, watched Pablo's enigmatic eyes, looking for and concentrating on each movement for some clue to his treachery. "Show me the money, and I show you the goods. Comprende?"

His voice sounded as dry and abrasive as coarse sandpaper.

Bryce's stomach tightened with tension. Something about his mannerism did not bode well or fit together properly in his mind. Instead, he seemed to be agitated.

Pablo, staring at Bryce with eyes like daggers, slowly backstepped toward the car, where the hooded Heriberto reached out and handed him a brown leather attaché case through the dark tinted window.

Without taking his eyes off Bryce, Pablo slowly shambled back, standing no closer than three feet in front of Bryce. Bryce backed up a foot as Pablo seemed to have a serious case of halitosis. Bryce looked him straight in the eye, his jaw tense. "Open it," he demanded

Pablo kneeled down and opened the briefcase, which was presumably filled with stacks of unserialized US currency. Bryce slowly backstepped to the rear of the Jeep and lifted out a dark L. L. Bean backpack, then walked back, placing it on the ground in front of Pablo.

Pablo opened the backpack, and using a knife he had been keeping in a wristband, he cut a small hole in one of the plastic bags, withdrawing a microsample, and sniffed it.

"Una buena cosa," he said.

Inside the backpack was five kilos of cocaine with a street value of $250,000. Having confirmed the quantity and purity, Pablo nudged the briefcase over to Bryce's feet.

Just after Pablo had picked up the backpack and started to walk back to his car, he stopped in midstride several feet from Bryce, rounding on him at a pitched angle with a pistol in hand. Austin, at the exact moment having spotted the silver barrel of a gun now pointing out the open driver's window of Pablo's car, yelled reflexively from the Jeep, "Down! Gun!" and all hell broke loose as a convulsive hailstorm of rapid gunfire erupted from the two vehicles, echoing the ensuing bedlam over the mountaintops.

Bryce's stomach clenched. His response was visceral and immediate. With lightning-fast reflexed speed honed by years of field experience, he pivoted and rolled away, pulling his glock from his holster and firing at Pablo and his driver as he retreated toward the Jeep with bullets sizzling by his head. Pablo, clutching the backpack and his pistol in his right hand, took a bullet in the right shoulder and instantly dropped the backpack and gun as he took a nosedive into the pavement. Whipping around and shouting Spanish deprecations, he crawled across the pavement on all fours under blistering fire and desperately bolted pell-mell to the driver's side of the car, screaming in agonizing pain as he had caught another bullet, this one in the ass. With his left hand, he ripped open the driver's door with a primal burst of savagery, yowling and screaming a volley of wicked Spanish expletives, and yanked a now limp, mortally wounded Heriberto out of the driver's seat, tossing him to the pavement.

In the blink of an eye, he threw the vehicle into drive and slewed around, spitting gravel, doing a 180, then gunned it, roaring out of the parking lot like a bat out of hell lunatic with wheels screaming and fishtailing across the asphalt.

Bryce wasn't overly surprised to note that it had no license plates. He stood there for a moment, awash in thought, as his adrenaline leveled off.

* * *

Bryce

We didn't follow the oaf. Fortunately, as the gun echoes withered, neither of us was hit, but we couldn't say the same for Pablo's Mexican confederate yahoo. Austin squatted to check for a pulse. No movement and no guttural moans were coming from Heriberto. His eyes were open, bluish green, now fading to translucent brown. Blood dripped from his mouth and nostrils. He was dead. According to Austin, the Mexican beast of burden was an undocumented roofer and muscleman who belonged to the Maduro Operation. He was now face down, splayed on the payment in an expanding pool of blood, having been shot several times, once in the head. Two bloodied pistols lay on the pavement. Both would go through ballistic testing back at the lab, along with fingerprint testing of the spent shells, and both would be DNA checked and recorded.

Holstering our guns, we quickly scanned the area before securing the money and drugs back in the vehicle.

There's a saying that one should always be prepared for the unexpected and the best-made plans are thrown out once the shooting starts, but that's actually only half-true.

Having done our recce the day before and fully obviated a possible ambush somewhere down the road, we had located an unmapped passageway on the opposite side of the mountain, which we used. Reaching the bottom of the mountain on the lee side, I contacted the FBI office. I requested they get a chopper up on the mountain quickly, remove the body, and clean up any residue before the local authorities got involved.

"I'm sure someone heard the shots being fired as they echoed in the mountains," I told them.

"Like a flame for a moth," I said. But fortunately, Pablo had made an unfortunate mistake and was going to feel the heat.

Pablo would have much explaining when he returned to the Maduro compound. He had not only taken a bullet in the shoulder and lost a foot soldier with even fewer scruples than him, but his ineptness had also woefully resulted in the loss of $100,000 in cold cash and five kilos of cocaine worth over $250,000 on the street, with nothing to show for it. I thought Maduro would go ballistic, and Pablo's future didn't look promising.

Austin agreed.

Hugo was furious and almost homicidal, shaking his head ruminatively. They had upset his imperturbable equanimity. Rage was pouring through his veins, swamping every other sensation.

Having lost over $350,000, Hugo would now be in a heightened state of alert and have his cohorts beating the bush looking for us, as he knew that we were still in the mountains. He would have his men scanning the airports and bus stations for two Mexicans trying to leave the country in a hurry.

Austin and I didn't waste any time exiting and destroying the costumes before we made a beeline back to Charleston and disposed of the Jeep at the cell parking lot of the airport. The bureau had already deposited a nondescript vehicle for our return to the hotel. We wouldn't underestimate Hugo: Mr. Hugo Maduro wanted us both dead.

I was carefully building a case against the Maduro organization, and the entire transaction was recorded on a video camera mounted in the Jeep grill. Maduro and Libya were exchanging more than oil.

The Maduro organization provided military-grade weapons to Libya that could proliferate throughout the Middle East.

I explained, "As he rises in power, he's being entrusted with more and more sensitive state secrets. He's involved in an unfathomable amount of weapons deals, oil-for-cash deals, missile information, human trafficking, kidnappings, rapes, ultraviolent murders, prostitution, and a proliferation of other crimes.

"He takes orders from the Mideast for young girls thirteen years of age and up and then orders their kidnapping, meeting specifications from all over Mexico and South America. A smaller number have been kidnaped from right here in the United States and Canada."

Soon, I would be forced to exercise restraint, standing face to face with a killer and a child abductor. If I found him, I would act as judge, jury, and executioner.

Austin looked at me and, I could tell, saw the unfathomable concentration in my face. He had never seen anyone with such fierce, decisive resolve to take down a criminal organization.

The situation was fluid and constantly changing. However, we had an inside contact feeding us up-to-date information, allowing us to adapt to the evolving variations in political and law enforcement operations.

"We know that he has his people plan the extractions well in advance and that they require significant prior preparation. They use stun guns to subdue their victims, and they employ nitrous oxide to sedate and keep them either semiconscious or unconscious during transit, usually in cages.

"He has recently begun kidnapping young teenage girls, and most recently, to our knowledge, a young wife of a politician in Kentucky. Having a politician's daughter and/or wife guarantees the politician's cooperation in approving whatever the Maduro organization wants.

"We know he has access to confidential information on each of his victims before he kidnaps them. We need to determine how he has access to that information. We also want to find out where he gets his nitrous oxide, as this is not an over-the-counter item. He may have control of a doctor.

"We already have suspected and connected that link. It's Senator Davis and/or Senator Assad. Both are under Hugo's absolute control.

"The agency checked the identity of the dead Mexican, and it turned out that he was illegal and not in the database, which meant that he was a recent transplant."

"Any tattoos associated with a cartel?" I asked.

"No, but he had psoriasis on his arms and legs so bad he looked like he was molting."

The early evening came with a light rain that dampened the streets. Later, a heavy rain and fog ushered in the night, wiping out all traces of the confrontation.

CHAPTER 30

Two weeks later, Nuna had capitulated, finding that his ebullient smile, his whimsical wheedling and cajoling were too disarming to continue her token resistance. They'd crossed paths a half dozen times, slowly building a relationship of trust. Her father had always said that a good soldier knew when to surrender with dignity.

Nuna now recognized her defeat and gave in to it most graciously with zest. She also knew that things were happening between them at a whirlwind pace. All day she had been in a state of anticipation, looking forward to having dinner and spending a relaxing evening with Bryce. She added gold loops to her ears after washing her hair and letting it dry naturally. She stared at herself while slipping into black French lace lingerie under a wisp of a dress: thin spaghetti straps, a hem that brushed the top of her knees. She desperately wanted a relationship with a man. A real vibrant man. This man!

Not bad, she thought, preening critically at the harried image in the bathroom mirror. Nuna was as jittery as a girl going to a prom with a football star. She had gone to Fayetteville in the morning, where she had made an appointment with her hairdresser, getting coiffed and manicured.

The sound of the doorbell chime gave her heart a jolt as she struggled with the zipper at the back of her skirt, fastening the hook and eye. Her heart now fluttering like a hummingbird's wings. A significant departure from her fastidious, prim, and proper no-nonsense business look. She needed to catch up by applying her eyeliner in the mirror. Eight o'clock on the dot. She had spent the afternoon rifling through the dresses, skirts, blouses, and other outfits hanging in her closet, looking for a seductive look for their date. Also, one that would contrast with her flaxen hair and fair complexion. Some still had the tags attached, indicating a possible return. Having tried on fewer than a dozen articles, she chose a skirt and blouse ensemble she had purchased at the beginning of last summer and still needed to wear. It still perfectly fit her figure, with the blouse accentuating her breasts like a second skin. Tonight she decided to forgo her usual inhibitions and test the waters.

Bryce was punctual, as she should have expected. The sun was waning in the sky, and the first vestiges of dusk began to appear over the mountains. She was taking a couple of deep breaths, trying not to hyperventilate as she ran through the bedroom and downstairs into the living room in stockinged feet to open the front door for him, barely containing her glee.

"Hi," he said with simple casualness and a beatific smile as he made a final adjustment to his collar.

Then, with warm sparkling eyes, having reclaimed her composure, she gave him a warm, flirtatious welcoming look and rose up on her toes, kissing him on the cheek. He followed her into the parlor with riveting eyes rapaciously admiring every inch of her natural dewy skin. The expression on his face when she had opened the door said it all, dispelling any lingering qualms she might have had about him.

He whistled. "Nuna, you look ravishing. No, you look sensational!"

He looked at her body, all of it, from head to toe, but with a subtlety that suggested admiration, not lust.

She explained that she was running a little behind and needed a couple of minutes to complete her priming.

Bryce checked his wristwatch. "Not a problem. How much time do you need?"

Nuna sighed with resignation. "Give me ten minutes."

"Relax, take what you need," he said solemnly.

Nuna looked stunning. Absolutely radiant.

She only wore a soupcon of makeup, but what was there was artfully applied. First, she smoothed a blushing gel onto the hollows of her cheekbones and gouged out a measured half spoonful of peached-flavored lip gloss, which she applied to her lips. Then, upon whisking her wand along the tips of her long black eyelashes, she gave herself a final appraising glance, lightly misted herself with Obsession, and gazed at a smiling, ecstatic reflection. At the base of her throat lay a single band of pearls. Pearl studs from her mother adorned her ears.

Bryce stepped into a nicely twilit decorated living room and took a seat on a comfortable couch facing a fireplace as Nuna dashed back upstairs to her bedroom. Everything was off-white with just a tinge of yellow. There were fresh flowers in a vase. A small stack of cordwood was piled near the fireplace along with a pail of kindling. The windows were shaded with off-white wooden shutters. He couldn't help noticing that her house was spotless and that she had an extensive collection of novels nesting in a massive bookshelf. She also had a number of pictures of her parents and late husband, along with the triangular flag prominently displayed on the mantel above the fireplace. The black-and-white photographs of her parents glowed with warmth, intelligence, and kindness as she stood between them beaming at her first communion. he studied and paid close attention to the photos of Nuna with Chris. The photos of Chris confirmed the association that he had had with her husband. There were also several vintage pictures of her mother and father at the altar and of her with her parents and a young child. Deep inside him was a simmering anger about what he'd learned of Chris. Setting his expression and concentrating only on his purpose for being there, he moved from one photo to another.

Still, with the vindictive thoughts edging into his thoughts, he sternly cautioned myself against losing sight of the mission. Nuna was a woman who was sure of herself, who she was. With considerable insight, she could and would be willing to be a good listener and help others in need. Chris, on the other hand, would not even extend a hand.

Having stepped into her shoes, she misted herself again with another touch of fragrance and critically surveyed the results of her time in the bathroom. She smiled at the image and decided it highlighted her best features and was as glamorous as she was going to get. Nuna felt a flutter of excitement. Butterflies took flight, overtaking her stomach, and her heartbeat was anything but normal.

Returning with a twinkle in her eyes, having completed the last ministrations of her ensemble, she said, "Shall we go?"

Bryce froze with an unconcealed appreciation of Nuna upon watching her delicately descend the stairs holding on to the banister with her left hand, beaming and sashaying in her heels.

"Nuna, you're beautifully luminescent in that dress." She was provocatively dressed to kill with the merest hint of makeup.

"Why thank you, Bryce," she said with gaiety in her succinct, laid-back West Virginia drawl. "That was my goal."

Having descended the stairs, she slowly pirouetted in a tight saucy twirl and curtsied for Bryce, crinkling her nose coquettishly and employing all her womanly wiles. With just a mild timidity in her voice, Nuna sounded like she was going out on her first date.

Beautiful was an exaggeration, but considering she hadn't had a date like this in years, she looked better than she had any right to expect.

Ready, she gathered her handmade crocheted shawl and beaded evening purse and said, "Let's go."

He ushered her out the front door as she locked it, leaving the front light on.

"Do you have a burglar alarm system?"

"No, not yet."

"You should. This is a house on a deserted street with lots of ways for a thief to break in and burglarize."

Since it was a warm, celestial starlit night with a full buck moon casting a blueish glow over the mountains, she asked if they could walk instead of driving to the restaurant. Bryce didn't hesitate to agree: it was an exotic evening, and they were still a few minutes early for their reservation. The crystal clarity of the night air was evocative with the fragrance of her perfume and reflected off Nuna's skin translucently, her eyes sparkling and lupine.

Bryce held out his arm, and Nuna quickly slipped her hand through it, intertwining her fingers with his. "I thought chivalry was dead," she whispered.

"Actually, it's in intensive care with occasional signs of life."

They strolled arm and arm under the twilight, talking about the history of the river with the mellifluous sounds of the falls cascading on their left side as they walked up the dimly lit pathway to the historic restaurant.

Nuna was feeling euphoric, and there was a suffused twinkle in her eye. The warmth of his hand seemed to had penetrated gently into her bones.

They were having dinner at the Glen Ferris Inn in Glen Ferris, about a thirty-minute walking distance from her house on the Midland Trail in Gauley Bridge.

While the restaurant was somewhat dated, it was upscale by Gauley Bridge standards. Surprisingly, Nuna had walked the grounds several times and had casually browsed inside the two-hundred-year-old historic inn a couple of times. Still, she had never eaten at the restaurant, which overlooked the impressive Kanawha Falls. The place was originally built as a private residence in 1810 before evolving in its final iteration as one of the finest inns in West Virginia. The vintage antebellum brick exterior and white Grecian columns supporting a large balcony spoke of the period in which it was built. Over the years, two Civil War generals and four United States presidents had stayed at the inn and dined in the eatery.

The upscale four-star restaurant had fifteen or so tables inside and a half dozen tables on the enclosed patio. All were either taken or reserved. Actually, the restaurant was the only fine dining establishment in the area and was booked out a month in advance. They, however, got lucky as they secured a table at the last minute due to a cancellation on the patio.

Nuna noticed that Bryce had also dressed to the nines for the evening and was devastatingly scrumptious. A fact that didn't seem to go unnoticed as several envious women were turning their heads as they wended our way to our table. She had never seen him dressed in anything but jeans and Western boots. Now Bryce showed evidence that he had spent enough time at the gym to test the seams of his custom-cut suit. His appearance left her breathless and bespoke his masculinity. He was wearing polished black shoes, a well-tailored dark suit, a white shirt, and a tie that was actually part of the bureau's de facto uniform. Bryce's Polo fragrance settled in her nostrils and made her unsteady on her feet. His darkly tanned, chiseled face contrasted nicely with his white teeth when he smiled like he was doing right now. He gallantly opened the mahogany entrance door and held it open for Nuna to pass through; she entered the vestibule. He didn't say a word. He didn't have to. His complacent smile spoke volumes.

Bryce then let the obsequious maître d', with his synthetic conspirator smile, blithely escort them through a maze of tables in the dining room to the outside enclosed patio festooned with small romantic lighting, where he gave her a warming smile before pulling out a chair for her with etiquette redolent of old-world "Southern hospitality." The décor was simple and the atmosphere congenial. Nuna smoothed the fabric of her dress over her knees, realigning the hem. They sat in cushioned wrought-iron chairs at an intimate table covered in a starched white linen tablecloth with white napkins, gleaming silverware arranged next to cut crystal water glasses. Flickering in the middle of the table was a single guttering votive candle, adding to the serenity as they gazed at each other. The restaurant was comfortably packed with a generally affluent and well-dressed dinner crowd.

They had an unimpeded view of the Kanawha River Falls and the looming mountains as a resplendent backdrop under a quarter moon high in the vaulted sky with thousands of twinkling stars set around it. Soft, romantic ambient music filled the air, along with the sounds of peals of laughter from the other diners. The twilight had settled in, and the temperature was a pleasant seventy-something. It was lovely to be enjoying the midsummer evening outside, corralled by flaming citronella tiki torches on the railings. More miniature twinkling white lights festooned the bushes around the patio. They made small talk until the waiter came tableside.

The waiter, with an easy grin and incipient beer belly that made it look like he was in his third trimester, sauntered over to their table, giving them a cursory look before pausing and lighting the single candle centerpiece. Then he set down a basket of warm mixed slices of bread and a small bowl of olive oil. He introduced himself as Jeffry and announced that he would be their server. He then handed them menus, recited the chef's daily specials, and unfolded the menus for their perusal. He quickly retreated several feet from the table after making eye contact with Nuna. Just as he stepped back, a young waitress hurried over to fill our glasses with bottled water.

Nuna, having perused the sections, chose a Cajun salmon and shrimp alfredo. Bryce ordered filet mignon with all the trimmings. The waiter, hovering nearby with a pen and tablet in his hand, returned to the table, took our entrée orders, and discreetly withdrew just as the sommelier appeared with a wine list, which was a veritable treasure trove of fine wines.

He was smiling obsequiously and proffering affable blandishments. Bryce asked Nuna if she had a preference. She responded in kind by saying, "Everything. I'm a connoisseur of experience." Bryce chose a bottle of Sauvignon Blanc from New Zealand.

"Would you like the wine decanted, sir?"

"No, that won't be necessary."

"Yes, thank you, sir."

Bryce spoke after the sommelier left. "I'm not exactly a wine aficionado, but I like practicing the process.

"You'll love this wine. It originates from New Zealand's Marlborough region and will very much complement your Cajun salmon and my filet mignon."

"I know, Bryce. It's one of my favorites also."

The sommelier returned and presented the bottle, which Bryce sampled, giving a thumbs-up approval of its effervescence, and he poured two long-stemmed glasses and placed the liter in a chiller sleeve before fading away into the chattering crowd. They raised and clinked glasses in salute, savoring the moment and the conversation at a leisurely pace. She took a sip of her wine and wiped her lips with her napkin as she traced the rim of her wineglass. Her eyes were wild with abandon. Zesty gooseberry, flowery peach, and passion fruit exploded across the surface of her tongue.

They were seated at a narrow corner table on the edge of the patio with a full view of the cascading falls and river below. Nuna deliberately sidled over and leaned into Bryce so that their bodies touched. Then, as he smiled, Bryce's hand found its way between her legs just above the knees under the table and he began the coaxing excitement of sex arousal.

Nuna instantly tightened her legs, her thighs feeling like melting wax, but wasn't objecting as she looked furtively around the dining area before looking up at him with a reassuring mischievous smile and a dulcet mew indicating that he might get lucky tonight.

Nuna was well-appointed and seductive tonight. Her flaxen hair was full and fell into a full mane that framed her face and delicately cascaded silkily over her unblemished sleeveless shoulders. She was a paragon of femininely, embracing a less-is-more approach with a black cotton skirt revealing more of her long slender legs sheathed in seamed nylon stockings and her slender figure, which Bryce would surely be attracted to. Her diaphanous blouse, with its scooped neckline, was a silky rose that only accented her voluptuous body and highlighted her magnificent breast. Her shoes were high-heeled, open-toe, no straps, red leather, high-class. A few traces of makeup, deftly and subtly applied, little more than eyeliner and lip gloss, accentuated her large liquid blue eyes and prominently displayed cheekbones. Around her neck, she wore a solitaire diamond necklace that truly enhanced her scintillating natural beauty: a graduation gift from her father upon receiving her master's degree.

Her attire tonight was provocative and was a far cry from the androgynous professional business attire her work demanded. Tonight, she was making every effort for Bryce to be outrageously sexy and coyly move the relationship to the next level, feeling a few little frissons of excitement. She was even thinking of possibly sleeping with him. With his looks, he wouldn't stay celibate for long. Nuna conjured up a picture of Bryce lying in bed with her cuddled helpless beneath him. Her heart was pounding abnormally, and she knew she now needed and wanted a man-woman relationship. She had been solitary and reclusive much too long.

Just then, she silently berated herself for thinking like a slut. She was a mature woman and shouldn't be thinking about him being naked and caressing every naked inch of her body. But there was a free-spirited woman in her longing to be released. A sensual, sexual woman trapped in an invisible cage of circumspection. An incredible geyser of desire shot through Nuna.

The heat in Bryce's eyes was piercing straight through hers and causing her heart inadvertently to surge and go pitter-patter as she watched the candlelight flicker on his face. His rock-hard body was so close to hers that she wanted to snuggle into his large arms. She was mesmerized by the magnetism of his eyes and somehow had become oblivious to everything happening around them. His rugged face radiated more heat than the candle, and she was being drawn to the heat. She had almost forgotten what it was like to be a woman and feel the magic and masculinity of a man like Bryce Tucker. She wanted the mouth centered on his granite square jaw to wrap around her lips; she wanted him to take possession of her body and take her to his bed. She was sure that this guy liked her and more than that, that he wanted to sleep with her and begin a long-term relationship. This highly desirable and respectable man was exactly the kind of guy she could see herself having a long-standing, mutually loving, and supportive relationship with. He was uncompromising, law-abiding, kind, genuinely independent, uncomplicated, and the kind of phenomenal man she would be unerringly very happy to spend the rest of her life with.

She had been swept off her feet and was falling in love, and as far as epiphanies went, this one was unmistakable. The seeds of an exciting relationship were in her hands. She thought they needed her personal feminine nurturing, however.

A decadent platter of dainty hors d'oeuvres of sautéed calamari on a bed of spinach, meant to excite the palate, arrived at their table, compliments of the chef, for their delectation, and they spent the next few minutes limply toying and picking at it as they inanely exchanged stories and spoke of life and their hopes and nebulous visions for the future.

Their prattling slowly dropped to an intimate pitch. Her lips parted in delightful laughter, and her blue eyes twinkled in mirth as she slowly ran her manicured finger around the rim of her wineglass. Bryce broke off a piece of bread, soaked it in the dish of olive oil, and then took a sip of his libation. Dolly Parton was singing softly about life in the mountains, followed by the limpid notes of a song about a girl named Jolene.

With no more than a thimbleful of wine left in their glasses, Bryce refilled both, and they both took a sip, pausing as the waiter aptly placed their entrées in front of them. Then he smiled at Nuna and added, "Bon appetit." The service at this restaurant was impeccable. They both enjoyed a bodacious dish of snowy chunks of lobster bisque flecked with small salted croutons delivered unhurriedly before moving on to the main event.

Bryce speared medallions of filet mignon with drizzles of béarnaise sauce, complemented by asparagus vinaigrette. Nuna picked up her fork and knife and slowly went to work on her Blackened salmon dish, nestled in a tangle of chopped collard greens, with learned grace.

"Want to try a piece of steak?" he asked, lifting a forkful of the succulent filet mignon toward her mouth. "I'd like you to share a sample of yours. Your dish looks awesome."

Bryce guided his fork to her lips, and she gracefully closed them around the tines of the fork. Then, with the fork coming away clean, he watched Nuna's lips as she chewed languidly. After that, they continued to chat about inconsequential things as he speared morsels of steak and she morsels of salmon.

After finishing a delectable dinner and satiating themselves with after-dinner cappuccinos, they diagonally laid their knives and forks on their plates. They talked about their favorite music, hobbies, weather, sports, and life. The waiter appeared and began clearing the dishes from the table, and Nuna softly put her fork down, dabbed and blotted her lips with her napkin, and folded it on the table before graciously pushing her chair away from the table. Leaving behind a mostly uneaten plate, she stood and scooped up her small purse, excusing herself, saying she would be right back, and sashayed to the ladies' room. With Nuna in the powder room, this was an opportune time for Bryce to relieve his bladder.

He returned to the table in time to see her opening the door.

Having freshen up her makeup in the mirror with just a touch of perfume and lip gloss and checked for any discomposure in her appearance, she exited the powder room. Her legs were a little unsteady, but she managed to gird her loins and recovered nicely after a couple of steps, wending her way back to the table. Several men in her path turned their heads conspiratorially to get a glimpse of her proud lissome carriage, the unaffected natural sway of her hips, her well-shaped legs, and her firm breasts. She strolled by their tables, incurring the possible wrath of their dates.

Bryce watched her return, breathing in the lingering wake of her perfume as she casually made her way around the table. She was happily relieved that she wouldn't have to listen to dessert-tray recitations. Instead, she smiled at Bryce, who was in the process of thanking the waiter as he bused the table and voicing accolades to the chef for the sumptuous meal. Having satisfied the check and handed it back to the waiter, he stood up as she was about to sit and softly asked her for a dance.

Several other couples were already dancing at the far end of the patio, and she didn't overlook that several women on the floor were scoping

Bryce out. They were all holding each other close and sashaying to the soft rhythms of "Facts of Life" by Calvin Richardson. Then the music segued into another sample of the classical repertoire. This was all taking place under an astral blanket of twinkling mountain night sky filled with happy vibes and romantic ambiance.

Looking into his eyes with unwavering gaze and gazing up at the moon above with an impish twinkle dancing in hers, she said enthusiastically, "I'd love to."

She loved to dance, but living alone in the mountains didn't give her much opportunity. Bryce took her hand, leading her out on the floor at the farthest corner, where she turned and ardently melted into his arms in rapture, her body going liquid. Nuna had forgotten how good it was to be held possessively and desired by a man who showed that he was more concerned about her pleasure than his own. His hands, with the subtlest pressure and hardness, followed by his gifted fingers, evocatively embedded themselves in the small of her back as she succumbed to his grasp, swaying to the music, her eyes closed languidly. Not having danced with anyone since losing her husband, she was burning inside as he slowly pulled her in by small degrees to his masculine chest. The sultry air embraced her, his virility searing through her clothes, leaving her as a pliant as quivering jelly in his powerful arms. Bryce enthralled her.

With his arm tightly wrapped around her slender waist, Bryce pulled her into his hard, masculine chest, and they nimbly swirled and swayed to the lulling notes of the music in gay abandon, as one, under the gloaming light of the moon. His hard thighs moved against her inner thighs with devastating effect. His hips cradled hers as they swayed across the floor, giving her a feeling of being Ginger Rogers.

The flirtation of masculinity with femininity gave her an out-of-body experience. She was warm, dewy, and fragrant, and she could feel the pressure of his large hand splayed possessively across the small of her back as they swayed to the music. Yes, it was intimate, sensual, and unmistakably romantic as the notes danced about, adding a dreamlike quality to the evening. The anticipation of his lips pulled her body tight against his with unmistakable, spine-tingling lust.

Bryce thought, It feels perfect to be with her and have her in my arms. Everything about her, the color of her hail polish, the timbre of her laugh, speaks of a remarkable woman.

Bryce whispered in her ear, "You're delectably beautiful, Nuna, and you have the softest skin and the most succulent lips I've ever laid eyes on." He was exulting in the sensation of having the curves of her body pressed against and harmonized with his. She moved with such femininity and grace to the music that it took his breath away.

After a prolonged moment, he inhaled deeply. "I also love your scent."

Nuna, holding her breath, was tingling with a swelling fervor all over her body as she bent like a willow in his arms from thigh to chest.

Tilting his head downward, he tipped and angled her head back, exposing her soft, pliant, and delectable lips. Her mouth was a warm, sacred cavern to be audaciously explored by the agilely of his tongue, which stroked the inside of her mouth up to the roof, her teeth, the inside of her lips, until her breaths were nothing more than short, light gasps. He kissed her soft, dewy lips, not chastely but masterfully and possessively, and she responded feverishly in the only way she could, pressing her body tight against his, taking his mouth hard, and kissing him back passionately in a delirium of carnal longing.

It had been way too long since she had allowed a man to kiss her, and she was now feeling gloriously alive as their mouths melded and tongues plundered each other deeper and deeper. The alignment of their bodies at the waist only got better. *God, did it ever.*

She knew the reason for the delicious, exhilarating zinging sensations spiraling through her every time the front of his trousers brushed against her buttocks.

She was dancing with a man she could love and pushed hard against him, pulling him closer to her full breasts. She reveled in having the freedom to touch him and let her inner deviant out to play. She'd been thinking all evening how handsome he looked and how consequential. The provocative grinding of his hips robbed her of breath. She continued to hold him tight. Bryce was not looking at her but into her as the candle flames danced in his eyes.

He could feel the cadence of her heart pounding between them. Nuna had known a few men over the years, but none had affected her as much as she was affected tonight, in Bryce's arms.

It was a wave of yearning that she couldn't understand or control. Lust was running through her. Greedily, her hands caressed him, and he took liberties with her until she was almost frantic with need. Through his suit, she could feel the heat of his body luring her closer.

His lips were hard, hot, and hungry and molded to hers like they were two parts of a whole. His legs felt powerful as they moved with hers.

"Oh God." With a sudden amorous urge, Nuna folded into him, unconsciously wrapping her arms fervently around his back and pressing a cheek into the crook of his neck. Her ears rang with a cacophony of sound, and she quickly realized that the drumming was the pounding lust of her own heart. She had never heard it before.

Bryce felt good. He was good, and with the electricity arcing between them, she knew deep in her heart that she was falling deeply in love with him. He made her heartbeat and breathing accelerate.

His arm tightened around her waist, and she tilted her upper body, arching unwillingly as his breath ghosted over her ear, reducing her to a quivering heap of raw nerves. They were gracefully swaying together and moving slowly across the polished hardwood floor in natural, pulsing rhythms. They meshed perfectly, with her body fitting his phenomenally well.

Bryce's caresses grew bolder and more deliberate. He was inebriated by her flamboyant exuberances. His hand slowly slid down, splaying possessively below her waist, not quite on her derriere, but beseechingly working its way there. With their bodies pressed tightly against each other, she could feel the explosive heat and the male excitement growing below his belt as he pulled her inexorably closer. Nuna whimpered but didn't repel the need to ardently kiss him back as she mindlessly fitted her femininity to his complementing masculinity. Without knowing it, she moved invitingly. His lips were brushing her ear, and she could feel the warmth of his breath blowing sweet nothings on her neck.

Looking up into Bryce's hot-for-her eyes and admiring the clean line of his square jaw, she struggled to restrain herself and whispered with fluttering eyelashes, "Didn't your mother ever tell you that classy Southern women don't let men feel them up on a public dance floor?"

"Oops," he said mirthfully. "I must have forgotten that testosterone lesson," he whispered, back-tilting his head with a simpering, unrepentantly impish grin. He didn't take umbrage, but it wreaked havoc on his erogenous zones.

She laughed with a quizzical smile and poked him in the ribs, disarmed by his mischievous charm. "Bryce, I have to reckon you're incorrigible."

"Vertical foreplay to music?" he chortled with a sappy grin.

His lighthearted mood was infectious, and she found it difficult to hold back her laugh.

He kissed her again, and she couldn't help but feel her eyes roll heavenward.

Sliding her hand along the width of his shoulder with closed eyes, she was enjoying the sensation and could feel herself warming up inside as her libido intensified. Her heart was pounding with anticipation. She began to feel a pleasurable throb as she wiggled and experimentally pressed her breast hard against his chest.

Impulsively, she was thrilled that she could provoke an intimate reaction from such a virile man. Her hips moved seductively against his. Her thighs pressed his thighs.

Her firm breasts strained against the thin fabric of her blouse, and she pressed her body against his muscular chest and could feel the firmness beneath the smoothness of his shirt.

Deep inside her body, her pulse began to accelerate. She tried to ignore the sudden acceleration of her pulse and the tingling rapture that coursed through the erogenous part of her body. Her nipples suddenly felt all hot and prickly as they pushed against her bra and blouse, which inexplicably seemed to have gotten a couple of sizes too small. She felt a warm dampness inside her panties.

Her firm breasts swelled and flattened against the unyielding muscles of his chest; she could feel the savage desire as her nipples tightened. She pressed and nested her hips more intimately against his with a wish that the dance would never end and the music never stop. Deep inside, her body quaked and was on fire.

Nuna found Bryce's neck and pressed her lips to the smooth, warm skin. He emanated heat and felt awesome. She was getting turned on as she threaded her fingers up through his hair.

"Nuna," Bryce whispered huskily, "I want to make love to you."

She lifted her head, and he cupped it between his hands, tilting it back as he kissed her lovingly on the mouth, stealing her breath. Her lips parted in surrender, and moaning and swaying slightly, she reached for his. Not a full-out French kiss, as they were on a public dance floor. Nuna's heart was beating so hard it frightened her. This man knew how to kiss a woman, and he meant business. Her stomach fluttered with the same lassitude as the rest of her body. Her knees went weak, and her earlobes throbbed from infused passion, sending a tingling sensation from her lips, initiating a tide of heat through her body that pooled between her thighs.

His words fell as smooth, emphatic puffs of air against her lips.

When the song ended on a poignant refrain, Nuna, sleepy-eyed and yawning, whispered, "It's getting somewhat late. Would you mind taking me home?" Her body slumped against his in surrender.

The flaring of Bryce's eyes was the ocular equivalent of a *hell yes*. He moved quickly, cupping the back of her neck, his mouth capturing hers. His eyes sparkled with devilment.

"It's time, isn't it?"

For the briefest of moments, Bryce thought he was about to get lucky, but Nuna saw the come-hither carnal gleam in his eyes and was conscious of feeling slightly nettled. She knew masculine sex on the brain when she saw it, and Bryce was exhibiting all the classic symptoms.

He was a veritable mountain of sleek, powerful muscle, pure sex-on-a-stick.

That in and of itself, she told herself, was exactly what she wanted.

"Great idea," Bryce amorously whispered in her ear.

Nuna burst out in full-bodied laughter. He was utterly impossible and way too sensually stimulating. Secretively, her body was on fire with yearning and her loins pounding with lust. Her blood was tingling through her body, and her mind was purring with erotic desire. Men, she thought savagely with a smile as they slowly strolled hand in hand, side by side, back to her house under a full celestial moon surrounded by a glittering shelter of scintillating stars. Nuna was ecstatic over their nearness.

A warm, misty breeze lapped at her face as they walked back along the deserted sidewalk of the river's edge with their hands tightly entwined, his fingers caressing hers, bantering jovially as they strolled. Nuna had little doubt that he knew about the heartfelt warmth he was spreading through her. Holding his hand, she had never felt safer than she did right then. Yet, at the same time, she was a little tipsy. They couldn't have been more in touch. A musical chorus of frogs sang from the morass as they walked aside the river's edge.

While the evening was still warm, she wished she had brought a shawl as the night air was cooling and the humidity had vanished. Bryce noticed her chill, removed his jacket, and draped it around her shoulders.

She opened her handbag, rummaging through the contents, finally digging her keys out myopically, and then cursed silently when she dropped them. Bryce graciously picked up the keys and unlocked the door for her. Nuna stepped inside and turned at the threshold to face him. "I enjoyed tonight, Bryce.

Bryce braced one hand on the outside of the doorframe, studying her through the screen. "I'd like to see you again, Nuna."

He stepped forward and pulled her into his arms and kissed her. A deep, hungry kiss that sent tremors of warmth radiating through her body. Not having put on a bra, she felt her nipples begin to pout beneath her blouse.

Wrapping her arms around his neck, Nuna kissed him back with reckless abandon.

"I'd like that," she said succinctly.

The cool night air and breeze had destroyed her hair, but she was heedless of it.

A deep sense of longing and hunger swept through her body as she attempted to close the screen door.

"So am I not coming in?" Bryce asked with a wolfish smile and a moue.

She looked up into the lean, dark face of the absolutely-perfect-for-the-life-she-wanted man standing so close to her.

"We're taking it slow, remember?" she said, smiling apologetically at Bryce.

He was suddenly deflated, but only for a second did Bryce's face reveal his disappointment and dejection.

"Drat," he said, softly kicking the porch railing. "Slow," he went on bleatingly with a coaxing voice and an almost hypnotic bedroom expression. Then he smiled a little wryly at her. "I've got it. Slow." He was pouting adorably in turn, and she gave him a mischievous smile.

Then he cupped her face with both hands and gave her a long, lingering kiss good night. His eyes penetrated hers. He had been honest in that he would take it slow, but he'd been equally honest in that *slow* to her and *slow* to him were vastly different avenues of thought.

Gripping his wrists, Nuna responded with lots of tongue and infectious enthusiasm.

When he released her from an inflaming kiss, teasing the corners of her mouth, she drew a deep gasp of air into her lungs as she stared up at him. To lambaste him for taking such outrageous liberties was totally out of the question. On the contrary, she enjoyed every second of it.

Nuna swallowed hard and pouted as she smothered a laugh and glanced down, taking notice of the impressive bulge between his thighs, which was probably as hard as marble.

When at last Bryce let her go and said a chaste good night, she smiled at him, sweetly apologetic. Then, with a brusque motion of his hand, he gave a jaunty wave and a naughty grin. He turned and sauntered down the sidewalk back to his jeep. Still wide awake, braced by the cool mountain air, he climbed in and left, intentionally avoiding a glance into the rearview mirror.

Before leaving, he gave Nuna one more good night kiss. He'd laughingly called it a flyby kiss as he squeezed her ass complacently. She'd threatened to smack him for taking liberties with her. He had no idea where she'd come up with such an old-fashioned term.

"Oh baby," he groaned, tilting her head back for one more delicious kiss. "You have no idea what liberties I'd like to take!" He laughed dryly and unrepentantly. Bryce understood her stance and was going to give Nuna the space she needed and wanted. But as she watched him drive away, she suddenly realized that keeping her distance should have been the furthest thing from her mind.

It would be a long drive back to Charleston.

For an abbreviated space of several seconds, Nuna watched as he pulled out of the driveway and faded away. Her eyes misted as she braced herself at a slant against the doorjamb, feeling forlorn, and watched until the swirling darkness absorbed the glow of his taillights as his jeep crossed over the Gauley bridge. Pulsating heartbeats thundered through her body as unbearable heat consumed her. She strained her ears with hope that he had turned around and was coming back to her.

What if he never came back to her? The fleeting thought terrified her.

He had learned tonight that Nuna was sexually passionate, a romantic, but also a no-nonsense woman that he now respected to the limit.

Nuna, crestfallen with the door still ajar as he drove away, waited for a single tingle to wear off before closing the door slowly and turned the bolt lock. It didn't. She felt her heart explode in an overpowering wave of infuriating anger at him as well as herself. The taste of his lips and tongue still lingered on her throbbing lips, and the feel of his tough sinew and muscular body was indelibly imprinted in her mind. Her curves had molded pliantly to his manliness.

His sudden withdrawal was more than tactile.

A tremor of remorse knifed through her as she drew in several restorative breaths, placing her arms around one of the two columns supporting the roof over the front porch. Regret pinched her heart as she wiped eloquent tears away from her face.

"Damn you, Bryce! For heaven's sake, he didn't even wave as he pulled away."

The curse startled her. Full tears clustered in her eyes.

He should have been more aggressive, she thought, taken her to bed, and made passionate love to her. She was starved for his masculinity. But no, he had to be the benevolent gentleman and had hardly even touched her where she wanted to be touched. All along, she was melting and, without question, malleable and willing to capitulate and participate in anything he wanted. He knew it, and so did she. Deep inside the chambers of her traitorous mind, she had an almost atavistic longing to be taken by him in the worst kind of way. He hadn't only roused slumbering erotic sensors that had gone dormant and been forgotten but awakened then with a rampant explosion of titillating lust.

Bryce was a gorgeous hulk of a man, sexy in a dangerous way. She was well aware of it now. He had drawn her out of her shell to a point where she didn't recognize herself anymore.

Never in her life had she met a man who was capable of turning her placid life inside out and causing her to go into a tailspin. She had been attracted to him the moment he smiled at her, and he was going to be the turning point in her world, giving her a zest for life again.

He unquestionably had a seductive magnetism that titillated every cell in her body. Bryce had an intoxicating essence of danger about him and sheer sexuality that was drawing her toward nirvana. The men she had met over the years were unremarkable and forgettable, and once she bade a date good night, she rarely, if ever, remembered what he had worn or what he had even looked like. While she was no longer a virgin, she had been celibate since her marriage to Chris.

The intoxicating Bryce Tucker wasn't going to be forgotten! No waffling on that, she chided herself with a pouty face. She averred, taking a deep breath of determination that she was now going to use all the feminine wiles in her West Virginia Southern arsenal to bring him back into her arms.

She was misty-eyed as a kaleidoscope of emotions flickered across her mind. She was trembling with anticipation. Her knees felt weak, and her stomach was in knots.

She was falling in love with him, and he seemed to reciprocate her feelings in ways she wasn't accustomed to. She knew right from wrong but was now dreaming of a fervent night of uninhibited fornication with him.

She was flabbergasted and laughed with self-derision. Her love life since Chris had been a barren wasteland, which had been acceptable. It wasn't anymore. Providence was compensated for that. She couldn't remember how long she stood there in the doorway with her arms wrapped around her chest before pivoting on her heels, but she finally closed the door and locked it, a bit deflated.

Having forsaken her wish not to submit to him tonight was no longer as desirous, but it was too late to recall it. She had erected a protective boundary in her mind that she had to take down quickly. Her excited expression became crestfallen. He had already left, and she bemoaned her instinctive reasoning and despondency. Bryce had awakened the sleeping passion in her as no other man had or could. He was, magically, her prince. Something was happening between them, and she could feel the almost tangible chemistry, tiny embryonic seeds of attraction that might be very special. She had known him for only a week and had allowed him to go further with her than any man had in a long time. Her feelings for him were frightening, to say the least. Where in her befuddled brain were all her protective epithets? He was exciting and the most interesting man she had ever had a conversation with.

Feeling a pang of guilt for pushing him away, she dabbed her eyes as she switched off the kitchen lights and then dispiritedly made her way upstairs. She couldn't get him out of her mind as she brushed her teeth. One thought led to another, and it didn't take long before she was picturing herself naked in his arms. Her sobs shook her petite body. Copious tears streamed down her face as she groped her way to the bedroom. Removing her blouse and shimmying out of her skirt, she stepped into the shower's hot spray, allowing the hot water to sluice over her body. Then she dried her body with a warm terry-cloth towel, wiped the mist from the mirror, and blow-dried her hair. She assessed her nakedness over the basin and screamed at the reflection in the mirror and the walls around her.

Yes, I still had the image of a young, desirable woman with strong West Virginian virtues, she thought. The ravages of time on this thirty-year-old woman were minimal, considering she had been climbing mountains and up trees since she had known better. Her breasts were firm, her stomach flat, and her flaxen blond hair cascaded in waves to below her shoulders. Her blue eyes were still her most arresting feature.

Folding back the quilted comforter and fluffing up the pillows, she collapsed onto the bed, curling up and pulling the covers tightly around her, falling into a dream where Bryce was tightly holding her as she ruefully indulged in her recollections of the enchanting evening.

As she lay on her back, stretched out, still sobbing and staring up at the ceiling, all kinds of erotic endearments and conjectures were flashing back and forth in her head. She turned off the bedside table lamp. For an hour or so, she tossed and turned on her bed, frustrated and unable to sleep and completely unaware of the fact that back in Charleston,

Bryce Tucker was doing exactly the same thing. She quickly discarded the platonic thoughts. Bryce was in all of them. Bryce should be here with me, she thought, as she closed her eyes and relived the evening dancing with him as he held, caressed, and kissed her. She felt depression settling down upon her like a suffocating blanket before she succumbed to a torrent of tears.

Then, Nuna lay cradled in her bed naked in a state of euphoria for a first time in a long time, lost in a salacious trancelike delirium of sex. He was in love with her, not for what she could do for him but for what he wanted for her. Images of his hardness pressing against her and her pressing her body to his faded. The thoughts of Bryce were morphing into more urgent fantasies and revivifying a lust for life that she had thought she had lost. He had created an out-of-body hunger that no man before him had. His epitomized male masculinity in its rawest form. The darkness didn't dispel or flush away any of her electrifying thoughts. She lay on her back long into the darkest hours of the night, which seemed like an eternity, crying silently to a blissfully, happy indefinable, immeasurable sleep.

Yet if anything, her thoughts intensified as she wrapped her arms around her pillow and envisioned all kinds of deliciously wicked things. She needed to take inventory of the night and ached for Bryce's lips, even though she somehow felt that his only interest in her was as a conduit for information in the Maduros.

* * *

Bryce, having clipped his seat belt, reversed out of the driveway and drove slowly back to Charleston. It was after midnight when he reached the hotel and parked his car. After alighting from the jeep, he gazed at the darkened night sky. So many stars shone above, but they were far from providence. Having entered his room, he cracked open the windows, removed his boots, stepped out of his jeans, and slid in between the sheets of his bed. With his hands clutched beneath his head, he stared at the ceiling fan twirling overhead. He lay awake until the wee hours of the morning, thinking of her and unable to rid himself of her image. Everything about the woman was sexy. Even the way she ate was sexy. He had paid close attention to the way she licked her lips with her tongue after every bite and then daintily touched them with her napkin. Nuna was an absolutely amazing woman who had instinctively aroused his manhood. It took every ounce of his willpower to control his instincts and remind himself why he was with her in the first place. Still, there was no denying that there was chemistry between them. He coveted every waking moment he had with her.

When he finally fell asleep, slipping out of reality, his dreams were decidedly erotic: he was being drawn to her incandescence and wanted the relationship to blossom into an obsession.

Unfortunately, Bryce wasn't about to lose sight of his objective and his present emotional baggage. So putting the peddle to the floor, he made a quick trip back in the darkness. Thunder sounded in the distance, rumbling long and low over the mountains with a northerly wind picking up. Within a few minutes, a light rain began to fall, then it began to pour with intensity. Still Bryce continued to drive to his hotel room in a leisurely mode, the rain, lightning, and wind not affecting him at all.

* * *

The following morning, as she made her way out to the front porch with her first mug of coffee, Nuna was surprised to find a arrangement of two dozen roses interspersed with fern and baby's breath in a tall lead crystal vase sitting just inside on her steps.

A single card lay waiting for her viewing: "Thank you for a beautiful evening. Bryce."

He'd gone to a lot of trouble and expense of having the flowers delivered to her home this early in the morning. She sat in her slider and kissed the card with one hand covering her left breast as though to still a pounding heart as her ire evaporated. That night was memorable, but it would not be the last.

CHAPTER 31

Her pathetic wails echoed through the halls of the windowless villa basement. Her name was Shandell Daniella Noosa, and she was a beautiful and shapely ebony-colored fifteen-year-old teen. Her left wrist was shackled to the bedpost as she was beaten, tortured, and raped by a masked man. Her warm blood was now on the pillow and sheets of the bed. She had been abducted from her Havana high school after-hours sporting event in the parking lot, kicking and screaming, without a trace. Her name eventually faded from the news.

She woke up crying, which was strange because she had never had a dream scare her so much. Then, finally, she squandered another deep breath and screamed, "Help meeeeeeee!" She now realized that her nightmare was real. Unbeknownst her to, her father had been in debt to a local drug lord and had his throat cut. She had been seized as compensation and given to Chris Vallarta as a gift for the gambling debt being dismissed.

"Shut the fuck up, bitch," Chris yelled at her. Then, wrapping his white cotton robe around him, he left the bed, walked over to the patio door, and threw it open, stepping outside into the warming afternoon sunshine. Raising his head to the blue sky and taking a deep breath of fresh air, he turned and looked at the young teen, still wailing and suffering involuntary convulsions on the bed. He smiled and said, "Better that I took your virginity rather than some ignorant peasant."

Today would be a beautiful day. A bright blue sky rose over the landscape of Havana. It was indeed a beautiful place to be. Both he and Hugo had greased the hands of anyone who mattered on the island. Yes, he was safe and very secure in his island paradise.

Shandell would be cleaned up and redressed by the staff before the delicious delicacy was presented to him on the outside terrace. It was pointless for her to fight anymore, as she lacked the strength to run. I'm going to subjugate and fuck her again, and this time sodomize her without mercy and consume her fecund womanhood, he thought. Then she would be sold to the highest bidder among the local pimps of Havana.

Two weeks earlier, having been locked in the basement of a building somewhere in the private sector of Havana, she had attempted a daring escape.

She had been put into one of five small dark, windowless rooms with heavy wooden doors. The planked floor was rough to the touch. Pain flamed across her raw knees as she silently crawled along the floor. There was no light of any kind, only darkness.

One night, several days after being kidnapped, she had been placed in the room, where a big man raped her. It had gone on most of the night. He had left drunk and had forgotten to lock the door. The faint rectangle of the doorway beckoned.

Silent as a ghost, she opened the door. Her senses heightened to a fever pitch, and she crept down the hallway and onto the porch. A battered raincoat lay over the railing. It was oversize, but it was something. At the base of the steps, she paused again to listen, but all she heard was the sounds of the sea in the darkness. These sounds were nearly eclipsed by the roar of fear in her head.

She could feel her knees quaking as she came to a juddering halt: her hands were all sweat and unsteady as she held the railing. She tried to calm herself; fear manifested on her swollen and bruised face. Finally, she closed her eyes to the darkness and the terror.

Only a quarter moon lit her way as she sprinted across the yard down to the pebbled shore. A profound sense of liberation engulfed her as she raced across the stones with her bare feet.

The night swallowed her, taking her into its darkness. A heavy wind chased her for a few yards before tapering off. She ran and ran deep into the darkness, careful to avoid a large piece of driftwood on the beach.

Finally, after what seemed like hours, she stopped at a wooden pier and knelt down on the ground to catch her breath.

Upon straightening, she glanced behind her. A feeling of relief rippled through her as she found that the shoreline was empty. No one was following her.

"I'm free. I did it. I'm free," she panted.

Elation drove her movement, and she began jogging forward further down the coastline. Not looking back, she found her rhythm as the waves crashed along the beach. Finally, she came to a river flowing out into the ocean, and for another one hundred yards or so, she followed the path that paralleled its banks. Her lungs burned and her muscles screamed with pain as she stepped up the pace.

She found the backyard of an apartment building and crawled up next to the porch. She pulled off a sheet hanging on a clothesline and covered herself with it. Just as she was about to return to the river's edge, the rear lights came on, and two men came running and tackled her to the ground. With their hands holding her head, one climbed on top of her. The other ripped off the sheet and then the raincoat. She fought back, slapping and clawing at their faces with both hands, but to no avail.

Now the first man had pinned both her arms with his knees and, having drawn his right hand back, slapped her several times until she lost the urge and strength to fight. Finding that she was stark nude, they made a call, and within a few minutes, a car came and two men took her back to the windowless dungeon.

Two of his female staff brought the young girl out of the dank, lamentable confines of the dungeon, down the sepulchral corridors to the terrace, and stood her trembling body in front of him.

He waved his hand, and they immediately bowed and retreated back into the villa, closing the door without saying a word. Neither approved, but having been selective captives themselves for several years, the subjugation of Stockholm syndrome had kicked in, and they obeyed, knowing that to do otherwise would mean their death.

"Pleeeeeease?" she begged in a voice barely audible.

The minutes ticked by with torturous slowness.

Shandell was cleaned, her hair brushed, and dressed in lace transparent black baby doll lingerie with matching panties and standing in four-inch open-toed stilettos. With the exception of a couple of welts on her cheeks, her face still had some of the softness of childhood. He was already aroused.

He removed the linen gag knotted around her mouth and the manacles securing her wrist behind her back. Her teeth ached from biting down on the gag. She was limp and numb.

She had a large purple bruise on her stomach where he had punched her after she tried to kick him in the groin.

"Say it," he gasped as he leaned back on the pillows. "You know how to make me happy. Say it."

"Meow, meow…" she finally whimpered in a capitulating whisper, her feigned smile pained.

"Keep saying it," he demanded.

She complied with a slight degrading whimper, making little meowing sounds.

"Meoow, meoow, meoow, meoow."

With a sense of invincibility, he chuckled at this image of absolute submission. His every command was carried out with no hesitation. After he placed a plastic food dish on the floor before her, she began eating voraciously.

Several guards below the terrace, armed with automatic weapons, were passing the time idly and indolently, resting against the wall sipping cold Tropicanas. Hearing the girl's sobbing cries for help, they looked up but offered no assistance. Their job was to protect Mr. Vallarta from any outside intrusion, not question his moral turpitude. The fate of his guests was of no importance to them.

Chris stood up, stepped in front of the cowering *muchachita*, and whispered in her ear, "Stop your fucking whining." He slowly undid his robe, feeling aroused once more. "Shandell, come here and serve your master."

She pursed her lips and cursed at him in Spanish. Then, with a good understanding of the language, Chris rushed forward and slapped her savagely across the face, sending her backward and crashing onto the floor. He slipped off his robe, lifted her off the floor by her hair, and literally tossed her onto the Chatham double chaise lounge. He climbed on top of her, pinning her arms behind her back. He held her tightly by the wrists as she struggled, kicked, and thrashed beneath him. He stared at her perfect, succulent breasts, trembling, her young pussy twisting and pressing against his manhood.

"Yes, I think a good fucking is exactly what you need. But first, a drink is in order."

"No?"

"Of course you do."

He had laced her drink with methamphetamine to increase her sexual arousal.

Chris forced her head back with the palm of his hand and upended a bottle of Jack Daniels, slowly pouring it into her mouth and down her throat.

Shandell's body was found three months later in a fetid canal about a mile or so away on the outskirts of Mariel Bay. She was found in a discarded trunk in pieces. For the short time that her pimps had possession of her, she was beaten into submission daily by her johns, who kept fucking her and demanding her absolute obedience. After she was finally sent back to her chamber for refreshing, the *mamacitas* overseeing her ignored her agony and sobbing cries for mercy. Instead, she was treated as raw meat, broken and crippled, physically and psychologically, and sent back to the wolves.

CHAPTER 32

It was now after seven, and the daylight was fading fast. The wind came up, whispering a sough through the canopy of the trees silhouetted by a slender unambitious sliver of a moon alongside the house and carrying with it the fermented scent of the river. Outside, the low clouds shrouding the mountaintops created an eerie darkness, and the air smelled of a storm brewing. The temperature had cooled down from the oppressive afternoon heat earlier, and the evening coolness was more pronounced. Unfortunately, the oppressive humidity still hung heavy in the thick air.

The weathermen had been predicting a late afternoon thunderstorm. Typical in the mountains this time of year. It wasn't long before she heard the first rumblings of thunder echoing through the mountains as she witnessed a bolt of lightning crack through the darkened night sky outside her kitchen window. The dewy petrichor scent of rain wafted through the open window, pulling the drape down as she closed it. More inclemency was just about to hit. Just then, the gentle patter of rain that had been tapping the tin roof escalated and turned into a discernable monotonous torrential downpour, buffeting the window panes and pouring down the gutter drainpipe outside the kitchen.

As Nuna was at the stove stir-frying her supper and visualizing the face of Bryce Tucker, a frantic pounding on the back door drew her attention away from the stove, snapping her out of her reverie and forcing her to look, startled, toward the door. She had never had anyone knock on her door, never mind pound on it.

Whoever was now braving the thunderstorm and pounding peremptorily on the door had to be in distress. She shut off the stove and slowly but perseveringly made her way over to the door with a frisson of fear and cold sweat descending her spine; she peeked out through a small crack in the venetian blinds. A lightning flash revealed a young girl with bloodied hands pressing against the door. She was as naked as the day she was born. Gaunt and pale, rain-soaked, and with overt terror on her face, the young girl stared in at her through the diamond-paned window in the door.

"Help meeeeeeee, pleeeeeeease!" The disembodied voice of a girl screamed hysterically as she pounding the entrance repeatedly. "Please, let me in," she cried piteously, wailing and frantically freeing the words from her mouth in a quavering voice of distress.

Nuna quickly noticed that the young girl as skeletally thin and had a battered face with blood running down both sides.

Aghast, Nuna pursed her lips and felt a cold chill to the marrow.

"Hurry!" the girl cried hysterically, rattling the doorknob incessantly with her left hand while her other hand continued to pound on the door, now more emphatically. "Please, please have mercy. Let me in! Please!"

Nuna, throwing caution to the wind, her heart thudding heavily in her ears, commiserated. Her fingers closed around the smooth brass knob, and she unlocked the door, opening it wide to the wailing wind but never taking her eyes off the girl.

"Goodness." Nuna was momentarily speechless.

The young, terrified girl, clearly discombobulated, burst headlong through the doorway, past Nuna, as if the devil were after her. Then, she literally threw her emaciated body into the kitchen.

"Apure, pro favor!" she wailed.

She found traction and crawled across the kitchen floor, trembling on her bare dirty hands and sinewy knees, bawling and breathing in deep, gasping sobs. Her hair was a tangled mess littered with twigs and leaves, remnants of her apparent escape down the mountain.

The gangly girl had a sallow complexion and questionable hygiene; she was pale and enervated and flailing uncontrollably on the kitchen floor. "Muchas graciassss. Thank you. Gracias mil veces." She let out an anguished cry.

She looked at Nuna, still bawling. Her furtive eyes were bleak, pleading, and apologetic, her lower lip quivering uncontrollably with stark fear. Her ribs and shoulder bones protruded from malnutrition.

Her voice, etched with pain, was little more than a nearly inaudible whine.

Given the dire circumstances, why she was apologizing was a mystery. Her eyes were empty, dead, depleted of energy. There was blood on her parched lips, and her front tooth was broken to the gum.

There were cuts and welts all over her face; both eyes were black and blue and swelling. Her voice was colored with fear as she spoke with a wheezing breath and began to flush. She threw her head back, and a terrible laugh spilled from her quavering, bloody mouth. "No one can save me."

Nuna kneeled on the floor and palpated the back of the girl's head, back, skeletally thin legs and arms. It didn't seem like she had sustained any serious injuries, but she was bruised and had bloodied scratches all over her face and body, having run through countless wild thorned blackberry bushes on her way down the mountain. Her hair was a jumble of tangles. She also had several puncture marks on both her arms, some of them oozing with puss, most likely from being injected with drugs.

Lying supine and seemingly disoriented, she first put her arms atop her head and then on her stomach, lacing her white knuckled fingers.

"Police department," came the voice on the other end of the phone. "How can I help you?"

"I need help! Pleeeeeease," Nuna pleaded, shaking her head vehemently.

"Missy, calm down and tell me what's wrong."

Nuna took a deep breath, finding it difficult to articulate her words. She finally regained her composure and explained the situation the best she could, along with the girl's condition, to the dispatcher.

"Missy. What is your name?"

"Nuna, Nuna Polinski," she cried.

"Nuna, what is the address? Nuna, is there anyone else there?"

"No, just the young girl!"

"Ms. Polinski, lock your doors and don't allow anyone in. Two units of State Police and an ambulance are en route."

She ran through the house, ensuring all the doors and windows were locked.

"It's OK. No one is going to hurt you," Nuna crooned, kneeling next to the girl. Slowly Nuna began to remove vines from the girl's body. "Shhh…" she whispered. "Help is on the way."

Time had never passed so slowly as she held the bawling girl, having survived wiles and horrors she couldn't dare to think of, in her arms, waiting for the police to arrive.

If a killer had been out there tracking the girl, he was still out there. All the trees on the mountain of her backyard now seemed eerily quiet and alien. Fear rippled down her spine.

Nuna grabbed the girl's trembling hands and held them tightly in hers.

She pulled away sharply and lifted what was left of her blood-splattered top to show me the large bruises on her breasts. Then, lifting her hair, she showed the raw place where her captor had pulled out a clump of her hair as he dragged her.

She canted her eyes to the ground and sighed deeply.

"I kept wondering if the police were looking for me even though I knew they weren't. I was kept in a shed for over six months."

Nuna was unaware of any reports of a missing girl, and to the best of her knowledge, there hadn't been any posters stapled to poles or taped to a store windows giving mention of her disappearance.

Nuna had given her a hairbrush. The girl looked at her, and dropped it to the floor. Nuna watched her pulling her hair free from the brush she held.

Long strands spilled over her shoulders. "It's scary," she replied. The girl looked so sad.

Nuna wanted to hold her and put her arm around her, but in her frail condition, she feared she might hurt her. Her heartbeat, which had been erratic, was coming back to normal now.

While it was only about five minutes, it seemed like forever before she heard the wail of approaching sirens coming into the holler. Within minutes, her yard was swarming with West Virginia State Police. Two firetrucks and an emergency ambulance from the Gauley Bridge Volunteer Fire Department with paramedics joined them. In all, there were a half dozen cruisers.

Two male and two female officers, guns drawn, knocked on the door. "Hello, Ms. Polinski, are you OK?"

"No!" she cried, slowly unlocking and opening the door before bursting into tears.

"Easy, easy, Ms. Polinski. You've had a bad experience tonight," one of the female officers said, sounding genuinely sympathetic. "Where is the girl?"

"She's sitting on the kitchen floor against the wall. She needs desperate medical attention!" Nuna screamed.

The place was now crawling with uniform police and detectives. Having searched the backyard where the girl had descended from the mountain, they had found nothing significant except the blood on the kitchen floor, already beginning to congeal. A detective told Nuna the ambulance would transport her to the Montgomery General Hospital in Charlestown for medical treatment and observation. Since she was underage without guardianship, she would be given protective status by the FBI in Charleston.

Just then, a dark Crown Victoria pulled up on the street, screeching its brakes, with the driver storming out quickly and running up the hill before walking into the open door of the kitchen.

"Tom, I heard the call on my radio and thought I better get involved."

"Lieutenant, this is Ms. Nuna Polinski," one of the male officers said, pointing to the woman sitting on the floor with the girl. "She's the homeowner who made the 911 call."

"Ms. Polinski, I'm Detective Doug Roddy with the West Virginia State Police Department. Ms. Polinski, please stay where you're at, and try to relax."

Nuna covered her trembling lips with her hands, which were now cold, clammy and bloodied. Tears welled in her eyes.

"We'll take over from here," the female detective said. She was kneeling on the kitchen floor, quietly talking to the girl, who was now holding her head between her legs and crying. "Just point us in the direction that you came off the mountain."

She at first didn't respond but eventually pointed to the kitchen door.

"Nuna, Detective Ellyn Doughty will stay with you and the girl while we work our way up the path that she came from."

The detective and a couple of other uniforms disappeared around the corner of the house and having found the bushes she had broken through, headed up the narrow footpath. They came back down a couple of hours later, after what seemed like forever, and acknowledged finding her footprints and bloodied leaves leading down off the mountain but nothing else.

The young girl and Officer Doughty had already left in the ambulance to the hospital.

Detective Roddy asked if Nuna was up to talking. Nuna just shrugged, knowing that they needed her information. The detective was not only aggressive but irritating with his questioning. He wanted to know when she got home today, where she was during the day, and the time when the girl started pounding on her door. "Ms. Polinski, why did it take you almost thirty minutes after letting the girl in to call 911."

She told him she had already answered these questions with Officer Doughty, but he wasn't listening.

"Tell me now, or I'm taking you to the police station." Just then, he pulled out a cigarette and was about to light it when she stood up and told him to take it outside.

"This is my house, and there's no smoking in it." He looked at her, startled, and then put the cigarette back in the pack.

Reluctantly, she retold her story in brief before requesting a lawyer.

As she finished telling the detective her story for the second time, he inappropriately put his hand on her shoulder and apologized for grilling her. "Take your hands off me," she screamed.

He immediately removed his hands and stepped back. "Unfortunately, Ms. Polinski, I need you to promise not to tell anyone about what happened here tonight. For now, I want to keep it under wraps." She slowly nodded that she understood.

Somehow word of the kidnapped girl was already out, and the following morning a half dozen reporters from the news media were at her house trying to get her to divulge the details surrounding the girl's rescue.

Later that morning, Bryce called, and Nuna shared everything that had happed with him. She desperately needed his support. "That girl was put through hell!"

Bryce was at her door within the hour, having driven at warp speed out of Charleston through the winding mountains.

Austin, maintaining his undercover as a photo reporter, was just minutes behind Bryce, en route. He was already in touch with his contacts at the state police department and the FBI in Charleston, gathering available data. It was then that he learned that the FBI had not yet been contacted by the local marshal or state police. Given that this was a kidnapping, he was assured that three agents would be immediately dispatched to take over the investigation.

Both were under the auspices of the *Charleston Gazette*. Both were fully aware that local law enforcement in West Virginia, especially southern West Virginia, might have been seriously compromised. Both had already observed undercurrents of alliances and rivalries between the local departments.

For the next twenty-four hours, after being admitted to an emergency trauma center at the Montgomery General Hospital, Danielle refused to speak a word. She only screamed and screamed. A team of doctors and nurses were assigned to her care. Her body was a patchwork of welts and cigarette burns. By morning the following day, the staff, having cleaned and treated her and treated her flesh wounds, had been able to calm her. With the doctors and nurses still examining her, Captain Shawn Russell of the West Virginia State Police, along with Special Agent Eileen Muniz of the FBI, entered the room, introducing themselves.

"Danielle, I'm Captain Shawn Russell of the West Virginia State Police; this is Special Agent Eileen Muniz of the FBI Charleston office."

Both of their faces blanched, as if they were looking over the abyss into hell's lair. Had they rescued a girl or only the shell of one? They knew that they had to trod carefully with this girl as she had suffered and was still suffering the effects of long-term trauma. It took over an hour before Special Agent Muniz finally got Danielle to respond to her own name.

"We realize you're in pain, but we have to ask you a few questions. So we will keep it brief. Danielle, who did this to you?"

When she stared at them plaintively with faraway, puffy eyes and didn't respond, they understood that it was much too painful for her to speak. Danielle stared at them, and they looked back at PTSD personified

"Danielle, don't try and talk. Just nod or shake your head."

She simply looked up with a desolate expression.

They didn't want to interview her right then, but they needed to elicit the information while it was still fresh in her head.

"OK?"

She returned the nod. "Sí," she whispered.

"You were kidnapped and then abducted somewhere in the Charleston area and imprisoned up on the mountain by several Mexicans?"

She nodded.

"Was there anything you could have done to prevent your abduction?"

She shook her head vehemently. A nurse in a blue smock sitting next to her wiped a stray tear from Danielle's eye.

"You, along with a group of young girls possibly numbering in the twenties or more, were stripped, tortured, and raped by these Mexican predators, in hour after hour of depravity. Many of them were sold and exported as sex slaves to foreigners."

She nodded.

"Are the people who abducted you the same as the ones that abused you?"

A nod.

"Danielle, could you identify these Mexicans from a lineup?"

A hesitant nod before her expression filled with fear again.

"Danielle, you're going to recover and get well in this hospital," the agent said plaintively. "We have multiple FBI officers outside your door, and they're going to remain there 24-7 until we capture the monsters who did this to you. I resolutely promise that no one is going to hurt you again. You have my word!"

Agent Eileen Muniz stroked the top of her head with a tender touch. "Danielle, whoever this monster is, he won't get near you again." She nodded slowly, but the horror would take a long time to fade. "Danielle, an officer from the West Virginia OVC victim advocates office will be with you shortly. She is just outside being briefed by FBI as we speak."

Pleading tears ran from her rheumy eyes as she watched us leave the room. It would take months for the ligature marks to fade from her ankles and wrists. Her memory of the ordeal might never heal.

Eventually, the authorities began to gain her trust with short visits and piece her story together bit by bit. On the morning of the third day, Danielle began slowly telling a story of horror.

"You were forcibly taken by a Mexican with a large scar on his face, shackled, ball gagged with duct tape, blindfolded, and forced into the back of a van, having just left a vacant building?"

"I want go home," she cried as her voice softly trailed off.

"Where is home?" the female detective asked.

"The *barrio bajos* of El Mirador," she cried.

The detective later identified El Mirador as a small farming village just west of Tijuana, Mexico.

"My father sold me to men from Tijuana for medical supplies to care for my sick mother."

The detective hesitated before posing his next question.

"Why do you want to go back to El Matador?"

With her head in her hands, she convulsed, collapsing to the floor from her chair in pain.

"It's the only place I know," she cried.

She had been kept with four other girls in a dank cellar of a stone carriage house up on the mountain. One by one, the other girls were taken out at night and never returned. Finally, the following night, he came for her and having removed her shackles, took her out behind the house. She assumed that he was going to kill her. Suddenly, a huge bear appeared out of the darkness, and her captor dropped her on the ground and escaped into the woods. Weak and without any clothes on, she took advantage of the situation and started running toward the woods in the opposite direction, eventually finding what looked like a path leading down the mountain.

The marshal and three deputies searched the mountain but could not locate the carriage house. What they did find, he said ominously, was a human femur sticking out of the dirt. Closer inspection of the area revealed several skeletons buried naked in shallow graves along a creek.

She was a young Panamanian woman in her late teens or early twenties who spoke fluent Spanish and only limited English. She should have been running free and living life to the fullest. But, unfortunately, she was now lost in a catatonic state and completely traumatized.

She had been working as a waitress in Charleston for the past year and a half before being snatched off the street on her way home and kidnapped.

Lying on the examination table, trembling in abject fear and pain, the petite young girl had olive skin and black hair. Dressed in a blue smock, she had a severe concussion, moderate to severe soft-tissue injuries to her back and chest, and two broken ribs. Her face and arms were badly bruised and scratched with some wounds requiring butterfly bandages. She looked at them with two black eyes wide, accentuated by stress and terror. Her right jaw was severely swollen, her left arm broken below the elbow and now in a cast, and she had a fractured ankle. Two nurses were attending her, and every time one would touch her, the pain would spike into her fragile cranium, causing her to squeeze her face into a taut grimace.

She was only fourteen or fifteen years old. She had run away from home in Pineville, escaping family abuse where her stepfather would quietly enter her bedroom at night and molest her regularly. Her mother not only turned her head but offered her out for money to buy drugs. Her name was Danielle Kooza. Having reached her obvious nadir, she had been sleeping in a muddy morass under a bridge in Charleston, covered in a thin army blanket, when a pimp snatched her. He raped and beat her for several weeks before putting her out with several other underage prostitutes. She was plunged into a terrible purgatory of degradation, drugs, sex, and despair. With no home to return to, she only had a handful of abandoned homeless girls to depend on; they congregated beneath an underpass to exchange smokes, lies, and drugs. She hallucinated vividly in her captivity, believing that she had been born in purgatory or hell, that she had been condemned to suffer for the rest of her life, and that the pimp that came through the door every night was actually the devil. Finally, one night, as a wave of panic threatened to overtake her rage, she slipped out of an alley under cover of darkness, escaped, and ran for miles before collapsing into a ditch. She was terrified but couldn't return home and face her parents' wrath. Having escaped her captivity, she was utterly alone, with nowhere to go. Her freedom didn't last long.

A couple of months later, having escaped from her pimp, she was forced into a van that was parked in front of a vacant building just outside Summerville.

"A Mexican with a large scar across his face put a large knife to my throat and forced me into his van before tying me to the floor and ripping off my blouse. He covered my mouth with a rag, and I guess, I passed out. Sometime later, he dragged me into a cabin and handcuffed me with police-styled handcuffs over my head, hanging me against a wall me in a dark, windowless room. An hour or so later, her strapped me to a bed. With his weight on top of me, he pinned me to the mattress spread eagle, crushing me as he raped and slapped me repeatedly, telling me I was his property now. He slapped and punched me to drive home the point, then forced me to look into a movie camera and smile.

"Then, as I thrashed against my bindings, he put a leather horse bit over my head, strangling my breath. My wrists were tightly bound in handcuffs to the metal headrest, and my ankles were manacled to the floor, making me utterly immobile. Helpless and muzzled, unable to scream, I moaned, hearing the sound echoing hollowly in a narrow basement corridor."

She cringed as her captor used a warm, damp towel to clean her vaginal area, whispering, "More to come, my *bonito-do*. You make a great movie. I sell the film for lots of money." His touch no longer repulsed her. She felt nothing. She no longer knew night from day. The room had no windows.

"He would sit me up and feed me once a day. The meal was simply a can of tuna and a water bottle to keep me hydrated. The only other time I was unshackled was when he allowed me to use the bathroom, which had no door."

Agent Muniz interrupted, "Danielle, do you remember what he looked like?"

"The room was dark, but he was big, naked, and spoke Spanish." Her eyes were filling with tears.

"Danielle, we know that this is painful for you. Just take all the time you need."

"He was staring down at me where I lay huddled on a mattress in the darkness in nothing more than a tattered, sodden T-shirt."

Her eyes had now adjusted to the darkness of the dank room where they were kept shackled in dark isolation. His eyes were different than before. He had always looked composed and unflappable. Now his expression was evil and angry.

"You are nothing bitch," he taunted. "You will be used and abused and possibly die here, *muchachita*, should no one else care to buy you. As of right now, no one is coming for you. No one cares."

Suddenly, he turned and walked over to another bed.

"Ah, there you are," he said in a hushed but curiously menacing voice.

He taunted the young girl on the bed as he positioned his camera.

He wasn't angry with Danielle. She would live a little longer, another day of no consequence.

"Mummy," she gasped, closing her eyes, and her tears came gushing out, and her whole body shook with them. "Help me."

Within minutes, she could see his shadow and hear him raping the girl in the darkness not more than a few feet from her. The girl, who an anorectic, emaciated look, was bucking violently against him, crying and screaming, "No, no! Pleeeeeease." Her undulating, insufferable screams ricocheted around the room as he forced himself upon her and impaled her repeatedly, making strange grunting sounds.

"Mama," she wailed repeatedly, and Danielle couldn't help to hear her protracted screams.

He was choking her with his bare muscular hands, letting her breathe and gag as she thrashed against him, then choking her again as she desperately gasped for air.

Over and over, he was saying to her that she had absorbed him and had now subjugated herself to his will forever.

"I'll be good," she started keening, her voice morphing into a whimper that rose to a cry of deflated pessimism. "But please," she pleaded, "me do anything you wish. I'll never tell anyone." She continued to sob, desperately gasping for air every time he relaxed his grip on her throat.

He laughed with evil audacity, "That is very well true, bitch. You will be silent forever. Before I sold your mama, you starred in a special movie with her, among your many appearances. But no one wants you now that your stomach is growing, and I've become bored."

He pulled her off the bed and punched her in the stomach. She crumpled to the floor.

Danielle saw the dark face of evil standing up and lifting the limp body of the naked girl off the floor to her feet by her hair like a halter, exposing her neck for the serrated knife he held in his right hand.

"Please…don't kill me…pleeeeeease," she whispered the words like a mantra. "Pleeeeeease!" The arterial spray of blood from the plunge of the heavy blade flooded the floor as her curdled scream erupted from her open, bloodied mouth.

And then there was a hollow dead silence. She was dead.

Danielle heard him drag the girl outside and shortly afterward come back and lock the door.

Later that night, while Daneille was still bound spread-eagle on the bed, he again put the horse bit over her head and, this time, covered her eyes with black blinders.

"Sleep well, my minion. Me fuck you in morning."

She closed her eyes, knowing she would refuse to give in to the madness.

Nothing she could do would alleviate her predicament and prevent what had happened to the girl. There was no way out. Any thought of an escape plan evaporated into the darkness. He would have no compunction about using me before killing me in the morning.

"Sometime later that night, I felt the presence of a woman who smelled like a flower enter my cell as I lay there on the bed, tied up like a chicken. She untied the knotted nylon rope from my bound, chafed ankles and wrists and slowly sat me up. My entire body was trembling like leaves in the wind as I felt her remove the horse bit and blinder and then touch my face with her soft fingers. The woman was wearing a mask and a dark shawl.

"She lit a small candle and handed me a plastic fork and whispered, 'Eat,' putting a paper plate of cold ravioli in tomato sauce in front of me. As she sat with me in the darkness, I speared every piece of ravioli on the plate and put it into my mouth, chewing hard. As she stood up in the darkness, her chair scrapped on the cement floor. She said, "Get dressed' and silently left the room without locking the door or reshackling me to the bed. On the bed were a T-shirt, a pair of shorts, and a pair of used sneakers. Pawing with trembling fingers along the bench in the dim light, I quickly donned the clothes left for me."

"Danielle, go back to that moment."

"Quaking with fear and sweating like a stuffed pig, I opened the door into the darkness of the night and swiftly sprinted, practically dove into the darkness of the forest behind the cabin, not knowing where I was running to."

Adrenaline-propelled, she had run hither and thither for two days and two nights, blending into the rugged wilderness and running across miles of dry leaves and pine needles through walls of briar bushes lining the forest. Her arms and legs took the brunt of the thorns, causing her unrelenting pain as she tripped and stumbled over logs. It was dark and gloomy under the trees and cooler.

Several times she had an unsettled feeling as she slogged her way up the side of a mountain and thought she heard someone running behind her, crunching dry leaves and pine needles, getting closer. The thought and sounds of pursuit gave wings to her bare feet. Branches slapped her in the face. She was sobbing, trembling, terrified that at any moment the big man would find her and take her back, and weariness and bone-deep fatigue began to suffocate her. She had to stop and catch her breath. Winded and panting, she collapsed, crawling into the undergrowth and covering herself with the thick padding of fallen leaves for concealment.

"Turning my head and checking over my shoulder frantically, I squatted close to the ground and picked up a sharp rock. Unfortunately, my vision was going a little cloudy from the tears welling up and maybe my panic. Finding cover on the ground behind a tree, I lay flat in the damp underbrush and slowed my breathing until the sound faded away. Whoever it was had remained hidden. Then there was silence as I stood up, still holding my breath. I stepped carefully, moving with care not to break a branch, pausing every few steps to listen until I was sure that whoever was out there had passed. The carpet of fallen pine needles hid the sound of my footsteps as I made my way through the buggy, steaming forest. Vines were everywhere, wrapping and hanging from the trees. The air smelled of damp earth. At the bottom of a mountain, I slid down a steep bank of moss and found myself wallowing around in the swamp water."

She had landed face first, panting, and now having found her footing, was knee-deep in the muck of a swamp. Somewhere in the distance, she heard thunder, and within minutes, the sky opened up.

Slowly she footed one step at a time through the muddy slough, which seemed to be forever. Suddenly, a branch snapped back, catching her in the side, eliciting a cry of pain. She fell hard face first in the mud with pain splintering through her body. Lying there like a broken doll, she wiped at her lips with the back of her hand, removing some of the mud from her mouth, each breath more painful than the last. The marsh grass was dense with clustered clumps of skunk cabbage seemingly floating on the water's surface. Branches swished high and low. Insects droned, and small rodents scurried before her. Crawling and finding dry ground, she wiped the greasy mud from her eyes, crawled, and flailed out of the bog up a steep bank before collapsing under a tree for the rest of the night.

The next day, as the first gray light of morning showed, soaked, filthy, hungry, and in terrible pain, she slowly trudged forward barefoot through a thick forest choked by weeds and thorny vines that tore at her bare skin. She stumbled into an almost invisible spider web. In absolute pain, she wiped the clammy web from her face and kept moving onward. And then, just when she thought she wasn't going to make it, she heard rushing water and saw faint lights of civilization in the distance. But at the same time, she heard, or at least she thought she heard, the Mexican yelling out to her back in the woods.

Gasping for air and catching her breath in panic, she dropped the rock and began running, tripping on roots and other stuff and sidestepping down the slope, crossing over a rushing creek and grabbing onto saplings on the steepest parts, easing herself down the bank. Suddenly she saw flickering lights in the distance. She began running in terror, sucking air into her burning lungs and oblivious to the pain of her scrapes and bruises; she bolted from the thicket crossing the backyard and began banging on the kitchen door.

Danielle was sure that if the Mexican caught her, he would kill her just like the other girl.

Austin had gotten a response back from the Mexican authorities in Tijuana, and the jacket wasn't good. Pablo had been arrested numerous times for dealing drugs and pimping, with his most recent arrest for breaking a bottle of liquor over a sixteen-year-old hooker's head, reshaping her face with the jagged handle of the bottle, and sending her to a hospital in a coma. He spent two hours in jail and was bailed by the seemingly unimpeachable Maduro organization. The charges were dropped as it was logged as self-defense: the hostile adolescent girl had attacked him with the bottle as he sat having lunch. He had a history, and few of his victims had ever been found; those that were chose not to press charges.

She survived the worst. She had been brutalized by a monster, drugged, tortured, raped, and there was a possible murder of another girl.

The salient fact was that she escaped and was alive.

An hour or two later (hard to tell), she was taken from the van and imprisoned in a large metal container, maybe a trailer with several other girls. It smelled terribly of urine. Still blindfolded, she could only hear their feeble whimpering. The next day, they were put in a van and taken to a warehouse where their blinders were removed before they were told to strip naked, relieve themselves, and shower, one at a time. Finally, coming out of the shower stall naked and wet, they were led over to a wooden wall dripping wet and shackled to hooks with their arms above their heads.

She went on. "Their English was about as good as my Spanish, but while we cried a lot, we spoke little. The following day, we were taken down from our hooks and led to another room where to our shock and utter astonishment, no less than twenty naked girls and a group of four boys that had to be around our age were shackled by their left wrist to a purple velvet lined wall being held as prisoners. Listening to their Spanish cries and pleas, I believed most to be Mexican. For two days, we were left hanging by our left wrists with nothing to eat and nowhere to go to the bathroom. The smell was abominable, a mix of rancid bodies, putrefied sweat, and urine collected in a metal pail that sufficed for a commode.

"A few times during the night, a couple of other girls were brought in, crying and moaning as the Mexicans shackled them. Twice they came that night to survey us. Finally, they unshackled two girls and took them to another room. We could hear their screams as they raped them over and over during the night. They were never seen again. The room smelled terrible, and three more girls were about to be added.

"An hour or so later, we heard heavy footfalls; two Hispanic yahoos came into the room and took a pressure hose to each of us, spraying us with ice-cold water. We were ordered to face the center of the room and watch as a third Mexican entered the room. Randomly, one of the yahoos, who they called Pablo, would choose a willowy brunette with long hair and force her to give him pleasure orally while she was being washed. He then forced her to kneel on the floor in front of all as he choked her, spread her legs wide, and thrust himself into her squirming ass. Screaming and begging for mercy, she was punched many times in the face before her screaming and moaning went quiet. Finally, he picked her off the floor by her hair like a rag doll and took her away. She was never seen again.

"An hour after the washing, as we dripped dry, they brought in cans of Campbell's and Progresso soups, handing one to each girl and boy to eat straight out of the can.

"One of the girls accidentally dropped her can. The man slapped her in the face repeatedly before unshackling her trembling arm. He then forced her to her knees and made her lick the spilled soup off the floor like a dog until it was cleaned.

The next several days followed the same torture routine until a group of well-dressed businessmen and three well-dressed women arrived that she had never seen before. They all spoke in a Middle Eastern dialect, but she couldn't be any more specific. A big man with a thick beard, a large gold chain around his neck, and a South American accent stood before the group of twenty naked girls shackled to the wall. After chewing on a large lit cigar, he took it from his mouth and blew perfect rings of smoke into the air. With ceiling lights turned on, this huge man with dark predatory eyes exuded raw power, not one the Mexicans would challenge. They had whispered that he was a *demonio* in the darkness. Again, she had not seen him before this day, and now he walked the line with a lopsided grin, barking orders and examining each girl and boy with his hand as he described their bodily assets to the assembly of men and women.

The teenagers were being individually auctioned off with a green tag placed around their necks that identified their name, age, gender, lineage, state, and country of origin and the location they were taken from. By the end of the day, most of the girls and boys had been auctioned off as *putas* and taken away. Danielle and another negro girl who had been beaten severely in the face were left hanging helplessly from the hook.

Can you describe the building where you were kept?

"Sí." She nodded, her hands shaking. "The first building was a shack with no bathroom or water. The second building I was brought to was much larger, with a bathroom and running water. A building with many rooms and many girls and boys shackled to the walls. We were left there for days without food or water and nowhere to go to the bathroom. The room smelled terrible. The last was a log cabin with no bathroom, and it also smelled like a cesspit. Nothing else."

The following morning, prompted by Danielle's escape and rescue, an alert was sent out. Having methodically studied the topographic maps of the area, the entire force of active and retired Gauley Bridge police officers, along with a team of state police, canine units, and local

volunteers met at the trailhead in Nuna's backyard and began searching
the rutted north-facing mountain slope, following a backcountry game
path that was hardly a path anymore through a towering thick forest and
a undergrowth of fir, blackberry bushes, wild mountain laurel, white
pine, and ash. They slowly followed the dogs along a steep, arduous trail
of broken branches and plants that Danielle had trampled and left behind in the woods during her escape.

Finally, on the third day, following the scent of evil around jagged
rock formations and tangles of exposed roots, they came upon an abandoned oversize Quonset hut. It was set back in a swale between two treed
ridges just off an abandoned forest service road about five miles into the
forest. A set of fading ATV tracks led into the forest before disappearing
on the service road. The siding of the ramshackle structure was sullied by
the elements, sun-bleached a mottled pale gray. The metal roof was also
showing signs of fatigue. Streaks of rust lines from each nailhead could
be seen where the galvanizing had been compromised by the elements.

When they stepped up over the rotting threshold and turned the
knob, opening the door and letting it swing open, a nauseating odor of
death rushed out from the rotting interior. The stench of stale urine, fe-
ces, and body odor was nauseating; they knew from Danielle's summary
this was the cabin she had described. From the vault of rafters overhead,
a horned owl swiveled its head like something on a greased bearing to
better see his intruders below before spreading his wings and gliding
soundlessly out. Using flashlights, they saw the walls were covered with
shackles and blood splatter. A half dozen chains hung from the rusted corrugated ceiling. The place was seemingly designed and made to
be a temporary holding facility. Filthy mattresses were strewn about the
room, some with bloodstains on them.

At both ends of the room were two cots with shackles attached. They
could only imagine the girls suffocating inside, tethered to the wall. The
place was filthy, with trash everywhere: magazines, old newspapers, candy wrappers, and beer cans.

The detectives stepped out of the cabin and sucked deep breaths of the fresh mountain air. They had been in the cabin longer than they realized. A crowd of onlookers and reporters began to clog the forest service road, forcing the police to push back the crowd and cordon the road out of the forest. About a hundred yards into the thick woods, the dogs located four shallow graves, each containing a female skeleton wrapped in a skirt with her hands hogtied behind her back.

The officers began searching several pathways leading away from the cabin. The cadaver dogs found what they were looking for and more. They also found what looked like a half dozen shallow graves fifty yards out from the cabin. The team had dug down and unearthed six skulls. They stopped and now waited for proper exhumation. A petite young girl no older than maybe fourteen was found close by under a pile of leaves, her body stiff with early rigor mortis and a glob of congealed blood, leading them to believe that her murder was very recent as the pathetic serial killer hadn't yet had the time to bury her. Her body had been scourged severely with a metal chain, and she had been savagely beaten prior to her strangulation. A medical anthropologist and coroner had been summoned and would give a more precise estimate of her time of death along with answers to a litany of horrific questions that would follow. Early evidence suggested that she had been forced to engage in antemortem intercourse prior to her throat being cut. Ants were already working on her, and her bloodied facial expression showed a nightmare countenance. She had been a pretty girl. Now she was a sad pile of rotting, decomposing flesh. Her body had been brutalized, showing overlapping lacerations, ligatures on her wrists and ankles, and contusions from head to toe. Her throat had been cut ear to ear with a jagged knife. She had been young and died an agonizing savage death.

Evidence of torture and rape was present in the cabin. But, unfortunately, so much of it had been compromised. The police chief lowered and shook his head. What kind of person does this? he thought. Having a young daughter himself, he felt ill at the depravity of the individuals who had committed these acts.

The following morning, Austin and Bryce met for breakfast and watched *Breaking News* on Fox 61. The political corruption in Washington was being presaged by a sudden horrendous headline story: as with every other channel in the state, this one was focused entirely on the murders in the West Virginia forest. Austin suddenly asked the waitress to turn up the volume. The anchor announced that at a surprise news conference held just moments ago at police headquarters, there had been a break in the disappearance of a couple of young girls in West Virginia. As the story unfolded, there were stunning details of the find and close-ups of the cabin, now surrounded by yellow tape, and all the official activity that had taken place at the crime scene. The facts were slim, but the descriptions of the bodies and skeletal remains were lurid and pointed to a serial killer. Everyone was talking about the murdered girls in the forest, and the Gauley Bridge Police hadn't set up a press conference yet. All available manpower was being assigned to the case, including the state police and the FBI. Austin would stay in touch with his inside contact at the FBI regional office in Charleston, as it was imperative that he and Bryce remain undercover.

Autopsies on the victims would be initiated immediately.

But even more disturbing was the report of three other teens from across the state who had not been seen for over three months but had never officially been declared missing. While an active investigation was ongoing, all were now presumed dead. The story about the three missing teens seemed like it was never going away. But in fact they might have just been found.

CHAPTER 33

The morning dawned with an overcast gloomy sky. Pablo was wishing that some whim of nature might prevent today's meeting with Hugo from taking place. That wasn't to be. He took in deep mouthfuls of air as if hyperventilating.

Hugo had gone ballistic upon being told of losing his money and the drugs it was supposed to buy. Still reeling, he was becoming incandescent with implacable white-hot smoldering rage by the minute. He stood at the window gloating about what he was going to do with Pablo as he watched a steady rain fall outside. He ran his fingers through his hair from sheer aggravation. He was waiting for Pablo to arrive in a state of adamant agitation, anxiety, and bitter self-reproach for giving the Mexican the errand he had failed to execute. As far as he was concerned, the whole damn valley below him could drown in the Elk River. He couldn't care less about the locals. They were too relaxed, too friendly, too submissively polite, environmentally conscious, and fucking noisy.

But nothing was more infuriating than listening to the recalcitrant Mexican explain the clusterfuck by which he had lost $150,000 in cash and over $250,000 in cocaine. Hugo had a memory like a hard drive and was obsessive about power and control. Having been slighted, he would never forgive, and they would be enemies for life.

Unenthusiastically, Pablo arrived at the Maduro compound just before 1:00 p.m., knowing that there were going to be repercussions for losing the drugs. What he didn't realize was how severe the consequences would be.

"Hola," he said as he walked up to the unsmiling guard masticating an apple at the main security gate. He knew the guard and had drunk with him for several years on a number of occasions, but today the guard took pause and didn't immediately open the gate. To the contrary, he put down the apple and barely even deigned to look at him.

"*Buenos días*, Pablo. Is Mr. Maduro expecting you?" His voice held no inflection at all.

"Yes. What the fuck is going on, asshole?" He flashed a mirthless smile. "Open the fucking gate! I'm getting wet." Pablo was nervous, and a bead of unwanted sweat came to his forehead.

The armed guard gave him a caustic look as he conversed with someone up at the main house and then sourly addressed Pablo.

"Mr. Maduro will see you now, Pablo," he said with chilly politeness, and after a protracted silence, he added, "You will have to check your weapons here."

Pablo blanched briefly, hesitated, and scowled at the guard, who shot him a venomous look as he surrendered his gun and knife. "But, Pablo, I also need the pistol in your boot." Growling, he bent down and removed the beretta from the inside of his left shoe.

Having secured the weapons, the stone-faced guard, his voice becoming more strident, pushed a button on the console and opened the heavy metal gate, allowing Pablo to cross through the stone archway and into a small entrance equipped with an electronic military-grade full-body scanner and camera.

Hugo left nothing to chance when it came to his personal security.

He still considered himself a valuable asset of the Maduro organization, having lived almost twenty years on the US side of the border and speaking English fluently with just a lilt of Spanish. He fully understood the "Norte Americanos" way of living and how to maneuver within it. His take was delusional. As he limped from the guardhouse up the hill, the gardeners and other groundskeepers, who all knew him, looked gravely before turning their heads. Rumor had run rapidly through the estate that he had screwed up a significant business transaction and cost Mr. Maduro a ton of money.

Unshaven and with bated breath, Pablo slowly shambled into Maduro's carpeted Zen garden reception area, which had recessed lighting. He was warmly greeted by Paula, Hugo's voluptuous private secretary, who raised an eyebrow as he entered. He leered at her, giving her a lascivious grin before advising her that he was here to see Senor Hugo. He was vaguely unsettled always but especially today.

Her cheeks flushed as she smiled absently in his direction.

"Please take a seat, Pablo," she said, gesturing to him with her hand toward the leather couch. "I'll let him know you're here."

She lifted the phone, pressed the button, and called Hugo, informing him that Pablo was in the lobby. Hugo tolerated zero risk, and Paula had a loaded Taser in her side desk drawer and knew how to use it if necessary.

The light on the intercom panel lit up on Hugo's desk, and the intercom buzzed from the front desk. He pressed the receiving speaker button.

"Yes, Paula."

"Pablo is here," she whispered without further ado.

"Send him in," he responded. "And Paula, hold my calls."

"Yes, Mr. Maduro." She turned to Pablo. "Mr. Maduro will see you now," she said politely, her voice now languidly contemptuous. Preening her skirt with her hands as she got up from her desk and stepping aside, she opened the double oak doors to Hugo's sanctum for him to pass through. He stood up and thanked the *senorita* before stiffly walking into Hugo's office with a pronounced limp. He was trying to acquire a piece of Hugo's sympathy and favor and possibly avoid his expected rage. He paled significantly as he entered the room.

Paula quietly closed the doors behind her as she retreated back to her desk.

Pablo's pulse skittered, his brow sweat, his breathing was shallow and smelled of badly metabolized garlic, and the skin on his pale oval face was clammy. He was trembling and dithering with raw fear and trepidation.

"Como estas, señor?"

Hugo sat stolidly in his commodious tucked-leather wingback arm-chair behind his desk, swirling and clinking the ice cubes in two fingers of amber single malt scotch in his favorite chunky glass. It was a skillful act of repose that he had mastered long ago. His demeanor was disdainfully calm as his face assumed a hard, contorted cast; his salt-and-pepper hair was well groomed. He was used to projecting a feigned façade during these times of apoplectic rage. This was definitely one of those times.

His feet planted firmly on the floor, he was also puffing on a fat Cuban cigar just removed from the humidor on his desk when the door opened. A large framed painting of him showcased his chiseled looks in uniform at an earlier time. The cuffs of his starched white shirt were rolled up to just below his elbows. His three top buttons were undone, revealing a mascu-line chest. His singed loafers were polished to the point they looked new. He had been sorting through a small pile of cut diamonds and other gem-stones on his desk as Pablo walked through the doorway.

Hugo raised his head and glowered at him with malevolence as he took another sip of his drink, as if summoning his resolve.

His sharp, insolent eyes, cold and cruel, alighted on Pablo and held him there like a magnet on iron metal as he gnashed his teeth with ma-lign rage.

"Well, well. So come in, Pablo," he said in a deprecating stentorian tone, raising a scathing slash of eyebrow in his direction. "Take a seat," he added acidly.

Pablo blanched, wiping his sweaty palms down the side of his pant legs. He then sat down, squirming uneasily in a chair in front of Hugo's desk, fidgeting with his hands and twining his fingers so fiercely that he was in danger of breaking them.

He glared at the pile of glistening gems, but his gaze never left Hugo. Instead, he cleared his throat nervously.

After a moment of protractive silence, Hugo felt his incipient incendiary anger building as he released his stippled fingers and began crushing them. Then, finally, florid with rage, he rolled his chair back behind his desk, rose up, practically levitating off the chair, slammed his glass down, pulled out his .38 caliber revolver, and put it to Pablo's forehead.

His explosive Mexican temper couldn't be constrained as he turned hard eyes on Pablo, his cowl fearsome.

"What the fuck went wrong?" he said testily. Rage rose as he shouted. The impotent ineptitude, he thought. "Did you not comprehend the planning that went into this?"

Hugo had expected a quick surgical hit. Instead, the killing looked like a parking lot drug deal gone wrong with a dead illegal Mexican. No clues, no witnesses.

"Failure is not tolerated within the Maduro organization," Hugo said. He was as brutally cold as a glacier and didn't give a dot about Pablo's pain. Instead, white-hot apoplectic rage, infused with anger at losing the cocaine and cash, twisted through him. He now despised Pablo and fought the urge to kill the sicario on the spot with everything he had.

Unfortunately, at the moment, there wasn't anyone else with his talent for killing and taking care of business that he could trust. He would change this very soon. No one was irreplaceable, especially a pathetic factotum like Pablo.

Hugo sat back down and put the gun on the desk in front of him, intrigued by a thought. He lifted the glass of scotch to his lips and took a long, indulgent pull.

Pablo's face paled with a spasm of fear crossing his face as he felt his bladder releasing, and the wetness in his crotch began to run down his leg as he tried to explain that he had no choice but to run for my life.

"Please, Señor Hugo…please. He brayed…I assure you that it will never happen again…I swear on my mother's grave. Like a *padre*…you have been so good to me.

"Heriberto, that fat-assed hombre, missed his target and exposed me to a hail of gunfire. Had I taken another second to retrieve the case, I would be dead also. So I had no choice but to get the fuck out of there."

Hugo sailed past the interjection. He gritted his teeth for a moment before answering as his lips drew into a cruel mirthless smile.

"Pablo, you do understand that you failed to meet my expectations?" There was no empathy in his voice. He puffed on his cigar as he watched the wastrel quiver through a cloud of smoke. "Pablo, you were given an exact and specific assignment. It was not to be a hit. Who knows what shit this is going to release."

"Senor Hugo, please…" Pablo shrugged, unaware that spittle was leaking out of his mouth as he interjected. Trembling like a leaf, he looked at the small puddle on the floor. "Señor…I find and kill Del Loco Estrada…" he said as Hugo cut him off with a gesture.

"Bullshit," Hugo grated through his teeth. "I want to know exactly whose fault this was, you fucking dirtbag! Suppose we start by you expounding in detail what exactly happened up there."

"Sí, señor."

No matter how meticulously he planned, Hugo still had to rely on his men. Their vagaries and failings them drove him over the edge.

He told, as best he could, colloquially, how he and Heriberto were parked at the summit parking area at the top of the mountain. "Del Loco and his driver pulled in about fifteen minutes later and parked several slots away from us. I had given Heriberto, one of our undocumented men, explicit instructions that if the opportunity should arise and there was absolutely no possible chance of missing Del Loco, he was to shoot to kill him and his driver. Unfortunately, the homey missed the mark, and Del Loco's driver instantly opened up with a hail of bullets, and all chaos broke loose.

"Heriberto was killed immediately in the hailstorm of bullets, and I ran for the car with the backpack in my right hand. Halfway to the car, I took a bullet in my right shoulder, causing me to drop the backpack. Before I could bend down and pick it up, I took another bullet in my ass and instantly ran for the car. I yanked Heriberto out and escaped down the mountain.

"Senor Hugo, if I had stayed a second longer to retrieve the back-pack, I would be dead and the backpack would still be there on the ground." Pablo felt a quick twinge of panic. "*Por favor*, let me find…and kill Del Loco before he escapes!"

Pablo was sweating and amped up, impervious to his pending peril, his bravado gone.

Hugo stood up again, walked around the desk, and leaned negligently on its corner before Pablo.

He riveted his blazing eyes on Pablo. "Estás lleno de mierda, Pablo." You are full of shit.

Trapped between raging thoughts and words, with one swift and fluid motion, he made a fist with a brass knuckle in his right hand and drove it into Pablo's face twice like a blistering sledgehammer, sending Pablo sprawling across the floor. He was now lying on the floor, whimpering in a bleating voice, with two fewer front teeth, and blood flowed out his mouth onto his white wifebeater.

Hugo, blind with rage, stared fiercely at Pablo, pulling him up by his greasy hair.

Pablo's cascade of words ceased. "Your mettle and enthusiasm is noted, but I'll decide whether or not you get a second shot at Estrada. Right now, get your fucking shoulder and ass fixed before I put a bullet in the other. You look like shit and smell worse." Hugo was sure that the rank odor of putrefaction had begun to leak from the untreated wounds of the miscreant. Blood trickled from Pablo's mouth and broken nose as he looked up at Hugo from the floor in stark terror. Hugo was not a sympathetic employer and had difficulty channeling his explosive volcanic rage at Pablo's effrontery. Driving his fists into Pablo's face was his catharsis.

Pablo, not having had time to dodge the blow, ground his teeth in pain as his face wizened, rattled by the implied threat. He looked petrified. Then, not wanting to irk Hugo anymore, he composed himself, his nerve endings frazzled; he lay quiet in mortified silence, cowering on the floor, and kept his swollen mouth shut. Every capillary in Pablo's body was expanding, and his homicidal bravado was wavering under the ferocious incendiary glare of Hugo, glowering over him. Finally, furtively knowing that he was on thin ice and expendable, he decided that he had better start making his plans.

"Now get your dumb ass the fuck out of my sight."

He flounced out of Hugo's office, snarling with indignation. His face was shattered, making him look like a mangy dog, and he was bleeding from the nose and mouth. He closed his hand into a tight fist. His ignominious dejection turned to sardonic outrage. He immediately noticed upon leaving that Hugo's secretary and another assistant turned their heads and sneered at him as if he had something they could catch. Wraith-like, he exited the building, grousing and muttering deprecations under his breath in Spanish, and then left the grounds like a bat out of hell.

Addled, he extended his middle finger. "Adios, you mother fuckers!"

The next day, Hugo, having thwarted Pablo and done his due diligence with his wife, summoned Maria's personal guard, Glenn Nunez, to his office. Of course, he preferred having a man on his payroll whom he had vetted personally. Still, Maria highly recommended Glenn, and he wanted him to supplant the duplicitous Mexican immediately.

"Glenn, you're now to assume the position as my right-hand man in this West Virginia operation. It's imperative that you recover the money and property that Pablo lost in the fucking debacle."

"What about Pablo?" Glenn asked.

Hugo, without any moral turpitude and with a somewhat cavalier attitude, gave him an arch look and grinned wolfishly, picking a fleck of tobacco off his upper lip.

"I've shitcanned him!"

Hugo had discovered through one of his accountants that Pablo had been skimming drugs and cash from his warehouse stash. His trusted "soldier" had betrayed him, and there would be severe consequences as disloyalty was unforgivable.

"He was paid well, yet it wasn't enough. I would be a fool to let the clusterfuck continue thinking he was outsmarting me." Hugo looked at Glenn and asked without preface, "Do you think you might be smarter than me, Glenn." Hugo laughed scoffingly, his eyes narrowing.

Glenn looked at Hugo as he sat across from him at his desk. "No," he said briefly, "but I'm more intelligent than Pablo, and I have no desire to be disloyal to either you or Maria and die at your hands."

Hugo smiled saucily, but his expression was less than desirable. "Bravely spoken. That fractious pissant will be fertilizing watermelons if I don't crack his dumbass head like a piñata first."

His droll remark brought a smile from Glenn. They both laughed.

"Glenn," he said with a rictus of a bolstering smile, "I also want Del Loco Estrada and his minion dispatched and eviscerated. Since Pablo is now off the payroll, I want you to eliminate both him and a small liability for me. You remember her name: it's Nuna, the bitch from the bank that used to process my transactions. Arrange for her to have an accident. *A fatal accident.* I want her silenced soon."

At the same time, Pablo, devoid of all illusion, exited the compound like a rat abandoning a sinking ship. He quickly began to articulate the fiery internal rage within him into a raging apoplectic mania and began to salivate as he plotted a revengeful recourse.

"Fuck Hugo!"

Affronted and intentionally belittled, he would never forget the insult and the feeling of being a disposable cockroach. He was blitzed, and having finished venting over the pompous unrelenting bastard, embittered and in a funk, he tore out of the parking lot and drove recklessly back to his saloon. He parked in the rear of the pub and used the back stairs. He poured himself several shots of tequila and then hunkered down on the sofa and began setting out a plan to fuck up Hugo's money transfers. He had watched Nuna's movements for a week now and was ready to take her in the word's full meaning. He was going to force her into submission, subjugate her utterly, then strangle the bitch slowly and sensually until she was extinguished. The ferocious beast inside him was now in a frisson of excitement and anxious to get the hottie on her bed, hog-tie her, and rape her over and over and over before he strangled her.

"Nobody fucks with Pablo. Nobody fucks with Pablo," he recited over and over through sullen lips and now through gritted teeth. "Nobody…"

His nostrils pulsated as the adrenaline rush of the moment accelerated his breathing.

"He wanted to hurt the heinous bastard badly and then fuck the bitch before silencing her forever." While he had a limited command of the English language, he effectively used his gutter vernacular.

He was now excited and intrigued by the malicious nature of his belligerent thoughts, which came from his dark animus. It had already been a week since his cantankerous meeting with Hugo, and the area around his left eye had run the gamut of colors; it was now a jaundiced yellow. The urge to step into a new sinister dimension was almost irresistible. Hugo would rue the day he was born.

The following day, Glenn using a secured line and gave Austin an update on Hugo's drubbing of Pablo and what was taking place at the Maduro residence.

Austin immediately alerted Bryce verbatim of the new development. Pablo was a psychopath, deranged by Hugo's rejection, and was now a ticking time bomb.

Having left the Maduro residence in disgrace, Pablo became unglued and retreated back to the Red Dog and began a drinking jag. Four empty longneck beer bottles graced the bar top before him. Consuela slid a near-lethal glass of Jack Daniels to him.

And then another. He cursed savagely, slurring his words, and polished off a third in one gulp.

He was hammered like nothing she had seen before.

A broad grin fell across Pablo's leathery face as he raised his rheumy eyes to Consuela. "The hell you looking at, bitch?" Nobody fucks with me," he muttered with a skulk, "not Hugo or anyone else." He repeated the words that now had become his mantra several times. With bestial ferocity, he ordered Consuela to remove the two bullets still in him.

"*Muchas gracias*, bitch," he said laconically as she set another glass of whiskey before him. She slowly removed the bullet from his right shoulder and then the other on the right side of his ass. Going to the hospital was out of the question. He finally surrendered to his lethargy and passing out where he lay.

CHAPTER 34

Bryce was in the living room cleaning and oiling his glock 23 at some predawn hour when Austin knocked on the door before using his card. Bryce answered the decorous knock with "Come in, damn it!'"

Austin stepped in, closed the door, and handed Bryce a Redweld accordion folder that had just arrived by special messenger from the admiral. The envelope, marked *Classified/Confidential* contained three packets of preliminary info from the crime lab and two dozen grotesque photos of the corpses and the crime scene, including forensic evidence taken by the Elkins Police Department and the West Virginia State Police Crime Scene Unit. A number of them were close-ups, while others were from varying distances and angles. The second packet was a postmortem summary from the medical examiner. There followed a pregnant moment of uncomfortable silence.

His eyes turned glacial, and his nostrils flared. Responding to Austin's no-nonsense timbre, Bryce, perplexed, began getting dressed, buck naked without a modicum of modesty, with maximum efficiency. Still unshaven, he grabbed his gear before hunching into his jacket, and they headed for the station. Unfortunately, several police cars were still blocking the street, keeping a circle of media vans at bay from the mobile crime unit.

Two uniformed officers stopped them, requesting their purpose and to see their IDs. Instead, they held out their badges and asked to proceed to the crime scene. A cheerless drizzle blurred their view of the bodies.

The absence of identification and the putrefied condition of the wretched, sodden bodies left the cause of death open to conjecture and speculation. It took a week for the medical examiner to join the dots and identify them as federal agents. The third packet contained a paucity of witness interview summaries, which didn't amount to much. Being that they were federal agents under deep cover and now in a high-profile murder investigation, the Charleston FBI Bureau was currently directly involved in the atrocity. Their team was prohibited from assisting or breaking their cover and encroaching on the investigation.

They were to remain undercover and never forget for a moment that the Manduro operation was rife with danger. Synapses were rapidly firing in Bryce's brain, and a tide of raging anger washed over him as he held back a silent scream of outrage. Somehow he would finesse the information needed from the feds without compromising their cover.

The grotesque flash images from the medical examiner's autopsy captured the vicious horror now frozen in time by the rigor mortis that had set in. What he saw of the mutilated bodies sent a shiver of revulsion racing through him. Each had had their fingers and ears severed before death, and the damage to their lungs suggested that they had been subjected to waterboarding. Their mouths, filled with a mass of maggots, hung open, as if they were screaming, exposing smashed and missing front teeth. Welts and cigarette burns scared their swollen faces. A cold fire erupted violently in his mind.

The decomposing and decomposing bodies of Dominic Formosa and Ken Carrabba had been found bobbing half underwater, covered by flotsam, by a couple of fishermen on the edge of a bank of the Elk River just north of Dry Fork, West Virginia. They had been brutally beaten, with their hands bound behind their backs, stabbed, and their throats cut. Their eyes bulged in their sockets, peering up through the murky river water from swollen faces. Their weed-shrouded corpses were bloated, and their mottled skin had changed to a pallid shade of green. The site was an hour and a half north of the Maduro compound on US-219. No water was found in their lungs, so drowning was ruled out.

Judging from the forensic evidence of decomposition and rigor mortis, they had been in the water for several weeks. Based on the marks and lacerations on their bodies, it was clear both had been tortured and then executed, shot once in the back of the head with a large caliber weapon before being tossed into the river. It was pretty isolated up there.

After viewing the gut-wrenching images and placing them face down on the tabletop, Bryce pushed my chair back, stood up in stoic silence, and slammed his fist onto the table.

Austin explained, "The state police believe they need better quality surveillance footage from a service station a couple of miles from the scene of a suspicious vehicle that may be useful. The faces are blurred, but enhancements are being worked on. The images, as usual, were grainy and barely recognizable.

"Four men in a black Tahoe, two in front and two in back. The driver, wearing a hoodie, got out, inserted a credit card, and pumped gas while the other three stayed in the ar. The two men in the back don't seem to move. Having filled the vehicle, they left the station, driving north. The credit card used turned out to have been stolen several hours earlier during a mugging of a tourist at Hawks Nest State Park. The vehicle was abandoned and torched in a parking lot next to the river."

Bryce was now back in his room, his laptop humming on the desk, its screen saver an ever-changing montage of photos shot by Austin over the past several days.

It was almost two in the morning, and Bryce was still pacing the room, feeling his blood pressure amp up higher with every step but still maintaining an admirable sangfroid. He couldn't sleep or shut his eyes for more than a few seconds, his mind smoldering with images of the bloated, tortured bodies of the agents and the tall grass behind them ebbing and flowing in the wind. His head felt like a pressure cooker about to blow; raw anger coursed through him. He took a long, deep breath and dragged his hand over his mouth and chin, muttering silent deprecations to whoever had done this.

"Who killed you? Who murdered you?"

Anger lanced through every molecule of his body, and he silently made a visceral pact with himself that he would not let the torture and murder of these two agents go unavenged. There was something about them being dumped in the brackish dark water of the river that felt extra evil. Somehow, somewhere, he was going to go back and run some kind of postmortem into what went wrong with their operation. They had been murdered in cold blood with malice aforethought. The horror of what they had endured could not be undone, but at least they were at peace now, on terra firma, providing him with a degree of solace.

The investigation into the murder of the two agents continued to weigh heavily on him. A flame of anger rose in him like a smoldering ember glowing with renewed life. He thought, I will get the coldhearted bastard who did this if it is the last thing I ever do. He was surprised at the vehemence of my thoughts. He could use a whisper of divine intervention at this time. He was filled with a renewed sense of foreboding. Looking out the window, he could almost reach out and touch the raw danger lurking in the air.

CHAPTER 35

Overnight, a new weather front barreled across the mountains. The eastern sky was awash in incandescent orange and yellow with just a smattering of wispy clouds. The Weather Channel was predicting a hot, humid day with a 50 percent chance of a thunderstorm.

The alarm went off at five, too early for the complimentary breakfast. However, the room coffee and complimentary croissant would suffice.

Having stopped to fill the tank of his car at a nondescript truck stop just outside of Charleston with several queues of pumps available, Bryce parked, shut off the engine, got out, inserted the credit card, and began pumping. The sun was scorching hot, and the air reeked of gas and diesel fumes. The sound of approaching thunder could be heard in the distance. The service station had seen more prosperous days. It had once been painted white, but stains, smog, and sun had weathered it over the years, with ferns running down off the roof. He had just topped off the tank and was in the process of rehanging the tattered nozzle on the pump, oblivious to the impending danger, when he felt the cold, hard steel of the barrel of a pistol against the back of his head. The slothful gas station attendant who had come out to wash his windshield was now holding a revolver.

"*Señor*, you get behind the wheel very slowly, and keep both hands on the steering wheel," he said, unaffected, in a deep, hoarse, inebriated voice. Then, as Bryce got into the front seat, he slid into the back, never taking the gun from Bryce's head.

God damn it, I should have questioned it, he thought. Instead, his only cogent thought was that no one was washing windows anymore. But the realization had come too late.

"Start the car and go," he shouted in a gruff disembodied voice with a Spanish lilt. "*Señor*, keep both your fucking hands on steering wheel, or I put big hole in your fucking head, *comprendo*? You and me are going for a short drive out in the country to discuss your future." His voice was low and throaty. "One bad move from you, I shoot you in head right here."

Bryce sedately started the car and drove out of the Mobil station, turning left, following the Mexican's instructions. As he began encountering morning traffic, he could feel the barrel pressed harder against his right temple. "What is it that you want from me?"

"You, *señor*, should not have stuck your nose into something not your business. Señor Maduro is very upset with you."

He instructed Bryce to go faster and didn't say any more. Then, finally, the needle touched eighty, and the countryside became a blur as they sped along the two-lane country roadway, leaving the Charleston city limit behind.

Taking a quick slanted glance in the rearview mirror, Bryce noticed that the man wasn't wearing a mask, which meant that he didn't feel he would need one with Bryce dead. He had seen this hombre before in the Red Dog Saloon. He was one of Pablo's thugs, and the heavy scent of alcohol told Bryce that the guy had been drinking. He probably had just downed a pint of Canadian whiskey before drawing his gun. He had sharp features; long, dark, matted, unwashed hair to his shoulders; a long nose that had obviously been broken more than once; several missing front teeth. He had gone several days without a shave. His unblinking eyes were dark and bulging like those of a lizard.

Without giving warning, Bryce cut across a labyrinth of lanes, accelerating and weaving in and out of slower traffic as a cacophony of horns blared and obscenities filled the air, cutting across more lanes, brakes screeching, angling for the highway, blitzing forward, fishtailing down the highway, slowing down, and watching the mirrors. Nobody had done anything to tickle his suspicions. Just then, the sky opened up, sending a downpour on them. The hot pavement was steaming and glistening from the soaking.

"Where are we going?" Bryce said, keeping his voice low key and calm as he increased the.

His mind was racing. He casually reached for the radio knob before feeling the barrel of the pistol slam him in the head. "Get that hand back on the wheel, or I shoot!"

"Hey, that hurt, damn it!"

He came to a red light at a four-way intersection with his arm draped over the steering wheel, and a bunch of kids pulled up in the next lane as the car sat at idle. Even though his windows were closed, their radio blared loud enough to set the jackal on edge. The light turned green. Bryce pressed the accelerator and nonchalantly looked in his rearview mirror. From the expression on the Mexican's face and the timbre of his voice, it was clear he was stressed out in a big way.

The Mexican was obviously a phlegmatic Manduro hitman but not exactly a professional. In his rush to leave the gas station, he never frisked or even asked Bryce if he was armed. Under his jacket was his glock, nestled in his shoulder holster, with the barrel facing the back of the seat.

He would have difficulty reaching it with both hands on the steering wheel and visible to the hitman. Not ready to take a chance, he would wait for the right moment of distraction in the back seat.

* * *

Bryce

Leaving the sprawling suburbs of Charleston behind, I could sense the nervousness of the Mexican as he casually watched me in the rearview mirror. Again, I asked him where he was taking me.

"Somewhere where we can talk business in quiet. Take next left," he ordered as we encountered a construction rerouting that had built up some traffic congestion in a school zone. His voice was an octave higher than before.

I slowed for the approaching intersection and turned left onto Kelly's Creek Road. I knew full well that talking was the last thing on the Mexican's agenda.

The wheels were turning, and I was in full combat mode, considering my options as I powered out of town, revving the engine, exceeding the posted speed limits with my hands draped over the steering wheel. I knew I could initiate a countermeasure by speeding up and slamming on the brakes, spinning the wheel in the wrong direction. But it would have to be quick as I didn't doubt for a second that the Mexican wouldn't hesitate to blow my head off. I depressed the accelerator to the floor, and the needle surged past ninety as I blitzed down the highway unimpeded except for one car, which I sped past, prompting the driver to honk.

The wheels smoked and squealed before regaining purchase on the hot asphalt. I was going so fast I could tell the pickup in front of me thought that I would rear-end him. Pulling into the passing lane as the car felt light beneath me, I passed him like he was standing still before pulling back into the lane. His horn blared, but I didn't have time to allow myself to care. I was sure the other driver expressed a few choice words, though.

"Take that left," my captor yelled hysterically.

I slowed at the entrance and pulled into what seemed like a deserted open parking verge overlooking the Pocatalico River. That all changed in seconds when over forty children and about ten adults came out of the woods carrying tubes.

The Mexican yelled, "Let's get the hell out of here, now. Get moving. Go right!"

As instructed, I pulled out of the parking lot with wheels squealing on the payment. An elderly women walking the perimeter of the lot with a cocker spaniel gave me a disapproving stare. The roadway along the river was lightly trafficked in both directions. I barreled down the road another mile or two at high speed, working the accelerator and brakes, hugging the curves of the river before the guy again yelled, "Take this right."

We pulled onto a small deserted dirt road and made a sharp turn, throwing up dirt and dust, making one leaning telephone pole lean a little bit farther as the tires bit into gravel before finding the road again.

Pulling into another vacant parking area on the riverbed, the Mexican ordered me to park in the far corner of the lot. I could smell hay and manure. In the periphery of my vision, I saw that he was desperately scanning the area for a spot to assassinate and dump me without being seen. He was also nervously surveying the lot for any activity as we slowly crossed the clearing, looking left and right, then he turned his head quickly to glance out the back window to nothingness. We were on a hill with views of open farmland with several large mounds that might be discerned as unnatural-looking undulations in the sweeping landscape. My guess was that they were large piles of cow manure. Just then, feeling some of the pressure of the barrel against my temple momentarily let up, I made my move.

Without notice, I stealthy slipped my left hand off the steering wheel and, with blinding speed, secured the glock and blindly squeezed the trigger four times in rapid succession, firing four shots through the seat. Four ear-shattering explosions filled the car's interior as the bullets ripped through the seat. The looming question was whether I had hit him. I got my answer in a nanosecond as the gun fell away from my head. As I spun around, ready to fire again, I saw the Mexican slouched in an ungodly way on the back seat with the pistol still in his right hand. A diaphanous cloud of gun smoke hovered above. Half his face was missing. I was out of the car while the dust around the wheels was still rising.

Dark, thundering cobalt storm clouds were skidding across an otherwise clear sky.

The air was hot and humid and heavily laden with moisture. A light drizzle began to fall, forcing me to turn on the wipers. A looming storm was imminent.

I called Austin to advise him of what had taken place and my current situation and requested a rendezvous with another covert agent to dispose of the car and the corpse in the back seat. A half hour later, a black Tahoe pulled in behind me. The driver identified himself as Special Agent McGee and told me he would take care of the disposal as he pulled a body bag from the truck and covered the body on the back seat. No one was going to miss him or give a rat's ass about his whereabouts other than the son of a bitch who had hired him. Tossing me the fob for the Tahoe, he told me I was to take the Tahoe until a replacement vehicle arrived. So much for an otherwise routine morning turning into a calamitous one.

I returned to the hotel and met Austin in the parking garage. After I discussed the attack and the attacker's evil intent to send me to a better world, we both called it a night, with Austin retiring to his room. Long evening shadows crept through the bedroom window. It was drizzling outside. Unable to sleep, I got up and brewed another cup of coffee, then pulled out my gun cleaning kit on the kitchen counter.

As I had fired the glock four times against the seat cushion, it needed cleaning.

And then it suddenly occurred to me: if I was now a target and being connected to Nuna, she would also be in danger. Hugo Manduro was on the move, and when dealing with organizations like the Maduro operation, it was better to err on the side of extreme caution.

Austin had a signed warrant for a wiretap in hand on the Maduro West Virginia facility the next day. CIA operatives were monitoring Maduro's encrypted outgoing and incoming communications 24-7 from Norman's Cay and Cuba via satellite. Maduro's phone calls were being routed through a small, windowless room on the fifth floor of Langley.

CHAPTER 36

The sound of the back door opening flooded Nuna with relief as she rushed back to the kitchen from the living room, where she was watching the news on TV.

"Kate, is that you?" she asked, looking at the clock hanging on the wall in the kitchen as it chimed at the four o'clock hour. Her neighbor Kate was notoriously early. She had already disarmed the security system, expecting Kate for dinner.

She had just unloaded the clothesline, where she had struggled with the bedsheets and linens that seemed to want to take flight in the brisk wind whipping through the holler. Having retrieved the last of the errant clothespins from the lawn, she began folding the clothes as she watched TV in the living room. While she did have a working dryer, she liked the fresh, airy smell of linens and bedsheets being hung outside under a bright azure sky. She a hopelessly old-fashioned West Virginia gal.

The mailman rang the doorbell and greeted her as she came out the front door. He commented on the humid weather they'd been having, and she took the two pieces of junk mail soliciting subscriptions to magazines she'd never heard of. Ten minutes later, the doorbell rang again and she opened the door wide, thinking it was the mailman again.

A haggard barrel-chested bulk of a man in a filthy canvas chore coat, tattered carpenter jeans, and combat boots stood in the doorway, his face a scant foot away from hers.

"Pablo!" she screamed in a high-pitched shrill. "Pablo, you scared the hell out of me," she added with undisguised asperity. "Whatcha doin' here?" Her jittery eyes were wide with fear.

All her senses were now on high alert. Her skin was on fire, her heart was pounding, and she couldn't seem to get enough oxygen into her lungs.

"Where is Mr. Maduro?" she asked timorously. "Why didn't Hugo come with you?"

What she was feeling was a sense of foreboding. If she had learned anything in her life in the mountains, it was to pay attention to her instincts.

Then, before she could blink, he pushed her into the kitchen, hooking his left arm around her neck, whirling her to the kitchen floor on her back and jamming a handgun into her ribcage. He then aimed it at her forehead; she was looking directly into the lethal barrel of the .38 caliber revolver.

She cringed, lapsing into a hostile silence.

Her eyes skittered to the door and back at him. She felt a fission of unease as a prickling slide down the back of her neck.

"Because I didn't invite the hombre, *mamacita*," he retorted, grinning maliciously, his cockiness in full flame, shooting poison glances at her.

He looked at her with a menacing rictus that made her skin crawl. Nuna returned the fish-eyed look, aghast.

Her stomach knotted with incipient fear as he emitted a bark of laughter. Terror, raw and primitive, skittered down her spine, her heart pounded, and her breathing accelerated. His voice was slurred as innuendos came through his repulsive yellow-stained teeth.

He had been hiding in the underbrush of the backyard for almost an hour, waiting for his moment.

"This nice private place, *señorita*," he said in a sibilant whisper," me been watching it for several days now. Has great view of the road and river below, no?"

Nuna, feeling hideously vulnerable, tried to close the door, but he insinuated himself between it and the frame.

While he wasn't that tall, maybe 5-foot-6, he was muscular and at least 220 pounds. Nuna prickled with fear, stock-still, with her mouth agape, and screamed as he breached the door. She was caught in that state of suspended animation for a few seconds, coming to terms with the fact that the terrible event that was taking place in her kitchen was real and not a bad nightmare. Her facial expression was one of haughty contempt.

The disheveled Mexican had come through the door at the speed of a cougar; too dumbfounded, she didn't even have time to flinch back in fear, much less strike back and defend herself. His dark, menacing, evil gaze fixed on her, scorching the flesh right off Nuna's bones. She instinctively backed away, looking for a weapon to fend him off.

He lunged at her, hooking his left arm around her neck and clamping his right hand over her mouth. Then, whirling her around and pinning her to the floor with his blood-smeared right hand, he jammed the barrel of a handgun into her ribcage hard. She struggled hysterically, wriggling, twisting, and desperately trashing her arms and legs on the floor until he pressed the pistol to her head. Panic sluiced through her, leaving her trembling so hard the veins in her neck were throbbing in repugnance. Now looking directly into the lethal barrel of the .38 caliber revolver, she froze with such diluted animosity that she quavered on the inside.

She suddenly became more cooperative, silently whimpering and sobbing beneath the shadow of Pablo. Her ears were ringing as panic set in, and she could feel tears welling up in her eyes. He was straddling her with his broad chest, firmly clutching her throat with his left hand blocking her from any further movement. She could feel and smell his foul breath as his tongue licked the side of her face, her mouth, and then her earlobe; he then nestled his head along the side of her neck. The taste of him on her mouth made her sick. With his strength, she had little chance of escaping his manacling grip on her. No one was there to help her. She was at his mercy now, and she knew it.

Overcome with the reality of her situation, her eyes now blurry, her audible breath ragged, her heart pumping like a turbine, she again scanned the room for an escape before making a futile attempt at struggling and brazenly jostling and flailing against the deranged maniac. Her left hand grabbed for Pablo's face. Her face was contorted, her fingers on her right hand curled into claws. But his hold on her only became more tenacious. Crying, screaming, and pleading had no effect on him. Pablo had slurped his slimy, disgusting tongue all over her mouth, after having done the same to her face. She was shaking in fear with revulsion.

"Now, now," he said with a wicked smirk on his pockmarked face. Her mind was racing; she swallowed convulsively. "No need to be unfriendly, my sweet *señorita*." He gave her a hideous smile, laughter underlying his words.

A sharp bite on her earlobe punctuated his words before he ran wet, sloppy kisses down her neck. "We'll have much more fun if you follow my instructions, yes?" Her blood ran cold as she heard a chuckle and he blew in her ear.

"Let's keep some of that fighting spirit of yours for me later. I thought we possibly could chat for a little while," he said casually. "Do you understand me, *señorita*?"

He was delusional.

Terror-ridden, she deliberately didn't look at him. Instead, she meekly averted her gaze and hunched her shoulders, nodding her head in surrender, fearing that he felt his machismo was at stake. Her hair was disheveled from her struggle, and her quivering face was smeared with mascara and eyeliner that had descended down her cheeks through her flood of tears.

Her face did not hide her contempt for him as she read the open hostility and scorn in his voice.

"That's a good girl," he said, getting up from the floor and pulling her up by the roots of her hair with him. He smiled triumphantly as she winced at the pain. "You're a fast learner," he added, tucking her hair behind her ears as his hand lecherously circled up around her shoulder, pulling her to lean against him.

She struggled against him and with all her adrenaline in force, drew up her right knee and pistoned her leg into his groin like a prize fighter. He bent over in pain, but only for a moment, before catching her face with his fist, sending her across the kitchen floor. He then pulled her up by my hair again and slapped her several times in the face for no apparent reason other than to leave his palm print on her cheeks.

Nuna, now in pain, stared into his dark, menacing eyes for a brief moment, horrified at the sudden realization and full comprehension of her situation. She looked at him stonily, her face a mask of pure melancholy and horror, and goose bumps lined her arms. She was his prisoner and was in sheer terror of what he might have planned for her.

"Shh!" he hissed directly into her ear. "Be still, or I'll have to hurt you real bad."

Nuna stopped struggling but steeled herself against feeling anything but venomous contempt for him.

"That's more like it," he said.

His hand encircled her wrist like a manacle before he jerked her back down beside him.

"What could we possibly talk about?" she hissed quietly with revulsion at the blatant violation.

His casual tone continued; it was as if he were talking to a friend. He advanced on her with a predatory gait. "*Señorita*, we could talk about many things, the weather, music, sex…" He trailed off. "For another thing, I've noticed that you have a set of great tits and a killer ass, *señorita*, yes?" A bemused, inebriated smile crossed his lips. "Tsk-tsk, my sweet *señorita*. I think you always looked down at me as if I were trash. You're not looking down at me now."

He turned and locked the kitchen door and closed the curtains before turning back to her with a stern face as he closed the distance between them. Nuna tried to back away from him, but he caught her with his right hand around her waist and his left hand gripping her jaw. A red handprint was clearly visible on her cheek from his manhandling of her.

"You have to learn the rules, *señorita*!"

"What rules, you bastard?" she asked haltingly.

"Rule number one: you're mine, and you will be obedient and do exactly as I tell you, or you'll be punished.

"Rule number two: you only speak if I ask you to, or you'll be punished.

"Rule number three: you address me as Señor Pablo, or you will be punished.

"Rule number four: you answer me with the truth when I ask you a question, or you will be punished."

Pablo looked at her expectantly and stroked her hair lightly, prompting her. "Get my drift?"

Sarcasm dripped from every syllable.

Nuna, petrified, her heart thudding, whimpered and stared back at him with a blank expression as she tried to quell the horror of the moment.

She grimaced and nodded slowly. "Yes, Señor Pablo."

Her horror was amplified when she realized what was yet to come.

"Who else is here? Where's your husband?"

Nuna's vocal cords were faltering with intensifying fear; petrified, she couldn't speak.

Unnerving tension sizzled through her as she swung her fist at his head.

He struck her hard in the midriff with his fist and slapped her hard across the face, sending her backward, crashing onto the floor.

"Please, don't kill me!" She got up and, cradling her face, she screamed in abject fear of her attacker as he clutched the back of her neck.

He pulled back the hammer of the gun and squeezed the back of her neck, then said again with a more threatening emphasis, "Who else is fuckin' here, *señorita?*"

He was only an inch or so away. She could smell his breath.

With an uneasy sense of foreboding, Nuna felt a prickly chill of galloping fear run down her spine.

"No…one," she cried, whimpering with a ragged breath at his feet. "I'm a widow."

He shot a baleful look at her. "You better not be fucking lying to me, bitch! If there's someone here, I kill you first. Get my drift?"

"Yes," she nervously mumbled. She didn't want to die.

He backhanded her with deliberate brutality, bouncing her head hard off the floor as he laughed maniacally. Just then, a ringing sound came from the living room. The phone rang and rang and finally went to voicemail. It took several seconds before she realized the shrill sound was the ringing of her cell phone, which she had left on the couch lying out of sight under the antimacassar. Pulling her up by the neck, he pushed her into the living room.

* * *

Nuna

"Pick it up and turn it on speaker." Without a word, he removed his hand from around my throat. Still trembling, my quaking legs barely able to support me, I picked up the phone. "It's my mother," I cried.

His gun was pointed at the back of my head, and he was browbeating me as I listened to her voicemail message. My sister-in-law had called my mother, telling her that my brother had just had a massive heart attack and was at the Montana Medical Center. My mother was flying to Montana that evening to be with my brother and give my sister-in-law support. She said she expected to be there for at least a couple of weeks or until my brother returned home.

He deposited the phone in his back pocket.

He bound my wrist together behind my back with plastic ties. I tried to twist my hands free but gave up the effort. He gestured with his hands. "Get over there and sit! Move it" he screamed when I hesitated.

With faltering steps, I was jolted back into horrible reality as I made my way to the kitchen. I settled on the chair, looking at him anxiously with fear. "Please don't hurt me," I pleaded. Then I whispered, "I beg you. Pleeeease…I have a couple hundred dollars and some jewelry in my desk drawer." I was babbling now. "You can have it all. Please don't hurt me." I squeezed my eyes shut with my heart pounding, praying that I could somehow wake up from this living nightmare from hell.

He began to prowl back and forth between the kitchen and living room, seemingly collecting himself.

"Your keys, where are they?"

"Go to hell!"

"Your keys, bitch," he said, slapping me hard in the face.

"In my purse," I cried.

"Where's your purse?" He growled in my ear. "Don't piss me off!"

I cried, "It's on the floor next to the living room couch." He shoved me forward onto the sofa with the barrel of the pistol in my back, eyeing me mistrustfully with a hard, threatening look.

"Your guns, where are they?"

"I don't have any." I lied.

With a scowling look, he slammed me with his right fist, grabbed me around the ankles, and with my wrists shackled, he dragged me to the bedroom. I started screaming incessantly and desperately tried to kick and break away, but with my hands tied behind my back, it was useless. He was all muscle. He picked me up off the floor and propelled me onto my bed face down on my pillow and told me to shut the fuck up, not to move a muscle. "No one is going to hear you." I could hear him rummaging through the drawers and closet, looking for something.

Returning to the bed, he untied my hands and turned me over on my back, only to retie my arms to the head post with my nylons. Tears of pain and fear were stinging my eyes. "I'm going to take a piss' don't do anything fucking stupid."

He then secured my legs to the baseboard, leaving me spread eagle, before leaving the room and shutting the door behind him. I breathed a sigh of relief as he left the room, relieved that he didn't pounce on me.

Tears filled my eyes, pouring down my cheeks. Then, finally, I closed them, reflecting back on the events of the morning. I had risen early, showered, dressed, put on my makeup, spritzed myself with perfume, made breakfast, and had gone to Mabscott to drop off a monthly care package at the fire department and do some grocery shopping at Kroger before returning back home. Having taken two weeks' vacation from the bank, I had been planning to spend some quality time working on my next book and was anxious to return.

I was terrified. Chills and pain were now rapidly blistering through my body.

I writhed and fought back wildly trying to loosen the nylons by pulling on them with all my muscle, but it was useless.

I heard his footfalls in the hallway outside my door just before the door opened, and he stepped in, holding several dried lace delicates and two of my black bras with unabashed curiosity. Looking around the room, he then turned and walked toward me.

"Buenas noches. Did you miss me?" he asked with twisted lust and his sleazy reptilian smile. "I'm askin' you a question, bitch! You miss me?" He laughed a hyena laugh.

My hackles rose instinctively, and my cheeks flared with color at the word *bitch*. "You're vile!"

* * *

His forty-five-year-old cock was tented in his pants like a flagpole.

"Noooo," Nuna said meekly. She tried to regain her composure but was terrified. "You've got to be out of your fucking mind, you effing pervert."

His glittering predatory eyes widened as she thrashed and flailed. "A feisty little one! I love it. Me like a good fight from a *puta*."

His heavy body pinned her, his chest rising and falling with exertion. And then he mashed his mouth to her lips. His mordant breath caused her to gag.

He was amused at her fight, drooling like a Saint Bernard in heat as his hands went from her breast to her buttocks and took up purchase there.

"Before I'm finished with you, you will beg me to get between your fine legs, yes? I going to fuck you hard, *señorita*! Si?" Pablo wrapped his hand in her hair and yanked her to his face. Panic and fear exploded through her veins. The bastard's eyes reddened with sick arousal at what he planned for her.

She smelled his acrid scent. He reeked.

"I knew that you might want it rough." He ran his fingers into her cleavage, yanked most of her blouse off, and removed her bra with one deft flick, baring her breasts.

He ripped off her panties, baring her pubic womanhood to his eyes. He smashed his lips over hers with disgusting savagery.

"Ah." With a sadistic glean in his mischievous eyes, moving over her caustically, he went on, "Your body, now my treasured *puta*, yes?"

"Please Señor Pablo," Nuna pleaded as she flailed under the despicable Mexican. Her whole body prickled with the fear of him raping her.

He untied her feet and then her hands, standing over her and pointing the gun at her head.

"I'm warning you," he said, "don't even think of trying to escape. Give me your word, *mamacita*."

"Pleeeease, I promise," she cried.

"Good, now we have an understanding. Get up," he demanded as he walked slowly around the bed.

Nuna grimaced with pain and struggled to roll off the bed, with every muscle in her body aching. She obeyed as he instructed her to walk slowly to the kitchen and sit at the table. Each step was slow and painful. However, she didn't dare escape as he was walking behind her.

"Can I use the bathroom?" she asked submissively without turning around to face him.

He rolled his eyes and gestured with his head upward in disgust. "OK, but the door stays open, and I'm going to be right outside the doorway. So take it or leave it, like it or not, you have no options, bitch."

He gave her a shove with the palm of his hand, sending her through the door opening. "Remember," he said, "stupidity can be a capital offense!"

Trembling in front of the basin, she turned on the water and cupped a couple of handfuls, scooping them up to her flushed face. She was a sad sight: her face bruised, her makeup dripping, her hair a tangled mess, and her clothes torn and barely covering her.

He heard the commode flush and pounded on the half-open door. "Your time is up!" he grunted. Nuna looked at herself one final time in the mirror, collecting herself before leaving the sanctuary of the bathroom. He stood right in front of the door framing the doorway and struck her again, sending her backward, crashing, onto the bathroom floor.

"Get up, bitch," he yelled.

She carefully wiped away her tears with her right hand and gripped the doorknob with her left, pulling herself up from the floor. The right side was now bruised and swollen from his fist. She had a black eye and a bloody lip from grappling with him with fear and desperation.

She couldn't hold him off, and she knew it. She had never been subjected to such gross abuse and indignity in her life and was now scared of what this lunatic might be capable of. He obviously had a callous indifference to her suffering, as his evil eyes never left her face.

Having dragged her back to the kitchen, her body quaking with fear, he yelled that he was hungry and instructed her to cook him a meal. If only I had some rat poison in the cabinets, she thought. He pulled up a kitchen chair at the table, straddled it, rested his arms on it, and kept looking at her.

Nuna pulled three burger patties and a bowl of refried beans from the refrigerator and placed them in the microwave. She gave him two cheeseburgers and a bowl of beans three minutes later. She noticed that while she was tied to the bed, he had removed all the knives from the kitchen and consumed the bottle of wine she had just purchased in Mabscott. He wolfed down both burgers and the beans with the dining manners of a hyena, using nothing more than his bare hands. He then took her burger shamelessly without a word, flushing it down with a bottle of beer before burping and wiping his hands on his pant legs.

"I'm so sorry, missy." His laugh was now maniacal. "Nuna, you must have been a naughty girl." His lips twitched as he smiled.

Her eyes were wide with terror. She began whimpering helplessly, making a mewing sound, expecting to be hit again. Before she could react, he reached across the table, hooked his hand around her neck, and pulled her forward across the table, bringing her mouth up to his.

He began to forcefully assault her lips, with his tongue stabbing and prying her lips apart. She pushed and pounded his chest, fighting him like a wildcat, but it didn't stop him as he squeezed her neck and plumbed her mouth.

Suddenly, he released her and pushed her off the table, crashing her to the floor. He grabbed a handful of her hair and yanked, lifting her up as she screamed in excruciating pain. "Vámonos," he said, pulling her into the bedroom.

He bound her to the bed, tying nylons around her hands and feet. She was trashing around violently in terror, wondering what he would do to her. He's more than capable of killing me. What else could he do? He couldn't walk away and set me free, she thought. She pondered the possibility of a psychological approach, convincing him that she wouldn't tell anyone if he gave her freedom.

No, that wouldn't work, she realized in an instant. He's obviously desperate and certainly doesn't want to go to prison. He was beginning to get handsy, reaching for her face and squeezing her breasts and kneading her nipples.

"Surely you must have man in your life," he said solicitously.

"Not for a while," I said with anger in my voice.

"I can tell you're the type of woman with much love to give a man. But all work and no play is no fun at all, yes?

"Nuna, you a beautiful woman, and we're going to sleep on this bed together. I do my best to keep my hands to myself. But you'll learn soon enough that my best exceeds all expectations."

He stretched, arching his back and pulling his filthy shirt off, revealing his muscled chest, dark nipples, and the hard line of his abs. He then unbuckled his belt, unfastened his jeans, and stuck his hand inside them lasciviously. "By the way, I always sleep in the nude."

"Thanks for the warning," she said.

There was a sprinkling of freckles along his left shoulder and a narrow scar that ran low on his right hip, a line that drew attention straight to the taut curve of his ass. The sound of his sigh prickled the back of her neck as she writhed on the bed.

"Time to be honest. If you think I can throw caution to the wind and stop after thirty minutes, you are reading me wrong."

Her smile widened. "Now that I'm glad I was wrong about," she said.

He went into the bathroom and took a long shower with the door open, allowing steam to escape as the water sluiced over his bare skin amid his low aimless humming. Coming out with slicked-back hair, showing his repulsive hairy chest, he walked around to the left side of the bed and slipped under the sheets with a contented sigh like he didn't have a care in the world. He believed hundreds of women would sell their firstborn child to be with him in bed. His libido was screaming delight.

He placed his hand on her leg, ran it up to my inner thigh, and then whistled sibilantly, "Nice legs, *minino!*"

Nuna's bravado deserted her.

She closed her teary eyes in shame and swallowed convulsively before she began to thrash violently, spasmodically, screaming at the top of her lungs. As if another force altogether had taken possession of her body, the concentrated will to survive was transmuting into a primal muscular response. She writhed and flailed against the restraints.

He began to fondle her ass, squeezing the buttocks with his hard, rough fingers. She went rigid.

"You know, *señorita*, after being with my whore, your firm white ass is looking really good."

Pablo's eyes glinted evilly as he smiled and forced a cruelly jubilant kiss on her pale lips. She turned her head away from her obscene, deviant, possibly insane captor as he continued to grope her.

She pulled against her restraints in mortification as he ripped open her blouse in the most demeaning way before stripping her of her slacks. "Don't. Please."

"Why?" he asked, laughing gloatingly.

"Because I don't want you to." Her voice quavered in protest. Her back arched off the bed.

"Yes, you do," he said insolently with audacious conceit. Rubbing against her suggestively. "You a woman who will respond to a real man."

"No, No," she screamed, biting her lower lip and violently rolling her head from side to side while bucking her hips.

She began to cry. Her eyes were now dilated and welling with fear.

"Shut up, bitch! Me going to put fire between your legs, *mamacita*." He tried to wedge his hand between her thighs, but she kept them clamped. Finally, he slapped the side of her head left to right several times, and she screamed in pain. "Open your fucking legs," he growled, squeezing her throat with his right hand as she gasped for air.

He let go of her throat before she passed out.

"Don't, please," she whimpered, her head lolling back against the pillow.

He stepped out of his boots and dropped his jeans without a modicum of modesty, tossing them on the floor.

He twisted a handful of her blond hair around his fists and forced her to look at his erection. "Yes, you do," he repeated with audacious conceit. "Open your mouth, bitch! If you bite me, I'll friggin' cut your tits off, and then I'll pull every fucking tooth you have out, one by one. Understand, bitch!" She tensed, but he brooked no resistance. "Me going to fuck you really good. Comprende?"

With blind terror, she vacillated and surrendered, simpering. "Yes… Señor Pablo, I understand," she whimpered, alert for opportunities and being obsequious to buy herself time." "Please don't hurt me."

Tears, weeping humiliation, streamed from her eyes as she surrendered.

"You might as well participate," he rasped, feeling her body tense. "The longer you resist, the longer it will take me to fill your pussy."

Most of his pleasure came from watching her surrender and submit her body to him. His eyes were maliciously teasing. Her sassy mouth was working hard, trying to suck and take him deeper and deeper down her throat. His disgusting groping on her naked body kept her gasping with shock and outrage. He fucked her unmercifully for the next couple of hours before finally collapsing alongside her.

Nuna was passed out on the bed, and he was snoring loudly. She was out cold.

He was soon lulled into a deep slumber. But his sleep was sporadic.

He woke up at six that evening groaning with a raging hard-on. He had dreamed of this day of having Nuna for himself. He loved to watch her breasts jiggling under her blouse, her behind proud and sassy, her long, slender legs walking proudly.

Nuna, drained by fatigue, sleeplessness, and trauma, was doing her best to hold it together. She would endure Pablo's rape of her body.

"Your eyes look a little droopy. Did you have a good rest last night, *señorita*?"

The whole arrangement was turning into a quid pro quo, though he couldn't bring himself to care. "How much I wanted to climb up your body and ride you until your legs gave out." He went on, "I'd like a cheeseburger on a English muffin with the works, and leave out the peppers."

Nuna looked stunned. "With or without ketchup?" she screamed, pacing back and forth in the kitchen before throwing the open bottle at him. Her heart was pounding as she frantically looked about for a possible weapon. She stared at him with unabashed hatred as she nervously cut her burger with a plastic knife and fork and started to eat. He quickly stood from his chair and punched her in the face before grabbing her by her hair and throwing across the kitchen floor into the wall. Then, enraged, bleeding from the mouth, and still seething with impotent fury, she stood up facing him in her robe, her spine and arms rigid, her chin tilted up in absolute defiance, and she threw a hot steel frying pan at his head. Pablo quickly maneuvered his head out of the path.

Nuna was already repressing a shiver when the hiss of wind blew in through the open window, carrying the scent of rain with it. She could

see that the downpour had eased and was now little more than intermittent sprinkles. But the cloud cover remained, with the thick, tangled
shadows obscuring the moon and extending the darkness of the night.
The sense of violation and vulnerability that she felt was suddenly immense. The sanctuary of her home had been invaded. Her body had been
invaded and abused, leaving her little hope.

CHAPTER 37

Glenn had alerted Austin and Bryce by a secure phone about the latest information coming from the Maduro camp concerning the alienation of Pablo. He also informed them of the hit being initiated and placed by Hugo on both Nuna and Pablo. A frisson of heightened concern rattled Bryce.

Cognizant of the coming darkness, he knew that he would move heaven and earth to protect Nuna. A glint of the half-quarter moon was becoming visible in the thick haze of the sky but was barely discernible with a low-hanging fog boiling up off the river. Twilight was fading quickly as a CSX train was slowly making its way to the railyard in Charleston. Through some unexplainable intuition, he sensed that Nuna was in serious trouble at her house, and his pulse quickened as he willed his mind to turn cold. Antsy, he holstered his fully loaded 9 mm glock on his belt with the extra clip and grabbed his keys on the way out the door, apprehension melding with a sense of cruel irony over his sense of protection of her.

Bryce, with a foul temper, told Austin to continue monitoring his equipment. Throwing caution to the wind, he secured his weapon, ran down the hallway, jumped into his jeep, engaged the gears, and put the pedal to the metal, careening out of the hotel parking lot and onto the highway, into the two-lane mountain passage at warp speed, squealing tires swerving sideways on the turns with a barely controlled ferocity as he jounced reflectively through the mountainside roller-coaster turns.

Austin also had concerns and second thoughts as he followed his boss out of the parking lot. He was no more than twenty minutes behind, speeding through the dead-man turns, rock walls, and forest on one side and thin air on the other.

With his headlights casting twin beams into the darkness, search-ing cautiously for precarious pullouts, Bryce conquered the entire thir-ty-eight miles through a bug-splattered windshield from the hotel in Charleston on winding Route 60 to the town of Gauley Bridge in a flat, interminable thirty-five minutes, with only Nuna on his mind.

Austin, having confirmed the situation back to Glenn, wasn't far behind him.

Still not sure, Bryce parked the car some hundred yards from the house along the side of the road and literally flew up the hill at a blister-ing pace under the cover of darkness on foot before finding a body of a woman lying prone on the lawn. He quickly turned her on her back and checked her for a pulse. She was dead. Her throat had been slit ear to ear. It wasn't Nuna. He quickly recognized her as Nuna's next-door neighbor.

Adrenaline and fear pulsing through his veins, he pushed up and literally flung himself through the neighbor's privet hedges like a bull out the shute before sprinting across Nuna's backyard. He maintained a brisk pace and crossed the lawn in the backyard at warp speed without breaking stride, setting his sight on the back kitchen door. Mainlining his adrenaline, his nerves and sinews taut with tension, he could feel the amped-up aggression flowing through his veins as he threw his legs over the fence. He then landed firmly on the ground. Just off the deck in a squatting position, he scanned the deck before spotting his target in the kitchen.

Pablo was visible in the kitchen through the rear door window, vi-vaciously holding Nuna in a chokehold. He pulled out his glock, having registered the danger that Nuna was in within milliseconds; he had a natural radar for aggression, fear, and turmoil. He covered the distance between the first step and the deck in three long strides before smashing headlong through the rear kitchen door with the sureness of a Roman gladiator. There was a thud, then the shriek of splintered wood sending splinters of glass and broken hinges everywhere as he shouldered through the kitchen door with murderous eyes on Pablo.

The reverberation from the door smashing into the wall sounded like an explosion. Nuna, petrified at first, sprang into action. Her feisty heart went into arrhythmia when she espied Bryce coming through the doorway at a light-face pace with crazed primeval anguish on his face. Without thinking, she went ballistic, experiencing a frisson of terror, and started violently twisting and vociferously screaming manically in hellish torment. She spun and clawed at his face, and when he raised his hands, she drove a fist into his groin with all the force she could muster. She fought him like a wild mountain animal.

She felt Pablo's hand release the pressure on her neck fractionally, and coughing, wheezing, and gasping for air with a dry mouth, she immediately spun around. With the raw force of a scorching August heat, she started pummeling him pathetically in the face with her fists. Then, with adrenaline shooting through her veins, she began kicking at his kneecaps with everything she had, squirming frantically for release.

Bryce found Pablo swinging around in shock as he continued to hold Nuna around the neck in a chokehold with a large seven-inch KA-BAR knife fisted in his right hand against her throat. Reacting with complete surprise and without forethought, before he could process the intrusion, he dropped the knife, pivoted, and lunged for his 9 mm Smith & Wesson next to him on the counter.

"You fucking son of a bitch!" he yelled.

The knife went skittering across the floor, and fueled by abject fear, Nuna dove for it.

Pablo screamed at Bryce, "*Mierda*, you goddamned fucking son of a bitch!"

With adrenaline spiking, his nostrils flared, his eyes glittering with anger, his senses hyperfocused, Bryce didn't wait for Pablo to lift the gun and fire. Instead, he just squeezed the trigger on his twice, firing off two shots in rapid succession from his glock, hitting the wild-eyed Mexican point blank in the chest and throat, severing his carotid artery and splattering blood everywhere. The kitchen reverberated from the two high-caliber thunderous explosions. The fisted gun fired one more round harmlessly into the floor before he dropped it. With petrified shock and pain sweeping his face, Pablo squinted in disbelief as both hands clutched the exploding holes of scarlet gore in his chest and neck; he felt the blood pouring out of him. He tottered slowly, holding onto the edge of the refrigerator door before crumpling to his knees in a kneeling position, his head sagging sideways. His eyes were wide, his legs writhing violently, his last breath of life escaping his useless prostrate body with utter stupefaction.

Trembling in disbelief and deafened by the explosion of the gunshots at such close range, Nuna blanched, letting loose an ear-piercing shriek while she stabbed Pablo several times in the chest as he lay on the floor before breaking for Bryce. Her nightgown was covered in the Mexican's blood.

Bryce's mind working tactically and logically, he scooped her up, spinning her around as if he were holding something sacred, and drew her into an all-encompassing embrace. Her face and arms were covered in bruises. She pressed her body flush with his, and they held each other tightly as he quickly slewed about and carried her out of the kitchen into the living room, away from the bloody carnage. Her brimming tears flowed down her cheeks and were absorbed by the bloody cloth of his shirt.

Relief welled up inside her knowing Bryce was there for her. Typically she would have resented a man's protective hug but not this time. She was hanging on to him with every ounce of strength she had in her body.

Just then, she felt wetness and removed her hand from Bryce's leather jacket. Her hand was covered in warm blood as she glanced up at him. She opened the front of his jacket; his white shirt had an expanding ghastly crimson stain.

"Oh my God!" She screamed in an octave she had never heard out of her mouth before. Bryce had been hit and was bleeding copiously. "You've been shot; I've got to stop the bleeding."

Gritting his teeth in excruciating pain with blood soaking his shirt, he yelled, "Not now."

"Sit down," Nuna cried.

"Not now!" His truncated voice went perilously shrill as adrenaline coursed through him.

Then she hyperventilated and caught the unmistakable stench of gasoline overtaking the acrid smell of gunpowder, then heard the crackle of flames and the smell of smoke just as the shrill sound of her fire and smoke alarms began to squeal from down the hall.

Bryce, with his glock still in hand, moving on pure adrenaline, counterintuitively took hold of her wrist and, without uttering another word, pushed Nuna straight out the front door and followed her cannonballing off the porch away from the house just as the inside of the house burst into a flash of heat and flames, propelling them both to the ground. Unclipping his phone from his belt, he reluctantly came off the ground on one knee, regaining his purchase, dialing 911, and following that call with a speed dial to Austin for assistance as he desperately shielded Nuna from the searing oven-like waves of heat passing over them. His experience and training had given him the ability to ignore the physical and mental agony of the moment.

Nuna, kneeling beside him, gulping and sucking in air, reached out, removed his thick suede jacket, and ripped open his bloodstained shirt. The ropy muscles of his left side were a bloodcurdling mess.

Unable to find the wound quickly, she used her fingers to feel for the source of the bleeding. Then, having found the gaping wound, she ripped off her a section of her nightgown and wrapped it snugly around his rib cage.

The house was now fully engulfed in flames. Bryce spotted blurred movement through his peripheral vision, bringing him to full alert. Illuminated by the ghostly light of the half-moon, a Maduro assassin of imposing height and girth, looking like a Neanderthal from the Stone Age, came around the corner of the house faster than a rattlesnake, striking with a large automatic Magnum .357 caliber pistol in his right hand, and began blazing heedlessly. Then there was an abrupt pause. His gun jammed, and he screamed incoherently. Summoning every last ounce of steeled determination, seemingly impervious to the pain he had left, Bryce rose up, and with blinding speed, he went limbic, pushing himself off the ground. He shoved Nuna out of his line of fire as he stood with his gun in an isosceles brace with both hands and rapidly fired off four to five successive deafening rounds at the assassin, catching him several times in the chest and once in the forehead.

The fleshy-faced, bearded Mexican let loose a bloodcurdling scream into the darkness from where he had materialized; it was like something born in the horror of a nightmare. He then stumbled, teetered forward, twitched spasmodically, and turned and fell backward on the ground. He stayed down, writhing briefly in final agony but not before another explosion; Bryce took another bullet from a second Mexican to the left shoulder. Like a cougar in the night, he instantly charged the other assassin, who was almost on top of him. With lightning speed, he drove his hardened right fist into the guy's chin, breaking his jaw and sending the assailant stumbling backward unceremoniously to the ground, screaming. When the guy made the mistake of getting up, Bryce drove his iron fist into his gut, followed by two more undercuts. Rolling on the ground, bleary-eyed with blood spilling out of his mouth, the assassin drew a gun, and Bryce, having recovered, instinctively shot the monster three times at point-blank range: one in the chest, one blowing off the assailant's gun hand, and one in his left knee. Just then Bryce pitched forward and collapsed on the lawn.

Overwrought, wheezing, and gasping for breath, Nuna pushed herself off the damp ground in terrifying shock, her ears still ringing from the deafening volley of rapid-fire explosions. She covered her face with her bloody hands to block the ominous searing heat and thick, blinding smoke that was filling her lungs and clogging her nostrils. Coughing and gasping for air, she kept crawling in the grass, screaming and calling out for Bryce with a trembling voice. The roar of the intense fire was so loud that it drowned out all night sounds and presumably Bryce's voice as well. "Bryce, Bryce, pleeeeeease." And just then, she heard a low groan somewhere in the blackness over the fire, which now sounded like a freight train.

The twenty-foot arborvitaes that lined the side yard were now entirely engulfed, sending searing flames high in the sky. With unbridled emotions and stark terror welling inside her, she followed the low bellow of agony, crawling on her hands and knees about fifteen feet to her left. Finding him on his back and barely breathing, she kneeled over him with clenched teeth and a mouth dry as sandpaper. She frantically ripped open the front of his shirt and saw blood gushing profusely from two wounds in his chest. His chest was solid and firm with muscle like she had never seen before and now covered in slippery blood, too much blood. His neck vein was still pulsing, but the pulse was growing weaker. Terror grabbed her heart at the thought of him dying. Straddling him and shaking like a leaf in the wind, she began applying all the compressive pressure she could muster to his wounds.

She was hysterical and desperately trying to staunch the warm sticky blood flow with her hands as she began coughing up a vile mucus. Her heart shattered in a million jaded pieces. She could feel his heart beating against her palm and his chest shuddering as he gasped for precious air. His right hand moved, and his fingers lightly touched her arm and attempted to squeeze but couldn't. Blood colored his lips as he tried to breath. His eyes struggled to open but couldn't hold their focus. "Nuna? Are you OK?" While his graying lips were moving, his voice was fading away.

"It's going to be OK, Bryce," she said with garbled words drowning in tears. "Hang on, Bryce, damn you." How often did a woman find a man willing to take two bullets for her? "No, please, God no! I love you. Don't leave me."

Adrenaline was expelled by fear and a tsunami of grief-driven tears, leaving a numb despair in its wake. Looking down into his eyes, she saw a passion so fierce she felt an electrical charge run through her body like none she had ever felt before. She looked down at him while her heart pounded and her pulse raced. Her face touched his. Bryce was looking up at her, his breathing unevenly faint. If pain showed in her eyes, Bryce knew better than to acknowledge it.

This couldn't possibly happen after finding a man I truly loved, she thought. While Bryce was still alive, he was in dire need of medical help and was passing in and out of consciousness. She pulled out his phone from his jacket pocket, dialed 911, screamed, Man shot, and my house is on fire!" and gave her address, almost indecipherable in her frame of mind. The operator answered, her voice the maddening epitome of calmness. She didn't know that the 911 dial on Bryce's phone was linked directly to Glenn and Austin in case an emergency arose. She held fast to Bryce's wounds, her ragged breathing suspended. A plume of hideous flames was raging out of the top of the house.

As a fire from hell burned behind her. She began screaming, screaming, screaming into the night for help. Dark, dense gray noxious smoke billowed and mushroomed over the lawn, and the intense heat was almost blistering. With tears welling in her bloodshot eyes, she was terrified that he might fade out at any moment. She could feel Bryce's chest heaving against her as she sucked in fresh air and desperately compressed her lips to his and blew into his mouth in her best effort at CPR. The advancing wailing sounds of discordant, blaring sirens indicated the cavalcade, amped and echoing in the distance; the minutes waiting for it were glacially slow and interminable but brought desperate solace to her palpitating heart.

He smelled of smoke, and she presumed she did as well. Her skin was damp with sweat, and she was gasping for breath as if she had just run a marathon.

By the time the EMTs arrived, she was covered from head to toe in blood, but she had miraculously slowed down his blood loss.

Headlights and lights flashing blue like sporadic sapphires were now washing up the driveway. In the distance, she could see red and blue pulsars ablaze, creating a kaleidoscope of patterns in the darkness, ascending and slicing down toward the river and up toward the house perched on the banks above it. Every police officer in Fayette County seemingly had heeded the 911 call. Four cruisers, two fire engines, and an ambulance arrived in rapid succession in her driveway and on her lawn, and there was the sound of screeching tires, radio staccato, and doors slamming. A small gathering of people from the immediate neighborhood clustered under umbrellas in an amorphous, murmuring group, agog, having most likely heard the reports of the gunshots, now craning their necks in the direction of the calamity unfolding before them. The overwhelming sirens were almost loud enough now to drown out the roar of the flames.

Police cruisers quickly erected barricades, blocking all traffic from both directions, and kept the media trucks at bay and away from the scene. The scent of gasoline, still foreboding, hung in the air. As soon as the first responders arrived, Nuna's eyes were wide and blurred by an endless flow of unchecked tears, and mascara streaming down her blackened, soot-covered cheeks; she began screaming in a trembling voice for medical help. She was crouched down on the ground alongside him, crying, drenched in blood, with a galloping heart pounding like a kettledrum in her chest, asking why.

"This way. Hurry!" she cried.

Two large male EMTs ran to her, gently touched her shoulders from behind, and lifted her. Her knees were wobbly, and if the EMTs hadn't been supporting her, she would have fallen back to the ground. Satisfied that she hadn't been shot or hurt physically, they moved her gently to the side. Startled, she looked up and felt an oxygen mask being slipped over her face by a female paramedic and then began inhaling fresh air as her lungs ached. She whispered to the female EMT that she had been raped by a Mexican earlier. Two other paramedics put an oxygen mask over the face of Bryce and then stripped him to the waist and began checking his vitals.

The EMT screamed out, "No heartbeat!" They immediately wiped his sun-scorched chest clean and began zapping him with a defibrillator until they regained a pulse. His chances of survival would be touch and go. They quickly stabilized him and did an immediate triage, placing him on a gurney, putting an IV in his right arm, and attaching EKG sensors to his chest. Both were momentarily stunned by the number of bullet and knife scars on his chest.

"Sir, are you able to move? Are you in pain?" His tone was measured and uncharacteristically reserved.

Still lucid, Bryce responded by expelling a weak but long and reedy breath. "Absolutely, feels like a semi has hit me, but I've suffered a hell of a lot worse on the battlefield, believe me," he said, trying to express a twinkle of conviction ruefully.

"Get an oxygen mask on him."

His bloodied face was pale and flaccid. He grimaced with excruciating pain. He was constantly going in and out of consciousness.

Bright lights, masked people, tubes and lines being inserted into him. Then, mercifully, darkness closed over him, and he momentarily lost consciousness and passed into the darkness. A portable generator had been set up on the street where a line of yellow emergency work lights on tripods was throwing a couple of thousand watts of halogen light and water on the hillside scene. They found two people, one still alive with gunshot wounds, and a female who had been stabbed to death on the other side of the shrubs.

They injected a small about of morphine into Bryce's IV to reduce his pain and then started fluids and plasma while subduing the external bleeding. Finally, satisfied that he was stabilized enough to be transported, the two EMTs lifted him onto a stretcher, strapped him down, hooked him to a monitor, and lifted him into the ambulance. Having risen to her feet, Nuna watched, her heart suddenly in her throat, thudding painfully.

While Bryce would never have admit it, he was in dire straits due to his exsanguination.

The paramedics had already called the hospital, alerting them of the incoming patients, one with two bullet wounds to the chest and the other a rape victim. While his vitals were fair, he had lost a lot of blood and was in excruciating pain. All around him, his world went silent and dark. Despite her fierce resolve, Nuna's nauseating dizziness swept over her in cascading waves.

The local police and fire department had been on the scene within ten minutes of her 911 call, with Austin and a half dozen FBI agents following right behind the phalanx of stroboscopic flashing lights. As they put Bryce into the ambulance, one of the local officers secured her by her shoulders and attempted to restrain her from going into the ambulance with him.

"Are you his wife?" the officer asked peremptorily.

Anguished, she turned and looked up at his steeled face with the briefest of pauses. "No, I'm…" Nuna was weeping copiously. Fear clogged her throat as she screamed in anguished desperation. "Bryce!"

Austin and another FBI agent, standing next to the ambulance, immediately saw that she was desperate, scared senseless, and adamantly inconsolable, refusing to let go of the open door of the ambulance. They immediately stepped in and rectified the situation with authoritative voices. The officer took a second look at Nuna in earnest as her blood pressure rose and immediately capitulated, now realizing her excruciating mental pain and now sounding sincerely sympathetic. "Please let me help you get in, Miss," he said solemnly as the female EMT came to her aid.

Despite the night's low-seventies temperature, she could see the sheen of sweat on Austin's brow. Having noticed that she was suffering from spasms of pain in her contorted face, bruised and bloody, he took off his jacket and wrapped her nightgown-clad body with it as he lifted her into the ambulance. The doors closed with a metallic clang.

Two paramedics fitted a new oxygen mask to Bryce's face and hooked him up to an IV. The female EMT sat next to her with her arms around

Nuna, giving her some warmth and understanding. The ambulance jolted forward with sirens blaring as they sped toward Charleston with a state police escort requested and authorized by Austin. A second ambulance transported the wounded Mexican to the hospital; he was handcuffed and under police guard. Austin couldn't chance another attempt on Nuna's life. The last couple attempts on Bryce's and Nuna's lives had merely confirmed his skepticism in the benevolence of fate.

The paramedics continued to monitor and bustle around their patient all the way to the hospital, paying little attention to her or the two FBI agents sitting next to her. Nuna, reaching frantically, her blouse, hands, and face covered in his blood, held Bryce's hand to her breast all the way to the hospital in Montgomery, which was a twenty-minute, harrowing ride. She took a couple of deep breaths to calm herself. Panicking was not going to help Bryce. She kissed his cheek and tasted his blood, her features distorted by grief.

"Bryce," she said, her expression as discombobulated as her thoughts, "please don't die." She looked at pallid face, his stillness. To her surprise, two FBI agents, one male and one female, had climbed in right behind her and were accompanying her and Bryce to the hospital.

Bryce opened his eyes briefly and looked up at the blurred face above him. He moaned so softly that the words were barely audible, but she heard them as he opened his eyes: "I love you." He then collapsed into a sea of darkness. Out of the darkness came the nightmare.

Austin had already begun gathering information that this was not just an attack on Nuna and Pablo but a coordinated attack on Bryce. Bryce and Nuna had now become significant targets of the Maduro organization. For a short while, they were quiet before realizing that Bryce had mercifully lapsed into unconsciousness.

The firefighters fought the blaze till around one in the morning, and it was a total loss. Several local uniformed police officers, along with two FBI agents, cordoned off the crime scene for the rest of the night.

CHAPTER 38

Wrestling with fleeting sleep and fighting for a few moments of release, Bryce closed his eyes and let the horrific iterations of superimposed memory flashback with ghosts of the past crowding into his restless mind with renewed nightmarish vigor. The pain, the smells, and the faces of evil brought him back to the unforgiving Vietnam jungle scene by rote, back to a place that he would have rather forgotten. Back to a place as far removed as possible from the warmth of the fire in his home in the Adirondack Mountains of West Virginia.

The morning light beckoned with the rising orange sun turning to yellow, forcing its way through his tightly closed eyelids. He begged for it to go away, but it always radiated its way in. He was back in Vietnam, back to the tidal swamps of the Mekong Delta and the most hellish moments of his life.

We were idle as the sun radiated off the shimmering rice fields. A half dozen undernourished workers on the port side bent low in the ankle-deep water, picking at rice stalks in the luscious green patties like chickens pecking at corn. Having worked in the rice fields most of their young lives, they were inured to the violence taking place all around them.

His gunboat had been ambushed while on a search-and-destroy patrol as part of Operation Game Warden in the northern Mekong Delta. Now wounded and in the water, he watched in horror as the boat blew up, having been hit by a rocket-propelled grenade. No one on the boat would have survived the explosion and the following explosions as the ammunition locker on board blew up.

Bryce struggled to find his breath. His back ached terribly from the bullet that had taken him over the side of the 120 Mk PBR on which he had been going up a tributary of the Mekong Delta to Prey Veng before returning to base camp. As his head broke the surface of the water, he witnessed the heavy *fire of green tracers from the elephant-grass-lined riverbank going over his head, cutting the boat to ribbons, and then the deafening explosion of the boat ten to fifteen yards from him. He couldn't hear the explosion, and time was in slow motion as he frantically made his way to the river's edge. It had been most likely hit by a couple of RPGs that found the mark. The horrific scene under a full moon in the dark of the night before him was surreal. Suddenly, it seemed that his brain was talking to him from all his nerve endings.*

The brutal scene snatched him by the brain and took him back to where he didn't want to be.

The torrential rains were relentless. The Special Operations mission was routine and basically quiet, but this day would be anything from routine, and it would be a long time before it was quiet again for Lieutenant Bryce Tucker.

His mind fumbled for his M14, and finding it smashed, he then went for his .38 Smith & Wesson, only to find an empty leather holster with his bloody right hand. Due to the loss of the chief petty officer for PBR 139 at Tinh Binh in the Mekong Delta, the base command had temporarily assigned Bryce to cover the position. Bryce's mind was strained, and his aching body refused to cooperate as he attempted to respond. He wanted to scream but couldn't. He closed his eyes and forced himself to focus on surviving and living for the next two months. Having made his way to the edge of the muddy riverbank, he began a slow crawl along the bank when he felt the butt of a rifle slam him in the right side of his head, rendering him unconscious.

One of the VC had seen him go over the side of the boat and found his position on the riverbank. Bryce, an expert in hand-to-hand combat, didn't have a chance to escape into the jungle, and with two bullets in him, his only recourse was to surrender. Not that he had much choice at the moment. His last thought as he caught another rifle butt in the face was that he would die on the west bank of the Vam Co Dong River.

When he regained consciousness, he found himself hanging upright with his wrists tied together and strung up from a stout tree branch. Opening his blurred eyes slowly for a moment, he became aware of his surroundings and believed that he was in a clearing surrounded by a peat mangrove deep in the jungle. A rope had been looped around his ankles, anchoring him in place and rendering him helpless. Nowhere were there any members of his crew. He had to assume that they had all died in the explosion.

His head hung down as he stared at the soggy earth a foot or two below his feet.

Surveying the scene around him, he saw about a dozen or more black-pajama-clad VC were huddled and congregating around a firepit, created more to give light and ward off mosquitoes than to provide heat. A couple were standing and walking the perimeter, constantly watching him and looking into the darkened jungle as if waiting for an attack. There was no way that they would have known that a rescue attempt had even been initiated as communications had been terminated with a kill shot to the communications. The humidity was such that rivulets of sweat were running down Bryce's body. He began to convulse involuntarily as blood from his wounds dripped, mixing with his sweat and forming a small pool on the muddy ground below his feet.

Most of them were in their early twenties, a couple of them rangy, indigenous, and elderly, a couple wearing NVA uniforms, and all were nervously milling around, staring at him with evil intent. They seemed apprehensive and nervous, speaking in low, soft, but excited tones that mixed with the surrounding sounds of the jungle around them.

Bryce had no idea what the VC had planned for him, but as dusk fell, his future looked dim. He sucked in as much of the fetid swamp air as he could get into his lungs just to stay alive. It hurt to breathe, it hurt to move, and it even hurt to think. Knowing that the VC never stayed long in one location, he had a gnawing feeling that they would either take him with them or leave him for the animals. With two bullets still in him, he would be a weight they would not want to drag around for sure. He received a ritual of predictable daily beatings administered like clockwork for his captors' amusement.

Slowly, as he hung there tethered from the tree under the faint glow of the moon like a piece of low-hanging meat, enduring the sadistic ritual beatings, a new pain overtook the place of the pain in his chest from the bullets. Being *suspended for almost an hour was taking its toll on his joints and nerve end-ings. The pain felt like thousands of needles being injected into his shoulders, twisted for maximum effect.*

He wanted to survive, and to do that, he had to conquer his fear, main-tain his wits without sleep, not surrender, and not give the enemy the satis-faction of knowing of the pain he felt, which was gradually overtaking him. His mind had to resist the biorhythms that were telling him it was time to succumb and shut down.

Without provocation, one of the uniformed NVA suddenly stood up stiff-ly and came at him with a wild look and a large knife, gleaming off the fire. Taking one swipe, he sliced his chest from left to right before slicing the rope holding me to the tree. Bryce dropped face-first into a bloody, writhing heap of mud. He fought to breathe as several gooks turned him upright in the muck and took turns kicking and beating him with a vengeance.

Somewhere in the process, he went unconscious.

Sometime later, Bryce regained consciousness but kept his swollen eyes closed. He found himself crammed in a four-by-four bamboo cage at the base of the thick tree trunk that he had been hanging from. The air was hot and unrelentingly humid. His hands were tied behind his back, and his ankles were tied together. Slowly, he took a quick inventory of what he had and found that they had taken everything except his torn, olive-drab T-shirt and pants. One of them was most likely wearing his socks and boots. The NVA soldiers were nowhere to be seen, and the others were about forty feet away, huddled in a circle under a palm tree, oblivious to the unrelenting torrential rain. A canvas tarp covered their weapons from the incessant deluge. While it was still light out, darkness wasn't far away. The bottom of the cage was now in three inches of water. Mosquitoes were buzzing everywhere, biting him re-lentlessly. But he didn't dare utter a sound. He didn't want them to know that he was awake, for they would surely beat him again if they knew. It was the middle of the night and still hot and humid as hell in the backwater swamp. Bryce instinctively knew that if he survived, he would have to endure much more pain at the hands of his captors.

At the first hint of the rising orange sun the following morning, the two NVA soldiers were back, with a third one barking orders to the VC. The morning sun felt like a blast furnace, and beads of sweat ran down his bloodied forehead, the harbinger of an insufferable day. Within moments there was a flurry of activity, and everybody was moving and scurrying about. He felt a flutter of panic as handles were attached to his cage. Four gooks with their AK-47s and small rucksacks slung over their backs took hold and put a rope around his neck, lifting his depleted body off the ground as they began their rigorous trek north.

After an hour or so of carrying him along a path skulking through a quagmire of dense jungle, humus, and mud interspersed with jutting rocks, they dropped the cage and cut it open, spilling him out on the soggy ground. His exposed skin was scraped, gouged, cut, bruised, and lashed. Two of them pulled him up to his feet, and a third jabbed him in the back with an AK-47, mercilessly pushing and dragging him forward, sloshing him along the trail deeper in the jungle. With his hands hog-tied behind him, he hobbled and stumbled forward like a wounded animal on a leash, struggling to keep pace in his bare feet. When he could no longer stand, two of the VC would lift his between them, feet dragging.

The pain in his body caused by the forced marches brought him back, back to hell. His physical condition had deteriorated considerably over the past six or seven weeks, with a fractured right leg, a dislocated left shoulder, deep bruises, and numerous cuts all over his body, caused by the constant beatings and relentless lashings by his captors. Fortunately, when the others were occupied with camp chores and other predawn activities, one of the elderly VC would sit down with him every couple of days and use the point of his knife to remove tiger leeches that had attached themselves to his arms and legs during the forced marches. Regardless of the motive behind it, this vague act of kindness was readily received.

His mind rebelled and took him back to back to a place in his mind as far removed as possible from the safe, warm space in front of his fire hearth in the Adirondack Mountains.

Back to a time when a protective mental mechanism within his mind was used to escape agony and find a better place, a place without death, without war. A place without pain.

A sudden spasmodic twitching in both extremities jarred him from his musings and brought him back to his nightmare. Time no longer really had any meaning.

He had been sloshed through waist-deep swamp most of the afternoon, and it began to get dark. The head honcho gave the order to make camp as they found a small clearing of wet marshland languishing just off the footpath. He was pushed into the muddy ground by the two VC as the NVA regulars scurried about setting up camp. He began to reflect on the thoughts he had retained over the past six weeks that he had been held prisoner. One of the VC soldiers had some medical training, and he had removed one bullet from his chest as the other one had seemingly exited his back. The pain in his chest was excruciating as he closed up the wounds with a thread. Perspiration ran down his face as he held back his agony.

The NVA captain, Nguyen, whom Bryce had learned to fear, had Bryce placed face first against a tree and had him secured with his arms draped around the tree spread eagle. He was about to be interrogated again by this sadistic son of a bitch, for the tenth or twelfth time. He was given a dozen lashes each time for refusing to provide the captain with information beyond his name and serial number. It had become a painful ritual at the end of each day, and the captain enjoyed testing his capacity for pain. His back looked like a road map. At this point in time, while Bryce wanted to live, he wasn't sure if death was such an unpalatable alternative. He had lost a lot of weight and was rapidly losing more, with several broken ribs now showing in his chest. Periodically, in the early morning hours just before daybreak, the elderly doc would come over to his cage and pour a peroxide solution over his back to reduce or stabilize his wound infection.

Even with the injuries to his body, he never stopped looking for a means to escape.

It was early in the morning, just before the rising orange sun proclaimed a new day, when they roused him from a sound sleep by prodding him in the side with sharpened bamboo sticks. After his captors had eaten, he was thrown a piece of dried cassava manioc root and a small rancid ball of rice, both covered with ants. He had learned to eat food immediately and swallow it quickly as they would drag him out of his cage without waiting for him to eat what he had been thrown.

He was untied from the tree, pushed, and punched down a hillside path that seemed lightly traveled away from the campsite. It was another day of an unrelenting deluge of rain, mud, and swamp.

In his weakened condition, he fell frequently, and his guard would beat him on the back with his bamboo whip, which he always had ready. They marched from daybreak to nightfall, traveling about six to seven clicks a day without stopping or sharing any of their food with him. The day was surreal. When he fell and stumbled into the forest muck, they would pull him back up to his feet by his hair and ram the AK-47 into his back, forcing him forward. This process would repeat itself a dozen or more times before he would finally fall for the last time as the sun fell and darkness took hold.

As darkness fell, he was dumped in a small clearing along the side of the footpath underneath a magnolia tree, where he collapsed in exhaustion. After that, eh could only stare off into the night. Dark shapes in his peripheral vision danced here and there as clouds passed before the moon and he drifted in and out of consciousness. One of the VC again brought him a manioc root and a ration of rice packed into a ball about the size of a man's fist, which was barely enough to keep him alive and his muscles from atrophying. his couldn't move very much in my cage anyway.

As the days went on, they would force him to eat anything put before him. On a good day, he would be given leaves with dead bugs on them or raw fish heads and leftover frog guts for the entertainment of his captors. Bryce had learned to understand that protein was protein no matter how pungent and unappetizing the morsels were. He gobbled it down quickly as his captors howled.

They quickly fashioned another bamboo cage for him that night, and he willingly crawled into it and curled up in a fetal position like an abused dog. Several guards would assume their positions surrounding the cage and watch his every move. While his captors secured cover from the elements for the night, he was left exposed to the incessant downpour. Having gotten accustomed to sleeping in the elements over the past weeks, he fell asleep within minutes.

The following days were the same, marching from daybreak to sunset, except that the beatings were becoming more frequent.

On a couple of occasions, when they stopped at a friendly village, Captain Nguyen allowed villagers to beat him with thick hemp rope about three inches thick and three feet long. He was tethered and pinned to the ground face first and spread eagle; they began with his neck and methodically worked their way down his back to his buttocks and the backs of his thighs. The beating ritual typically lasted about twenty minutes, and was followed by kicking him in the kidneys and groin. Somewhere during the punishment, the doc must have stepped in and stopped the beating. This was the worst beating he had endured since being captured, and he didn't know if he would have survived had it gone on much longer. His back was now an aching, bloody piece of raw meat, and the constant rain that poured over his neck, back, and legs was the only relief he got from the stinging pain. There was no antiseptic available, and no one would apply it if there were. They dragged his limp, bloody body back to the new bamboo cage, again a three-by-three-foot cube preventing him from moving at all.

When the pain became overwhelming, he would close his eyes and mentally retreat into his safe place, refuge, and sanctuary, impervious to the pain. Somewhere along the way, he had learned that his mind was a forceful tool, one that would enable him to escape unbearable pain, turn garbage into fine cuisine, and make the unbearable tolerable.

Suddenly, an NVA soldier burst through the dense brush, branches breaking directly behind him. He was panicked, sweating profusely, nostrils flaring, his eyes terrified. There was gunfire coming from two fronts, and the VC and NVA soldiers were trapped and running in all directions into the jungle. Not knowing what was taking place, he quickly mustered all the energy he could, crawled, and rolled into the dense brush.

He hadn't counted on Captain Nguyen holding back and following him into the bush. Standing over him in the slippery muck with a sadistic smirk on his face infused with blind hatred, he pulled his pistol from his holster, cocked it, and pointed it at my head.

He forced himself to stand, refusing to die lying on his back before this monster. Just then, he tripped on a root, and his legs gave out; he fell headlong into the forest floor muck. Turning over on his back in the mud, he felt he was finished as his body had abandoned him.

The next sounds he heard were two short blasts distinctly from an M16, and he saw Captain Nguyen, mouth open in horror and disbelief, falling in a heap on top of him. Bryce lay on his back for what seemed like an eternity in the quagmire as the captain bled all over him from multiple shots to the head and chest before two American soldiers in camouflaged uniforms pulled the SOB off him and lifted his skeletal body out of the mud. Trying as he could, he wasn't able to take a single step before collapsing.

The soldier looked at him with clenched teeth, seemingly stupefied for a second that seemed more like an eternity before vaulting the body of the NVA captain off him. Then he, along with another soldier, lifted him out of the mud, put him over a shoulder, and carried him over to the extraction chopper. Forty-eight hours later, he was on a C-130 and flown to the US Naval Station Hospital at Subic Bay in Manilas, the Philippines.

With that, acrid smells of the firefight that had preceded the extraction no more than several moments earlier were no longer present. Captain Nguyen was dead, and all Bryce felt was rapture.

There were only a few cries, moans, and screams of the dying, mingling with the acrid smell of gunpowder in the jungle. Some of the fallen had a single gunshot to the head. They had all paid the ultimate price for what they had done to him, and he would see another day to serve.

Suffering from starvation and severe dehydration, he was lifted by a chopper, cleaned up a little, and stitched as necessary before being flown out to Da Nang for immediate medical treatment. He had wanted to live for only one reason: to kill every last one of them for what they had done to him.

Mission accomplished. He would live another day and cope with whatever came from it. Period.

Bryce rested for another four weeks, slowly regaining his strength. However, he was far from perfect when he volunteered for another mission.

He was carried to a chopper and extracted from the southern Cambodian border.

If he kept his eyes closed, the afterimages of his torture and deprivation were still very much alive.

As he was shackled inside the nightmare, the ticking clock on the wall wasn't measuring the time of the dream; it was creating it and replaying it in an endless loop as he waited out the night.

It was a measure of infinite distance to painfully understand and lacerate the traumatic horror that he had endured. Nam was now a misbegotten mélange of savagery, a near-death experience forever lodged in his memory that could not be banished.

As the recurring nightmare engraved in his memory began to evaporate into the morning light, he found himself drenched from head to foot in now damp sheets. Tangible evidence that his virtual ghosts could be very deliriously real and of the erstwhile nightmare that still plagued him and drew him back to the unending stream of horror like a siren to a sunken boat. He shook his head haltingly to vaporize the last vestiges of the nightmare. He was pursued by both virtual ghosts of the past and those now real. Bryce was a survivor and always on guard, isolating the reprieve from the pain he kept so deeply buried inside of himself. He would never discuss it.

A voice inside his head began its usual hypnotic litany: "You're a warrior. Never give in. Never give in. Never, never, never, never—in nothing, great or small, large or petty—never give in, except to convictions of honor and God sense" (Winston Churchill).

Bryce staggered to the bathroom, took a piss, and rinsed his face with cold water, then towel-dried, not wanting to go back to bed and risk immersing himself back in the nightmare. He lay down on the edge of the bed and forced himself to breathe slowly and take control of his out-of-control pulse. Relax, he told himself, just relax. Then he was catapulted back to the smell of disinfectant.

CHAPTER 39

They reached the porte cochere of the hospital emergency room. Nuna, her mind still reeling in the aftermath, refused to let go of his hand and ran alongside the gurney in bare feet under the harsh fluorescent lights, through the double doors and all the way down the long tiled antiseptic hallway to the ER. No less than fifteen blue-scrub-covered professionals were present attending to Bryce. Hospital smells permeated the air: under intense ceiling lighting, she could detect harsh, vaguely nauseating disinfectants, antiseptics, alcohol, and she could only imagine what else. Wheelchairs, mobile beds, oxygen tanks, and women in sea-green hospital scrubs abounded, conveying the seriousness of his condition.

As they reached the ER and passed through double doors, she gave him a chaste kiss on the forehead before the doctor told her that it was time for her to leave him with them. The doctor gave two nurses instructions to care for her and promised to keep her updated on Bryce's status before sternly yelling, "Let's go!" His vitals were critical but stable. Her sodden eyes swollen from crying and covered with watered-down blood and mascara, she leaned down, trembling, and gently gave him another kiss. His eyes opened ever so briefly, giving her a catatonic stare.

Austin, having exited the ambulance along with a state trooper, immediately began issuing orders to a dozen officers setting up a security net around the hospital.

Nuna looked ashen, her eyes disconnected and vague. She went silent. She felt the heavy weight of guilt settle over her and press down on her lungs. The love of her life was close to death's door. She knew it was useless to try and follow Bryce as they wheeled him through the polished double doors. She nervously found an isolated corner in the colorless waiting room, shimmering with anguish, her throat aching with immobilizing emotion for the next couple of interminable hours. She kneeled on the floor and prayed and prayed. Tears, running copiously from her eyes, blended with Bryce's blood on her wet cheeks. Her strong Catholic faith had always been paramount in her upbringing, and while she rarely asked for divine support, she now needed it and was calling in desperation for divine help. Not for herself. She wasn't important. She was down on her knees and pressed the palms of her hands together.

"God, Bryce is a good man. Please, don't let him die. Please, I beg you. I need him desperately. Pleeeeeease! Pleeeeeease!" she cried. Copious tears of anguish ran down her cheeks in full display.

She had ceased to exist when she saw Bryce take the second bullet on the lawn and the blood splatter his chest. The two nurses, understanding her excruciating pain, took a moment, kneeled, and prayed with her. She had a hollow, wasting ache in her stomach as if an insidious virus were destroying her from the inside. She hoped her faith would imbue him with enough strength to pull through.

The hours crawled on as she consumed several bottles of Poland Spring. She had been treated for smoke inhalation and several minor burns to her back that had resulted from flying sparks. Otherwise, she was medically fine, except for a thumping headache that wouldn't go away.

The usual supplicants of ER at this hour occupied the uncomfortable waiting room chairs. The junkies, indigents, intoxicated drunks, and bleeders. The chitchat in the room was mostly inconsequential. The double doors opened, and an elderly man in a walker pushed through with the help of a younger woman Nuna presumed to be his daughter. Nuna had never felt comfortable in hospitals, and now shew was even less so as she sat in the far corner with an army blanket around her shivering body lapsing into convulsive sobs. Her arms hugged her chest; her head dropped low in a vain effort to divert attention from her tears of internal suffering.

Moments later, Austin, along with a female doctor and two sympathetic ER nurses, appeared out of nowhere and immediately cleared the room. Taking notice that her face and arms were seriously bruised, not to mention she had been sexually assaulted and was covered in blood all over her semiclothed bedraggled body and was unaware if she was injured or not, they immediately took hold of her, put her in a wheelchair, and wheeled her trembling body from the waiting room, down several busy corridors into an emergency evaluation room.

With a shell-shocked, stoic expression on her face, Nuna sat trembling with noticeable palpitations, staring at the now-closed door. She was then wheeled into a private room next to the ER, where two other nurses in nondescript scrubs began helping her out of her blood-soaked clothes. Distraught, she sat quietly and plowed her fingers through her blood-caked blond hair. She began to pray again like never before as blurriness overtook her. A couple of women and one man, in a dark jacket, his tie loosened, stood vigil, surrounding her. They tried to comfort her, to little avail. The night dragged on interminably.

A female doctor and two critical care nurses put her up on a gurney and began to work on her. She couldn't get the stench of blood and smoke from her soot-clogged nose. The same two nurses, after getting instructions from the doctor still examining her, took the necessary pictures of her bruised body and facial wounds, which included two black eyes, before taking necessary samples of semen from her. They then took her to a shower to wash off the blood and smoke and clean her up. They awkwardly dressed her in a clean patient gown and slippers one of the other nurses had gotten for her. Miraculously, she had walked away from the night's horror mostly physically unscathed. Mentally, she was hurting inside. Will Bryce still want me after he finds out what Pablo has done to me? she asked herself. Will he look down at me as white trash, damaged goods? Nuna quietly cried deep within herself.

The next several interminable hours passed in a blur of confusion, heartache, and fear as she pleaded for the umpteenth time for information from the nurses' station. Finally, she asked, and they accepted her donation of blood to replace what he had lost. She stood up and began to feel woozy, disoriented, and nauseated as the room started to swirl around her. She staggered, closed her eyes as a wave of dizziness swept over her, and then she passed out, caught by nurse before she could fall to the floor and potentially slam her head onto the tile. She felt as helpless as a zombie as several nurses in white uniforms immediately rushed to her aid and lifted her onto another gurney, screaming for a doctor, fearing a possible stroke.

Over and over, she relived the night, that split second when Bryce crashed through the door and the guns discharged in the kitchen. She kept trying to reconstruct what had happened, to make some sense of it.

Over and over and over again…

The mental review served no purpose. The sequence of events did little to alleviate the torture and helplessness she was feeling.

Even with the lateness of the hour, it didn't take long for all of Nuna's neighbors to spill out of their houses and congregate on the street facelessly in the dark, staring at the fire, the activity of the fire engines, ambulance, police cruisers, and the kaleidoscope of flashing lights, huddled in small groups and watching the mayhem in horror and fascination. Finally, one of the locals commented to a news reporter yelling for information from ten yards away, "Nothing like this has ever happened in Gauley Bridge." The fire had completely devoured the house. All that was left was the smoldering fetid wreckage.

It didn't take long for Nuna to realize that the story that Bryce had embroidered about being a reporter for the *Charleston Gazette* was a ruse. A kaleidoscope of images passed through her mind. Although, in hindsight, she should have seen it coming. At the same time, the astonishingly advanced medical attention and the phalanx of white-coated nurses and doctors attending to him was way beyond the norm. They immediately stripped him and hooked up an IV.

Within an hour of their arrival at the hospital, two medical specialists and anesthesiologist from Walter Reed Medical, along with two military nurses, were flown in on the orders of the Admiral to take over his surgery and recovery in the now heavily guarded ICU. A room adjacent to Bryce's was assigned to her, and one of the nurses graciously brought her a clean change of clothing amounting to fashionable blue hospital scrubs. Two FBI agents had been assigned outside her room also.

Nuna was twisting a damp handkerchief in her hands. Tears spilled from her eyes. Her bruised and battered face was raw and red from crying. Then, shortly after she took only one or two bites of a hospital dinner plate, her legs buckled, and she fell backward, collapsing to the floor.

She and Bryce would be sequestered at the hospital for a week or more. Both uniform and undercover federal security stood outside their rooms; the security was ultra tight. Unbeknownst to her, she had been sedated for almost ten hours and hooked up to an oxygen regenerator to clear her lungs of inhaled smoke.

Nuna tried to relax in the hospital bed that night, but it wasn't going to happen.

She rolled and twisted the better part of the evening, reliving the heartrending nightmare. She was sentient and surprised that she was alive and physically unhurt. All she could do was pray that he lived. Then, unknowingly, per an order from the doctor, she was given another sedative in her glass of water and was soon in a deep sleep.

A new day came with a golden haze of a rising sun, but Nuna was unaware of it, just staring with gritty eyes at the acoustic tile ceiling above her as she massaged the searing headache out of her temples. She felt the pain of her nightmare last night. Her body was stiff and her muscles sore. Last night, she'd been too caught up in shock and adrenaline to feel any pain, but now that had all faded away, leaving her with plenty of aches. With a sigh, she eased her bruised body out of bed and went to the bathroom to splash water on her face, wetting the washcloth several times, wiping her face before retreating back to the bed. Just then, there was a knock on the door of her room, snapping her out of her musings.

Austin and a female federal officer brought her coffee and breakfast from the hospital café. She cried pitifully from her two blackened eyes, emptying a box of tissues as she told them in a strangled voice what had happened. She wasn't hungry, but her body begged for a jolt of caffeine.

"Nuna," Austin said in a crooning, soothing voice, "you have to eat to keep your strength up." But he knew that she was still suffering terribly inside. She was in shock from everything she'd been subjected to, seen, and survived in the past twenty-four hours. The steaming foam cups of coffee were the only pleasant scents emanating among the cornucopia of antiseptic hospital smells in the room.

"I'm not hungry," she said with a brittle smile. She knew that she had no appetite or desire to eat. The only thing she was thinking of was Bryce. Regaining her equilibrium, she stepped out into the hallway and grabbed the arm of a nurse as she walked by, pleading with the nurse to let her see Bryce.

The nurse responded by saying he was still unresponsive and in a critical condition, having had two .38 caliber bullets removed from his chest. "Mr. Tucker has been diagnostically tested, X-rayed, and examined carefully by two top military surgeons," she explained. "While they found no signs of internal injuries to any vital organs, he hasn't yet regained consciousness and is still comatose, having lost a lot of blood before reaching the hospital.

Nuna stifled a cry that almost manifested. The clock ticked.

"Ms. Polinski, I'm sure that when he wakes up and his condition stabilizes, Dr. Monroe will let you see him. But until then, y'all will have to be patient." The nurse smiled wearily.

Nuna whispered thank you and turned away, resuming her unwavering forlorn vigil in her room, slumping into a chair and covering her face with her hands. Her voice trailed off despairingly, and to her dismay, she could feel her eyes start to well up again as she desperately fought to regain her composure. Her bruised lips began to tremble uncontrollably. It was going to be an interminable wait for her as the afternoon slid into night. The febrile sparkle in her eyes seemed to confirm her sleep deprivation, for everyone, but especially her. There was no clear definition of day or night. The doctors and nurses going back and forth through closed doors continued.

Twenty-four hours later, the doctor came out and told her that he was still in the ICU but she could go in for no more than a minute. He advised that neither of the bullet wounds was a walk in the park but neither was catastrophic or life-threatening at this point. Having dried her eyes and regained her composure, Nuna followed the doctor into the operating room. The soles of her hospital-supplied slippers squeaked on the vinyl tiles as she crossed the room and approached his bed. Bryce was lying flat in a morphine haze covered with a blue sheet tucked in and around him with a macabre ensemble of CRTs monitoring his life vitals: heartbeat, blood pressure, oxygen saturation. The ICU was a sterile chamber with a decoupage of clear tubes and green and red flashing lights and machines beeping and chirping ceaselessly. The steady beep of the monitors provided a modicum of reassurance to Nuna as she kept vigil beside his bed. She knelt and cried next to him softly, entangling her fingers with his and saying a prayer before kissing him on the forehead.

"Hi, Bryce. It's me, Nuna," she whispered, wiping the tears from her eyes. She hoped for some sign of acknowledgment that he heard her, but there was no twitching of his lips or movement of his eyes beneath his lids, no faint shift of his finger now interlaced with hers. "Bryce, I love you. I love you so much…" Her voice was a ghost of a whisper. "You came when I most needed you, and you fought for me when I no longer had the strength to fight for myself. Please, pleeeeeease come back to me." Tears coursed down her black-and-blue cheeks.

He was still unconscious and extremely pale but holding on. A quick rap on the door presaged the arrival of his critical care nurse, advising Nuna that her time was up and Bryce needed his rest. As she hazarded one last glance at Bryce, the nurse gave her a warm and encouraging smile.

They would be at the hospital another week or two. Night turned to day, and day turned to night. Nuna prayed to God for a miracle.

Austin stayed with her, ushering her back to her room. When they entered it, he closed the door behind him. Taking a seat next to Nuna and gripping her shoulder, he looked her straight in the eyes. "Bryce is a living legend still walking. He's the toughest man I know, and if anyone can pull through, he can. Nuna, Bryce is an aberration, a suspension of the rules of physical being."

"Austin, I know. He came to my rescue and, risking his own life, saved me from certain death," she cried.

With the admiral's authorization, Austin had made contact with Ray, his only living relative. With that authorization, Austin began to briefly impart who and what Captain Bryce Tucker was and the reason for all the high-level security. With Bryce's incapacitation, Austin was now in command of the operation, which now was at idle pending Bryce's recovery. While he wasn't at liberty to openly discuss the operation or Bryce's part in it, he felt that she had to know under the circumstances, with her now being a target in the crossfire. She now knew that Bryce was a highly decorated Vietnam combat veteran and a legendary senior covert undercover operative with CIA Special Operations. His sole mission at the moment was to take down the Maduro Operation both here in the States and offshore. She also now knew that he had served three and a half tours in Vietnam and had received enough medals to fill the chest of a uniform during that time: five Purple Hearts, two Silver Stars for gallantry in combat, a Bronze Star for heroic achievement, and the coveted Navy Cross for heroism in combat while severely wounded himself in bringing forty-two wounded men out of battle and back to a naval base on a boat that barely floated on the water.

Captain Bryce Tucker was an unsung formidable hero with an iron constitution and was a legend to his team, exhibiting dedication, integrity, and honor. Men of his ilk were by nature required to be unquestionably fearsome and patriotic. Austin didn't mention that Bryce was captured on a mission in Laos and tortured for over three weeks until rescued, barely alive, by a SEAL Recovery Team. The scars on his stomach and back bore testament. It was because of his capture during the Vietnam War that he was hardened to the cruelty one person could inflict on another. "His fearless character, as you witnessed, was formed in the heated crucible of war. He's brilliant and relentless, going from a young navy lieutenant fresh out of college to a captain with Navy SEAL Team One to the FBI and now CIA Special Operations."

"That's quite a segue," she said.

"Nuna, one other thing," Austin said, noting her uncomfortable look. "Please, and I repeat, please don't bring up any questions concerning his time in Vietnam. Bryce's military service in Vietnam remains terra incognita. He will not talk about it."

Nuna knew he was special. Now she was positive that he was a higher-caliber man than any other man she had ever known.

Bryce woke to darkness, pain, and the continuous humming and chirping of the machines before lapsing back into unconsciousness. His breathing was slow and measured, and when he closed his eyes, he again drifted off into a night of sleep. Nurses and doctors came and went. They would check his vitals and charts and then disappear behind the white hanging curtain. A velvet oblivion of darkness had claimed him again.

The next time he opened my blurry eyes, eh could sense activity around him. He started blinking. It felt like he had sand on his eyeballs they were so dry. The same with his dry throat. He tried to swallow, but there was nothing to swallow. A young nurse hovered over him, removing an oxygen mask from his face and asking him if he could sip some water. He didn't remember giving an answer, but his mouth was wet and he felt water running down his throat like a waterfall. He felt dizzy, nausea began overtaking him, and he slipped into darkness again.

The next time he woke, he blinked his dry eyes again before turning his head, his eyes focusing, narrowing, and roaming. The walls seemed to sway back and forth sickeningly. A chrome light bar was streaking where the curtains didn't connect. He was still in the intensive care unit, which was bereft of color. His eyes adjusted to the blurred shapes around him. Still in a daze, he could hear a soft female voice with an accent asking me if he could see her. With the room now coming back in focus, he could see there was a nurse in blue surgical scrubs and a doctor in a white coat. In the private hospital room with its view of the Charleston skyline, Nuna was hovering over him with affecting docility, rubbing a damp towel across his forehead. Holding his hand gently, she whispered a prayer and thanked God for saving his life. She looked like an angel as she covered his forehead with soft kisses.

For a big, surprisingly formidable man, he looked pale, except that his five-o'clock shadow was giving him some color. His hair was damp across his forehead and beginning to wave off the back of his muscular neck. He also looked tired.

"At least it wasn't my last rites," he deadpanned. "How long have I been out?" he strained to ask in monosyllabic words, still very disorientated.

"This is day fourteen," she whispered.

The doctor appeared in a white lab coat, standing by her side, taking my pulse.

"Hello, Mr. Tucker; I'm Dr. Johnansen. I've been working on you along with my colleagues for the past two weeks. You're a lucky man. You had lost a lot of blood by the time they got you here. For the record, you died twice: once in the ambulance, and you again flatlined on the operating table. Both times the code blue was initiated, and both times the medical teams did their magic and brought you back from the grave."

"Nuna?" Bryce asked.

"Nuna is fine now also," the doctor said, hovering close to him, a stethoscope hanging around his neck. "But she's been begging to hold your hand, crying and praying for you every day, morning, noon, and night.

"She's fine now, Bryce. She's one remarkable woman. She saved your life, and you should be aware that she also gave you two liters of her own blood the night they brought you in." The doctor quietly increased his medication, manipulating the flow into his system. He turned to Nuna and went on, "I've increased the pain medication to get him back to sleep. Nuna, the last thing we need is for him to become agitated and begin pulling the tubing. His body went into shock a couple of times from the loss of blood. Now he needs to rest, and I will update you on his condition. Trust me, he has the best of medical care."

Bryce had been drifting in and out for days and had no reference of time. The days had bled into each other.

He was released six days later, all bandaged up, still in a hospital smock, with strict instructions to rest. There was a collective sigh as he had been in the hospital almost three weeks, two weeks comatose in intensive care and on the brink of death. Tears flowed from Nuna; she had her miracle.

A male nurse had helped him shower and shaved him the morning before he was released from the hospital. The following day, they were brought to the helipad on the hospital roof, where a military chopper waited to lift off and fly the captain and Ms. Nuna Polinski home to Fayetteville under the tightest security measures. Intelligence had intercepted a rouge communication from Mexico that a $250,000 assassination bounty had been placed on the heads of the captain and Nuna. Glenn confirmed that it most likely originated from the Maduro operation. Unfortunately, his personal safety was not paramount in his line of work. Nuna would be a potentially significant material witness to the financial transactions that had taken place during her employment with the bank and the Maduro organization. Now that she was seemingly under the protection of the FBI, it was in both the bank's and the Maduro organization's best interest to have her silenced quickly.

CHAPTER 40

They left the hospital together. Having stepped into the chopper, ducking low under the idling whirling blades, Nuna followed Bryce, who had been lifted aboard by two male nurses. The *whup-whup* sound of the blades had her heart pulsing rapidly as she was scared out of her mind. Suddenly the lazy *whup-whup* of the idling blades changed to a centripetal *whip-whip-whip* as the chopper lifted off the hospital roof rising into the air with its rotor blades glinting like the wings of a fantastic insect and then tilted, turning north. The ground spun dizzyingly below her. Nuna had never been in a helicopter before, never mind flying in one in nothing more than hospital pajamas.

The helicopter rose straight up one thousand feet, retracting it wheels before drifting right, dipping its nose down, sweeping over the treetops high and fast, nearly clipping the tops as it flew away. It was too loud and the vibration too intense to have a civilized conversation, so Nuna spent most of the short ride holding his hand and raining kisses all over his beautiful face when she wasn't staring out the window at the expanse of the Monongahela forest below. It wasn't long before she spotted the New River Bridge below. The mountaintops glowed orange on the slopes, which faced the setting sun, and dull tan in the hollows.

While their voices were drowned out by the deafening roar of the blades, they occasionally gazed at each other, their eyes relaying plenty. The chopper vectored in, banking and maneuvering through the mountain ridgelines, keeping a low profile, and came to a stationary hover before setting down in Bryce's open backyard.

"Oh my heavens!" she exclaimed when the fully lit house on the summit of the mountain cliff came into view below with all its austere beauty. The chopper was put down on its runners in the backyard clearing, and several heavily armed camouflage soldiers flagged it down. As they dispatched the chopper, the soldiers went first and disappeared into the forest with stealth, lying low in the underbrush. Their orders were to lie in wait and keep watch on Captain Tucker's house. Per intelligence gained from the surviving Mexican, now confirmed, it was open season on the Captain and Nuna.

Nuna was relieved to be on the ground, away from the thumping rotors and the nerve-rattling vibration and downdraft of the chopper. As soon as they had alighted from the helicopter, it took off in a cloud of rotor wash dust.

According to the doctors, Bryce's wounds were serious: the two .45 caliber bullets broke a rib, nicked some blood vessels, and collapsed his left lung. Still, fortunately, they missed his heart, and no organs had been damaged. He would be laid up for a couple weeks or more recuperating with limited mobility and have another couple of interesting mottled scars to add to his growing collection of puckered mementos. Otherwise, he was exceptionally healthy, and there was seemingly no permanent damage.

"Unfortunately, Ms. Polinski, Captain Tucker is no stranger to pain, and I expect that he will become less ambulatory every day," the doctor had warned. "Nuna, you saved his life as he otherwise would have bled out before the paramedics got to him."

That was easy for them to say, she thought. She, unscathed physically but not mentally, would never forget the horrific moments of degradation while being raped by Pablo and what followed that hellish night when Bryce shot and killed two men and took two bullets for her. The horror and fear that had seared through her when she realized that he'd been shot a second time only a couple minutes after being first shot and was dying in front of her would haunt her to the end of her existence. Nuna wasn't a fragile person, but she dropped to her knees and her head spun; she felt overcome by vertigo. Tears gathered in her eyes as she looked at and smoothly traced the scars on his chest. Two of them had been meant for her.

Four stone-faced FBI agents, heavily armed, were already on the ground conversing with Ray, whom Nuna immediately recognized when they landed. Her understanding was that they would be posted outside the house 24/7 for several weeks covering the grounds.

Ray, standing just outside the torrent of wind, yelled, "Hey, y'all." He came over to them and smothered Nuna in a whopping mountain bear hug, the likes which she had not experienced in a long time, not since her daddy had hugged her similarly. She couldn't help to notice the tears welling in his eyes as he wiped them with his red sweat rag. Then, breaking the embrace apart, he effusively proffered his weathered hand out and introduced himself to Austin as Bryce's cousin before leading the medical team and the rest of the group into the house.

"Y'all be needing anything doing, just holler, and I'd be obliged to take care of it." He guided Austin to the upstairs loft where he would take residence and set up his geek equipment with an unobstructed electronic view over the mountains.

Soon after, he came back down, giving Bryce a second look. Ray rested his hand on Bryce's shoulder and shook his head in surrender.

Bryce opened his eyes, rolled them in a haze of pain, and slowly said, "I'm going to do nothing."

In his usual inimitable way, Ray gave him a placating look of suspicion. "I reckon you're not. You best not, or I'll be personally fixin' to kick your ass, ya hear?" he said anxiously, in his most jocular tone. "And why didn't you just tell us what needed doing and stay put in the hospital like you was si-posed-tew do?" Ray asked lamely without reservation, giving Bryce another frowning once-over. "You look like shit, bro. T'ain't funning either." That was so typically Ray, Nuna realized later.

Bryce, looking defeated, closed his eyes and went silent, slipping into drowsiness.

"Oh dang," Ray said in his unpretentious drawl as he left the room. He then took control of the outside professional landscaping crew, which was quickly being scrutinized and processed by the FBI, allowed to continue their mowing of the premises and other landscaping duties. The discerning smell of fresh-cut grass permeated the air.

What stuck Nuna first was how cool the inside of his log house was compared to the sultry heat outside. And then she was immediately awed by its sprawling size. Ray closed the door quietly behind them as they moved Bryce across the lacquered floors in the wheelchair, forward to the wide spiral staircase with polished oak handrails leading to the second-floor bedrooms. He had already disarmed the alarm system. Acutely aware of the direness of the situation, Nuna stayed fast, knowing that she had to be alert and to think quickly on her feet, none of which seemed remotely possible at the moment.

Two military medics carried him up the stairs on a Stryker cot and slowly lifted and laid him onto his bed. They pulled back the covers, laid him down gently between two king-sized overstuffed pillows, and then gave him two Percocet for pain. Nuna thanked them, saying that she would take it from there. Placing a pillow behind his head, she asked if she could get anything for him. Nothing came from his languid lips. He had already passed out from the drugs. Nuna didn't leave his side for the rest of the night.

Bryce unconsciously did not attempt to cover himself. Nevertheless, it was impossible to conceal her reaction when he turned over. She stopped just short of gasping out loud when she looked at his backside and now understood what the doctor had alluded to. Bryce had been viciously tortured: whipped, burned, stabbed, and shot a half dozen times in the back and legs.

She now understood his hardness and tough resilience to physical pain, but he was also gentle. Of course, he could be absolutely dour, but that only made his occasional jokes and smiles more precious. Her heart ached for him.

He seemed to have an awkward issue with expressing emotions, leading her to believe that he hadn't received much tenderness growing up. But having personally witnessed his unnerving bravery in saving her, she now knew beyond a shadow of a doubt that he was capable of deep feelings and wouldn't hesitate to act on them.

Bryce turned over again and opened his eyes, then gave a weak smile.

Overwhelmed with compassion for the agony he must have suffered, she gently traced several of the raised purple scars with her fingertip. "Do they still hurt?"

"Sometimes."

Reaching up ever so slowly with his right hand, he touched her cheek. She took his hand to her mouth and tenderly kissed the palm and each of his fingers.

Ray, exhausted, tired, and somewhat disheveled but feeling the need to stay close, stayed the night in his private guest room. Nuna reckoned that Ray was now feeling reasonably secure that Bryce would be convalescing in good hands. In a somewhat jocular mood, Ray said, "I'm calling it a night and getting out of y'all's hair." Opening the fridge, he removed a fifth of moonshine. "Helps me sleep," he said before going upstairs. "I'm an early riser, and I will serve up breakfast in the morning. We have a ton of catfish in the fridge. I will be serving fried catfish, eggs, and grits off the grill. Y'all be hungry in the morn, hear?"

Nuna gave Ray a hug and went back to Bryce's bedroom; finding him still asleep and deeply snoring, she kissed his forehead softly before pulling over a small bedroom chair next to his bed. She closed her eyes and let exhaustion claim her for the rest of the night. Thor, realizing that she wasn't a threat, took residence next to her and nuzzled her knee before lying on the carpeted floor between the bed and the chair. Nuna patted his head gently before quietly saying good night to the dog.

* * *

The following morning, she woke early to find that a throw blanket had been put around her and a pillow had been placed under my head. Having left the hospital in just a smock, she was sans bra and panties. There was a pair of jeans, boxers, and an oversize sweatshirt on the nightstand, most likely all from Bryce's closet. The hospital had disposed of her bloody clothing, and her guess was that one of the female agents had donated the jeans. Sometime during the night, Ray obviously had come into the room to check on them and done the honors. It wasn't long before she began to understand Ray, finding him to be unquestionably the salt of the earth. He was a man of few words and obnoxiously gentle with his Southern backwoods words. However, there wasn't one thing that he couldn't or wouldn't do to protect her or make her secure and comfortable in her new home.

Thor, having seemingly taken up sentry duty next to Bryce's bed during the night, gave a growl low in his throat before trotting over to her at a slow, easy gait, his tongue lolling, tail wagging slowly before resting his head on her knee. She stroked his neck as he looked up at her with sad, serious eyes.

She could easily tell that Bryce was the center of his world.

Taking a deep breath, she took in the surroundings of the bedroom. The room was, amazingly, tombstone quiet, with a nearly soundless air-conditioning system keeping it cool. His domicile wasn't at all typical of bachelor digs. There was a large walk-in closet and a huge, beautiful bathroom of polished granite and marble with double gleaming white porcelain sinks, a marble Jacuzzi tub, and a separate oversize shower stall behind a glass wall. The four strategically mounted nozzles spouted jets of hot water, massaging the fatigue from her body.

Having towel-dried herself and briskly dried her hair under ceiling heat lamps, she slipped into the oversize clothes Ray had left for her. Barefoot, she padded downstairs to the kitchen, where she found Ray feeding Thor.

While she realized that her thoughts were sexist, she was surprised to be looking at a bachelor's home that was absolutely spotless. *Impeccable* was a better description. The entire interior smelled like fresh mountain flora. Nuna figured that Bryce had a serious cleaning service.

* * *

The following day, Austin, along with a couple of hardened yet sympathetic undercover agents from the FBI and DEA, requested that she accompany them and drove her back to the crime scene and remnants of her home. She was greeted by the scorched outline of the roof against the blue azure sky; her heart sank as she swallowed hard with fear and trepidation. Blinking away incipient tears, she steeled herself, remembering the house as it was. All her worldly possessions—car; computer; photographs of her childhood, college, and her parents—were lost. With the exception of her life, she had lost everything. With the grace of her God, she wasn't going to lose Bryce.

Tears pressed against her eyes as she got out of the car and began walking slowly up the hill with the assistance of Austin. She began sifting through the rubble, hoping to find something to salvage out of the mayhem. Everything was gone. What little remained offered scant evidence that her home had stood in that spot. TV camera crews, having been shepherded to the other side of the river, were filming the scar of burnt earth from the street below, barred from coming any closer. Crime scene tape cordoned off the yard from the street and adjacent yards, but Austin lifted it for Nuna to skirt under and followed suit. It stung her hard as she stoically looked upon a brutalized skeleton of her house, now in a rutted lawn surrounded by burned and scorched fauna.

A team of FBI agents, along with the Gauley Bridge sheriff, fire marshal, and West Virginia State Police captain, were already there going through the burnt-out shell and clearing the carnage of any evidence of a shoot-out and the fatalities that had taken place. The Gauley Bridge sheriff stood a couple of feet from her and asked if she had any relatives in the area or a place to stay.

She lowered her head and began silently crying. Who? She asked herself. She had no living relatives that she knew of; having recently moved to Gauley Bridge, she didn't have a single friend she could call on. "No," she said. "There's no one." She shook her head sadly.

Austin, walking back from conversing with a couple of agents, noticed her distress and quickly came to her aid, informing the sheriff that
from this moment forward, any and all questions related to her or the
crime scene would have to be communicated through the FBI office
in Charleston. A hazmat team was working with the fire department
cleaning up kitchen and garage chemicals in the aftermath. A lone sharp-
shinned hawk perched on a power line with watchful eyes as a broad-
winged hawk soared in the thermals above.

Nuna shed more tears as she stared at the burnt remains and realized
that she had lost all her belongings in the fire, including cherished memories of her past. She always loved the street in front of her house with its
antique gas-lamp-style streetlights. The gingerbread houses were set back
from the sidewalk, usually with a discreet white picket fence marking the
property lines. The backyards were less peaceful with railroad right ways
carved into the landscape by active coal-train tracks running south to
north out of town.

The police photographs of the scene had been taken by the time of
their arrival. The bodies of her next-door neighbor Kate and the would-
be assassins had been quickly and quietly removed last night and sent to
the morgue in Charleston for temporary storage. The local police had
located Bryce's jeep and contacted Austin for instructions. Any evidence,
in terms of bloodstains or the grim carnage that had taken place on the
lawn, had been washed clean. The fire marshal confirmed that the fire
was arson, having found a couple of empty cans of gasoline in the back
rooms of the house. A knot of people—neighbors, curious seekers, and
passersby—peppered both sides of the street outside the yellow tape in
the aftermath, asking questions of the posted uniformed officers denying
them access. All were being told that there had been a house fire last
night and that no one was home when it happened.

Nuna couldn't believe her eyes. The house she had cherished just a
couple of months before had now been reduced to a burned-out shell in
a muddy quagmire. Everything that she owned had gone up in flames.

The following day, the *Fayetteville Tribune* ran a short, bare-bones article on the third page covering the Gauley Bridge house fire. It simply reported that there had been a house fire and that the fire marshal of Gauley Bridge had suggested that the fire was most likely caused by an electrical short in the basement and while it was a complete loss, there were no injuries.

With the assistance of Glenn, Austin quietly terminated both Bryce's and his own hotel agreements, vacating the suites. The following day, they packed and removed all of Bryce's gear and personal belongings from the hotel. Together, over a cup of coffee, they fieldstripped Bryce's glock, taking their time to clean it to pristine condition. Having used his badge and federal authority, Austin had quickly secured the weapon on the ground and blocked the local police from taking the glock as evidence in the shooting of the two men. He would be relocating to one of the five guest rooms in Bryce's house. Being that the hoes was located on the top of a mountain and forty miles closer to Maduro's residence, it would enhance his ability to create algorithms in his digital netherworld to monitor Maduro's communications with his array of high-tech satellite computer enhanced audiovisual equipment.

He quickly began accumulating significant correspondence between Hugo, his offshore shell companies, and his associate in Cuba. Austin also added extra electronic protection inside the house, should it be needed. He was well aware that it was Nuna that was the intended target, not Bryce. Rather, Bryce was in the right place at the right time. Glenn was to stay away from the hospital and continue deep undercover surveillance at the Maduro compound.

The following day, Austin completed the relocation of his equipment to the room at the back of Bryce's home overlooking the forested mountains. He organized and reset his surveillance equipment, which now overlooked Slaty Forks via satellite. His six computers were on laminated tables monitoring activities closely and logging data from multiple locations, including those coming in from satellites monitoring activities on both Norman's Cay and Puerto Rico. All of it coming in from Langley and being recorded to his command center at a rapid pace. When not walking the grounds and conversing with the agents on the perimeter, Austin was sitting in a swivel chair in front of the computers, digesting and logging the info crossing the screens.

CHAPTER 41

Nuna, having lost her home in Gauley Bridge and with Bryce needing her to help him get back on his feet, had taken up residence in a guest room next to Bryce's. She wasn't even considering cohabitation, but Bryce was in serious need of attention and Ray, sprouting a benign smile, had insisted on ensconcing her in Bryce's home to look after him. She knew that this arrangement also afforded her maximum protection as someone was out to kill her.

The horrible memories of that night tore through her mind. As much as she wanted to, she realized there was no escaping the horrific moment of terror at her house. The face of evil lurking in the world had once again, in a pregnant instinct, invaded her life without warning.

With the exception of the blue-striped hospital patient suit she was still wearing, she had nothing, not even a toothbrush to call her own.

"Ray, I appreciate y'all letting me stay here till I find another place of my own. I really do. Thank you," she said. Then, without getting too maudlin, she kissed Ray's ruddy cheek as they sat at the kitchen table. Nuna sipped her coffee and set the cup down carefully, though her fingers trembled somewhat as she inhaled deeply and savored the tangy scent of cedar all around her.

Quietly, she had also become a loving nurse of Bryce's sandpaper jaw in the morning as she gently tiptoed to his bedside crooned and laved him with a warm soapy wash cloth and towel. With her hand, she brushed back a few vagrant strands of his hair from his forehead. Having listened to her footfalls, he said, "I could get used to this," adding a little levity to the moment. She laughed, bending down and giving him a loving kiss. She was still awestruck by his seminakedness, her eyes taking in every nuance of his corded muscular frame, and she was still shocked by the purple scars that dotted, meandered across, and crisscrossed down his chest, back, and legs. His chest and stomach, now wrapped in fresh bandages she had debrided earlier, were rock hard and now partially covered in dark curly hair that was stretched out taut across his abdomen. His legs were solid muscle and tanned like the rest of him, which made her mouth water. He had seven older bullet wounds, two shrapnel wounds on his legs, and now two new bullet wounds, one stab wound, and a dozen scars on his back, seemingly from what looked like a barbed whip.

He grinned. "I've been around a bit, but it isn't all that bad once you get used to it."

"I wouldn't have expected it," she replied honestly.

Bryce and Nuna smiled at each other. It had been a long time since she had given so much thought to the male anatomy, but she was now fully aware of the latent strength beneath his rugged bronze skin.

Her summer tan had faded, and her eyelids were now heavy. The recent events had taken their toll, but hopefully the horrific memory would recede.

Ray had taken the liberty to light a fire in the huge stone fireplace in the great room and give her and Austin a cursory tour of the sprawling, airy, rough-hewn loft-style house. He made sure that she knew where everything in the place was and had everything she needed, including a toothbrush and all the other necessities. Then he bade her good night, affording her some coveted breathing room on the couch. She gently patted Ray's arm, smiling good night to him. Austin also rose and said good night as he was turning in also.

"Good night, Austin," she said, "and thank you both for everything."

Nuna opened the damper a little more and added a couple more logs, stacking them to allow for airflow. It wasn't long before they began to catch, and she added a third. Within a couple of minutes, the oak logs were giving off heat, and she stretched out on the floor before the fire holding and hugging Thor. He had cuddled up next to her and put his head in Nuna's lap. Stroking the dog's smooth head was comforting to him, but Nuna knew it was good for her too. The flickering fire made shadows dance around the huge open room. This wasn't her first rodeo with the operation of a fireplace.

They stared into the fire for a few more moments. The fury of the fire had abated and now leisurely worked on the blackened logs with only a few blood red embers remaining.

* * *

Thor panted at her heels as he followed her movements around the house, wagging his tail. "Hey, boy." She scratched his head as she went to her knees. Thor took to her almost immediately, licking her face. She had forgotten how much she had loved dogs, a fait accompli.

The cedar house was huge, open, and airy. The cathedral living room wall was impressive at twelve feet high, with an exposed massive granite stone fireplace set between four floor-to-ceiling vertical windows offering a panoramic unobstructed one-thousand-foot vertiginous view of the New River Gorge and the spectacular white-water river below. It was like stepping into the pages of *Architectural Digest*. The house had been designed for comfort, convenience, and security, with not one amenity spared.

She stood silently, drinking up the scent of the wood. Through the bulletproof armored glass window, she spotted a bald eagle soaring above the river. A large thick glass coffee table sat before her with a fresh bouquet of flowers, uncluttered by not a single magazine. The mammoth gourmet kitchen with its dining area was professional-grade with its granite counters extending out. It was equipped with every conceivable built-in appliance one could dream of set on a terrazzo tile floor. Upstairs were five spacious bedrooms, all with polished hardwood floors and panoramic views, each with its own adjoining bathroom. Only three of the bedrooms had been furnished, one for Bryce and the other for Ray and the third for whoever stayed over. The furnishings in the sumptuous master bedroom were somewhat austere by her standards, but the beauty lay in their cozy starkness. The room was dominated by a California king bed that she was sure had never been slept in. It was still wrapped in the manufacturer's plastic.

In her own room, Nuna had taken note of the skylighted, high, sawed-wood-beamed ceilings, the large bay window overlooking the gorge, the large walk-in closets, and the oversize bathroom with a walk-in glass-enclosed shower. But nothing in the room detracted from the spectacular scenery beyond the picture window glass. Having lost everything she owned in the fire, she had nothing to deposit in her room.

Outside, behind a three-car garage, there was an awesome heated pool with a waterfall grotto connected to a hot tub churning bubbles. The sprawling, palatial home was built almost exclusively of glass and local hardwood, blending harmoniously with the forested setting. She had grown up in a modes home, and so this one felt light years away from what she was used to.

While the cordon of security was invisible along the rustic split-rail fence at the far end of the pasture, no one was able to encroach upon the home without FBI detection.

With Ryan watching over Bryce like a bald eagle over a fledging spring nest, she, with two undercover federal female officers at her side, was able to slip out early and go to Charleston to shop for clothes and other necessities at reasonably upscale boutiques and shops. She had lost her wardrobe, along with everything else, in the fire that night. Bryce, having noticed Nuna was wearing some of his clothes and that her hair was singed terribly by the fire, and only now realizing that she had lost everything in the fire, gave Austin instructions to get her taken care of immediately. Austin instructed the two federal officers to use their government credit cards and make Nuna whole again before the day's end.

"C'mon, this is an assignment to be enjoyed," said Karen, one of the two special agents assigned to protect Nuna 24-7.

The first task of the day was to find a salon and a stylist to salvage her scorched and singed hair. They found one, and before Nuna could object, the stylist began whacking and cutting the hanks of her blond hair. Having closed her eyes as she moved toward the shampoo basin, she glanced down and saw her former mane lying on the floor to be recycled into a wig. After seeing the carnage, she was moved over to one of the workstations for final shaping.

Over the sound of the hair dryer, the stylist said, "You're going to love your new look." She turned off the dryer, combed, sprayed, and made a few adjustments for Nuna and then placed a mirror in her hand. "Now look. You look beautiful, Nuna, and this is the perfect style for you."

Her hair fell to my shoulders, full and glossy, turning slightly at the ends. She looked into the mirror and blossomed. She loved it. The agents upped their tip, leaving a hundred dollars on the table to show their appreciation.

As they drove from one boutique to the next, she couldn't help but notice that the two officers were constantly checking their rear and side mirrors for any vehicles taking an overt interest in our vehicle. Austin, using his FBI status, had a new driver's license and a credit card issued to her by the end of the day. He had also made arrangement with the Gauley Bridge Police Department to release and deliver Bryce's jeep to the residence. Nuna, having lost her car in the fire, would be needing it now. Before leaving Fayetteville, the two agents made a quick stop at the Gauley Bridge Post Office and had Nuna's mail diverted to Bryce's address in Fayetteville. Bills still had to be satisfied.

Having returned to the house, she went to her room and closed the door. Feeling a growing pain in her heart, she sat down on the bed as tears threatened to explode from her. She let it happen.

Getting her emotions under control, she slowly began unpacking the few items she had purchased

The next day

The sun was up when Nuna awoke the next morning. She darted awake, suddenly aware of how late it was. She had things to do, and Bryce came first. While he was neat even by her anal standards and even had a cleaning lady in twice a week to dust, vacuum, et cetera, the house resembled a bachelor pad, with the iconic pool table in the dining room.

Why wouldn't it? she thought. Let's face it, he is a bachelor. An organized bachelor.

The only sign of what had been a family was framed photographs of him and his parents and a couple others at a youthful age with his grandparents. Other than a recent one of him, Ray, and Thor relaxing on the porch, that was it. Bryce didn't have much family left, and neither did she. Nothing on the walls gave a sense of his past life: no graduation pictures, no military medals under glass on display or pictures of him in uniform, no pictures of female friends from the past. Neat and memory free, his home was sparse but cozy. And there was certainly no evidence of his horrid wartime experience.

Having been given carte blanch by Bryce to decorate as she saw fit, she would be applying a woman's touch. Within a week of having met, Nuna and Maria, his cleaning lady, had turned the kitchen and dining room upside down and rearranged dishes, flatware, pots and pans, and everything else. Nuna liked Maria. She was feisty, forthright, and had her own aesthetic. Nuna asked Maria if she might be available to work several hours, five days a week, at the house. Maria, a middle-aged married Filipino with a young daughter at home, gave Nuna a big welcoming hug and graciously accepted the offer. Nuna looked at Maria and smiled warmly. Maria returned the look for a brief moment before lowering her head. She could only smile when she discovered that the dining room table covered with a large white tablecloth was actually Bryce's billiard table with a hardtop cover and a half dozen gray Samsonite folding chairs statically placed around it. In talking to Ray, Nuna had learned it had never been used either as a pool table or a dining table.

Given Bryce's profession, he needed more time and occasion to entertain. So Nuna decided that she would change this. Now, everywhere you looked, there was evidence of Nuna slowly waltzing barefoot and rearranging the internal landscape. Again, there was a striking feminine impact, including vases and bouquets of blossoming wildflowers from the gardens filling the house with heady fragrances. Several slowly dying houseplants rallied to her touch as she had watered them just right and moved them to better locations.

Around midafternoon, the two women decided to cook a gourmet dinner for everyone.

Maria made a luscious multicolored garden salad with a mustard vinaigrette topped with thinly shaved parmesan. Nuna boiled two boxes of pasta before draining and coating them with a fine coat of olive oil and stirring basil, oregano, and garlic into a thick tomato sauce. A delicious platter of twenty homemade meatballs was warming in the oven. It wasn't long before a divine marinara aroma filled the kitchen, magnetically drawing in both Ray and Austin to the dining/pool table. After dinner, with Austin providing surveillance assistance, all six FBI agents took turns leaving their station and coming to the kitchen table for a delicious hot meal complimented by chunks of warm Italian bread and ice-cold Southern ice tea.

Later that day, the surveillance supervisor gave them notice that this was the best surveillance operation he and his team had ever been on. "Thank you," he said.

Maria loved working with Nuna and commented to Ray that she was indeed the epitome of genteel Southern decorum.

Bryce had changed Nuna: she was no longer the shy and staid country girl she had been before meeting him at the Maduro gala. While she was still a West Virginia gal, her life in the last three months had taken on new meaning. She was going to savor the love and security that Bryce had brought into her world. Her love and devotion to him would forever be.

Later that evening, with the dishes cleared and having cleaned the kitchen with the help of Maria, Nuna quietly tiptoed into the bedroom to check on Bryce.

Unfortunately, under doctors' orders, he wasn't able to eat solid food yet. His bed stand light turned on; Thor was at the foot of the bed. Bryce was in his bed, looking all the more masculine. She stopped in front of him, her breath caught in her throat.

His eyes slowly opened, and he had that mischievous smile on his face as he was entranced with the cadence of her voice.

Nuna was placing feathery kisses no heavier than a butterfly in flight across his lips as she redressed his wounds, having already given him his nightly body washing.

"How did you feel when you woke up?" she said.

"I hurt all over," he said brusquely.

"The doctor said you would. Did Ray give you your painkillers?"

"He did, and I didn't argue with him."

"Good boy." She chuckled, looking at him askance as she was kneading his shoulders with capable hands. "How do you feel now?"

"Must be good drugs as I now feel all nice, warm, and fuzzy." Rolling slowly onto his side and pulling back the covers, he added, "Thanks for taking care of me."

She leaned down and kissed him on the lips. "I'm going to be staying real close to you, Bryce Tucker."

He let out an occasional grimace from time to time as the pain in his chest was still present. Holding up the covers, he patted the mattress, beseechingly favoring his wounded left side, occasionally grimacing at the pain. "Now, Nuna, and don't tell me you don't want to," he said with a twisted smile. "The doctor's instructions say I need to get some more rest and recharge my batteries. I want to do it knowing that you're lying on the bed beside me.

She couldn't refuse him and got up and shut the bedroom door, shedding all her inhibitions, undressing and slipping into her new chemise. She went willingly, yearning for his love and to feel secure in his arms. She only existed for him. She could feel the heat radiating from his body and seeping into her as she pulled the covers up and nuzzled, gently spooning up to him. Her fingers strummed the placket of his pajama top.

Bryce took her into his arms, holding her tenderly and ever so gently. Tears welled up in her eyes as he began to give her long, slow, sensual kisses, one right after the other. As she closed her eyes, he gently massaged the back of her head with his huge hand.

With her eyes closed and her head touching his, she said wearily, "Bryce?"

"Mmm?"

Her voice went up an octave as she blinked away tears. "I'm scared."

"I know you are. I am too."

Her voice faded to silence, and she fell fast asleep. Nuna had been caring for him 24-7 with little sleep, and she was fading. A fierce surge of protectiveness rippled through him; he knew he would do anything to see to it that she could sleep safely for the rest of her life.

Staring up at the ceiling, he knew only one way to keep her safe: to kill Hugo and take down all his henchmen, including the two senators. But first, he would follow orders and bring them all to justice. After that, their futures would be short-lived.

He downed a couple of pain pills with his bottle of water and, within a few minutes, drifted into a relaxing, deep, fuzzy sleep. Her fingers drifted across his stomach, not quite touching his manhood but flirting with the idea.

"Young girls can get in a lot of trouble doing that to men," he growled, keeping his eyes closed.

With a mischievous gamine grin, she giggled and quietly whispered. "That's what I'm counting on."

Her lips covered his carnally, silently before they both drifted to sleep.

A light drizzle and a dark gray sky accompanied the dawn.

CHAPTER 42

Seven weeks later

The weekly therapy and daily walks were improving Bryce's stride, and his stamina was also increasing. Nuna's care and patience during his convalescence had eliminated any possibility of atrophy. Since arriving home almost six weeks ago, he'd climbed gingerly out of bed only a few times to answer nature's call. Little by little, he began walking on legs that were lethargic from him lying down for weeks on end. In the quiet of the moment, he surveyed his injuries. The headaches had faded away, and he was thankful for that. There was still a tightness in his rib cage, but the pain was considerably less, and the ache of bruised muscle rose and fell with each breath.

Eight weeks later, unable to sleep, he poured himself two fingers of a double scotch and went outside, glancing toward the guest room's French doors. All was dark as he took a couple moments in the silence to stretch the soreness out of his muscles and joints. Standing against the railing, half-hidden in the shadows, he was in no hurry.

He gazed up at the sky; the waxing moon looked pale and low. The hanging rain clouds saturated the night air with moisture and brewing trouble, but he had yet to feel a drop. Instead, the atmosphere was electrically charged, and for sure, there was a storm brewing in the distance.

No sooner had the thought crossed his mind when a loud roar of thunder rolled through the mountains and a proverbially blinding flash of lightning sizzled across the darkened sky just above the mountaintops. Thunder rolled continuously, sounding both close and far away.

Hearing the huge crack of thunder, Nuna snapped into a sitting position just as a jagged bolt of lightning split the sky outside her window. Sliding out of her bed, still unfamiliar with the furnishings, she cautiously walked across the room, taking in the shadows and looking out the thick glass of the French doors. The wind was blowing angrily, howling and baying like a wolf at a full moon in a darkened sky. Suddenly, another fork of lightning, brilliant and buzzing with magnificent electricity, flashed majestically across the distant mountains.

That's when she spotted the silhouette of Bryce, limned by the bolt of lightning, standing foursquare on the deck before her. He was leaning against the deck railing, dishabille, bare-chested, barefoot, and audaciously looking straight at her with steamy lambent eyes, visually feasting on her soft sultry body.

He looked dangerously primitive with a grin that could have been Satan-inspired.

She was immediately arrested by the sight of him and felt a feminine orgasmic aphrodisiac wave embrace her; she couldn't move and seemingly went into full deer-in-the-headlights mode. Then, somewhere within her mind, she heard a whisper: "I like savagery and the lure of the forbidden." It was at that moment she wanted nothing other than to be cosseted, caressed, covered, conquered by this man.

Without a word, having unerringly zeroed in on her breast, he pushed himself away from the railing and sauntered toward her with a slow, measured, voracious, predatory gait radiating aggression.

So much for the chaste sleeping arrangements. Her carefully arranged resolve scattered. She was now shivering with sheer, unadulterated sexual desire.

They were right at this moment at the brink of consummation. Tears glistened in her eyes, and she swallowed visibly as she stared back at him.

His eyes made several rapid sweeps, taking a tour of her, then slowed to a leisurely casual search, drinking in every detail of her texture, shape, and color. She was wearing only a temptation of a silk ecru chemise that emphasized, rather than concealed, the swell of her voluptuous breasts, clinging to her like an affectionate ghost. The slithering silk molded to and delineated the delta between her thighs, contributing to the carnal seduction. Her spirit had never felt more elevated. She was ready to love and be loved. She didn't deter him. She wasn't going to be left on a sacrificial altar. She was going to be as untamed as a lioness, tawny, and provocatively savage.

She wasn't going to be idly submissive, and there would be no false modesty tonight. Her eyes skittered downward to his tented shorts. She now understood that being a good country girl was nothing more than a social trap. Dazzled and mesmerized by his arresting masculinity, she unlocked and swung open the sliding glass doors and began moving toward him in wild, feral haste in the midnight wind. With every primitive erogenous zone of her body exploding and on fire, she would satisfy her mate's lust. The sheer curtains billowed into the open room, filling like sails and capturing the coolness of the night air.

The lacy garment was gratuitous, evanescent, and came free, and he effortlessly peeled it away. She felt him stiffen and swallow hard as she blinked away tears. Then she felt his mouth, warm, wet, and loving. *Loving her.*

She moved toward him without the slightest compunction; her gossamer, unfettered breasts swayed with enticement, her nipples forming taut peaks. No longer tentative or hesitant, he delayed no longer. He had regained his strength and countenanced no resistance to Nuna. He took hold of her arm, pulled her toward him, framed her face with his large hands, and crushed his mouth to hers. The kiss was feral, provocative, hungry, possessive, demanding, and persuasive. There was no preliminary investigation, subtle teasing, or time for her to protest the onslaught coming even if she wanted to. Bryce forced his thrusting tongue between her lips and plundered her defenseless and responsive mouth over and over, feathering and caressing the roof of her mouth with his. He rapaciously devoured her, and she melted in his arms, returning his kisses with greed. And she didn't want to slow down. She wanted him with a ferocity that until now had been completely alien to her. The electricity passing through them became like two parts of a throbbing whole.

"Nuna. I want you so damn much." His warm, wet satin tongue brushed her navel and then her breasts until they were glistening with torturous pleasure. A flair of intensifying pleasure ran between her legs as she pressed and squirmed against him.

His strong fingers delved into her disheveled hair and held her head steady, forcing her eyes to look into his. His touch elicited delicious tingles all over her body. Her legs quivered and nearly turned to jelly, but he steadied and held her tight. Another kiss followed, just as urgent! She held her breath when he stepped out of his underwear. His erection bobbed upward, straining and rigid. The man was beautiful to look at.

His overpowering tongue claimed and plundered her mouth with a possessive fury, and she was more than ready for it. Her mind exploded in a riot of color and light as she welcomed the pillage and their bare torsos met. Her body was yearning for his virility, and her breathing and heart rate escalated. She felt the tendrils of desire twine through her.

He was so fucking hard, so fucking ready to ram his cock inside her mouth and then her womanhood. She was going to let him have whatever he wanted tonight.

Her arms slid under his, pulling his rippling abs against her breast tightly.

His agile tongue, working her dusty nipples, torched and inflamed every cell in her body, now surging with renewed life and riotous excitement. Her heart started pulsing as fast as the frenzied wind, and when he was within arm's reach, she threw herself at him, taking his face into her hands and tenaciously drawing his lips toward hers, the passion urgent, primal, untamed, and almost desperate.

Desperately wanting to please him, she shed all her inhibitions; tonight she was going to give him more than he could have ever dreamed for. Like him, she had become oblivious to everything except the undulating, swelling sensations of lust that had engulfed them. Never had she felt such raging want.

"Nuna, I want you!"

She bent her knee and provocatively nudged his groin. He was hard. "Hmm?"

He heeded her silent yearning and melded their lips together. His possessive tongue slid deep into her mouth and prowled at will, awakening her body in a potent, earth-shattering kaleidoscope of explosive desires.

Driven by a craving to get closer to him, she took unconscious steps toward him, her full breast rising and falling with accelerated breathing.

"I love how you laugh and how you make me laugh."

He put his hand on her waist and seesawed her up and down.

"I like the way your body is put together."

He lowered his head and nuzzled her ear.

"The shape of your luscious lips."

He worked her lips repeatedly until they parted, begging to be possessed.

He was bigger and stronger than she was, demanding, all muscle, unmistakably, overwhelmingly male, complete with washboard abs, and she wasn't going to let him escape. He didn't give her any other choice or chance to protest as he drew her up, pulled her into his muscled chest, and laced his fingers together on the back of her head. She slid down his chest and kneeled before him. Her mouth opened wide in anticipation of him gracing it with his huge, pulsing cock. Her overzealous tongue shamelessly flicked out to lick the bead of moisture off his tip, the flavor of his manhood exploding on my tongue. She moved her head up to face his.

"Nuna, tonight you're my woman."

"Yes," I panted, nuzzling into his groin. Tonight, she would unleash all her sexual fantasies on a man that she truly loved and make him her man. She shivered with incredible sexual pleasure as she opened her mouth wide and took his hot shaft deeper and deeper.

Bryce was definitely the aggressor, but Nuna was more than willingly compliant as she next entwined her arms around his neck and let her tongue riot deep inside his mouth. They were now breathing deeply in tandem without conscious thought.

She allowed him all the liberties he seemed to take as his due with unchivalrous fervor as he rapaciously devoured her neck, paying it homage. Hers was a greediness stemming from raw desire and unbridled deprivation. Her breast tingled, eliciting thrilling feverish sensations throughout her naked body as she luxuriated in the out-of-body experience against his. She ran her tongue across his shoulders and chest, carefully avoiding his wound. His mouth, so unapologetically hungry and consummately male, overwhelmed hers. His kiss was plundering, robbing her of any thoughts or regrets she might have had. They were like starving people who couldn't get enough of each other. Nuna wanted this man to fill her womanhood, ridding her of the emptiness in her life that she had endured for so long.

She could feel his stubble on her forehead. Their ardent kisses were intimate and sensuously erotic. His mouth was commanding as it conquered hers, robbing her of will. Nuna closed her eyes and reveled in the sensations his roaming fingers and soothing palms elicited.

Bryce splayed his hand across the small of her back, holding her flush against his chest, commanding without equivocation, "I want you now."

The kiss only deepened. His hands drifted from the outside of her arms down to their tender undersides, then to the shallows of her armpits and down the outer sides of her breast.

"Feel good?" he whispered.

"Oh yeah," she whispered in affirmation.

Their mouths dissolved together.

"Nuna, your breasts are beautiful, and your perfect nipples are delicate and sweet."

Nuna hadn't known kisses could be so adoring, unhurried, and so ardent as he continued to play upon her breasts.

She was swirling in an effervescent ocean of erotic feelings between her legs, morphing into a pulse of throbbing need.

He pulled her against the unyielding muscled wall of his chest with the force of the next roar of thunder, melding her body with his. She was enthralled by the warm security of his muscular hands, moaning in erotic supplication. A small, satisfied moan, like as birdcall, issued out of her throat as his hands slid in between her thighs, finding her pliant and moist. She purred and panted in contentment, and her breasts stood up full and firm, with her bewitching nipples proudly erect, begging for the merest attention. She felt the touch of her silk nightgown against his skin, the tautness of her nipples against him, and the dampness between her legs. The kiss he ground upon her mouth was both firm and dry and was as ruthless as the relentless wind outside. It claimed and explored every nuance of her mouth.

His hands were plundering her body in ways she had only dreamed about. She was just as insistent and hungry, kissing him full on the mouth, her tongue twirling around his, her arms wrapping around him, crushing him tightly against her breasts.

"Nuna, you're beautiful." His voice was low and deep, sending shivers down her spine.

It wasn't long before kissing her wasn't enough, and his hand moved to her waist.

"I want you, Nuna," he growled, his breath short and shallow.

As he rasped out the words "I'm going to fuck you," she trembled with arousal, and her breast heaved with remnants of fiery passion long since forgotten.

Purring her desire, she lifted her hips an inch above the mattress and wiggled out of her panties.

As she lay on her back, Bryce stretched out and positioned his body on top of hers, plowing his fingers through her thick flaxen pubic hair, and held her in place with his lips taking control of hers, their bodies meshing and molding in perfect harmony.

Nuna stared into his face with molten eyes and speechlessly nodded in silent acquiescence as she rhythmically massaged him between his thighs. Her eyes closed as he erotically massaged her breasts and kissed her nipples gently in a sensual cadence until he got the reaction he demanded. A primal moan escaped her lips, and her naked body writhed in lustful response. His sensual caressing between her thighs was bringing her to a pitch of arousal that she had never experienced before.

With Nuna's arms tightly holding on to him and her legs curling around his hips in an all-encompassing embrace, Bryce stepped inside and closed the doors to the steady thrum of rain hitting the glass doors, locking them behind him. Bright flashes of lightning streaking across the darkened sky outside glowed through the glass doorway, illuminating their silhouette. He kissed his way down her throat.

Her knees liquefied and went weak as a hot throbbing deep inside her screamed with abandon. She closed her eyes and tilted her head to one side, enabling him to feather her earlobe with his warm breath, and his tongue found and caressed the tender curve between her neck and shoulder on his way down her neck. He was much bigger than she was, far stronger, and he was giving her notice.

She was totally aroused with unbearable heat; her entire body was literally on fire.

"Oh God, I want you to fuck me, fuck me hard. Pleeeeeease," she cried. "Yes, yes," she moaned, begging him as her hips arched up to meet his thrust.

"Ah, Nuna," he groaned, lowering himself on top of her again. He buried himself in the welcoming silk of her womanhood. She felt his muscular spasms deep inside her.

Her legs went tight, convulsing around him reflexively with pleasure at the simple decadence of touching her warrior's body.

"Say you want me," he said, his fingers touching the warmth between her slender thighs, which bespoke an entreaty all their own.

"Yes, I do," she moaned as she went limp against his masculinity.

The moans and cries of pulsing ecstasy that raged between them rivaled the roar of the storm outside.

The touch of his marauding tongue on her nape sent a cataclysm of shivers of delight up and down her spine. Heat raced through her body like a flash fire. Her loins clenched with rioting arousal. Holding her hip bones and turning her into him, she went into shock as he kissed a path from her mouth down her body to her breasts. He licked and sucked at the peaks, working her into a frenzy before moving across her flat belly and going lower down the cleft between her legs and softly kissing her there. Using his mount and his aggressive tongue, he was igniting wildfires inside her like she had never experienced in her life. She was in a frenzy, writhing with helpless pleasure. He toyed with the sensitive area between her legs, savoring and enjoying the shivers that quaked her body as he tongued the shallow indention. Using his fingers, he slowly parted her folds, already slick from her arousal. He devoured her clit, savoring her feminine essence.

Nuna's world exploded with a kaleidoscope of lights. She knew she was ready—more than ready—for him. And if he didn't make his move soon, she was going to take matters into her own hands and ravish him until he begged her for mercy.

The heat. Oh God, the heat radiated from the forest of thick curly hair on his chest, titillating her nipples as she pressed her body against his, demanding and beseeching at the same moment in time. She was now making mewling sounds of pleasure. Bryce was kissing and stimulating her forbidden erogenous zones with a raw hunger that made her burn with intensity deep inside, driving her to the brink of delirium.

Lifting her, he masterfully carried her to the bed and laid her down. He was incredibly strong and self-confident. His massive hands settled around her lower back, over her taut and incredibly cute derrière, and he pressed his erection against her cleft. She felt the mattress sink with his body weight as he lay down beside her and curved his body. Removing one strap and then the other of her chemise, baring her firm breast. His mouth found her nipple; he closed his lips around it and madly laved it with his tongue. Soft moans escaped Nuna's parted lips until he silenced them with his.

She smiled and adjusted her position on the bed to make her breasts more accessible.

She traced her curled fingertips down the hard flesh of his chest, caressing and filling her palm with his thick forest of hair.

He was aroused. "Nuna, Nuna, Nuna, I want you.

So was she, and she was burning inside erotically. "Oh my God, Bryce…yes, yes, yes," she cried out.

She made a slight sound of abject surrender into his ear as his fingers moved down over her taut, flat stomach and brushed over her sensitive spot, and when he did it the second time, she turned to jelly and melted in his arms. Bryce gently lowered himself over her until they were chest to breast, masculine muscle to feminine softness, rolled her onto her back, and braced himself over her with his elbow, staring into her eyes.

"No one will ever love you the way I will."

She quaked as his tentative fingers probed her womanhood.

His right knee insinuated its way between her thighs. It met no resistance as she lay with a pulsating heart in an attitude of breathless anticipation of his sensual persuasion. She arched her malleable body to his, wrapping her legs around him, feeling his unquestioning current of blissful affection, and pulled him into her body.

"Prove it. Bring out the beast."

He took her hand and placed it on his manhood.

After a couple more seconds, her silk crotch-grabbing camisole in tatters, they were both naked, and she took hold of his rock-hard masculinity. His arms pulled her closer, her ample breasts swelled against his chest, and her ruby nipples tightened and yearned.

She cried out, tremors exploding inside her, her fingers and toes tingling with excitement, and she gave him everything she had. As he covered her with his body, she felt the massive throbbing evidence of his manhood against the insides of her thighs, filling her completely.

She welcomed the weight of his body atop hers and his moans of gratification.

He gave it all back and more.

He weighed 225 pounds, and she wanted every ounce of it on top of her. His hand was cupping her surging breast, caressing her, and she was quaking and melting inside.

The ferocity of the storm was fully upon them now. The fierce wind howled. Lightning flashed, and thunder cracked. Rain fell in torrents, with sheets pounding against the French doors. They were mindless of it all. His caresses went on and on until she was spinning in geysers of erotic sensation all along her nerve endings.

He made a low, erotic sound and began cupping, caressing, and kneading her breasts; she wasn't going to do anything to stop him. Instead, she pressed against his six-pack abs and offered herself whole to him.

"Nuna, you're by far the most beautiful, courageous woman I've ever known." She stared wistfully at Bryce as he whispered loving endearments and accolades.

Her cool, ethereal beauty turned haunting in the moonlight that slid through the curtains. Where did he come from, and how did I get this lucky? she thought. "Make love to me, Bryce," she cried as she raised her mouth toward his, blindly seeking his lips. She called out his name as she came with an intensity that she had never even begun to imagine she was capable of.

Involuntarily, her naked hips pressed against his solid manhood with all the fervor of her passion, bringing his hardness fully against her. The contact was electrifying, and she rode him with escalating intensity. She was experiencing the most erotic throbbing feelings she had ever felt in her life. A hot, intoxicating, pheromone-infused tide of sexual excitement spread through every cell of her body.

Bryce said nothing as he reached for her, pulling her naked body against his chest with a pang of desperate hunger, his fingers lightly caressed her pussy lips, inciting a raging desire. Nuna moaned with every cell in her body, responding to Bryce's touch. She clutched at him as he expertly sucked her nipples and ran his tongue down her belly all the way to the distended heart of her sexuality. He reawakened her femininity with his tongue, and she fell back under his body and let his weight consume all of her grasping cries of pleasure.

Nuna felt the warmth of his fingers and the wetness of his tongue and cried out with joy when he knelt between her thighs and thrust himself into her, impaling her with urgency replacing delicacy as he rocked inside her all the way to her womb. She was blinking frantically as she became oblivious to everything except him. She lost focus and now felt wild and insatiable. Gradually, almost reluctantly, she felt her body building to a climax and desperately tried to fight it, to prolong the moment of arousal as long as possible until it was no longer something she could control. Bryce's slow and controlled yet relentless plunges into her rendered her mindless with burning desire. Finally, she cried out again, her nails digging into the flesh of his buttocks, pulling him deeper inside her. She writhed beneath him, moaning. Bryce had made sure that she climaxed before him.

Seconds later, impossible-to-bridle, uncontainable, Bryce allowed himself to climax. Again, she felt his warm cataclysmic release surging deep inside her as she squeezed him tight.

"Deeper," she cried. He drove deep inside her one last time and finally, shuddering, found his own release. She began to shake uncontrollably, gasping with every thrust before letting out a long cry of lust.

Replete, they collapsed against one another, his head lying against her breasts, her legs wrapped around him as she snuggled against his naked body, fondling his firm nipples. Lying on her back, she bucked upward, her hands flying to his head, digging in her nails, gulped in the air, praying that her heart wouldn't burst out of her chest.

Their bodies were covered in a thin coating of well-deserved sweat, and she was grinning like a crazy loon looking at him as she curled one of his chest hairs with her finger.

"Nuna, you're insatiable."

Mirth shone in her eyes, and she held him tightly. "And aren't you the lucky one. Take me again, Bryce." She squirmed underneath him, begging.

Bryce's eyes were closed, his breathing slowly returning to normal. He held her tightly until the aftershocks gracefully dissipated. "Nuna, I love you," he said and kissed her with love and with a warm passion.

"Seems like it was as long in between for you as it was for me," she said, her lungs still gasping as he nuzzled her breasts, her legs wrapped around his waist, her fingers holding on to his mane.

She lifted her quivering breasts for his delectation, her hips wide for his for his taking. "Take me again, Bryce!"

As she looked beyond his scars, his dark, glistening tan looked golden, and his broad shoulders, powerful back, corded arms, narrow hips, tight ass, and long, strong-looking legs were beyond anything she could have dreamed of to have in bed. Nuna ran her finger down his leg, stopping at the pink raised scar on his thigh, where he had taken a bullet that nicked his femoral artery during the war. As he turned to look at her, she saw his huge biceps sported military tattoos, but his full-frontal chiseled chest with some pronounced six-pack abs really fascinated her. Bryce exuded magnetic energy and was absolutely all male where it counted. She couldn't take her eyes off him.

The nuances of his kisses had become an excruciating addiction to her, and she wanted more. Docilely, she offered her mouth for his carnal pleasure. But she was insatiable. Finally, she couldn't take the torment anymore. With a mischievous glint in her eyes, she pushed him onto his back, straddled him, perching her firm derriere on him, and then proceeded to drive him insane. Nuna straddled his hips, impaling herself on him, while his hands pressed against her waist, moving her gently up and down, each time driving her in deeper, deeper, and penetrating her by smaller escalations of urgency until there was a tiny wail rising out of her throat. When they had reached the pinnacle of ecstasy and she finally climaxed, she collapsed on top of his ample and perfect body.

"Bryce," she sighed in a state of euphoria replete with love, "I'll remember this night forever."

The rain from the heavens above continued through the night, and so did their copulation.

Following the sublimity of the evening of romance and sex, Bryce was haunted by the lingering scent of Nuna's intoxicating perfume. For several long moments afterward, they lay next to each other exhausted, spent, in blissful devastation. Then, having pulled the sheet up over them, they fell asleep entangled and coiled in each other arms, exhausted and spent from a breathless evening of lovemaking that was long overdue.

He swore in a hoarse whisper to himself the sorry bastard would not be hurting her again.

Deliciously languorous, they held each other and fell into a brief rest

He woke drowsily an hour or so later, finding Nuna looking at him. He turned, levered himself on his elbow, and looked down at her. "Was I rough?" he asked with loving concern.

"No," she whispered as she looked at him and gently touched the scar on his eyebrow with her fingertip. "Bryce, no one has ever made love to me like you did tonight. My nipples are still quivering from the treatment you gave them."

She leaned over and kissed him. He was totally depleted and totally spent. She sliced her fingers through his hair before they drifted into a deep postcoital bliss after a joyous night of sex.

They rose late the next morning, sated, stark naked, basking in a remnant of satiated postcoital glow. They showered together, taking turns soaping each other under the steaming water. Within minutes they were having sex again as the water sluiced over them. A thought crossed her mind. Had Bryce seduced her, or had she seduced him? Never in her life had she had a night of incredible sex with a man she was now falling in love with and climaxed five times.

Standing in front of the bathroom mirror, she couldn't help but notice that her breasts were chafed in several spots where Bryce's stubble had abraded her. Instead of feeling angry, she melted at remembering his masculine aggression and intoxicating kisses. Her face bore further traces of lovemaking and required a touch of makeup. For the first time in years, she was actually thinking of the future in optimistic overtures.

Her window was open, and there was a bright, breezy late-July Appalachian mountain fragrance of rhododendrons and mountain laurel wafting in the air. Without opening her eyes, just a little bit disoriented, she reached over and groped his hard, masculine shoulder as she listened to the soft rhythmic cadence of his breathing. Then, opening her eyes, she smiled, rolled over, and burrowed voluptuously against his furry chest, making herself smaller and needier in his warm embrace. She didn't utter a word as there was nothing either could say that the other didn't already know. Bryce wrapped his arms around her, embracing and cocooning her just long enough for time to evaporate. Snuggled in his arms, she was daydreaming about last night and was instantly mortified as she kneaded his body. She had told Bryce that she had never had an unbridled orgasm until last night and that he was the only man she had slept with since losing her husband.

"Don't worry," he said. "Many, many, many more to come," he added as he feasted on her glistening nakedness. Bryce was insatiable, giving and demanding with each thrust, and continued forever. Bryce was an animal, and she had quickly learned that she was too.

Bryce fell asleep, her breath synchronized with his with a replete sigh, and she, too, fell into a deep sleep. They'd earned it.

Nuna knew that the night was far from over as she felt tiny capsules of energy exploding inside her, filling her body with enthusiasm for living. She couldn't sleep anymore and slowly emerged from the postcoital glow, wiggling out of his embrace and touching the floor. Her body was tingling with a new, electrifying sensation of life. This night had spoiled her. She now needed his strength during the night and the security of his arms, to listen to the sound of his breathing. She wanted this intimacy to last forever.

She was lying face down on top of the sheet with her face turned toward him, and he ran his hand down her back and over the rise of her butt. "Women don't understand how beautiful they are. They don't understand it. They get beauty confused with personality, charisma, or a friendly smile. They don't see the simple beauty of this." His hand glided again over her bottom. "It's a goddamned tragedy that you can't see it. And it's just so beautiful."

She pulled up the sheets as they cuddled and began to cool in a slow, almost timeless, ecstatic, magical rhythm. It was the most wonderful feeling Nuna had ever experienced. She yawned broadly and lay there a moment longer, utterly sated, her body deliciously sore, before considering getting up. Pushing the fresh sheets back, she slowly swung her feet to the floor and vaulted off the sanctuary of the bed to the bathroom shower. She shook her mane as she stepped into the shower and let the hot water work its magic. Then, with her lustful passion now temporarily slaked, she left the bathroom and quietly approached the front of the bed, taking in the heavenly image of Bryce seemingly still asleep with a mischievous smile, unabashedly stark naked. He was her man. She smiled and winked mischievously at the beautiful man before her.

Scampering barefoot into the bathroom again, she stood before the mirror, checking herself out. Running a brush through her wet, wild mane of hair wasn't doing much to alter the fact that she had experienced a fantastic night of never-to-be-forgotten sex. Her breast hurt with pent-up emotion. Several minutes later, she dressed in a pair of her new jeans, put on a new sweatshirt, and padded her way down the hall to the kitchen. She wore no makeup.

The world as she knew it was fading. She was in love and had been transported into Bryce's sphere, where he ruled and dominated every twinkling star in her universe. The lonely life she had lived by herself without warmth, color, or love was now behind her.

I'm sure it's illegal to be this happy, she thought.

The communion was immediate and forever.

She turned around and looked back at him with luminescent eyes. He was the man she had always dreamed of and wanted; tall, powerful, hard as granite, intelligent, soft, and humorous. The union of their bodies had been both erotic and glorious. The view of his hard cock pretty much cemented her desire to spend the rest of her life right there between his legs.

She looked as though she had just been thoroughly fucked, which caused her to smile. Very thoroughly, to tell the truth, she thought. She snuggled into his side and pillowed her head on his shoulder. He stroked a finger over her cheek. "Go to sleep, baby," he said, his body blanketing her, warm and so reassuring. They both felt secure and comfortable, like they'd been lovers for years. They molded.

An electrifying thrill of anxiety and the delicious echo of erotic pleasure pulsed through her. She now had the awesome feeling of being a real woman. *Bryce's woman.*

The morning dawned warm, clear, and bright. Bryce was awakened by the aroma of fresh coffee and breakfast on the stove. He put on his housecoat and slippers and went down the hall to the kitchen. Nuna was lost in thought at the counter, wearing his apron, singing cheerfully to herself, preparing breakfast. She was prancing barefoot around his kitchen, apparently playing the role of the happy vixen housewife with aplomb. Looking over at him as he stood on the threshold leaning against the doorjamb, filling the doorway, she smiled.

"Ah, Sleeping Beauty awakens," she said, smiling.

She had quietly slipped out of bed an hour earlier. Having performed a cursory ablution of her face and hands, she had then brushed her teeth and haphazardly brushed her hair, putting it into a ponytail with the only barrette she had.

"Mmmmmmm. Something wafting from the kitchen smells delicious, besides you, of course," Bryce said softly, giving her a predatory grin. "Sex has a unique way of giving one an appetite."

In self-introspection, he was confident that no man, not even Chris, had kissed her with the same degree of intimacy that he had. No one knew the taste of her lips as he did.

They laughed at each other like naughty children who shared a secret of having committed some playful transgression and gotten away with it.

Indeed, they had.

"The coffee smells good."

"How would you like your eggs?" she asked. "Scrambled or sunny-side up?"

"Scrambled," he said with a kiss to the back of her head.

The dining room table was set for three. Austin had yet to come down.

She whirled around in the kitchen, laying out a spread of pancakes, cornmeal grits, English muffins, and scrambled eggs with Canadian bacon, set down a mug of coffee on a trivet.

"Delicious!" he pronounced after taking his first bite. "Where did you learn to cook like this?"

"My mother taught me the basics, and I took it from there with a cooking class in college."

"I'm sure you were at the top of your class," he said. "You're not eating breakfast with me?"

"No, I've been nibbling a little bit of this and that," she said, pointing to the sausage, bacon, and home fires. "Watching my waistline."

"Nuna, I've been watching it for you, and you don't have any reason to worry." Watching her at the stove as she tended the skillet, he noted that she was stunning from the back as she was from the front. "What waistline?"

She laughed and sank into a chair next to him.

They sat at the kitchen table for almost an hour with an easy camaraderie growing between them. They talked about everything and nothing. Finally, she told him that she had become her father's cook after her mother passed away.

It was like they had known each other for a very long time and the effervescence was growing. They talked about the past, the present, and everything in between. She was gradually allowing herself to understand that she and Bryce were becoming a couple. Bryce was feeling the same and, for the first time in his life, wanted a real commitment, a commitment that went beyond the bedroom.

As he watched her from the table, she began again busying herself, putting together a series of breakfast platters of scrambled eggs, bacon, sausage, peppery golden home fries, grits, and a stack of pancakes with fresh coffee in new thermoses provided by Ray for the federal security agents outside. For the next half hour or so, she walked back and forth carrying covered platters to each of the seven FBI agents at the front perimeter facing the river and the backyard, which was five acres wide. Ray took care of the two federal agents at the bottom of the mountain, joining them for breakfast at daybreak.

"Bryce, I've been doing this since the day you were brought home three and a half weeks ago. Ray and Wanda, the female FBI agents, have also taught me daily lessons and how to shoot your glock 19M, should I need to protect you."

"I've gotten pretty good, so they all tell me. I also now have a federal license to carry. Bryce," she said with tears in her eyes, "I will protect you with my life if I have to."

Bryce couldn't help but give her a warming smile.

He pulled her up close, wrapping his arms around her, and gave her a loving hug. "Nuna, in the short time you've been here, you've done wonders in this house, and it feels so right having you here."

Bryce, unfamiliar with waking up in the guest room, uncoiled from the twin bed and did his morning pandiculation before the sliding glass doors, looking out across the backyard. With the eyes of an eagle, he quickly spotted the faint glint of an FBI agents binoculars at the far corner of the forest perimeter. Then, picking up a pair of binoculars off the end table, he quickly located a second agent about 100 to 150 yards out, standing upright in Ray's elevated deer blind. Security was tight, but at the moment, both agents were casually scoping a pair of yearling bucks carousing in the open field before heading back into the thicket.

Outside, bright sunlight was already filtering through the trees and casting wavering patterns against the house. Birds were chirping happily with squirrels chasing each other across the lawn. Blue jays and robins reminded him of brightly feathered arrows as they darted in and out of the trees.

He had awakened this morning with a nagging sense of something left undone that could have potentially serious consequences. His personality type contradicted sitting on his ass for very long.

While he was a dangerous man, he was also low-hanging fruit.

CHAPTER 43

Bryce knocked softly at Nuna's door. Having already dressed, she opened it quickly. She was freshly bathed and fragrant with shampoo and Dove soap.

"I've been waiting for you, Bryce. I walked past your room a couple of minutes ago," she said as he entered. I overheard you talking on the phone. No. Don't tell me. I won't ask; I know: *when the time is right.*

"Bryce, you don't have to explain yourself to me," she said querulously. "I already know who you are. Austin has already told me that you and he are both CIA special agents working with the DHS."

Bryce sat down on the couch, marshaling his thoughts. He had been dreading this moment.

There was an awkward moment of silence. She noticed that all jocularity had faded from his face. She looked at him askance. The corner of his mouth lifted in a semblance of a smile, but the expression on his face was dead serious and his gaze inscrutable. Bryce had decided to forego the subterfuge any longer and apprise her of the status of the current investigation. Hindsight was nobody's friend, least of all his.

"Nuna, hear me out. He didn't tell you all of it," he said gravely. "Look at me," he continued, barely above a whisper. "Please, just hear me out." Nuna looked at him in an attitude of listening. "Yes, we're both CIA special agents, but we're also deep undercover agents. So what I'm going to say to you has to remain confidential. Is this agreeable?"

Nuna stared at him in perplexity. "Yes, absolutely," she responded stoically.

Bryce took a deep, labored breath, marshaling his professionalism, his voice rueful at first, then spoke as best he could in a strong portentous voice of eminent authoritative reasonableness, parsing his words. He desperately wanted to censor himself but could no longer. Of course, he would have to lend plausibility to the implausible story he was about to tell her, sparing any sensitive disquisitions on the mission. His occupation did carry certain strictures.

Bryce laid a file on the table and began foisting out photos of the Manduro facilities and operations both in West Virginia and the Bahamas and incontrovertible evidence of criminal operations as precisely as he could, in a composed voice, without any irrelevant platitudes or other information compromising the operation.

Desensitized to violence, he laid out the facts the way a mason laid his bricks, methodically, one at a time.

Nuna had a look of incomprehension on her face. She listened avidly as he described the various aspects of Maduro's modus operandi—his documented pattern of gun running, money laundering, kidnapping, human trafficking, rape, torture, and murder.

"Nuna, two of our agents were sent down here last year undercover to investigate the Maduro operation. Unfortunately, both disappeared without a trace. Their tortured bodies were just recently found floating in a river. Well, I think the time is right," he said, and he immediately felt a burden on his conscience being lifted, almost a physical sensation of finally being able to breathe deeply after so long being deprived of oxygen.

Nuna was listening with rapt attention. The look on his face communicated the gravity of the situation: he was about to give her a sobering, unvarnished summary of his mission.

Bryce pulled a thin leather wallet from his pocket, flipped it open, and handed it to her. A gold badge with a blue, red, and white Department of Justice emblem was in the center. It also contained a photo of Bryce identifying him as *Special Agent Captain Bryce Tucker, FBI, Special Operations Division.*

"This is who I am," he said curtly.

All her trepidation drained as she handed the wallet back to him. There was no escaping the situation; he was about to unravel his secret.

"It almost looks like you're staking me out," she said.

"Well, that's what I'm here to talk to you about."

"Pray tell," she said in her Southern West Virginia accent, batting her eyelashes and grinning.

Choosing his words carefully, he spoke, telling her of things that he had kept pent-up for months. The last thing he wanted to do was obfuscate his purpose by explaining it too rapidly.

Finally, he confided that he had a mission: to infiltrate the Maduro organization, capture and arrest Hugo and his associates, and then precipitate the dismantling of the organization. "It's a indubitable fact that Hugo Manduro is the mastermind behind the crime syndicates, and he and he alone put the smuggling and distribution system together and enforced it all with an iron fist."

Bryce brought Nuna through the mosaic of incontrovertible evidence against Hugo. She listened, wide-eyed, taking it all in. Then she got to her feet and began pacing the room.

The operation was top secret due to Congressional sensitivities, which needed a nucleus on which he could focus all his energy. It didn't lend itself to a swift and fatal attack, at least not yet. Instead, it was mercurial, constantly changing. It was a multilayered and complex conundrum involving families, businesses, individuals, money, power, and emotions. A complicated mix as it involved two senators, one from Kentucky and the other from right there in West Virginia.

Pensive, she shook her head in disbelief. She went to the dressing table and, visibly distraught, began fumbling with her small black leather handbag, rummaging through it, finally pulling out a lipstick tube. She applied a dab of color, blotted her lips with a tissue, then put the lipstick back.

"I realize that there's no such thing as a guarantee of privacy anymore. Still, I'm shocked that the government had the utter gall and cavalier disregard for my privacy to investigate and create a file on me. I thought it might.

"Bryce, why are you really here?" She exhaled resignedly.

"It's a long, complicated story," he responded. "Nuna, first, how did you get involved in the Maduro investment operation?"

"I swear to you, Bryce," she said, shaking her head in disbelief, "that I didn't know the actual operations of the Maduros."

Then, thinking there was nothing to lose, she told him her entire story. "While I've come to believe they can be despicable, I would have never thought them drug dealers, murderers, and sex traffickers."

How could she have been so naïve? Why hadn't she even questioned where their money was being generated? Not once did it occur to her that it might be criminal. She had been so dazzled by the job, and their magnetism, that she hadn't thought of looking beyond the obvious. She had felt privileged to be under the tutelage of such a global businessman. The warmth they had shown her in the early days of her employment was a sham.

"Nuna, tell me a little about your personal life."

Her gaze became opaque. Nuna, now with a drawn, wilted look on her face, closed her eyes as they welled up in tears. Softly, she answered; her tone became wan.

"I'm sure you and the CIA already know that I don't have many friends. But you can be assured that it wasn't always that way. I was actually quite popular in college and got along well with my classmates. I had my small special group of friends, the ones you would spend all night chatting with, eating pizzas and discussing boys. For personal reasons, I kept my private thoughts to myself as I didn't have much angst regarding male relationships. While I kept in touch with a couple of girlfriends after getting married, I let them drift after my husband was killed in Vietnam. There were other reasons also. My husband, before enlisting, became antisocial, and we never seemed to go anywhere with others.

"I would sometimes wonder if he had stopped loving me. There wasn't a whole bunch of arguing or physical confrontations and never any unkindness. Just a slow fade from sunshine to gray and then blackness as the intensity of his obsessions seemed to be escalating like a disaster about to happen."

Nuna explained her recent explosive encounter with Hugo and Maria earlier in the week and her resignation from the bank. She couldn't imagine a worse day, but unknown to her, it was about to come. She also explained to Bryce that during the past month, she had received strange phone calls during the course of the night, after midnight. When she reached over to pick up the receiver, all she heard was some heavy breathing before the phone went dead.

"Nuna, again, my assignment is to dethrone Hugo Maduro and the entire insidious Maduro operation, ending his unmitigated evil empire globally and here in West Virginia. Having never been arrested in the United States or even charged with a crime, he is associated with suspicion and insurmountable evidence of criminal activity. Hugo Maduro, a shady character, is the linchpin figure linked to everything from counterfeit money to money laundering, drugs, human trafficking, illegal organ transplants, prostitution, pornography, extortion, arms sales, and other contraband.

"Hugo Maduro is a ruthless, blithe, dangerously evil force with no moral scruples or integrity," he opined. "None whatsoever. My job is to thwart the nefarious ogre's ambitions and take him down permanently before he ravages West Virginia and the rest of the country. The Maduros look good on the outside and seem successful and respectable, but without the many masks they wear, they're insane and evil to the core. Hugo kills without a smidgen of remorse.

"Austin and I, along with Special Agent Glenn Nunez, who you know as the entrance guard, have stealthily infiltrated the Maduro organization in West Virginia. While he has a lot of wealthy and well-connected friends in both West Virginia and Kentucky, he will be derailed.

"Hugo isn't going to be a free man much longer."

He eyed her sympathetically. "Hugo Maduro has quite a well-documented storied past with absolutely no reverence for the law." Bryce jump-started the conversation elucidating the reasons for his actions, no longer able to skirt the issues.

Nuna shook her head in bafflement. "I don't..." She went on, "So you just banged me to get to Hugo? You bastard!"

Bryce could see the undisguised anger flashing in her eyes. He cautiously responded, his tone etched with pain, "I can understand why you might think that."

"Your damn understanding doesn't cut it!"

She moved to slap him, but he caught her right hand. He said, "But of course, that wasn't the intention at all, and what you don't seem to understand is that many lives are at stake, including your own."

"I don't understand."

"Let me explain," he said. "Hugo's public reputation is that of a legitimate businessman. But his actual intentions are inhuman, and he is capable of evil, criminal barbarism. He has committed many atrocities with inconceivable savagery. He is a madman. He is uncommonly bright and unflinchingly ruthless and aims to have despotic power.

"His charisma managed to conceal his underlying face of evil and sadistic nature. But his evil enterprise has no geographic boundaries." Bryce stared at her across the coffee table. "But, Nuna, I've also been dealing with one hell of a coincidence out of my past, and it's been weighing on me terribly."

"What's the coincidence?" she almost whispered.

"You," Bryce responded.

She set her glass down in the center of her cocktail napkin and stared at him, nonplussed, with an unwavering expression. Yet what he had said caused her to moderate her tone and made her blood run icy cold. A heavy, palpable silence filled the room as she gauged the veracity of what was being said. Misgivings assailed her, a premise unbidden and unwelcome was insinuating itself into the mentality of her mind.

"OK," Nuna said with chagrin, thinking that she was about to fall down the rabbit hole.

Bryce gave her a serious look with the confidence of a man who was sure he was holding all the right cards.

"Nuna, I was given this operation by high command as it concerned national defense, but it's become much more sinister." The gravity of his eyes alerted her to his conundrum. "Nuna, I knew your husband in Vietnam." He enunciated each word with care. "I was only a few klicks downriver from him when his boat was blown up."

She hesitated a moment, looking at him in utter incomprehension before her mouth fell open and her chin began to quiver in seismic shock. She stiffened and froze at his words. The implications associated with what he had just said rushed at her like a swarm of killer bees. Her heart plummeted to the pit of her stomach. A wave of numbness moved slowly through her body as she covered her head with her hands, digested his words, biting her lower lip, forcing down the scalding bile filling her throat. The words pierced her as no others could have. She shot him a look of naked anguish.

"How could that be?"

There was a moment of ominous silence between them.

She lowered her head, not wanting him to see the tears that flooded her eyes and coursed uncharted down her face. She almost choked on her food. Her heart began to pound, and she gave Bryce a horrified look. She felt a weird, practically lightheaded sensation. She was so stunned by his admission that shock reverberated through her, and it took her a few seconds to find her voice.

She stared at him with cold surmise.

"Is this your idea of a joke?" she asked finally.

"No." He watched her with his striking, enigmatic eyes.

"He's alive, isn't he?" she asked him, not even believing it as she said it. "Chris is still alive?" Her face went pale. A tidal wave of anguish and regret washed over her. Swaying slightly, her eyes closing and her knees giving way, she fell to the floor in a swoon. She was turning into a basket case before his eyes. The shell of anger and ferocity she had built slowly began peeling away. What remained was utter emptiness.

He sat on the couch beside her and put his hands on her heaving shoulders. Nuna folded herself into his knees, holding his legs tightly for emotional support.

Quickly standing up and summoning up all his strength to lift her up before she unraveled, he turned and faced her closely. Looking her straight in her tearing eyes, he said, "I believe ominously that Chris is alive. Nuna, I've recently uncovered some very disturbing evidence that Chris of this. We have documented intelligence that he somehow escaped the carnage of Dung Ha." He was giving her the unvarnished truth about her late husband, not glossing over the aspects that she would find disturbing. "He's alive, but he's not the man you knew." Tension flooded his body.

Her ears were filled with a rush of her blood. Her heart began to accelerate as she fought to regain composure.

What she was hearing was far worse than she had expected or feared. Befuddled, she clamped her fingers around the arms of the chair as she fought back the compulsion to scream. Tears welled in her eyes; her lower lip quavered as she began a meltdown.

"His name is now Chris Vallarta, and he is being sought by several Asian international authorities for his baseless savagery; dastardly, unspeakable vile acts of cruelty; and horrific violence against young Asian girls. He's depraved, divorced from his soul, and has turned absolutely amoral, killing young girls with no conscience"

He let that reverberate for a few moments before continuing. That in itself struck her hard, and the bile rose again in her stomach. She stared at him in mystification as his face became hardened.

"This Chris Vallarta is a heartless zealot currently working for Hugo. Both belong to the cartel syndicate. Together, they are responsible for a global prostitution ring, taking young girls from Europe, Asia, South America, and even here in West Virginia and selling them worldwide to the highest bidder with the one goal of lining their pockets.

"Nuna, we've also uncovered information that Hugo and Chris might have been instrumental in arranging your father's death. Your father died under strange circumstances, a fact you know well, as his car careened over a cliff. The same cliff that Chris's parents went over four years earlier. It's believed that your father might have learned of something the Maduro organization didn't want anyone to know about."

"Why?" she asked.

Bryce chose his words carefully. These revelations, if true, could prove devastating to Nuna. But unfortunately, the past has a way of catching up with all of us.

"To stop him from going to court and presenting his evidence. Your father had already notified the police just before the accident. We've identified the detectives that interviewed your father, and it's been learned and documented via security cameras that they have been seen a number of times visiting the Maduro complex and meeting with Hugo in their off hours. It's also been learned that they never logged your father's complaint. Both of their bank accounts have been audited. It was discovered that substantial deposits were made in their accounts following your father's death. Both are about to be arrested on murder one charges as coconspirators in your father's death."

Benumbed and fighting for control, Nuna clenched her hands and remained calm, hiding her emotions deep within her heart. A cavalcade of mortifying recollections flashed through her mind. She had always suspected her father's death wasn't an accident.

It would be impossible to imagine a worse set of occurrences. From the shock of hearing that Chris was still alive, living in a dark world, to being a victim of a carefully planned crime. Nuna couldn't imagine a worse day. She also now understood that if what she was hearing was true, she had wasted all these years grieving over a man who couldn't have cared less about her love for him. She had been in love with an image arising from the ashes of her decimated ego.

Slumping against Bryce, she acknowledged the magnitude of her folly. He wrapped his arms around her and held her close as she cried.

Bryce showed Nuna the picture. "Take a closer look."

"It's impossible."

"Is it?"

She looked at it again and couldn't believe what she was seeing. The man in the photograph was so dissimilar to Chris physical appearance, perhaps as much as a hundred pounds heavier than the man she remembered. While she couldn't see his face, he seemed a damaged person. His reptilian eyes were like daggers lacking any radiant warmth. Still, there was something familiar about the posture of this man.

While Nuna had not seen his cremation, she had, with her own hands, scattered his, or someone's, ashes across the Kanawha River off the Gauley Bridge. Now she had to believe that she had scattered the ashes of another person.

After a brief but disquieting staring contest, she said, "I'll admit there's a resemblance."

"Nuna, our intelligence supports that Chris may have survived the battle and intentionally evolved or taken the identity of someone else in his escape during the chaos of that battle."

"I know that this man is ferocious and has done many terrible things and hurt and killed many people. Untold are the reaches of his barbarities, uncounted the number of his treacheries, beyond belief the unbridled conceitedness of depravity of his actions."

Bryce took her in his arms and supported her while her tears trickled inky stains down the front of his shirt. Then, dipping her knees, he curved one arm beneath her legs and swung her up into his arms. He carried her into the living room and lowered himself into an overstuffed chair. Keeping her on his lap, he wrapped his arms around her and held her close, tucking her head safely beneath his chin. Then he did nothing but let her cry. He indulged each racking, cleansing sob. Her tears ran out before his patience did. Even then, he sat still and silent while she hiccupped against his chest.

"He's not worth crying over, Nuna."

She blinked away her lingering tears and brought him into focus. "I know. But whadaya want me to say?"

Sitting silently with her in his arms, he compassionately wiped away her rivulets of flowing tears.

"Feel better," he said with a coaxing voice, and she began to snivel, looking sad. Then, with his finger, he tilted her chin up and her head back. "Chris isn't worth crying over."

"I'm not crying over him. I'm crying for wasting all these years mooning over him."

Nuna knew only the gnawing agony deep inside her and the hollow emptiness that lurked on the outer perimeter of her soul, threatening to suck her into its fathomless chasm.

She found the deeper she reached for her memories of Chris, the more indistinct and nebulous they became. One thing was certain, though: if Bryce was right, if Chris was who Bryce now believed him to be, then she had never actually met that man she married. His unfaithfulness had been so well-hidden that she'd never even imagined such a thought. Her tongue soured, and her throat burned with reflux as she ingested the thought of Chris kidnapping and raping innocent adolescent girls. Long-buried images of her past with Chris rose, blurry at first, then gradually coming into focus, all deeply disturbing. She now realized that she had seen only a small part of the man's carriage, the part of him he'd allowed her to see.

"We'll have plenty of time for me to tell you how this all played out, how you fit into it." Nuna was in his arms now, and he listened to her laugh, a sound that penetrated his being like a warm salve. Despite the gravity of the moment, Bryce managed to give her a smile.

Nuna turned to face him. A ponderous moment of silence passed, and her expression softened as she mustered a fleeting smile back. She now understood his focus, and he discerned things she had allowed the passage of time to obscure. His breath ghosted over her tear-streaked face.

"Bryce, I'm not frightened; I'm terrified. If this is indeed Chris, I now also want to consign this monster to hell." She moved close, nestling against him, savoring and drawing upon his strength. "I've made my decision. I'll cooperate with your mission and give you my unswerving support and cooperation."

Bryce squeezed her hand as he watched her capitulate and her acceptance registered. There was no deception in her expression. Her eyes were earnest and blatantly sincere.

Bryce shared a few memories that he had with Chris during the war, but he remained vague about most of the details, focusing on trivial stuff like the humidity and the jungle.

"Nuna, the dream, not the nightmare, that makes its way into my head sometimes has caused me to lose sleep many nights. Once again, I'm forced to relive the events that led to the deaths of twenty-three men. I fully believe that if Chris and his other PBR had led us out, the engagement would have been much different and many lives would have been saved.

"I'm saying that Chris will disappear the second he knows we are onto him." He looked at her, eyes clear. ""We're going to take this monster down."

At that moment, she knew what he was proposing.

The angry flush on her face was swept away, and a look of clarity replaced it. She nodded.

"I'm not even going to ask, Bryce. I want you to know I'm with you and will do whatever it takes. Do you hear me? Do you understand me?

"I now regret that I ever met Chris Polinski. I loved him, Bryce. Or thought I did. I was married to him. I wanted to have his children. How could I not have seen that he was a monster? You weren't looking. He didn't have any keepsakes or photographs, except one of his mother and father with him as a boy. He was never in touch with old friends. He never reminisced. He said he preferred to live in the present rather than visit the past, and I stupidly accepted that explanation without question. It never occurred to me that he was hiding something. Occasionally I saw traces or glimpses of selfishness and self-absorption and his evil alter ego with grave misgivings."

"Don't be too hard on yourself, Nuna. You weren't the only one he hoodwinked."

"No." Nuna smiled thinly. "That's where you're wrong. I know exactly what you have to do, Bryce. And I'm already involved." She picked up his photo. "He was my husband. Do you know what I'm going to do to him?" She nodded. "Yes. I want him dead also!"

He looked at her imploringly. "Are you going to help me?"

"But of course. I'll help you."

Bryce placed a kiss to her forehead. "Trust me, Nuna. Let me and my men handle this. I want you to stay in this house, where you're protected 24-7. We already know you're a Manduro target."

"OK." She sighed, reluctantly nodding in agreement. Then she asked, "So tell me how you became a CIA agent."

Since he knew almost everything about her, it made sense that she wanted to know more about him and what made him tick.

"It was either FBI agent or a lawyer," Bryce said. "They lured me in with a great salary. And the hours. They clinched the deal when they told me that occasionally people might shoot at me with a gun."

Nuna laughed. She loved him. And she felt safe with him. His integrity was beyond reproach.

Bryce thought reflectively that had this operation not come about under his command, he would have lived the rest of his life without ever meeting Nuna.

"So did you pick your team, or were Austin and Glenn assigned to you?" Nuna asked.

"They were assigned to me. Both speak several languages, which is what we needed."

Scooping her up in his arms, he knew he was holding someone sacred. Then he lowered his head and kissed her. His tongue slipped between her lips, gently at first, but instantly the kiss turned wet and hot, infinitely sexy, brimming with evocative promise. His beard stubble abraded her, but his kiss was soft. She welcomed his kiss along with the warm dampness of his lips. He placed his hand on the small of her back and drew her up flush against him. They kissed for endless minutes, never breaking contact. "Nuna, I'll love you as you've never been loved."

Nuna untucked his shirt and started to unbutton it.

She decided that would take too long, so she grabbed it and yanked it open, sending buttons flying everywhere. Bryce was the antithesis of Chris. She peeled the shirt down over his shoulders and discarded it on the floor.

She ran her fingers up and down his chest, sending tingling electrical sensations throughout his body. She was wearing a loose-fitting blouse and skirt. She was unaware that each time she drew in a deep breath, her breasts would lift and swell, emphasizing their fullness and unspoiled beauty. He reached down, ran his hands up her legs, and slowly unzipped the back of her skirt and let it drop to the floor. She stepped out of it and stood before him in only her bra, underwear, and cowboy boots.

Her skin smelled like Obsession. He lowered his head and kissed the swell of her breast, hoarsely whispering in her ear, "Nuna." Pulling her closer, he kneeled above her and kissed her flat stomach, navel, and pelvis above her panty line. She sat on the edge of the bed and held up a leg. He took off her boots one at a time, rolled the socks off her feet, and stood back up, and she undid his belt and slid his pants down. She took off her bra, tossed it aside, and slipped off her underwear before scooting back on the bed, her body bathed in milky moonlight.

Nuna said, "Make love to me, Bryce. Make love to me as you've never made love to another woman before."

He slipped into bed and covered her mouth his before nibbling at the fragile, sensitive skin of her flat belly and working his way down her beautiful body, his tongue flirting with her navel as his hands moved masterfully behind her to palm and take hold of her derriere.

She wrapped her naked legs around him, and he slid into her cloud of blond hair; she was caught with a bolt of electricity surging through her body. It was a wakening, and they both felt it. They were made for each other.

They sat on the couch, both of them ruminating on the future.

"Trust me, Nuna, I'm going to take down both the Maduro Operation and Chris Vallarta." He removed the tissue from her hand.

She stared at him with one arm draped casually behind his head and her left leg sprawled across his legs. "OK."

She was no longer taking sedatives, and when she did wake up in the night, she did so bolting up, gasping for air in panic, screaming in terror. "Bad dream, baby?" he would ask.

"Sort of, I guess," she would say, then fiercely whisper to herself, "Suck it up."

Watching movies together at night had become the norm, and she would eventually succumb to sleep. Or was it her therapy? Holding on to Bryce's stalwart presence gave her instant reassurance.

When she snuggled up to him and slithered up his body, his warm and solid being gave her everything she needed. She would fulfill his every need and make fulfilling hers a lifetime challenge that Bryce would look forward to.

The next thing she knew, Bryce was nudging her awake. "By the way, did you know you snore?"

CHAPTER 44

As befitted the tenor of his day's activities, heavy dark clouds settled low over the mountains and a steady nurturing rain had been falling for several hours now. One could almost cut the humidity with a knife.

Senator Schiff had agreed to meet with Bryce at 9:30 a.m. at his ostentatious office in Charleston overlooking the Kanawha River. Having arrived ten minutes early, Bryce opened the front door and was hit with a blast of air-conditioning. A polite young woman in the front lobby with magenta lips greeted him with a vapid smile and asked if he had an appointment. He advised her that he did and was told by her that the senator was running late and would arrive shortly.

Bryce took a seat; he wasn't known for small talk. The air in the room was scented with an artificial bouquet spray, impossibly sweet. Nothing in nature has ever smelled like that, he thought. The senator finally arrived thirty minutes late by design with an imperishable chip on his shoulder, wholly unapologetic for the delay. Punctuality, it seemed, was beneath his station. Without noticing Bryce sitting in the waiting area, he blithely walked past him, giving his secretary a disparaging glance, and entered his office, closing the door behind him. Fifteen long minutes passed before his receptionist, with a rueful grin, announced that the senator would now see him, and she opened the door and led him into his office.

The dandified Senator Schiff was complacently seated across the room, rocking back in a leather wingback chair behind a sizable burnished mahogany desk, talking on the phone with a unlit cigar clamped between his fingers. His jacket had two buttons and narrow lapels with French cuffs fastened by gold links inlaid with emerald jade. The silver-gray hair just above the temples gave him a very distingue appearance. The room reeked of stale cigar smoke. The senator was in his midfifties, with doughy pallor, medium height, medium build and mien, and scowling with a receding hairline of streaked graying hair brushed back to cover his baldness. His brooding ferret-brown eyes, covered by nerdy glasses, were set slightly askew over a long, thin nose centered in a vulpine face radiant with confidence. He wasn't at all that impressive, and Bryce was utterly underwhelmed. What he didn't look like was a senator from West Virginia. He didn't even deign to look up as Bryce entered the room.

Bryce didn't know much about the senator, but from what he had learned and his perspicacity about his political actions and support for the Maduro organization, he was the quintessential example of an opportunistic titular politician chameleon bought and paid for.

During his visit to the library, Bryce had scrutinized his faux public record and had come away with a negative impression of the smug and sententious senator.

Having strong, distinguished, stiff-necked Southern Baptist liberal family political connections seemed to be his sole qualification, and it had been nurtured to get him elected. But, of course, Schiff's vaunted family tree was well-oiled in Charleston's old money and big prestigious law firms, rooted deep in West Virginia coal mines. He had never entered one, presumably as it was below his social standing to enter a cave with a bunch of coal-mining hillbillies.

He was a Southern West Virginian by heritage and inclination, and according to available data, his forebears had walked into the West Virginia mountains as indentured servants in the early 1800s. By the mid-1800, they had created a cabal of several conservative Democratic legislators and risen to the rank of respected patrician landholders of a half dozen coal mines. By 1863 the cabal had denounced the Confederacy upon seeing its fall and sided with the Union. Senator Alan Schiff had been bred to be a Southern politician. Nevertheless, he retained the style and charismatic grace of the well-to-do family into which he had been born.

His conscience had been truly cauterized, with his reputation less than sterling.

Bryce was beginning to see a pattern of possible family temerity, corruption, and enough Orwellian cachet and money to buy a congressional seat. In Bryce's thoughts, this place was one of the last refuges of anathema aristocracy in America. If you weren't the son of one of the upper-crust families, then you, for all intents and purposes, were invisible in the hive of ordinary life.

The senator's inner sanctum was decorated in the same opulent style as the office of a major Wall Street bank president. One wall was covered in gold-tinted plate glass looking over Charleston proper. In contrast, the two opposing walls were festooned with a vast array of prominently displayed diplomas, citations, certifications, and pictures of him posing with the governor, the town council, the mayor of Charleston; there were also plaques commemorating questionable accomplishments. He was a political schmoozer, for sure. To the left of his desk, a dark mahogany bar stocked with Grey Goose, Johnnie Walker Black, Dewar's, and a bottle of Knob Creek. A bottle of Butchertown Brandy sat on his desk. To the right was a matching credenza. On his desk, he had a couple of file folders, an overflowing ashtray, and several framed photos of his family and of himself with his trophy wife. A sizable Persian carpet covered an Italian marble floor adorned with expensive French oak furnishings.

Without so much as changing his tone, he winked, glanced up at Bryce with a detached, preening expression, then ostentatiously looked at his watch as he tilted down his thick spectacles and motioned him to take a proffered seat.

"Please come in and sit down, Mr. Tucker," the senator said dismissively in a haughty insouciant tone of voice, pointing imperiously with an unctuous wave of his trembling hand to a chair in front of his desk.

Bryce, now with a strong aversion to the senator, didn't proffer him his either but did thank the senator for seeing him on such short notice.

Bryce seriously loathed the senator and his cavalier attitude. The late-morning rays of sunlight were streaming through the venetian blinds, casting slats of shadows across Schiff's desk. Bryce's instincts were firing on all neurons.

The spineless West Virginia senator, who had an inflated view of himself, was having a hard time looking Bryce in the eye and maintaining his somewhat insouciant appearance straightening his trademark bowtie, tidying up his desktop, squaring all the pads, pens, and paper on his desk before demurely folding his hands on his belly. That seeming procrastination in itself galled me and put me on high alert that what he was about to tell me I probably would not find comforting. Knowing his reputation for chicanery, I had to assume that his office was anything but not sterile and I would be choosing my words carefully.

"Can I offer you something to drink or smoke," he asked with an ingratiating smile as he reached into an ornate cigar box on his desk, picked out a panatela, rolled it, and lit it. The senator turned the cigar band around his finger. "It's Cuban."

"Thanks, Senator, but much too early for me, and I don't smoke," Bryce said perfunctorily. He didn't appreciate his cavalier attitude at all.

The senator poured two fingers of the 124-proof brandy from an expensive decanter for himself with shaking hands, studied the libation for a second or two as he swirled it in his glass, and then took a tentative sip before tossing it back and bibulously swallowing it like a shot before pouring another. Looking up from his newspaper and then opening a file on his desk, he met Bryce's discordant glare with a disingenuous facsimile of a smile. Raising his left hand, he checked his gaudy Cartier wristwatch with casual insouciance. "I'm sure you realize that I'm a busy man and can appreciate how valuable my time is, Mr. Tucker."

With a thin, reedy voice, coupled with a carefully cultivated enunciation, he spoke ungraciously with a sardonic expression on his face before launching into a disingenuous monologue about the weather with the confidence of an oracle, noting how hot the summer was in the mountains.

The sanctimonious son of a bitch smiled at Bryce without warmth, his flittering eyes stoically wandering over his, his hands fidgeting with a cigar trailing ashes. "I'll come right to the point." His stilted voice was expansive and brazenly smooth with insouciance; he moistened his lips and averted his eyes. "I've been informed by an anonymous source that you might be investigating a possible connection between the Maduro organization and the Charleston Planning and Zoning Commissions. As senator of the Seventieth District, I find these accusations are asinine. There is absolutely no connection between the two organizations, and any allegations of impropriety are preposterous! With that being said, I'm ordering you to cease and desist your investigation immediately," he drawled brusquely. His tone was as hostile as his expression.

A weighted silence set in between them. Bryce's anxiety was simmering as his eyes fixed on the senators; he stared him down skeptically and weighed his falsity. Bryce was not easily intimidated and had a burning aversion to taking this politician down.

The senator's pompous directive was so dogmatically cavalier and given with such stilted and unflappable conceit that his initial inflamed reaction was to strangle the unmitigated son of a bitch right there in his office. But just as quickly, Bryce sucked in a grimace, and the urge subsided.

He stood up, bristling and unfazed by the senator's political prominence, and shot a glance over his shoulder at the closed door. Then, his rancor boiling and creasing his broad upper forehead, he planted both his hands securely on the top of the politician's desk and gave him a piercing fulminating stare, matching his hauteur. Bryce wanted to hit the sanctimonious prick but instead locked unflinching gazes with him, verbally lambasting and telegraphing his disdain with overwhelming impetus. The senator cowered under Bryce's fierce Viking glare, turning away, and went silent as Bryce recoiled.

"Senator," he said in a conspiratorial whisper, "perchance can you enlighten me on the identity of your most recent paramour? More direct, are you having a sexual relationship with Senator Assad?"

He vehemently denied it.

There was a sharp undertone of disgust in Bryce's tone as he stared at and dressed down the rabid senator with unflinching eyes. The senator's duplicitous face suddenly turned pale as he surged to his feet, then collapsed back in his chair as Bryce put one of the photos taken by Glenn in front of him. The two had taken the risk of cavorting in the nude in full view of the cottage's bare windows. Indignant, he looked up in utter shock but was now looking at Bryce, who was holding another photo with rapt attention.

His head went still, but he did something inside his mouth that caused his upper lip to quiver and drained the brandy in his glass. He played with the ring on his finger absentmindedly.

"Yes, Senator, my informants have confirmed that you have, on several occasions, stayed overnight with Senator Assad at the Maduro Estate and the Roadway Inn in Charleston." With acerbity, he stared at the senator. "What would your constituents or even the electorate think of your sordid assignations with a married senator? What would your wife think of your indiscreet trysts?

"And Senator, shifting gears, another shattering revelation has recently come to light. Two years ago, Hugo Maduro called you at your office and asked if you could rectify an unfortunate issue that Senator Assad was dealing with. As you know, her son was arrested in Knoxville for speeding and carrying a brick of heroin in his car. We've recently discovered through an electronic retrace that you desperately made a number of phone calls that night. Young, ambitious as hell, and very well politically connected, you were calling in political debts and unsavory favors from across the county, inveigling friends and political allies to have the charges dropped and the arrest record officially expunged by the following day. Your supporters, prosecutors, and local cops, most as unethical as you are, were most likely paid off by taking a bribe and making the case disappear, Senator. I believe that the boy was a carrier making a delivery for Maduro.

"'Obstruction of justice' is the phrase that will be bandied by the media, who will soon lose confidence in anything you say. Understand, Senator?" The strychnine disdain in Bryce's voice was unmistakable, with the muscles in his corded throat starkly defining his anger.

The senator looked at Bryce warily.

Bryce took a piece of paper out of his pocket and gave the disingenuous senator a glaring look, peppering his voice with truculence. "Another indiscretion of interesting malfeasance has come within the purview of our investigation. A union official has now been arrested and placed in protective custody due to a recent threat to his and his family's lives. We've known for over a year now that with possible deluded political help, Maduro has been conspiratorially and surreptitiously skimming millions of dollars off the top of construction profits, employing undocumented workers, and using substandard materials and bribing a city inspector to approve and stamp them. With the arrest and this individual's cooperation, extortion is being added to the list of criminal indiscretions committed by you and Maduro.

"The witness vehemently claims that you have been squeezing him on building contracts through your intercession, Senator Assad, and the Maduro organization for the last two years, taking ten to fifteen percent payouts in suitcase drop-offs. He also stated that if the flaccid union organization wanted to mix union and nonunion labor to cut costs, the payout would go up another five to ten percent. Extortion, Senator?" he said snidely, looking down at him reproachfully, with skepticism.

Bryce folded the paper twice and slipped it into his breast pocket. "While I was involved in several interviews with the union representative, nothing that was said dovetailed with the political squeeze exactly. With the uptick in construction projects in West Virginia, there has to be more going on behind closed doors."

The senator gave him a bristling stare as he began to dither and stutter; it was as if he had just developed a speech impediment. The senator's agitation flared in his jowls as he again drained the brandy from his glass and replaced it with a balled white-knuckle fist. And then, like a crazed animal, he surged to his feet again, splayfooted and cocksure, slamming his clenched fist down on the polished top of desk, sending papers and documents flying. His previous arrogant complacency and theatrical glare vanished, replaced with a wild, crazed look of panic in his eyes. Red-faced and glowering with anger, he again, with a visceral reaction, slammed his fist down hard on his desk; he should have broken his damn wrist.

The senator was dismissive. "Unrelenting," he hissed, giving Bryce a hostile glance. "How dare you impugn the integrity of my office with this goddamned bullshit based on these unbalanced and ridiculous accusations!" he said, exasperated, practically levitating off the floor with his temperature rising. "Can you appreciate the embarrassment that a lengthy investigation based on nothing but wild conjectures and aspersions like these could cause my family and me?" he bellowed indignantly in a loud, clipped voice, showing no remorse for his indiscretions.

"Maybe you should have thought of that before you started surreptitiously hobnobbing and perfidiously screwing around and sullying the privileges of your soulless office." Bryce stood up, looked down at him disparagingly with a sardonic grin, and asked, "Is your family involved in your nefarious activities?" His voice was as hard as jagged granite.

The senator flew up from his desk, unrepentant, angry, and scared. He was shaking like a leaf in a strong wind. "This is all preposterous, and I want you out of my damn office now," he said haltingly, "Get the hell out."

"So would drug dealing, arms, and human trafficking qualify as besmirching the family's reputation?" Bryce's voice was stern, his body tense, and his right hand curled into a hardened fist. The senator snorted derisively.

Without another word passing between them, Bryce allowed himself a wry smile. He turned to walk out the door with the smile of a Cheshire cat. The arrogant devil-incarnate effrontery of the man defied belief.

"Yes, Senator, your nose is growing. You've become Pinocchio," he said blithely with a quelling look and left the room without a commiserating backward glance. The senator was frozen in his chair, denigrated and seething. The bluff was audacious but made with enormous certitude and therefore was quite informative, even if he was a pathetic and despicable parasitic asshole.

"Actually, I couldn't give a rat's ass for protecting his feckless reputation," Bryce muttered as he exited the rogue senator's office and walked back to his car. The hair on the back of his neck bristled.

Bryce's meeting with the senator niggled at him all the way back to the hotel as he muttered a couple of expletives. He immediately knew he had to take down this asswipe before he could alert Manduro of the covert operation. So he was going to take him down tomorrow at any cost. Period. It was ironic that with all the money in the Schiff family, the senator was now a pawn, bought and paid for by Hugo Maduro.

The senator wouldn't contact Maduro tonight as he was out of the country on business with an associate in Cuba and wouldn't be returning until the day after tomorrow. So he had to calm down and think this out quickly and with a cool calculation of political interest. Implicating Hugo Maduro and two United States senators in a web of international corruption, subterfuge, and lust without a plausible explanation would surely make national headlines as a significant tawdry scandal and result in his disappearance.

Bryce also knew that to take down and arrest a sitting senator, he would first have to have an order from the Senate. The only exception was if the senator was apprehended in flagrante delicto, and Bryce had cogent proof of the senator's crime.

He called Austin shortly after leaving the senator's office and set up a rendezvous for noon the next day. They would follow the senator's every move. In the meantime, Austin requested a team already on the island to set up a discreet camera and audio system throughout the mansion. As requested, Austin had already attached a transmitter and an audio receiver to

Senator Schiff's and Senator Assad's cars that morning to glean additional information on their activities. They learned that Maduro now possessed over a million dollars of heroin and a million doses of fentanyl. Through an informant doing surveillance at the site, all of it was being stashed in a remote, heavily guarded warehouse at the far end of the island.

To their surprise, Senator Schiff called Senator Assad on his cell phone while driving home and asked her how much they had taken in the last month. "Five million here and about the same offshore," she said.

"Great," he said in a strangled whisper. "That should satisfy the boss's bon vivant."

He arranged to pick her up at her condo for dinner the following night, but she chose to drive herself instead.

Austin requested his assistance with Glenn having the day off at the Maduro compound.

CHAPTER 45

Bryce

I would not be stymied by the power of the senator. Following him into Charleston proper in a bland-looking repurposed van, Austin, Glenn, and I caucused behind a hedge line at the periphery of the parking lot and watched as he valeted his newly purchased Jaguar and alighted from it. Within seconds, Senator Assad pulled in and parked her Mercedes in the lot; having left her car, she sauntered across the lot, meeting Senator Schiff at the entrance. Together, they entered the haute subterranean Black Sheep nightclub on West Quartier Street. It was an elegant beamed restaurant just off the thriving business district, surrounded by terraced hills that made it ideal for clandestine local political meetings. It seemed that he had calmed down measurably. While most restaurants of this caliber employed security cameras, the Black Sheep did not. Obviously, someone had introduced the senators to its patrician offerings.

We gave them a half hour to unwind and get settled. Glenn stayed with the van as Austin and I casually walked into the five-star eatery. Slipping the hostess a twenty, we assured her we were joining another couple already seated. Carefully, we worked our way around the perimeter of the dimly lit lounge. The restaurant was, fortuitously, almost empty, and "Coal Miner's Daughter" was jamming out of the sound system. Austin counted about a dozen other occupants, four older gentlemen sitting at the bar enjoying and comparing single malts, a young couple in a booth, and a family of six occupying a table.

We found the senators ensconced in a dark corner booth at the far end of the dining room. Schiff was about to raise his hand and hail the cocktail waitress for a second round of Glenlivet fifty-year-old vintage single malt scotch, which went for $29.50 per glass. Senator Assad was licking the rim of her empty glass. The ardent intoxicant, along with the gourmet meals before them, was surely being proffered by the Maduro organization, which was all too accommodating in proving two senators of their standing with anything they wished.

Austin and I both obscured ourselves, snagging a couple of stools at the far end of the bar, just far enough away from the booth, giving us a hidden vantage point where we surreptitiously watched them using our peripheral vision. We ordered two double Absoluts and casually listened to the low murmurs of the restaurant crowd and the soft rattle of our ice cubes in the heavy crystal glass as we watched askance from the bar. Meanwhile, the loathsome senators ate their meals. We watched several couples come and then go out the front door. After finishing dinner, Senator Assad went to the restroom with a confident stride, then quickly returned to her seat as Senator Schiff engaged in chitchat with the young waitress serving their table.

Seeing that he had just signed the check and they were imbibing the last of their drinks as the waitress walked away from their table, Austin and I made our move, having barely touched our drinks, feigning nonchalance. We hadn't received our bar bill and had no time to ask for one, so I left a few bills on the bar, more than enough to cover our tab. The sound of laughter came from the other end of the bar where they sat. We casually came up behind them, and I slapped a hand on Senator Schiff right shoulder as Austin, with the smile of a Cheshire cat, took the seat and sidled over to the demure Senator Assad with his gun in hand just below the table.

"How are you, my friend?" I asked with a sarcastic smile.

The senator blanched and spun around in the leather seat, and as he did so, I offered my hand; in a reflexive action, he accepted it.

"We're leaving, senators," I said, whispering discretely, peremptorily abandoning preliminaries and pulling him out of the booth.

Then, recognizing me, he began to protest, saying, "I'm not going anywhere with you," until he heard the click of the hammer and felt

the cold steel of the barrel of my glock jammed in his side, which un-
nerved him.

With that, he slowly got up and gestured a wave, saying goodbye
to the bartender, who was too busy with another couple of bar patrons
to see him or respond. With Austin still holding a gun against Senator
Assad's side, both senators were savvy enough to understand the seriousness of the situation. They walked hand in hand calmly with us to the
entrance and out the front door.

Fortunately, the host wasn't at her station as we were leaving, so no
one witnessed our exiting the restaurant, and we quietly avoided any
potential bedlam.

Following the conversation through his earbud, Glenn had the black
nondescript Tahoe waiting outside with its rear door open and the engine running.

Austin escorted Assad to the rear driver's side with the glock semiau-
tomatic still in her back. At the same time, I assisted Schiff into the rear
passenger side, with both of us closing the doors simultaneously.

"Where are your car keys?" I said peevishly.

"In my pocket," the senator said dryly, looking up at me with rage
and apprehension in his eyes.

"Give them to me," I bellowed in a galvanizing drill sergeant's command voice.

Having reached into his pocket, he handed me the keys, clenching
and unclenching his hands spastically at his side; I immediately cuffed
them behind his back. Austin, taking no chances and nothing for grant-
ed, did the same, immediately cuffing Assad's hands behind her back.

"Why are you doing this, and where are you taking us? This is a kidnapping and a federal offense," Schiff yelled belligerently.

"Not necessarily," I hedged, giving him a jaundiced eye. "And I'll ask
the questions, Senator. You're nothing but a fucking pathological liar,
but this afternoon you're going to be telling me nothing but the truth.
Or so help me, I'm going to kill you.

"We're not kidnapping you, Senator. We're apprehending you. Actions such as this have a lengthy precedent and are legally recognized."

Dusk was falling, and the neon glitter was beginning to light up the Charleston landscape.

Before either of them could say another word, we clamped plastic masks against their faces and held them firm until they were both incapacitated by the chloroform.

An hour later, having dealt with heavy rush-hour traffic on the freeway, reducing our speed to a snail's pace, we pulled into an abandoned brick fire station just outside the town of Beckley that the government owned and the CIA used periodically as a safe house. Glenn dialed in the code on his cell phone, and the doors opened and closed behind us as we drove into the large, cavernous room.

Grabbing the senators by the collar, we exited the SUV. We proceeded upstairs to a recently refurbished office and interrogation room, where Schiff's left hand was immediately manacled to a chair. His right was left free to gesticulate. Our footfalls echoed loudly, bouncing off the bare walls and high ceilings. All the windows had been replaced with double brick, preventing any light from getting in and eliminating any means of escape.

Without preamble, Austin took Senator Assad down the hall corridor to another drab interrogation room, a spartan chamber with no clock on the wall and no windows. It had two video cameras and a concealed tape recorder under the table to record the interview, as well as a steel table, gunmetal gray, with four straight-backed steel chairs, deliberately uncomfortable.

Two of the chairs were occupied by Special Agent Wanda Garcia and Special Agent Austin. They did a quick pat down before Assad was secured in a metal chair, lashing both her legs to the legs of the chair before washing her face with a wet towel and bringing her back to consciousness. They left her there, staring at blank walls and nothing more.

Austin had already arranged for Agent Garcia to see to her needs while we interrogated Schiff. She arrived within the hour. Glenn, having completed a pat down of Schiff, sat him shackled upright in a straight-back metal chair bolted to the floor with both his legs bound to the legs of the chair. Austin repeated the process by slapping him in the face with a wet towel, one side to the other, to revive him. The senator was now twisting with a yowl of pain, shaking his head and staring at me in bafflement.

Glenn drove Austin back to the pub to retrieve the senators' cars. We would store them here in the basement garage until some future date.

I gave the Senator a penetrating, effective, menacing look as he sat down in the chair with splayed fingers on the desk.

"Senator, you are one narcissistic, opportunistic jackass!"

"Fuck you!" Schiff spat the words at me for the umpteenth time, becoming argumentative and belligerent.

His arrogance became his only protective carapace.

I let the insult pass and continued the questioning without intonation.

Senator Schiff's lips compressed. He shifted uncomfortably in his seat.

"Senator, I'm going to lay out a brief scenario of events based on what we currently know about your nefarious activities, and you're going to fill in the blanks." But, truth be told, I was going to get the information out of him or make him regret the day he was born.

I pushed myself back, stood out of my chair, and started slowly walking around the senator in silent circumspection, summarizing my incontrovertible information on him.

"Senator, last month you took a two-month extended vacation from Congress for personal medical reasons. Two weeks ago, you traveled to Bermuda as a guest of Hugo Madura and his wife via the *Lady Maria*, a private yacht owned by Madura International Enterprises. Two days later, you flew from Maduro's private island of Norman's Cay aboard his private Learjet to Havana, Cuba, where you met with a General Armando Chaos and a Maduro associate by the name of Chris Vallarta at the storied Hotel Nacional de Cuba before continuing on to Caracas, Venezuela. There, the three of you were met by a military attaché at the airport and were made the personal honorary guests of the ignoble secretary general, Carlos Andrés Pérez, staying at the presidential suites of the five-star Hotel Altamira. And from what we've been able to gather so far, this was also an all-expenses-paid trip compliments of the de facto Venezuelan government.

"Among other intelligence we've gathered, we've learned that during your stay in Caracas, you all met and dined several times with Pérez and several high-ranking members of his staff. What was the agenda, Senator?"

"This is preposterous!" he snapped in a rapid-fire, guttural, sardonic voice. "I don't give a rat's ass about your intelligence!

"Where is Senator Assad?" He was sidestepping my question. "What have you done with her?" he said with a waspish tongue.

He was struggling to break out of the bonds securing him to the chair. But he was locked in like an unfortunate insect trapped in amber.

"Where the hell did you get this bullshit information from?" the senator yelled again and again in a loud, irritating falsetto voice.

"Let me clarify, Senator. I never reveal my sources, and the evidence we now have is irrefutable."

"I had recently learned that Agent Bomen, compliments of the CIA, had a literal army of shallow informants and state-of-the-art camera and audio techies spread out worldwide at his disposal.

"If I were you, I'd be taking extra precautions from here on out when taking a shit. Get my drift, asshole! Senator, that in itself is a really big doo-doo. Your congressional buddies have sanctioned both from doing any business with the US or its allies. That includes accepting gifts such as the humidor of Cohiba-Behike cigars valued at fifteen-thousand dollars that General Chaos presented you as a gift from President Castro during your overnight stay in Havana. In addition, since 1963, the US government has banned all American citizens from visiting or having any contact with them.

"Please clarify for me, Senator, and explain why you think you're above that law."

I had already constructed his line of questioning. With instinct, I laid my trap and anticipated the senator's lies in advance.

"We would also be interested in why a deposit of a million dollars was recently made at the Scotiabank in the Cayman Islands in your name, Senator. What would your colleagues think of your shadowy international cabal and your newfound wealth? Ergo, might treason fit the bill, you gutless son of a bitch? Think of the ramifications. Bribery and noxious blackmail. The two flagrant cardinal virtues of illicit political influence-peddling."

Full of indignation, I cast a sharp, skewering look at the senator, and my expression turned grim. "Yes, Senator, despite your vaunted reputation, you will be ostracized after the press vilifies you. You're a bumbling amateur who has passed the Rubicon and now is in deep shit! We can have an arrest warrant within the hour, charging you with wiretapping, extortion, conspiracy to commit treason, and much more."

Cutting to the chase, I opened a brown manila envelope and splayed the contents on the table before him. "The CIA has received a trenchant collection of excellent photos of your trip, haven't they, Senator?"

The smile bobbled and vanished, and his mouth fell open in consternation as he stared with haunted eyes at the collection of photos displayed before him.

"Do you remember General William Garcia, Senator?" I pointed out a half dozen photos of the senator poising with the unscrupulous Venezuelan and Cuban generals. "What was your business with the generals, Senator? Please explain."

Unknown to the senator, General Garcia, who was second-in-command of the Venezuelan Army, was corrupt and, having accepted several substantial bribes, had been compromised by the CIA a year earlier. However, because of the intelligence being on a "need to know only" basis, I didn't mention that the general and his wife were summarily executed by being slowly beaten to death with a baseball bat at their home a week after he left.

I went on, "Fortunately, the general had already emailed the photos to his handler. Unfortunately, the word was that the general had gotten greedy and embezzled from the Venezuelan government over twelve million dollars in bearer bonds which he electronically forwarded to your account, Senator."

I also advised him that another compromised official had come forward in the last few days and provided us with information that the general had spilled his guts on the heinous details of the plot before being murked by his assassins. He had sold out the senator's name, and the senator was now an encumbrance on a hit list of individuals to be whacked. All the information was undeleted on his laptop, confirming Schiff's involvement. The senator was now a loose end that had to be eliminated before he began to sing like a canary. The regime had most likely already dispatched agents to eliminate him.

"Getting the picture, hotshot?" I asked. "You've been at this now for over a year, and like all crooks, you grew sloppy and complacent. So I've been sent here to put a bullet in your fucking head before they do if you don't give me the information that I want. You weren't aware of that, were you?"

I placed his foot on the chair next to the senator and leaned in, staring directly into the senator's eye.

"Senator, I want some quid pro quo, and I want it now. Start talking now, or I'll put your ass out there so fast that it'll leave a vapor trail."

The senator's demeanor suddenly changed, and he squirmed in his chair. He quaked and was now somewhat red-eyed and becoming anemic with more than a hint of fatigue darkening his face, which wasn't surprising considering that it was now well after three in the morning. He had been handcuffed to the chair, being interrogated, for over eight hours.

"Oh shit!" Considering his diminishing options, the senator lamented. There would be no magic elixir washing away his culpability. Biting the bullet of recognition, he gave me an unwavering stare, knowing now that he had no other choice but to come clean about the diabolical plan and divulge what he knew and to cooperate.

It was apparent we knew everywhere he had been and everyone he had contact with.

The operation was in full play mode, but the genesis of the malfeasance was now unraveling. He could feel the handcuffs and now envision himself incarcerated in an orange jumpsuit as a convict, indicted, divorced, and disbarred with his mug shot in the newspapers for all to see. A shadow of mental anguish and resignation etched in his eyes betrayed that maybe he had said too much.

Now shaking like he had Parkinson's disease, the senator, with downcast eyes, began to sputter and verbosely vomit out revelatory information, including the well-established particulars of the Maduro modus operandi and why the Venezuelan secretary general Pérez had an advanced payment of a million dollars. In addition, there would be another payment of five million euros in bearer bonds upon the successful delivery of a shipload carrying twenty-four thousand tons of Russian and American artillery, tanks, rockets, weapons, and ammunition to the Port of La Guairá.

Schiff explained, "Upon completing the transaction, I would transfer the money in hundred-thousand-dollar increments to Maduro's choice of offshore banks or other investment accounts. Thereupon, I would receive a ten percent commission for each successful transaction and a hundred-thousand-dollar bonus upon completion of the financial transfers."

Everything he did was carefully orchestrated with precision. While some transactions with rebels wouldn't involve cash, they did have large stashes of gold, blood diamonds, and control of petroleum wells. Maduro would exchange and monetize these into rands out of South Africa and then launder them into US currency on the international market.

Dejectedly, I rose to my feet and pandiculated as I slowly walked around the table. "What's the endgame, Senator?"

"There isn't one," he opined, unblinking, with dead eyes. He heard his voice quavering but knew he was out of options. "Once you're in, you're in until death do you part," he said in a hollow vibrato. He went on, "Hugo Maduro is known by the sobriquet the Merchant of Death. He has a vested interest in international chaos. His power is absolute and he rules without contention.

"He's an implacable, loathsome bastard of a man, obdurate in his determination, who uses lethal, sanctimonious coercion and a constellation of other men and women as if they were wrenches in his toolbox to commit his heinous crimes. He destroys careers and callously crushes anyone who stands in his way as he increases his power. Believe me, atrocious power to Hugo is his greatest aphrodisiac. He truly believes he has a license to kill at will if thwarted and remains indifferent and unruffled. He is ruthless, without a hint of empathy, and cunning as a fox, leaving no trail back to him.

"He is a psychopathic killer, and his handprints are everywhere from the Middle East, to Mexico and South America—in shell companies, arms, munitions, drugs, assassinations, girls, prostitution, porn, your name it. He'll buy and sell anything or anybody for the right price.

"Hugo Maduro can be and is gratuitously cruel. He is also ruthlessly short-tempered. Several years ago, he had a dispute with a local fisherman on Norman's Cay. The indigent fisherman refused to sell his plot of land. So Hugo had him, his wife, and their teenage son locked down in the galley of the fisherman's small wooden lobster boat and towed out to sea, where the boat was doused with gasoline and set afire. Without any witnesses to the horrible murders, Hugo had the land classified as abandoned and took possession. This is just one of the known horrific atrocities he committed without a second thought.

"The depravity of Hugo Maduro and his blithe disregard for others knows no bounds. He's ruthless. Maduro has long since put his disreputable past behind him, but he is still a certified badass with a gigantic ego. Maduro and an unknown Russian oligarch have also invested in a half dozen cruise ships, floating hotels, casinos, brothels, and prisons. Three are currently docked in the Mediterranean, and the others are sailing in the Atlantic from South America to the Florida coast flying the Libyan flag.

"A couple of women are taking in the sun in lounge chairs beside the swimming pool on this boat. There is Susan, a trim, pale-freckled-skin redhead, and Debra, a slim, tall, sharp-featured African American woman.

"Heinous crimes have been orchestrated, crimes are in process, and crimes are in the planning."

I responded, "If you don't start talking, I'm going to drag you across the street and put you in the ladies' room and strip you fucking naked and leave you handcuff you to the toilet while I call the *Charleston Gazette*."

Maduro had ensnared the congressman in a web of bribes, blackmail, and money laundering, and I knew it.

Schiff said, "There will be a significant exchange of goods between the Venezuelan Cartel of the Suns and the Maduro organization. The Maduros have sent a messenger requesting the delivery of fifty-five virgin girls, all class A stock, between the ages of thirteen and sixteen, to be delivered via two private jets to a remote airstrip on the Punta Cana coast by the end of the month. That's where the exchange will take place. Five girls will be chloroformed, loaded on Maduro's yacht, and delivered to Norman's Cay for processing by his madams. The others will be medically sedated with an amnesiac, transferred to a Liberian ship, and delivered to Senator Assad's brother, a Somalian trafficker, as part of the fifty-million-dollar arms deals with a billionaire from Dubai.

"The Maduro organization prefers moving their human goods via private jets, but on occasion, they will employ a cargo ship. To protect his products, every male crew member delivering the product is certified neutered. Once out in the open water and just south of Norman's Cay, the girls will be transferred to his yacht, which will take them to the island. In exchange, the Maduro enterprise will pay five thousand dollars per head and supply the cartel with seventy-five cases of new AK-47 rifles along with one hundred cases of ammunition out of his deep-water warehouse in Mariel Bay, Cuba."

"What else, Senator?"

"A substantial financial transaction is going to take place later this week in the climes. Maduro's Contract agent, Chris Vallarta, will authorize the rapid-sequence transfer of two billion dollars through commingled bank accounts and secret banking channels.

"Are you talking about money laundering?"

"Yes. Mr. Vallarta will be acting as a conduit for Hugo, with the money being transferred from Dubai through the Bank of Venezuela and again through the Central Bank of Cuba. Ten million dollars will be transferred to the brother of Sahra to cover the down payment for a shipload of excess military-grade weapons and explosives, which is now supposedly already in transit. Sahara's brother is the president of the Dara-Salaam Bank in Somalia.

"That's, that's…all I know," he stammered.

"Senator, I now want you to tell me all about Chris Vallarta, whom you've spent much time with at his villa in Cuba."

"No, no," he whined, "he will kill me."

"Senator, your life doesn't mean shit to me, and it will mean even less to them if I let you loose and let Maduro know you've made amends with the feds."

That in itself scared the bejesus out of him. The senator put his head down and began to cry.

"What was he to Maduro?" I rephrased the question. "How would you describe him, Senator?"

"Vallarta isn't from Cuba." He quivered. "I believe that he was, like me, born and raised in southern Virginia or West Virginia. His soul is twisted, ruthless, and evil. In his own words, he doesn't feel pain. I swear that he has homicidal urges. He wears a mask and gloves due to an unfortunate accident while he was in the military stationed in Vietnam. It seems that his boat was blown up while he was several yards away on shore taking a piss in a latrine hole. He jokes that it was the healthiest piss he ever took. Anyway, he was burned over twenty-five percent of his body, with his face and hands taking the brunt of the injuries. Somehow, by an act of God, or more likely the devil, under an incessant din of swirling helicopter blades and the cadence of machine gun fire and artillery explosions, miraculously he managed to survive the attack by covering himself with debris when the VC and NVA pulled back. In excruciating pain, according to his story, he crawled back to the boat and switched his dog tags with a corpse on one of the burning boats and somehow escaped to safer ground, slithering into the jungle unseen where, for the next several months, he nursed himself back to health by eating rodents and insects. His upper body was bruised and burned and shredded.

"After he could stand upright and walk, he limped across the border into Laos. He said he didn't want any part of the war or the United States from that day forth. In his own words, he had escaped from ruins and, with his talent, survived in the muck of the fiercest jungle in the world for over a year. Almost as a joke, he bartered the dog tags that he stole for a tarp from a Vietnamese rice farmer before crossing into Laos. I've never seen his face or hands, and I doubt anyone else still alive has either.

"He has several aliases, Chris Vallarta being his latest. There are no boundaries or barriers between him and self-gratification. His stories were horrific and fiendishly terrifying."

"Did he ever mention whether he was ever married?"

"Never, and that question was never even thought of." The senator busted out in a fit of bacchanalian laughter. "Knowing his narcissistic self-absorption and deranged proclivities toward sex and drugs, I doubt he would ever consider an attachment to a female. He is misogynistic, and to him, females are only temporary somatic pets with breasts and vaginas for his entertainment and profitable distribution."

Chris had obviously abolished any memories of his wife.

"He's a major whoremonger, notorious for dealing in women and especially a leach for young ones. Mr. Vallarta sees them as pleasurable assets to be exploited in any way he wants.

"He's catnip to females. On any given day, he will have a dozen or so mistresses of varying flavors housed in his basement harem for his pleasure and that of VIP guests. No, without a scintilla of doubt, Mr. Vallarta is not the marrying type and has only malice toward women. He's also a clever opportunist with a violent eruptive disposition and an unimaginably rapacious appetite to kill.

"While I didn't actually see it, he described one egregious event that shocked the hell out of me. One of his drug deals had gone sour a couple of years back, and he had invited the dealer, his wife, and his daughter to have dinner with him. After dinner, he took the family on a tour downstairs to his special chamber. At gunpoint, he chained all three to chairs around a table. The dealer and his wife, who owned a butcher shop in Havana, watched in horror as he stripped and defiled their fourteen-year-old daughter and continuously raped, beat, and tortured her, screaming on a bed next to their table, until she passed out. He then forced the dealer to watch in abject horror as his wife suffered the same fate, which also included forced fellation. When he finished, he used a cigar cutter and severed each of the fingers off his wife, one by one, without a qualm before slowly flaying her chest in thin ribbons. He castrated the husband before killing both of them and had them hung on meat hooks in their shop. It was a sadistic warning from a deranged killer to other dealers. He gave the daughter to another drug dealer as a gift and literally walked away from the atrocity.

"Mr. Vallarta is beyond cruel. He is an angry, pathetic nihilist who believes in the netherworld of drugs, sex, and crime at any level, including murder for hire. He has the power and influence to demand the loyalty of his subjects, including his suppliers and distributors. He is not someone to be trifled with. Even his gunmen fear him.

"Believe me, during the time I spent with Mr. Vallarta, I found the amoral son of a bitch to be a man completely without compassion. Like Maduro, he kills without conscience or remorse. Looking back at the incident that I just told you about, I am reminded he is sadistic, remorseless, and vindictive and he has the raw instincts of a carnivorous vulture. On several walls inside his villa, there are montages of women and young girls in various stages of undress.

"One night when he had drunk one drink too many, he told me how his father used to beat his mother in the bedroom as an aphrodisiac. He had a visceral hatred for both his parents and killed both of them one night by opening a gas line in their basement and lighting the stove as he left.

"He and his old man had fought a lot over his alcohol and drug use, and his father had threatened to disinherit him."

Now feeling a wave of smoldering, impetuous anger growing hotter by the minute, I recoiled at the dysfunctional nakedness of it all.

"Where else does Senator Assad fit into this transaction, Senator? Don't fucking lie to me!" I said.

"Honestly, I don't know, but I did overhear Chris Vallarta on his cell phone one night talking to someone and saying that Sahra was facilitating the transfer of the girls to Somalia.

There hadn't been any defectors or informants from the Maduro organization until now. The senator, now despondent with a tired hangdog look, had confessed, hoping outlandishly for a prison sentence less than life. He continued to talk unbidden.

A lot of planning was going to be required to rescue the girls and take the Maduro Enterprise down. However, I was beginning to break the Maduro code of silence and was committed to seeing it all the way through the denouement.

I went silent for a couple of moments, and I could almost hear my synapses firing as I considered the possible unctuous statements from the senator.

"It is high time Hugo Maduro gets his comeuppance," I said.

CHAPTER 46

Six hours later

Having arrived shortly after we took possession of the venomous Senator Assad, Special Agent Wanda Garcia arrived from CIA headquarters in Langley, Virginia, and began babysitting the testy senator for them while they interrogated Senator Schiff. Wanda took the senator to the restroom and searched her handbag and body for any weapons. As with a plot synopsis, Austin went through the formalities and, with studied indifference, filled her in on the operation as succinctly as he could, noting that some of the information was still somewhat sketchy. Wanda was irritable and anxious to put the petulant senator in her place and didn't miss a beat. She made no attempt to offer euphemisms or otherwise be polite.

Pushing the slim, diminutive senator up against the concrete wall, Wanda again frisked her from head to toe before finding a small stash of cocaine packed in her panties. *Babysitting* was not exactly a fitting description as she was kept awake strapped to a chair for over six hours in a miserable, barren six-by-eight-foot room with only a faux metal table and two uncomfortable metal chairs under a blinding fluorescent light as Garcia tried to elicit some useful information out of her. No windows, no clock on the wall, no pictures, nothing to allow you to escape mentally.

There was a video camera in the ceiling monitoring the activities. Every so often, when she began to lower her head and retreat into a cocoon and close her eyes, Agent Garcia immediately responded with a stern and indomitable expression as solid as a block of granite. Not being as deferential as Austin had been, she yanked her head back up, and slapped her hard across the face with unstinting intensity, knocking her off her chair onto the floor, face first.

"Bitch, that was my weak arm," she said in an uncompromising cadence.

With a slight, mirthless smile and a paroxysm of unbidden anger, she tossed a paper cup of ice water in the senator's insolent face to revive her. Assad's unrepentant barracuda expression slewed in her direction.

"You don't sleep on my watch, Senator!" Garcia said sarcastically in an acerbic tone, giving Assad a jaundiced smile as she glanced anxiously at her watch.

The senator mentally harrumphed as her loathing gaze wandered around the room.

Austin stepped in, telling Agent Garcia to step back and breathe. He reset the chair upright with the senator still handcuffed to its metal frame and a sizable welt blooming on her cheek. He tried to let the ameliorating factors leaven her mood. They didn't.

Seething with raw, abject hatred and still disoriented and smarting from the slap, she would open her eyes and squint against the harsh white lights of the interrogation room.

The senator was soaked from her hijab, now hanging off the back of her head down to her waist, when Austin and Wanda opened the door. Her bouffant hair bun was in complete disarray. Still strapped to the chair, hunching her shoulders cantankerously, she wasn't a pretty sight, but she had been trained to resist and had a steely determination not to crack under pressure.

Bryce suddenly appeared in the doorway, taking the brooding senator by surprise as he stepped into the room and took the seat directly in front of her.

Without uttering a word, he smiled tolerantly as he tented his fingers on the table.

Looking at Austin and Agent Garcia, he asked, "Has she been Mirandized?"

Austin responded curtly, "Not yet."

"Screw you," she screamed without preamble, giving Bryce a fulminating glare. Her perverse sass was noted.

Bryce immediately noticed the angst in the senator's eyes. "I'm getting the hint that you're going to be obtuse."

She shot him a look of virulent annoyance.

"Where did you learn your oratory skills, Senator?" Bryce asked. "They are quite eloquent," he added in a disparaging tone.

The senator, seething, fulminating, with the eyes of a raptor, scowled and let out a furious hiss through her pole-axed clenched teeth and then spit her venom at him across the table but missed widely. Special Agent Garcia and Austin smiled from the far ends of the table at her unsurprising querulousness as Bryce gave an ostentatious sigh. He stood and walked slowly around the room, his hands clasped firmly behind his back.

"That wasn't very ladylike of you, Senator," Bryce said sagely with a modified sadistic attitude as he scrutinized her.

"I remember you, you bastard," she retorted loudly with a string of scathing profanities. "You're the newspaper photographer from the Manduro gala." She again spat at him, and again she missed.

"Are you sure you want to play it this way, Senator? Be advised that this isn't the attitude I was expecting from you, and I will be honest with you, I can be exceptionally nasty," he said with derision and a sardonic tone.

She gave Bryce an evil look. "Go to hell," she replied icily.

"An uninspired riposte."

Bryce paused, possibly seeing an unspoken acknowledgment in the senator's contemptuous face. But instead, she gave him a sarcastic smile as her perfectly painted lips gnashed in anger.

Bryce's call to the admiral an hour earlier, giving updated information on the inchoate bombshell on their hands, had likely already set off all sorts of alarms. The CIA had no doubt already dispatched operatives to Somalia and the Cayman Islands and would exert overwhelming political pressure on Cuba to disrupt the transactions.

Bryce took a seat at the head of the table, angled back and precariously propped against a wall. "Senator, I'm sure that you're aware of the gravity of your actions and that I wouldn't have taken these measures if

I didn't have overwhelming and undisputable evidence of your nefarious involvement in the human trafficking of a group of young teenage girls to your brother's harem in Somalia, which includes a large sum of illegal cash also being deposited in his account. The irony of this, Senator, is that all of it has been directed and authorized by you, a United States senator of Arab ethnicity who took the oath to serve and protect."

She bared her teeth with asperity and gave Bryce an ugly, insolent smile.

"Fuck you. I'm not going to listen to your bullshit," she screamed.

"Again, for a United States senator, your elocution is excellent."

Her gaze was mutinous and icy. "You are a bastard," she screamed acerbically in a high-pitched, uncontrolled tantrum, adding a couple more invectives. "Your threats cannot harm me. I'm a United States senator! Your threats are nothing more than vaporous, unprovable lies."

Bryce nodded slowly in a phlegmatic manner. "Senator, have you ever heard the proverb 'you reap what you sow.' Probably not…but if I were you, I'd give it some considerable thought."

"When I'm freed, I'll see that you're arrested, and you'll never see the light of day as long as you live!" she screamed defiantly.

She looked up at the ceiling camera sarcastically and stuck her hostile tongue out, laughing mirthlessly. "Fuck off!" she screamed.

Unruffled by her glib histrionics, Bryce nodded again, snarling blithely. "Your brother isn't a US senator, and we both know that if you don't cooperate, he will most likely spend the rest of his life in a Somalian prison hellhole for his heinous perfidy.

"And Senator, you will reside in a similar hole when convicted for giving aid to, counsel to, and abetting a terrorist."

He pointed his finger directly in her face to accentuate the point in a no-nonsense manner. Her eyes went wide, and she bared her teeth, snapping them together, imitating a dog.

"Do you want to throw him under the bus? Don't you have any contrition in your heart for him?" Bryce said.

She was exhausted, and her vehement intransigence was now waning under the pressure. There was a fractional eeriness to the silence in the room. Her face now contorted with pain at the thought. He let her marinate in her thoughts before he continued. He, Glenn, and Wanda looked at her, measuring her up.

She rolled her head once, then quickly, with the facsimile of a shrug, said, "What are you talking about?"

Just then, we went into a staring contest, which she lost. She cast her eyes to the table and didn't raise them again until Agent Garcia approached her and threw another cup of ice water in her face.

Bryce could sense her vacillation, and it was time to push her down the rabbit hole. He glanced at Wanda, who took her cue and stepped in. Austin and Bryce had filled her in on a few details earlier.

Wanda made an exasperated sound.

"Senator, if these girls can be saved and your brother is willing to cooperate with us, he will most likely be acquitted of the crimes. However, I know that you know that this laundered money is going to be used to fund fanatical terrorism in the Middle East, and should that happen, the blood of innocent people will be forever on your hands. Hugo Maduro, besotted with his wealth and power, is, without a doubt, funding and orchestrating terrorist organizations. I also have information that he is funding a significant portion of your campaign, Senator."

"That's fucking bullshit!" she screamed defiantly, continuing to prevaricate about the issue. "You're the terrorist. I'm a United States senator, and you kidnapped me," she screamed again, sloughing off the issue of terrorism in a breathy voice.

"We're wasting our time with this one." Wanda stood up, and Bryce and Austin did the same, letting the moment of silence pull her deeper. "Obviously, there must be a problem with my diction, or we're not dealing with an intelligent woman."

Then, adroitly, they shifted the scope of their interrogation. Laying a conciliatory hand on her shoulder, Bryce said, "Senator Schiff has a much more enlightened view of his future. Senator, he's even come clean about this nefarious scheme, not relaxing one iota, debasing you about your promiscuous escapades with him in Maduro's guest cabins. Senator, we also have you both in flagrante delicto, compliments of Maduro's surveillance cameras, and you've been a naughty girl.

"As a hypothetical scenario, if you were in bed, no pun intended, with a corrupt politician on the take from the Manduro Organization, they may assume that you're being detained as a witness to their operations and might be cutting a deal with the government and ratting them out for protection. If you have even a modicum of common sense in your head, Senator, you will see your predicament as precariously lethal. Hugo Manduro will see you as a liability that has to be eliminated." This added the visceral punch that he knew was needed.

"What do you mean?" Senator Assad blanched. "What's that bastard saying?" she screamed dejectedly with a harrowed, stultifying look. Every leering set of eyes in the room was on her as she began to waffle.

She tried to put power into her words, but her words went arid and came out in a hollow vibrato. She began to hyperventilate. Desperation replacing defiance was now evident in her voice. Equally evident on her face was the irony of the imbroglio as she was now beginning to understand the gravity of the situation.

All three agents were still standing. Bryce stepped forward and said, "Talk to me." His jaw tightened. "Senator, I want details of the pending transfer of the girls, and I want the names of the shell companies where the funds are being channeled and the account numbers and passcodes used in the wire transfers now!" he snapped.

"But I don't have any of that information. Senator Schiff is the lead coordinator, not me," she cried, emitting crocodile tears with only a hint of a plausible explanation. "I know only a fragment."

"I'm waiting, Senator." Three sets of reproaching eyes were fixed on her. "Senator, I absolutely despise your mendacity. Senator Schiff has already confessed to the plot and his casual dalliance with you." After a moment, he whispered, "OK, we're wasting our time" just loud enough for her to overhear his instructions to Wanda and Austin to get word back to Maduro that she was cooperating with federal authorities.

He gave her a minute or two and let the thought percolate. Then, just as the three of them turned and began to leave the room, there was a scream in the back of the room.

"No!" Sensing her capitulation, we knew that the pregnant moment of her full confession had arrived. Her rebellious anger quelled.

The haughtiness suddenly disappeared from her face as she returned to terra firma.

There was an attenuated silence as she lowered her head in wilted mortification and began to sob before our eyes. The jauntiness had been struck clean from her.

"I don't want to die." She was breathing heavily, furiously, and whatever fragile ground she had stood on was shattered. "Stop!" she gasped, crestfallen, apoplectic, and now ashen, stammering and quivering uncontrollably. The senator was approaching a panic, her lower lip quivering. Her mind was going helter-skelter, flooding and overwhelming her with calamitous implications. All pretense of senatorial gravitas was abandoned as she was despairingly crushed with trepidation. She was now trembling and perspiring heavily, having plunged from soaring indomitability to an unconquerable abysmal lassitude. Real tears of anguish welled in her downcast eyes as she quickly became cognizant of the magnitude of her idiocy.

"Please," she implored, vacillating with indecision.

Bryce gave her a hard stare. "Senator, this is a quid pro quo situation. I need information from you in return right now. Otherwise, you're free to go. It would behoove the senator to not lie to me."

"No!" She hazarded a glance up at Bryce. "The information you're looking for is on my laptop back at my condo," she cried. "It's locked in the safe."

"Give Austin the password code," Bryce said.

She gave him the code as her voice trailed off. The senator, her eyes wide with abject fear as she faced the inexorable consequences for being a snitch, was well aware that her confession had now made her expendable and that Hugo would never believe that she was set free without betraying him. Much to her chagrin, her steeled resolve seemed to pour out of her with each tear shed as she quailed in abject fear. He would know that the organization had been penetrated. She would become shark bate and expunged. Loose ends tended to disappear in the Atlantic, the well-known price of betrayal in the iniquitous Maduro organization.

The senator, now petrified with fear, took on a cast of seriousness as she lapsed into a sullen silence, staring at the floor and muttering something in Arabic under her breath. Several moments ticked by as she was held transfixed by the intensity of Bryce's voice and the hypnotizing power of his glaring stare. He couldn't help but see the angst on her face as she gave a resigned sigh and lowered her head.

He and Austin were being careful not to contaminate fingerprints and were back within an hour with the laptop in hand. They found two unused syringes inside the wall safe, along with several bottles of oxycodone, several vials of cocaine, and twenty-five boxes, each containing six bottles of what they presumed to be heroin and fentanyl. If all the boxes contained the same amount, the street value would be approximately $10 million. She was definitely not only a user but also a major dealer for the Maduro operation. They also found a small .25 caliber beretta with the serial numbers filed off and concealed in a small black purse secreted at the back of the wall safe.

Of particular interest was what Austin stumbled upon while surfing her data. Senator Assad had numerous research files containing personal and confidential information and clippings on addictions, past brushes with the law, et cetera, concerning local and state authorities, including their families and close associates, all the way up to the Senate. She was obviously collecting and using the information and any dirt that she could find to blackmail these people as needed. But, unfortunately, this find would be just the tip of the proverbial iceberg.

The senator had now betrayed everyone with whom she'd ever had illegal dealings. It was all on her laptop. It had the names, photographs, bank transactions as they played out, dates, and even potential witnesses. A senior financial bank officer by the name of David Siniscalo was a computer whiz. He had been involved in a tryst with the senator and an underage girl at the Manduro compound. He had been shown the film clip and was now being blackmailed by Senator Assad into servicing the Manduro organization. She had the names of his wife and two children on file, along with the name of the school the children attended. At the instruction of Hugo, Siniscalo would digitally move money all over the world, leaving no trail.

Having gleaned valuable information off her hard drive, Bryce and Austin had an elasticized view of what the operation would entail. They were now going to be taking down and making cases against some very naughty people.

Wanda stepped forward, giving the hinky Senator her Miranda rights with limited enthusiasm.

Having completed the interrogation and packed up the evidence, they took both senators to be processed at the Charleston FBI facility. They walked out of the building with Senator Schiff and Senator Assad in handcuffs, led by Wanda on the right and Austin on the left.

Just then, four rifle shots rang out from somewhere in one of the abandoned buildings across the lot. Senator Assad faltered momentarily and fell dead onto the asphalt pavement, having been shot in the head with a high-caliber bullet. Her head had ruptured in a spray of crimson and gray gore. The three agents grabbed Senator Schiff as one of the bullets whizzed by Bryce's face. They dove for cover behind the van as two more shots rang out, taking out the van's windshield. Drawing their weapons and scanning the rooftops from left to right, they looked for a target, but the assassin escaped without a trace. With no more shots fired, Austin and Wanda quickly ran to Senator Assad to check for a pulse. Unfortunately, none was found. Detritus and pith from her head oozed into a puddle on the concrete pavement. Senator Schiff was still alive, breathing stertorously and moaning in pain, having taken a bullet in the left shoulder.

Angered, Bryce yelled emotionlessly for Austin and Wanda to carry both senators into the van and to call for emergency backup.

Having rose unsteadily, Bryce levered his head left and then to the right. He ran toward the nearest building to confront the assassin, but as he reached the top, the assailant was nowhere to be found, having escaped down the rear emergency exit ladder attached to the rear side of the building. Four 30 mm shell casings lay on the floor.

Ten minutes later, an unmarked Secret Service helicopter landed in the parking lot to retrieve the senators and clean up the crime scene. Fifteen minutes later, there was only grim silence. Something savage and unyielding burned deep in Bryce's gut. He turned and grunted, "Shit!"

CHAPTER 47

Three tedious days had passed. Hugo was having a raging conniption over what Pablo had attempted and failed to do. From what he had gleaned from the newspaper's front page about the home invasion, Pablo was shot and killed at the scene in Gauley Bridge by an FBI agent. This in itself was especially concerning. Why had an FBI agent been at Nuna Polinski's house? Hugo's instinctive skepticism led him to assume that Nuna had contacted the authorities.

He instructed Glenn to clean up Pablo's mess and not to forget to terminate the girl. "I don't want any connection to either," he said. What Glenn hadn't known was that Hugo had secretly instructed another yahoo to kill both Pablo and Nuna this night.

Sensing that Senator Schiff and the incompetent Senator Assad had also been compromised, he had instructed one of his best snippers to eliminate both of them quickly. From what he gathered from *Breaking News*, an FBI agent was shot and had been hospitalized in serious critical condition and wasn't expected to live. The fucking FBI and state law enforcement will be all over these mountains before morning, he thought. In the meantime, following his instincts, he was going to take a hiatus and make a quick exit out of the country to the outlier island until this all got sorted out.

Hugo's 300 foot super yacht *Blue Moon* was docked at the Cape Charles Yacht Club on the Chesapeake Bay just north of the bridge. From Shady Forks, it was a good hour's trip by chopper. He called ahead to have the crew assembled. When the helicopter touched down on the yacht club pad, Hugo and Doc were chauffeured to the vessel docked at the marina, where Captain Garcia and seven Mexican crew members were lined on the dock next to the gangplank for inspection. He was dressed in Bermuda shorts, sandals, and a floral tropical shirt. He carried a leather briefcase and a concealed .38 caliber Smith & Wesson in a holster on his belt.

"Good morning, Senor Maduro," Captain Garcia said. "May we take your luggage?"

"No luggage; we're traveling light. Let's shove off," he said emphatically.

"Yes, sir."

"By the way, Captain, maintain strict radio silence."

Captain Garcia frowned. "Radio silence? Yes, sir, but what if…"

Hugo responded, "Just do it."

The captain had already received instructions from Hugo, and the weather was forecasted to be almost perfect with calm seas all the way to Norman's Cay.

Captain Garcia had been the captain of the Maduro's yacht for just over ten years and was fully trusted. Hugo had purchased it in Cuba and had it delivered to Norman's Cay for his exclusive use.

Hugo smiled behind dark Armani sunglasses, giving the crew a quick inspection.

The sky was overcast with a slight drizzle falling, the salt infused air heavy with the staunch smells of fresh fish coming from the fish market on the pier to the left and diesel fuel from the fuel dock to the right. Seagulls were squawking above their heads, squabbling for morsels of fish. A half dozen boats, including catamarans and luxury cabin cruisers, bobbed in the rolling waves along the weathered waterfront businesses in the marina, which included a fishing and tackle shop on the wharf, a seafood restaurant, and a yacht brokerage firm that Hugo had recently acquired.

A Coast Guard cutter and a harbor patrol boat were stationed and moored some fifty yards away. Hugo had packed a small bag. Among the many perks of sailing on your own yacht was that you could bring anything on board with you: weapons, explosives, sexual slaves. He had all three.

Hugo and Doc boarded and stood on the teakwood deck with margaritas in hand. They watched as the crew untied from the moorings and prepared to cast off. Finally, with the generators already operating at idle, the captain received approval from the harbor master to exit the harbor entrance. Twenty minutes later, having cleared the stone pillars that marked the harbor entrance, the captain throttled full. The *Blue Moon* was on its way. The vessel slowly sliced the turquoise blue water heading out of the harbor, sounding a loud claxon horn as it approached the open harbor buoy, commanding everyone within sound distance to take notice. Easing through the marina's sapphire blue-green water at a leisurely two-knot clip, they looked out and glanced down at the water skimming past the hull as they sailed past the seawall, the water spreading into a wake as the boat picked up speed. A cloud of seagulls was following their departure.

Agent Nunez had alerted Bryce and Austin of the unscheduled trip. Bryce had in turn arranged for a SEAL team to monitor the departure from a Coast Guard cutter and to follow the vessel out of the harbor at a distance. A second SEAL team was already in position on the island, with a third on a nondescript fishing trawler just off the island's leeward side.

Hugo and the Doc stood at the stern and watched the harbor grow smaller and smaller. Having made his escape and now feeling comfortable, Hugo took Doc on a tour of the ornate teak upper decks of the yacht. Before going below into a sumptuous main saloon decorated in Spanish décor, he made several phone calls. His aura flashed with impatience and dark energy. Hugo had lavished a considerable fortune on his boat as it was one of his prized processions. It was equipped with the most advanced electronic and communication equipment on the market. All deck lighting, furniture, and curtains were of the highest quality. All deck railings, staircases, cabin doors, and paneling were constructed of expensive and beautiful teakwood. Three imposing-looking Mexicans in black suits were standing guard outside the bridge.

The *Blue Moon* was a vessel like nothing else on the water, and Hugo felt confident and unconquerable as it rolled up and down in the swelling waves, slicing through the sea. It had a luxuriously appointed master suite with a huge bathroom, Jacuzzi, sitting room, and private office fully equipped with the latest electronic communication equipment. Behind his desk was an electronic board showing the current position of the yacht. Thick sliding stained glass doors opened from the master suite onto an outside deck furnished with a chaise lounge and a table with several chairs where he would enjoy breakfast on warm mornings.

The yacht had five guest staterooms with large windows, private baths, and Jacuzzis. The dining room could seat twelve guests. The vessel's paintings were expensive, exquisite, and erotic. Hugo also had a large selection of pornographic movies for his perusal.

"Well, Doc," he said as they stood on the bridge, "you've seen most of it. I'll show you more tomorrow, but first, I want to thank you for taking care of that senator. I only wish that you had also killed the other one."

"Mr. Manduro, he will not survive my next shot."

"Make sure of that," Maduro said. "The steward will direct you to your stateroom. As a gift, I've requested that a recently acquired young female from Kentucky give you comfort during the trip. She has been prescreened but not yet broken in; she will share your room and provide you with all the pleasures of sexual lust. She just turned fifteen, and I'm sure you'll teach her to be sensitive to your needs." She had been delivered to his room, her head down, shivering and whimpering. "In the meantime, I have some business to attend to. Enjoy yourself."

"Siempre," Doc said with a smile.

No one came to her aid when she began screaming. It didn't last long after he shut the door.

Hugo checked the GPS for the current location of the yacht before he excused himself and took the stairs down to his suite. Based on the current readings, given the fair weather, they would arrive at his private pier on Norman's Cay in two days.

At his request, another young girl was brought to his suite and shackled to the wall. Having beaten and fucked the girl during the night, he had her brought to the deck screaming just before daybreak.

"Captain, cut her up and throw the body overboard. Sharks will take care of rest."

The captain did exactly as Hugo ordered. He knew better than to protest.

They were one hundred miles out, paralleling the ribbon of the eastern coast, tacking starboard, as he attended to his computer, pressing his thumb to the ID pad, booting into his encrypted network connection to the alliance. They were approaching the Bahamas, steering a course to the leeward side of the islands. As they approached the island's coastline, Doc was on the bridge, taking in the impressive sight of the island surrounded by a tranquil sea. Seagulls were squawking and squabbling over scraps of fish bate, their cries loud and brash in the faltering twilight.

Hugo was in a foul, pensive mood. A troubling premonition was creeping up his spine, but he couldn't yet put his finger on it. Though he lived the good life of a very successful capitalist, in his heart, he believed that in using his leadership position and power, he should also rule over all others. He had been a leader in Venezuela, and he would be a leader here in the Bahamas also. In his mind, he had never been wrong.

A ship would be arriving from Iran in the morning carrying tons of armament, which would be exchanged for cash, drugs, and eighty-five virgin teens of various nationalities, including five vivacious blondes from West Virginia. The men they would meet to negotiate and complete the transaction made him uneasy as they were of an unknown desert tribe and, as such, unpredictable. Consequently, his men were on high alert. The negotiated price for the product was $15,000 for Asians; $20,000 for Mexican, Venezuelan, and Brazilian beauties; and $25,000 for European and American virgins.

A quick calculation brought a smile to his face; it would be $2 million for the girls alone. Another $1 million for the drugs. While it was less than he had wanted, it was still a desirable profit, and there were three more shipments in the works.

This transaction would not take place, however.

CHAPTER 48

Norman's Cay, Bahamas

A moonless black night shrouded Norman's Cay. A strong easterly ocean wind blew across the island as a twenty-two-foot reinforced fiberglass assault boat slowed, throttling back as they reached the western shore on the leeward side of the island. Another boat of the same caliber was in the turquoise surf on the eastern side waiting for the signal from the platoon leader of SEAL Team Two to enter the marina just below Hugo's villa. Two dozen SEALs were already just off shore on both sides of the island, hunkered down in black rubber rafts waiting for orders to move forth and begin neutralizing the guards and relieving them of their weapons. That was the plan, and it was the lull before the storm, Bryce thought. While they would take over the island with overwhelming firepower, the rules of engagement were minimal collateral damage and dictated a caveat of the nonlethal takedown of Hugo Maduro along with his soldiers if at all possible. This made the execution of the developing operation much more dangerous than it could have otherwise been because their teams were in a "no fire zone" and were not to use lethal force unless fired upon first.

The island was a well-armed fortress with thirty-five to forty Mexican cartel guards armed to the teeth with AK-47's. Half were at various strategic guard towers around the island, with a dozen roamers going from station to station. Maduro's mercenaries were hired Mexican thugs, wearing tan fatigue pants, wifebeater tops, and combat boots. They openly patrolled the streets and shores around the island. The plan was to insert at high tide so the SEAL teams could quickly move up and cross several sandbars leading to the beach before striking across the island.

Bryce, Austin, the admiral, and the SEAL commander had methodically mapped every inch of the island and produced a floor plan for each facility. A SEAL team unit had been deployed from an underwater naval submarine two miles off the island two weeks earlier to reconnoiter the island and identify any manmade or natural obstacles offshore. Several target beaches were located as insertion points for the amphibious assault. The admiral gave Bryce his usual conspiratorial smile. With lives at stake, there was no margin for error and the orchestration of the operational teams and units had to be flawless.

At the first light of dawn, all the resources and equipment were in place. Bryce had taken out his new Sig Sauer P320. He withdrew it from its holster, switched the safety off, and pulled the slide back slightly, prechecking the weapon to see the hollow-point round in the chamber. Returning it to safe position, he reinserted the weapon in the holster and clipped it to his waist belt.

The raid would take place from four island sections and be executed meticulously, with the precision of open-heart surgery. Though it wasn't exactly going to go that way.

Bryce and Austin were sitting in the back of a Boeing CH-47 Chinook that harkened back to the Vietnam War era. The Chinook approached the island from seventeen feet, then dived and banked, positioning us between two sandbars approximately thirty klicks off the eastern shore without touching down. It was a trick resurrected from the Vietnam War, pulling up at the last possible moment. They exited via the aluminum ramp in the back of the cargo bay meeting up with a mobile naval amphibious unit just offshore. They rode the rest of the way on an inflatable raft with four SEAL team divers rowing. As soon as the bow brushed the sand, they exited, pulling the raft up onto the beach. The divers went back into the water, moving slowly just off the beach. Bryce and Austin began crawling for cover as we made our way to the target.

Bryce radioed the four helos north of us to set down at 0600 hours and deploy their troops and begin a quiet sweep of the island. One bird was to stay in the air at one thousand feet monitoring the raid and deliver support if needed. At exactly 0600 hours, the choppers swooped in and hovered several feet off the ground. Special ops troops dropped from both side of the choppers, rifles at the ready, before taking cover. From what Bryce and Austin saw, the men in the guard towers started dropping like flies. The snipers, using silencers, were doing their jobs to perfection.

A satellite photo of the secluded compound taken twenty-four hours before gave them the complete layout of the island. There was an adequate twelve-hundred-foot runway for light aircraft and a helicopter pad to the left of it. A gleaming Gulfstream was located on the tarmac just south of the terminal hangar facility and was guarded by three armed men. A SEAL team was tasked with taking down the guards quietly and removing the cowling of the left engine, effectively disabling it from taking flight. Hugo Maduro had been spotted on the island and was to be considered armed and assumed to resist violently. It was also reported that an associate named Chris Vallarta was living on the island visiting. Like Maduro, he was to be treated as armed and extremely dangerous.

Two unmarked high-altitude drones had reconnoitered the island several times during the past couple of hours, taking aerial photographs of targeted sights and specific landmarks, including two inconsequential-looking warehouses that seemed heavily guarded. The plan had a welter of moving parts, and the probability of a screwup was always there.

A sizable glitzy party had taken place at the mansion last night and had given the four SEALs the opportunity to move about unheard and unnoticed. The two roaming guards along with their dogs at the marina were neutralized without incident, and three wireless cameras were discreetly mounted to monitor the event. They learned that these weekend paloozas took place a couple of times a month as the product was delivered.

Austin commented, "Looks like a great party: food, music, dancing. And to think that the surprise guests have yet to arrive.

"So we're surprise guests?" Bryce whispered, grinning at Austin.

A gull cawed from a distant mooring. Several expensive yachts were tied up and bobbing in the marina. One belonged to Hugo, and another belonged to Vallarta. The third belonged to an unknown guest of unknown origin. It wasn't in the marina two days ago. Having hacked into the camera feeds inside the mansion, which were wired for maximum surveillance, they saw there were people snorting coke, screwing in the bedrooms, and doing other drugs openly. A number of naked underage girls were spotted in a large studio engaging in sex acts on the floor with both men and women.

Chris Vallarta had concluded his meeting and dinner with Hugo at the main house and retired to the opulently appointed villa that Maduro had offered to him for his infrequent personal visits to the island. Vallarta, lounging in a leather Utter Bliss recliner in front of a propane fireplace wearing only a white silk robe, felt the heat of passion beginning to rise within his body.

Having worked with Maduro for several years, he expected only the finest in accommodations, including entertainment provided by Madam Zagar to service his pleasures as requested. At precisely 9:30 p.m., as he sat at the table overlooking the sea, the doorbell chimes rang, announcing the expected arrival of two young Kentucky-bred countrified virgin fillies. Gifts from Hugo.

He opened the door; two stunning young fifteen-year-old teens were standing at the threshold, each carrying a small duffel bag.

"My name is Polly," the striking, statuesque blonde said breathily.

"And my name is Sherry," the lithesome raven-haired girl said. "You like what you see?"

Chris closed the door behind them. He grinned widely. "Yes, I like," he said.

Polly spoke. "We are sisters. We hope you'll not be disappointed."

"I'm sure I won't," Chris responded with lustful anticipation.

"We'll change in another room?"

"Yes. What do you girls want to drink?"

"We'd both like a Cabernet."

Maduro's Madam Zagar, as she styled herself, was a repossession of a failed Portuguese transaction that had cost her husband's life. Now working for Maduro, she proffered the very best training of young virgin fillies without advertising her service as she had done in Lisbon for her husband. Hugo now owned her, and he alone dictated who got to enjoy her offerings. Having passed the medical examinations, the girls would be tattooed with the Maduro rose on their wrists, showing ownership. They were then turned over to Madam Zagar for eight to sixteen weeks of hospitality training, which included a rigid exercise schedule, hygiene and dietary requirements, feminine beautification, and discretionary obedience training. All body crevices were irrigated and scented, legs and pubic areas waxed, skin exfoliated and moisturized, feet pumiced, nails filed and painted, eyebrows and eyelashes tweezed and colored as necessary. Upon completion of the course, Madam Zagar would personally inspect and allow the girl to entertain her in her private office before they were certified for appointments or for sale. The girls were well aware that failure to meet Madam Zagar's expectations could result in their untimely disposal at sea, as shown in the many films they were exposed to during their training period.

An hour later, Vallarta was nude and staring at them in stupefaction, sitting on the floor against the side of the bed, handcuffed to the bedpost and sedated by the two girls.

Sherry pulled the hooded mask off his head and screamed with both her hands covering her mouth. They were looking at the most grotesque-looking guy alive. A Face of Evil.

No, he was a monster from hell.

"And I think a final pleasure for you, Mr. Vallarta," Sherry whispered in his ear as she looped a razor-sharp wire around his neck. He groaned just as the garrote sliced through his esophagus, and he spoke no more. Polly watched as his head slumped forward. This was how he ended her mother's life four years ago.

Her mother had sold her for $2,000 and a bottle of Chanel No. 5. Polly had planned the murder for a week after learning that they would be entertaining Mr. Vallarta. She had run through every detail a hundred times. Yet she had never lost sight of what it would feel like to kill the monster and hopefully escape on one of the boats. It was the only thing that kept her moving forward. Everything else in her life was lost.

Havana, Cuba

With the takedown operation imminent, SEAL Team Two, armed to the gills and looking like black ninjas in scuba-masked gear, had already received the go-ahead from the admiral before ascending the seaward walls of Vallarta's villa. At exactly 0600 hours, they stealthily breached the dark front entryway and were already inside the Cuban compound before the four security guards and staff could respond and trigger alarms. Having located Vallarta's private office, they downloaded his two computer hard drives, along with a number of documents and thousands of photos of young girls being tortured, abused, and raped both by him and others. All of it was sent electronically back to Langley for processing.

They had also found and photographed an octagonal sex chamber with a massive bed in the middle. Strapped on the moiré walls were whips, handcuffs, leather hoods, and other assorted devices that Vallarta had employed to elicit pain. A ceiling-mounted camera to record the activities was deactivated permanently and secured for processing. Amid the operation, they rescued a half dozen girls being held in the basement. All were unshackled, dressed, and quietly brought out of the building by female FBI agents, then taken down to the rubber raft tied to a quay at the rear of the villa. Four of the SEALs slithered back into the surf and swam along the thin sliver of concrete, a perpendicular extension 150 feet out into the Atlantic, before making their way over to the warehouse and quickly disarming the three security soldiers there permanently before entering the warehouse. Having taken photos of the armament and munitions found inside, they wired the building to explode one hour after their extraction by a naval sub waiting just offshore.

Austin and Bryce, having gotten into their camo, blackened their faces, secured their gear, and were ready. A constant stream of communication buzzed over the secure satellite radios.

There was a lot of logistics and personnel to coordinate. A Coast Guard cutter was stationed twelve klicks off the eastern shore of the island. Two Apache gunships armed with M240 machine guns were now in the air, hovering in wait for orders.

We were bobbing off a remote sandbar one thousand yards east of the airfield. The smell of salt water and sand was intense. We would slowly move the rest of the way into a dredged canal offering easy access to the marina, where we would begin moving in tandem through the moonless darkness. The low hanging fog was an impediment but also a cover. A large pile of couch shells and stacks of lobster traps provided immediate cover.

On Norman's Cay, under strict radio silence and under the command of Admiral Connelly, the island and its spine of back streets and alleyways had been cordoned off by Special Operations Delta Force, consisting of CIA, NSA, and FBI agents, along with Special Forces operatives, all exits had been blocked, and all logistical docks had been secured. Over the last several months, they had slipped in an undercover bartender, a gourmet cook, and two dishwashers at the Buccaneer Lounge, Hugo's favorite restaurant on the island. Well, it was the only restaurant on the island, and it was learned that the Maduros and their guests never fraternize with the help. The few local civilians that still inhabited the island had been cowed; their movements were furtive in their daily activities. They also had an undercover Hispanic cleaning lady keeping tabs on the activities inside his villa and the heavily guarded warehouse. This particular building had bars on every door and window. The admiral had also arranged to have Apache helicopters available on both Highborn Cay to the north and Shroud Cay to the south to give air support if needed without notifying local authorities. A couple of the tourist choppers had been acquired and were being used to periodically watch for any unusual activity on the island.

The seven guest cottages, desalination facility, radio towers, and guard shacks had been discreetly secured. All twelve of the highly trained Dobermans surrounding the three concrete warehouses had now been tranquilized with a neuromuscular incapacitated. Two of the warehouses, with a half dozen forklifts outside, contained a large stockpile of military armament and munitions. The guards panicked, but it was too late.

In the predawn murk, the five men, equipped with night-vision goggles, approached the island at 0600 hours by boat. The timing was perfect as there was a heavy fog coming in off the sea. The waters were calm. The air was brisk, smelling salty and tangy. Bryce was familiar with the sounds of the sea: the morning gulls searching for morsels of food, the lapping waves.

The enclosed double perimeter concertina razor wire fence had already been peeled back and breached in several locations by an advanced SEAL team, who took up observation positions. Several dozen heavily armed federal agents would hit the island from four locations. Bryce and Austin would lead the first boat into the marina before breaking off with another operative and going up the beach to cut off any chance of Hugo escaping to his helo. The second wave would consist of medics and other support groups for the children.

The three bulky coastal guards on the dock, toting submachine guns, were caught by total surprise and taken out with little resistance. Within twenty minutes, the force dispersed and took out the rest of the startled internal security force that had been corralled.

Bryce focused on the main house through his binoculars, where Hugo was expected to be. The twenty-four-thousand-square-foot vintage Mediterranean house with cream-colored walls and a bright turquoise roof showed no sign of life from his vantage point; the house was dark, and all the curtains were open. Several German shepherds roamed the grounds, and they were quietly put to sleep for the next couple of hours. Suddenly, Bryce spotted a flash in the top turret of the house. It was a ray of sun gleaming off the lens of someone's binoculars. Then it was gone.

"Hugo may have seen us," he yelled to Austin.

In reduced light, with an umbrella drink in his hand, Maduro watched the action on the pancake landscape through his Big Eye vision scope mounted in the crow's nest atop his mansion.

Dressed in blue Bermuda shorts, knee-high white socks, and a blousy white shirt, he was prepared for a relaxing morning on the island and had a bottle of Jamaican Bhakta 1990 rum to celebrate the new shipment of fresh pleasures. The Doc, standing next to him, having just exited the shower, listened to Hugo boast about the multimillion-dollar transaction that was about to take place. He was also enjoying his second morning rum cocktail. He commented that the transfer of product seemed to be going smoothly and like clockwork. Hugo nodded imperiously but had a momentary and fleeting sense of foreboding as he looked across the water. He was a man who demanded perfection and expected nothing less than success. Three vans were parked and waiting for the *Pelora* to drop anchor and begin delivering the girls. It would be a short drive to the barracks, where the Doc and his assistant would begin examining the girls. Unfortunately, two FBI agents had mistakenly overtaken the van drivers earlier than planned. Three agents immediately replaced them, donning their uniforms.

To Bryce's team's surprise, two of Maduro's men had slipped into the salt-marsh cattails and began firing AK-47s indiscriminately at the agents.

Bam! Bam! Bam! Bam! Bam! Bam!

The stillness and the ocean's rhythmic pounding on the shore were shattered when the heavy whoop of helicopter gunships began shaking the ground, raking the marsh with pummeling firepower. The automatic weapons from the marsh went silent. The helicopters were flying in from the north, crossing the island to the south quadrant.

Complicating the operation was the spotting of a large container ship flying a Liberian flag that had suddenly materialized out of the fog during the early morning, looming two football fields in length from stem to stern. ETA for US CCG *Hamilton* to intercept was 0645 hours, and all communications were being sent and confirmed in code. The ship's exterior had seen better days and was now looking barely seaworthy. It was anchored with its dark, ominous hull deep in the water ten nautical miles east of Norman's Cay, just far enough outside the Bahamian territorial waters to render it free to do business unconstrained by merchant laws.

There wasn't any activity on deck. Little did they know that this covert operation had been given unlimited latitude and unconstrained by rules or the ambit of territorial laws. The ship was loaded with forty-five cubic yard corrugated metal containers stacked two high and five across from bow to bridge. Two of the four containers on the deck were labeled *Class One Explosives*. The other two were marked *Composition C-4*. The fact that the ship was riding low in the water signified that it was carrying possibly five to six times I the holds what it was carrying on the upper deck, and that was a cause for serious concern.

Two Black Hawks without markings were now circling the ship, with a third preparing to land on the helipad atop the darkened forecastle. Scuba divers from SEAL Team Two had already boarded the ship, rounded up and secured the ten-man crew, and shut down the engine room quickly. It was found to contain tons of illegal weapons and explosives. The twenty-cubic-yard containers were packed with Russian and Bulgarian AK-47 assault rifles, Israeli Uzis, sniper rifles, night-vision scopes, anti-tank weapons, automatic pistols, crates of ammunitions, land mines, grenades, mortars, and surface-to-air rockets including sidewinders and Javelins. The ship was an arsenal superstore ready to supply an army of Islamic terrorists. The girls were just icing on the cake, at a price.

After they quickly secured the captain, it was learned from the ship's logs that the ship was under contract with the Maduro organization to deliver produce from Mexico. The vessel originated in Venezuela and following inspection and the loading of the girls would be bound for Iran, with Hugo's authorization.

There was the soft, distant boom-and-shush of waves crashing, and the palm fronds rasped in the wind. It was hot when they began the assault this morning and was even hotter now, at high noon, as they raced across the sand under the merciless sun.

Barely twenty-four hours ago, at the Port of Punta Cana in the Dominican Republic, the girls had been placed aboard Maduro's seventy-five-foot super yacht the *Pelora*. They had been delivered to Punta Cana aboard a private plane out of Venezuela. The plane and pilot wouldn't be returning to Venezuela as the plane now had some serious mechanical issues, grounding it for an extended period of time, compliments of the CIA. Another confiscated private jet to be added to the CIA fleet. The pilot, having been arrested for human trafficking, began divulging the entire operation rather than face twenty to twenty-five years of imprisonment in the DR. The information was quickly transmitted to CIA Intelligence. The pilot and plane were flown to Florida for disposition.

During its stay at Punta Cana, the yacht had been quickly refurbished with 30 cells below deck. With a tonnage capacity of 5,500 hundred tons, she could comfortably carry 30 passengers and a crew of 8. So the yacht was carrying 30 girls, all show model quality, in their early teens, and a crew of 8 men, with a half dozen girls being forced to work with the staff. Five of the girls were Korean, 5 were Venezuelan, 5 were Mexican, 10 were from Bangkok, and 5 were Brazilian. The *Pelora*, exceptionally fast, could accelerate up to a speed of 20 knots with a cruising speed of 15 knots.

Arriving at the island's eastern side, just south of the marina, at 0700 hours, shortly after sunrise, they dropped anchor offshore and lowered the rigid-hulled inflatable equipped with a high-performance outboard. The yacht was too large to enter the marina. The plan was to transport ten girls at a time to shore before returning for another lot. When all thirty girls were on shore and accounted for, the yacht would depart for Havana, where the crew would await further instructions. A UDT team of SEALs would interrupt the plan. The girls were to be transported from the dock by van to their holding barracks just west of the runway.

Having been given a signal from shore to begin the transfer, they pulled away from the *Pelora*. The sun now high in the sky, gave off a bright oppressive glare. A crew member on the upper deck was squinting his eyes under the brim of his Mexican flat cap, scanning both the sea and the sky with high-power binoculars for any possible threats to the transfer. He didn't have long to wait as a SEAL team had already breached the gunwales of the yacht and shot the crew member dead. A single distress signal was sent from the boat.

"Commandos!"

Just then, the transmission was killed, and the radio in the yacht went silent. The Venezuelan crew, along with the guards, was immediately overtaken. Unfortunately, several were shot and killed after firing on the SEALs. The girls were found below cuffed and in shackles. With the *Pelora* now secured and anchored offshore, the Coast Guard cutter pulled alongside, and the girls were all safety transferred off the yacht.

Now sweating profusely, Hugo slapped at a monster horsefly that had bitten his right shoulder. Now staring out the turret, his eyes thunderstruck and stretched wide, his mouth gaped open, looking visibly pained, Hugo turned to the Doc in utter shock and began to hyperventilate.

"What the fuck? We're fucking being invaded!" he screamed. Fury and rage piqued in his eyes and in his aura. "How could this happen?" he groused.

A bolt of terror ripped through him in a rage of self-absorption as he drew his hand across his lower lip. His teeth clicked together; his face became instantly taut with fury.

Doc responded lamely, looking out the window, lifting his right hand to shade his eyes from the rising sun, "We have a traitor in our mists, maybe an infiltrator. The operation was compromised."

Hugo went ballistic. His brow furrowed, his lips quivering in repressed rage, he threw his drink against the triple-paned window.

Suddenly, the beach was overtaken by fifty or more soldiers fanning across the eastern beachhead. He then realized that a vastly overwhelming force surrounded him. What he didn't know was that a similar force was coming ashore from the western side of the island.

Bursts of automatic gunfire were taking his men down rapidly. Then the gunfire stopped, the bloodcurdling screaming went silent, and the raw silence that followed was eerie.

For the briefest of moments, Hugo stared out the corner of the window weighing his options. His eyes seemed to catch fire, boring into Doc's. He didn't have any options as his fear hit critical mass. His stony expression had shattered into a million shards of wrath. He immediately went to the wall safe, stuffing all he could into a bag, including his gun. His eyes were wild and crazed.

"This way," he yelled tersely, pushing ahead and bending low, motioning the Doc to do the same. In one swift moment, Hugo and Doc descended the loft and quickly entered a secret chamber connected to his study behind a bookcase.

"Shit," exclaimed Hugo. "Stay close!"

He and Doc did a helter-skelter run down the narrow pitch-dark stairwell to a steel door. After closing and locking the entrance door behind them, they grabbed battery-operated lanterns and armed themselves before quickly steeling themselves and looking into the looming pitch blackness before them. The fetid odor of the musty narrow passageway was almost overwhelming. But without hesitation, they both descended the steep stairs and began slogging along a long two-hundred-yard, dark, filthy, and stifling coral subterranean escape passageway, evidently not disturbed for years, leading underneath the airstrip that hugged the shoreline.

The damp, rodent-infested tunnel with exposed wiring in the ceiling had almost a foot of brackish water on the floor, and with the exception of their feet sloshing through the water, the tunnel was dead silent. Being severely claustrophobic, Doc had an anxiety attack within minutes of entering the tunnel. He began to tremble and could not swallow as his heart went arrhythmic. Fetching and gasping for air in absolute throttling terror as his steps began to falter, he staggered and stumbled before collapsing into the dank, rat-infested putrid water. His sentience failed him in the dark; he could no longer see the corridor before him as he made a wallowing splash. Hugo made a grating sound as he turned around and lifted him by the collar of his shirt, pulling the panicked Doc forward. "Shut up, asshole, and get a fucking grip!" he yelled.

Crawling on hands and knees in some places, sloshing erect and stoop-shouldered in others, when the room allowed, they moved quickly, navigating forward as Hugo was determined to egress and escape. Unfortunately, there was no sunlight or electricity to operate internal lighting. Hugo could only see an inch or so into the pitch-black darkness. The heat in the tunnel was brutal. Hugo scorched the tunnel walls with echoing curses and disparagements. Somewhere near the midpoint, a colony of bats took flight and began attacking the intruders. Using both their hands, they fought off the unbidden vampires as they continued their escape. The passageway had been initially built by Carlos Lehder, known by the moniker Crazy Carlos, back in the seventies when the Medellin cartel used it in their cocaine cornucopia trade. Hugo had just been in it. And right now, he had only one focus of attention: to get to his chopper and get the hell off this island.

The splashes of their footfalls echoed throughout the tunnel's empty interior as they ran with the long, angry strides of men bent on swiftly escaping. Both were sweating profusely, and their breath was soughing loudly in the darkness. Upon seeing a flicker of dim light ahead, Hugo exultantly stumbled toward it, Doc on his hands and knees following right behind. They quickly realized that they were looking at the proverbial light at the end of the tunnel. The ray of sunlight was coming through a small leaded glass window in a rusted metal door at the tunnel entrance. Both of them, now hyperventilating and breathing erratically from the exertion and lack of oxygen, eyeballed the corroded locking mechanism on the door. They tried to turn the wheel on the locking device but couldn't get any purchase. Finding a rusted shovel next to the door, the two pried the sliding bolt on the door loose, opening it only a crack and peering out, looking to their left and right. The iron door squeaked and protested loudly as they forced it open just enough to slip through the opening. Suddenly, the heavy door slammed shut behind them, leaving no other avenue of escape but straight into the sweltering heat. There was no means of opening it from the outside. Stopping and hunkering down in the sand for a moment, their sodden ripped clothing clinging to their bodies, they had to quickly adjust to the intense brightness before them. They were squinting their eyes as they emerged to orient themselves to the bright flaming orange orb of sunlight. They cautiously looked over the top of the crumbling concrete wall. The wind had begun to whip the sand into a frenzied maelstrom.

The runway looked clear, and his helicopter was still strapped on the helipad. Just then, two dark silhouettes suddenly appeared ten to fifteen yards outside the tunnel entrance wall, heading straight at them.

Hugo's lethal eyes burned with maniacal defiance as the two were confronted at the end of the hidden tunnel in front of the control tower by Bryce, Austin, and another agent perched behind a high sand dune. They bided their time. Bryce and the others were dressed in black combat fatigues and strapped down with adequate weaponry. Hugo heard the disembodied voice of Bryce, who ordered both of them to lay down their weapons. Hugo was voicing a well-enunciated string of profanities in Spanish before they actually saw him and the Doc.

* * *

Bryce

Hugo was ensnared at the end of the tunnel, and we knew that he would try to get to his helicopter via the tunnel.

Without any other avenues at his disposal, Hugo locked eyes on us gringos, raised his gun, and yelled in a crazed voice, "You are not long for this world, pig! I'm going to fucking kill you."

The agent next to me yelled, "Federal agents!" just as Hugo dove into the sand and came up, firing two rapid shots as he exited the narrow opening. It was their only escape avenue. Bullets ricocheted between the walls, sending chips of concrete everywhere.

He and Doc threw themselves behind the concrete storm wall and fired at us repeatedly. The volleys being fired in rapid succession created a scene of total bedlam. I dropped to one knee and returned fire at Hugo. It was then that I realized that Randy Keen, the FBI agent flanking me, was on his back in the sand. Blood was gushing from a bullet wound to his forehead and gurgling from another to his chest.

Seeing the ominous red puddle in the sand, I instantly knew he was dead.

Hugo dashed across the naked sands helter-skelter, following the Doc, zigzagging back and forth across the beach, desperately trying to reach the chopper. The soft sand was giving him limited traction, hampering his escape, as he was moving left and right across the soft white beach on all fours, tripping as he went. Austin and I took off after them, firing a half dozen shots in their direction as we ran in pursuit. Unknown to Hugo, the chopper wasn't going anywhere as it had already been disabled during the night.

The Doc pivoted in a half circle and fired back. A second later, a bullet exploded in his throat, followed by another in his crotch. His head bolted forward, and then there was a roaring sound before he went face down in the sand, twitching violently with one hand on his neck and the other holding his groin before going still.

I shouted, "Federal officers! Hugo, stop or I'll shoot." I saw Hugo's gun spurt fire twice, exploding in my direction. A deafening burst, orange flashes, and I felt the bullets fly by my head. Hugo lost his glasses in the foray but didn't skip a beat and continued his escape, running right over the Doc. Austin, having taken a bullet in the shoulder, stopped and stayed with the Doc to give aid. It wasn't necessary, and the Doc didn't have time to say his act of contrition.

I yelled again for Hugo to stop as he ran amok on the beach. He didn't. I squeezed the trigger several more times, firing at his legs, and either the second or third bullet slammed into his left thigh. By rote, with the precision I'd learn from twenty years as a SEAL, I took the thirty-yard shot at his moving legs. Hugo buckled, dropped to the sand on his right knee, and pivoted around, firing shots back at me with the shots zinging by me with musical notes as he pushed himself up out of the deep sand, cursing, calling me a fucking bastard as he recovered his gait, dragging his leg in a towering rage in his bid for freedom.

Unyielding to the pain, he held his leg and kept going, dragging the leg like some crazed, desperate animal searching for an escape. Every ten to fifteen feet, he would stop, kneel, ram another magazine clip into his gun, and fire his pistol back at me. A bullet whizzed by my head, slamming into the concrete wall behind me. Closing the distance, Hugo was only fifty or so yards ahead of me, limping and utterly determined to reach the chopper.

Having caught up with him within twenty feet, breathing deeply, I took aim with both hands. "That's far enough!" I yelled. "The next shot will find your fucking head!"

His blood-red eyes glared with raw hatred, and his nostrils were receding and expanding like twin bellows from hell.

Hugo crumbled, going down slowly, splaying on his stomach to an exhausted stop face down in the sand. He slowly raised his hands in the air as he turned over. A mocking grin was etched on his face despite his leg wound.

He had somewhere lost his gun in the sand, and I could see in his eyes that he was searching for it. Now looking like a penitent before an altar, with his knees deep in the sand and his hands raised above his head, he was pleading for me not to shoot him.

Suddenly, he rolled over on his side and with his right hand jetted into the sand, came up, throwing a handful of sand into my face as he leaped and charged forward, launching a scything roundhouse punch toward my head. Moving sinuously, I sidestepped, ducked, and drove my elbow into Hugo's side as he spun around, landing on his left knee with a flailing arm. Hugo then sprung up again and lunged forward, yelling obscenities and launching wild punches with both fists. I blocked one, and then as he went to parry the second one, I found that it was too late to nullify his speed. Hugo's fist blasted past my raised forearm and smashed into my chest. The force knocked the wind out of me as I went backward, landing on my back. Just as Hugo was about to pile his foot into my head, I sprang to my feet, spun around counterclockwise, and slammed a kick into his balls. He staggered back before doubling over and falling on his good knee. Getting up again and regaining his balance, he came at me like a crazed animal. He was fast, slamming into me with his left shoulder in an attempt to hit me with a right hook. I stepped to his right, and as he passed, I drove my fist into his temple with a second punch into his throat, crushing his larynx. His mouth was now gushing blood. The sordid bastard lay on his side, clutching his neck desperately, uttering a guttural moan and trying to suck air. The surrounding sand became purple as he continued to bleed from his leg.

No spurting, just a venous seepage. A curious gull soared overhead.

My head felt like it was ready to explode! This filthy piece of shit had cost us three men, maybe four. I walked up to him and slamming the barrel of my glock to his forehead. He continued to gasp for air and taunt me with his fucking mocking grin.

Just as he made a lame attempt to get up, I slammed the glock against his skull, and he fell back with his head landing hard on the ground. He lay with his back in the sand and just laughed, and he again made an attempt to get up. With that, I hit him with a snap kick square in the head, using all the power I had left. Turning 180, I again delivered a boot into his chin and another to the bridge of his nose, smashing the cartilage. The ruthless scumbag now howled in pain as he collapsed on his back again in the sand, bleeding out like a stuffed pig and sucking air. The bastard lay in the sand inert and didn't move a muscle this time.

I stood back to survey his condition before flipping him on his stomach and cuffing his hand behind his back. Rolling him over, I yanked him up off the ground.

"Maduro, you're under arrest. We're all going to walk back slowly, nice and slow."

Austin stepped forward and frisked him and found a mini .38 caliber inside a belt holster.

"You're going to spend the rest of your fucking life begging guards for smokes in Guantanamo." My orders were to take him alive, but I couldn't resist my urge to do him damage. I put two bullets in his knees and gave him a couple of swift kicks, gouging his groin with all my torquing, strength sending his vulnerable testicles climbing. I hauled the screaming bastard all the way back, and I was less than gentle about it. Hugo looked feral. He was still retching when he was placed in the military chopper under ultra tight security for his one-way trip to Guantanamo. He would rot in hell. The only reason he was still alive was I had given my word to the admiral that I wouldn't kill him.

We opened the door and entered a dark room.

Turning on the lights, we found a workbench with a number of vials filled with blood. A second section held hypodermic needles, and a third section wadded-up tubes with a single tongue floating in a mud mixture.

Obviously a souvenir.

Hugo's cool and meticulous appearance had deteriorated into an edgy, unshaven mess now, with manacled wrists and shackled leg irons clanging together, being helped by two guards.

Even with this, I wouldn't rest until Hugo was securely ensconced in hell.

Taking down Hugo Maduro and his organization was a triumphant moment.

A warehouse had been raided and was found to have been constructed with a series of rooms with clear Plexiglas doors on three levels.

The lower level had a large open area with a bar and linen-covered tables surrounding a raised section of floor resembling a stage for entertainment. Each room was equipped with a bed and a folding chair and table, nothing else. To our surprise, sixty of the rooms were occupied by teenage girls, all manacled, gagged, and dressed in yellow jumpsuits. When we interrogated the guard, it was found that they had been purchased and were awaiting a ship today to transport them to an unknown location in the Middle East. The extraction plan was to place the girls on the CCC anchored off the eastern side of the island and deliver them to federal and health authorities in Florida.

The admiral had been advised that over eighty-five girls had been rescued in the operation. However, due to their physical and mental conditions, they would have to be flown back to FBI headquarters in Langley for medical treatment. Their processing would follow as they recovered from the harrowing treatment they had endured. A number of them had been chained and shackled in the warehouse for over a month.

Bryce and Austin, having returned on an earlier flight, gazed back at the girls disembarking from the C-130 cargo plane. An army of medical and other personnel were already positioned on the tarmac to provide the girls with immediate medical assistance and social services. The girls, naked when rescued, were all wrapped in military blankets and being protected by a number of female FBI and DEA agents along with medical personnel. Seven of them were recovering from being drugged and raped by the Venezuelan and Mexican guards.

Slaty Forks, West Virginia
The perimeter of the Maduro compound at Slaty Forks would be secured by CIA, ATF, and West Virginia State Police by tomorrow, with a second group of undercover operatives securing the perimeter of the base of the mountain. The raid, a frontal assault under the command of Lieutenant Nunez, had left nothing to chance, and nothing would be going in or out of the compound without him knowing about it. Moonlight trickled

down and slanted through the dense trees on the mountain. There were fifteen armed security guards wearing black facial masks and five guard dogs patrolling the grounds with a dozen off-duty guards housed in a barrack facility at the rear of the property. Agent Nunez simmered with impatience as everyone reported in one mile from the Manduro compound.

"Got the warrant, Agent Nunez?"

"I do." He held up the document.

"Then lock and load."

"Let's light the fuse," Agent Nunez said, "and stir up the hornet's nest."

After he made a quick call to command and receiving final confirmation to move forth, the raid was on.

The first order of business was to tranquilize and silence the dogs, giving them an unscheduled nap for a couple of hours. After that, the phalanx of armed guards would be taken down quickly by the DEA, ATF, and state police SWAT teams already in place. At the same time, the fifteen sleeping guards in the barracks were neutralized, with several flash bombs being tossed at both ends of the building. One of the guards managed to escape through a side door, and in the dark ran straight into Glenn. Glenn hit him once in the gut and then again in the face before the guard knew what was happening. Fast and hard! The guard buckled and fell to his knees. Glenn, recognizing the guard as one of the hired rogue bullies, picked his spot and hit him a third time, a solid blow against the side of the head. He was now sprawled out on his back, inert, unconscious, bleeding heavily from a broken jaw and nose. Glenn stepped back and actually enjoyed the confrontation. He reached down and opened the guard's coat; the guy was wearing a leather shoulder holster with a loaded glock 17 that he never got the chance to use. In his waist belt was a pair of stainless steel handcuffs, West Virginia Police issue. Glenn dug through the guy's pockets and found his wallet and badge. He was the chief of police of Gauley Bridge, moonlighting and providing security for the Manduro Organization in Slaty Forks. He was quickly cuffed and taken away by a DEA agent.

Adjoining the Maduro estate three miles west of the main gate was a US Forest Service garage facility for government vehicles. This was the epicenter of the operation, with the entire assault team being housed there, along with NSA agents that were equipped to terminate all electronic communications from both facilities. All were functioning on adrenaline as the sun began to rise. Glenn and a DEA agent surprised the guard at the main gate and stuck a hypodermic needle in his neck with an appropriate dose of ketamine to keep him out for several hours. A trooper took his place. Finally, he and the other fifteen guards were cuffed, shackled, and taken away to a holding facility at the garage, now staffed by West Virginia State Police. Five hours remained before their strike time at both locations. With the Maduro security personnel secured, the SWAT teams spread out over the premises from end to end, securing the compound just as the sun began to rise.

Having heard a noise downstairs, Maria quickly threw on her housecoat and opened the bedroom door only to find two men dressed as ninjas pushing her back through the door and securing her. She screamed, screamed, screamed for her security, thinking this was a home invasion until she spotted two West Virginia state troopers entering the room. They ordered her to turn around, and she was placed under arrests, cuffed, and read her Miranda rights. No, this has to be a nightmare, she thought woodenly. No one came to her aid, and she collapsed, shaking uncontrollably in a hellish spasm like she had been electrocuted.

The following day, in the hangar next to Hugo's chopper, they found a hidden vault with a cache of hundreds of bricks of cocaine and other drugs worth millions on the open market.

All told, it was a successful operation. The body of Chris Vallarta had been found in a guesthouse on the island and had been identified as matching that of Chris Polinski.

There were over two dozen investigators and support staff from the CIA, FBI, DEA, ATF, and Homeland Security doing investigative work, searching buildings, bagging photos, collecting transaction evidence, and scanning every inch of the island with drug-sniffing and cadaver dogs searching for hidden graves. Not one was found. The same process was taking place at the Maduro compound in West Virginia. While the Castro regime was unaware of the raid that took place in Havana until a week later, they declined to cooperate with the investigation of Chris Vallarta and his operations on the island. The Mexican authorities, on the other hand, were more receptive and stepped up their investigation south of the border

Having wrapped up the operations in West Virginia, Norman's Cay, and Havana, I, along with Austin and Glenn, filed our detailed After Action Reports to the Admiral. Austin spent the next week in the hospital healing from his shoulder wound.

Hugo Maduro would be tried in a federal court for murder, conspiracy to commit murder, human trafficking, tax evasion, money laundering, arms trafficking, and drug smuggling. Having breached his wall safe in his office, authorities were now aware of his front shell companies, domestic and foreign business names, and political contacts going back several years. The intelligence was a devastating hit to the organization. The political ramifications would reverberate across the globe for years. He was possibly facing the death penalty or, at the least, would suffer in perpetuity in prison and would never see the light of day again.

The t population of Slaty Forks tripled in the weeks ahead, with federal, state, and local law enforcement officials and personnel. Every newspaper in West Virginia, the paparazzi, and mainstream media converged and joined the gaggle of international media surrounding the Maduro estate. All looking and eager for gore. When the news of the involvement of the Gauley Bridge chief of police and two corrupt senators broke, the people of West Virginia were aghast. The collapse of the international Maduro organization was a rabid headlining media flash fire.

Also competing for front-page coverage was the federal arrest of Senator Adam Schiff and Chase-Webster Bank president David Siniscalo for their criminal involvement in the Maduro organization. Both would be serving long prison sentences.

It was breaking news around the world, with every news outlet on the planet reporting. Every motel for miles was filled to capacity.

With restaurants in the area unable to satisfy the demand, food trucks were lining the streets and parking lots, selling their offerings, from tacos to country fried chicken and hot dogs. The twenty-thousand-square-foot mansion would soon be listed by Sotheby's. Still, even after all the authorities and journalists had evaporated, it would be a long time before the small town of Slaty Forks returned to some semblance of normalcy.

After they secured the island, a search of Maduro's mansion revealed a treasure trove of evidence of his criminal activities.

Having found another huge wall safe in his basement and cleared a half dozen codes, including two fail-safes, investigators found it to contain somewhere between $550 million and $660 million in crisp bills, some of it foreign currency. Along with that were deep shelves of cut diamonds, emeralds, and other glittering high-value jewelry nestled in black velvet sleeves.

The day after the takedown, the questioning of Hugo Maduro began. We watched anxiously from a small observation room with a one-way window into the interrogation room. Since Hugo, with a black hood over his head, was being held at Guantanamo Bay Detention Camp on the Island of Cuba, he was not entitled or allowed to have a lawyer present. He was not going to be subject to an extradition treaty. His trial would be secret and keep him indefinitely while the wheels of military justice spun in the mud.

He would be incarcerated and spend the rest of his life a hundred miles south of Denver, Colorado, at the ADX Federal Correctional Complex, a supermax prison. He would die here; that is, unless he initiated a Methuselah.

Hugo Maduro, who once commanded an empire, now sat on a hard bed in his ten-by-six-foot reinforced cinder block cell on the fifth floor of ADX Florence. He was convicted and sentenced to six life sentences without the possibly of parole. He would never see the light of day again.

There was loud noise all around him coming from hard-core prisoners as he lay on his hard bunk bed. Meal carts squeaked and squealed as they rolled across the concrete floor. Heavy metal barred doors were opening and shutting, stinking commodes flushing, echoing up and down the corridor. His dinner of dry chicken, watery sweet potatoes, and a slice of bread would be slid into his cell on a tray. Instead of silver utensils, as he was accustomed to, he now used plastic.

Having been given official notice by the Justice Department, David Siniscalo, along with several others officers working at the Chase-Webster Bank, were eviscerated by the bank for their roll in the Maduro money-laundering operation. Nuna gave expert testimony, putting the final nail in their future. Maria was relieved of all her financial assets and sentenced to five years in a federal prison. Having been stripped of her citizenship as part of her sentencing, she would be deported back to Brazil. Senator Alan Schiff was impeached by the Senate majority and immediately arrested by federal marshals for his role in the money-laundering and international human-trafficking operation. Police Chief Clay and two of his officers were sentenced to twenty-five years to life in state prison for their role in child sex trafficking and murder. Because of the human remains found at the cabin in the woods, all the others were convicted and sentenced to life without the possibly of parole and would be housed at ADX Florence. In all, their existences would consist of endless torment and an eternity of suffering, all compressed in single cells with each torturous moment being the same.

After wrapping up operations and participating in the sentencing of the faces of evil, I flew home and quickly embraced Nuna in the threshold. "It's over!"

CHAPTER 49

Nuna studied Bryce. "Have you ever considered living an ordinary life?"

"On occasion, though it's difficult to return to what I was," he replied. "It's hard. There are days that I envy ordinary civilian people, but I feel so detached from them."

"Are you seeing anyone?" she asked

"No."

"Me either," she said.

"We could take it slow together."

"Maybe," she replied, and Bryce laughed. "You sound like you might be a little gun-shy."

"Just a little," Nuna replied.

"Some bad relationships, huh?"

Nuna nodded. "A couple."

Bryce chuckled ruefully. "I hear ya. I've had a couple that fizzled too. How about we start with dinner again, the first chance we get?"

Returning his smile, Nuna registered how handsome he was. He would make any right-minded woman drool with his dark, even-featured face and hard, athletic body. Plus, she thought he was sweet and intelligent, and *I like him a lot.*

"I'd like that," she said. Bryce's eyes moved over her face. Then, to her surprise, he slid a hand around the back of her neck, pulled her closer, bent his head, and kissed her.

Nothing about the kiss fell under the heading "taking it slow." Instead, there was tons of tongue action, tons of heat. They both shivered with sensual vitality from the top of their heads to the toes of their feet. It was a *Twilight Zone* moment as they stepped into another life. A life so much different from the one they lived.

Her heart was pounding. She kissed him back and thoroughly enjoyed the pleasant slight tingle of excitement that chased around inside her. Her heart pounded like a timpani, her pulse quickened, and her stomach fluttered like hundreds of butterflies were taking flight.

Giving her a seductive smile, he whispered to Nuna, "I don't suppose you'd want to stop by my room for a drink from the mini fridge?"

Despite the semihopeful tone, it was so obviously said with no expectation of her taking him up on it that Nuna smiled.

"No," she said.

"Ahem, got it. We're taking it slow."

They had reached her room by that time. Bryce waited while she opened the door and walked inside.

"See ya," he said, smiling with the memory of that kiss in his eyes.

It was a lovely kiss. One she wouldn't mind repeating.

"Good night," she said and closed the door.

On a more exciting note, one Sunday afternoon, they had decided to participate in one of Ray's four-hour white-watering adventures on the New River. The innocent adventure started gently enough until the river began to pound and wind itself around the base of the Fayetteville Mountain and start a breathtaking series of deafening four-to-nine-foot vertical drops in the white-water rapids. Having landed on a sandy side of the river six miles south of where they had started, they got out of the raft, soaking wet and glad to be still alive. With a look of ecstasy on their faces, neither could keep their hands off the other, and they made passionate love right there on the river's edge.

Bryce rolled over onto his back. Nuna could see his hard profile, the firm musculature of his chest and the flat plane of his abdomen, the bulge in his bathing suit, and the powerful length of his legs. God, I want him. The thought came out of nowhere, and she was helpless against it. She wanted to crawl up on with him, wrapping herself around him and letting him do anything he wanted to her while she sated herself with that hard body.

There was a hot, insistent throbbing deep inside her body, the too-rapid beating of her heart, and every other physical manifestation of her inner-slut-where-he-was-concerned. He would now and forever be the bulwark of her life.

Aside from the marvelous sex, she also liked his solidness and admired his practical viewpoint and unmitigated honesty, even considering his shortcomings. He appealed to her physically, cerebrally, and emotionally. He was as close as she'd ever come to the one.

He wanted to know more about her, but as with a flower, he had to wait for the petals to unfurl on their own. He didn't want to push.

Sleep came quickly that night.

CHAPTER 50

Twelve months later, standing in the gazebo overlooking the New River Gorge, he found the setting truly romantic. He took and squeezed her hand, letting the ambiance seep into her as he genuflected.

"Nuna, I'm in love with you. In this case, it's really personal. I didn't start falling in love with you that first day in Shady Fork. I fell all the way, Hard. I knew you were the one the minute you turned and looked into my eyes."

He was fervently whispering, even though no one was there. Mutely, she stared at him. There was a ponderous silence. She didn't say a word as she was mesmerized by his eyes and the sincerity she read in them.

She looked dee into his eyes, stunned. "You did? "Lil' ol' me? Oh my god," she responded, rolling her eyes with her rolling mountain cadences. The hillbilly accent that she usually tried to hide dripped from her lips.

"Marry me, Nuna. I've spent all day preparing this proposal. Believe me when I say every word is heartfelt."

She was speechless and dumbfounded. A wave of ecstasy coursed through her body.

For the briefest moment, they looked at each other with a measuring gaze.

Bryce was holding her close, so she had to go up on tiptoes and tilt her head back to meet the depth of his lulling sky-blue eyes. She was more alluring and more intoxicating than ever.

"You're serious about this, aren't you?"

"I love you" Pressing her face between his hands, he gave her the sweetest kiss she had ever known in her life. This was a kiss of devotion.

This was the magical effervescence she had been praying for all her adult life and hadn't had in a long time.

Nuna's angelic eyes misted with tears. Her heart began tap-dancing in her chest.

"Nuna, marriage is one subject I take very seriously. You're immeasurably precious, and I want to love you forever."

She drew in several deep breaths, trying to retain a hold on the moment. This couldn't be happening, and it was happening so fast. "We've only known each other for a year, under very stressful circumstances."

"You do know that you want me, though, right?"

She squeezed her eyes tightly shut as tremors of rioting lightning bolts shot through her body. "Yes, I want you, Bryce Tucker. More than I've ever wanted anything in my whole life." Nuna didn't recognize the frail Southern voice as her own. Her eyes were luminous and alight with effervescence and anticipation. She knew in her heart that she was standing in the arms of the man she loved, hoping that he would be able to hold her this way forever.

"Nuna, all I want going forward is for you to be what you are: smart, talented, self-confident, and self-reliant. And most importantly, for us to be deeply in love and together for the rest of our lives."

Nuna wiped mirthful tears from the corners of her eyes. Framing his face between her hands and looking into his eyes, she said, "I love you too, Bryce," kissing him softly, sealing the vow. "I love you more than my next breath."

For Nuna, there would be no prenuptial jitters this time around. The salient fact was that, without a doubt, she was in ecstasy and totally in love with Bryce Tucker, who would be her life partner. Finally, she was ready to make that sappy lifetime pledge she had always dreamed about. This was truly the most momentous night of her life.

While Bryce had some serious issues, they would work on them together over time. If he was willing to let her help him, they would put his past behind him. She knew he loved her and he would.

For Bryce, it had all started with a phone call from the admiral.

* * *

The following two months were filled with frantic preparations for the wedding. Wanda Garcia was enlisted to be maid of honor, and Ray was Bryce's best man.

News of the forthcoming nuptial festivities spread like wildfire through Fayetteville as the locals were atwitter. Bryce Tucker was now the most popular figure in Fayetteville County.

Bryce wasn't deeply religious, but he had an off-and-on sense of communication with the Almighty in a loose-casual form that worked for him.

It was a sparkling clear June afternoon, and the church was filled with long-stemmed red roses and white carnations.

"Everything is perfect." Nuna beamed. "This is truly the best day of my life."

"Me too," he whispered.

With that said Bryce reached into his pocket and pulled out a small suede jewelry pouch.

In it was a four-carat diamond ring and a diamond brooch hosting a five-carat oval on a string of pearls that had been left to him by his mother in her will. He moved closer and clasped the strand around her neck. Nuna's eyes smarted with a fresh batch of tears as he slid the ring onto her finger. "You're beautiful, Nuna, and now I'm yours."

"It's beautiful, Bryce," she said, her smile beaming as she stood back from the reflection in the mirror.

News of their betrothal became the top story overnight in West Virginia.

It was a glorious Saturday afternoon. Bryce and Nuna were married at Fayetteville Baptist Church on the edge of the scenic New River Gorge. Pastor Daniel Miramant from Nuna's hometown of Coalwood stepped up to the pulpit, proud, and happily officiated the ceremony.

The pastor had known the bride and her family since her birth. With the prenuptial chaos and a flurry of activities to address, they had hired a professional wedding planner from Charleston to cover the event, and the church abounded in baskets of flowers and candelabras.

Bryce thought, I haven't been to church in years, and kneeling and praying feels strange. Since leaving Vietnam, I've had difficulty finding solace in religion and believing in God. Witnessing the horrors of war, corpse after corpse after corpse that once was a living human being, didn't sit well with my religious thoughts and made me question the existence of God. Nuna, a devout churchgoer and a very religious woman, has changed my thoughts. As a result, I have never been happier in my life.

Nuna put on an elegant but unpretentious floor-length white lace and satin wedding gown with a full skirt, a sweeping avalanche of tulle, matching heels, and long white silk gloves. Her resplendent coiffure turned many a head that morning, especially Bryce's.

He thought she was the loveliest and most beautiful woman in the world. He know that he always would.

With the exchange of rings at the altar, the pastor smiled as he delivered the invocation.

"Nuna, Bryce, you've asked your family and friends to gather here today to witness your exchange of wedding vows and to celebrate your love for each other.

"By the authority vested in me by Almighty God and the state of West Virginia, I now pronounce you husband and wife.

"Captain Tucker, you may kiss your bride."

The wedding guests, all in their Sunday best, gave an overwhelming standing applause followed by an eruption of laughter as Bryce drew Nuna into his arms and kissed her beyond the expected chaste token.

"Ladies and gentlemen," the pastor intoned, "may I present Mr. and Mrs. Bryce Tucker for the first time."

Nuna kneeled, expressing a beatific smile, and genuflected, crossing herself. Bryce did likewise.

Walking down the aisle with Bryce, the blushing bride held a stunning cascading bridal bouquet of purple peonies, lilacs, and baby's breath and became Mrs. Bryce Tucker.

Bryce was dashing in his black satin Armani tuxedo and looked like the happiest man in the world.

Along with his best man Ray, a half dozen FBI and local police officers served as groomsmen and bridesmaids.

"I don't attend Mass as regularly as I should," he said.

"We'll work on that," she said, squeezing his hand.

Standing first in line, Ray took her in his arms and embraced her. "Nuna, welcome to our family. You're a godsend as we needed a West Virginian woman like you in the family."

Nuna kissed him on the cheek. "Ray, you're so nice to say the things you say."

"Oh, josh, another jug."

Nuna and Bryce had originally planned it to be a small wedding. Still, by the time the guest list was complete, the church was filled to capacity with local friends and a veritable who's who of local law enforcement, Navy SEALs, FBI, and CIA agents from West Virginia to Washington, DC. For sure, it was the most protected wedding anyone could remember. Nuna had an angelic look and wore a beatific expression as she slowly walked out of the church with Bryce.

Both the wedding ceremony and the elegant reception, held at the Tamarack in Beckley, went off flawlessly. The two female federal officers that had been protecting Nuna stepped in and served as her bridesmaids. Ray was the best man, with Austin and Glenn being the groomsmen. Nuna was utterly taken by surprise when Bryce introduced her to FBI Special Agent Glenn Nunez.

The wedding gifts were amazing. Law enforcement had stepped up, knowing that Bryce had been a bachelor and lived the lifestyle of one. His billiards table was also his dining room table, after all. However, all of that was about to change. Their gifts included Wedgwood china, Waterford crystal, and Lenox Gorham flatware. A new dining room table would be forthcoming.

Now they had only moments before they made their obligatory fare-wells to the last of the two hundred guests in the Tamarack's humongous ballroom. The party passed in a blur for Nuna and Bryce. The lavish, boisterous wedding was finally over. The dancing, toasts, schmoozing, and photographed kisses and smiles over the cake. Now it was just the two of them with the rest of their lives to live together, from now to eternity.

When they returned to the house, Nuna was ecstatic and in a state of pure euphoria as Bryce lifted her and carried her across the threshold of her new home. While she had been living there for over six months, this moment was special. It was the first time that she had been carried over the threshold of this beautiful house as Mrs. Nuna Tucker. She was going to celebrate, and her heart had been filled with overwhelming ecstasy. A dream fulfilled, she would live here in this magnificent house with the love of her life, and they would love each other forever and gracefully grow old together.

Bryce set her down just inside the entranceway and, with arms wide, she pivoted 360 degrees, taking in her new home. She was going to make it a beautiful home with an abundance of love.

"Mind if I remove this?" Bryce asked, gently lifting her bridal veil.

"Not at all."

They kissed, and he held her with the possessiveness she desperately wanted, unfastening the zipper at the back of her dress, letting the neck-line gently fall just below her shoulders. Then the tops of her breasts.

She wiggled out of his muscular grasp, backing toward the master bedroom, a mischievous smile in her liquid blue eyes. God, he loved those eyes.

Having stayed in bed for longer than they should have, with an in-satiable lust for each other, they dressed and made it to the airport with an hour to spare as Bryce had to drag Nuna out of bed that morning.

Fortunately, she had laid out all her clothes the day before and was completely packed except for her makeup bag and accessories. The drive to the airport could only be described as NASCAR, for he was doing over eighty miles per hour all the way to Charleston. He had already decided that if he got pulled over by a local officer, he would show his FBI badge. Federal agents were at least entitled to one get-out-of-jail-free card.

Nuna didn't take notice that Bryce was armed until he showed his credentials at the security check-in. His office had already notified Jet Blue and customs that he was a CIA special agent, and their carry-on suitcases were wisped through the concourse to the flight gate without incident.

One year to the day of that memorable morning when she met Bryce, they were man and wife, on a romantic sojourn honeymooning in Saint Lucia.

While Bryce drew some attention from travelers for both his mannerisms and the fact that he had a gun holstered at chest level, it was Nuna that was turning heads as they walked the concourse to the departure gate. Although dressed for the Caribbean, she was wearing a fitted blouse and a long-flowing skirt, and just about every guy in the terminal either turned or craned a neck to get a second look at her. As he held her hand, it was like she was sashaying down a runway.

Bryce was glowing as he knew that she was oblivious to the googly-eyed passersby giving her exclamatory looks.

They were traveling first class. The attendant graciously took their jackets and carry-ons, storing them in the bins above. Nuna took the window seat, while Bryce sat beside her, holding her hand. Having had little sleep, she leaned back, latched her seat belt, closed her eyes, and let the predeparture activity lull her. She was sound asleep, lost in a world of her romantic thoughts before the plane even lifted off. The plane then began its southeastward turn over the Atlantic.

Nuna didn't open her eyes until the pilot announced they were descending and preparing to land at the Hewanorra International Airport in Saint Lucia. Their descent and disembarkation were carried off without a hitch. A limousine waited in front of the airport for their arrival.

His teeth were a sparkling white against his ruggedly handsome tanned face. The island sun would only enhance the color of his skin.

After he retrieved their luggage and began schlepping it through the airport, Nuna made a quick stop at the ladies' room to freshen up. Bryce was leaning against a railing, waiting for her as he read a travel brochure on things to do in Saint Lucia. Nuna had her own plans. Bryce would take her in his massive arms and suavely carry her to a nearby palm tree, undress her, and make passionate love to her until she and he climaxed and climaxed and climaxed. The travel agent had told her before they left that it only rains in Saint Lucia a dozen days a year. So far, they had missed them all.

Nuna got her wish.

The couple spent their honeymoon secretly ensconced in Saint Lucia relaxing, frolicking in the waves, and taking long walks on the warm white-sand beach by day. Then, after enjoying a gastronomic Caribbean dinner of cold lobster and ceviche with a chilled bottle of Chardonnay in the evening, they would moonlight bathe in the warm waves. Finally, they were cloistered in an evocative, candlelit over-the-water-thatched-roofed bungalow, making exquisite love and listening to the rhythmic pounding of the ocean surf with a brimming flute of leftover bubbly. The darkened night sky was crystalline with stars; the air was faintly redolent of salt.

With both of their bodies having been burned to a deep copper tone by the tropical sun in just a couple of days as they lay on the beach, they fell prey to the magical masseurs and their tropical twin massages. But, unfortunately, they only had seven days in this paradise as they had an important appointment in Langley: his official retirement party.

CHAPTER 51

One year later

Having received a healthy settlement from the Maduro organization and the Chase-Webster Bank for the attempt on her life and her burned-out home in Gauley Bridge, Nuna decided to sell the two acres of land she owned to a young couple that wanted to build their own home.

Nuna was now living in Bryce's beautiful home atop the rim of the New River Gorge, and the botanical views were breathtaking. She had never pined for a life of luxury but was now looking forward to using her exceptional culinary skills in her kitchen for Bryce. The log cabin and the setting formed the most beautiful place she'd ever seen. That thought was validated every morning when she looked out over the majestic gorge. She loved the gorge's peace, solitude, tranquility, and the occasional burst of song from a resident mockingbird. Her mind was now as clear and calm as still water. Her life was now a reflecting pool. No worries and no anger. Again, like looking into a reflecting pool, only reflecting pure love.

Bryce had given her the mission of decorating the house from a feminine perspective, and she gave him a crash course in decorating.

She no longer turned on the TV or listened to the news. It was all bad, filled with conflicts, violence, hatred, racism, and bigotry being committed by terrible people. Yet her world was now full of bliss and sublime peace. What will I now do with all this free time? she thought to herself. What will *we* do with all this time? Use our imaginations, and maybe take some time to talk.

She smiled mischievously. She loved it!

Nuna had turned down a manager position with the Chase-Webster Bank and decided it was time to pursue her lifelong aspiration of becoming an author of children's books. She didn't want to work for anyone ever again. No more bureaucratic conflict and the morning pile of paper crowding her inbox. She now had the freedom to write, the time to do it, and most importantly, the support and blessing of her loving husband. She was now the obedient and submissive wife of a man she had only dreamed of, and she literally tossed away the last vestiges of circumspection. Bryce, with her input, built a beautiful library studio on the upper level of their home with an unobstructed view of the river.

Bryce took a step back and semiretired from the CIA. Having done her diligence, Nuna convinced him that undercover FBI agents' mortality rate wasn't high. But as he already knew, it was high for senior undercover FBI special agents acting in the capacity of CIA agents and he should resign. Bryce had already known that having served fifteen years, he was on borrowed time, and his occupation was unforgiving. The admiral reluctantly accepted his resignation; Bryce would now be an acting consultant as needed. He finally decided to let the younger agents do the shooting and globe-trot. We wanted both stability and a home life. Within two months, he accepted the position of sheriff. Fayetteville had a new sheriff in town.

Bryce had an overwhelming sense of valor and a deeply ingrained penchant for protecting others.

* * *

The grandfather clock chimed six times in the distant living room, announcing 0600 hours.

Bryce opened his eyes to a sunny morning, feeling relaxed and refreshed. It was one of those serendipitous days when everything was going to be picture-perfect. Nuna was stirring beside him but not yet awake. Or so he thought.

Suddenly her legs encased him, and the bedroom was instantly filled with the effervescent energy of a new life.

As Nuna looked out from the front upper deck of her new home in her stocking-clad feet, she was awed by the natural scenery and the stark, sugary beauty of the landscape before her. A couple of does were foraging for food at the far tree line. How different this all was from where she had been. The backyard was bathed in silvery sunlight. The air was clean and crisp, and the sky was ablaze up into the heavens.

Nuna had slept late this morning and awoken to the sounds of chirping birds and the sibilant whisper of his breath. She was floating in white clouds, with a thick white comforter, puffy pillows, and a thick white bedspread piled at her feet. The king-size bed was topped with a white canopy and by far the most comfortable she had ever slept on. She lay there trying to convince herself she was really there. There was no jarring alarm clock, no harried rush to shower, dress, and hurry through the frantic rituals of getting to the bank. This was the way she would live out her life. Knowing that Bryce was close, she could now lie abed, naked, and not worry about danger.

Bryce kissed her.

"You're incredibly nice to wake up to," he said.

"You too," she said with an impish grin, running her hand down into his briefs. "Might something be growing down there?"

"Nuna, You're a hell of a perceptive woman," Bryce said, rolling on top of her.

She gazed up at him with her melting mountain girl look that made her man as hard as steel but as malleable as putty.

With reluctance and in boxers only, Bryce had already left the clouds and begun his morning maintenance. Lathering his face over the bathroom sink, he couldn't believe he was married to the prettiest woman he had ever known. Without a doubt, she was all woman, passionate and unquestionably sensuous. Having shaved, he stepped into the shower and turned the faucets on full blast. He soaped himself, besotted with the beguiling image of her vividly imprinted inside his mind. Her scent was so familiar to him now that he savored it in his dreams. Turning the water off, he stepped out of the shower, drying himself with a thick oversize towel as he padded naked around the bathroom. He was having a hell of a time stuffing his oversize and now swollen manhood into his Tommy Johns. He frowned as he stifled a yawn.

Slapping his face with a splash of Polo, he dressed and went for a run with Thor.

* * *

Nuna slipped out of her robe and headed for the bath. She had begun the morning languishing in a bubble bath for a half hour before stepping into the steaming shower and luxuriating.

The water in the shower was heavenly as she closed her eyes and let the spray pound over her body.

She lathered more lavishly than she usually did, sliding her hands over her body with a renewed appreciation she had never felt before. The scent of floral shampoo wafted in the air.

It sluiced over her body as a delicious morning pleasure. She could feel the pores of her skin reacting to the refreshing cleansing. It was mornings like this when she felt infused with everything beautiful about living in the mountains of West Virginia with Bryce.

He opened the shower door and stepped in, closing the glass door behind him.

"Bryce," she yelled. "You're getting all wet."

With his big hands, he pulled her in and captured her, framing her face.

"Yes," she whispered. "I remember."

Bryce unzipped his jeans and stepped out of them, dropping them in a puddle.

Nuna looked down with appreciation at his jutting penis, startled to realize that he was now fully erect. A wave of sizzling heat rushed through her as she encircled his penis with her hand and softly stroked it, rolling her thumb over the massive bulb.

"What are you doing?"

"I can't resist you when you're all wet and under the showerhead. It gets me hot. Then again, Nuna, everything about you gets me hot."

"You're amoral, Bryce."

He winked.

"I know, but I'm only shameless with you, my love."

Time arrested all thought. One minute turned into ten.

She had no chance before his mouth took possession of hers. The shower had become an orgy of naked skin, warm water, curious hands, and insatiable mouths. Her lips were pliant against his. His tongue was like that of a marauder, maneuvering with limber skill. He was running his hands with precision over her skin, touching and caressing every erogenous zone on her body, stimulating and sending a thrill of pleasure through her.

Pure hedonistic gratification that released a bloom of warmth suffused her body, leaving her limp. She was now his captive. All she could do was make helpless little mewling sounds deep in her throat in an orgy of excitement. She kissed him back with a burning intensity that she had never known existed in her.

With his big, possessive hands, he gripped her ass and lifted her straight off her feet, cradling and pinning her against the shower wall tiles as the warm water sluiced down her body. She was oblivious to everything as his soapy hands caressed her body. Instinctively, she clutched his shoulders to steady herself and, at the same time, wrapped her legs around his waist. She plastered her breasts against the muscled wall of his chest, arching her body to meet his incredible length. She could feel the intense heat radiating from his body and the warmth of his breath gently blowing in her ear.

His lips were hot and urgent and mind-blowingly arousing. The moment's excitement created an erotic thrill, sending tremors through every inch of her body.

She was now becoming a pathetic primitive creature, encasing him between her thighs and kissing him with reckless abandon. He held her in place with one arm around her back. With his other hand, he teased her mercilessly until she was desperate for him to enter her.

He sandwiched her against the wall and then impaled her with his turgid penis, driving deep inside her womanhood. She was feeling a mind-blowing, delicious sensation inside her body that she had never felt before. The feel of him rhythmically pumping inside of her was a mindless pleasure and a blast of torrid heat. She sank her nails into his shoulders as he stroked rapidly in and out.

His phenomenal release rocked her body, leaving her breathless. When he climaxed, she knew he had deliberately held back, waiting for her to reach her pinnacle first.

When it was over, they remained locked in each other's arms for several long, tremulous moments, breathing hard and recovering. Finally, Nuna squeezed her eyes shut; she literally wanted him to stay nestled in her forever.

Then, very deliberately, Bryce lowered her to her feet and began toweling her first. His act of chivalry. He tenderly adjusted the robe around her, gave her an understanding smile, and softly patted her bottom.

"I agree," he said. "You need time to get attuned to the idea of having me around."

Nuna shook her head with a naughty glint in her eyes. "Oh yeah."

She was absolutely beautiful when she stepped out of the shower and dried herself in the mirror. She had not a hint of makeup on. Her nose was prominent, her lips full, all enhanced by wide blue eyes that were warm, intense, and playful. Nuna smiled and replayed the scene over and over in her head as she recalled every precious morning moment. She had never known what true love felt like, but she truly understood the treasured feeling now.

"Bryce. Make love to me again."

With purpose, she slowly stroked his penis and pressed her hips up against him while provoking him with a persuasive tongue.

His heartbeat began to accelerate, and his manhood became turgid.

As Bryce reentered her, Nuna moaned and murmured something incoherent. Her whole body and soul quivered as Bryce buried his face in her hair and she surrendered to his explosive release.

"Bryce, I'm with you forever."

As they now lay entwined under the covers, she pulled him in tightly against her breasts.

"I'm hungry," Nuna said from the bed, now sitting up against the headboard with the sheet pulled up to her neck.

Bryce grinned at her with his mischievous eyes. "What kind of hunger are you referring to?"

"Bryce Tucker, you have an insatiable appetite for sex. That's a good thing," she said with a devilish smile."

"Ohhhhhh, you mean food. We may have just burned up several thousand calories in the past hour.

Nuna blushed prettily. "I can't think of a better diet plan."

She surreptitiously found her panties and slipped them on as she stepped out of bed.

Bryce exited the bed behind her, pulling on his jeans with quick, disjointed motions.

The splendor of last night would be forever burned into her memory bank.

Their morning shower together became a ritual of love. Unashamed and uninhibited, their hands explored slick skin, caressed and massaged, amid murmurs of pleasure and sighs of fulfillment. His lathered fingers moved provocatively through the silky tuft at the top of her thighs. Their coupling was exquisite and seemingly timeless.

* * *

He was smiling with a comical leer, and the sunlight pouring in through the bay window spilled over his tall, powerfully built body as if he were as solid as the house itself. His broad shoulders and wide-muscled chest stretched out the white T-shirt in a way that made her take notice. The muscles of his arms and a six-pack abdomen with narrow hips mounted on long powerful legs all screamed "all-American man!"

Having finished his morning ministrations, Bryce walked out onto the deck and embraced her. The leaves were falling from the trees, twirling slowly and mournfully. October now delivered cool nights. A mist slipped silently through the mountains as softly as a spider's silk, confirming the end of summer and foretelling of another West Virginia winter. She had a fresh, citrusy, just-out-of-the-shower scent to her. He turned and smiled at her, and her heart swelled with love. He kissed her, and when their fused lips parted, she looked up at him, her angelic eyes wide and glistening. She cupped his jaw with her hand and beheld him as if she were memorizing every nuance of his face.

"I love you, Bryce Tucker. I've never known a man like you."

"I love you, Nuna."

She smiled.

At the edge of the thick glade of trees, there was a doe and her tiny foal nibbling on grass in the misting morning rain. Nuna, holding her cup of coffee in tranquilly, held her breath and watched them before they slowly meandered back into the forest.

Now an author of children's stories, Nuna was going to make a new life for herself and Bryce in which corruption was part of her past, not her present and not her future.

That part dazzled her.

Having already made the bed, Nuna was now bending over the couch in the living room, arranging and fluffing the cushions and some throw pillows. He just leaned against the archway, enjoying the view.

When Nuna stood up, she noticed him with a shit-eating grin on his face. "How long have you been standing there?"

"Just long enough to admire your heart-shaped derrière in those tight jeans."

"My jeans aren't tight."

"They are when you bend over. Care to show me again?"

"Another time." She laughed.

"Of course," he said.

* * *

He was freshly shaved and smelled of cologne and just a faint hint of peanut butter on his breath. He had on clean but well-worn Levi's and a plain white shirt. A Western tooled-leather belt and cowboy boots. She needed and wanted the support of his touch. She might still feel vulnerable, but she damn sure wasn't going to feel it alone anymore.

Reality climbed up on his chest and stared him in the eye. "Bryce, please don't make me a widow again," she said. "I'll be furious with you if you make me a widow."

He rolled onto his side and riffled his fingers through her wild blond hair. "Sweetheart, I'm going to keep that in mind."

She touched her fingertips to his cheek and gave out a soft sigh. "I love you."

The sounds and smells of breakfast emanated from the kitchen, along with the sounds of a woman humming. She had already set the breakfast table. The smell of coffee, bacon, eggs, and fresh homemade buttermilk biscuits overwhelmed my senses. He stood sentry, waiting for the toast to pop up. Then, as if that wasn't enough, she had made a delicious fresh peach cobbler and placed the crockery with a scoop of vanilla ice cream for dessert on the table. Nuna loved her kitchen, and they both sat down and enjoyed a leisurely breakfast. From the kitchen bay window, she had an unimpaired view of the mountains in the distance.

Absently looking at her, Bryce polished off the cobbler and licked the last dripping of ice cream off his spoon, licking his lips with his tongue.

His ritual was turning on the morning news and leafing through the *Fayette Tribune*. Not because he liked to listen and read the news; he didn't. Instead, it reflected Bryce's need to stay in touch with the developments in the world they had left behind. It only took a minute or two before he muted it as he couldn't stand the chatter and the incessant commercials.

Nuna, holding onto her old-fashioned mountain ways, preferred washing the dishes by hand, seasoning the skillets, and wiping down the granite counter. When the kitchen was spotless, she would drive down into town and get a local newspaper. She would arise early and go for a swim in the heated pool before relaxing in the churning bubbles of the hot tub. She loved the tranquil solitude of her home. Time permitting, she would ride her horse down through the mountain holler with Thor close to her side and breathe in the fresh Appalachian morning air while watching a hawk pirouette freely in the currents above before galloping back up and finding Bryce nesting in front of the deck fireplace, drinking his second cup of morning coffee on the back porch. This had become their morning MO.

Later that afternoon, as dusk seemed to be gathering, Bryce took her hand. "Care to take a walk?" he asked.

They walked a narrow ridge path up a steep incline through the verdant forest that she hadn't yet known about. Thor was right ahead, seemingly providing protection from chipmunks and other rodents brave enough to scurry across the path. Bryce explained that an ancient Shawnee or maybe a Cherokee passage led to a forgotten outcropping in the forest overlooking the spectacular gorge from the eastern rim.

When they crested, she paused, catching her breath and looking out across the abyss before taking in the scenery; she could see in the distance the Hawk's Nest on the other ridge of the gorge. The immense stone precipice was of ancient limestone and it hung off the side of the mountain, reflected in the translucent water below. Stepping out to the edge, she felt like she was suspended in the open air. It was majestic and beautiful, with wave after wave of rolling Appalachian mountain vistas stretching beyond the horizon.

He took her hand, looked at her with his hypnotic smile, and yelled into the george, "I love you, Nuna!" The echo returned with an incredible resounding approval.

So passed their days together. Nuna soaked in the pleasure and joy of life all the more because she was now Bryce's wife forever. She loved to work in her kitchen, making Bryce home-cooked meals, and Bryce became the captain of the grill on the deck. When not cooking, they would dine out in local eateries or pack picnic lunches and either walk hand in hand, jog a mountain path, or ride their horses down to the river's edge and wallow slow and lazy in the cool mountain water. It had become obviously clear to Nuna as she kept a pace that she was a better runner than Bryce had expected. Thor would curl up under a weeping willow on the bank when not in the river and always be alongside, protecting them from vicious squirrels and curious rabbits.

John Denver got it right when he coined the phrase "almost heaven."

They spent many of their evenings ensconced on the porch swing in the cool mountain air, talking and listening to the crickets. Somewhere out in the woods, a coyote was yipping in anticipation of a possible meal.

Ray stopped over just before noon with his tackle box, three rods, and a Styrofoam cup filled with bait, and they let him browbeat them into going fishing. "Come on, you two, let's get these poles in the water." They grabbed a six-pack, and off they went.

Ray led us to his favorite spot where catfish ran. It would be catfish for supper tonight. We spent several hours fishing on the riverbank, landing a few decent-sized catfish and a couple of healthy largemouth bass.

While she prepared a garden salad, Ray and Bryce did the filleting and prepping of the beer-battered fillets, cooking them on the grill along with a half dozen cobs of corn fresh out of our garden. While Bryce removed the corn off the grill, Ryan, emperor of the gridiron, carried the golden platter to the table. Thor sniffed the grilled fish wafting in the air, licking his chops in anticipation. With the combination of sun, fresh air, fishing, and Guinness, it didn't take Bryce long to fall into a slumberous sleep in the slider.

Having finished supper and cleaned the dishes, Nuna joined him. Ray left with a promise that they would go fishing again next week.

EPILOGUE

Two years later

Autumn came, and the cool nights grew longer, with the weather seesawing back and forth. The air smelled of burning firewood. A brisk wind warned of cold days to follow. The deciduous trees were already beginning to turn. It wasn't quite seven o'clock yet, but nightfall came early in the mountains, especially at this time of year. The night sky, without light pollution, was brilliant with stars. The ground began to be covered in a kaleidoscope of wind-driven autumn-colored leaves. Having finished an elaborate dinner of tenderloin Kobe steak with mushroom sauce and garlic mashed potatoes that began with a Caesar salad followed by Maryland crab cake appetizers, they feasted on her homemade hot apple pie topped with vanilla ice cream for dessert.

Nuna was an excellent cook, for sure.

After dinner, Bryce cleaned up and cleared the table while Nuna stacked the dishes and silverware in the dishwasher, which he would always rearrange before turning it on. With the kitchen in order a few minutes later, they migrated out to the rear deck, and Bryce lit a cheery fire to enhance the evening. She was sitting on the bench cushion with her shoes off and her feet tucked under her. The October sun angled behind the mountain ridgeline, leaving in its wake a broad ephemeral ribbon of ruby-infused amethyst twisting through the indigo sky. She held her wineglass in both hands and stared over the rim of it into the fire. The glass was still nearly full in her hands. The flames moved in the fireplace, and one of the logs settled. A bubble of residual moisture, squeezed by the heat, oozed out the end of one of the logs and vaporized in an audible hiss.

Bryce sat beside her, leaned back a little, stretched his legs out toward the fire, and put his arm around her shoulder. he could tell that she had

598

just showered. She smelled good, like soap, powder, and woman. They sat quietly for a while. It had been a perfect relaxing autumn day as she curled up on the sofa with soft, soothing new age music playing throughout the house. Thor had switched allegiances and was lying content and vigilant, sprawled below her. Then, with the gloaming of the ambient night sky fading into a somnolent darkness, there was the familiar call of the whip-poor-will deep in the woods followed by the soft, sonorous cry of a great horned owl that must have been nesting.

Fireflies lit up the darkened back lawn. Because Bryce was now in her life, everything was new, exciting, and wonderful. She thought she could sit there on the back deck talking to this man with his grinning five-o'clock shadow for the rest of her life. The evening was charming and now in full-throated song. A lone bay of a wolf could be heard somewhere in the forest. Invisible creatures celebrated in the darkness: frogs, crickets, and nightingales.

The almost full hunter's moon was the only light in the sky. Bryce poured her a scotch from the enclosed bar, turned on some slow music, and then poured one for himself. He clinked her glass, and they both took a celebratory sip. They just sat there watching fireflies in the grass, talking about growing old together. In the distance, there was a shirr of cicadas and the croaking of a couple of bullfrogs adding to the nocturnal chorus.

"Nuna, you're a remarkable woman, and I will love you forever."

She swayed to the soft music and sashayed over to him in her slinky peignoir with its loose, cleavage-barring neckline held up only by two satiny spaghetti straps. The shimmery peach negligee clung to her full, prodigious breasts, leaving little to the imagination. Her nipples stood up in taut supplication beneath the thin silk.

He had to know, as she did, that they were like that because of him.

"Bryce?"

"Hmm?"

"That was an eloquent *hmm*," she whispered. "This is all I've ever wished for."

"As what might that be?" he asked.

"Blissful normalcy," she whispered languidly.

Neither said a word, and all was silent until Bryce spoke. "Any other wishes you might want to consider?"

"Great sex whenever I want it." Nuna, now a little randy, kissed his lips, did a little bit of spin, and then glided back to the bedroom, creating a sublime invitation. "Bryce, I'm so glad I stumbled into your woods."

Walking away from the fading ghost sex she had shared with her late husband, she was now in a wave of heat and ready for some mind-blowing hot sex with her man.

Turning on the gas-fired fireplace in the bedroom wall, going over to the huge California king bed, she pulled back the thousand-thread-count Egyptian cotton sheets and then stripped back the thick silk floral duvet, piled high with plush coordinating shams and throw pillows and the scent of lavender sachets.

Her life with Bryce was going to be one full of love and enduring happiness.

His unleashed sexual desire percolated into Nuna, and she responded willingly. It blossomed and spread through her now sun-kissed body like an approaching storm of lust.

They were naked, lying on the bed. Nuna was on her back, and Bryce was on his side, leaning over her. She was staring deeply into his eyes, and crickets could be heard through the open windows where sheer curtains ruffled in the night breeze.

Bryce whispered, "Your mine."

"Bryce, I was once affronted by a man's possessiveness. I'm not anymore. Your assertion is only half-right, though," she said.

"Why?"

"Because you're my man. And I take that very seriously," she said with some asperity.

He cupped and kneaded her breast before sliding his hand down affectionately to her knee, moving the hem of her skirt slowly and bunching it around her hips. Her slender and shapely legs were sheathed in pale fishnet nylon stockings connected by lacy suspenders to a garter belt.

He slipped his hand inside and began caressing the inside of her thigh. Nuna was purring. Tremors of white-hot carnal flames rippled through her as her head thrashed back and forth on the pillow; she was crying out his name.

She flung her head back, her lips silently appealing to his ardent kiss. Bryce was all too obliging to grant her wish. He reached over and placed his hand on her breast, cupping the fullness inside her slip. Caressing her delicious body and abrading her skin was truly erotic.

Day faded, and twilight gave in to darkness. They fell asleep facing each other in peaceful quietude with arms enwrapped.

Bryce enjoyed the languidly sublime aftermath of making love with Nuna. He kissed her, stroked his hand through her hair, and then pressed his forehead against hers, enjoying lying face-to-face with her in blissful lassitude. He lay quietly, finally hearing her breathing slip into la-la land. He finally allowed himself to succumb, and they became one in body and spirit.

She put her arms around his neck. "How do you do that?"

"Do what?"

"Look ominous and dangerous and incredibly sexy all simultaneously."

He appeared to give that a moment's serious contemplation. "Damned if I know.

"It's a gift." She laughed and pulled him closer.

He felt the vibrant energy of love shimmering and knew that Nuna felt it too. They would share it for the rest of their lives.

"The government doesn't grant sabbaticals. It's time to take my life back. I'm talking about retirement."

Nuna offered no resistance as he slid her scanty garment down her thighs. She didn't waste any time stepping out of her panties.

While Bryce was fierce and unrelenting as an operative, he was a very nurturing person at home. Nuna loved that part of him. He was caring and had a gentle spirit, and she loved his tenderness.

They lay in each other's arms for a long time that night after they made love, with a full moon shining in their bedroom window. With their naked bodies still fused together, they felt a sense of breathless repletion. And after he fell asleep, she lay next to him and watched him. And all she could think as she looked at him was how lucky she was to have him. He was all she needed and wanted and always would.

* * *

Bryce would relax on the rear deck with a beer in one hand and a cigar in the other. Other times, he would be in the garage working on the engine of his latest acquisition, a treasured classic 1963 Corvette.

Walking into the kitchen, he stopped and inhaled a whiff of shellfish, tomatoes, and saffron. "What is it you're making for dinner? It smells delicious," he said with a grin.

"It's a dish that I saw on a menu last month. It's called paella, a popular Spanish dish you'll love."

Bryce responded that the aroma alone would secure his presence in the kitchen.

Over dinner, they opened a bottle of prosecco and clinked our glasses. The paella was a hit, just as she said it would be. After dinner, he began to help clean up, stacking dishes in the sink until she told him to stop, insisting that this was her domain. It didn't take him long to learn that everything in her kitchen was planned and equipped in fastidious detail. He liked it.

She opened a lower cabinet and tied a full trash bag. "You can take this out to the garage."

"Happy to, my love."

"Thanks, Bryce," she said with loving sincerity. She finished hand-wiping a pot and fiddled with the hem of a dish towel.

The next morning, she moved the covers and slipped out of bed like a wraith, moving soundlessly out of the room, grabbing and wrapping herself in her robe as she went.

Bryce woke with a start to the sound of Nuna singing in the kitchen. He threw on his plaid flannel robe and stepped into the kitchen to find her bending over, pulling a tray of blueberry muffins out of the oven.

He took a deep breath, drawing the delicious aroma into his lungs. Then, he waited until she set the pan on the marble counter, not wanting to startle her.

"Smells great!"

She whirled around in surprise, looking at him with his hair tousled and a sleepy smile on his handsome face. "I didn't mean to wake you, but I sometimes sing in the kitchen and wanted breakfast ready for you when you awoke."

"Nuna, you have a beautiful voice."

She poured him a cup of coffee, then moved to the stove to fry some eggs and sausage. The scent of home fries was already wafting in the air.

The hot months of July and August gave way to September. A crispness came to the air in the mountains, and ever so slowly, the lushness of the West Virginia woods began to suggest the coming of riotous color, a last blast of activity before the snow. So it was fall. A single robin curved in past some trees and settled on the lawn and cocked his head, listening for a worm. He heard none and, having made several short hops across the lawn, flapped his wings and flew away.

A blustery winter wind was coming way too early for October. Bryce was out blowing leaves off the walkway, inhaling the fullness of the brisk mountain air.

Indulging in a moment of peace, Nuna curled up on the couch, propping a soft blue throw pillow against the sofa's arm under her ribs.

A life of morning sunrises and roses, friends aplenty, quiet moon-light evenings, and a strong, protective dog. Life was good!

Two hours later, they found their way to the house and watched the news for all of five minutes before she proposed watching a movie. "Action, romance, or comedy?" she called out as she sorted through her DVD library. She was on her knees, sending out a hot vibe, her skirt hiked up and now barely covering her ass.

"*After Dark*," he said.

Nuna inserted the disc, dimmed the lights as silvery moonlight poured through the living-room window, then kicked off her heels, grabbed a quilt, and joined Bryce on the couch, burrowing into him. She wedged and wiggled and snuggled and pulled the quilt over them, and when she was finally situated, there was a lot of sultry contact. And then there was touching. Bryce sniffed her hair and thought how easy this was.

Warmed by the quilt, the wine-induced euphoria, and each other's bodies, they watched the movie for all of ten minutes. After, they could not determine who fell asleep first.

* * *

After Nuna cleared the dinner dishes, they stepped outside on the porch and listened to Kenny Rogers croon "Islands in the Stream." Then, they slowly danced under the full moon.

The next morning was bright and sunny, and he was already dressed in his running gear and doing his morning stretches as he waited for her to come out the door.

"Beautiful morning, honey," she said as Bryce smiled at her, still stretching her arms and adjusting her exercise bra. The forest was spectac-ular. The sun was rising over the mountains in a blaze of glory. The tem-perature was in the low sixties with zero humidity with just a light breeze coming through the trees. As usual, they did a short morning warm-up in the gym and then, with Thor by their sides, went on a two-mile jog, trotting down the mountain with a metronomic rhythm, huffing at a deliberate pace to the bridge until they began to sweat. Small critters skittered away as they passed, and every so often, a startled doe leaped back into the shelter of the forest, with Thor giving a brief chase.

"No, I stand corrected." Bryce began to sweat. Nuna began to glisten. She refused to acknowledge her soaked outfit, now stuck to her body, or her dripping ponytail.

As their breathing became more pronounced, they would do a 180-degree turn and then begin a leisurely walk back up, discussing this and that. Thor would be in the lead, protecting them from angry squirrels or rabbits. Bryce kept pace with Nuna and Thor easily, even when they upped the pace, needing a healthy dose of endorphins. He didn't even breathe hard. By the time they got back up, she would be panting with her hands on her hips, trying to catch her breath and remembering that they were both in shape at thirty-five with both their bodies in tone.

She hadn't been using any birth control for years, thinking that she could not have a child. Her body continued to cycle as regularly as the morning sun rising. For a week or so lately, she had been experiencing what she believed to be a mild morning sickness. She hadn't wanted to say anything to Bryce until it was medically confirmed. Finally, she made an appointment with her gynecologist, and he confirmed that she was indeed pregnant and in the early stage. Now, she couldn't hold back any longer.

That night, as they sat before the fireplace, she was beaming with a thousand-watt smile as she looked at him. "Bryce, I have something to tell you." In an effort to contain her excitement, she turned and gripped his collar. "I'm pregnant! We're going to have a baby!" she cried out a with a level of excitement that she had never experienced before.

Bryce looked at her with a sincere longing. With tears of instant elation in his eyes, he took hold of her and hugged her lightly but firmly. "Nuna, you're absolutely glowing. Motherhood becomes you, and I love you all the more for it."

A single cricket sang its lonely two-note melody somewhere in the darkened night.

Nuna had brains, brawn, and beauty—how could he ask for more? Their goal was to raise their child together on the top of the mountain, play with their grandchildren, and grow old gracefully together on the mountain. What more could a mountain girl born and raised in West Virginia ask for? Nuna leaned over and kissed him, a soft, effectuate kiss that contained all the sweetness that was her. Bryce closed his eyes, savoring the moment, one of the many to come in their lifetimes. Their love for each other would be the essence of a full and wonderful life.

She smiled. "Good night, Bryce."

He laughed. "Good night, Nuna."

THE END

ABOUT THE AUTHOR

For years, Richard "Rick" Nicholson Jr. dreamed of writing an action-adventure novel—complex, multigenre, with a narrative and plot that would intrigue the reader.

Face of Evil is his debut novel.

Nicholson has lived in Connecticut most of his life, having served three years on the muddy rivers of Vietnam. He received a bachelor's degree in business from Teikyo-Post University, and his professional career centered on corporate leadership roles in purchasing management. Having married his lovely wife shortly after returning home from Vietnam, he quickly learned the profession of fatherhood. After his wife passed away from cancer at an early age, he brought up his two sons by himself. Since retiring several years ago, he has become an avid reader, reading no less than sixty novels annually.

Milton Keynes UK
Ingram Content Group UK Ltd.
UKHW040909191024
449793UK00013B/109/J